Praise for these bestselling authors

Linda Lael Miller

"Sensuality, passion, excitement, and drama
are Ms. Miller's hallmarks."
—*Romantic Times*

"Her characters come alive and walk right off the pages
and into your hearts."
—*Rendezvous*

Carla Neggers

"Brimming with Neggers's usual flair
for creating likeable, believable characters...
she delivers a colorful, well-spun story..."
—*Publishers Weekly* on *The Carriage House*

"No one does romantic suspense better!"
—Janet Evanovich

Lori Foster

"You can pick up any Lori Foster book
and know you're in for a good time."
—*New York Times* bestselling author Linda Howard

"Lori Foster has a reputation for warm, engaging
characters combined with sizzling sexual tension."
—Amazon.com reviews

LINDA LAEL MILLER

CARLA NEGGERS
LORI FOSTER

under his skin

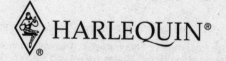

TORONTO • NEW YORK • LONDON
AMSTERDAM • PARIS • SYDNEY • HAMBURG
STOCKHOLM • ATHENS • TOKYO • MILAN • MADRID
PRAGUE • WARSAW • BUDAPEST • AUCKLAND

HARLEQUIN BOOKS
225 Duncan Mill Road, Don Mills,
Ontario, Canada M3B 3K9

ISBN 0-373-83588-4

UNDER HIS SKIN

Printed in U.S.A.

CONTENTS

SNOWFLAKES ON THE SEA

Linda Lael Miller

1

The bare semblance of a smile curved Nathan McKendrick's taut lips as he stood at the living room windows looking down at the measured madness in the streets below. Cars fishtailed up and down the steep hills, and buses ground cautiously through the six inches of snow that, according to the doorman, had fallen since morning. The stuff was still coming down, in great lazy slow-motion flakes, like flour from a giant sifter.

Nathan sighed. The people of Seattle didn't really *believe* in snow—though they were certainly acclimated to rain—and they were always caught off guard when it came. The timid closed down their businesses and cowered at home, while the more adventurous braved the elements.

He focused his dark gaze on the distance. The harbor was invisible, through the swirling storm and the cloak of night, except for a few flickering lights, and the rugged Olympic Mountains beyond were blotted out entirely. The Space Needle, a modern tower commemorating a past world's fair, appeared as a patch of blue light in the gloom.

Depressed, Nathan turned from the scene and sighed again. The penthouse, sumptuously furnished in rich suedes and velvets, was close and confining that night, even though it occupied the entire top floor of the building and had been carefully designed to seem even more spacious than it was.

Where was Mallory? The question played in Nathan's exhausted mind and stretched his waning patience thin. He began to pace the empty living room in long, fierce strides, expending energy he didn't possess. A six-week concert tour, followed by the endless flight back from Sydney, had left him physically drained.

He paused, looking down at his travel-rumpled clothes—tailored gray slacks and a lightweight cream-colored turtleneck sweater—and grimaced. The garments felt scratchy against the lean, muscular length of his body, and the rough stubble of a new beard stood out on his face like tiny needles.

Though the penthouse boasted no less than four bathrooms, it hadn't occurred to him until that moment to take the time to shower, shave and change his clothes; he'd been too frightened, too desperate to find Mallory. Oblivious to everything except the state of his wife's health, he'd caught a cab at the airport and hurried to the hospital, where he'd been summarily informed that "Ms. O'Connor" had been treated and released.

The nurses had told him so little, and he hadn't been able to reach Mallory's doctor, Mallory herself or any of her friends. Finally, when he'd frantically dialed his sister's number, he'd gotten a recorded voice telling him cheerily that Pat couldn't come to the telephone at the moment.

Though he'd tried the penthouse number and gotten no answer, he had hurried there hoping that Mallory might have left a note.

Now, having made all the same fruitless calls again and left a rather direct message on his sister's answering machine, he was nearly overwhelmed by weariness and frustration.

Softly, furiously, he cursed. Then, with consummate control, Nathan brought himself up short. Mallory was *all right*—Pat's cable had said that much, at least, and with characteristic certainty. Pat was never wrong about anything.

He ground his teeth and went back to the window, only to turn away again and stride toward the master bedroom and the sumptuous bathroom beyond. There, he stripped and stepped into a pulsing, steaming shower.

By the time he'd finished scouring his tense flesh, shaved and gotten dressed again, he felt better. He tried Pat's number once more and got the same mechanical spiel he'd heard before. Muttering a curse, he dialed the island house and was informed by a harried operator that the lines were down.

At that moment, the doorbell rang. Nathan bounded over the plush carpet and wrenched open one of the heavy double doors.

His sister stood impatiently in the hallway, glaring up at him. "You shouldn't say things like that on the telephone, Nathan!"

He remembered the colorful message he'd left for Pat and laughed gruffly. "And you should be at home when I want to talk to you," he retorted, arching one dark eyebrow.

Pat sighed, placated by his off-the-cuff comment. She looked tired as she ran one slender hand through the copper and gold strands of her long hair and blinked her wide cornflower blue eyes. "Could we start over here?" She smiled, stepping around her brother to enter the penthouse. And then, without waiting for an answer, she cleared her throat and began again. "Hello, handsome. Rough trip?"

Nathan shook his head distractedly. The grandfather clock in the living room chimed a soft reminder of the hour. "Pat, I'm going insane while you make small talk. What's the matter with Mallory, and where the hell is she?"

Pat stood on tiptoe to kiss her brother's freshly shaven chin. "Relax," she said gently. "Mallory is okay. After they released her from the hospital, I took her out to the island so she could have some peace and quiet."

He took his sister's arm, ushered her somewhat roughly toward the living room. "Why was she in the hospital, damn it?" he snapped, impatient and scared.

Pat settled herself on the suede sofa and crossed her shapely legs. "She collapsed on the set last night, Nathan, and they called an ambulance. Somebody from the show got in touch with me and I cabled you as soon as I'd seen Mallory and talked to the doctor and everything."

Nathan stiffened, then leaned back against the long teakwood bar Mallory had bought in the Orient several years before, and folded his powerful arms in stubborn outrage. "I've been going out of my mind," he growled. "They wouldn't tell me anything at the hospital—"

Pat lowered her expressive blue eyes for a moment, regrouping, and then raised them intrepidly to her brother's face again. "Mallory's producer threatened them with mayhem if they gave out any information to anyone. Nathan, let it go."

With a harsh motion of one hand, Nathan reclaimed the brown leather jacket he'd tossed into a chair earlier and slipped his arms into it. Mallory was his first concern—at the moment, his only concern.

As he turned to leave, Pat rose from the couch and caught his arm in one hand, gently but firmly. "Nathan, don't hassle Mallory about the name thing or the soap opera, all right? She's a wreck, frankly, and she doesn't need it."

"Right," Nathan agreed crisply.

Pat reached up to touch his dark still-damp hair. "One more thing, love—stop worrying. Everything is okay."

Nathan laughed, even though nothing in the whole damned world was funny, and walked away from his sister without looking back.

Mallory O'Connor loved the island house, though she didn't get back to it much, now that she was working in Seattle. Often, the sturdy, simply furnished structure seemed to be the only real thing in her life. Now, standing in the huge old-fashioned kitchen, with snow drifting past the polished windows, she drew a deep breath and allowed herself to feel the sweet, singular embrace of the one place that was really home. Then, comforted, Mallory began selecting fragrant, splintery lengths of kindling from the box beside the big wood-burning stove to start a fire. She'd slept for a while after Pat had raced back to the city, and now she was pleasantly hungry.

Pride filled Mallory as the blaze caught and began to heat the spacious kitchen. Her mother had been right—there *was* a certain satisfaction in doing things the old way, a satisfaction she'd never found in the posh Seattle penthouse she and Nathan shared between his long and frequent absences.

Mallory sighed. She loved Nathan McKendrick with an intensity that had never abated in six tumultuous years of marriage, though she couldn't have honestly said that she was happy. At twenty-seven, she was successful in her out-of-the-blue career, and Nathan, at thirty-four, was certainly successful in his. But there were elements missing from their relationship that caused Mallory to hunger even in the midst of opulence.

Money and recognition were pitiable substitutes for children, and the hectic pace most people considered glamorous only made Mallory's heart cry out for simplicity and peace.

Outside, in the silent storm, Mallory's Irish Setter, Cinnamon, began to howl for admission. Mallory smiled and went out onto the screened sun porch to welcome her furry and much-missed friend.

Cinnamon whimpered and squirmed in unabashed delight as Mallory greeted her with a pat on the head. "What do you say we just hide out here from now on, girl?" Mallory asked, only half in jest. "Nathan could go on with his concert tours—the darling of millions—and we'd exist on a diet of oysters and clams and wild blackberries."

The dog abandoned its mistress to sniff and paw at a large, unopened sack of dog food leaning against the inside wall of the porch beside the screen door. Mallory began to pry at the stubborn stitching sealing the bag. "So much for living off the land," she muttered.

While Cinnamon crunched happily away on the dried morsels wrested from that recalcitrant bag, Mallory heated canned chicken soup on the cookstove. There was very little in the house to eat, but shopping could wait until morning—Mallory would get her car out of the locked garage then, and drive to the small store on the other side of the island.

The wooden telephone on the kitchen wall, actually a modern replica of the old-fashioned crank phone, rang in pleasant tones, and Mallory left the soup simmering on the stove to answer. When she and Pat had arrived, there hadn't been any phone service at all.

"Hello?"

Pleased feminine laughter sounded on the other end of the crackling line. "Mall, you *are* back!" cried Trish Demming, one of Mallory's closest friends. "Thank heaven. I thought I'd fallen short in my dog-watching duties—I called Cinnamon until I was hoarse."

Mallory smiled. "She's here, Trish—safe and sound. I tried to call you, but the lines were dead."

Trish's voice was warm. "No problem. Actually, I should have looked at your house in the first place. Even when you're gone, Cinnamon is always dashing over there. What's going on, anyway? I thought you were all involved in taping that soap—er—daytime drama of yours, Mall."

Mallory sighed. "I'm having an enforced vacation, Trish. Brad isn't going to let me back on the set until I have a doctor's permission." She didn't add that she was relieved to have a respite from the crazy schedule; Trish wouldn't have understood.

There was a short silence while Trish considered the implications of Mallory's statement. "Honey," she said finally, concern ringing in her voice, "you're not sick, are you? I mean, you must be, but is it serious?"

Mallory touched the top of the yellow-enameled wainscoting reaching halfway up the kitchen wall and frowned at the smudge of dust that lingered on her fingertip. "I'm just tired," she assured her friend, glad that Trish couldn't see the dark splotches of fatigue under her eyes or the telltale thinness of her already slender figure.

For a while, the two women discussed the plot line of "Tender Days, Savage Nights," the first soap opera ever to be produced in Seattle. Brad Ranner, the show's dynamic creator and chief stockholder, had brought it out from New York a year before, partly because of lower production costs and partly because of a desire to use more outdoor scenes. The spectacular vista of sea and mountains and lush woodlands gave the program unique appeal.

Most of the original cast had balked at leaving New York, however, and open auditions had been held in Seattle. On a whim, Mallory had gone, along with a horde of other applicants, to read for a part. Anxious to accomplish something strictly on her own, she had given her maiden name and prayed that no one would recognize her as the wife of a world famous rock singer.

No one had, and furthermore, Mallory had been selected, despite an embarrassing lack of acting experience, to play the role of Tracy Ballard, a troubled young woman who devoted boundless energy to destroying long-term marriages. The part had been a small one at first, but Mallory had played it with a verve that pleased sponsors and viewers alike. Her character on the show took on interesting dimensions, and suddenly, Mallory O'Connor McKendrick was a success in her own right.

And how empty it was.

She promised to visit Trish soon and rang off, frowning. Her hand lingered for a moment on the telephone receiver. Mallory was rich now and, in her own way, even famous, if "famous" was the proper word for a notoriety that caused strange women to confront her in supermarkets and department stores and even libraries, demanding that she stop interfering in this or that fictional marriage.

Nibbling at her lukewarm soup, Mallory considered her life and, for perhaps the ten-thousandth time, wished that it could all be different. Her hard-won teaching certificate had never seen a day's use, and she longed for a child of her own to love and nurture.

She was rinsing out her empty bowl and placing it in the orange plastic drainer beside the sink when a pair of headlights swung into the yard, their golden light speckled with glistening flakes of snow. Mallory leaned close to the cool, damp window, trying to recognize the car.

When that proved impossible due to the storm, she ran her hands down the worn red-and-blue-plaid flannel of her shirtfront and hurried out onto the screened porch. Cinnamon danced at her heels and then wriggled gleefully against the legs of her jeans.

The slam of a car door echoed, mingling with the nightsong of the tide, and Cinnamon's magnificent tawny head shot up, suddenly alert. Before Mallory could grasp her collar, the dog propelled herself through the outside screen door and bounded into the ever-deepening snow, yipping hysterically.

Nathan laughed and reached down to greet Cinnamon with the customary pat-and-rub motion that made her ears flop about in comical disarray. "Hello, you worthless mutt," he said.

Mallory stood in the doorway, her mouth open, just staring. Would she never get over feeling as though she'd just been punched in the solar plexis whenever Nathan McKendrick came striding back into her life?

Standing in the stream of light coming from the kitchen, Nathan forgot the dog and raised his eyes to Mallory. They made their way over her trim, rounded hips, her small waistline, her high, firm breasts to settle at last on her face.

Mallory fell against the doorframe, watching him in stricken silence. Snow glistened in his unruly ebony hair and on the straining shoulders of his jacket, and he put his hands onto his narrow, powerful hips and stared back.

There was a charged silence between them for a long moment, threatening to melt the snow and raise steam from the buried earth. Mallory's traitorous heart caught in her throat. She'd known that he would come, known that Pat, ever the loyal sister, would contact him, alert him to the fact that his wife had been hospitalized. And yet she had hoped for more time, even as she had longed to be near him again.

Nathan executed a mocking bow. "Good evening—Ms. O'Connor," he said in a sardonic drawl.

As quickly as that, the strange spell was broken. Mallory lifted her chin in answer to his challenge and replied, "Good evening, Mr. McKendrick."

Nathan's jawline tightened with immediate annoyance, and some unreadable emotion glittered in his dark eyes as he strode toward her. Before Mallory could move, he had lifted her out of the doorway and over the two snow-laden steps beneath it.

Her insides rioted with involuntary need as he held her, suspended, his face between her ripe, inviting breasts. Even through the heavy flannel of her shirt, she could feel the warmth of his breath.

Slowly, he lowered her, so that the throbbing fullness of her chest was crushed against the hard expanse of his own. Then, his hands cupping the roundness of her bottom, he pressed her to him, to the ready demand of his manhood and the granitelike wall of his thighs.

Good Lord, Mallory thought with remorse. *I'm as bad as any groupie—if he wanted to take me right here in the snow, I'd let him!*

Nathan must have known what havoc he was wreaking on her straining senses, but he said nothing. His mouth came down on hers in a kiss that was at once gentle and demanding. Deftly, his lips parted hers for the sweet invasion and searing exploration of his tongue. Mallory responded with hungry abandon, shivering violently in the force of her need.

Then suddenly, Nathan was thrusting her away, holding her at arm's length. His eyes glowed as they touched her lips and trailed, like the touch of a warm finger, to the pulsing hollow at the base of her throat. He turned her around and propelled her toward the house.

Mallory's face was hot as she turned to watch her husband enter behind her, Cinnamon rollicking exuberantly at his side.

Nathan closed the door quietly, his eyes working their singular magic again as they moved idly over Mallory's body, assessing her, stirring primitive reactions as they passed. "I've missed you, lady," he said in a low voice.

Crimson color stained Mallory's cheeks, and her pride caused her to thrust her head back, so that her dark taffy hair flew over her shoulders in glossy profusion. Her round, thickly lashed eyes flashed with sea green fury born of his ability to inflame her so easily, and she did her best to scowl.

He laughed. "You *are* an actress, pumpkin," he allowed, approaching her slowly. One of Nathan's hands cupped Mallory's breast, the thumb stroking the bare nipple beneath her old shirt to hard and undeniable response. "Your body betrays you," he said hoarsely. "You don't hate me nearly as much as you'd like me to believe."

Of course I don't hate you! Mallory wanted to scream, but her pride wouldn't allow that, so she lifted her chin in stubborn, wordless defiance. But a small cry escaped her as Nathan's hand released her breast to undo one of her shirt buttons, and then another. Her entire body pinkened as he bared the rounded sweetness of her to his lazy inspection.

Mallory abandoned her act when her husband lowered his lips to one waiting nipple to nip at it, ever so gently, with his teeth. She moaned aloud and arched her back slightly so that he could feast upon her.

He chuckled in gruff triumph and flicked the rosy, pulsing center of her breast with the tip of his tongue, teasing. His hand slid between Mallory's legs to caress the taut, womanly secrets of her inner thighs.

"Bastard," she whispered, but there was a catch in her voice and a caress in the word itself. Her hands entangled themselves, without conscious instruction from Mallory, in the thick richness of his dark hair, pressing him closer. With sudden hunger, he devoured the freely offered breast, answering Mallory's groan of ancient pleasure with one of his own.

Presently, he turned to sample the other breast, again teasing and nibbling, again driving Mallory nearly insane with the need of him. She would not beg him—she *would not*—but even as she made this decision, desperate pleas were aching in her throat.

At last, Nathan pressed her against the wainscoting lining the wall, and the lean, inescapable hardness of his body joining hers revealed the force of his desire. He stood back only long enough to divest Mallory of her flannel shirt and kiss her flat, soft stomach in a tantalizing promise of further kisses that would drive her beyond passion into the paradise they had visited so many times.

He unsnapped her jeans, and she felt the zipper give way, the fabric slide down over her hips. She shivered as her panties, too, were lowered. Lips parted, she awaited loving that always bordered on the deliciously unendurable.

Nathan nuzzled the silken shelter of her womanhood; the warm promise of his breath and his searching lips made her tremble. One plea broke past her resolve, and it took the shape of his name.

Slowly, he revealed the small, yearning nubbin. In desperation, Mallory caught his head in both hands and thrust him to her. "Oh, God," she breathed, mindless now in her wanting. "Oh, God, Nathan, *please—*"

At the invitation he had purposely forced from her, Nathan partook hungrily of her, and his tender greed brought her to swift and searing release. She shuddered reflexively, her fingers moving in his hair, and moaned as he nibbled at her at his leisure, demanding a fiery encore to the performance just past.

Bared to him, and so deliciously vulnerable, Mallory whispered words of gentle, desperate encouragement as he tormented the bit of quivering flesh with soft kisses. She writhed, gasped with delight, when he took his pleasure yet again, bringing his tongue into play this time, sampling her and then suckling as though to draw some sweet nectar from her. "Don't—stop—" she pleaded, her wanting now as naked as her hips and her thighs and her stomach.

He drew back, just slightly. "Sweet," he whispered in a ragged voice, and then he enjoyed her in long, warm, delicious strokes of his tongue. Savage pleasure convulsed Mallory, and her triumph came in a cry that was half shout, half sob.

It was then that, in the snowy silence outside, an engine roared. One car door slammed, and then another.

Nathan swore harshly and straightened, while Mallory, cheeks burning, frantically righted her clothes. Feet were stomping heavily on the porch outside, and Cinnamon began to bark in somewhat belated alarm.

"Just a minute!" Nathan growled, closing his eyes in an obvious effort to control his roiling emotions and frustrated need.

As embarrassed as though the visitors had seen the impromptu love scene staged in the McKendrick kitchen, Mallory turned to the stove to hide her flaming face and occupy her hands with the task of brewing fresh coffee. After another moment of preparation, Nathan answered the door.

"Oops!" Trish Demming blushed, sizing up the situation with her usual gentle shrewdness. "Alex, I think we interrupted something."

Trish's good-natured, bespectacled husband pretended to rush for the door. He was Nathan's accountant and one of his closest friends.

"Sit down," Nathan ordered humorlessly, and Mallory felt his hot gaze touch her rigid back. Out of the corner of one eye, she saw Trish set a covered baking dish down on the counter.

It was several minutes before Mallory gathered enough composure to join the others at the kitchen table, and, even when she did, it was clear that Nathan wasn't going to give her an easy time of it. His dark eyes seared her breasts whenever the opportunity afforded itself, and lingered on her lips until she thought she'd shout with frustration.

Still, it was pleasant to spend time with dear friends, and Mallory genuinely enjoyed the lively conversation touching on everything from Nathan's last concert tour to the ban on gathering oysters along the island's rocky shores. Trish had brought one of her highly acclaimed peach cobblers, and they all ate a hefty slice with their coffee, Trish and Mallory bemoaning the astronomical calorie count.

Mallory was fairly trembling with hidden exhaustion and anticipation when Trish began to make sincere noises about leaving. Goodbyes were said, and the Demmings bundled up in their practical island coats and braved the snow piling up between the house and their car.

Mallory and Nathan exchanged a look of resignation when they heard the car's motor grind halfheartedly, and then die. Nathan's eyes moved over Mallory's body in a sweep of hungry promise, and then he swatted her gently on the bottom and bent his head to nibble briefly at her earlobe. "I'll be back soon," he said, and strode out onto the sun porch, rummaging through the collection of battered coats that had belonged to her father.

Mallory needed to sink languidly into a warm, scented bath and go to bed. She was so tired that sleep would come easily, but not before she and Nathan had reached the breathless heights of love they always scaled after they'd been apart.

And we're apart so much, she thought, her weariness reaching new and aching depths.

A moment later, there was a stomping sound on the porch, and Trish reappeared, looking embarrassed and apologetic. "Nathan and Alex are trying to get the car started," she mumbled, unconsciously rubbing her chilled hands together. "Ace mechanics they're not."

Mallory grinned at her friend and firmly ushered her closer to the stove. "It's all *right,* Trish," she cajoled. "There's still plenty of coffee, if you'd like more."

Trish shook her head, and her soft blond hair moved delicately with the motion. "We shouldn't have barged in here like that," she said ruefully, and then her blue eyes moved to Mallory's face. "I'm so sorry, Mall—it's just that I was worried about you, and, of course, we had no idea that Nathan was home."

Mallory hugged Trish warmly. "You were being thoughtful, as always. So stop apologizing."

Trish's pretty aquamarine eyes were pensive now, seeing too much. "Mall, you really look beat. Are you okay?"

Suddenly, Mallory had to look away; she couldn't sustain eye contact with this friend she'd known all her life and say what she meant to say. "I'm fine," she insisted after a short pause.

The tone of Trish's voice betrayed the fact that she was neither convinced nor mollified, but she spared Mallory her questions and gave her a gentle shove in the direction of the bathroom. "Go and take a nice hot bath and get yourself into bed, Mrs. McKendrick. I can look after myself until the men get our car going again."

Mrs. McKendrick. Mallory blanched, unwittingly giving away something she hadn't meant to reveal. She longed to be known by her married name again, and yet, it sounded strange to her, as though she had no right to resume it.

Trish laid a comforting hand on her shoulder. "Get some rest, Mall. We'll have a good, long talk when you're up to it."

There was much that Mallory needed to confide, but this was neither the time nor the place. "I—If you're sure you won't feel slighted—"

Trish's eyes were sparkling with warmth and controlled concern. "Just go, will you? I'm not such an air head that I can't entertain myself for a few minutes!"

Mallory laughed, but the sound was raw and mirthless. Reluctantly, she left her friend to her own devices and stumbled into the bathroom, where she started running hot water in the tub.

While it ran, Mallory hurried through the doorway that joined that room to the master bedroom and began to search wearily through the suitcases Pat had packed for her earlier at the penthouse. There were jeans and sweaters, always necessary for winter visits to the island, but nothing even remotely glamorous had been included. Mallory thought of all the silken lingerie left behind in Seattle and sighed. She had so wanted to look especially attractive for Nathan, but Pat had either not foreseen that contingency or not considered it important.

With resolve, Mallory ferreted out her least virginal flannel nightgown and carried it into the steam-clouded bathroom. Over the roar of the water, she heard Trish and Alex's car start up.

Smiling to herself, Mallory stripped and climbed into the tub. The warmth of the scented water was heaven to her tired muscles, and she sank into it up to her chin, giving a soft sigh of contentment as total relaxation came at last.

Home, she thought happily. *I am home.*

The heavy enameled door of the bathroom squeaked open then, and, suddenly, Nathan was there, his dark eyes taking in the slender, heat-pinkened length of her body. Beneath the suntan he'd undoubtedly acquired in Australia, where it was now the height of summer, he paled.

"My God, Mallory," he swore. "How much weight have you lost?"

Mallory shrugged as she averted her eyes. "Maybe five pounds," she said.

Nathan was leaning against the chipped pedestal sink now, his arms folded, watching her. "More like fifteen," he argued, his voice sharpened to a lethal edge. "You were too thin when I left, but now—"

Mallory squeezed her eyes closed, hoping to press back the sudden and unaccountable tears that burned there. Was he saying that he didn't want her anymore, didn't find her physically attractive?

She felt his presence in the steamy bathroom, heard him kneel on the linoleum floor. When Mallory opened her eyes, she was not surprised to find him beside her, the knuckles of his powerful, gifted hands white with the force of his grasp on the curved edge of the bathtub.

"Mallory, talk to me," he pleaded hoarsely. "Tell me what to do—how to change things—how to make you really happy again."

One traitorous tear escaped, trickling down Mallory's slender cheek and falling into the bathwater. "I am happy, Nathan," she lied.

Nathan made a harsh, disgusted sound low in his throat. His eyes burned like ebony fire. "No," he countered. "Something is chewing you up alive, and the hell of it is, I can't do a damned thing about it if you won't trust me enough to be honest."

Mallory's voice was small and shaky with dread. "Do you want a divorce, Nathan?"

He was on his feet in an instant, turning his back on Mallory, shutting her out. His broad shoulders were taut under the soft gray fabric of his shirt.

Unable to bear the oppressive silence placidly, Mallory reached out and grasped the big sponge resting in an inside corner of the tub. Fiercely, she lathered it with soap and began to scrub herself so hard that her flesh tingled.

"I would understand," she said, when she dared speak.

Nathan whirled suddenly, startling her so badly that she dropped the sponge and stared at him, openmouthed. His face was rigid with suppressed fury and something very much like pain. He folded his arms in a gesture that, with him, signaled stubborn determination.

"Understand this," he said in a low and dangerous tone. "You are my wife and you will remain my wife. I don't intend to let you go, ever. And you will warm no one else's bed, my love—not Brad Ranner's, not anyone's."

Mallory felt the words strike her like stones, and it was all she could do not to flinch with the pain. "What?" she whispered finally, in shock.

Nathan's face was desolate now, but it was hard, too. "You've been wasting away ever since you signed on with that damned soap opera, Mallory. And there has to be a reason."

Mallory lifted her chin. There were reasons, all right, but Brad Ranner wasn't among them, nor was any other man.

"I've been faithful to you," she said stiffly. And it was true—she had never even been tempted to become intimate with another man, and she had come to Nathan's bed as a virgin. She couldn't bring herself to ask if he'd been as loyal; she was too afraid of the answer.

Nathan sighed, the sound broken, heavy. "I know, Mallory—I'm sorry."

Sorry for what? Mallory wondered silently, sick with the anguish of loving a man who belonged to so many. *Sorry for accusing me like you did or sorry that you have a number of nubile groupies to occupy your many nights away from home?*

"I'm very tired," she said instead.

"I see. You weren't tired in the kitchen tonight, were you?"

The sarcasm in his voice made Mallory's cheeks burn bright pink. "That was a long time ago," she snapped, not daring to meet his eyes.

"At least an hour," Nathan retorted.

"Leave me alone!"

"Gladly," he snapped. Then, slowly, Nathan turned and left the room. When the door closed behind him, Mallory dissolved in silent tears of exhaustion and grief.

Nathan stood at the bedroom window, looking out. There wasn't much to see in the darkness, but the storm had stopped anyway. That was something. Behind him, Mallory slept. The soft meter of her breathing drew him, and he turned back to look at her.

The dim glow of the hallway light made her fine cheekbones look gaunt and turned the smudges of fatigue beneath her eyes to deep shadows. She looked so vulnerable lying there, all her grief openly revealed in the involuntary honesty of sleep.

Nathan drew a ragged breath. How could he have urged her to surrender her body the way he had, when she was so obviously ill? And what had possessed him to imply that she was attracted to Brad Ranner, knowing, as he did, that that kind of deceit was foreign to her nature?

Quietly, he approached the bed and pulled the covers up around her thin shoulders. She stirred in her uneasy sleep and moaned softly, intensifying the merciless ache that had wrenched at Nathan's midsection since the moment his press agent, Diane Vincent, had thrust Pat's cable into his hands after the last concert in Sydney.

The night was bitterly cold. Nathan slid back into bed beside his wife and held himself at a careful distance. Even now, the wanting of her, the needing of her, was almost more than he could bear. Raising himself onto one elbow, Nathan watched Mallory for a long time, trying to analyze the things that had gone wrong between them.

He loved her fiercely and had since the moment he'd seen her, some six and a half years ago. Prior to that stunning day, he'd prided himself on his freedom, on the fact that he'd needed no other person. Now, in the darkness of the bedroom, beneath the warmth of the electric blanket, he sighed. If he lost Mallory— and he was grimly convinced that he *was* losing her, day by hectic day—nothing else in his life would matter. Nothing.

She stirred beside him. Nathan wanted her with every fiber of his being and knew that he would always want her. But there was one thing greater than his consuming desire, and that was his love. He fell back on his pillows, his hands cupped behind his head, his eyes fixed on the shadowed ceiling.

Her hand came to his chest, warm and searching, her fingers entangling themselves in the thick matting of hair covering muscle and bone. "Nathan?" she whispered in a sleepy voice.

Despite the pain inside him, he laughed. "Who else?" he whispered back. "Sleep, babe."

But Mallory snuggled against him, soft and vulnerable. "I don't want to sleep," she retorted petulantly. "Make love to me."

"No."

Her hand coursed downward over his chest, over his hard abdomen, urging him, teasing. "Yes," she argued.

Nathan was impatient. "Will you stop it?" he said tightly. "I'm trying to be noble here, damn it."

"Mmm," Mallory purred, and her tantalizing exploration continued. "Noble."

"Mallory."

She raised herself onto one elbow and then bent her head to sample one masculine nipple with a teasing tongue.

Nathan groaned, but he remembered her thinness, her collapse on the set in Seattle, the hollow ache visible in her green eyes. And he turned away, as if in anger, and ignored her until she withdrew.

2

The telephone was ringing when Mallory awakened the next morning. She burrowed down under the covers with a groan, determined to ignore it. If she waited long enough, Nathan would answer it or the caller would give up.

But the ringing continued mercilessly, and Mallory realized that her husband wasn't nestled between the smooth flannel sheets with her. Tossing back the bedclothes with a cry of mingled irritation and disappointment, she scrambled out of bed and reached automatically for her robe.

The house was pleasantly warm, and Mallory smiled, leaving the robe—and an aching recollection of Nathan's rejection the night before—behind as she made her way into the kitchen and disengaged the old-fashioned earpiece from its hook on the side of the telephone. "Hello?" she spoke into the mouthpiece, idly scanning the neat kitchen for signs of Nathan. Except for the heat radiating from the big woodburning stove, there was nothing to indicate that he'd been around at all.

"Hello," snapped Diane Vincent, Nathan's press agent. "Is Nate there?"

Mallory frowned. *Good question,* she thought ruefully. *And where the hell do you get off calling him "Nate"?*

"Mallory?" Diane prodded.

"He was here," Mallory answered, and hated herself for sounding so lame and uncertain.

Disdain crackled in Diane's voice. "One night stopover, huh? Listen, if he happens to get in touch, tell him to call me. I'm staying at my sister's place in Settle. He knows the number."

Mallory was seething, and her knees felt weak. She reached

out awkwardly for one of the kitchen chairs, drew it near and sat down. She despised Diane Vincent and, in some ways, even feared her. But she wasn't about to let anything show. "I'll relay your message," she said evenly.

Diane sighed in irritation, and Mallory knew that she was wondering why a dynamic, vital man like Nathan McKendrick had to have such a sappy wife. "You do that, sugarplum—it's important."

Mallory forced a smile to her face. "Oh, I'm sure it is—dearest."

Diane hung up.

Outside, in the pristine stillness of an island morning, Cinnamon's joyful bark pierced the air. Mallory hung up the phone and went to stand at the window over the kitchen sink, a genuine smile displacing the frozen one she'd assumed for Diane Vincent. Nathan and the enormous red dog were frolicking in the snow, their breath forming silvery white plumes in the crisp chill of the day. Beyond them, the towering pine trees edging the unpaved driveway swayed softly in the wind, green and snow-burdened against the splotchy sky.

Mallory swallowed as bittersweet memories flooded her mind. For a moment, she slid back through the blurry channels of time to a cheerful memory....

"One of these days," her father was saying, snowflakes melting on the shoulders of his checkered wool coat and water pooling on the freshly waxed floor around his feet, "I'm going to have to fell those pine trees, Janet, whether you and Mallory like it or not. If I don't, one of them is sure to come down in a windstorm and crash right through the roof of this house."

Mallory and her mother had only exchanged smiles, knowing that Paul O'Connor would never destroy those magnificent trees. They had already been giants when the island was settled, over a hundred years before, and that made them honored elders.

With reluctance, Mallory wrenched herself back to the eternal present and retreated into the bedroom. There would be time enough to tell Nathan that Diane wanted him to call, she thought, with uncharacteristic malice. Time enough.

Mallory crawled into bed, yawned and immediately sank into a sweet, sound, dreamless sleep.

When she awakened much later, the sun was high in the sky, and she could hear the sizzle of bacon frying and the low, caressing timbre of Nathan's magical voice. Grinning, buoyed by the sounds and scents of morning, Mallory slid out of bed and crept to the kitchen doorway.

Nathan, clad in battered blue jeans and a bulky blue pullover sweater, stood with his back to her, the telephone's earpiece propped precariously between his shoulder and his ear. While he listened to the person on the other end of the line, he was trying to turn the fragrant bacon and keep an eager Cinnamon at bay at the same time. Finally, using a meat fork, he lifted one crispy strip from the pan, allowed the hot fat to drip off and then let the morsel fall to the floor. "Careful, girl—that's hot," he muttered. And then he moved closer to the mouthpiece and snapped, "Very funny, Diane. I was talking to the *dog*."

Mallory stiffened. Suddenly, the peace, beauty and comfort of the day were gone. It was as though the island had been invaded by a hostile army.

She went back to the bedroom, now chilled despite the glowing warmth that filled the old house, and took brown corduroy slacks and a wooly white sweater from her suitcases. After dressing and generally making herself presentable, she again ventured into enemy territory.

Nathan was setting the table with Blue Willow dishes and everyday silver and humming one of his own tunes as he worked. Mallory looked at the dishes and remembered the grace of her mother's hands as she'd performed the same task, the lilting softness of the songs she'd sung.

Missing both her parents keenly in that moment, she shut her eyes tight against the memory of their tragic deaths. She had so nearly died with them that terrible day, and she shuddered as her mind replayed the sound of splintering wood, the dreadful chill and smothering silence of the water closing over her face, the crippling fear.

"Mall?" Nathan queried in a low voice. "Babe?"

She forced herself to open her eyes, draw a deep, restorative breath. Janet and Paul O'Connor were gone, and there was no sense in reliving the brutal loss now. She tried to smile and failed miserably.

"Breakfast smells good," she said.

Nathan could be very perceptive at times—it was a part, Mallory believed, of his mystique as a superstar. The quality came through in the songs he wrote and in the haunting way he sang them. "Could it be," he began, raising one dark eyebrow and watching his wife with a sort of restrained sympathy, "that there are a few gentle and beloved ghosts among us this morning?"

Mallory nodded quickly and swallowed the tears that had been much too close to the surface of late. The horror of that boating accident, taking place only a few months after her marriage to Nathan, flashed through her mind once more in glaring technicolor. The Coast Guard had pulled her, unconscious, from the water, but it had been too late for Paul and Janet O'Connor.

Nathan moved to stand behind her, his hands solid and strong on her shoulders. It almost seemed that he was trying to draw the pain out of her spirit and into his own.

Mallory lifted her chin. "What did Diane want?" she asked, deliberately giving the words a sharp edge. If she didn't distract Nathan somehow, she would end up dissolving before his very eyes, just as she'd done so many times during the wretched, agonizing days following the accident.

He sighed and released his soothing hold on her shoulders, then rounded the table and sank into his own chair, reaching out for the platter of fried bacon. "Nothing important," he said, dropping another slice of the succulent meat into Cinnamon's gaping mouth.

Mallory began to fill her own plate with the bacon, eggs and toast Nathan had prepared. "Diane is beautiful, isn't she?"

Nathan glowered. "She's a bitch," he said flatly.

Mallory heartily agreed, in secret, of course, and it seemed wise to change the subject. "My contract with the soap is almost up," she ventured carefully, longing for a response she knew Nathan wouldn't give.

"Hmm," he said, taking an irritating interest in the view framed by the big window over the sink. The dwarf cherry trees in the yard looked as though someone had trimmed their naked gray branches in glistening white lace.

Mallory bit into a slice of bacon, annoyed. *Damn him, why doesn't he say that he's pleased to know I'll have time for him again, that we should have a child now?* "Well?" she snapped.

"Well, what?" he muttered, still avoiding her eyes.

Mallory ached inside. If she told him that she wanted to give up her career—it wasn't even a career to her, really, but something she had stumbled into—it would seem that she was groveling, that she hadn't been able to maintain her independence. "Nothing," she replied with a defeated sigh. She looked at the food spread out on the table and suddenly realized that the makings of such a meal hadn't been on hand when she arrived the night before. "You've been to the store."

He laughed at this astute observation, and at last he allowed his dark, brooding eyes to make contact with her green ones. "My dear," he imparted loftily, "some of us don't lounge about in our beds half the day with absolutely no concern for the nutritional needs of the human body. Which reminds me—" His wooden chair scraped along the floor as he stood up and reached out for a bulky paper bag resting on the kitchen counter. From it, he took six enormous bottles containing vitamin supplements. Ignoring his own rapidly cooling breakfast, Nathan began to shake pills from each of the bottles and place them neatly beside Mallory's orange juice. Finally, when there was a colorful mountain of capsules and tablets sitting on the tablecloth, he commanded sternly, "Start swallowing."

Mallory gulped, eyeing what amounted to a small meal all on its own. "But—"

Nathan merely leaned forward and raised his eyebrows in firm instruction, daring her to defy him.

Dutifully, his wife swallowed the vitamins, one by one. When the arduous task had been completed, Mallory had no appetite left for the food remaining on her plate, but she ate it anyway. Clearly Nathan meant to press the point if she didn't.

Once the meal was over, they washed and dried the dishes together, talking cautiously about things that didn't matter. As Mallory put the last piece of silverware into the appropriate drawer, however, she bluntly asked a question that had been tormenting her all along.

"Nathan, why didn't you make love to me last night?"

He looked at her, and their eyes held for a moment, but Mallory saw the hardening of Nathan's jawline and the tightening of his fine lips. He broke away from her gaze and once again took a consuming interest in the cherry trees outside.

"I was tired," he said after a long pause. "Jet lag, I guess."

Mallory was not sure whether what she felt was courage or just plain foolishness. "Are you having an affair, Nathan?"

He whirled, all his attention suddenly focused on Mallory's face. "No," he bit out, plainly insulted at the suggestion. "And in case you're wondering, I still find you as desirable as ever, last night notwithstanding, even if you are a touch too bony for my taste."

"Then what is it?" Mallory pressed, crumpling the damp dish towel between her hands. "We haven't been together in six weeks and—"

Nathan pried the cloth out of her hands, tossed it aside and drew Mallory very close. The encounter of their two bodies, his, hard and commanding, hers, gently rounded and very willing, set off an intangible, electric response in them both. "You don't need to remind me how long we've been apart, pumpkin," he muttered, his lips warm and soft at her temple. "This last tour was torture."

Mallory throbbed with the dreadful, ancient need of him. "Make love to me now, Nathan," she whispered.

But he stiffened and held her away, and the only contact remaining was the weight of his hands on her shoulders. "No," he said firmly. "You're tired and sick.... I don't know what your doctor's orders were, but I'm sure they didn't include a sexual marathon."

Mallory's chin trembled slightly. Was he really concerned for her health? Or was he fulfilling his needs in someone else's bed? He'd denied having an affair, but it didn't seem likely that he would admit to anything of that sort when he knew his wife had been hospitalized only a few days before.

Taking no apparent notice of her silence, Nathan kissed Mallory's forehead in a brotherly manner and released his hold on her shoulders. "There's a nice fire going in the living room," he said, sounding determinedly cheerful. "Why don't you curl up on the couch and read or something?"

Mallory had several "or somethings" in mind for the living room sofa, but they certainly didn't include reading. With a proud lift of her chin, she turned and marched out of the kitchen without a word.

The living room was a warm and welcoming place, however, with its window seats and sweeping view of Puget Sound. Mallory couldn't help feeling soothed as she entered. She stood still for a long time, looking out at the water and the snowy orchard that had been her father's pride. When he wasn't piloting or repairing his charter fishing boat, Paul O'Connor had spent every free moment among those trees, pruning and spraying and rejoicing in the sweet fruit they bore.

Presently, the snow began to fall again. Mallory took a childlike pleasure in the beauty of it, longing to rush outside and catch the huge, iridescent flakes on her tongue. Too tired for the moment to pursue the yearning, she perched instead on a window seat, her knees sinking deep in its bright polka-dot cushions, and let her forehead rest against the cool dampness of the window glass.

She sensed Nathan's presence long before he approached to stand behind her, disturbingly close.

"I've got some business to take care of, pumpkin," he said quietly. "I'll be back later."

Mallory's shoulders tensed painfully, and she did not turn around to look at her husband. She had a pretty good idea of what kind of "business" he had in mind, but she would have died before calling him on it. If she was losing her husband, she could at least lose him with dignity and grace.

But she was entirely unprepared for the warm, moving touch of his lips on the side of her neck. A shiver of delightful passion went through her, and she was about to turn all her concentration on seducing Nathan then and there when he suddenly turned and strode out of the room.

Mallory closed her eyes and didn't open them again until she'd heard the distant click of the back door closing behind him. She cried silently for several minutes, and then marched into the bathroom and splashed cold water on her face until the tears had been banished.

On the back porch, Mallory exchanged her sneakers for sturdy boots and pulled on one of the oversize woolen coats that hung on pegs along the inside wall. The garment was heavy, and it smelled comfortingly of pine sap, salt water and tobacco. Wearing it brought her father so near that Mallory almost thought she might turn around and see him standing in the doorway, grinning his infectious grin.

Outside, the tracks in the deep, crusted snow indicated that Nathan had brought his Porsche to the island the night before. The car was gone now, and so was Cinnamon.

Mallory crammed her gloveless hands into the pockets of her father's coat and frowned. "Rat fink dog," she muttered.

A stiff wind was blowing in from the Sound, churning the lazy flakes of snow that were still falling in furious white swirls. Mallory turned her back to the wind and started toward the wooded area that was the center of the island.

Here, there were towering pine trees, and more of the Douglas fir that lined Mallory's driveway, but there were cedars and elms and madronas, too. Under the ever-thickening pelt of snow, she knew, were the primitive wild ferns, with their big, scalloped fronds.

Privately, Mallory thought that the ferns were remnants of the murky time before the great ice age, when the area might well have been a jungle. It was easy to picture dinosaurs and other vanished beasts munching on the plants while volcanoes erupted angrily in the background.

Mallory marched on. The mountains were minding their manners now, with the exception of one, but who knew when they might awaken again, alive with fiery violence? Unnerved by Mount Saint Helens, many scientists were pondering Mount Rainier now, along with the rest of the Cascade range.

As Mallory made her way through the thick underbrush, a blackberry vine caught at her sleeve, eliciting from her a small gasp of irritation and then a reluctant smile. How many times had she ventured here as a child, armed with an empty coffee can or a shortening tin, to pluck the tart late-summer berries from their wicked, thorny bushes?

The thought made Mallory miss her mother desperately, and she hurried on. The motion did nothing, though, to allay the loneliness she felt, or banish persistent memories of Janet's warm praise at the gathering of "so many very, very fine black-berries." After the fruit had been thoroughly washed under cold water, Mallory's mother had cooked jams and jellies and mouth-watering pies.

At last, Mallory emerged on the other side of the island's dense green yoke, and Kate Sheridan's A-frame house came into view. She should have called before dropping in on this busy woman who had been her mother's dearest friend for so many years, she realized, but it was too late to consider manners now. Kate was standing on the deck at the back of the house, smiling as she watched Mallory's approach.

She waved in her exuberant fashion, this trim, sturdy woman, and called out, "I *knew* I was right to wrench myself away from that wretched typewriter and brew some coffee!"

Mallory was warmed by this enthusiastic greeting, but she

was chagrined, too. Kate Sheridan was the author of a series of children's mystery novels, all set in the Puget Sound area, and her time was valuable indeed. Pausing at the base of the snowy path, Mallory deliberated. "I could come back another time," she offered.

"Nonsense!" Kate cried, beaming. "I wouldn't dream of letting an interesting guest like you escape. But I warn you, Mallory—I intend to pump you for information about the things that nasty character you play is planning!"

Mallory assumed a stubborn look as she tromped up the wooden stairway leading to Kate's deck, but she knew that her eyes were sparkling. Her friend's undisguised interest in the plot line of the soap opera amused her deeply.

"My lips are sealed," Mallory said with appropriate drama, knowing all the while that she would tell Kate everything if pressed.

Kate laughed and hugged her, but there was a brief flicker of concern in her intelligent hazel eyes. "You look tuckered out, Mallory," she observed in her direct way.

Mallory only nodded and was infinitely grateful when Kate let the subject drop there and pulled her inside the comfortable house.

Kate Sheridan's home was a lovely place, though small. The opposite wall of the living room was all glass and presented a staggering view of the Sound. At night, the lights of Seattle were often visible, dancing in the misty distance like a mirage.

There was a small fireplace on the back wall near the sliding glass doors that opened onto the deck, and a crackling fire danced on the hearth. The furniture was as simple and appealing as Kate herself; the chairs and sofa were shiny brown wicker, set off by colorful patchwork-patterned cushions. Kate's large metal desk and ancient typewriter looked out over the water, an indulgence the gifted woman often bemoaned but never altered. She was fond of saying that she spent more time gazing at the scenery than working.

Of course, her success belied that assertion; Kate's writing obviously did not suffer for her devotion to the magnificent view. If anything, it was enhanced.

"Sit down," Kate ordered crisply as she took Mallory's bulky coat and hung it from a hook on the brass coat tree near the sliding doors. "Heavens, I haven't seen you since Christmas. It's about time you had some time off."

Mallory, settling into one of the wicker chairs, didn't point out that not even a month had passed since Christmas. She was comforted by the presence of things that were dear and familiar, and she watched Kate with overt affection as the woman strode purposefully into the tiny kitchenette to pour the promised coffee, looking terrific in her gray flannel slacks, white blouse and wispy upswept hairdo. The maroon sweater draped over her shoulders, its sleeves tied loosely in front, gave her a sporty look that suited her well.

"How is the new book coming?" Mallory called out, over the refined clatter of china and silver.

Kate's scrubbed face was shining as she carried two cups of coffee into the living room, placed them on the round coffee table and sat down in the chair facing Mallory's. "Splendidly, if I do say so myself. But tell me about *you*—why aren't you working?"

Mallory lowered her eyes. "They decided I was too tired."

Kate sat back in her chair and crossed legs that were still trim and strong, probably because of her penchant for walking all over the island. "You do look some the worse for wear, as I said before. Is it serious?"

Mallory shook her head quickly. "I'm all right, Kate," she promised in firm tones.

The older, quietly elegant woman took a thoughtful sip from her coffee cup, watching Mallory all the while. "I don't think you are," she argued kindly. "You look about as unhappy as anybody I've ever seen. Mallory, what in heaven's name is wrong?"

Suddenly, Mallory's throat ached and her eyes burned with

unshed tears. She lifted her chin. "Everything," she confessed, in a small, broken voice.

Kate raised a speculative eyebrow. "Nathan?"

"Partly," Mallory admitted, setting her own cup down on the coffee table and entwining her fingers. "Oh, Kate, our marriage is such a joke! Nathan is always away on tour or recording or something, and I'm working twelve- and fourteen-hour days on that stupid soap—"

"Stupid?" Kate asked, with no indication of opinion one way or the other.

Mallory's chin quivered. "I'm afraid I'm not very liberated, Kate," she confessed. "I wanted to prove that I could have a career, and that I could be important as someone other than the wife of a famous man. Now I've done that, I guess, but it isn't at all the way I thought it would be." She paused, reaching for her cup. It rattled ominously in its saucer, and she set it down again. "I'm so miserable!"

"I can see that," Kate replied calmly, resting her chin in her hands in a characteristic gesture. "What do you really want, Mallory?"

Mallory turned her head, not quite able to meet her friend's wise, discerning eyes, and examined the familiar scene in front of Kate's house. The beach looked strange under its blanket of snow, and the waters of the Sound were choppy. "I want to be a wife and a mother," she muttered. "And, maybe, someday, use my teaching certificate—"

"Rash thing!" cried Kate, with humorous, feigned outrage. "You want to be a card-carrying *woman!*"

Mallory was gaping at her friend, speechless.

Kate laughed. "You were right before, Mallory—you aren't very liberated. Liberation, you see, is the freedom to do what you really want to do, not some immovable directive requiring every woman on earth to carry a briefcase or wield a jackhammer!"

Mallory was still staring, but something very much like hope was beginning to flicker inside her. Kate Sheridan was the most "liberated" woman she'd ever known, and here she was, saying that wanting to make a home with the man you love was all right. "I thought—"

"I know what you thought," Kate broke in with good-natured irritation. "You thought it was your duty as a modern, intelligent young woman to set aside your real inclinations and devote all your energy to something that doesn't begin to please you."

Mallory reached for her coffee cup, this time successfully. Her thoughts were in a pleasant tangle, and she didn't try to talk.

Kate bent toward her, balancing her own cup and saucer on her knees. "Mallory McKendrick, you march to your own drumbeat," she ordered. "Your life won't be worth a damned thing if you don't."

Mallory laughed softly in relief; it felt so good to be addressed by her married name again. "I love you, Kate."

"I love you, too," the woman replied briskly. "But there have been times when I wanted to shake you. You do a creditable job as an actress, Mallory, but you weren't born to it. I've always seen you as a crackerjack mother, myself."

"Are you just saying that because you know it's what I want to hear?" Mallory challenged, grinning.

Kate laughed. "My dear, you know me better than that. Hot air belongs in balloons, not conversations between people who care about each other."

Mallory was pensive again. All right, she'd decided that she wanted a more settled life, children, maybe a chance to teach, when the time was right. But how would Nathan react to all this? They hadn't discussed any of the options, really, and they had grown apart since Mallory stopped accompanying him on tour to pursue a career of her own.

Kate's hand rested on Mallory's. "These things generally work out," she said with uncanny insight. "*Talk* to Nathan. He loves you, Mallory."

The two women chatted about less pressing things after that, and, when the snowstorm began to show signs of becoming really nasty, Mallory reluctantly took her leave. She was on automatic pilot during the walk home, her mind absorbed in all the things she needed to say to Nathan.

But as she came out of the woods and onto her own property, Mallory was jolted. Beside Nathan's silver Porsche sat Diane Vincent's bright red MG roadster.

Mallory paused, alarmed on some instinctive level that defied reason. All her assurances to herself that she was being silly blew away on the winter wind. After drawing a deep breath, she made her way purposefully across the yard and onto the screened porch, where she was met by a delighted Cinnamon.

"Don't tell me how glad you are to see me!" she admonished the squirming dog, even as she reached down to ruffle her lustrous, rusty coat. "You traitor!"

The back door squeaked open as Mallory was hanging her father's woolen coat. Nathan appeared in the doorway, his eyes even darker than usual, and snapping with challenge and controlled fury. "Where the hell have you been?" he demanded.

It seemed now that the sensible, reassuring conversation with Kate Sheridan had taken place in another lifetime. Mallory thrust out her chin. "I've been walking," she retorted.

"In this blizzard?" Nathan's jaw tightened in annoyance.

Mallory pressed her lips together, unable to shake the unsettling idea that Nathan's obnoxious mood had something to do with Diane Vincent's presence. Was he having an attack of conscience?

"Kate's house isn't that far away," she said. "And blizzard or no blizzard, Nathan McKendrick, I'll go wherever I want, *when*ever I want."

His granitelike features softened a little, and he even managed a halfhearted grin. "I'm sorry, Mallory—I was worried, that's all. Next time, will you at least leave a note or something?"

Too busy bracing herself for another encounter with Diane

Vincent to answer him, Mallory simply brushed past her husband and entered the kitchen.

Diane looked sensational in her tailored pale blue slacks, white silk blouse and navy blazer. Her long, blond hair, so pale that it was almost silver, shimmered on her shoulders in a fetching profusion of curls, and her clear blue eyes assessed Mallory in a way that was at once polite and disdainful.

"Hello, Mallory," she said sweetly.

Mallory nodded. "Diane," she responded, already moving toward the stove. The kitchen was the heart of all island houses, and coffee was offered to every guest. Being a relative newcomer, Nathan had overlooked the gesture.

Diane seemed profoundly amused when Mallory raised the old-fashioned enamel coffeepot in question. "No, thanks," she said in a soft but cutting voice, one manicured nail tapping expressively at the less provincial drink Mallory hadn't noticed before. Diane's gaze swung fondly to Nathan, moving over his impressive frame like a caress.

Nathan scowled and tossed a beleaguered look in Mallory's direction that brought his earlier one-word appraisal of Diane swiftly to mind. *Bitch.*

Mallory smiled, and for a while at least, she was no longer afraid of this woman, no longer in awe of her beauty and her sophistication and her undeniable charm. "Nathan?" she asked, again indicating the coffeepot.

He nodded, and Mallory grinned as she filled his cup and set it before him.

"That's bad for you!" Diane complained, frowning and reaching out to grasp Nathan's arm.

Nathan pulled free, raised the cup to his lips and winked at his wife. "Allow me this one vice," he said. "Since I'm temporarily denied my favorite."

Mallory felt her face flush, but she didn't look away. Nathan's gaze lingered at her lips for a long moment, causing her a sweet, singular sort of discomfort.

"So," Diane said, too cheerfully, "how is it that the noto-
rious Ms. O'Connor isn't cavorting before the cameras?"

Mallory felt strong and confident for the first time in weeks,
though she couldn't decide whether the quality had its roots in
the long talk with Kate or the way Nathan was quietly making
love to her with his eyes. Both, probably.

"The name is McKendrick," she said pleasantly, with a
slight lift of her chin.

Something changed in Nathan's eyes; there was an earnest
curiosity there, displacing the teasing hunger she'd noticed before.

Diane looked mildly upset. "I thought 'O'Connor' was your
professional name," she said in an argumentative tone.

"O'Connor was my maiden name," Mallory replied sweetly,
with a corresponding smile. "I *am* married, you know."

Nathan raised one eyebrow, but he said nothing. He merely
toyed with the handle of his coffee mug.

Diane was obviously at a loss, but she recovered quickly.
Leveling her devastating blue eyes at Nathan, she seemed to
forget that Mallory was even in the room. "What have you
decided about that television special, Nathan? I think it would
be great to go back to Australia again, don't you? And the
money is fantastic, even for you—"

Mallory suddenly felt bereft again, shut out. Those feelings
intensified when she saw a sparkle in Nathan's dark eyes. What
was he remembering? The beautiful, awe-inspiring Australian
countryside? Walks along moon-kissed beaches with a warm
and willing Diane?

"The people are so friendly," he mused aloud.

Especially the ones who wear Spandex jeans and lip gloss,
Mallory thought bitterly.

Diane laughed with unrestrained glee and clapped her elegant
hands together. Her whole face shone with appealing mischief
as she smiled at Nathan. "I thought I would *die* when you were
presented with that kangaroo!" she sang, and her voice rang
like music in the simple, homey room.

Nathan grinned at the memory, but then his eyes strayed to Mallory, just briefly, and darkened with an emotion she couldn't quite read.

"They gave you a kangaroo?" Mallory put in quickly, in an effort to join the conversation. "What did you do with it?"

He shrugged, and his gaze was fixed on some point just above Diane's glowing head. "I gave it to the zoo."

"And then there was that great Christmas Eve party," Diane trilled, tossing a look of triumphant malice in Mallory's direction. "My God, the sun was coming up before *that* broke up—"

Nathan frowned, clearly irritated by the mention of the holidays. Or was he warning Diane not to reveal too much? "Ho, ho, ho," he grumbled.

Mallory lowered her eyes to her coffee cup. Her shooting schedule hadn't permitted her to join Nathan at Christmas, and while they hadn't discussed that fact in person, the subject had generated several scathing exchanges over long-distance telephone. She said nothing.

But Diane went mercilessly on. "You can't imagine how *odd* it seemed, swimming outdoors on Christmas Day!" There followed a short, calculated pause. "What was it like *here,* Mallory!"

The shot hit dead center, and Mallory had to work up her courage before daring to glance at Nathan. His features were stiff with resentment, just as she'd feared.

"It was lonely," she said in complete honesty.

Diane was on a roll, and she knew it. Cloaking her animosity in sweetness, she smiled indulgently. "Now, Mallory, don't try to convince us that you sat at home and pined. Everybody knows what super parties Brad Ranner gives, and I read that you celebrated the holidays in a romantic ski lodge high in the Cascades."

Mallory had forgotten the write-up she'd gotten in the supermarket scandal sheets over Christmas week. One had borne the headline, McKENDRICK MARRIAGE CRACKING, and linked Mallory to a country-and-western singer she'd never even met. Another had, just as Diane maintained, claimed that she had carried on an interesting intrigue in the mountains.

Neither claim was true, of course, but she still felt defensive and annoyed. Why did people buy those awful newspapers, anyway? If they wanted fiction, books were a better bet.

Diane giggled prettily. "No comment, huh? Is that what you told the reporters?"

Mallory clasped her hands together in her lap, felt the color drain from her face as she glared defiantly at Diane. She did not dare to look at Nathan. "I didn't talk to any reporters," she said stiffly, hating herself for explaining anything to this woman. Inwardly, she realized that she was actually explaining, left-handedly, the facts to her husband. "Those stories were utter lies, and you damned well know it, Diane."

Diane sat back in her chair, apparently relaxed and unchallenged by Mallory's words. She shrugged. "Sometimes they get lucky and print the truth," she threw out.

Nathan's voice was an icy, sudden rumble. "Shut up, Diane," he said. "None of this is any of your business."

A smile quirked one side of Diane's glistening pink mouth. "They should have been watching *you*, shouldn't they? I can just see the headlines now: ROCK STAR CAVORTS DOWN UNDER."

Mallory flinched and bit her lower lip. She could feel Nathan's rage rising in the room like lava swelling a volcano. Any minute, the eruption would come, and they'd all be buried in ash.

"How about this one?" he drawled, leaning toward Diane with ominous leisure. "PRESS AGENT FIRED."

For the first time, Diane backed down. A girlish blush rose to pinken her classic cheekbones, and real tears gathered in her eyes. "I was only teasing," she said. "Where *did* you spend Christmas, Mallory?"

"In Outer Slobovia, Diane," Mallory replied acidly. "With fourteen midgets and a camel."

Nathan roared with laughter, but Diane looked affronted. "We could get along if we tried, you know," she scolded in a tone that implied crushing pain.

"I seriously doubt that," Mallory retorted. "Why don't you leave now?"

"Good idea," Nathan said.

Diane bristled. "Nathan!"

Nathan smiled and stood up, gesturing for silence with both hands. "Now, now, Diane—no more gossip. After all, the camel isn't here to defend itself."

Diane flung one scorching look at Mallory and stormed out, slamming the kitchen door behind her. A moment later, the outer door slammed, too.

"Thank you," Mallory whispered.

"Anytime," Nathan said, sitting down again.

"Those stories about me—"

He reached out, cupped her chin in one hand. "I know, Mall. Forget it."

Mallory couldn't "forget it"; there was too much that needed to be said. "I was here, Nathan—right here, on the island. I spent Christmas Eve with Trish and Alex, and the next day with Kate Sheridan. I—"

His index finger moved to rest on her lips. "It's all *right,* Mallory."

She drew back from him, more stung by some of the things Diane had implied than she would have admitted. "What did *you* do over Christmas, Nathan?"

He looked away. "I drank a lot."

"No Christmas tree?"

"No Christmas tree."

Mallory sighed wistfully. "I didn't put one up, either. But Trish had a lovely one—"

Suddenly, Nathan was staring at her. She knew he was thinking of the beautiful tree ornaments she'd collected in every part of the world, of the way she shopped and fussed for weeks before Christmas every year, of the way she always threw herself into the celebration with the unbridled enthusiasm of a child. "No tree?" he echoed in a stunned voice that was only part mockery. "No presents?"

Mallory had received a number of gifts—a silk blouse from Kate, books from Trish and Alex, a gold chain from Nathan's sister Pat—but she saw no point in listing them aloud. The package Nathan had sent was still stored in a guest room closet at the Seattle penthouse, unopened.

She lifted her coffee cup in a sort of listless toast. "Just call me Scrooge," she said.

3

Fortunately, Nathan dropped the touchy subject of that Christmas just past—the first Christmas since their marriage that the McKendricks had spent apart—and said instead, "Your turn to cook, woman."

Mallory glanced at the small electric clock hanging on the wall near the telephone, and started guiltily. Lunchtime was long past. "And cook I will," she replied.

In the next few minutes, Mallory discovered that her husband had done a remarkable job grocery shopping; the cupboards were full. She was humming as she assembled sandwiches and heated soup, regardless of the fact that she had absolutely no appetite.

While Mallory labored over that simple midday repast, Nathan fidgeted at the table. He looked almost relieved when the telephone rang, and moved to answer it with a swiftness that injured his wife. Was it so hard for him to talk to her that he was grateful for any excuse to avoid it?

"Hello," he muttered, and then, as Mallory watched, she saw him turn his back to her, saw the powerful muscles stiffen beneath his shirt. "Yes, Mrs. Jeffries," he said in a low voice. "Yes, Diane is supposed to stay there. The band is coming, too—they'll all be there before nightfall, I suppose. No, get extra help if you need it—"

Mallory set the sandwich plates down on the table with an eloquent *thunk* and whirled angrily to ladle hot soup into two bowls. Nathan was talking to his housekeeper, giving her orders to make Diane Vincent and the others comfortable in the sprawling Spanish-style villa on the other side of the island. *His* villa.

"Damn!" she muttered. She should have known that there

would be no private time for the McKendricks—Diane and the band would see to that.

"Right," Nathan said, turning to scowl at Mallory, as though reading her inhospitable thoughts. "Hell, I don't care. Whatever's in the freezer—"

"What?" Mallory grumbled. "No lobster? No filet mignon?"

"Shut up!" Nathan rasped, and then he colored comically and glared at Mallory. "No, Mrs. Jeffries," he said into the telephone receiver, "I wasn't talking to you. Well, they usually bring their wives, don't they?"

"Whip out the satin sheets!" Mallory said, gesturing wildly with a soup spoon in one hand and a tuna fish sandwich in the other.

Nathan gave his wife an evil look and then grinned. "Oh, and one more thing, Mrs. Jeffries—put satin sheets on all the beds."

Mallory stuck out her tongue and sank into her chair at the table with as much visible trauma as she could manage.

Clearly, Nathan was enjoying her tantrum. She knew that she was behaving like a child but couldn't seem to stop. He ended the conversation with an additional order, meant to make his wife seethe. "We'll need lots of towels for the hot tub, too."

"We'll need lots of towels for the hot tub, too!" Mallory mimicked sourly. "God forbid that Diane Vincent should have to *drip-dry!*"

Nathan was chuckling as he bid his housekeeper farewell and hung up. "Mellow out, Mall," he teased, grasping the back of his own chair in both hands and tilting his magnificent head to one side in a mischievous manner. "I'm not planning an orgy, you know."

"Why should you?" Mallory shot back. "The stage is already set for one!"

Nathan's eyes darkened, and the mischief faded from their depths, displaced by impatience. His voice was a sardonic drawl, and he made no move to sit down and share the lunch he'd all but ordered Mallory to prepare. "This is enlightening. I didn't think you *gave* a damn what went on at Angel Cove. You so rarely condescend to put in an appearance!''

Mallory swallowed miserably, all her saucy defiance gone. It was true that she avoided the magnificent house at Angel Cove— there were always too many people there, and there was always too much noise. "Sit down and eat," she said in a small voice.

Surprisingly, Nathan sat down. There was a short, awkward pause while he assessed the canned soup and slap-dash sandwiches. The fare was no doubt much more appetizing at Angel Cove.

Mallory mourned, feeling wearier than ever, as she dragged her spoon listlessly through her soup. She felt Nathan's gaze touch her, and involuntarily looked up.

"You didn't decorate a Christmas tree?" he asked incredulously.

There was no point in trying to skirt the issue; she had known it would come up again. She swallowed the pain that still lingered from that lonely holiday and answered the question honestly. "No."

"You?" Nathan pressed, no trace of his earlier irritation showing in his handsome, sensitive features.

Mallory nodded. "As far as I'm concerned, Christmas just didn't happen this year."

His eyes searched her face. "What about the things I sent? Did you get the package?"

Mallory managed a stiff smile. "I put them in one of the guest rooms, in a closet," she said, thinking of the large parcel she hadn't had the heart to open. "You got your gifts, didn't you? I mailed early—"

"Good Lord," Nathan breathed, shaking his head. It was clear that he either hadn't heard her question about the carefully chosen gifts she'd sent to him or didn't mean to answer. "Which closet?"

Mallory shrugged, though nonchalance was the last thing she felt. "You are a man of many closets," she remarked lamely.

"Mallory."

She frowned at him. "The room Pat sleeps in when she stays at the penthouse."

Nathan looked thoughtful, and a long silence followed. Finally, when both husband and wife had finished pretending to eat, he stood up, scraping his chair against the linoleum floor as he moved. "I don't think you're up to greeting the band," he said in a voice that was gruff and tender at the same time. "Not tonight, at least."

I'll bet you were counting on that, Mallory thought, but she only nodded, relieved that she could deposit the remains of her lunch in Cinnamon's bowl and spend some time gathering her scattered thoughts and emotions. "Say hello for me," she mumbled, holding back tears as Nathan bent to brush her cheek briefly with his lips.

When he was gone, Mallory ambled aimlessly into the living room where she went through the contents of several bookshelves and found nothing she wanted to read. She was being stubborn and stupid, and she knew it. Damn, anybody with any guts at all would have gone over to the villa on the other side of the island and—

And what?

Mallory flung out her arms and cried out with self-mocking drama, "God, I'm so depressed!"

There was no answer, of course, but Mallory's gaze fell on the video recorder hooked up to her portable television set, and she remembered her favorite remedy for depression—old Jimmie Stewart movies.

Five minutes later, she was curled up on the sofa, immersed in the opening, snowy scenes of *It's a Wonderful Life.*

The cold press of Cinnamon's nose awakened her with a start, and Mallory sat up on the sofa, alarmed. The house was cold and dark, and she knew without making even the most cursory search that Nathan was nowhere within its walls.

Patting the dog's head in quick reassurance, Mallory scrambled to her feet. She turned on a lamp and turned off the video recorder and the TV and saw by the glass clock on the mantel that it was nearly three in the morning.

Poor Cinnamon hadn't had any dinner at all.

"I am a dog abuser," Mallory said sleepily. Then, her thoughts churning, she made her way into the kitchen and quickly refilled Cinnamon's dishes with food and water.

Where was Nathan?

Mallory found her purse and rummaged through it until she found the medication her doctor had given her when she had been released from the hospital. She took one capsule into her palm, glared at it for a moment, filled a glass with water and assured herself of hours of deep, undisturbed sleep. If Nathan was at Angel Cove, making music with Diane Vincent, she didn't want to know.

It was late morning when Mallory awakened, and the house was filled with strange sounds and smells. It took her several moments to identify them. She sat up in bed, wide-eyed with disbelief. Turkey? The house definitely smelled of roasting turkey, and the lilting notes of Christmas music filled the air.

Mallory tossed back her covers, frowning in curious consternation. Deck the halls? What in the world was going on?

Wearing only Nathan's old football jersey, which she had put on in the wee hours of the morning after taking the sleeping medication, she made her way out into the kitchen. A glance at the window revealed yet another snowfall, this one lacking the fury of recent storms.

"Nathan?" Mallory ventured, still frowning. The kitchen table was littered with eggshells, onion skins, bread crumbs, wilted celery leaves and an assortment of dirty mixing bowls. "Nathan!"

The recorded Christmas music came to a sudden and scratchy halt, and Mallory wandered toward the living room to investigate. Her mouth fell open in wonder, and her third call of her husband's name died on her lips.

Nathan was standing in the corner beside a fully decorated Christmas tree, grinning like a little boy. With a flourish, he flipped a switch, and the tree was suddenly alight with colorful, glistening splendor.

"Merry Christmas, pumpkin," he said.

Mallory's sentimental heart twisted within her, and tears of delighted surprise smarted in her eyes. "Nathan McKendrick," she whispered, "it is the middle of January!"

He smiled, the Christmas tree switch still resting in one hand. "Not in this house it isn't. Aren't you going to open your presents?"

Mallory's blurred gaze dropped to the base of the fragrant evergreen tree and a number of brightly wrapped packages. In that instant, she knew where Nathan had been during the night, and how badly she had misjudged him.

"You went all the way to Seattle!"

Nathan shrugged. "It seemed the logical thing to do."

"Logical!" Mallory choked, beaming through her tears. And then she raced across the room and flung herself into the arms of her own private Santa Claus.

Their embrace subtly changed the mood. The brief melding of their two bodies sparked a charge that lingered long after Mallory had opened the beautifully wrapped gifts that Nathan had originally mailed from Sydney.

Sitting cross-legged on the hearth rug, still clad in the soft-washed and somewhat shabby red football jersey, Mallory made a sound that fell somewhere between a chuckle and a sob. "There aren't any presents for you!" she mourned.

He arched one eyebrow and folded his arms, and a wicked grin curved his lips as he assessed her speculatively. "I can think of one," he teased. "And I can't wait to unwrap it."

Mallory turned the color of her football jersey, but her heart sang with the desire this man stirred in her. She looked at the glittering litter surrounding her, the sumptuous gifts, the Christmas tree. Finally, she dared to look at Nathan, who was perched on the arm of the old-fashioned sofa, looking even more handsome than usual in his dark blue velour shirt and gray flannel slacks.

"I love you," she said, as awed by the intensity of her feelings as she had been the day she first faced them, more than six years before.

Though he was a tall and muscular man, Nathan moved deftly. Within a moment, he was kneeling on the hearth rug, facing Mallory. Gently he traced the outline of her cheek with a warm index finger. His voice, when he spoke, was hoarse with emotion. "I hope you mean that, lady."

Mallory shifted to her knees with as much grace as possible, and wrapped her arms around Nathan's neck. Her answering pledge was in the kiss she gave him.

Tenderly, without breaking the kiss, Nathan pressed Mallory backward until she lay supine on the large oval rug. His right hand stroked her collarbone, the hollow of her throat, and then slid beneath the neckline of the jersey to close possessively over one warm, rounded breast. She groaned as his thumb brought the rosy center swiftly to a sensuous peak.

The kiss ended, and Nathan's lips strayed, warm, to the sensitive place beneath Mallory's ear and then to the pulsing hollow of her throat. She moaned once again as he drew the neckline of the jersey down far enough to expose a breast.

Idly he surveyed this first sweet plunder of his conquering, as though it were some rare and special confection, to be savored and then consumed slowly. After what seemed like an eternity to Mallory, he lowered his head and nipped gently at the peak awaiting him, causing his wife to writhe. She gasped with shameless pleasure as he softly kissed the pulsing morsel and then tasted it.

He laughed, his breath warm on the tender globe he fully possessed. "You like that, don't you, pumpkin?" he teased in a rich, baritone voice.

Mallory nodded feverishly, unable to speak.

Nathan circled the pink fruit of her bounty with a warm, tormenting tongue. "Umm," he murmured as his right hand moved over Mallory's knee and then beneath the jersey to her firm, satiny thigh.

She squirmed, instinctively parted her legs in an early and desperate surrender. Her hands moved of their own frantic accord, to explore the muscular hardness of his back, beneath his shirt.

He shuddered with pleasure at her touch, and as his mouth closed hungrily over the breast that had grown warm and heavy for him he caressed her inner thighs with gentle fingertips and then tangled them in the nest of curls where sweet, ancient secrets were hidden.

Mallory whimpered as he parted the silken veil to pluck gently at the treasure sheltered there, bringing it to the same throbbing response as her distended nipple. "Yes," she gasped as he drew the football shirt ever upward, unveiling the spoils of his impending conquest. "Yes—"

And suddenly she was totally bared to him, the jersey flung aside. She was grateful when he wrenched off his shirt and hurled that away, too. She could touch him then, entangle her searching fingers in the crisp dark hair curling on his chest, feel the loving, countering warmth of him.

Easily he lifted her, so that she was sitting on the edge of the sofa. Then, kneeling, he gently parted her knees, stroked the tingling, delicate flesh along her inner thighs. A primitive groan of surrender escaped her as he lifted one of her feet, and then the other, placing them so that the heels were braced on the sofa. This accomplished, he pressed on the insides of her knees until she was totally, beautifully vulnerable to him.

This time it was Mallory who drew back the sheltering veil, baring her mysterious, aching self to him. She cried out in throaty ecstasy when she felt his breath, pleaded raggedly until he took timeless sustenance at the waiting feast.

Her fingers entwined in his thick hair, her breath coming in tearing gasps, Mallory reveled in his hunger, in the warm strength of the hands holding her knees apart, so that she could not close herself to him. As his tongue began to savor her in long strokes, Mallory shuddered and gasped a plea and loosed her fingers from his hair to again spread the veiled place for his full satisfaction and her own.

Tremors, both physical and spiritual, rocked Mallory's entire being as he brought her to a release so savage that she sobbed out his name. Quivering with molten aftershocks, she was too stricken to speak again, or even move.

"I love you," he breathed against the moist smoothness of her inner thigh.

Finally, after at least a partial recovery of her senses, Mallory met his eyes. She did not need to speak to relay her message; she wanted to be filled with him, to sheathe him in the rippling, velvety warmth of her and hear his familiar, rasping cries of need and violent, soul-searing satisfaction.

Understanding, his eyes dark with a wanting to match Mallory's own, Nathan moved back a foot or so, still kneeling on the floor, and moaned as his wife slid from the sofa's edge to face him. He trembled, closed his eyes and tilted his head back as she opened his slacks to reveal his straining manhood. For the next several minutes, Mallory enjoyed his magnificence at her leisure, with her eyes, her fingers, her mouth. Her spirit soared at his words of tormented surrender.

In a smooth motion born of passion and desperation, Nathan grasped Mallory's slender waist, lifted her easily and then lowered her onto the pulsing pillar that would make them each a part of the other.

They moved with a rhythm as old as time, increasing their pace as the swelling crescendo building within both of them demanded. When the explosion came, it rocked them, and they shouted their triumph in one voice.

They were still one person, still shuddering with their fierce mingling, when Cinnamon began to bark in the kitchen and they heard the back door open with a cautious creak. "Nathan!" called Eric Moore, the lead guitarist in Nathan's band. "Hey, Nate—I know you're in here somewhere! Mallory?"

Nathan cursed and scrambled to his feet. He was fully dressed again before Mallory had managed to wriggle back into the discarded football jersey.

"Stay where you are, Eric!" Nathan ordered in ominous tones as he strode out of the glittering, cluttered living room without so much as a backward glance. "And next time, knock, will you?"

Still sitting on the floor, Mallory cowered against the front of the sofa, trembling with resentment and a wild, inexplicable loneliness. The conversation taking place in the kitchen was couched in terse undertones, and she understood none of it. She sighed. Understanding the exact situation wasn't really necessary anyway. The fact was that, once again, Nathan's dynamic, demanding life was pulling him in another direction.

Mallory was thoroughly annoyed. She had been planning to give up her role in the soap opera in order to devote more time to a marriage she knew was failing. And all her efforts would mean nothing if Nathan could not or would not meet her halfway.

She stood up slowly, feeling hollow and broken inside. Was Diane really the threat she appeared to be sometimes, or was Nathan's career his real mistress?

Mallory stooped to recover the toy kangaroo that had been one of Nathan's gifts to her and then held it close. She could hold her own against a flesh-and-blood woman any time. But how could she compete with thousands of them? How could she hope to prevail against the tidal wave of adoration lavished upon Nathan McKendrick every time he sang his soul-wrenching compositions?

Still clutching the stuffed kangaroo, she sank to the sofa in dejected thought. Obviously the physical passion between her and her husband was as formidable as ever. Still, Mallory knew that a lasting marriage required more than sexual compatibility, more than romance.

She sensed, rather than saw or heard, Nathan's return to the room. He stood behind her, and though Mallory knew he wanted to touch her, he refrained. His voice was a low rumble and caused tremors in Mallory's heart like some kind of emotional earthquake.

"I've got to go to Angel Cove for a little while, Mallory," he said. "Diane is doing one of her numbers again. Do you want to come with me?"

Mallory did not turn to face her husband; she simply shook her head.

"Babe—"

Mallory held up both hands. "No—I'm all right. Just go and straighten everything out."

"We'll talk when I get back," he muttered, and Mallory could tell that he was already turning away. "Pumpkin, there is so much to say."

Yes, Mallory thought, *there is so much to say, and it is all so painful.* "I'll be here," she said aloud, wishing that she could crawl inside the pouch of the toy kangaroo and hide there forever. "Nathan?" she whispered, on the off chance that he was still near enough to hear.

He was. "What?" he asked, somewhat hoarsely.

"I love you."

He came to her then, bent, brushed her temple with his lips. A moment later, he was gone, and the glistening beauty of the decorated room was a mockery.

Mallory sat very still for a long time, absorbed by her own anguish and confusion. It was only the smell of burning turkey that brought her back to her senses.

She took Nathan's awkward attempt at culinary competence from the oven before wandering into the bedroom to dress. When the telephone rang, she was standing in the kitchen, trying valiantly to salvage at least a portion of the incinerated fowl.

"Hello!" she snapped, certain that the caller meant to make yet another impossible demand on Nathan's time.

"It's me," said Pat, Nathan's sister, in a placating tone. "Mall, I'm sorry if I'm intruding—"

Mallory loved Pat, and regretted the tart way she'd spoken. "Pat," she said gently. "No, you're not intruding. It's just—"

"That plenty of other people are," Pat finished for her with quiet understanding.

"Right," agreed Mallory, who had learned never to try to fool her astute sister-in-law. At twenty-two, Pat was young, but her mind was as formidable as Nathan's. "Shall we start with the band, and progress to Diane Vincent, press agent *extraordinaire?*"

Pat sighed heavily. "Please," she retorted. "I just ate."

Suddenly, inexplicably, Mallory began to cry in the wrenching, heartbroken way she'd cried after losing her parents.

Pat drew in a sharp breath. "Mallory, honey, what is it? How can I help?"

The warmth in Pat's voice only made Mallory sob harder. She felt stupid, but she couldn't stop her tears, and she couldn't manage an answer, either.

"Sit tight," Pat said in brisk, take-charge tones. "I'm on my way."

Mallory sank into one of the kitchen chairs and buried her face in her hands. The telephone receiver made an accusing clatter as it bounced against the wall.

It was a full fifteen minutes before Mallory regained her composure. When she had, she dashed away her tears, marched into the bathroom, ran a tubful of hot water and tried to wash away all the questions that tormented her.

Was Nathan's casual dislike for Diane Vincent really part of some elaborate ruse designed to distract Mallory and everyone else from what was really taking place?

"Diane is doing one of her numbers again," Nathan had said just before he dashed off to handle the situation.

Mallory slid down in the hot, scented water to her chin, watching the slow drip fall from the old-fashioned faucet. Diane wasn't really the issue, she reminded herself. It was just easier to blame her, since she was so obligingly obnoxious in the first place.

Grimly, Mallory finished her bath and, wrapped in a towel, walked into the adjoining bedroom. As she rummaged through her drawers for clean clothes, she regretted not asking Pat to stop by the Penthouse for more of her things.

Once dressed in a pair of jeans and a soft yellow sweater, Mallory went to the bedroom window and pushed back the brightly colored cotton curtains to look outside. The snow was still falling, already filling the tracks left by Nathan's car.

Mallory returned to the bathroom to brush her teeth and comb her hair and apply a touch of makeup. Unless she was on camera, she needed nothing more than a dab of lip gloss. Her eyelashes were thick and dark, requiring no mascara, and, normally, because of her fondness for the outdoors, her cheeks had plenty of color. Now, staring at herself in the old mirror over the bathroom sink, Mallory saw the pallor that had so alarmed her friends and co-workers of late. Because she hadn't brought blusher from the penthouse, she improvised by pinching her cheeks hard.

In the living room, the lights on Nathan's Christmas tree were still blazing, and with a sigh, Mallory flipped the switch. The glorious tree was dark again, and the tinsel dangling from its branches whispered in a draft.

Mallory closed the door leading into the living room as she went out. The January Christmas was a private thing, and she did not want to share it with anyone other than Nathan—not even Pat.

In the kitchen, she sliced off a piece of turkey and gave it to an appreciative Cinnamon, but she had no appetite herself. She cleaned up the mess Nathan had left behind and put the half-charred bird into the refrigerator.

Mallory was brewing fresh coffee when she heard the sound of a car motor outside. Knowing better than to hope that Diane's crisis, whatever it was, had been resolved so soon, thus freeing Nathan, she didn't bother to rush to the window and look out.

The visitor was Pat. Her trim camel's hair coat glistened with snowflakes as she rushed into the kitchen, shivering. "Good Lord," she complained, hurrying to stand beside Mallory at the stove. "It's *cold* out there!"

Mallory laughed, somewhat rawly, and began to divest her

sister-in-law of her coat and knitted scarf. When the things had been put away, the two women sat down at the kitchen table to sip coffee and talk.

Pat's shimmering blond hair was swept up into an appealing knot on top of her head, and she looked slim and competent in her tailored black suede suit and red silk blouse. Her blue eyes searched Mallory's face as she warmed her hands on her coffee mug.

"You were pretty shook up when I called, Mall. Are you okay now?"

Mallory nodded. She was tired of all the solicitude, and besides, there was really nothing Pat could do to help. In any case, she had no intention of complaining about Nathan's demanding life to his sister. "I—I'm all right, Pat—honestly. And I'm sorry if I frightened you. C-couldn't we talk about something mundane—like the weather?"

Pat gave her a cynical look, but she wasn't the type to pry; that was one of her most endearing qualities. "You and Nathan assured me," she said, arching one golden eyebrow, "that the weather on Puget Sound was *mild*. Do you realize that it has been snowing for almost a week?"

Mallory shrugged, grinning. "What can I say in our defense? Every few years somebody up there forgets that it isn't supposed to snow much here, and we get buried in the stuff. Seattle must be wild."

Pat rolled her eyes. "We are talking blatant insanity here!" she cried. "When I drove onto the ferry, I was amazed that I'd made it through town in one piece. People are slipping and sliding into each other over there, with and without cars."

"You like Seattle, Pat," Mallory challenged kindly. "You're not fooling me one bit."

Suddenly Pat was beaming. Her cornflower blue eyes sparkled, and her face glowed. "You're right," she confessed. "I love it! The water, the mountains, the trees—"

Mallory laughed. "Not to mention the fresh raisin bagels they sell at Pike Place Market."

Pat shook her head. "I've sworn off bagels, along with lottery tickets and cigarettes."

"How about Roger Carstairs?" Mallory teased. "Have you sworn off him, too?"

Pat seemed to shine like the Christmas tree hidden away in the living room at the mention of the handsome young attorney she'd met while acquiring property for Nathan's growing corporation. Since then, Roger's name came up a lot. "No way. I don't make a habit of swearing off hunks, Mallory."

Mallory's green eyes danced with mischief. "Patty Mc-Kendrick, you're in love!"

The guess was correct; Pat blushed slightly and nodded her head. "Don't tell Nathan, though. I don't want him doing one of his Big Brother numbers—demanding to know Roger's intentions or something."

Mallory laughed. That would be like Nathan; he was fiercely protective of his sister, partly because their parents, like Mallory's, were no longer living. "I promise not to breathe a word!"

"Good," Pat said. "How is Nate, by the way? He looked pretty undone at the penthouse the other night."

Mallory laid her hand on Pat's, quick to reassure her. "He's fine." *I'm the one who might have to be carted off in a padded basket.*

Like her brother, Pat could be uncannily perceptive at times. "Mall," she began cautiously, "I love you, but you really look like hell. Have you told Nathan that you're thinking of dropping your contract with the soap?"

Mallory's eyes strayed to the window, and she pretended an interest in the incessant snow. "No."

"Why not?"

Cinnamon came to lay her head in Mallory's lap and whimpered sadly. Probably she was feeling abandoned, since Nathan had left her behind this time. Her mistress patted her reassuringly. "I'm not sure how he'll take it, Pat."

"What do you mean, you're not sure how he'll take it? You know he hates the demands the show makes on you, and, well…'' Pat paused, and when Mallory glanced back at her sister-in-law, she saw a reluctant look in her eyes. ''Mallory,'' she went on at last, ''it hurts him that you don't use his name anymore.''

''I know,'' Mallory nodded, thinking back to Diane's visit the day before, when she had announced her intention to drop ''O'Connor'' and call herself Mallory McKendrick again. She hadn't had a chance to explain her decision to Nathan—or was it that she hadn't had the courage? Now, she wasn't sure which was really the case. ''I guess, in the back of my mind, Pat, I'm afraid that taking back my married name isn't going to matter to Nathan. His life is so fast paced, and I'm not sure I can keep up anymore.''

''*Talk* to the man, Mallory. Make him listen, even if you have to throw a screaming fit or insult his band to do it!''

It was the only sensible course of action, and Mallory knew it. Too many times, all during her marriage to Nathan, she had stepped aside when other demands were made on him, however intrusive and unreasonable, content to wait her turn. A hot blush of anger crept up from her collarbone into her cheeks, and she drew a deep breath.

Her turn had come.

''I see I've gotten through,'' Pat said, rising purposefully from her chair. ''He's over at the other house, I assume?''

Mallory nodded, the high color of outrage still pounding in her cheeks.

Pat collected her coat and scarf from the hall closet and came back into the kitchen. ''I'll spend the night over there, since I can't quite face fighting my way through downtown Seattle tonight. And you, Mrs. McKendrick—you get Nathan on the phone and tell him to get over here, in no uncertain terms!''

Mallory felt some of her determination drain away. Nobody *told* Nathan McKendrick to do anything, and Pat knew it as well as she did. ''But if he's busy—'' she wavered, hating herself all the while. *Busy doing what?* taunted a voice in her mind. *Holding Diane's trembling hand? Soaking in the hot tub?*

Pat pressed her lips together in undisguised annoyance. "Stop with the peasantlike awe, will you, Mallory?" she snapped. "Nathan is a man, not a god. It's high time he turned some of his energy into his marriage, and if you don't tell him that, I will!"

Mallory bit her lower lip, but she was already making her way to the telephone when Pat left the house. Her hands trembled a little as she dialed the number that would connect her with her husband.

One of the band members answered in a lazy drawl. "Yeah?"

"This is Mallory," Mrs. McKendrick said bravely. "I would like to speak to Nathan, please."

"Oh—Nate. Yeah. Well, he's not around right now."

Mallory felt a growing uneasiness quiver in the pit of her stomach. "Where is he?" she asked stiffly.

There was a long, discomforting pause. "Diane was freaking out, so he took her back to Seattle."

Mallory drew a deep breath and let her forehead rest against the kitchen wall. "What do you mean, 'Diane was freaking out'?"

"I don't know—like, she was just losing it, you know? Really coming undone."

"There must have been a reason," Mallory insisted.

Another pause. "Like, I'll have Nate call you when he gets back, all right?"

"Don't bother," Mallory snapped. And then, without pausing to give the matter further thought, she left the telephone receiver dangling, strode into the bedroom and began flinging the few things she'd unpacked back into her suitcases.

Twenty minutes later, with Cinnamon sitting happily in the back seat, Mallory drove her sleek black-and-white Mazda onto the passenger ferry that would carry her back to Seattle.

The huge vessel, capable of transporting both pedestrians and motorists, had always reminded Mallory of an old-time riverboat, with its railed decks and dozens of windows. Normally she loved to stand on the highest deck, watching the magnificent scenery pass and feeding chunks of snack-bar cinnamon rolls to the gulls, but today it was bitterly cold and she didn't even bother to get out of the car and climb the metal stairs leading to the lower deck. She simply sat behind the wheel, Cinnamon patient behind her, and stared beyond the other cars parked in the bowels of the craft to the water ahead.

The snow was still falling, and Mallory watched in aching silence as the huge, intricate flakes, so beautiful and perfect, came down to the salty waters of Puget Sound and were dissolved. The snowflakes, like the love she and Nathan shared, were at once breathtakingly beautiful and temporal.

Mallory lowered her head to the steering wheel, and she didn't lift it again until the great horn sounded, announcing that Seattle was just ahead. When the ferry docked, Mallory collected her scattered emotions and concentrated on the task of driving. Navigating in the storm-plagued city would require all her attention.

Pat had certainly been right about the traffic conditions, and the next half hour was harrowing. Mallory was pale with exhaustion when she finally drew the small car to a halt in front of the expensive apartment complex in the city's heart and climbed from behind the wheel.

The doorman, George Roberts, rushed toward her. "Ms. O'Connor! I thought you were on the island—"

With an effort, Mallory returned the man's warm smile. She saw no need, the way things stood, to correct his use of her name. "Is Mr. McKendrick at home?" she asked, hoping that the vast importance of the matter didn't show in her face.

George shook his head, and wisps of powdery snow flew from the brim of his impeccable visored hat and shimmered on the gold epaulets stitched to the shoulders of his coat. "No, ma'am, he isn't," he answered, stealing an unreadable look at Cinnamon, who was whining to be let out of the car.

Mallory turned her head to take one more look at the busy, storm-shrouded Sound. *Snowflakes on the sea,* she thought, aching inside.

4

Mallory hooked Cinnamon's leash to her collar and flipped the seat forward so that the dog could leap out onto the paved driveway and wriggle in the joy of sudden freedom. "If you would?" she said to George, indicating the car.

George Roberts nodded, smiling. "I'll have it parked for you, Ms. O'Connor. Is there any luggage?"

Mallory was already leading a delighted Cinnamon toward the well-lighted, posh lobby of the building. "There is," she called over one shoulder. "But please don't worry about it now. I'll get it in the morning."

No one inside the building looked askance at Mallory and her canine companion, and no comments were made during the elevator ride either, though there were a surprising number of people crowded inside. Mallory liked to think that they were being kind—pets other than birds or tropical fish were strictly forbidden by general agreement—but she knew the real reason was simply deference to Nathan. After all, he owned the building.

On the top floor, Mallory fumbled with the keys for several seconds, her hands numbed by the cold outside, and then managed to open the double doors leading into the penthouse. She paused in the lighted, marble-floored entryway, her eyes rising to the polished antique grandfather clock opposite the door. It was still very early—what was she going to do with the rest of the evening?

Mallory sighed as Cinnamon whimpered beside her; in her turmoil she'd forgotten how very inconvenient the high-rise apartment building would be for the poor creature, who was used to roaming the island at will. With glum resignation, Mallory locked the penthouse again and pushed the button that would summon one of the two elevators serving the building.

The doorman raised a curious eyebrow when Mallory and Cinnamon stepped out into the snowy night so soon after going in. But he said nothing.

Mallory walked Cinnamon until she could bear the stinging cold no longer, and then went home again. After feeding the dog two cans of liver pâté in the enormous kitchen, Mrs. Nathan McKendrick marched down the hallway to the plush master bedroom and began shedding her clothes.

Looking up at the huge skylight over the bed, at the shifting lace of glistening snow, Mallory felt tears smarting in her eyes. How many times had she and Nathan made love in this bed, with the sky stretched out above them like a beautiful mural? She swallowed hard, tossed back the covers of the oversize round bed and crawled between icy satin sheets. Cinnamon settled companionably at her feet with a canine sigh, her nose resting on her red, shaggy paws, her great weight causing the mattress to slope slightly.

In spite of everything, Mallory laughed. "You lead a tough life, dog," she said, reaching out to switch off the lamp beside the bed. "Sorry we were out of caviar, but such is life."

Cinnamon made a contented sound and went to sleep.

Mallory, however, spent several hellish hours just staring up at the moving patterns of eiderdown snow on the skylight. She'd been wrong to leave the island without a word to anyone; she knew that now and guessed that she'd known it all along.

The thing was, she just hadn't been able to face another night of waiting for Nathan.

So what do you call this? she asked herself ruthlessly. *Aren't you waiting, even now, for him to call or show up? Preferably with some convincing reason for leaving the island with Diane and not even bothering to let you know first?*

Mallory turned restlessly onto her side. Why should she have left word for him? Hadn't he been equally thoughtless?

Her stomach twisted into a painful knot. It was possible that

Nathan wouldn't even know she was gone for hours yet, and that was the hardest thing of all to bear.

She buried her face in the smoothness of her pillow and cried until her throat was raw. Then, fitfully, she slept.

Nathan glanced at the clock on the Porsche's dashboard and grimaced. Damn, it was late.

Diane flung a petulant, sidelong look in his direction as he guided the car down the ferry ramp and into the still-crazy Seattle traffic. Her face was pale and pinched with residual shock, and her hands were clasped, motionless, in her lap.

High drama, Nathan thought bitterly. *God, she should have been an actress.*

"This is all a bad dream," she said in a stricken, whispery voice.

Nathan shifted gears and reminded himself that she'd had a hard night. She'd been so upset by his decision that he'd taken her from the island to Tacoma, where her parents lived, thinking that she needed to be close to someone who cared about her. But her parents had been away, and they'd missed the connecting ferry to Seattle finding that out.

He sighed. "Listen, Diane—I'm sorry you had to hear the news from the guys in the band. I really am—"

Diane drew in an audible breath calculated to inspire guilt and lifted her chin in theatrical acceptance of a cruel fate. "One way or the other, we're all fired. I don't see what it matters that I heard it from them and not you."

Nathan had no answer for that; he concentrated on the road ahead. The traffic lights were mere splotches of red or amber or green, dimly visible in the swirling snow, and the tires of the Porsche weren't gripping the pavement all that well.

"You're doing this for Mallory, aren't you, Nathan?" Diane demanded, after some moments of silence.

Nathan stiffened but didn't look away from the traffic. "Mallory is my wife," he replied flatly.

Diane made a disdainful sound. "Wife! Good Lord, Nathan, you're insane to give up your career for *her!*"

Nathan tossed one scathing look in Diane's direction. "Watch it."

She subsided a little. "Why? Nathan, just tell me why. If she loved you, she—"

"I'm tired, Diane," he broke in, and his tones proved it. "I've got more money than I can spend in a lifetime, and I've done everything I set out to do, musically, at least. Now I intend to straighten out my marriage."

"You have no marriage!" Diane cried in a hoarse, contemptuous whisper. "You and Mallory are a joke!"

Nathan's fingers tightened dangerously on the leather-covered steering wheel, but he maintained control. "Your opinion of my marriage couldn't matter less to me, Diane."

There was still a tinge of hysteria in her tone when she spoke again. "So you're doing the farewell concert here, and that's it? No television specials, no tours, no records?"

"I'll record, and I suppose I'll write songs, too. But I'm through chasing fans all over the world."

"How do you plan to make records without a band?" Diane demanded, her voice rising.

Nathan sighed. "If the guys are available, we'll work together." He looked again at Diane and saw exactly what he'd feared he would—hope. Why couldn't she just find another job and let the thing drop? She was a gifted press agent, and she wouldn't be out of work long. Although Nathan had always disliked her on a personal basis, her recommendation would be a good one.

"Then I could keep doing your press work—"

"No."

Diane seethed in electric silence as Nathan guided the car up a slight hill into the residential section where her sister lived. Because Diane's work kept her in Los Angeles most of the time, she didn't need a permanent place in Seattle.

When he drew the Porsche to a stop in front of her building, he faced her. "Good night, Diane. And I'm sorry."

Diane's lower lip trembled, and she tossed her magnificent

head of hair in a kind of broken defiance. The motion filled the chilly interior of the car with the flowery, somewhat cloying scent of her perfume. "Not half as sorry as you're going to be, Nathan McKendrick," she vowed.

Nathan rested his head against the back of the car seat, sighed and glowered up at the leather upholstery in the roof. "What is that supposed to mean, pray tell?"

There was a note of relished power in her tone. "I built you up, Nathan. I can tear you down."

"How melodramatic," he retorted in sardonic tones. "For all the world like a scorned lover."

Diane wrenched open the car door and scrambled out to stand, trembling, on the snowy sidewalk. Her eyes glittered, scalding Nathan in blue fire. "How long do you think that naive little wife of yours will last under a full-scale press attack, darling?"

An explosive rage consumed Nathan's spirit, and his jaw tightened until it ached. Still, he managed to keep his hands on the steering wheel and his voice even. "If you do anything to hurt Mallory, Diane—*anything*—you'll spend the rest of your shallow little life regretting it."

Diane smiled viciously. "Or savoring it. Good night, handsome."

Wondering why he hadn't fired Diane years ago, Nathan watched until she had disappeared inside her sister's apartment building. Then another glance at the dashboard clock made him groan. Why the hell hadn't he called Mallory before leaving the island? God knew what she was thinking by now.

Turning the Porsche back toward the waterfront in a wide, deft sweep, he swore under his breath. He could stop and call now, however after-the-fact the gesture might be. But Mallory was probably asleep. No, he would just get back to the island as soon as he could and they would talk in the morning.

Seething, Diane Vincent unlocked her sister's front door and stormed into the apartment, not even bothering to turn on a light. In the room Claire kept just for her, she flung down her purse, wrenched off her coat and angrily punched out a familiar number on the telephone beside the bed.

"I know it's late!" she seethed, when the recipient of her call grumbled about the time. "Did you find someone?"

The affirmative answer made Diane smile. Without even saying goodbye, she hung up.

Cinnamon awakened Mallory early the next morning, bounding up and down the length of the big bed and occasionally plunging an icy nose into her mistress's face.

Grumbling, Mallory crawled out of bed and stumbled into the bathroom. It was as large as the living room in the island house with its garden tub, hanging plants, cushioned chairs and gleaming counters.

After a quick shower, Mallory dressed in gray wool slacks, a red turtleneck sweater and boots. Two more cans of pâté were sacrificed to Cinnamon's hearty appetite, and then it was time for another walk.

The telephone on the hallway table rang as they were going out, but Mallory didn't answer. In fact, she didn't even look back. But a half an hour later, with Cinnamon's morning walk accomplished, Mallory found herself at loose ends. Still shivering from the bite of the winter wind, she choked down one slice of whole wheat toast and a cup of tea.

After that, she went into the study, a spacious room equipped with two glass desks that faced each other, and flipped on the television set. "Tender Days, Savage Nights" was on, and she watched herself steal a diamond bracelet and the heroine's husband, all in the space of an hour.

And then Cinnamon was hungry again. She stood by, watching, as the beast happily consumed two cans of imported lobster.

"This will never do, you know," she informed the Setter as she poured scalding water over the dish the dog had eaten from and placed it inside the dishwasher. "So don't expect gourmet fare. From here on out, it's good old canned dog food, all the way."

Cinnamon whimpered and tilted her beautiful red-gold head to one side, as if to protest this projected change in the menu.

Mallory reached down to pet the dog and sighed. She'd kept all thoughts of Nathan carefully at bay, but now they were suddenly streaming into her mind and heart like some intangible river.

She wandered into the mammoth living room, with its massive ivory fireplace and thick silver-gray carpeting. Snow drifted past the slightly rounded floor-to-ceiling windows overlooking Seattle's beleaguered downtown area and the waterfront.

Her thoughts spanned the angry waters to the small island, invisible in the fury of the day. Surely Nathan was there, angry but safe—

The shrill jingle of the telephone made Mallory start. She steeled herself. This time, she would have to answer it.

The walk to the telephone table beside Nathan's favorite chair seemed inordinately long.

"Hello?" she ventured, turning the cord nervously in her fingers.

"Hi, babe," Brad Ranner greeted her, his voice full of pleased surprise. "How long have you been back in the big city?"

Mallory swallowed, sank onto the sturdy suede-upholstered arm of Nathan's chair. "Since last night. Why?"

"Mallory, haven't you heard? There isn't any phone service to the island, and the ferries aren't running, either. I called on the off chance that you might have come back to town earlier than you planned."

Mallory felt a swift stab of alarm. Except during labor strikes, the ferries *always* ran.

Brad seemed to sense her agitation. "Relax," he said. "You're back in civilization yourself. That's what counts."

His insensitive comments taxed Mallory's strained patience. "Brad, I have a number of friends on that island, and I think Nathan is there, too. What if someone is sick or—or—"

Brad's tone was soothing. "Honey, take it easy. The Coast Guard will check things out. You know that."

Mallory did know, and she was comforted. Besides, the islanders were independent sorts, and they would look after one another. "How are things on the set?" she asked in order to change the subject.

"Everybody is excited. Mall, I have *great* news. That's one of the reasons I called. I'd like to tell you in person, though. Is it all right if I brave the treacherous roadways and drop in?"

Mallory closed her eyes for a moment, summoning up her courage. "Brad, about the show—I—"

"We'll talk when I get there," Brad broke in cheerfully. And then, before she could say a word in response, he hung up.

Will we ever, Mallory thought, one hand still resting on the telephone receiver. *And you're not going to like my end of the conversation at all.*

Two minutes later, Mallory was in the bathroom, applying makeup. No sense in greeting Brad with her wan, tired face and having to endure the inevitable you-haven't-been-taking-care-of-yourself lecture.

The cosmetics transformed Mallory from a very pretty woman to a beauty, but they could do nothing to mask the weariness in the depths of her green eyes. In hopes of drawing attention away from them, she brushed her lustrous dark taffy hair and pinned it up into a loose Gibson girl.

Once again, she felt pain and remorse; Nathan loved her hair in that particular style.

Where was he now? Stranded on the island, with no idea where his wife had gone? Lying in some love-rumpled bed with Diane Vincent? Mallory brought herself up short. She had enough trouble without borrowing more.

She went back into the bedroom and sat down on the edge of the neatly made bed, hurriedly dialing the number of the house at Angel Cove. Maybe Brad had been wrong about the telephone service being out. But an operator broke in to say that emergency line repairs were being made.

So Brad had been right, after all. Frustrated, Mallory wandered back to the living room and distractedly petted a whimpering

Cinnamon. She had wanted so badly to reach Nathan, to hear his voice, to apologize. Now, it might be hours, or even days, before she reached him.

Mallory went to the windows and, for the first time in her life, cursed the snow.

Cinnamon made a low, whining sound in her throat, and then barked uncertainly. A moment later, Mallory heard the opening and closing of the front doors. She turned, frowning, from the windows, expecting to see the woman who came in to clean twice a week.

Instead, she was confronted with a scowling, disheveled, un-shaven Nathan. His dark eyes swept over her, leaving an aching trail wherever they touched.

"I chartered a boat," he growled, neatly dispensing with the first question that rose in Mallory's mind. "What are you doing here?"

Mallory's throat closed and, for a moment, her mind went blank and she honestly didn't know what she was doing there. "I—I—" she stammered.

Nathan slid out of his suede jacket and ran one hand through his rumpled hair. "Damn it, Mallory, what is going on with you? Everybody on the island is out of their mind with worry—"

Suddenly, Mallory found her voice. Hot color pounded in her cheeks. "Was that before Diane's latest crisis or after?" she snapped.

Some of the fierce anger drained from Nathan's lean, towering frame, and he sank into a chair. "Is that why you did the dis-appearing number, Mallory? Because of Diane?"

His tone was so reasonable that Mallory felt ashamed of her outburst. She dared not approach him, but she did try to match his decorum with her own. "Yes," she admitted. "I called y-your house—at the Cove. One of the guys said you'd taken Diane back to Seattle. I—I know I was hasty, but—"

Nathan thrust himself out of his chair and made a hoarse, contemptuous sound in his throat. "Spare me, Mallory. I'm tired and mad as hell and I really don't think this is a good time to discuss your paranoia about Diane.''

Mallory was instantly furious. Her *paranoia!* How dare he shift all the blame to her, when none of this would have happened if he hadn't been so quick to come to Diane's aid! ''Damn you,'' she swore. ''Nathan McKendrick—''

But he was striding around her, on his way toward the bedroom. By the time she recovered enough composure to storm in after him, he was in the shower.

Outraged, Mallory pounded at the thick, etched-glass doors with both fists. Through the barrier, she could see the shifting blur of his tanned flesh.

''Nathan!'' she yelled, in anger and in pain.

Suddenly, the shower doors slid open and, with a lightning-quick motion of his hand, Nathan pulled Mallory under the pounding, steaming spray. Water plastered his ebony hair to his face and dripped, in little rivulets, down over his muscular, darkly matted chest. Mallory dared look no farther.

''You wanted to talk,'' he shouted over the roar of the shower. ''So talk!''

Mallory's makeup was smeared, and her hair clung to her neck. Her sweater, slacks and boots were all drenched. She threw back her head and shrieked in primitive, unadulterated fury.

Gently, Nathan thrust her backward against the inside wall of the shower and out of the spray of water. His hand caught under her chin and lifted. ''So I *can* make you feel something, lady— even if it is rage.''

Mallory stared up at him, stunned by his words, by the situation, by the alarming proximity of his naked, beautifully sculptured frame. Her throat worked painfully, but she could say nothing.

Nathan bent his head to kiss her, and the sea-breeze scent of his wet hair caught at her heart. His lips moved gently on hers, at first, and then with undeniable demand. She trembled as his tongue laid first claim to total possession. ''Mallory,'' he rasped, when the devastating kiss broke at last. ''I want you.''

Mallory stiffened and thrust him angrily away, even though a desire equal to his was raging inside her. She turned, let her forehead rest against the water-speckled tiles lining the inside of the shower stall. "Don't, Nathan. Don't touch me—don't talk—"

But his hands were hard on her shoulders as he turned her back to face him. "Listen to me, Mallory. We've played this game long enough. I didn't spend the night rolling around in Diane Vincent's bed!"

Mallory arched one eyebrow and looked up at him in silence.

His muscular shoulders moved in a defeated sigh. "I was wrong not to call you and let you know what was going on, and I'm sorry."

Mallory believed him. She looked down at her soaked clothes and laughed, at herself, at Nathan, at the ludicrous insanity of the situation.

And he kissed her again.

The ancient heat began to build in Mallory's slender body, just as she knew it was building in Nathan's powerful one. She trembled as he removed her sodden garments, her boots, the few pins that had held her hair in place, and discarded them in the separate world beyond the shower doors.

Nathan surveyed her waiting body for a long moment, missing nothing—not the full sweetness of her firm breasts, the narrow tapering of her waist, the trim but rounded lines of her hips and thighs. Making a sound low in his throat that must have dated back to the beginning of time, he reached out for her again.

His tongue traced the pink hollow of her ear, flicked briefly at her lobe. Mallory shuddered with reflexive pleasure as he nibbled at the softness of her neck and kissed the tender hollow of her throat. She arched her back and cried out when the warmth of his mouth strayed over the rounded tip of her breast and then claimed the waiting nipple. With one hand, he cupped the breast he was consuming, with the other, he sought the very core of her womanhood. When he knelt, Mallory entwined both her hands in the thick darkness of his hair to keep herself from soaring away on the crest of her own fiercely undeniable need.

Her release was so savage in its force that it nearly convulsed her.

She was in a spell as Nathan turned off the spray of the shower, as they dried each other with soft, thirsty towels, as her husband lifted her into his arms and carried her into the adjoining room to the bed, where the final and most intimate sharing would take place.

They lay facing each other, naked and still warm from the shower, and Nathan groaned as Mallory circled one masculine nipple with a mischievous tongue. She worked her own magic, loving him fully, savoring the responses she stirred in him.

When the outer boundaries of ecstasy had been reached, she lay back to await his claiming. A low moan escaped her as he parted her legs with one knee and poised above her, and she saw the reluctance in his eyes, along with a fathomless need.

"Mallory, if you don't feel—"

She shook her head, almost feverishly, and clasped his taut buttocks in her hand, urging him to her. She gasped with delight as their two bodies became one.

Nathan's control was awesome, his entry and withdrawal calculated to prolong the sweet misery for them both.

When she could bear the waiting and the needing no longer, Mallory lifted herself to him, prevented his retreat with strong, desperate hands. The steady rhythm of her hips caused him to plead with her in a soft, ragged voice.

Mallory's passion flared within her like fire, compelling her on to a fulfillment she couldn't have escaped even if she'd wanted to. In one glimmering moment, shattering release was upon them, flinging them as one beyond the charted regions and into a world of streaming silver comets and crimson suns. They drifted downward slowly, linked spiritually as well as physically among the fragments, their mingled cries of triumph echoing around them like music.

The insistent buzz of the doorbell signaled their return to the real world.

Nathan groaned, and Mallory laughed, soft and pliant beneath him, smoothing his damp hair with a tender hand. "Our public," she said.

Nathan swore, stood up and wrenched on a hooded maroon velour robe. "I'm coming!" he shouted angrily, and Mallory dissolved in a fresh spate of giggles.

If Brad Ranner had any idea what he'd interrupted, he did an admirable job of hiding the knowledge. When Mallory and Nathan emerged from the bedroom, one at a time and as subtly as possible, he made no comment. Of course, he couldn't have helped noticing that Nathan, now clad in jeans and a red T-shirt, had answered the door in a bathrobe.

His shrewd blue eyes did catch, just momentarily, the flush in Mallory's cheeks, before moving on to politely assess the silken lines of her pink-and-gold caftan.

Brad was a short, stocky man, and the uninitiated usually took him for a serious young accountant or a budding corporate lawyer. In truth, he was a dynamic and innovative entrepreneur, noted for his skill, insight and artistry.

"Mallory," he began without preamble, raising his glass in a dashing toast, "we're about to talk business, you and I. *Big* business."

Nathan folded his arms and raked the unflappable Brad with a scorching look. Then he nodded curtly in Mallory's direction, as though they hadn't soared in each other's arms only minutes before, and muttered, "This is obviously private. Later."

The crisp words and his immediate departure for the study made Mallory blush slightly. She was still floating in the warm glow of Nathan's lovemaking, though it appeared that her husband had already forgotten their brief, fiery union. Besides, she'd wanted him to hear the things she meant to say to Brad.

Brad pretended an almost clinical interest in his drink. There was no love lost between the two men, but they usually managed a sort of cold civility. "If you'd told me Mr. Superstar was here," he said softly, "I would have stayed away."

Mallory lifted her chin and offered no reply. When Brad offered, with a gesture, to make a drink for her, she nodded.

There was a short stiff silence, broken only by the clink of crystal, as Brad poured Mallory's customary white wine. Cinnamon, fickle to the end, had left the room with Nathan.

Mallory sighed as Brad handed her her drink and sat down on the sofa beside her. "So what's the big news?" she asked without any real interest, wondering how he was going to take her announcement that she had no intention of renewing her contract with the show.

Brad grinned and took a slow sip from his whiskey. "Cable," he said.

Mallory frowned. "Cable?"

"The show is being picked up by a cable network, Mallory, and they're opening with a two-hour movie. It will mean more money and extra exposure."

Mallory tensed, staring at her producer. "Exposure is certainly the applicable word. Brad, have you *seen* those cable soaps? Everybody is naked—"

Brad's eyes moved almost imperceptibly to Mallory's fine bust line, and then back to her face. "You don't have anything to worry about on that score," he said. "If you'll pardon the expression, love, you'd stack up against the best of them."

Mallory shot to her feet, and some of her wine sloshed over the rim of her glass and fell onto the rug. "My God, Brad—I can't believe you're asking me—do you really mean—I *wouldn't*—"

As usual, Brad was totally unruffled, absorbing her outburst without evident effort. "Calm down, Mall. It's true that cable soaps have nude scenes, but they also have some really challenging scripts. This is your chance to grow as an actress—"

"*No.*"

"Why not?" Brad asked reasonably, raising one eyebrow. "Think of it as an art form."

Mallory was pacing now, her glass clasped in both hands. "Art form! Bull chips, Brad. My God, Nathan would—"

Brad set his drink aside and folded his hands casually around one knee. "There we have it, don't we, Mallory? Nathan. Couldn't Mr. Macho handle the competition?"

Mallory stopped her pacing, too stunned to move. She gaped at Brad, who was watching her implacably, and then snapped. "This is *my* body we're talking about, Brad. Don't try to shift the blame on to Nathan. *I'm* the one who doesn't want to flash for America!"

Brad sat back, sighing a little. From his manner, they might have been discussing some mundane, everyday matter. "Bull," he said pleasantly. "You're afraid of what Nathan will say—or do."

Mallory's heart was pounding with anger, just as it had pounded with passion such a short time before, and her breath burned in her lungs. "Damn it, Brad, I wouldn't do what you're asking even if I were single!"

Brad stood up, walked to the teakwood bar, and set the drink he had just reclaimed down with a thump. When he turned to face Mallory again, his eyes were snapping, even though his voice was low and evenly modulated. "Mallory, we are talking about big, *big* money here—millions."

"I don't care."

"Damn it, I do!" Brad retorted. "If we have to recast your part, production will be delayed."

"Then production will be delayed!"

"Mallory—"

"No. Damn it, Brad, *no*. I wasn't planning to renew my contract as it was—"

Brad swore roundly. Then, without another word, he grabbed his overcoat and stormed out of the penthouse, slamming the doors behind him.

Having been wrenched, in just one morning, from one emotional extreme to the other, Mallory folded. She sank into Nathan's chair, set her drink on the table beside it and wept softly into both hands.

She caught Nathan's clean, distinctive scent just as he drew her up out of the chair and into his arms.

"What did that bastard say to you?" he wanted to know, but his tones were infinitely gentle.

Mallory could only shake her head and cry harder.

"Okay," Nathan conceded softly, his hand warm and strong in her hair, his lips brushing her temple. "We'll talk about it later. But if I see that guy again, he may have to order new knees."

Despite everything, Mallory giggled into the fragrant warmth of Nathan's red T-shirt.

Her husband caught one hand under her chin and tenderly urged her to look up at him. Briskly, he kissed the tip of her nose. "I believe we were conducting a rather interesting reunion before we were so rudely interrupted."

Sniffling and smiling through her tears and already warming to the hard, insistent nearness of this man she loved so fully, Mallory nodded.

Nathan laughed softly. "I'll be with you in a minute—just let me make a sign for the front door."

Mallory lay in bed, looking up at the black velvet expanse of the skylight. The snow was melting, leaving shimmering beads of water in its place. Beside her, warm and solid, Nathan slept the sleep of the exhausted. Tenderness welled up inside Mallory as she turned to look at him, to gently trace the outline of his strong jaw, his arrogant chin, his neck. He stirred but did not awaken.

Mallory smiled. Nothing would disturb his desperately needed sleep—nothing. If need be, she would have fought tigers to see to that.

Gently she kissed the cleft in his chin. "I love you, Nathan McKendrick," she said softly. Then, snuggled close to him, she slept.

* * *

The bright warmth of undiluted sunshine awakened Mallory the next morning, aided by the cold, wet nuzzling of Cinnamon's nose in her face. The dog whimpered as Mallory sat up, wriggled impatiently as she crept out of bed without awakening Nathan.

"Shh," she ordered, raising an index finger to her lips. "I know you need to go outside."

Cinnamon whined as Mallory scrambled into her clothes, again wishing that she'd left the dog behind on the island. Keeping the poor creature in a penthouse was inexcusable.

In the outer hallway as Mallory and Cinnamon waited for an elevator, Mallory made up her mind to correct the mistake that very day. Provided the ferries were running again, she would take the dog home.

Outside, the glaring brightness of the day greeted them, as did the inevitable clamor of a big city. Horns honked, boat whistles whined and cars rushed helter-skelter through the glistening slush on the roads.

Cinnamon was terrified.

In a grocery store some blocks away, Mallory bought two cans of dog food, having left Cinnamon to wait bravely on the sidewalk.

Because the weather was so beautiful and Cinnamon seemed calmer, Mallory decided not to go directly back to the penthouse. Even though Nathan would be there, the blue and gold day was simply too appealing to be abandoned so quickly.

They walked, woman and dog, back toward the waterfront. On Pike Street, where the road was paved with worn red bricks and merchants offered every sort of fish, fresh vegetable and pastry from open stalls, they bought bagels and cream cheese.

On the Sound, a passenger ferry sounded its horn, as if to remind all and sundry that no storm could stay it for long.

Mallory drew a deep, salt-scented breath. "We'll go home today," she said, as much to herself as to Cinnamon. "All of us."

Cinnamon yipped, as if in celebration, and then strained at her leash as a tame sea gull ventured too near, waddling over the brick street in search of scraps. Mallory was restraining the dog when she felt a hand come to rest on the sleeve of her Windbreaker.

She turned, smiling, expecting a friend or someone who had been following her misadventures on the soap. Instead, she met the snapping azure gaze of Diane Vincent.

After a moment, Diane allowed her eyes to sweep contemptuously to the dog, who still wanted to investigate the intrepid sea gull foraging nearby. "Hello," she said, her voice trimmed in sweet malice. "Out walking your—dog?"

"Obviously," Mallory replied.

Diane smiled acidly. She did look splendid, though, in her casual tweed blazer, yellow silk blouse fetchingly open at the throat and tailored designer jeans. "Let's have coffee, Mallory. How long has it been since we really talked, you and I?"

Not long enough. Mallory managed a stiff smile, though she couldn't have said why she made the effort. "I really don't have time, Diane." She patted the shopping bag resting in the curve of one arm, still holding Cinnamon's taut leash in the other hand. "When Nathan wakes up, he's going to be hungry, and—"

Diane tossed her head, so that the sun caught in her magnificent hair. "He's still sleeping—well, after last night, that figures."

Mallory visualized headlines in her mind. SOAP OPERA VILLAINESS MURDERS REAL-LIFE RIVAL....

"Diane," she said at length, and with commendable control, "if you've got something to say about last night, why don't you just say it?"

Nathan's beautiful press agent shrugged, and a hint of a malicious smile curved her lips and then shifted to her eyes. "We'll get together another time, Mallory," she said. "Give my regards to Nathan."

With that, the woman turned and walked away, leaving Mallory to stare after her, all her questions unanswered.

5

When Cinnamon began to tug anxiously at her leash, probably bored with the sea gull and ready for breakfast, Mallory, stunned, snapped out of her mood and started off in the direction of the apartment complex. When she reached the building, her earlier high spirits still tarnished by the encounter with Diane, Mallory found that the lobby was uncommonly crowded.

"What's going on, George?" she asked of the harried doorman, who was scowling at the bevy of reporters and photographers milling about.

George's suspicious glance turned to one of worried recognition. "Ms. O'Connor—they'll recognize you—" Before she could find out more, Mallory was being shuffled into the building manager's cluttered office, out of view, Cinnamon following cheerfully behind.

Inside, Mallory frowned and set her shopping bag down on the desk usually occupied by the woman Nathan retained to look after the building. "Where's Marge? George, what in the world—?"

"They're after Mr. McKendrick, from what I gather," George confided, looking very much like a beleaguered general barely able to stave off attack. "Marge is upstairs, talking to Mr. McKendrick."

Annoyed, Mallory reached for the telephone on Marge's desk and punched out the number for the penthouse. Oddly, it was Marge who answered. "Yes?" she demanded coldly.

"Marge, this is Mallory—I'm downstairs. Will you put Nathan on, please?"

"Are you in my office?" Marge blurted after a sharp intake of breath. "For God's sake, stay there—" For a moment, the middle-aged woman's voice sounded farther away as she spoke to someone else. "Yes, she's here—I don't think so—"

A moment later, Nathan was on the line, and the strange timbre of his voice frightened Mallory. "Mallory, listen to me. I want you to stay inside that office until I come for you. All right?"

Something shivered in the pit of Mallory's stomach. "Nathan, what's happening? There are reporters and—"

He broke in brusquely. "I'll explain it all in a few minutes, Mallory—*just don't leave that office.*"

"But—"

"Mallory."

"Nathan, you've got to tell me—"

"Do I have your promise or not?"

Even more alarmed, Mallory sighed in frustration. "All right, damn it, I promise."

"Good," Nathan snapped, and then the line went dead.

Just then, the office door burst open, and an avid-looking man was standing there, his small eyes raking over Mallory as though she were some curious museum piece, meant to be thoroughly examined. "Did you know about the girl, Mrs. McKendrick?" he blurted out, as an angry George lumbered toward him. "Has your husband admitted to an affair with her?"

Mallory could only stare at the man, and the office spun around her as George pushed the man out and quickly locked the door. The doorman was grumbling as he turned to face the woman he had so wanted to protect.

Apparently alarmed by the sight of her, he sputtered, "Now, Mrs. McKendrick—Ms. O'Connor—don't pay any mind to that scum! He's probably with one of those papers they sell in the supermarket—"

Mallory couldn't answer; her head was full of echoes. *Did you know about the girl, Mrs. McKendrick? Has your husband admitted to an affair with her?*

George caught her arms, thrust her gently into the chair behind Marge's desk and brought her a plastic cup brimming with hot, strong coffee. Five minutes passed, ten. Mallory managed the occasional sip of coffee, but only because George looked so worried. The stuff was like bile in her mouth.

Suddenly, she heard an unmistakable shout of annoyance in the area outside the office, followed by a terse invective that the reporters would probably choose not to print. George opened the door to admit a livid Nathan.

"Will you get rid of those creeps?" snapped Mallory's husband, addressing the doorman.

"I'll try," George promised somewhat uncertainly, making a hasty exit.

Nathan swept Mallory's trembling frame with dark, furious eyes, and then turned to lock the door again. Her hand shaking, she set aside what was left of her coffee and braced herself.

After a rather drawn-out battle with a very simple lock, Nathan turned to face his wife. "Are you all right?"

Mallory could manage nothing more than a nod. If he didn't explain what was happening, and fast, she would explode in a fit of shrieking hysteria.

Pale beneath his tan, Nathan took a newspaper Mallory hadn't noticed before from under his arm and thrust it at her. Despite what the reporter had said to her, cold, sickening shock turned her stomach as she read the headline. SINGER NATHAN McKENDRICK NAMED IN PATERNITY SUIT.

Mallory closed her eyes and swallowed the burning sickness that scalded in her throat. *These things happen all the time,* one part of her mind argued calmly. *It's gossip, it's trash—*

"Mallory." Nathan's voice broke through the fog of pain and betrayal that surrounded her. *This is no cheap scandal sheet. It's an important newspaper—*

"Mallory!"

She felt the angry, frightened strength of Nathan's hands as he grasped her shoulders, and opened her eyes to see the torment in his face. "Who is she?" she whispered.

Nathan flinched as though she'd struck him, and drew back. Head down, he thrust his hands into the pockets of his gray flannel slacks, and an awesome tension tightened the muscles in his shoulders. "I don't know."

"What do you mean you don't know?" Mallory cried out, wounded. Then, remembering the reporters who were no doubt still lurking outside, anxious to grasp any tidbit, she lowered her voice. "Nathan, damn you, start talking!"

As if insulted, he thrust the newspaper at her. "Read it for yourself," he snarled. "And then you'll know as much about it as I do!"

Hoping that she could trust her hands, Mallory unfolded the newspaper, winced inwardly as she read the headline again, and then turned her attention to the picture and article beneath it. The photograph showed Nathan standing in a crowd of delighted girls, clad in the flowing silk shirt and fitted trousers he customarily wore on stage. His arm curved easily around the waist of one particularly voluptuous young lady, and he was smiling.

Mallory forced herself to read the words printed below. *Eighteen-year-old Renee Parker, of Eagle Falls, Washington, has named singer Nathan McKendrick in a paternity suit, claiming that she and McKendrick have been intimately involved on a number of occasions. This alliance, says the attractive young waitress, has resulted in the conception of...*

Mallory could read no further. A soft cry of outraged pain echoed in the room, and she realized that it was her own.

"Read the rest of it," Nathan ordered, his voice a taut, anguished rasp, his arms folded across his chest.

She shook her head. "No—no, I can't."

"It ends with, 'Mr. McKendrick was unavailable for comment, according to his press agent, Diane Vincent.' Mallory, does that tell you anything?"

The tumult outside the office seemed to be building to a crescendo, rather than waning. Apparently, George had been unsuccessful in his efforts to get rid of the press.

"Eighteen," Mallory whispered, as though Nathan hadn't spoken. "Oh, my God, Nathan, she's only. *eighteen.*"

Nathan's magnificent features were flushed with outraged

color, and a vein at the base of his throat pulsed ominously. "God in heaven, Mallory, you don't seriously think—"

Before he could finish, there was an imperious knocking at the door, and Pat's voice rang out over the clamor in the lobby. "Nathan—Mallory! Let me in!"

After one scathing glance at Mallory, Nathan unlocked the door, easily this time, to admit his sister.

She spared a sympathetic look for her brother and then turned her attention to a stricken Mallory. "I see this morning's fast-breaking news story didn't go over well. Nate, I've talked to the press. They'll let Mallory pass if you'll answer some of their questions. If you don't, they're prepared to hang around until Nixon gets reelected."

Nathan's dark eyes, charged with fury only a moment before, were dull with pain as they linked again with Mallory's. "Tell them they have a deal," he said, in a voice his wife hardly recognized. "Just get Mallory out of here."

Five minutes later, Mallory and a very confused Cinnamon were in the safe confines of Pat's bright yellow Mustang, on their way to her condominium overlooking Lake Washington.

Pat looked pale as she navigated the slushy streets, and her knuckles were white where they gripped the steering wheel. "You know, I hope," she ventured, after they'd traveled some distance, "that that newspaper article is libelous?"

Libel. Mallory might have laughed if she hadn't felt as though everything within her was crumbling. "That's no gossip rag, Pat," she said brokenly. "It's a responsible, highly respected newspaper."

Pat said a very unladylike word. "You innocent. Are you telling me that you *bought* that garbage?"

"I don't know," Mallory admitted honestly, her eyes fixed on the blurred houses and businesses moving past the car window. And it was true—at that moment, she couldn't have said whether she believed Nathan to be innocent or guilty. She was still in shock.

There was a long, painful silence. Pat finally broke it with an impatient, "Do you want to go to the island, Mallory? To Trish or Kate? I could take you there right now—"

Mallory shook her head quickly. The island might have offered sanctuary during any other crisis, but, for the moment, it held no appeal at all. She wouldn't be able to think clearly there or in any other place she'd lived with Nathan. "You could do me one favor, though," she said tentatively, and the softening in Pat's face was comforting.

"What's that?"

Mallory reached back and patted the fitful dog filling the car's back seat. "Take Cinnamon back to the island. Trish will look after her."

"Are you sure you'll be okay—while I'm gone, I mean? Nathan might be busy for a while."

"I need some time alone," she said, and knew that her eyes were imploring Pat. "C-could you keep Nathan away f-for a few days?"

Pat sighed as she turned into the driveway of her condo. "I'll try, Mallory. But he knows where you are, and he's going to be very anxious to settle this."

Glumly, Mallory nodded. "I know, but I don't want to talk to him now. I've got to think—"

"You can't run away from this, Mallory," Pat said, not unkindly as she turned off the car's engine and pulled the keys from the ignition. "Rotten as it is, it's real, and avoiding your husband won't make it go away."

"Three days," Mallory pleaded. "Please—just three days."

Pat shrugged, but her blue eyes were filled with worry and reluctance. "All right, Mall—I'll plead your case. Just remember that I can't promise he won't come storming over here to have it out with you."

Half an hour later, Mallory had her wish—temporarily, anyway. She was alone in Pat's airy, sun-brightened condo, without even Cinnamon to disturb her churning thoughts.

She paced the sumptuously carpeted living room for some minutes after Pat's departure, looking blindly out at the view of

Lake Washington. Despite the miserable weather of the past few days, or perhaps because of it, the azure water was dotted with the colorful sails of several sleek pleasure boats.

Mallory was honestly surprised to discover that there were tears sliding down her face. Angry with herself, she brushed them away and approached the telephone. After a short, awkward conversation with a discerning Trish—surely the newspaper article was common knowledge on the island, too, by now—she replaced the receiver and wandered to the sofa. Bless her, Trish had asked no questions, probably sensing that Mallory couldn't bear to talk about the impending lawsuit just yet, and she'd promised to look after Cinnamon.

The telephone rang shrilly, startling Mallory, and she debated whether to answer it or ignore it. She didn't want to talk to Nathan yet, and she certainly didn't want to speak with any reporters, but this was Pat's telephone and it was most likely that the call was unrelated to Mallory's personal problems.

She answered with a spiritless, one-word greeting, and nearly hung up when she heard Nathan's voice.

"Babe, are you all right?"

Oh, I'm wonderful. You've made some groupie pregnant and she's telling the world and who could ask for anything more? "I'm fine," she lied. "How about you?"

He made an irritated, raspy sound. "I don't need the light repartee right now, sweetheart," he replied tartly. "I know what you're thinking."

"Then you know I need time, Nathan. Time and space."

"I'm not the father of that girl's baby, Mallory."

Tears were coursing down Mallory's face again, and she was glad of only one thing in the world—that Nathan couldn't see her crying. She wanted so desperately to believe him, but she was afraid to; it would be too shattering to find out later that he'd lied. "D-don't, Nathan—not now. I'm so tired and so confused—"

His sigh was a broken, despondent sound. "All right. All

right—just don't forget that I love you, Mallory, and that I don't sell out people who trust me.''

Mallory nodded, realizing that he couldn't see her. "I'll call you in a few days, Nathan—I promise."

"Is there anything you need?"

She thought for a moment—it was so difficult to accomplish even the simplest mental processes with her mind in such a turmoil. "My car. Could you have George bring my car?"

"Sure," he said, and Mallory was grateful that he didn't offer to deliver it himself. "Take care, pumpkin."

"I will," Mallory whispered, and her hand shook as she replaced the telephone receiver.

Twenty minutes later, George delivered Mallory's Mazda, handed over the keys without comment and left again in a taxi. Mallory made her way to Pat's guest bath, took a shower and appropriated a cozy-looking chenille bathrobe from her sister-in-law's bedroom closet.

She was curled up on the living room sofa again, trying to read, when Pat returned. With typical thoughtfulness, she'd stopped at the penthouse for a suitcase full of Mallory's clothes.

"Did you hear from Nathan?" she asked without preamble, setting the suitcase down at Mallory's feet.

Mallory nodded, but was, for the moment, speechless. Why in hell did she feel so guilty, when it was Nathan who had stirred up an ugly scandal, Nathan who had been the betrayer? Or had he? She saw an angry defense of him brewing in Pat's dark blue eyes.

"He was in pretty bad shape when I left him a few minutes ago, Mall."

Mallory felt a swift and searing fury flash through her battered spirit, but the emotion was tempered with self-doubt. Suppose Renee Parker's paternity charge was trumped up, as so many such cases involving celebrities were? Suppose Nathan was as innocent a victim as Mallory herself?

"Be more specific, Pat. 'Pretty bad shape' is a broad phrase."

Pat pulled off her coat in angry motions and tossed it aside.

Then she sank into a chair facing Mallory's and glared at her sister-in-law. "Will 'dead drunk' do? Damn it, Mallory, you're putting the man through hell for something he didn't do!" Sudden tears brimmed up in the blue eyes and then spilled over. "He's my brother and I love him and I can't stand what this is doing to him!"

Mallory shivered. Nathan, drunk? She'd never seen him intoxicated even once, in all the time that they'd been married, and she couldn't begin to imagine how he would look or sound in such a state. "Pat," she asserted, "you're not being fair! I'm not trying to hurt Nathan—"

Quickly, Pat reached out, caught Mallory's hand in her own. "I know, Mall—I know. It's just that—well—"

"I understand. A-are you sure he was drunk?" In her mind, Mallory was remembering the day she and Nathan had talked about their Christmas apart from each other, and he'd said, *"I drank a lot."*

A rueful, sniffly giggle escaped Pat. "He was on his lips, Mallory."

"Was he alone?"

Instantly, Pat was on the defensive again. "Did you think he'd send for Renee Parker, Mallory? Of course he's alone!"

"He shouldn't be."

Hope gleamed in Pat's misty eyes. "You'll go to him, then?"

Mallory shook her head. "I can't, Pat—not yet. But he shouldn't be by himself. Alex Demming is his best friend—I'll call him."

"Forget it," Pat said sharply, disappointment clear in her voice. "I'll ask Roger to go over there."

Mallory looked down at her hands, clasped painfully in her lap, startlingly white against the deep blue of the borrowed chenille robe, and wondered if she was being selfish in avoiding Nathan now when he obviously needed her. She did her best not to hear Pat's tearful conversation with her boyfriend and felt deep gratitude when Nathan's sister informed her, after hanging up the phone, that Roger was on his way to the penthouse.

It was a long night. Mallory soon gave up on the idea of sleep and got out of bed to pace the guest room, torn between the fact that she loved Nathan McKendrick with all her heart and soul, no matter what he might have done, and the counterpoint: her own pride.

No matter how deeply she loved that impossible, arrogant, wonderful man, she would never live with him again if he'd betrayed her. There would be no trust, and without trust, love meant nothing.

The sun was barely up when Mallory crept out of Pat's condo, yesterday's newspaper tucked under one arm. Sitting behind the wheel of her Mazda, she scanned the article just once more, to confirm her plans.

The girl's name was Renee Parker, and she lived in Eagle Falls, a small town about an hour from Seattle. Mallory had been in that community once, years before, with her parents.

And now she was going there again.

Nathan rolled over in bed and moaned. Nausea welled up in his middle, and blood pounded in the veins beneath his skull. He swore.

Roger Carstairs, Pat's boyfriend, appeared in the bedroom doorway, his healthy looks annoying. He was wearing the housekeeper's apron and stirring something in a mixing bowl. "Breakfast?" He grinned, his green eyes alight with malicious mischief.

Nathan swore again. "How much did I drink last night?"

"Let's just say I wouldn't throw a party, if I were you, without replenishing your liquor supply."

The telephone on the bedside table rang suddenly, jarring Nathan's throbbing head. "Hello!" he barked obnoxiously into the receiver. If it was a reporter, he'd—

It was Pat, and she sounded worried. "Nate, is Mallory over there?"

Nathan's jaw was suddenly clenched so tightly that it ached. "No—" He paused and looked questioningly at Roger. "Mallory didn't drop by, did she?"

Roger shook his head.

"No," Nathan repeated. "My lovely wife is not here, soothing my tortured brow. Did you call her place on the island or Angel Cove?"

"Yes, I called Kate Sheridan and Trish Demming, too, and they haven't seen her either."

Though he was trying to be angry, Nathan was actually scared. Mallory hadn't been in the best state of mind before the paternity charge, and the pain and confusion she had to be feeling didn't even bear thinking about. God, she might have left, might have walked out of his life forever. And the hell of it was that he was innocent; whatever other sins he might have committed, he had been a faithful husband from the first.

"She must have said something, Pat—*anything*."

"She said very little, Nathan. Her clothes are still here, if that's any comfort."

It wasn't. Mallory had enough credit cards to buy all the new ones she wanted. Forgetting his incredible hangover, Nathan threw back the covers on his bed and sat up, still cradling the receiver with his shoulder. He was reaching for a pair of jeans when he barked, "Damn it, if she's left me—she *promised*—"

"Oh," Pat marveled in the tones of one who has just had a revelation. "I think I know where she is."

"Spare me the dramatic pause, Pat!" Nathan snapped, struggling into the jeans. *"Where?"*

"Eagle Falls."

"Eagle what?"

"That little town where your alleged lover lives, dummy. Eagle Falls. Mallory went there."

The thought made Nathan sick. "What makes you think she'd do a stupid thing like that? What the hell could she hope to accomplish?"

"I'd do that, if I were in her shoes—that's what makes me think it. Nathan, you have been straight with me, haven't you? She's not going to walk into some hideaway filled with romantic mementos and candid snapshots of you, is she?"

Nathan was balancing the telephone receiver between his

shoulder and his ear, and wrenching on his socks. "On the basis of our long-standing relationship, sister dear, I'm going to let that question pass. It's too damned low to rate an answer!"

"All right, all right. So what do we do now?"

Instantly deflated and stung on some primary level, Nathan sank back to the bed, abandoning his previous hasty efforts to get dressed. He ignored Pat's question to continue angrily, "She *believes* it. God, after everything we've been through together, *she thinks I'd go to bed with someone else.*"

"Nathan—"

Rage and hurt made his voice harsh. "Damn her, she knows better!"

"Does she? Nathan, how would you have felt if that story had been about her? Well, I'll tell you how you would have felt, bozo!"

Nathan calmly laid the receiver down on the bedside table and walked away, and his sister's tirade was audible even from the doorway leading into the bathroom.

He heard Roger speaking placating words into the phone as he reached into the shower and turned the spigots.

Eagle Falls was smaller than Mallory remembered. In fact, it boasted only one gas station, one café and one grocery store. Behind this one-block business section, about two dozen shabby houses were perched on the verdant hillside, along with a post office, a tiny school and a wood-frame church. Remembering that Renee Parker was, according to the newspaper article, a waitress, Mallory headed for the café.

Inside that dusty, fly-speckled kitchen, she was informed by an eager-eyed fry cook that Renee lived in the pink house next door to the church. Like as not, the man imparted further, she'd be home, since she wasn't working in the café anymore.

Mallory nodded politely and left. What was she going to say to this Renee person, anyway, once they came face to face?— "Pardon me, but have you been sleeping with my husband?"

Angry tears were stinging her eyes when she slid back behind the wheel of the car, and it was a moment before she dared start up the engine again and drive. Damn it, she didn't *know* what she was going to say to the bimbo, but she had to see her. One look at her and she would know whether the stories were true or not. Just one look.

I could say I'm the Avon lady, she thought five minutes later when she drew the car to a stop in the crunchy snow rutting the street in front of Renee Parker's modest house. After drawing one deep breath, Mallory got out of the car and strode toward Renee's front door, exuding a confidence she didn't feel.

There was smoke curling from a chimney in the roof of the small house, and the front door was open, the passage blocked only by a rickety screen door. Inside, a young, female voice was lustily singing along with one of Nathan's records.

And in that moment, inexplicably, Mallory froze. Nathan was innocent. She was about to force her rigid muscles to carry her back down the crumbling walk when the screen door opened suddenly and a pretty girl appeared on the porch. "Ray—"

Mallory assessed Renee Parker—she looked much as she had in the newspaper picture—and mentally kicked herself. The girl was cute, and obviously pregnant, but she was too young to hope for more than passing notice from a man like Nathan. He was far more likely, if he strayed, to choose someone like Diane Vincent.

Renee paled, then her brown eyes darkened. "Tracy Ballard!" she gasped, reaching wildly for the handle of the screen door behind her. "Mom, Tracy Ballard is out here—"

Mallory lifted her chin. All this and a fan of the soap in the bargain. She nearly laughed. "I'm not really Tracy Ballard, Renee," she said, with dignity. "I'm Mrs. Nathan McKendrick."

Renee laid one unsteady hand on her protruding stomach. "Oh."

"Yes. Could we talk, Renee?"

The girl's eyes were suddenly very round. "I'm not taking back any of the things I said!"

Mallory advanced a step, trying to look ominous, though she hadn't the vaguest idea what she'd do if Renee called her bluff.

Fortunately, Renee didn't. She leapt behind the screen door, pulled it shut and flipped the hook into place, as though fearing for her very life. "This baby belongs to your husband!" Renee cried, "and that's the truth!"

"We both know it isn't, Renee," Mallory said evenly. "Who paid you to file that lawsuit?"

"Nobody paid me! Nathan was in love with me, he—"

"I see. Did you know he's planning to file a countersuit, Renee? This is slander, you know. His lawyers will make you appear in court, and it will be harder to lie there. You'd be committing perjury, and they can put you in jail for that."

"Jail?"

"Jail," Mallory confirmed, feeling profoundly sorry for the frightened girl before her. "Who put you up to this?"

Renee shook her head. "Nobody—nobody!"

"Very well. Then I'll see you in court. Goodbye, Renee."

With that, Mallory turned regally and walked back to her car. She was starting the engine when Renee appeared at the window on the driver's side, her face pinched and pale with fear. "C-could you wait a minute? Could we talk?"

Mallory managed a nonchalant shrug, betraying none of the jumbled nerves that were snapping inside her like shorted electrical wires. "I thought we'd said everything."

"J-just wait here—just for a minute—please?"

"I'll wait," Mallory promised, and when Renee had scurried back inside the small pink house, she allowed her forehead to drop to the steering wheel. Good God, what had she done? Nathan had never said anything about filing a countersuit against Renee Parker. What if Renee called Mallory's bluff?

Seconds later, when Mallory had composed herself again, Renee reappeared. She was holding a battered *TV Guide* cover in one hand, and there was a pinhole in the top, as though it had been affixed to a wall.

Mallory took the cover and was assaulted by her own smiling face. She had forgotten that interview; even though they'd used her picture on the cover, most of the writer's questions had been about Nathan. She looked up at Renee, truly puzzled. "What—?"

"Would you autograph it? Would you write, 'To Renee, from Tracy'?"

For a moment, Mallory could not believe what she was hearing. Was it possible that this girl would ruin her life, shake the very foundations of a marriage she treasured and then blithely ask her for an autograph? "You've got to be kidding."

Renee looked hurt. "I watch your show all the time—"

Mallory drew a deep breath, then fumbled through her purse for a pen. "Tell you what, Renee. I'm going to write a phone number on the back. If you decide to tell the truth about your baby, you call me."

"D-did you leave Nathan?"

Mallory lifted her chin. *In the lurch,* she thought. *Like a fool.* "I love him, Renee, and he loves me."

One tear glistened in the corner of Renee's eye as Mallory handed her the worn *TV Guide* cover, now boasting Tracy Ballard's signature and several phone numbers on the back. "I didn't mean to—it was so much money—"

Mallory's throat ached so badly that she couldn't speak. She could only look into this young woman's face and hope.

The girl bit her lower lip and stepped back. "I might call you soon, okay?"

"Okay," Mallory managed.

Renee looked down at the magazine cover in her hands and beamed. "Oh, boy, just *wait* till I show this to my mom—"

Mallory stopped herself from offering the girl a check that would exceed whatever she'd been paid to lie about Nathan and calmly drove away.

When she came to the gas station, however, she pulled up beside the rest rooms, ran inside the appropriate chamber and was violently ill. Afterward, she splashed her face with the tepid water that trickled from the spigot marked Cold and returned to her car. Again, she considered paying Renee.

She shuddered. If she did that, people would say she'd bought the girl off, and believe ever after that Nathan had indeed fathered Renee Parker's child. *Nathan.*

The name was like a plea, torn from her heart. *Forgive me,* she thought. *Oh, forgive me—*

He'd tried to tell her, and she hadn't listened to him—she hadn't *listened.* She picked up the newspaper, still resting on the seat, and read the article again, objectively.

And the last line quivered, jagged, in her mind like a wounding spear. *Mr. McKendrick was unavailable for comment, according to his press agent, Diane Vincent.*

"Fool," she whispered brokenly. "Oh, Mallory, you *fool!*"

With that, Mrs. Nathan McKendrick started the journey back to Seattle, and self-recriminations dogged her every inch of the way. Again and again, she heard Nathan recite that last line of the article, heard him say, *"Mallory, does that tell you anything?"*

She was crying when she surrendered the Mazda to a worried-looking George and rushed into the one elevator that would take her all the way to the penthouse.

Her hands trembled as she unlocked the door and stepped into the entry hall, and she knew that Nathan wasn't there long before she called his name and got no answer at all.

Pacing the study in his house at Angel Cove, Nathan was drawn to the telephone again and again. Where was Mallory now? What was she thinking? Feeling?

God knew what kind of reception she'd gotten from Renee Parker, whoever the hell she was. What if there had been some kind of ugly scene and Mallory was shaken up and driving? What if she'd been hurt? What if, even now, she was in some ditch along the road, bleeding—?

He caught himself on one raspy swearword, and started when the telephone rang.

"She's back," Pat said coolly. "I just talked to her, so why haven't you?"

Nathan sighed, sank into his desk chair and twisted the phone cord in his fingers. "She knows where I am," he bit out, his relief at knowing that Mallory was all right completely hidden by his tone.

"Nathan, you ass. Will you call the woman, please?"

"Hell, no. She wanted time—she gets time. *I*, as it happens, want time."

"For what?"

"To think."

"About what?"

"About whether or not I want to stay married to a woman who obviously has such a low opinion of my morals."

"It's your *brain* that I hold in question. Nathan, do you love your wife or not?"

He sighed as a savage headache gripped the nape of his neck. "You know I do."

"Then why don't you act like it?"

"Because I'm mad as hell right now, that's why."

"Poor baby," Pat crooned in an obnoxious manner that conveyed all her scorn. "Damn you, Nathan, *grow up!*"

Having imparted this message, Pat hung up with a resounding crash. Nathan glared at the receiver in his hand for a moment, and then chuckled ruefully. The hell of it was, he reflected as he replaced it in its cradle, that she was right. He was sulking.

Ten minutes later, Nathan was on board the ferry and on his way to Seattle.

After imbibing two glasses of white wine and stalking back and forth across the penthouse living room until she thought she'd shout with frustration, Mallory fell on the telephone that waited beside Nathan's chair and forced herself to dial his number. One ring, two, three—no one was there, not even Mrs. Jeffries.

Tears smarted in Mallory's eyes as she hung up and then tried the other number in desperation—the one that would ring in her own house on the other side of the island. There was no answer there either.

Mallory ached inside. *Good Lord,* she thought hugging herself in her anxiety. *If I don't talk to somebody, I'll die.*

Just then she heard a key in the lock and stiffened in sudden panic. As desperate as she'd been to reach Nathan, she didn't know what she would say to him now. She hurried to the bar and refilled her wineglass, and when she turned around, he was there, his dark eyes piercing her. But were they accusing or pleading?

His name caught in her throat and came out as an unrecognizable sound.

He came to her in long strides, removed the glass from her hand and set it on the bar with an authoritative thump. "Take it from one who knows, pumpkin—that stuff won't solve your problems."

"I—I saw her today—I talked to her," Mallory faltered miserably, needing to speak rationally with this man standing so disturbingly close. "Renee, I mean."

Nathan raised one dark eyebrow, his expression unreadable. "Does she have two heads?"

"Sh-she's a child, really. Scared—"

He was being stubbornly silent; refusing to make the conversation easier, to reach out. He stood still, his arms folded over his chest, waiting.

Mallory lowered her eyes. "I'm sorry," she whispered.

"Are you?" he drawled, and there was no love in the words, no warmth. "What, exactly, transpired in Eagle River?"

"Eagle Falls," Mallory corrected him, still unable to meet his eyes. "Nothing much happened. She insisted the baby was yours to the end. She also hinted that someone had paid her to say so."

"A contradiction in terms," Nathan observed blandly, still keeping his distance.

Mallory made a sound that might have been a chuckle or a sob, and dashed at the tears burning her eyes with the back of one hand. "Renee is nothing if not a walking contradiction. Would you believe she asked me to autograph that old *TV Guide* cover? She wanted me to write, 'To Renee, from Tracy.'"

Nathan placed his hands gently on her shoulders, drawing her close. His lips were warm in her hair. "Did you?"

Mallory began to tremble violently, and hysteria bubbled up into her throat and escaped in a series of racking sobs. Nathan lifted her into his arms, carried her to a chair and sat down, holding her in his lap like a shattered child. He continued to hold her until long after the sobs had subsided and the trembling had stopped.

"We're in a lot of trouble, you and I," he said, at length.

"I know," Mallory responded, her head resting against his shoulder. And she knew he wasn't talking about the paternity suit or Renee Parker, but about the chasm that had grown between them.

As the sun went down, they agreed to separate.

6

Even though the initial stir had died down, there were a few press people posted in the lobby that evening when Nathan and Mallory set out for the island. Nathan was coldly uncommunicative; he had never, under the best of circumstances, been overly fond of reporters. But Mallory recognized a number of these people, and considered them friends. There wasn't much she could say without betraying things that were necessarily private, but she did manage a few polite, if inane, words, and she kept her chin high and her shoulders square.

On board the ferry, Mallory and Nathan remained in the Porsche, dealing in silence with their thoughts and feelings. Mallory's car would be delivered in the morning.

The silence looming between them had reached ominous levels by the time Nathan drew the luxurious, high-powered automobile to a stop in front of the house they both thought of as Mallory's.

Was there nothing that was not specifically his or hers, but theirs? Mallory wondered brokenly.

Still at the wheel of his car, Nathan flexed his hands and sighed, his eyes carefully avoiding his wife's. "I still love you," he said, his voice so low that it was almost inaudible.

"And I love you," Mallory replied.

He turned his head slightly to study her with eyes that were both wounded and angry. "Then what the hell are we doing?"

Mallory couldn't answer. She got out of the car, thus forcing Nathan to do so, too, and her gaze locked with his over the black vinyl expanse of the vehicle's roof. Her throat worked painfully, and she swallowed.

"Is it okay if I come in for a little while?" Nathan asked gruffly, again avoiding her eyes.

Mallory nodded, despairing, and wondered why she couldn't talk to this man, why things couldn't be straightened out with a few rational words.

The next half hour was a tense time, and Mallory was grateful for the mechanics of reopening the house. While Nathan started a fire in the stove, she unpacked her clothes.

Though her back was to the door, Mallory knew immediately when Nathan entered the bedroom. She stood very still and did not turn around to face him.

He said nothing, and the silence again seemed infinite and eternal.

Mallory was both stricken and relieved when Nathan withdrew and busied himself in the living room. She could not bear to follow, but she knew that he was dismantling the January Christmas tree.

Long after the unpacking was finished, Mallory ventured as far as the kitchen. She was grateful that Nathan hadn't made coffee; it gave her something to do. All the same, an unbearable sadness clutched at her heart as she grappled with the small task.

Beyond the window, the dwarf cherry trees looked grim without their lacy trimming of snow, and the sky was a bleak and threatening gray. Mallory was sure that she would carry a jagged and hurting piece of that sky in her heart forever.

She was sitting at the kitchen table, sipping coffee, when Nathan came in. Without a word, he set the gifts he'd given Mallory on the far end of the counter and folded his arms.

Since even a screaming fight would be better than this blasted silence, Mallory said the first thing that came into her mind, and her voice was brittle. "Why do you suppose Diane didn't try to head off those reporters?"

Nathan went to the stove, poured himself a cup of coffee. "I fired Diane."

Mallory closed her eyes. So he did lay Renee Parker's lawsuit at Diane's feet. She wondered why that knowledge didn't make her feel better. "Oh," she said woodenly, when she wanted to scream, *Don't leave me, don't let this happen, I love you.*

"No cries of joy?" he pressed, without apparent bitterness, but Mallory was angered all the same.

For a moment, she forgot her anguish, her desperate need to make peace. "What you do with your employees is your business," she parried coldly.

Nathan came to sit at the table across from her, his hands cupped around his coffee mug, his dark, accusing eyes fixed on Mallory's face. "How long are we going to keep this up, Mallory?"

Mallory looked down at her own coffee; it was half-gone and she hadn't tasted it at all, had no conscious memory of drinking it. "How long are we going to keep what up?" she retorted.

Nathan spat a swearword, tilted his head back, closed his eyes. "Mallory, I didn't fire Diane for the reason you're thinking," he offered, in the tones of one offering sanity to a raving maniac. "I don't need her anymore."

"Define 'need,' if you don't mind," Mallory ventured, aware of the caustic note in her voice but unable to alter it.

The dark eyes were suddenly riveted to her face, hurting where they touched. "Damn it, talking to you is like sparring with a shadow! And kindly stop trying to switch this conversation off into all my imagined transgressions!"

Mallory sat back in her chair, folded her arms stubbornly across her chest and waited.

Nathan gave an irritated sigh and shook his head. "I'm trying to tell you that I don't need Diane because I don't need a *press agent.* I'm retiring, Mallory."

Nothing he could have said would have startled her more. Mallory's coffee spilled onto the tablecloth as she put it down with a jolt. *"Retiring?"* she choked. "Nathan, why didn't you tell me?"

He scowled, his gaze fierce, challenging. "If you hadn't rushed out of here in a huff, I would have. And then at the penthouse, if you'll remember, we weren't into heavy discussions.''

Mallory remembered all right, and she yearned for that stolen, glorious time. Perhaps, even if their marriage somehow survived this agreed separation, they would never soar like that again, never share souls and bodies quite so fully. She was mourning when she spoke again. "Aren't you a little young to retire?"

"Why shouldn't I retire?" he shot back sharply. "Do we need the money?"

Mallory might have laughed if the situation hadn't been so serious. Nathan had been wealthy long before their marriage, and money had never been an issue. "What do you intend to do with your time?" she hedged.

Nathan's eyes were brooding, defying her to discuss the subject they were skirting. "I didn't father that baby, Mallory," he said bluntly.

Mallory knew he hadn't; the confrontation with Renee Parker had convinced her of that much. But something inside her insisted that she deny what she knew to be truth, that she use the issue to keep Nathan at a safe distance.

"Mallory."

She met his eyes. "Assuming that someone really paid Renee to file that suit—"

"Assuming? Mallory, she as much as told you someone did! And that someone was, undoubtedly, Diane Vincent."

"She might have been scared—Renee, I mean—"

"The baby *isn't mine!"*

"Okay," Mallory said in a voice that was at once agreeable and frantic.

Nathan was obviously frustrated. "My God, you still don't believe me, do you?"

Suddenly, despite her earlier certainty, Mallory didn't know the answer to that question. All her instincts told her that Nathan was and always had been a faithful husband, but she could not fully trust them. Wishful thinking, in a situation like that one, was an easy trap to fall into. Maybe she'd done just that that morning, when she'd sought out Renee. Maybe she'd only believed Nathan innocent because she couldn't bear not to.

"We've been apart so much, Nathan," she said reasonably, sanely. "Women offer themselves to you as a matter of course. You'd be superhuman if you—"

But Nathan was on his feet so suddenly that his chair overturned with a crash, and his hand was hard under Mallory's chin. "I'll tell you about me, Ms. O'Connor!" he cried in a controlled roar. "I love my wife! And while I may have been tempted to bed the occasional groupie, I never have!"

Instantly furious herself, Mallory thrust his hand aside and stood up. "Damn it, Nathan. Stop!" she screamed. "You would hardly confess to an indiscretion when you have every reason to believe that I would fall apart before your very eyes!"

Something violent contorted Nathan's big frame; Mallory could feel it even though they weren't actually touching. When it passed, he spoke again, in ragged tones. "If I were callous enough to sell you out like that, Mallory, I wouldn't care how you reacted, would I?"

Now tears were smarting in Mallory's eyes. "Maybe you just didn't plan on getting caught!"

A muscle moved in Nathan's jaw, and ominous rage made his throat work, but he said nothing. He turned away from Mallory and stormed out of the house, slamming the door behind him.

Mallory sank back into her chair and dropped her head to her trembling arms, too shattered to cry. The separation of the McKendricks was off to a less than tender start.

Probably unable to refrain any longer, Trish knocked on Mallory's kitchen door bright and early the next morning. One look at her friend's tear-swollen face brought her scurrying across the uneven linoleum floor to offer an embrace.

Mallory cried, and so did Trish. But neither spoke until they had left the house and walked down the muddy path through the orchard to the Sound. The tide was in, and it did much, in its ancient and dependable way, to soothe Mallory.

After an interlude of reflection, Trish bent, slender in her worn blue jeans and red Windbreaker, to pick up a small piece of driftwood and fling it into the bubbling surf. "What happened, Mall?"

Mallory overturned a barnacle-covered rock and watched dispassionately as the tiny sand crabs living beneath it rushed in every direction. "I'm not sure," she said.

"What the hell does that mean?"

Mallory abandoned the pandemonium she'd created in the sand to sit down on a bleached-out log and wriggle the toes of her sneakers in a tangle of wet kelp. "You read about the paternity thing?"

Trish nodded, letting the low tide surge around her ankles. "You must know that's a crock," she observed, squinting in the springlike sun.

Mallory swallowed miserably. "The crazy thing is, Trish, I *do* know that. I think I knew it from the time the story broke. But instead of saying that, and standing my ground, I drove up to Eagle Falls and confronted her."

Trish sighed. "I guess I would have done that, too," she conceded finally, though she clearly disapproved. "Was Nathan upset about it?"

"He saw it as a lack of trust on my part."

"And?"

"And we can't seem to talk about it without fighting, Trish. My God, even when I wanted to say that I believed in him, I couldn't. It was as though that part of me had been shoved aside."

Trish came to sit beside Mallory, her hands cradling her knees. "Do you love him?"

Mallory nodded glumly.

Trish's soft blond hair danced around her face as she studied her friend. "But still you wanted to keep him at a distance, didn't you, Mallory?"

Mallory's mouth dropped open, but before she could say anything, Trish went bravely on.

"You know what I think, Mall? I think you're trying to hold onto your old life—the life you had when your parents were still alive. Look at you—you're married to a millionaire, for God's sake, and you *insist* on living in that little cracker box of a house because that way you won't have to let go of Mummy and Daddy.''

Mallory shot to her feet, her cheeks crimson, her throat closing and opening spasmodically over a surging fury. "That's a lie!''

"Is it, Mallory? You've been married to that man for over six years and I'll bet you haven't spent more than two or three nights at Angel Cove in all that time! And if it weren't for that damned soap opera, which everyone knows makes you *miserable,* you probably wouldn't set foot inside the penthouse, either! And then there's your name—''

"Shut up!'' Mallory shrieked.

Trish stood up calmly, faced her friend. "Your parents are dead, Mallory. Dead. Gone. And, baby, it's forever!''

Mallory was trembling; she wanted to turn and run away from Trish, from all the hurtful things her friend was saying, but she couldn't move. It was as though she'd become a part of that beach. Tears coursed down her cheeks, and her throat ached over screams of protest.

And Trish hugged her. High in the azure sky, a lone gull squawked in comment.

Mallory sniffled inelegantly and moved to dash at her tears. "How can you—say such—things—?''

Trish shrugged, her hands firm on Mallory's shoulders. "Mallory, grow up. You love Nathan—fight for him.''

Drawing deep restorative breaths, Mallory shook her head. "We've agreed to separate for a while, Trish. And I th-think we need the time apart.''

Trish shook her head in angry wonder. "You've had too *much* time apart already, don't you see that? Go to him, tell him everything you're feeling—contradictions and all.''

But Mallory was drawing back inside herself, refusing to hear the reason in Trish's suggestion, refusing to think that she didn't belong in the small house beyond the orchard anymore.

And after that, there was no reaching her.

Nathan stood at the living room windows in his own house, looking out over the peaceful vista of sea and sky and mountains. Angel Cove itself was sapphire blue and sun dappled that day, and boats with brightly colored sails bobbed in the distance. Beyond them rose Mount Rainier, snowy and impervious even as she favored lesser beings with a rare view of her rugged slopes.

"Mr. McKendrick?"

He started slightly, having forgotten that he wasn't alone. Even though the band was gone for the time being—some of them hadn't taken the news of his retirement any better than Diane had—the housekeeper was always in residence.

Mrs. Jeffries stood in the center of the spacious room now, carrying a china coffeepot with steam curling from its spout and looking nervous. The stains in her cheeks, no doubt, were the result of the scandal and shame served up by the ever-vigilant press.

"What is it?" Nathan demanded, none too politely.

"Th-there's a man at the door, asking to see you."

"Who?"

Mrs. Jeffries actually shuddered, and the coffeepot was in peril. "I think he's a process server!"

Nathan sighed, exasperated and weary. "Show him in, please. And put down that coffee before you burn yourself!"

The housekeeper obeyed, then scurried out into the hallway again.

Nathan looked at the coffee and distractedly shook his head, even though there was no one to see. He'd had too much coffee during the long night, and his nerves were crackling under his skin like high-voltage wires.

A moment later, a man in a sedate business suit entered the room and looked at Nathan with obvious recognition. "Nathan McKendrick?"

Irritated, Nathan simply held out his hand.

The visitor extended a folded document and then fled.

After parting with Trish, Mallory made her way back toward the house alone. Cinnamon met her in the middle of the orchard path, bounding and yipping in greeting.

The pat Mallory gave the animal was halfhearted, at best. Reaching the house, she filled Cinnamon's bowl from the dog food bag on the screened porch and set it down near the door.

The telephone rang suddenly, and the sound of it reverberated through Mallory's body to her very spirit. She crossed the kitchen floor with such speed that she bruised her knee on one corner of the big woodburning stove, and tears of physical pain were brimming in her eyes. "Hello!"

"Hi," Brad Ranner said, as easily as though they'd never argued, never shouted at each other over cross-purposes. "How's life in the wilds of Puget Sound?"

Mallory's disappointment was crushing; she had hoped, desperately, unaccountably, that the caller would be Nathan. "Wild," she answered in a peevish, dispirited whisper.

"I'm sorry about that scene at the penthouse the other day, Mallory—I really blew it. Forgiven?"

Mallory sighed, rubbing her throbbing knee and grimacing. "Brad, I haven't changed my mind. I'm still leaving the show."

Brad's voice was as smooth and warm as the fresh butter Mallory's mother had always served with steamed clams. "In view of Nathan's latest escapade, I'm surprised."

Mallory closed her eyes tight, but the gesture was no help against the sudden knotting pain in her stomach and the ache beneath her skull. "Brad," she responded evenly, "I don't care if my husband impregnates a *hundred* groupies—I'm still not going to take my clothes off on national television."

"Maybe we could work around that."

Mallory bit her lower lip and tried to think clearly, but she was simply too tired and too confused.

"Mall?"

She drew herself up, summoned all her flagging strength.

"I'm here. Listen, Brad—I'm not really an actress, you know? The show was a kind of a—well—a lark for me. But now I'm tired and I can't think and—"

"Babe, this paternity thing has really leveled you, hasn't it?"

Why lie? "Yes And I'll thank you not to make any more remarks about Nathan's alleged escapades, Brad."

He sighed. "I was out of line, and I'm sorry."

Even though she knew he couldn't see the gesture, Mallory nodded. "C-could we talk another time, Brad?"

"Of course, sugar. You'll think about renewing your contract, won't you?"

Mallory McKendrick was not sure of many things at that point, but she was sure about one in particular. She hated memorizing lines, standing under bright lights and before cameras, getting up before dawn to go to the studio to be smothered in makeup. "No, Brad. I'll finish out my commitment, but that's all."

"Fine," Brad said, his calm manner gone. "You're fired!"

"Thank you very much."

"Mallory!"

Mallory replaced the telephone receiver gently. She had no more than stepped back from it when she felt a wild relief. For all the things that were wrong in her life, she'd taken one positive step. Once the few episodes she was legally bound to do had been taped, she would be free.

Maybe too free, she thought as the fact that Nathan was living in one house and she in another displaced her momentary pleasure.

She turned, looked around the humble kitchen, and saw that it looked almost exactly as it had when her mother had walked out of it for the last time. Was Trish right? Was she trying to cling to two people who no longer existed?

I'm on some kind of psychological roll here, she thought with grim humor. And she knew then that, on some subconscious level, she'd been waiting here, all this time, for parents she knew could not return to her.

Mallory wiped away the tears that had welled up in her eyes and reached resolutely for the telephone again.

Mrs. Jeffries spoke in crisp answer, her voice harried and sharp. Undoubtedly, people had been calling from all over the world, shocked by the news of Nathan's retirement. Not to mention Renee Parker's accusation.

"This is Mrs. McKendrick," Mallory said wearily, her pride thick in her throat as she swallowed it. "May I please speak with my husband?"

There was a pause, perhaps to give the loyal housekeeper time to decide whether Mallory was really Nathan's wife or just some brazen fan. "He isn't taking calls now, Mrs. McKendrick—"

Mallory felt crimson fury pounding in her cheeks. It was bad enough to grovel, without being turned away like some salesperson or irksome reporter. "I want to talk to him *now!*"

Mrs. Jeffries reconsidered, and, a full two minutes later, Nathan ventured a cautious greeting into the phone.

Mallory didn't know where to begin; they'd made such a tangle of things that any one of half a dozen conversational threads could have been picked up. She drew a deep, shaky breath, closed her eyes and took the plunge. "Do you think we could go back to square one and start over, Nathan?"

There was a silence on the other end of the line, and then a rasped, "I'll be right over."

Mallory remembered the things Trish had said to her that morning on the beach, and the sense of it all was undeniable. "No, I'll come there."

His voice was hoarse, broken. "Mallory—"

She swallowed painfully, knowing how troubled he was, regretting every moment she hadn't spent at his side. "Shh. We'll talk when I get there."

"But—"

Mallory hung up the telephone.

The villa overlooking Angel Cove was of graceful, Spanish architecture, and Mallory admired it anew as she approached. It was enormous, boasting a terra-cotta roof and some twenty rooms in addition to a swimming pool and a plant-bedecked sun porch with its own hot tub. Holly trees grew in the yard, and the house looked out over the Sound and the private wharf where Nathan's boat, the *Sky Dancer,* bobbed on the water.

Mallory was so caught up in the ambience of the place that she was startled by her husband's voice.

"Hi," he said, and she looked up to see that he was waiting on the front step. For all his strength, he looked so vulnerable in that moment that Mallory's heart constricted.

"Hi," she replied, when she could speak.

He was standing up, striding toward her. When they were face-to-face at the base of the long flagstone walk, he brought gentle hands to her shoulders and bent to kiss her forehead. "I would have killed the fatted calf, but we don't have one."

Mallory smiled up at him, feeling shaky inside. What if they ended up hurting each other again? What if—

Firmly she caught herself. "I'd settle for a glass of white wine and a dip in your hot tub," she said.

He laughed. "You're on. The phones are unplugged, and Mrs. Jeffries has stern orders to tell any visitors that we're lost in the Cascade mountains."

As they walked toward the magnificent house, Mallory tucked under Nathan's arm and wondered how to begin straightening things out. She ventured a serious statement. "No sex, though— okay? Every time we try to talk, we end up making love and nothing gets settled."

He held up one hand, as if to swear an oath. "No sex," he promised. And then an evil light flashed behind the pain in his dark eyes. "For now," he added.

Less than five minutes later, they were both in the swirling waters of Nathan's hot tub, Mallory sipping the requested white wine. The black-and-white swimsuit she wore was one she'd left behind one summer day, and she was grateful that it was her own; she wasn't quite sure she could have dealt with all the questions that would have arisen in her mind if it hadn't been.

Nathan, his strong, tanned forearms braced against the tiled edge of the hot tub, watched her for several long seconds before he ventured, "Mallory, I was served with the summons today—it's official."

She wanted to avert her eyes, to look down at the warm water bubbling around her or stare into her wineglass. But she didn't. She forced herself to meet his gaze squarely. "I'm sorry."

He sighed, and his voice, when he spoke, was low and rough. "My lawyers want me to settle out of court."

"Do you plan to?"

Nathan shook his head quickly, but he didn't look affronted by the question. "No. That would mean an admission of guilt."

Mallory swallowed. "Nathan, you know you're not guilty, and I know you're not. Maybe it would be easier if you did settle."

Nathan brought one gentle hand to Mallory's shoulder, and his eyes searched her face. "Do you, Mallory? Do you believe I'm telling the truth?"

She nodded. "I guess I was just hysterical or something. I don't know. Trish made me see that I might be—well, kind of holding out on you and on our marriage—trying to keep one foot in the life I had with my parents and one in the life you and I share."

He said nothing; clearly, he was waiting for her to continue. She drew a deep, shaky breath.

"I—I never realized it before, but I think Trish had a point. I mean, I kept on calling myself 'Mallory O'Connor' and then there's the house—"

Nathan smiled, traced the curve of her right cheek with an index finger. "Lots of women are using their own last names now, Mallory. It's a sign of the times."

"Well, I don't feel comfortable with it."

"The choice is yours, Mallory. With your career and everything, it makes sense to call yourself 'O'Connor.'"

Mallory flushed slightly at his mention of her acting; here was another subject they hadn't even touched on. She'd been shocked to hear that he planned to retire, and now he'd be shocked, too. Dear heaven, when had they stopped telling each other their plans and their hopes and their dreams? "I'm not renewing my contract with the soap, Nathan."

He raised one dark eyebrow. "That's news to me. Did you get another offer or something?"

She could see by the expression on his face, guarded as it was, that he was hoping she hadn't. "No. I just don't *like* acting. If I did, it would be different."

He looked away for a moment, pretending an interest in the fuchsias, ferns and healthy ivy plants thriving along one wall of the steamy room. "So what do you plan, as you asked me, to do with your time?"

Mallory took another sip from her wineglass, then set it aside. "The first thing I want to do," she began softly, her hand rising, of its own accord, to his muscle-corded shoulder, "is my part to make our marriage work. Nathan, we've grown so far apart. We don't share anymore—we don't act like married people."

He laughed, and it was a gruff sound, a sound of agreement. "That is truly an understatement, my love. You should have been the first to know that I planned to retire."

"And you should have been the first to know that I did, too. Oh, Nathan, what happened to us? Why did things change?"

"Change is inevitable, Mallory. As much as I'd like to be a part of you, we're two separate people and we've simply gone our own ways."

"Do you think we can find each other again?"

"I know we can. But it's going to take work, Mallory, and time—not to mention understanding and patience."

"Then maybe it's a good thing our careers won't be pulling us apart." She paused to touch his steam-dampened, fragrant hair, and then frowned. "I'm sure quitting the soap is best for me, but I'm not so certain about your leaving the music business. Nathan, it's a part of you."

He shrugged, then drew her close, so that their bodies were touching beneath the lulling churn of the water in the hot tub. "Lady, for you I would quit the *breathing* business. Besides, I'm tired—for the time being, all I want is you and one hell of a lot of rest." He bent his magnificent head, sipped mischie-vously at her lips. "Admittedly, those two objectives are about as compatible as oil and water."

She laughed, drew back slightly in his embrace, and looked up at him with dancing eyes. "No sex, remember?"

He groaned, made his case by nipping seductively at her lower lip.

"Nathan."

He stepped back, looking comically chagrined. "Just how long did I agree to abstain?" he demanded.

She was trembling with a desire that equalled or even sur-passed his, but she managed a flippant toss of her head. "At least long enough to get upstairs. People don't make love in hot tubs, after all."

He chuckled and then made a growling sound in his throat as he wrenched her close again, trailed searching lips along the length of her tingling neck. "Don't they? Mallory, Mallory—you innocent."

She gasped involuntarily as his hand rose to cup her breast; it was a proprietary gesture, for all its gentleness, and it made her traitorous body yearn to offer itself in unqualified surrender. "P-please—stop—"

But Nathan drew down her strapless, elasticized swimming suit top to reveal just one delectable breast. The nipple pulsed as his thumb stroked it to an inviting hardness, and the tender flesh surrounding that pink nubbin was being caressed not only by his hand, but by the warm, soothing water.

Mallory tried to protest, but all that came out of her mouth was a sound that was part croon, part whimper.

"Please, Mallory," he whispered, his lips burning at her ear like fire. "Let me see you—all of you. Let me touch you—"

"M-Mrs. Jeffries—" she reminded him breathlessly.

He drew the swimsuit down deftly, baring her other breast, her stomach, her abdomen. She stepped out of the garment and immediately forgot that it had ever existed, as a pulsing, insistent warmth surged through her. She cried out softly as he closed hungry lips around the nipple of one breast, drew teasingly at its tip.

Her legs were wrapped around his waist almost before she knew what was happening, and she groaned as he took his leisurely pleasure at her breasts, leaving one only to devour the other.

Presently, he released her and set her back on her feet. She caught both thumbs under the top of his swim trunks and drew them down until he was as naked as she. Then, with gentle hands, she caressed him.

Nathan gasped with pleasure and stood with his feet planted wide apart so that he could be still more vulnerable to Mallory's touch. The passion she saw in his taut features made her want him desperately.

When he could bear the sweet torment no longer, he lifted Mallory out of the hot tub, climbed out himself and tenderly pressed her down onto a thickly padded chaise longue. He placed her feet gently onto the tiled floor, one on one side of the chaise, and one on the other.

She gasped and arched her back as he caressed the silken vee at the junction of her thighs, trailed soft, warm kisses over her rib cage, her stomach, the tingling flesh beneath her breasts.

He nibbled at the sweet peak of one breast. "Tell me what you want, Mallory."

She didn't have the breath to answer him; her body was doing that without words. Her hips moved in rhythm with the delicious torment of his fingers, and her hands clutched desperately at the ebony richness of his hair.

He mounted her gently, entered her just far enough to tease. "Mallory," he rumbled, his lips moist and commanding where her neck and shoulder met. "Tell me."

"I—I want you to f-fill me—"

Her reward was a swift thrust of his hips as he plunged deep inside her, filling her, possessing her and yet, at the very same moment, surrendering. They moved as one person, both gasping words that made no sense.

Finally, Nathan lifted Mallory's hips, so that his shaft stroked the very core of her womanhood as it entered and withdrew, entered and withdrew. And then she cried out, shuddering, as the crescendo of their loving convulsed her, took primitive pleasure in his echoing groan of total release.

When, at last, they had both caught their breath and drawn apart, albeit unwillingly, there was a timid knock at the door leading into the kitchen.

"What?" Nathan barked irritably, as Mallory blushed profusely and plunged back into the hot tub in search of her discarded swimsuit.

"L-lunch is ready," dared Mrs. Jeffries meekly, from beyond the door.

Mallory began to giggle unaccountably as she struggled into her suit, and the sound softened the awesome tension in Nathan's face and finally caused him to grin lopsidedly.

"We'll have it in the master bedroom," he replied, his eyes sparkling as he watched another blush rise in Mallory's cheeks. At last clothed—if somewhat more scantily than she would have liked—Mallory found Nathan's trunks and flung them at him furiously.

He caught them, but made no effort to put them on again. His grin widened as Mrs. Jeffries called out something and then went back to her duties.

Mallory bit her lower lip, annoyed with Nathan, annoyed with herself. "We'll have it in the master bedroom!" she mimicked.

Nathan laughed. "No doubt we will."

"I meant—oh, damn you—"

He arched one eyebrow. "Must be some kind of mating ritual," he mused.

Mallory crossed her arms over her breasts and stood stubbornly in the middle of the hot tub. "What are you talking about?"

"The way we always fight—before and after making love. It must have *some* significance."

"Why?" Mallory demanded sourly, her feet still firmly planted on the floor of the hot tub.

Idly Nathan pulled on his swim trunks, his eyes still full of mischievous musing. He slid easily into the bubbling, surging water again and approached her. "Why what?" he countered. "Why do our fights have significance, or why did I tell Mrs. Jeffries to serve lunch in the bedroom?"

Mallory retreated a step, wide-eyed and suddenly wary. "B-both, I guess," she faltered, stalling.

He grinned, and advanced toward her cautiously. "I think we fight because when we make love we both become so much a part of the other person that it scares us. And I want lunch in the bedroom because I want you in the bedroom."

Mallory trembled. There was much truth in what he'd said about their lovemaking; they were both strong willed people, both fierce individuals. And when their bodies joined in the throes of passion, she often felt as though she'd lost herself in the consuming fire, as though her separate identity had somehow been forged to his, creating a third person that neither of them really knew.

It wasn't surprising, really, to find out that Nathan had felt the same way. But as he drew too near, she was again aware of his incredible power over her, and she stepped back once more. "I—I for one intend to eat my lunch," she babbled inanely, trying to keep him at a distance. "I'm h-hungry and—"

He laughed, closed the space between them and caught her shoulders in strong, gentle hands. "Don't worry, pumpkin—you can eat undisturbed. I have, after all, a vested interest in seeing that you keep up your strength."

Just as he had probably intended her to, Mallory colored profusely. "Don't you ever think about anything besides sex?"

"Only rarely," he confessed in a gravelly tone that sent fresh desire stirring through her like warm butter. "Where you're concerned, it's a compulsion."

In spite of everything, she laughed into his damp, strong shoulder; in spite of everything, she listened as he told her, in gruff, sensuous tones, all that he meant to do to her in his bed.

And where he led, she followed.

7

They sat facing each other in the center of the huge, love-rumpled bed, Nathan clad only in a pair of cutoff jeans, Mallory wearing a lace-trimmed teddy that was, like the swimsuit, a remnant of some other visit to her husband's house.

A dozen feet away, a fire crackled romantically on the hearth of a small, ornate ivory fireplace, and a new snow was drifting past the windows over the head of Nathan's bed. Still dazed from the lovemaking that had consumed the whole afternoon, Mallory sighed with warm contentment.

"What do we do now?" she asked, stifling a yawn.

An evil light sparkled in Nathan's dark eyes, but then he laughed at her sudden blush. "You're as pink as that delectable bit of silk you're wearing. What is that thing, anyway?"

Mallory laughed and scooted back a little, as though to withhold herself from this man who could take her whenever and wherever he pleased. "It's a teddy—don't you know anything?"

He grinned, and with a warm, exploring finger traced the snow-white lace edging Mallory's bodice. "I know it drives me crazy. What I don't know is whether I like it better on or off."

"Lecher."

Nathan tilted his head to one side and chuckled. His finger slipped with tantalizing prowess into the warm, shadowed cleft between her breasts, then coursed upward, slowly, along the satiny length of her neck to the supersensitive place beneath her right ear.

Mallory shivered, though she'd never been warmer in her life, and then glared at her husband. "Will you stop that, you sex fiend?"

He laughed, withdrew his tormenting hand and bounded suddenly off the bed. The light from the fire shifted and danced in fascinating patterns on the sun-browned, muscular expanse of his naked back as he went to a closet and began rummaging through a variety of items stacked on the top shelf. "All right," he conceded in a teasing voice that set Mallory to wanting him all over again, "I am a man of my word. No sex for at least three hours."

"That is so big of you," Mallory retorted, somewhat petulantly, her eyes still fixed on the splendid play of the muscles in his back and his powerful thighs.

"Noble is my middle name," he said.

"Albert is your middle name," Mallory countered, an obnoxious grin curving her lips.

Nathan whirled from the shelf, a Monopoly box clutched in both hands, his face a mockery of outrage. "And if you ever tell, I'll shave your mink jacket," he threatened, approaching the bed with long, ominous strides.

"Rash words," she shot back, reaching out and grabbing the game from his hands. "You forget how many charge cards I have."

The bed sloped a little as Nathan returned to his former position, facing Mallory, his long legs crossed at the ankles, Indian-style, and opened the Monopoly box. "You have me there," he said. "But Monopoly is another matter. I'm warning you, woman—if you buy Park Place and Boardwalk again and jam them with hotels, it's over between us."

Mallory smiled evilly and arched one eyebrow. "Is that so, fella?"

He rummaged through the little metal game pieces tucked into a nook in the box. "Furthermore," he said, as though she hadn't challenged him at all, "I want the race car this time, and that's it."

Mallory sighed with mock resignation and reached into the box to claim her personal favorite, the tiny Scottie dog. "Look out," she said fiercely, and, within fifteen minutes, she owned both Boardwalk and Park Place.

* * *

"I'm having an underwear party," Trish announced briskly, her voice warm with humor. "It's this afternoon at two and you'd better be there, McKendrick."

Mallory yawned into the telephone receiver and snuggled down into the warm vacancy on Nathan's side of the bed. Hearing him singing in the shower, she smiled to herself. "Underwear?" she echoed, her mind still fogged by last night's lovemaking.

"You rich people call it 'lingerie,' daahling," Trish teased. "It's that silky, sexy stuff you wear under your clothes."

Mallory laughed, yawned again and stretched languidly in the warm bed. "Oh, *that,*" she said in the tones of one who suddenly understands a consuming mystery. "Isn't this short notice for a party? I'm trying to conduct a reconciliation here, you know."

As if on cue, Nathan came out of the master bath, wrapped in a precariously draped towel, the water from the shower beaded on his powerful shoulders, an evil grin on his face.

"Okay, so I didn't give you two weeks and an engraved invitation," Trish retorted. "Just be here, will you? I booked the thing so Candy Simpson could get a bathrobe for half price, and most of my guests are only coming because they think you'll be here!"

Mallory gasped as Nathan tugged teasingly at the covers, revealing one sleep-warmed breast, and then circled the nipple with a wanton finger. "A—bathrobe—for—half price?"

Nathan replaced the exploring finger with his tongue, causing Mallory's nipple to harden in eager surrender, and she moaned.

"What the devil's going on over there?" Trish demanded, never in her life having been accused of subtlety.

Mallory arched her back and swallowed a contented purr as Nathan nibbled mercilessly at her breast. "It would serve you right if I told you, Trish Demming—"

"T-two o'clock!" Trish sputtered in an obvious rush of understanding. "Candy's bathrobe is at stake!"

Nathan pulled the receiver from Mallory's hand and replaced it without interrupting his other enterprise at all.

There was a very becoming blush rising in Trish's cheeks as she opened her front door to Mallory that afternoon, but her blue eyes were sparkling with mischief. "How goes the reconciliation?" she whispered. "As if I needed to ask."

Mallory laughed. "Despite repeated interruptions, it goes well," she threw back.

Trish's modestly furnished living room was filled with familiar faces, including Kate Sheridan's.

"Did she give you that one about Candy Simpson's bathrobe, too?" Kate demanded from the leather recliner where Alex usually sat.

Mallory flashed a look of mock suspicion at Trish and nodded. "Was it just a ploy to get us here?"

"Of course it was," Trish confessed buoyantly. "Candy Simpson has more sense than the rest of us. She's in Hawaii, lounging in the sun and sipping Mai Tais."

Mallory shook her head as she shrugged out of her warm, snow-speckled jacket and thrust it into Trish's hands. "You rat. I thought I was on a mission of mercy!"

"You *are*," Trish imparted dramatically. "*I'm* the one who wants to get a bathrobe at half price!"

Despite the fact that she missed Nathan, despite the carefully veiled curiosity in the eyes of the half-dozen women in Trish's living room, Mallory enjoyed the lingerie party immensely. It felt good, after the rush of taping the soap every day for so many months, to participate in something so ordinary and frivolous.

"Have you heard about Trish's new business enterprise?" Kate Sheridan queried, once the party was over and she and Trish and Mallory sat alone in the Demming's spacious kitchen, drinking coffee.

Mallory raised her eyebrows and assessed her younger friend with teasing interest. "Don't tell me they've recruited you to sell underwear!"

Trish laughed, but her eyes were full of sparkling, earnest dreams. "I passed my real estate exam, Mall."

Admiration and genuine pride caused Mallory to reach out and touch her friend's arm. "Congratulations! Good heavens, I didn't even know you were studying for it."

Trish rolled her bright blue eyes. "It was a beast, but I managed. Starting next Monday, I'll be talking the tourists into cozy island hideaways."

"Great," Mallory said, honestly delighted. There was only one real estate agency on the island, but they did a brisk business among the summer people. "Are you going to give Soundview Properties a run for their money?"

Trish shook her head. "Heck no, I'd have to be a broker to do that. I'm working for them."

"Sensational. I'd like the honor of being your first client."

Trish leaned forward, nearly spilling her coffee, and widened her eyes. "What?"

Mallory looked from Trish to Kate and grinned at the startled expressions playing in both their faces. "I want to sell my house," she said bluntly.

Trish emitted an undignified whoop, and Kate beamed her approval.

"It's about time," observed the latter. "If I were married to a hunk like Nathan, I'd ride around in his hip pocket!"

Mallory laughed. "Kate Sheridan, I'm *shocked!*"

"That's progress," Kate retorted with tart good humor. "You've stepped up from stupid."

"Thanks a lot!"

Trish giggled conspiratorially and hunched her shoulders beneath her pink velour shirt. "Mall, you were terrific this afternoon! Those women were positively *eaten up* with curiosity, but you didn't give them one damned thing to talk about."

"They'll make things up to fill the void," Mallory said somewhat ruefully, turning her empty coffee cup in one hand.

"Who cares?" Kate demanded. "They would anyway."

Trish's hand closed over Mallory's, warm and reassuring. "I

really think you're doing the right thing, Mall. You love Nathan—I know you do.''

Mallory nodded distractedly; suddenly, it was as though Renee Parker had joined the women sitting around that homey table, and the glow of the afternoon just past was somewhat tarnished by her unseen presence.

"You and Nathan ought to go away somewhere," Kate interjected quickly. "Now that he's retiring—"

Mallory shook her head, drew a deep breath and forced a brave smile to her face. "We can't—not yet, anyway. It would look as though we were running away. Besides, he still has that farewell concert in Seattle next month. If I know him, rehearsals will begin any minute."

"After that, then," Kate persisted, a small, worried frown creasing the space between her eyebrows.

Mallory shrugged. "I can't think that far ahead. I still have an obligation to Brad, for one thing."

"Brad!" Kate scoffed dismissively. "That creep is half your problem, if not all of it. Break your contract, Mallory, and see Alice Jackson over at the elementary school. They're looking for substitute teachers to fill in whenever the regulars are sick."

Mallory was gaping at Kate. "Break my contract? I can't do that!"

"Why not?" Trish asked cautiously. "You said you didn't want to act anymore."

"Well, there is such a thing as loyalty, you know." Mallory bridled stiffly. "A contract is a promise!"

"There are exceptions to every rule," Kate said with staunch persistence. "And besides, I'll lay odds that Brad Ranner is behind this paternity suit."

Mallory was stunned; until that moment, she had placed all the blame for Renee Parker on Diane. "W-why would he do that?" she managed after a long, difficult pause.

Kate and Trish exchanged looks of exaggerated impatience before the younger of the two replied, "Mall, you dummy—Brad looks at you like you're made of spun sugar! If he thought he could get Nathan out of the picture, he'd do anything.''

Mallory had known that Nathan was jealous of Brad Ranner, though she'd never understood why. Their relationship was harmless—almost like that of a brother and sister. And yet, Brad had been so outraged that she meant to quit the show—

But that was business, of course. She glared at Trish and Kate in turn and lifted her chin. "Diane Vincent got Renee to say those things about Nathan," she said firmly. "Brad wouldn't do a thing like that!"

"Wouldn't he?" challenged Kate, who seldom interfered in the problems of other people. "Wake up, Mallory. I've seen him and Nathan together, and they look like two lions about to do battle over the same quarry."

"Diane did it because Nathan fired her!" Mallory insisted, almost desperately.

"When was that?" Trish pressed. "Yesterday? The day before? It takes longer than that to arrange a lawsuit, Mallory—this thing has been in the works for weeks."

"It could still have been Diane!"

Kate shrugged. "Maybe they arranged it together," she said. "I wouldn't put anything past that she-cat either. Just watch your step around Ranner, because he's not what he seems to be."

Mallory felt sudden, unaccountable tears smarting in her eyes. Why was it so important to her to blame Diane? Kate and Trish weren't meddlers, and they were both extremely intelligent. Had they noticed something in Brad's manner that she'd missed?

God, why did she have to think about Renee Parker and that stupid paternity suit, anyway?

Trish's pretty face crumpled with shared pain and deep concern. Unceremoniously, she dragged her chair closer to Mallory's and wrapped her friend in comforting arms. "I'm sorry, Mall. I should never have brought this up—"

Mallory sniffled, returned Trish's hug and drew back a little. "It's okay," she said bravely, dashing away the tears on her face. "You'll call me about putting the house on the market?"

Tears gleaming in her own eyes, Trish bit her lower lip and nodded.

Kate rose briskly from her chair. "Well, I've spent half of my next advance on lacy geegaws no man will ever see. I trust you earned your damned bathrobe!"

Both Trish and Mallory laughed, and the tension in that cozy room was broken, just as Kate had probably intended it to be. She laid a motherly hand on Mallory's shoulder.

"Come on, Mrs. McKendrick—I'll drive you home. If I know you, you walked over here."

Trish pretended to be very busy gathering up the coffee cups and spoons on the table. "Blizzards don't stop her. She has herself confused with the postal service. How does that go? 'Neither snow nor sleet nor gloom of night—'"

"You pitiable innocent," Kate broke in. "When was the last time you mailed anything?"

Mallory laughed. "Don't let Kate disillusion you, Trish. She has a running war with the post office."

Kate was shrugging into a heavy woolen sweater-coat. "Only because they deliver my manuscripts by skateboard. Let's get out of here before I *really* get on my soapbox!"

Knowing Trish's house as well as she knew her own, Mallory said goodbye and went off to find her jacket again. Kate was waiting in her car a few minutes later when she went outside.

The snow was falling in the gray twilight by then, and the air was bracing, but not really cold. Mallory almost regretted agreeing to the offer of a ride home; it would have been nice to walk.

"You're serious about selling your house?" Kate asked as she eased the small car out of Trish's driveway and onto the main road.

Mallory nodded. "I realize now that I've been using it as a hideout, rather than a home."

"You were happy there once. Naturally, you're fond of it."

Again, Mallory nodded. She wondered what advice her parents would have given her if they'd been alive. Would they have believed that Nathan deserved her trust and loyalty or would they have urged her to cut her losses and run?

The answer was easy. Janet and Paul O'Connor had liked and respected their son-in-law, after an initial wariness stemming from his unusual occupation, and they'd never been big on quitting.

"You're wondering what your parents would have thought about this paternity mess, aren't you?" Kate asked quietly.

Mallory chuckled. "Sometimes you amaze me. If you ever get tired of writing books, you could always become a mind reader."

"I'd probably make more money," Kate retorted with a wry grin. "I trust I can spare you the lecture about how you're a grown woman now and you should think for yourself?"

"I would be grateful if you did," Mallory said.

Kate's attention was fixed on the snowy road. "We didn't mean to upset you, Mallory—Trish and I. We just don't want you to be hurt anymore."

"You've never doubted Nathan since this thing started, have you, Kate? I don't think Trish has either. Tell me, why do you have so much confidence in him?"

Kate flipped on her windshield wipers and peered out at the snow-dappled night. "He wears his heart where his tie clasp should be," she said. "Love is an obvious thing, and I've never seen a more flagrant case than Nathan McKendrick's."

Mallory swallowed and looked out the window on her side of the car. "I wish I could be so sure as you are. S-sometimes I think he loves me, and other times—"

"Yes?" Kate prodded gently.

"Other times I think he can't possibly be interested in someone as ordinary as I am."

"Then the fault lies in you, not in him. You need to believe in yourself, Mallory."

Since no point on the small island was very far from any other, it didn't take Kate long to reach Angel Cove. During that brief time, however, Mallory seriously considered what her friend had said. It was true that she didn't have much confidence in herself.

The question was, why? Paul and Janet O'Connor had been wise parents—they'd raised Mallory to believe she could do anything. And she hadn't made such a bad showing. She'd gotten excellent grades in college, graduated with a teaching certificate, walked onto the set of a soap opera and landed a promising part.

In the warm confines of Kate's practical car, Mallory sighed. Nothing she might accomplish seemed very impressive beside the glittering success that attended Nathan's every move. But, then, who did she need to impress?

"Won't you come in for a few minutes?" Mallory asked a few minutes later when Kate drew the car to a stop in front of the brightly lit house at Angel Cove.

Kate shook her head firmly. "I'd like to, but chapter seven awaits. Besides, the last thing you and that young man need is company."

Mallory laughed and opened the car door to get out. After thanking her friend and saying goodbye, she bounded up the snow-dusted walk to the front door.

Nathan was just coming down the stairs when she walked in, and the house was deliciously quiet without the numerous members of his entourage. He grinned, as though he'd read her thoughts, and she blushed at the images his closely fitted jeans and soft, white sweater inspired.

"Hi," he said. "Where's your underwear?"

Mallory gaped at him, having forgotten all about the sales party she'd just left. "I beg your pardon?"

Nathan laughed, approached his wife and placed gentle hands on her shoulders. "I wasn't getting personal, pumpkin. Didn't you go to some kind of party at Trish's?"

Feeling foolish and oddly electrified by this man who had been her husband for six full years, Mallory nodded. "It's not underwear, it's lingerie. And you don't bring it home the same day like you would if you shopped in a store. You just order it."

His gifted fingers were kneading her tense shoulders, and she could feel their warmth, even through her jacket. "Thank you for clearing that up. I'll rest easier knowing the straight scoop about underwear parties."

Mallory gave him a slight shove, although the last thing she wanted at the moment was distance between them. "You're incorrigible. And by the way, you'd better give Alex a raise."

He lifted one eyebrow. "Yeah? Why?"

"Because the only reason Trish gave this party was to get a bathrobe for half price."

Nathan laughed. "Could we please drop this conversation? I've got a candlelight dinner all laid out in the dining room, and you're standing here talking about cut-rate bathrobes."

Mallory unbuttoned her jacket, and her flesh tingled pleasantly beneath her clothes as Nathan took the coat from her with practiced hands. "A candlelight dinner, is it? And we don't have to eat it in the bedroom?"

He feigned shock. "What? Eat on the very site of my ignoble defeat at Monopoly? Never."

Mallory smiled, wishing that their lives could always be this way—unhurried, romantic and private. "Tell me about this candlelight dinner. Did you cook it?"

"Yes," he said, guiding her out of the entry hall and through the doorway that led to the imposing formal dining room. "Mrs. Jeffries is in Seattle, visiting her sister. Therefore, I had no choice but to venture into the wilds of her kitchen and concoct a culinary delight unmatched even by your canned soup and tuna sandwiches."

"Was that a dig?"

Nathan pointedly ignored the question and ushered Mallory to a chair at the long mahogany table that was usually lined with band members, their wives and girlfriends, and an accumulation of diverse hangers-on. Candles flickered elegantly over a repast of hot dogs, white wine, and limp french fries.

Mallory sat down with dignity, biting her lower lip to keep from laughing out loud. The ploy was unsuccessful.

Nathan, seating himself next to her, looked properly wounded. "You have no appreciation for fine food."

"What on earth did you do to those french fries? They look positively anemic!"

He arched one eyebrow. "I put them in the microwave," he answered defensively.

"After taking them from the freezer, no doubt?"

"Of course."

"I see. Well, they're far more appetizing if they're browned in the regular oven."

"Thank you, Julia Child."

Mallory laughed and dutifully began to eat, and even though the french fries were still partially frozen and the hot dogs weren't much warmer, she couldn't remember a better meal.

"I'm selling my house," she announced, once the fare had been consumed, her eyes on the kaleidoscope colors the candles were casting into her wineglass.

There was a short silence, followed by the inevitable, "Why?"

Mallory swallowed, though she had yet to touch her wine, and met her husband's dark gaze. "Because it's foolish to hang around over there, waiting for my childhood to come back."

Nathan's hand gently covered both of Mallory's. "The place means a lot to you," he said, and she couldn't tell whether he was opposing her plans or approving them.

"I need to do it, Nathan—it feels right."

"Then do it."

"W-we have too many things that are yours or mine, and so few that are ours."

"Everything I have is yours, Mallory—I thought you knew that."

She felt tears burn in her eyes as she looked around at the huge dining room, with its elegant furnishings, its twin chandeliers, its oriental rugs. "I—I've spent so little time here, I feel like a guest."

"You still don't like this house, either, do you, Mallory? You're only here to please me."

She shook her head quickly. "I love this house, Nathan. It's so spacious and airy and elegant. It's just that usually—well—"

Nathan finished for her. "Usually, there are too many people here."

Glumly, Mallory nodded.

"That will change now," he said, and his gaze shifted from Mallory's face. "I'm retiring, remember?"

Though she knew that he hadn't meant her to, Mallory heard the reluctance in his voice. If he was reluctant now, how would he feel in a few weeks, a few months, a year? His career was understandably important to him. Would the loss of it make him bitter?

"I think one unemployed McKendrick is enough. Don't give up music because of me, Nathan. I couldn't bear to be the cause of that."

His eyes returned to her face now, but their expression was unreadable in the dim light. "I love you, Mallory—and I need you. Our marriage is more important to me than anything else in my life, including music."

"But you really don't want to quit, do you?"

He left his chair to stand beside hers, and his hand was gentle under her chin. "I'm not sure, Mallory. The only thing I really have a handle on right now is that our marriage is on shaky ground."

Mallory nodded in sad agreement and searched his face with wide, anxious eyes. "Nathan, please don't retire because of me. There has to be some other way."

He tilted his head to one side. "We need time, babe. Besides, do you think you're the only one who ever gets tired?"

Mallory had been to dozens of Nathan's concerts, and she was suddenly conscious of the incredible energy he expended when he performed. Add to that the constant travel and the endless rehearsals, and the formula for physical and emotional exhaustion was complete. "Then take six months off," she said quickly, "or even a year."

He looked away, considering. "A year," he said, finally. "I'll take a year off. At the end of that time, we'll talk again, Mrs. McKendrick."

Mallory offered a handshake to seal the bargain, but Nathan did not return the gesture in the usual way. Instead, he turned her hand and kissed the delicate, supersensitive skin on the inside of her wrist.

She trembled involuntarily, and Nathan chuckled in gruff amusement.

"Umm," he teased. "A year of candlelight dinners and love-making—I may never go back to work."

His tongue found the inside of her palm, teased it ruthlessly. "You'll—be—bored," Mallory managed, between gasps of helpless pleasure.

He drew her up and out of the chair, held her close. "Never that," he said, his lips at her temple now.

"Nathan."

His hands were drawing her sweater upward, making warm soothing circles on the small of her back. "I want you," he said.

Mallory shivered as both his index fingers found their way beneath the waistband of her jeans and circled her to meet boldly at the snap in front. It gave way, and so did the zipper.

Mallory gasped as he drew her jeans down over her hips, her thighs, her ankles. "Nathan," she protested, even as she stepped out of the jeans. "This is the dining room!"

He was kneeling before her now, and his hands were idly stroking her ankles, first one, and then the other. "How appropriate," he said.

In the morning, Mallory awakened to find that the snow had stopped. Humming, pleased that she had for once woken up before Nathan, she scrambled out of bed and made her way into the master bath. There, in the massive sunken tub, she took a long, luxurious bath.

She was about to get out of the tub again when she noticed

the froth of pink chiffon hanging, half-hidden, from a peg on the inside of the open door.

Do not jump to conclusions, Mallory, she thought. Slowly, she rose from the tub, climbed out and wrapped herself in a thick, thirsty towel. Her feet seemed reluctant to obey her mind as she forced herself toward the door and the bit of pink fluff hanging so naturally upon it.

It's probably mine, she assured herself. *I probably left it here, like the swimming suit and the teddy and—*

She took the garment down from its peg carefully, frowned as she turned it in her hands. It was a nightgown, short and tiered with lace-trimmed ruffles, and Mallory had never seen it before in her life.

She swallowed the aching lump that had risen in her throat and read the tiny gold label tucked away in one seam of the gown. The words stitched there made Mallory's eyes widen, replaced her rage with embarrassment, and caused her to stomp one foot and bellow, "Nathan McKendrick!"

He appeared as though summoned from a genie's lamp, peering with comical caution around the framework of the door.

"This isn't one bit funny!" she cried, waving the gossamer pink gown at him. "How long did it take poor Mrs. Jeffries to stitch 'Trust me, Mallory' onto this label!"

Nathan's broad, bare shoulders moved in an idle shrug. "Not long—she's a whiz with a needle."

She was still waving the nightgown. "I thought this was—I thought—"

"For shame, Mrs. McKendrick."

"Rat!"

He laughed. "Put your clothes on before I ravish you. We're spending the day in Seattle."

Mallory flung the nightgown at him, embarrassment still coloring her cheeks and quickening her breath. She couldn't have spoken if it had meant her life.

Nathan dodged the assault of pink ruffles and swatted her

playfully on the backside. "Where is your sense of humor, woman?"

Seething, Mallory swung one foot at him, trying to kick him in the shins. She missed, and her towel slipped unceremoniously to the floor, baring her to his delighted gaze. She went to retrieve the towel, but he was too quick—he grabbed it and waved it as though it were a matador's cape.

"Toro!" he yelled.

Despite her fury and her embarrassment, an involuntary smile tugged at one corner of Mallory's mouth. She kicked at him again, somewhat halfheartedly this time, and, in an instant, he had dropped the towel and caught both her elbows in his hands, pulling her close to him.

She wriggled, trying to free herself, but the motion only increased her awareness of Nathan's hard, masculine frame. "I th-thought we were g-going to Seattle," she stammered.

He laughed gruffly, and buried his face in her neck to nibble at the pulsing flesh there. The clean scent of his hair confused Mallory's senses, so that she no longer knew whether she wanted to be loved or left alone. "We are going to Seattle," he said. "Later."

They caught a midmorning ferry and enjoyed a certain amount of privacy, since the early rush was over. Mallory, publicly visible only on the soap opera, was not generally recognized anyway, but Nathan was known the world over, and keeping a low profile was not so easy for him. He managed it that day, for the most part, having dressed circumspectly in old jeans, a plaid flannel shirt and a denim jacket. Though there were the usual questioning stares, not one of the other passengers approached either him or Mallory.

"I think I'm losing my touch," he confided to Mallory, with a grin, clasping his gifted hands together on the snack-bar tabletop and leaning forward.

Mallory giggled. "Not likely, handsome." She stole a surreptitious glance at two teenage girls sitting in another part of the snack bar. Though they were trying to be subtle, their wide eyes kept straying to Nathan. "They can't be sure whether you're you or not. It would be humiliating, after all, to ask for your autograph and then find out that you're a crane operator from Bremerton."

Nathan laughed, softly, and there was something wistful in the sound. "Sometimes I wish I could be."

Mallory had been stirring her diet soda with her straw, but the motion stopped at her husband's words. "Really? Why, Nathan?"

But he was looking away now, and that wistful note that had sounded in his laugh and in his voice had stilled and risen to haunt his eyes. He watched the gulls soaring alongside the ferry, just a few feet beyond the window, and the muscles beneath the shoulders of his worn denim jacket were oddly slack.

Saddened for a reason she could not have begun to explain, Mallory reached out to cover one of his hands with her own. "Nathan?"

He sighed and turned back to her. "What?" he asked.

"Why do you wish you could be a crane operator from Bremerton?" she insisted.

He sat back in the unaccommodating plastic chair, and his shoulders were taut again. "I guess because their lives seem so peaceful and ordered to me. They go to work in the morning, come home to cold beer and good sex and the evening news. Some little kid in flannel pajamas tries to run over their feet with a plastic motorcycle that has pedals and—"

Mallory chuckled, though unaccountable tears were smarting in her eyes. "Do you wish we had children, Nathan?"

He looked down quickly at his coffee cup. "Maybe," he muttered after a long, painful pause.

Mallory looked out at the blue-gray sky, the water, the tree-lined shore in the distance. Inadvertently, she'd touched on a subject she hadn't meant to broach—children. Her arms ached for a baby of her own, a baby of Nathan's, but there had never been any time in their hectic lives to seriously consider starting a family.

Too, thinking of babies made her think, inevitably, of Renee Parker. Much of her pain, she knew now, had originated not so much in the fact of Nathan's alleged betrayal, but in his having a child that would not be hers.

With as much subtlety as possible, Mallory took a paper napkin from the table and dried the tears that glistened in her eyelashes. She drew a deep breath and forced a shaky smile to her mouth. "How dare you imply that only crane operators have good sex?" she demanded. "Not an hour ago, Mr. International Rock Star, you were pretty happy yourself."

Nathan laughed and made a growling sound, low in his throat, and, after that, they didn't speak of children again, but of their plans for the day.

Mallory loved her husband and was happy in this new wealth of time and closeness they were sharing, but she sensed a certain distance between them, too. Renee Parker was like a specter in their midst, unseen but always there.

After leaving the ferry, the McKendricks drove to a place they both loved—Pike Place.

The Pike Place Market, with its vegetable stands and open fish markets and craft items of every sort, was a big tourist attraction during the summer, but, now, in winter, it was less crowded.

After leaving the car, Mallory and Nathan ventured inside the large, aging building that comprised much of the market. Here, exotic parrots squawked in their cages, striking up incoherent arguments with the occasional wino. Shopkeepers sold everything from antiques to scrimshaw, dolls to old movie magazines. One merchant dealt in colorful kites of every size and shape, while another sold specially tinted photographs that made the posers look like fugitives from the distant past.

Nathan paused in front of this shop, his hand warm and strong over Mallory's, and studied the sample photographs on display in the windows. The men in the pictures were dressed, like the women, in period costume—some resembled outlaws, some lawmen, some cavalry officers. The women could choose from such nineteenth-century gems as long dresses with high Victorian collars and sweeping feathered-and-flowered hats, the delightfully skimpy garb of a dance-hall girl, or the calico-and-bonnet attire of a pioneer wife.

Nathan extended a crooked elbow in a gesture of grand invitation, his eyes sparkling. "Shall we, Mrs. McKendrick?" he asked formally, the merest hint of a grin tugging at his lips.

Mallory took the offered arm with decorum. "Oh, let's do, Mr. McKendrick," she replied.

The coming minutes were a delight of laughter and confusion—the McKendricks inspected costume after costume, before reaching a mutual decision. In the end, the photographer posed them as a lawman and a dance-hall girl—Nathan sitting sternly at a round table, a straight shot of pseudowhiskey in the curve of his gun hand, a remarkably authentic handlebar mustache stuck to his upper lip, a star-shaped badge gleaming on his rough tweed coat. He wore a round-brimmed hat that gave him a sort of menacing appeal, and his Colt .45 lay within easy reach on the tabletop.

Mallory, wearing a satiny merry widow and fishnet stockings, was posed beside him, one shapely leg resting on the seat of a wooden chair. Her hair, pinned up for effect, was half-hidden by a saucy little hat constructed mainly of satin, feathers and loose morals.

Both the marshal and the soiled dove had a hard time keeping straight faces until after the picture had been taken.

8

The crazy, quiet joy of that day notwithstanding, Mallory was still not well, and, once in her regular clothes again, she felt oddly deflated. Since there would be a twenty-minute wait for the special photograph, she sank gratefully into a chair at one of the tables in the wide hallway outside the shop and sighed.

Nathan gave her a gentle, discerning look. "Getting tired?"

She nodded. "I'll be all right in a minute, though."

Still standing, Nathan reached out and touched her face tenderly. "I'll scare up some coffee, pumpkin. Rest."

Coffee was one of Mallory's favorite vices—Nathan often said that it ran in her veins instead of blood—and a cup of that bracing brew sounded very good to her just then. "You drive a hard bargain, fella. Don't forget the artificial sweetener."

He laughed and turned away and, in only a moment, he had disappeared into the shifting, scattered crowds.

Mallory sighed and laced her fingers together on the tabletop, watching with interest as a little blond boy came bounding out of the nearby kite shop, clutching a colorful bag and beaming. He turned to look back at someone behind him and blurted, "Let's get ice cream now, okay? Let's get ice cream!"

"No way, Jamie," a very familiar feminine voice argued. "It's winter and I'm cold and it's hot chocolate or nothing!"

Mallory's mouth dropped open when Diane Vincent stepped into view. She looked away quickly, hoping that the woman wouldn't notice her, but she soon learned that she'd been unsuccessful.

"Hello, Mallory."

Mallory forced herself to look up, even to smile. *Might as well make the best of it, McKendrick,* she thought. "Diane," she said in greeting.

"It's incredible the way we keep running into each other, isn't it?" Diane asked, as Jamie drifted off to look at a display of space-war books in a nearby window. "Is Nathan with you?"

"Yes, as a matter of fact," Mallory replied. Now that the child, Jamie, was otherwise occupied, she saw no reason to be polite. "Did you want to see him?"

Diane bridled slightly, then recovered herself. She was casual elegance itself in her trim flannel slacks, turtleneck sweater and blazer. "It's nice to see that you're putting on such a brave front," she said, ignoring Mallory's question.

Mallory sat back in her chair, pretending to be relaxed, though inwardly she was seething. She let Diane's remark pass and glanced at Jamie, who was still admiring the bookstore display.

"He's my nephew," Diane offered, without apparent emotion. "When are you going back to the soap, Mallory?"

Mallory met Diane's gaze again, shrugged. "I'm in no particular hurry. Right now, I'm more concerned with my marriage."

Diane's pastel blue eyes sparkled with refined malice. "Now there's a hopeless pursuit, if I've ever heard one."

Swallowing hard, Mallory clung to her tenuous composure with all her strength. She could have kicked herself for giving Diane the opening she just had. "Speaking of hopeless pursuits, have you found a new job yet?"

There was a short, chilling silence, and then Diane smiled and tossed her beautiful head. "Oh, I'm in no hurry. Nathan was quite—generous—when we were together. I've got plenty of money. And now, plenty to do."

Mallory arched one eyebrow. *I should get an Emmy for this,* she thought. *Here I am, so calm and collected, when I'd like nothing better than to tear out this witch's hair, hank by shimmering hank.* "I'll bite, Diane. Why do you have plenty to do?"

"I'm planning to write a book—with a little help from a friend."

"Splendid."

"It's all about my affair with Nathan."

Mallory smiled slowly, acidly. "Oh, a novel. I would have expected nonfiction."

A fetching pink color rose in Diane's cheeks to complement the soft blue of her eyes. "You are so very good at deluding yourself, Mallory. That's probably how you're handling the paternity scandal, isn't it?"

"That suit is a crock, Diane, and we both know it."

Diane shrugged, and her eyes shifted briefly to her nephew before coming back to Mallory's face. "Maybe it is—she's a kid, after all. But I'm not, Mallory, and I've spent more nights with Nathan than you have. What do you think we were doing in all those hotel suites, all over the world—learning the languages?"

"Save it for your book, Diane."

"What book?" demanded a third voice, and Mallory looked up to see Nathan standing just behind Diane, a cup of coffee in each hand.

Diane squared her shoulders and faced him with a bravery Mallory couldn't help admiring. She ran one smartly gloved hand over the breast pocket of Nathan's denim jacket in an intimate, unpracticed-looking gesture and smiled. "I'm telling all, sugarplum. You don't mind, do you?"

Nathan looked, for just a moment, as though he would like to pour the coffee he carried down the front of Diane's sweater. "Of course not," he said, after a second or two. "Just make sure you get releases from all those bellhops and stagehands. That should take months."

Patches of crimson appeared on Diane's glamorous cheekbones. "Bastard," she hissed.

Nathan lifted one of the coffee cups in an insolent toast. "At your service," he said.

Bested, though Mallory suspected the condition was only temporary, Diane whirled away, collected her startled nephew from in front of the book shop and disappeared.

Mallory's hand trembled a little as she reached out for the coffee Nathan offered before sitting down at the table with her.

"Are you okay?" he asked after a moment.

Unable to look at him, Mallory nodded. "Sometimes I think that woman follows me around, just waiting for a chance to get under my skin."

"I should have fired her a long time ago."

Before Mallory had to come up with a reply to that, the clerk in the antique-photo shop came out and indicated with a gesture that the picture was ready.

They were inside the Porsche and well away from the Pike Place Market before either of the McKendricks spoke.

"Mallory, I'm sorry."

Mallory stole a glance at her husband, saw that he was looking straight ahead at the traffic. "For what?"

Still, he did not look at her; she would have felt his gaze if he had. "About Diane—about the paternity suit. All of it."

Mallory swallowed hard and laced her fingers together in her lap. "Do you have some reason to be sorry about Diane?"

"Nothing like you're thinking. I've never touched her, Mallory."

Closing her eyes, Mallory let the back of her head rest against the rich suede car seat. She couldn't help remembering the way Diane had touched Nathan back at the market. There had been some truth in Diane's words, too—she *had* probably spent more time with Nathan than Mallory herself. Could he have been in constant and close proximity with such a stunningly beautiful woman and never taken the pleasures she had surely offered time and again?

Weary misery squeezed Mallory's heart like a strong hand. Now, with her self-confidence at an unusually low ebb, it was so easy to think the worst.

"Mallory?"

She opened her eyes, stiffened in the car seat. Nathan was turning into the circular driveway of their apartment complex, shifting down, drawing the Porsche to a smooth stop. She stared at him in question, but said nothing.

"I think you need to rest for a while," he informed her, not quite meeting her eyes. "I'll see you upstairs and run a few errands while you're sleeping."

"What errands?" she retorted, and the words were rife with suspicions she hadn't meant to reveal.

Nathan's hands tightened on the steering wheel for a moment, then relaxed. When he looked at her, his dark eyes were snapping with sardonic fury. "I thought I'd go out and buy off all my former mistresses," he said coldly, "lest they write books. After that, I'll probably trip at least one old lady and roll a wino or two."

"Very funny!" Mallory shot back in a scathing whisper, as a delighted George rushed toward the car.

"If you're so worried about what I'm doing, Mallory," Nathan bit out, "why don't you hire a detective to follow me around?"

"That would make it too hard to keep on kidding myself!"

Before Nathan could reply to that, the doorman had reached Mallory's side of the car and opened the door to help her out. Her husband remained behind the wheel, glaring straight ahead, and when Mallory and George were clear of the vehicle, he shifted it into gear again and sped away, tires screeching on the slushy asphalt.

George cleared his throat but was careful not to let on that he'd noticed the obvious rift between the McKendricks. Graciously, he escorted Mallory all the way to the penthouse and left her only when she was safely inside.

Once she was alone, Mallory allowed the tears she'd been holding back in the name of dignity to flow unhampered. Damn it, she'd fallen right into Diane's trap, had allowed the bitch to spoil an otherwise delightful day.

Not bothering to dry her face, Mallory shrugged out of her coat and tossed it toward the brass coat tree just to the side of the doors, missing it completely and not caring. She paused to glance at the stack of mail waiting on the hall table. Even through blurred eyes, she could see that most of it was addressed to Nathan.

Except for one plain postcard, postmarked Eagle Falls. Mallory dashed away her tears and read the neat, flowing handwriting on the back with a sort of calm desperation.

I've been trying to call you. You're never where you said you'd be. My boyfriend got a job in Alaska, on a fishing boat. Could you get me a ticket to watch your TV show in real life?

Renee

At the end of the scatterbrained missive was a carefully printed telephone number. Mallory went to the closest phone—the one in the living room—and punched out the digits. After four rings, a woman answered.

"Is Renee there, please?" Mallory asked.

"Who is this?" the other party countered with tart suspicion.

"Mallory McKendrick," was the dignified response. *It's a good thing she can't see my mascara-streaked face,* Mallory thought. "Please—it's important that Renee and I talk."

There was a sort of irritated awe in the woman's voice as she called out, "Renee! It's that singer's wife!"

Mallory closed her eyes. *That singer's wife.* Well, at least she hadn't called her "Tracy."

"Tracy?!" chirped Renee, a moment later.

"Renee, my name is Mallory."

"Whatever. I've been trying to get ahold of you."

A minor ache began to pound beneath the rounding of Mallory's skull. "What do you want, Renee—besides a pass to watch us tape the show?"

"Just that. A ticket."

"What makes you think I'd be inclined to do you any favors?" The question was spoken calmly, evenly. Mallory was proud of herself.

"I never saw a real TV show before!" Renee wailed.

Instantly, Mallory was out of patience. Her dignity deserted her, and so did her determination to be civil. "Now you listen to me, you vacuous little bimbo, and you listen well. My husband is a good man, a decent man, and you've hurt him very badly with your lies. Furthermore, I don't give a *damn* that you've never seen a taping. Don't call me, Renee, and don't write to me—not unless you're ready to tell the truth!"

Incredibly, Renee began to cry.

But Mallory was not inclined toward mercy. She hung up the phone with a crash and was rewarded by the sound of applause from behind her.

She whirled and blushed hotly to see Nathan standing in the doorway of the living room, watching her. "Thank you," he said evenly.

A sob, sudden and raw, tore itself from Mallory's throat. "Damn you!" she shrieked, half-hysterical. "Why do you have to be handsome and famous and—and—"

He approached her cautiously, as one might approach a harmless creature flailing in a trap. Without a word, he drew her close, held her, tangled one soothing hand in her hair.

After a time, her grief abated a little, and the racking sobs that had been rising from the very core of her soul became sniffles. "Damn," she whispered raggedly. "Oh, damn—damn—"

Just then, the phone rang again. The sound so startled Mallory that she stiffened in Nathan's arms and gasped.

"I'll get it," he said gently, pressing the still-shaken Mallory into a chair before grasping the receiver and snapping, "Hello?"

Mallory watched as one of his eyebrows arched.

"How in the hell did you get this number?" Nathan demanded. His eyes, dark and unreadable, turned to Mallory as he listened to the caller's response. "She did? All right, so talk—yeah—? Thank you, Renee."

Mallory felt the color drain from her tear-smudged face as she saw the cold, murderous anger in Nathan's eyes. He hung up the telephone with a crash and started toward the door without so much as a backward glance.

"Nathan!" Mallory cried out, scrambling out of the chair "Where—what—?"

He paused but did not turn to face her. "Brad Ranner," he said, in low, frightening tones. "Brad Ranner paid Renee to name me as the father of her baby."

Mallory's knees felt as though they'd turned to sand. "My God," she breathed, stunned. "Why?"

"I'm about to find out," Nathan replied, biting off the words, moving again. A moment later, he was gone.

After only a short deliberation, Mallory lunged for the telephone. She talked to a receptionist, then a stagehand before reaching Brad himself. He sounded harried, and his greeting was crisp and impatient.

"This is Mallory."

There was a short silence while Brad absorbed that simple statement. Apparently he'd accepted the call without his usual demand to know who was on the line first. At last, he sighed, and Mallory could almost see him rubbing his eyes with a thumb and forefinger, his customary gesture of annoyance. "Ah—my prima donna."

Mallory's voice was unusually high, but carefully modulated otherwise. "This is important, Brad."

"I'm sure it is, princess. Tell me, have you come to your senses or am I in line for another spate of moral outrage?"

"What you're in line for, my former friend," Mallory replied calmly, "is orthopedic surgery. Nathan just found out why Renee Parker named him as the father of her baby."

Brad swore, then recovered himself admirably. "Wonderful."

"Brad, how could you?"

He sighed. "It's a long, complicated story, Mallory—"

"I'll bet it is."

"There were good reasons for what I did!"

"All of them taxable and very handy when the bills fall due, no doubt. You thought I'd be more likely to stay on the show if my marriage broke up, didn't you? Well you can take your stupid soap opera, Brad Ranner, and you can—"

"Mallory, for God's sake—"

She drew a deep breath. "Tut-tut, Brad, no time to quibble. If Nathan gets past studio security, you may find yourself in demand for body-cast scenes."

"You're calling from the island, right?"

"You wish. I'm calling from the penthouse."

Brad swore again and hung up.

Mallory replaced her own receiver slowly, pondering. Nathan would be furious that she'd warned Brad, but it had been the only thing she could do, in good conscience. When his storming rage had subsided, he would understand.

What would happen before that was anybody's guess.

Resigned, Mallory turned to walk away from the phone, only to be stopped again by its ringing. She stared at it for a few moments, and then answered with a sharp greeting.

"There you are," Trish said. "You rat, what are you doing in the city? We were supposed to arrange the sale of your house today."

Mallory sighed, relieved. "So arrange it. I trust you."

"Mall, are you all right? You sound funny."

She carried the phone to the teakwood bar, set it down and began the one-handed preparation of a stiff drink. "I'm fine. Wonderful. You and Kate were right—Brad Ranner did put Renee up to suing Nathan."

Trish drew in her breath. "Wow! Does Nathan know that?"

"Know it? He's on his way to the studio as we speak."

"No doubt planning to tattoo the whole ugly story on Ranner's face," Trish supplied.

"I hope he doesn't."

"Why?"

"Because I want to."

"Well, Mall, at least you're off the hook. I mean, now you won't have to go back and finish out your contract. Nobody would blame you if you didn't, not after—"

"Wait a second. A contract is a contract. I mean to honor mine, Trish."

"What?"

Mallory took a sip of her ineptly made drink and grimaced, setting the glass aside. "You heard me."

"Nathan will have a *fit!*"

"No, he won't, Trish. This is business and the other thing is private and—"

"And why don't you try rowing with both oars in the water for once, Mallory? He's going to *hate* that guy for the rest of his life, and I can't say I blame him! Do you really think he's going to want you *working* with the creep?"

"He might be mad at first, but—"

"Mallory, he'll be furious."

"Then he'll just have to get over it. When I promise to do something, I do it."

Trish made a disgusted sound and hung up on Mallory without further ceremony.

Mallory shrugged, hung up the phone and wandered off toward the bathroom. What she needed now was a hot bath and a long nap, and if the telephone rang again, she would simply ignore it.

It was dark when she awakened, and her stomach let her know how hungry she was. With a sigh, she crawled out of bed, wrapped herself in a short pink satin robe and wandered out into the darkened living room.

There was a light in the kitchen, and she paused outside the swinging door for a moment, gathering her courage. When she entered that spacious room, she found Nathan sitting at the table, his back to her. The muscles beneath his plaid flannel shirt were rigid.

"You warned him," he said, without turning around.

"Yes."

"Why?"

Mallory lingered in the doorway, not daring to approach her husband. "I had to, Nathan."

His powerful shoulders moved in a weary sigh, and at last he turned to face her. There was a beleaguered look in his eyes, and he was pale beneath his Australian suntan. "Right—I know you did. But I really wanted to tear him apart."

Mallory entered the kitchen, letting the door swing shut behind her. "I'm starved," she said, making her way to the refrigerator. "How about you? Did you eat?"

He laughed, but it was a rueful, tired sound, and it tore at Mallory's heart even as she ferreted cheddar cheese and an apple from the refrigerator. "I'm not sure of very many things right now, pumpkin, but I do know that if I tried to eat anything, the results would be disastrous."

Mallory took the cheese to the cutting board, sliced off a haphazard hunk and rewrapped what was left. When she had put that away, she joined Nathan at the table and bit into the apple with a lusty crunch.

"When do you start rehearsals for the Seattle concert?" she asked, hooking her bare feet in a rung of her chair.

Nathan rolled his eyes. "Soon. I wanted some time with you before we started, but between Diane and Renee and now Brad, things have gotten pretty complicated."

Mallory nibbled thoughtfully at her cheese. "I know," she mused. "Maybe it would be better if you just concentrated on the concert for a while. After all, I've got a few more shows to tape, and—"

He broke in sharply. "Hold it. What did you just say?"

"I said you should concentrate on your concert. You know, choose the songs, rehearse—"

"After that."

Cold dread niggled and twisted in the pit of Mallory's stomach. She knew what he meant, but she widened her eyes in deliberate innocence. "About taping the shows?"

"Bingo."

"I have to, Nathan—I have a contract."

"Break it."

"No! I agreed to appear in a certain number of shows, and that's what I'm going to do."

An ominous calm came over Nathan as he rose slowly to his

feet. "I don't believe this. After what that bastard did to us, you're actually going to *work* with him?"

Mallory bit her lower lip. So Trish had been right—all hell was about to break loose. "I'm not doing it for him, Nathan," she said quietly. "I'm doing it for myself. I don't want to remember it as an unfinished job all my life."

"How about our marriage, Mallory? How do you want to remember that?"

Fury stung Mallory like a giant bee, and the venom sent her surging to her feet, her late-night snack forgotten. "Are you threatening me, Nathan McKendrick?"

His face, so beloved, so familiar, was suddenly the face of an angry stranger. "Damn it, Mallory, haven't we both been through enough without this? My lawyers can break your contract."

"Don't you dare call them in!"

"Why are you being so damned stubborn? You've been an asset to that show, but it isn't going to fold without you. Why can't you just cut your losses and run?"

"Nathan, this is a point of honor. *You've* never broken a contract in your life—why do you expect me to do it?"

A muscle in his jawline tightened, and dark rage shifted in his eyes. "This is different."

"Is it? Why—because it involves my career, not yours?"

He turned away from her then in an obvious effort at self-control, and drew a deep, ragged breath. "If it's so important to you, Mallory, why are you quitting at all?"

"Because I have no desire to get naked in front of several million people, for one thing!" The words were spoken impulsively, and when Mallory saw the responding charge of unbridled fury move in her husband's broad shoulders, she regretted ever saying them.

He whirled to face her. *"What?"*

She lowered her eyes. There was no going back now; it was too late to hedge. "The show is going on a cable network," she said evenly, "and that means they'll have a lot more freedom. There will be some nude love scenes."

"Brad wanted you to do *nude love scenes?*"

"Will you relax, Nathan? I said no, and that's the end of it. I'm just going to fulfill my contract and leave the show."

Nathan was standing stock still. "Why, that—"

"Nathan."

His dark eyes were fierce on Mallory's face. "Call Ranner right now, Mallory," he ordered. "Tell him you're not coming back, ever."

"No."

Nathan's rage, like lava inside a volcano, was a frightening thing to behold. After raking his wife with one scathing, menacing glare, he turned and stormed toward the door without so much as a backward glance.

Mallory bolted after him. "Nathan, wait! Where are you going?"

His retreating form was a moving shadow in the darkness of the enormous living room. "Out!" he shouted back.

A second later, the front door slammed behind him.

Mallory had trouble focusing on the morning paper, and finally she yawned and tossed it aside in defeat. She hadn't slept the night before; she'd been consumed by rage one minute and racked by pain the next.

Nathan had never come to their bed at all, though she had heard him pass by in the wee hours of the morning on his way to one of the extra bedrooms. She considered all the places he might have been before that and flushed with helpless fury.

Just then, the kitchen door swung open and he walked in, looking surly and unshaven and rumpled. He was barefoot, though he had, at least, pulled on a pair of old jeans.

"Good morning," Mallory said stiffly, watching, with irritated fascination, the play of the muscles in his naked back as he opened the refrigerator door.

By way of an answer, he scowled at her and then turned back to his perusal of the refrigerator's rather meager contents. Finally, he extracted a quart of milk and set it down on the nearest counter with a thump.

Mallory watched with amusement as he plundered the cupboards, one by one, too stubborn to ask where to find the items he wanted. When he'd found cereal and a bowl, the ransacking began all over again.

"Top drawer beside the dishwasher," Mallory said.

He made a face at her, wrenched open the drawer and took out a spoon. Some of the milk slopped over the side of his cereal bowl as he set it down on the table.

"The rock star at home," Mallory observed wryly as he fell into a chair and ate a spoonful of cereal. "If only *People* magazine could see you now."

He grumbled something insensible.

But Mallory was in the mood to plague him. "I hope that milk isn't sour," she mused. "The housekeeper only buys it to put in her coffee."

Nathan glanced sharply at the milk carton and then went on eating. Just the slightest color rose in his face as he munched; she knew he'd been alarmed and then realized that he'd already tasted the milk and found it palatable. No doubt, he felt a little foolish.

Before Mallory could say anything else, the telephone rang. She went to the wall phone nearby and chimed a sweet hello into the receiver.

"Hi," Pat said in a breezy, yet conspiratorial voice. "I trust Nathan is home?"

"Yep," Mallory said, watching him out of the corner of her eye as he opened the milk carton and sniffed it questioningly. "And I must say, he's the first person I've ever known who didn't trust his own taste buds."

"I'll refrain from asking you to elaborate on that remark, Mall. Don't call him to the phone—I just wanted to tell you that he spent most of last night on my living room sofa."

"Ah," Mallory said. "I was wondering."

"I thought you might have been," Pat replied. "Just to keep

the peace, I wanted you to know the straight scoop. He's mad at you, and he's just ornery enough to try and make you think he was in the middle of an orgy.''

Mallory looked at her husband and, despite the rigors of the night just past and the painful battles of previous days, her eyes danced with mischief. "Why of *course,* Mr. Hefner," she gushed. "I'd *love* to be a centerfold! May? Certainly! I'll start undressing now!''

On the other end of the line, Pat laughed uproariously. Nathan shot out of his chair, realized that he'd been had, and sank, scowling, back into it.

"Give him hell, McKendrick," Pat said before she rang off.

Mallory hung up the phone, squared her shoulders and swallowed a giggle. "Where were you last night?" she demanded imperiously, fixing her husband with a steely glare.

Nathan slid his empty cereal bowl away and tried hard to look guilty. "Wouldn't you like to know, woman?"

Mallory took up her empty coffee cup and went to the electric percolator on the counter to refill it. With a dramatic toss of her head, she imparted, "Such is my fate—to share you with uncounted women."

He laughed, and the sound was warm and intimate and comfortable to hear. "This has gone far enough. I was tossing and turning on Pat's couch and you damned well know it—Miss May.''

"I'm holding out for October," Mallory said airily, coming back to the table with her fresh coffee. "I've always wanted to pose nude with seventeen pumpkins and a scarecrow.''

"Kinky," Nathan observed. "You're not going to break your contact with Brad, are you?"

Mallory sighed. No doubt, the light repartee was over and there would be another fight. "No," she said, bracing herself inwardly.

But a grin lifted one corner of Nathan's mouth, and he shook his head in bewildered amusement. "How the hell am I supposed to be a domineering husband if you won't ever give in?"

"I'm not being stubborn, Nathan," Mallory replied seriously. "It's a point of honor with me, that's all."

"Honor is wasted on the likes of Brad Ranner, but, for the sake of my sanity, I'm not going to fight you. Which is not to say I wouldn't like to fight *him.*"

Mallory shrugged. "Do to him what you will, oh avenging master—just don't get yourself thrown into jail. I've had all the separations I need."

Nathan looked away, toward the coffeepot, which emitted an electronic chortle. "I went to his apartment last night, before calling on my sensible sister."

"And?"

"And his housekeeper told me he was in Mexico, taking a vacation."

Mallory laughed. "He's in hiding!"

"If he's smart, he'll *stay* in hiding."

"Why did you go to Pat's house last night, instead of to the island or somewhere else?"

Nathan grinned. "I knew she'd make me see reason. Since when did she stop being my sister and become yours? She called me an idiot!"

"If the sombrero fits, wear it, *señor.*"

He grimaced. "Very funny. Open your bathrobe."

Mallory arched one eyebrow and brought a protective hand to clasp the robe shut at the neck. "I beg your pardon?"

"I want to see if you're centerfold material."

She stood up in mock outrage, bent on fleeing the scene to shower and dress. But Nathan caught her arm, without rising from his chair, and wrenched her onto his lap.

She struggled—albeit halfheartedly—but he subdued her easily and situated her so that she was astraddle his lap, facing him. Then, with an animal growl, he opened her robe.

Mallory gasped in pleasurable indignation as he caught both her wrists behind her, in one powerful hand, and pressed them against the small of her back, so that her full and pulsing breasts, now deliciously vulnerable, were thrust toward him.

She shivered as he bent his head to flick tauntingly at one nipple with just the tip of his tongue. The rosebud morsel responded with a fetching pout.

"Yum," he said, and his breath was warm against the tingling flesh of Mallory's breast.

Mallory moaned, and when she spoke, her breath came in soft gasps. "Will—I—do?"

He went to the other nipple, brought it to the same peak as its counterpart. "You definitely will," he rasped. "But not as a centerfold."

Mallory squirmed slightly in pleasure as he teased the chosen nipple, causing it to throb. "Why not?" she whispered.

Nathan laughed and opened her robe further, though he still held her prisoner, assessing her with smoldering approval. With his free hand, he touched her stomach. "There would be a staple here," he said, sliding fiery fingertips across her abdomen to the other side. "And here."

"We can't—ooh—have that—"

"Umm," replied Nathan, in a greedy purr. And then he chuckled as Mallory arched her back and tilted her head back, offering herself freely.

Slowly, sensuously, he drank his fill of her, his warm mouth tugging at one breast and then at the other, until Mallory was frantic with the need to join with him, to soar with him, to cause him the same tender torment he was causing her.

But Nathan was in no hurry. He feasted upon her until she was certain she could bear no more, and then he lifted her, so that she was standing, and feasted again.

And as he savored her, Mallory trembled, and her passions built to new heights. Whimpering low in her throat, she arched herself toward him and tangled her fingers in his dark hair. Again and again, he brought her to the very precipice of total release, only to draw back again, and bare her aching secret, and stroke it to maddening need with the tip of one finger.

"What do you want, Mallory?" he teased in a gruff voice.

In halting words, she told him, and he moved to the floor,

drawing her with him, but even then he would not grant her what she was willing to plead for. She knelt, and he slid beneath her, drawing her down onto the warm, consuming motions of his mouth.

Her knees were spread far apart and she was frantic and she writhed upon the long, tormenting strokes of his tongue. Savage release stiffened her entire body, and her cry of gratification echoed throughout the kitchen.

She moved to free herself, but he held her, helplessly impaled on the pleasure he offered. "No—" she whimpered, "oh, no, Nathan—not again—please—"

He lifted her slightly, only high enough to vow, "I'm not through with you yet, lady. Not by a long shot."

"N-Nathan—"

But he was again kissing her, nibbling her, tasting her. Fierce and jagged desire shot through her; she could not hope to escape him and even if she could have, she would not have tried. With a sound that was part sob and part croon, she leaned forward to take the only vengeance available.

He moved beneath her in frantic surrender as she repaid him, and as she soared skyward on the wings of a searing release, he followed. Their cries mingled, ragged and primitive, and became one sound.

And when it was over, they lay still, casualties of the same battle, unable to move for a very long time.

Finally, Nathan sat up beside a still-supine Mallory, and caressed the love-warmed, passion-heavy breast that welcomed him.

"Enough?" she managed in a labored whisper, not knowing what she wanted his answer to be.

He laughed hoarsely. "Dreamer. I could make love to you from now till the day I draw my first Social Security check, lady, and it still wouldn't be enough. I want more of you—a lot more."

Mallory had finally caught her breath, and she laughed, too. "You are insatiable."

He released her breast to lay his palm on the kitchen floor. "And you are prone to waxy yellow buildup. Since that would be an ignoble fate, I think I'll carry you into the bedroom and have my way with you."

"Again?"

He chuckled. "Pumpkin, consider yourself laid."

With that, Nathan stood, pulled Mallory after him, and lifted her into his arms. "I love you so much," he said softly, and his mouth was gentle as it touched hers.

Mallory pushed at him, though she made no move to free herself from his embrace. "Listen, mister—I love you, too. But maybe I'm tired of always being the submissive partner. Maybe I'd like to be the leader for once."

"Lead on," he said gruffly.

And just moments later, in the quiet comfort of their bedroom, Nathan proved how strong he was, how secure in his own concept of himself. He was strong enough to be vulnerable, strong enough to submit.

9

The next day was a momentous one for the McKendricks—
Renee Parker withdrew her lawsuit without comment, and Mallory's house was officially up for sale. Too, rehearsals for the
Seattle concert began in earnest. Nathan prepared for it, with a
renewed spirit, and the house at Angel Cove rang with laughter
and music.

Determined not to be a wet blanket, Mallory watched and
listened as the days passed, but she also called on the adminis-
trator of the local elementary school and offered her services as
a substitute teacher, read a backlog of books that she hadn't had
time for before, and spent happy hours visiting Trish and Kate.

After two weeks, she was fully recovered.

Of course, she was delighted when her doctor pronounced her
well, but there was a tiny tremor in the pit of her stomach, too.
She had almost a month left to run on her contract with Brad,
and she still meant to honor it, even though she dreaded every
line and scene.

Tanned and probably well aware that Nathan was occupied in
another part of the villa on Angel Cove, Brad Ranner appeared
within an hour of Mallory's return from Seattle and her doctor's
office, a new script under his arm.

Mallory met him in the main entry hall, her eyes on the script.
"The death scene, I presume?"

Brad grinned. "Nothing so predictable, sweetheart. Tracy Ballard is going to be arrested for shoplifting and see the error of
her ways. In the end, she'll be flying off to serve with the Peace
Corps, thus atoning for her many sins."

In spite of everything, Mallory laughed. "Whatever else that storyline is, it can't be called 'predictable.' By the way, how are you accounting for Tracy's absence now?''

Brad passed Mallory and walked, with studied casualness, into the large, empty living room. There, he put the script on a coffee table and sat down on the sofa. "She's being held captive in the attic of an old church by her lover's crazed ex-wife."

Mallory shook her head in amused amazement and moved to the butler's cart, where Mrs. Jeffries had left a pot of hot coffee only minutes before. "Coffee?"

Brad cast a nervous look around the room and nodded. "Enough bravado. Is Nathan around?"

Mallory took china cups from the cart and filled them with the fresh, steaming coffee. "Nathan is busy in the studio, Brad—they're rehearsing for the Seattle concert."

"Good." Brad sighed in blatant relief. "Mallory, I—"

She stopped him with an icy look. "I think it would be better if we pretended all that stuff didn't happen, don't you?"

Brad was flushed. "No, I don't," he answered hotly. "Mallory, there are things I have to explain."

Mallory sighed and dropped into Nathan's favorite chair, her eyes fixed on her coffee cup. "None of it will make a difference, Brad."

"It might. Mallory, the paternity suit was Diane's idea—I'm sick and tired of being the heavy in this melodrama."

Mallory rolled her sea green eyes. "That doesn't surprise me, Brad—both Nathan and I suspected Diane. But it doesn't excuse what you did either. You had to have set this thing rolling long before we had that row about my contract and the cable offer."

Brad spoke gently. "I did. It was a rotten and devious thing to do, I know—"

"You can say that again. Why *did* you do it, Brad?"

He looked away. "Because I love you, Mallory. I have since the day you walked into the studio and read for Tracy Ballard's role. I thought you were single, until the people in public relations clued me in." Brad returned distracted blue eyes to Mallory's face, and the high color of embarrassment burned in his cheeks. "When I found out you were Nathan McKendrick's wife, I considered jumping off the Space Needle. As time went by, I could see that you were ultraunhappy, so—"

"So you decided to sandbag my marriage."

Shame was clear in Brad's eyes. "Something like that. God, Mallory, I'm sorry. I was into the thing before I really thought—"

Either Brad Ranner was genuinely remorseful or he was working on the wrong side of the cameras. In any case, Mallory had difficulty sustaining grudges, and she saw no point in hating Brad when the time they had to work together would be so short. "Forget it," she said in businesslike tones. And then she reached out for the script.

After that, the conversation centered on the neat disposal of Tracy Ballard. Though Mallory's contract still had more than thirty days to run, her commitment would be completed in only ten. She knew that this was a conciliatory gesture on Brad's part, and she was grateful.

When Brad was ready to leave, she walked him out to his car, chatting companionably. She was unprepared for the swift, brotherly kiss he planted on her cheek before sliding behind the wheel.

"Watch out for Diane, okay?" he said gently. "I may have seen the light, but she's into vengeance in a big way."

Mallory folded her arms and shook her head. "Surely even Diane must have given up by now."

"Don't count on it. I heard she was planning to make an offer on that house you're selling."

Openmouthed, Mallory stared at Brad, unable to speak. Dear Lord, surely Trish wouldn't sell her house to Diane Vincent! The moment she could, she would call and make certain.

Brad lifted one eyebrow. "Stay on your toes, baby doll. Even if she can't buy that particular house, she could find another to rent or something."

Glumly, Mallory nodded. At that time of year, there were empty houses aplenty on the island. She swallowed and changed the subject. "What about the cable deal, Brad?" she asked, stepping back as he started the engine of his white Corvette. "Did it go through?"

Brad shook his head ruefully. "Not yet. You're not that easy to replace, button. And let's face it, Seattle isn't exactly rife with accomplished actresses."

"It shouldn't be so difficult," Mallory argued. "Mine was only a minor role."

He shrugged. "Maybe I'm waiting for another Mallory."

She looked away, uncomfortable, anxious to get Trish on the telephone. "I'm sorry, Brad."

"Don't be. See you Monday, my love—and thanks."

Mallory arched an eyebrow. "For what?"

"For not throwing that contract in my face," he answered, shifting the car into Reverse. His lips moved slightly, miming a kiss, and then he was backing out of the driveway, onto the main road.

Mallory waved, then hurried back into the house and made a dive for the hall telephone. She punched out Trish's number and tapped one foot impatiently while she waited.

"Good morning!" Trish sang after at least five rings.

"Don't sell my house to Diane Vincent!" Mallory blurted without so much as a hello to precede her words.

Trish laughed. "Mallory, I presume? She asked me and I told her we wanted a cool million, since you were semifamous and all. I do have a good offer from a young couple in Seattle, Mall—he works at Boeing and she's a painter—"

"Take it."

"Don't you want to know how much?"

"I don't care how much."

"See. Well, they want those trees cut down first—the ones at the edge of the driveway. Afraid they'll fall through the roof next time we get one of our bridge-breaking windstorms."

Mallory sighed. She'd loved those trees, resisted every effort Nathan made to persuade her to have them chopped down. "Okay. The trees go. Can you arrange it, Trish, or shall I?"

"I'll do it, you pay the bill. Hey, why don't you come over here and have lunch with me?"

"The big real estate magnate has time for lunch with a neighbor?" Mallory teased.

Trish laughed. "The magnate in question is wearing an old bathrobe and cleaning out her fridge. It's a horror. I don't mind when food starts growing fur, but when it tries to learn the language, I draw the line."

Mallory rolled her eyes. "You actually expect me to eat at your house when you've just made a remark like that? Come over here—the housekeeper made enough tuna salad to feed an army."

"Knowing you, you probably need to get out of there for a while," Trish retorted. "I suppose the band is there?"

"Along with wives, girlfriends and the occasional impressed relative. Let's strike a compromise and meet at the Bayview for clam strips and french fries."

"You have a deal, McKendrick," Trish replied. "Meet you there in half an hour."

Trish was waiting when Mallory reached the Bayview Clam Bar, the only restaurant on the island. She looked patently terrific in a soft blue cashmere suit.

"Glad you didn't wear your bathrobe," Mallory observed dryly, taking her place at their favorite table.

Trish laughed and preened just a little. "Don't I look great? Thanks to you and the couple from Seattle, I can afford this getup!"

Mallory set her purse aside and folded her arms comfortably on the table edge. "You really like selling, don't you, Trish? Have you got any other clients besides me?"

Trish was beaming. "Do I. Mall, I think I've sold that old farmhouse on Blackberry Lane—the one with the ghost. I showed it to a doctor from Renton, and he loved it!"

A waitress came, bringing water glasses and taking their orders, and wandered off again. "I hope you charged extra for the ghost. That's a definite plus, in my book."

Trish laughed, but there was something unsettling behind the merriment in her blue eyes. "Mall—"

"What?"

"After I talked to you, Herb called me from the office. He—he—well—"

Mallory was annoyed. "He what?"

"He wanted to know where the keys were for those new duplexes over on the Cove. His exact words were, 'a knockout blonde from Seattle wants to rent two bedrooms and a view.'"

Mallory frowned. "It might not be Diane, Trish," she said, somewhat irritably. "Surely she isn't the only 'knockout blonde' in Seattle."

"It's her, all right. Herb said she was driving a red MG roadster."

Mallory closed her eyes for a moment. If Diane rented one of the duplex units in question, she would be living just beyond Nathan's property line. In fact, she would be the McKendricks's nearest neighbor. "Damn," she muttered.

Trish was obviously torn. "I could ask Herb not to rent one to her, but he'll get a commission and he has a family and all—"

"No. Business is business. Maybe she won't stay long." When Mallory opened her eyes, she saw that Trish looked doubtful. As doubtful as Mallory felt.

"That bimbo," Trish declared. "I wonder what she hopes to accomplish."

Mallory didn't wonder, she knew. But she felt no compulsion to burden Trish with her suspicions, so she deliberately shifted the conversation on to another course. Throughout the remainder of the luncheon, the two women debated the existence of the ghost on Blackberry Lane.

Reaching the house on Angel Cove again, Mallory found that the rehearsal was still going on. Staunchly she gathered up the script that Brad had brought by earlier and, since the weather was springlike, ventured outside to study it. She was sitting on a fallen log, facing the Cove and within sight of the villa, when she sensed that she wasn't alone and looked up from the meaty lines she'd been trying to memorize.

Nathan was standing before her, his back to the sun-shimmered, blue and silver Cove, looking undeniably handsome even in old jeans and a battered blue Windbreaker. "Hi," he said softly.

Mallory swallowed and, even though it was the last thing she'd wanted to do, stole one wary look at the duplexes just down the beach. There was a rented trailer backed up to the front door of one, and Diane's bright blond head gleamed in the sun as she supervised the unloading of the vehicle. "Hi," she replied distractedly.

Nathan had followed her gaze, she saw a moment later, and the muscles in his jawline were bunched with annoyance. He muttered a swearword and started toward the scene, but Mallory leapt up from her perch on the log and caught his arm.

"Nathan, no," she said quickly, a plea in her voice. "There's nothing we can do."

He threw a menacing look in Mallory's direction, but he stopped. "That—"

"Nathan, we have to ignore her. Don't you see? If you go storming over there and make a scene, you'll be doing just what she wants you to!"

His broad shoulders moved in an irritated sigh, and she heard a raspy breath enter his lungs and come out again. "Damn it, I knew I should have bought that property when it was for sale."

Mallory smiled, albeit shakily. "You can't buy the whole world, you know. And if those duplexes hadn't been built, she would just have found some other way to get to us."

Nathan sighed again and touched an index finger to the tip of her nose. "You know something, lady? You're not only beautiful, but smart."

Mallory executed a sweeping bow and dropped the script into the soft, pungent carpet of pine needles cushioning the ground. Nathan's eyes fell to the familiar logo on its cover, and Mallory almost expected the thing to ignite under the fierce heat of his gaze.

"He was here," Nathan said in a rasp.

Mallory swallowed hard and nodded. "It's only ten days' work, Nathan."

Nathan's throat constricted, and he tilted his head back to glower up at the sky. "Starting when?"

"Monday. Nathan, don't worry, okay? He was contrite—he apologized—"

Nathan's gaze, when it came to Mallory's face, was scathing. "Sure he was. And you, of course, were forgiving."

"Nathan, I have to work with the man. I couldn't very well stir up a battle!"

"You don't have to work with the man, as you put it. Christ, Mallory, between Ranner and Diane, haven't we had enough trouble? Why do you insist on setting us up for more?"

"We've been all through this, Nathan. I gave my word, remember?"

Nathan muttered something and whirled away, and this time his attention was focused on Mount Rainier, towering in the distance. "I need you here."

"You don't, and you know it. I've got to be in Seattle on Monday, Nathan, and that's all there is to it."

He sighed, and his shoulders moved in exaggerated annoyance. "You know, Mallory, sometimes it seems that I'm doing all the compromising here. I'm giving up concert tours—television specials—recording dates. Can't you give up ten days of acting?"

The disparaging note he gave that last word was not lost on Mallory. She stiffened, then bent to retrieve the script. "Okay," she said coldly. "You give up the concert in Seattle, and I'll quit right now."

He turned to face her, stunned. "That concert has been promoted, Mallory—the tickets are already sold-out and I've signed contracts!"

Mallory grinned and held up one index finger. "Contracts. The magic word. Yours, then, are binding, but mine aren't?"

"Damn it!" Nathan spat, and then, without another word, he turned and stormed back down the wooded path toward the villa.

Though she wanted to follow after her husband and double up her fists and beat on his impervious back in frustration, Mallory was determined to be professional to the end. With great effort, she sat down on the log again, opened the script and went back to learning her lines.

The boathouse was dark, and Nathan didn't bother to turn on the light. Even though it had been hours since the latest confrontation with Mallory, he was still smarting from it. The shabby structure where the previous owner of the villa had stored fishing gear was the only place on the island where he could be reasonably sure of a few minutes' privacy.

Even after years of disuse, the place still smelled of oil and bait and kelp. There was no sound, other than the distant complaint of a ferry horn and the rhythmic lapping of the water beneath the filthy wooden floor. Nathan muttered an ugly word and felt better for it.

He sat down on the floor, wrapping his arms around his knees, and sighed. Just when he had thought he and Mallory were really linking up, really communicating, everything had gone to hell again.

Why did he have to corner her like that, when he knew the one thing she absolutely couldn't deal with was being ordered around? Why was he making such a big thing out of ten lousy days' work?

The answer to that question wasn't easy to face. Nathan knew it all too well, whether he permitted himself to confront the issue or not. He was jealous of Brad Ranner.

Just then, the door of the boathouse creaked open, admitting a shaft of weak, dust-flecked light. Without thinking, Nathan cursed softly and betrayed himself, and the beam of the flashlight swung immediately in his direction.

"Leave me alone," he growled, turning his head.

The intruder was undaunted, drawing nearer. After a second or so, Diane Vincent knelt beside him, impulsively tangling gentle fingers in his hair.

"You look rotten, babe," she commiserated.

Nathan deflected her hand roughly. "Go away, damn it."

It was as though he hadn't spoken. Diane's fingers found their way into his hair again, offering a treacherous comfort. She turned off the flashlight, and it rattled on the dusty board floor as she set it aside.

"I can make it all better," she crooned, and the exotic, specially blended scent of her perfume whispered against Nathan's raw senses like a caress.

For one insane moment, he wanted her. He even drew her close, and his lips brushed against hers in the darkness, seeking, not caring who she was.

Mallory. The name rang through him like the toll of some infinite bell. He thrust Diane aside harshly and sprang to his feet.

Diane spoke with disdain. "Still the faithful husband. Oh, Nate, baby, you *are* a fool."

Nathan wanted to leave the boathouse, but for the moment, he couldn't seem to mobilize the muscles in his legs. "Shut up," he snapped. "Just shut up and get the hell out of here."

Diane had never been easily intimidated. "Do you really think your gamine girl has been saving her sweet favors just for you?" she challenged in a silken voice.

Nathan closed his eyes and his midsection tightened into a steel knot. He tried to speak and failed.

In an instant, Diane was close to him again, pressing her thighs against his, moving her hands in circles on his chest. He pushed her away again in a furious need to be free of her.

It was then that the overhead light came on, glaring, blinding Nathan for a fraction of a second. When his vision cleared, he swore again.

Mallory was standing in the doorway, Cinnamon's leash dangling from one hand, her face chalk white, her green eyes emerald with pain. She took in Diane's triumphant grin, muttered something unintelligible and turned to flee.

Nathan bolted after her, shouted her name. But she kept right on running.

It was dark, and the wharf was treacherous with its coiled ropes and mooring rings, so Mallory dared not run her fastest, even though her heart urged her to keep pace with its frantic, stricken beat. As she scrambled up the slight, rocky hillside above the wharf, she knew that Nathan was gaining on her, felt his approach in every one of her screaming senses.

At the base of the lawn fronting his gigantic house, he caught her, and his hands were inescapable as they grasped her shoulders, harsh with controlled desperation as they turned her to face him.

"Mallory."

She looked up at him in the moonlight, too broken to struggle. His face was in shadows. "Damn you," she whispered in a ragged, tortured voice. "Damn you, you lying, cheating—"

Mallory could feel his pain as well as her own—it was a fathomless chasm between them, pushing them apart rather than drawing them closer.

"Stop it," he demanded.

Mallory was gasping now, trying to close her mind to what she had seen in the boathouse just moments before. They'd been alone there, Nathan and Diane, in the darkness—

Nathan's hands moved from her shoulders to her upper arms, and his voice was a gruff plea. "Mallory, listen to me."

Mallory's black, pounding rage made her need to kick and scream, but she couldn't move. It was as though someone had coated her entire body in plaster. She gave a small, strangled cry.

"Mallory, it wasn't—I didn't—"

At last, Mallory found her voice. "Don't say it, Nathan," she warned. "Don't give me that trite old line about how it wasn't what it looked like. It was *exactly* what it looked like, and we both know it."

A harsh sigh tore itself from his throat. "Everything I say right now will be a cliché, won't it?" he asked with raw, dismal resignation. "Mallory, I wasn't going to make love to Diane."

Mallory trembled, remembering a certain look in Diane's eyes. "You kissed her," she said, whirling in his grasp.

But he would not release her, and his grip was fierce as he wrenched her back. "You're not going anywhere until we settle this, lady. If I have to drag Diane over here by the hair, you're going to hear the truth!"

"The truth was all too apparent in the boathouse, Nathan!"

He shook her hard. "Damn it, Mallory, this is all a mistake!"

"You can say that again, handsome. I guess it's been that from the first—our marriage, I mean."

"What?"

"I want a divorce, Nathan."

He released her so swiftly that she nearly fell into the wet grass that had so recently been buried in snow. "No way!" he snapped.

Mallory turned and scrambled across the lawn, too stricken to consider dignity now. Nathan kept pace easily, and at the base of the porch, she faced him again. "Why fight it, Nathan?" she asked in a contemptuous, pain-laced whisper. "Now you won't have to lie and meet in boathouses."

Nathan didn't make a sound, and yet it was as though he had shouted. The night air seemed to reverberate with his rage and his frustration.

Mallory hurried across the porch toward the garage. For once, a bad habit stood her in good stead—her keys were in the ignition of the car.

She drove carefully out of the driveway, knowing that Nathan would pursue her if she didn't, and a few minutes later, let herself into the house that had been home all her life. The house that would soon belong, no doubt, to happy strangers.

Inside, she locked the doors and then sank down into a chair at the kitchen table, not bothering to turn on a light. Only then could she release the terrible, scalding sobs. They racked her, leaving her exhausted and mute when they finally abated.

Never had Mallory endured a longer night.

Though she took a long, hot bath and swallowed a sleeping pill, rest eluded her. She tried reading and couldn't retain so much as a sentence. Music was out of the question—she dared not turn on the radio for fear of hearing Nathan's latest hit, and the stereo might as well have been a thousand miles from the bed.

Again and again, Mallory relived the disaster in the boathouse, and the resultant agony was beyond anything she had ever experienced before.

In a far corner of her mind, a small voice pleaded a reasonable, rational case, but Mallory could not or would not listen. She couldn't afford to delude herself; she'd done enough of that.

With the gray, stormy dawn came more snow. Dispiritedly, Mallory packed a few clothes, called Trish to let her know that she was leaving Cinnamon behind in her care.

"What's going on, Mall?" Trish demanded, sensing that something was terribly wrong even though her friend was doing her level best to hide it.

Mallory sighed. "If I talk about it, I'll start blubbering. How about if I call you from the city, tomorrow or the next day?"

"Mall—"

"Please, Trish. I can't."

"Okay, okay. But what about the house? Is it still for sale, or what?"

"It's for sale. I—I'll have somebody come and p-pack up my things if that c-couple wants to buy it—"

"Don't worry about that," Trish admonished in a gentle voice. "Mall, honey, are you sure you want to sell the place? Don't go ahead with it if—"

"I'm sure, Trish. Really."

"You'll call tomorrow or the next day?"

"I promise."

"Take care, love."

Mallory couldn't say any more. Trusting Trish to understand, she hung up, left the house and drove to the island's small ferry terminal.

Diane's beautiful face was tear swollen, and her meticulously applied mascara made inky streaks down her cheeks. Her knuckles were white where they gripped the edge of her sofa.

Nathan, leaning back against the mantel of the fireplace that graced her small living room, felt no pity, no inclination toward mercy. He'd already shouted at Diane, and now he didn't trust himself to speak again; he wanted only to leave.

Diane swallowed convulsively. "I'll go to her, Nathan. I'll explain."

He made no effort to quell the cold hatred he knew was glittering in his eyes. "It's probably too late for that," he said in clipped tones as he made his way through the maze of half-packed boxes littering Diane's floor.

She caught at his arm as he passed. Her voice was small and peevish, and it chafed Nathan's already ragged nerves. "I'm sorry."

He wrenched open her front door. "Oh, thank you," he retorted sardonically. "I'll remember that when I crawl out of the courtroom, suddenly single."

Diane sniffled, lifted her chin in a theatrical gesture of martyrly acceptance. "Blame me if it makes you feel better, Nate, but it isn't all my fault and you know it. Your marriage was a shambles long before we met in the boathouse."

Nathan laughed, and it was a hoarse, cruel sound. "Before we *met!* You followed me!"

Diane's face seemed to crumble. "So I did. But you're a big boy, McKendrick, and you weren't forced into that kiss."

Nathan watched her for another moment, wondering idly if the show she was putting on might be based in real emotions. In the final analysis, he didn't care, one way or the other. He turned and strode away, leaving Diane's front door gaping open behind him.

He walked fast, with his head down, and nearly collided with

Jeff Kingston, his drummer, on the wooded path leading back to his own house.

Jeff was the only member of the band who had been with Nathan from the first. Because of that, there was a special empathy between the two men. "Hey, Nate—hold it. What's going on around here?"

Nathan stopped, braced himself against a tree with one hand and drew a deep breath. With his eyes carefully trained on the water, barely visible through the thickening curtain of snow, he told Jeff what had happened in the boathouse the night before. His tones were grim and concise.

When he'd finished, Jeff muttered a colorful word. "We're talking dumb moves here, Nate."

Nathan nodded distractedly.

"Have you called Mallory?"

Nathan shook his head. "She wouldn't talk to me if I did."

"Then go and see her."

Nathan turned his back to Jeff and ran one finger along the rough, cool bark of the tree he leaned against. "That wouldn't help either. I've lost her."

"There has got to be some way—"

Nathan turned suddenly. "What do I say to her, Jeff? That Diane has been throwing herself at me for six years and that I was confused and mad as hell and before I thought about what I was doing I kissed her?"

"Is that the truth?"

"Yes!"

"Then tell her that. Mallory is a class act, Nathan, and she loves you. She'll understand."

"I don't think so. Jeff, she's been through so much—the paternity thing, now this—"

Jeff sighed wearily. "Okay. Let her go, man. Ranner and about ten million other guys will appreciate the gesture, but it sure as hell won't do you any good, or Mallory, either."

"What the hell are you saying?"

Jeff shrugged. "If you don't want her, step out of the way. She won't be lonely long."

"God, you're a big help" Nathan roared, gesturing wildly with his arms. "I can't stand the thought of anybody else touching her, and you know it!"

Jeff's expression was somewhere between a smile and a smirk. "Then why don't you get your act together?"

"I thought it was," Nathan replied with less spirit. "I really thought it was."

"Why? Damn it, Nate, the rest of us have seen this coming since before the Australian tour. Mallory looks like a lost kid half the time, and you're always on edge."

"Doesn't it bother you that you're going to be out of work? That we're not going to be doing concerts after Seattle?"

"Sure, it bothers me, but I think it bothers you more. You don't want to quit the circuit, do you, Nate? The bottom line is, you just don't want to quit."

Nathan sighed and started walking toward the house again, his hands wedged into the pockets of his jeans. He could feel snow melting on his neck, but he didn't care. "No, I don't want to quit. But I didn't want to lose Mallory, either."

"Suppose you have lost her. What would you do?"

"Book more concerts. And I have, Jeff—this time, I *have* lost her."

"Maybe, and maybe not. If I were you, I guess I wouldn't even try to sort all this out until the concert is over and Mallory's off that soap opera. Then, old friend, take your wife away somewhere, alone, and work this out, one way or the other."

"It's hopeless," Nathan said in despair. "There are two ladies in my life—music and Mallory—and one of them has to go."

Sunday was a crummy day for Mallory, from start to finish. She stumbled through it blindly, ignoring both the telephone and the doorbell, knowing instinctively that none of the callers or visitors would be Nathan. She tried repeatedly to study the script Brad had brought to her, but the lines ascribed to her character made even less sense than they normally did. At the rate she was going, she thought dismally, she was going to have to ad lib every scene.

At dinner time, she made a quick search of the cupboards and was not really surprised to find them bare. The refrigerator contained only what remained of Nathan's carton of milk, and hot tears smarted in Mallory's eyes as she remembered how close she'd felt to him that day, how she'd soared in his arms.

Glumly, Mallory took the carton from the refrigerator shelf and tossed it into the trash compactor. Despite her jangled nerves and her heartache, she was hungry, and yet she certainly didn't feel like venturing out to a restaurant or even a grocery store.

After some moments of deliberation, she finally called her favorite Chinese restaurant and ordered a meal. She would shower and wrap up in a cozy bathrobe and, by the time her supper arrived, maybe she'd feel better. Maybe she'd even be able to learn her lines.

Her shower taken, her old, red corduroy bathrobe soft against her skin, Mallory was brushing her hair dry when the doorbell rang. "Dinner," she said with forced cheer as she pulled open the door.

"You shouldn't do that," Pat said, arching one eyebrow. "For all you knew, you could have been opening the door to a rapist or even a vacuum cleaner salesman."

"Horrors," Mallory replied, eyeing the cartons of Chinese food sheltered in Pat's capable arms. "Since when do you deliver for Chow May's?"

"Since I bribed the kid in the elevator. Mall, damn it, how come you aren't answering your phone or your door?"

"Maybe because I want to be alone," Mallory said archly, reaching for the cartons.

Pat withheld them and stepped past her sister-in-law to enter the penthouse. "Not so fast, hungry person. I charge one egg roll and two fortune cookies for my delivery services."

Mallory sighed and followed after Pat as she walked resolutely through the hallway to the living room. She put the cartons down on the coffee table and turned to glare at her brother's wife.

"What are you trying to do, Mall—scare all your friends and relations to death? I've been here twice and called four times, and I've been getting calls from Trish and Kate all day."

Stubbornly, Mallory folded her arms. "I don't feel guilty, if that's what you want from me."

"Far be it from me to inspire guilt," Pat retorted smoothly. "I mean, just because I thought you jumped out of a window and Trish thought you slit your wrists—"

"What was Kate's guess?" Mallory broke in irritably.

"She was going for the head-in-the-oven tactic. You and Nathan are on the outs again, aren't you?"

"Permanently," Mallory said, opening the sweet and sour pork and dipping in with a finger. "And don't try to talk me out of it."

Pat's bright blue eyes were flashing. "I wouldn't think of it," she said, taking an egg roll from one of the cartons. "You're both idiots, as far as I'm concerned, and I wash my hands of you."

Mallory made a face and then wandered off toward the kitchen for plates, knives and forks. And even though she and Pat didn't exchange a civil word while they were eating, she was still glad for the company.

10

Monday morning was a disaster.

Mallory arrived at the studio half an hour late, and all the makeup in the world wouldn't have disguised the pallor in her cheeks and the quiet torment in her eyes. To make matters worse, the set was crowded. Several fans had been admitted, and there were reporters and photographers from one of the magazines specializing in the doings of soap opera performers. Mallory's lines sounded wooden when she delivered them, and she couldn't remember her cues.

Finally, Brad shouted an order to the cameramen, and everyone took a badly needed break. His grasp was hard on Mallory's arm as he dragged her off the set, through a maze of cameras, light stands and thick electrical cables snaking along the floor.

"Damn it, Mallory," he seethed, glaring at her. "Is this your idea of revenge, or what? If you're trying to sandbag the whole production, you're succeeding!"

Mallory wanted nothing so much as to get the taping right and be done with television forever, and her zombielike behavior was anything but deliberate. Tears of frustration smarted in her eyes, and her lower lip trembled. But she couldn't manage a word.

Brad's tension seemed to ease; his bright blue eyes searched her face and then he sighed and raised tender hands to her cheeks. "What is it, button? What's happened?"

Even if she'd had a voice, Mallory would have been too proud to explain. She swallowed and shook her head in a reflexive gesture of helplessness.

It was clear in an instant, however, that Brad had read much of the situation in her eloquent eyes. "Nathan," he said with angry acceptance.

Mallory hadn't meant to cry, but, suddenly, she was doing just that. A terrible sob tore itself from her throat, and Brad drew her into his arms in a brotherly embrace. He was whispering gentle, innocuous words of comfort when his arms suddenly went rigid.

"Oh, Lord," he groaned.

Mallory's spine stiffened; without turning around, she knew that Nathan was in the studio, that he was striding toward her, that when she faced him, his expression would be murderous.

A throbbing silence descended, stilling even the jovial conversations of the light crew, the other actors and actresses, the writers and the camera people. When Mallory forced herself to turn from Brad to Nathan, she focused not on her husband's face, but on the reporters and photographers so obviously anxious to record whatever drama that might be offered.

"Call Security," Brad muttered to a gaping script girl.

Nathan laughed low in his throat, and it was a brutal, terrifying sound. "That won't be necessary," he said. "I promise to behave myself."

Mallory felt no fear—not for herself, at least. She peered in Nathan's direction, but his face was hidden in shadows, just as it had been during their last argument that night on the island. There was really no need to see his features; all his disdain had been evident in his voice.

"What do you want?" she demanded after a long, uncomfortable silence.

Nathan's powerful shoulders moved in a deceptively casual shrug. "A few minutes alone with my wife, if that can be arranged."

Pride made Mallory square her shoulders and stand tall. "Fine," she said stiffly. "We can talk in my dressing room."

Brad cleared his throat. "Mallory, I don't think—"

She cut him off politely. "It's all right, Brad—really."

Nathan offered his arm in a suave parody of good manners, and Mallory took it. The walk to the dressing room she shared with two other actresses was the longest of her life.

Nathan looked wan when she turned to face him after closing the dressing room door. His thick, dark hair was rumpled, and, as he folded his arms across his chest and leaned back against the wall, a shadow writhed in the depths of his eyes.

Mallory took in the blunt masculinity of his form with a dispatch that was entirely false. In truth, the corded muscles of his blue-jeaned thighs had a very disturbing effect on her determination never to surrender to him again. Beneath the expensive cream-colored sweater, his broad shoulders moved in another shrug.

"Aren't you going to compliment me on my self-restraint, Mallory?" he asked, his eyes raking over the revealing pink satin robe she'd worn in the last scene. "I didn't even comment on your—costume."

Mallory lifted her chin. "I trust you aren't here to demonstrate your boundless nobility."

There was a change in his face; the deadly white line edging his lips and his jawline faded, and there was a soft look in his eyes. "I love you, Mallory."

She would have found a bitter, scathing invective easier to deal with than this simple lie. "Don't."

"Don't love you or don't talk about it?"

Mallory bit her lower lip and refused to look at him, to speak, to react.

"It's true, you know. I've loved you since the day I met you." His voice was even, reasonable—so damned reasonable! "Mallory, that incident in the boathouse was a misunderstanding. It was innocent, like that hug you were just exchanging with Brad."

"*Innocent?*" Mallory whispered. "You *kissed* her, Nathan. You admitted that yourself! And even if you hadn't admitted it—"

"You would have known," he finished smoothly. "Mallory, I guess I did kiss her, if you can call it that—it was really more of a touch." He paused, drew a deep breath and flung his arms out in a gesture of frustration. "I needed somebody—anybody. And Diane was there."

Mallory was trying hard to hate him, but her love was so fathomless that it threatened all her thinking processes, all her desperate resignation. "In that case," she replied coldly, "I shudder to think what would have happened if I hadn't intruded."

Nathan's fingers drummed on the sweatered expanse of his upper arm, but that was the only outward indication of his impatience. "I think you know what would have happened, Mallory, whether you'll let yourself accept it or not. When I realized what I was doing, what I was throwing away, I backed off."

Mallory's resolve was wavering fast; she wasn't even sure it mattered whether or not he was lying. "What else could you have done, Nathan? Carried on as if your wife hadn't just walked in?"

A muscle flexed in his jaw and relaxed again. "Listen to your heart, Mallory. Forget all the garbage that's been programmed into you and listen to your instincts. Damn it, you *know* I'm telling the truth."

Mallory turned away, ostensibly to rearrange the jumble of creams and lotions and powders on her dressing table. In actuality, she was fighting tears and a growing need to believe him. "Please go," she said calmly. "Right now."

He said nothing, nor did he move. Mallory lifted her eyes, horrified to see that he'd been watching her reflection in the mirror, reading her real feelings in the tortured planes of her face.

In a fluid motion, Nathan crossed the small room and turned her to face him, trapping her against the vanity table with the hard pressure of his steel-like thighs, his stomach, his chest. The sound he made, deep in his throat, was somewhere between a moan and a growl.

And then he kissed her.

Mallory struggled at first, but then her body betrayed her pride, offering its own surrender. She opened her mouth to the plundering invasion of his tongue, then responded with her own. His right hand moved up her rib cage to cup her breast through the thin pink fabric of the robe. Even as that same hand strayed beneath the robe and the lacy camisole under it to claim the hard-peaked breast hidden there, Nathan did not break the shattering kiss.

Stormy winds of passion howled through Mallory's troubled spirit. Gasping, she tore her lips from his and buried her face in the soft, fragrant knit of his sweater.

He lifted her chin with a rough sort of gentleness. The knowledge that he could play her body in the same accomplished way he played countless musical instruments burned in his eyes, a savage, infuriating flame, and he made no move to free the imprisoned breast.

Sweet anguish affected every fiber of Mallory's being; the core of her womanhood was already preparing to receive him. Desire made her conscious of little other than the hardness of his need pressing against her.

And yet somehow, she found the strength within herself to thrust him away. "No," she said in a shaky voice. *"No."*

He shrugged, bent his head and nuzzled the satiny flesh on her neck briefly. Then he went to the door.

"You know where to find me," he said in a low, flat voice.

The insulted rage that seized Mallory in that moment was more than equal to the passion of seconds before. She snatched up a jar of cleansing cream and sent it whistling past his arrogant head, and flinched as it shattered against the door. Unruffled, Nathan turned the doorknob and assessed his wife with para-doxically tormented and amused eyes. He recited his phone number in matter-of-fact tones and walked out.

Mallory stood, hands clenched at her sides, trembling with impotent fury. "Damn you, Nathan McKendrick!" she screamed after him. *"Damn* you!"

It was then that a photographer appeared in the doorway and brazenly snapped Mallory's picture. Blinded by the flash and by renewed outrage, she screamed again and flung a hairbrush at the stranger.

She had no idea what she would have done after that, if Brad Ranner hadn't intervened just then. The possibilities didn't bear even the briefest consideration.

With admirable composure and aplomb, Brad cleared the set entirely, except for the necessary members of the cast and crew, and recruited two older actresses to put Mallory back together again.

Though she longed to sink into a screaming, mindless fit of hysteria, Mallory's anger sustained her. She would *not* give in; her self-respect was at stake.

All the rest of that day, Mallory got her lines right, and she gave the best performance of her short, crazy career.

Hours later, at home in the plush, lonely penthouse, she stripped off her clothes and stepped under a steamy shower, scrubbing her flesh with fierce motions, letting the hot, hot water soak her hair and stream down her face. Telling herself not to think about Nathan McKendrick was like playing the childhood game of telling herself not to think about blue elephants. His image raged in her mind and spirit like a brush fire.

When she could bear it no longer, she screamed in wordless fury, doubled her fists, and hammered wildly, senselessly, at the shower's tiled walls.

Eventually the hot water soothed her. She stepped out of the shower stall, dried herself methodically with a waiting towel, then slipped into a cozy terry-cloth robe and pink floppy scuffs. When she'd brushed and blow-dried her hair, Mallory walked aimlessly out into the living room. There, at the imposing teakwood bar, she mixed herself an unusually strong drink.

The aching tension in her shoulders and the nape of her neck eased a little as the bourbon burned her veins. But it did nothing for the frantic tremor in the pit of her stomach or the desolation in her heart.

She set the drink down with a forceful thud when the doorbell rang.

Stiffening her spine, Mallory ignored the incessant ringing until it stopped. Then, with resolve, she found the script for the next day's taping and began learning her lines and cues. She stayed up very late that night, working. When she knew her lines cold, she stumbled off to bed and fell, mercifully, into a dreamless and untroubled sleep.

She awakened to a stream of sunlight radiating from the huge skylight overhead and a spasm of incredible nausea. One hand clamped over her mouth, she scurried into the bathroom. After that, breakfast was out of the question; she couldn't even face coffee, and on the set she turned away in horror from the goopy doughnuts offered by the head writer.

"Are you feeling all right?" Brad asked idly, when she paled at the sight of the fast-food breakfast he was consuming.

"Flu, I guess," she said lamely, falling into a canvas chair and averting her eyes. But the scent of the scrambled eggs sandwiched between the slices of Brad's half-eaten English muffin suddenly sent her bounding across the cluttered studio and into the women's room.

She was just in time.

Never one to stand on custom, Brad was waiting when Mallory stumbled out of the stall and approached one of several porcelain sinks. He watched her in silence, his arms folded, until she'd recovered and begun drying her face with a rough brown paper towel.

"We can do your scenes tomorrow," he offered quietly.

Mallory shook her head. The color was coming back into her face, and she felt infinitely better. "I'm fine, Brad."

"Slightly pregnant, perhaps."

Mallory was stunned, and she gripped the edge of the sink for support. *Pregnant?* The word seemed to echo in the room.

She counted calmly, realized that she hadn't had a period since before Nathan left for Australia. "Oh, God," she whispered. "*Oh,* my God—"

"Uh-huh," Brad said, with crisp detachment. And then he considerately left the women's room.

Mallory tightened her grasp on the sink to keep her knees from giving way. Her emotions spun inside her, hopelessly tangled. She wanted the baby desperately—there was no question of that. But why couldn't it have been conceived when she still had a solid marriage?

She drew a deep, restorative breath. "Hold on, McKendrick," she ordered herself. "Maybe you're not pregnant. Maybe it was something you ate—"

And maybe it was that passionate farewell before Nathan flew off to Sydney, taunted a voice deep in Mallory's whirling mind.

She remembered, with both remorse and a sweet stirring in her middle. In early November, despite the forbidding weather, she and Nathan had spent a delicious, bittersweet weekend on his boat, exploring Puget Sound. Late that Sunday afternoon, probably dreading their impending separation, they'd argued.

And Nathan had flung Mallory's new packet of birth control pills overboard.

The action seemed significant in retrospect, as Mallory stood, stricken, in the studio rest room, trying to get a grip on herself. At the time, however, it had been nothing more than a gesture of anger.

Nathan had been trying to tell her, even then, that he wanted a child. Now that she was about to give him one, it was probably too late. Biting her lower lip, Mallory lowered her head and cried.

The rest of the day was ruined, for all intents and purposes, though she somehow got through it. She got no sleep at all that night—she spent it pacing, torn between calling Nathan and keeping her suspicions to herself.

In the end, she chose the latter course. After all, the pregnancy hadn't actually been confirmed, and the whole thing could be a mistake. She'd been to her doctor's office very recently, and it seemed to her that if she'd been pregnant, Dr. Sarah would have noticed it.

Noticed? She laughed ruefully as she refilled her coffee cup in the huge, gleaming penthouse kitchen. There had been no pelvic examination or lab tests, and pregnancy wasn't something people *noticed,* like a new blazer or a different haircut. Not in the early stages, at least.

With Brad's expansive blessing, Mallory drove to her doctor's office first thing in the morning. Her stomach was still quivering from another bout of raging nausea when she was squired into an examining room and told to undress.

Mallory obeyed, eyeing the examining table and its metal stirrups with dread. *Woman, the indignities you are heir to,* she thought wryly as she took off her black flannel slacks, her blue silk shirt, her lacy panties and bra.

She was wearing the obligatory scratchy white cotton gown when the doctor entered, smiling her most engaging smile. "Good morning, Mallory."

"Sarah," Mallory returned cordially, with a slight nod of her head.

"What's the trouble?"

Mallory grinned humorlessly. "I think I may have picked up a slight case of pregnancy."

"I see." The doctor frowned and ran one hand through her already-tousled gray hair. "Correct me if I'm wrong, but it seems to me that you've wanted a child for a long time."

Mallory lowered her head, pressing back the tears that burned behind her eyes. "I do—very much," she said.

"But?"

"Nathan and I are separated."

The physician permitted herself a sympathetic sigh. "Serious?"

"I asked him for a divorce."

Sarah Lester went to the shiny metal sink and began washing her hands. "Perhaps you can still work things out. In any case, Mallory, women everywhere are raising children on their own."

Mallory said nothing. She submitted to the examination, knowing all the while what the diagnosis would be, mourning the fact that Nathan wasn't pacing the outer office like a standard expectant father.

"Well," Sarah said, as she scrubbed her hands again and Mallory sat up. "We'll run the usual tests, but that's a formality. You've got a passenger, all right."

Mallory couldn't help feeling joyous, even though nothing else in her life was going right. She fairly floated back to the studio, mentally sorting through the prospective names she'd hoarded over the years.

The cast and crew were on a break when Mallory reached the set, but Brad was waiting at her dressing room door. The sight of him reminded her that her marriage was in ruins and sent her spirits plummeting.

"Well?" he asked gently.

"August," Mallory said in a tight voice.

Brad planted a brief kiss on her forehead. "Congratulations, love," he said.

Mallory lifted her chin, forcing herself not to cry. "Thanks," she said woodenly, turning to open the door. She was already late, and she still had makeup and a costume to deal with.

But Brad caught her arm and made her face him again. "Why don't you call Nathan?" he asked softly.

Mallory shook her head. "I can't, Brad."

"Why not? It's his kid, too—he has a right to know about this, Mallory."

"Since when are you so concerned with Nathan's rights?"

Brad laughed wryly. "I'm not. I think he's an obnoxious, arrogant bastard, but the fact remains that he fathered that child."

Mallory pressed her lips together and thought for a moment before she spoke again. "I don't suppose it's any big secret that Nathan and I are separated, Brad," she said evenly. "And it's probably equally obvious that I love him. If we can work things out, I want it to be because it's right for us to be together, not because he feels paternal responsibility."

"Responsibility?" Brad shot back. "Do you think that's all he'd feel? Listen, Mallory, I don't like the guy and he sure

doesn't like me, but I do know him well enough to be sure he cares about you.''

Mallory was not seeing Brad's face, or the studio behind him. She was seeing Diane and Nathan alone, in that darkened island boathouse. ''Maybe.''

Brad grasped her shoulders in a sudden and rather desperate grip and shook her slightly. ''Damn it, I love you too much to see you eaten up inside like this! I'm sorry—God, *so* sorry—that I let Diane talk me into that paternity suit scam. But Mallory, that's all it was—a scam!''

''That isn't the problem, Brad.''

''Then what is, pray tell?''

''Diane.''

Brad did not release her shoulders, and he tilted his head back, with a sign of frustration, to study the dark, high ceiling of the warehouse-turned-studio. ''I suppose you found them together somewhere,'' he said, his voice filled with affectionate scorn.

Surprised, Mallory nodded.

His fierce blue eyes turned to look at her face. ''Mallory, what did I warn you about, that day I came to the island? Didn't I tell you that Diane might try to do something to hurt you and Nathan both?''

Again, Mallory nodded, her eyes widening.

Brad swore in irritation. ''Sure as I'm standing here, she set him up.''

Mallory swallowed—*talk about wishful thinking!* And yet, the fact that Brad would offer that as a possibility, feeling the way he did about Nathan, gave the idea undeniable weight. ''He kissed her,'' she said, though she hadn't intended to reveal that humiliating tidbit of information.

Brad was clearly annoyed, clearly torn. ''Somebody tell me why I'm defending Nathan McKendrick. Am I losing my mind, or what? Mallory, maybe she got to him for a second—God knows she's been working on it long enough. What is one stupid kiss against a happy life together?''

Before Mallory had to answer, the other members of the cast

were straggling back, their break over. Gratefully, she escaped Brad and hurried in to change clothes and have her makeup done.

Again, as she had the day before, Mallory turned in an excellent performance. Somehow, she was able to shift her churning, confused emotions to another level of consciousness and concentrate on Tracy Ballard's outrageous pursuits.

For the first time, as Mallory left the studio at seven that night, she thought that she might miss performing—at least in one respect. It was certainly easier, and much less painful, to be Tracy Ballard than Mallory McKendrick.

The night air was brisk, though the snow was gone. Slush, muddy and slick, filled the parking lot, and Mallory made her way carefully toward her car. She was brought up short by the fact that Nathan's silver Porsche was parked beside her own sporty Mazda.

For a moment, Mallory considered rushing back inside the studio to hide. Before she could decide, one way or the other, however, Nathan was out of his car and striding toward her.

The lights rimming the parking lot didn't illuminate his face, but she could see that he was wearing tailored slacks, an Irish cable knit sweater and his favorite brown suede jacket. Without a word, he caught her arm in a gentle grasp at the elbow, and ushered her to his car. She was too overwhelmed to react until she was already seated inside the plush leather confines of the Porsche.

"Nathan—what—?" she stammered stupidly, unable to read his expression in the shadowed profile of his face as he slipped behind the wheel and slammed his car door.

"Dinner," he said shortly, without looking at her.

"Now just a minute, you!"

Nathan shifted the Porsche into Reverse with a smooth, practiced motion of his right hand, and the slush beneath the tires made a grinding sound as he backed the powerful car out of the parking space. "I've got an idea," he said, with gruff mockery grating in his voice. "Just for once, let's not argue. If that means saying nothing at all, so be it."

The spicy scent of his cologne was doing disturbing things to Mallory's carefully maintained defenses, and she could sense the hard strength of his body even though they weren't touching.

"Okay," she agreed.

They drove in silence for some minutes before Nathan slipped a cassette tape into the slot on the dashboard and Willie Nelson's voice filled the car. Mallory couldn't help smiling at the realization that Nathan never, but never, listened to his own recordings. And even though rock was his career, he enjoyed everything from Indian music and jungle drumming to the classics.

When both sides of Willie's tape had been played and they were still driving, Mallory shot an anxious glance in her husband's direction. "Where are we going?" she ventured. *Oh, and by the way, I'm pregnant.*

They'd left the heart of Seattle far behind by then, and joined the swift traffic on the freeway going south. "To dinner," Nathan answered irritably.

"Where?" Mallory snapped back. "In Wenatchee?"

Nathan tossed her a scathing look. "Peace—remember?"

Mallory sighed and bit her lower lip.

The restaurant Nathan had chosen was small and secluded and overlooked the dark waters of the Sound. Mallory could hear the unmistakable creak of a wooden wharf as they entered the tastefully rustic establishment.

Nathan spoke to the hostess who greeted them in a terse undertone.

"This way," the woman replied, proceeding across a carpeted, dimly lit and totally empty dining room.

"Where is everybody?" Mallory dared to ask as Nathan put one imperious hand on the small of her back and propelled her along.

"This is a private party," Nathan replied in a biting monotone.

"How private?" Mallory wanted to know, her eyes wide with mingled amazement and alarm.

"Very private. You and I add up to everyone."

"That's what you think," Mallory argued, only to regret her impulsive words instantly.

Nathan's gaze pierced her, impaling her for one shattering moment. "I'll thank you to explain that remark," he said in a low, even voice, standing stock-still in the middle of that elegant and deserted dining room.

Mallory felt betraying color rise in her face, and her answer came out in an unconvincing jumble. "I merely meant that—I mean—surely there will be other customers—"

A muscle in Nathan's jaw flexed, and an ominous white line edged his taut lips. "Not good enough."

Mallory closed her eyes. "Nathan—"

He took her arm again, roughly, and led her to the table selected for them. Then, impatient, he fairly thrust Mallory into her chair.

"Brad called me," he said bluntly, midway through the first course.

Mallory stared at him, a forkful of shrimp cocktail poised halfway between the glistening crystal dish and her open mouth.

Without waiting for her to speak, Nathan went on, his voice chafing Mallory's heart. "I can't tell you," he drawled in sardonic tones, "how I appreciate hearing news like that from Brad Ranner. Thank you so much."

"I'll kill him!" Mallory muttered, dazed.

There was violence in the forced stillness of Nathan's hands, in the crackling electricity of his ebony gaze. "You weren't going to tell me," he accused with quiet fury. "My God, Mallory, did you think you could hide the baby from me forever?"

Tears of pain and outrage stung Mallory's eyes and brimmed in her lashes. "Of course not!" she cried, leaning forward and slamming down her fork.

"When?" he demanded. "When will I be a father, Mallory? That is, if you consider it any of my business."

Mallory's throat ached savagely, and for a moment, no words would pass it. When they did, they were interspersed with little soblike catches. "August—the b-baby will be born in August. The t-timing is great, isn't it?"

With a harsh motion of his arm, Nathan slid his untouched shrimp cocktail summarily aside. His dark eyes were snapping, piercing Mallory's spirit like lethal swords. "Why weren't you going to tell me?"

She uttered the first retort that came to mind. "Because I thought you'd drag me back to the island!"

"Would that be so terrible? I know you're not crazy about me, but you've always liked the island!"

"We've got so many problems, Nathan! And a baby is the world's *worst* reason for two people to stay married!"

"Not to me, it isn't!" he snapped. Suddenly, his powerful hands closed over Mallory's wrists in an inescapable grip. "Listen to me, Mallory, and listen well. That child is as much mine as yours, and I *will not* be one of those fathers who conducts tours of Disneyland every summer and visits on alternating Sundays!"

Mallory swallowed hard but said nothing. She merely stared at her husband, wide-eyed and stricken by the force of his determination.

"Finish out your contract—whatever. But then you're coming back to the island—specifically to Angel Cove."

"I am, am I? You can't force me to live with you!"

He smiled, but there was no humor in the expression. His eyes, scorching Mallory only moments before, were now chilling. "Don't make me prove that you're wrong, sweetness. You don't have to sleep with me or even pretend that you're any kind of wife—but you *will* live under my roof!"

Mallory was fairly blinded with shock and fury. "Who do you think you are?" she challenged, keeping her voice down only by monumental effort.

His eyes slid with dark contempt to her breasts and then to her stomach; it was as though he were looking right through the table, right through her clothes. "I'm that baby's father," he answered, and the conversation was clearly over.

Mallory did eat her dinner, but she tasted none of the skillfully prepared food. She could think of nothing but the bitter, ruthless stranger seated across from her. He was, she knew, completely serious; he meant to drag her to his island house, if it came to that, and he would not let her leave with his child, be it born or unborn.

It was all so high-handed! Apparently, Nathan thought he could control independent human beings as easily as he hired restaurants and chartered airplanes.

The journey back to Seattle was made in numbing silence.

But when Nathan drew the Porsche to a stop in front of the apartment building and blithely tossed his car keys to the doorman, Mallory was furious enough to fight. She stiffened in the car seat and refused to get out, even after Nathan opened the door and the cool night wind rushed in to chill her.

He smiled savagely. "Think of your dignity, Mrs. McKendrick. Your *image,* if you will. How is it going to look if I throw you over one shoulder and carry you inside?"

With a small exclamation of frustration, Mallory got out of the car. In the elevator, she fixed her husband with a look as scathing and fierce as his own. "If you think we're going to live together, to sleep together, after all that's happened—"

Nathan touched her nose lightly. "I won't attack you, love, so don't worry." He shrugged in a manner that made Mallory dizzy with anger. "But, then, I probably won't have to, will I?"

Soundly, with all the force of her fury and her pain, Mallory slapped him. "I despise you!" she hissed.

"I know," he said.

Inside the richly furnished penthouse, Nathan gravitated immediately to the bar. Ignoring him as best she could, Mallory marched into the master bedroom, carefully locked the door behind her and began tearing off her clothes. Naked and trembling with rage, she strode into the imposing bathroom and wrenched on the shower spigots.

When she returned to the bedroom, a full half an hour later, wearing only an oversize T-shirt of Nathan's, she found him stretched languidly out on the bed, pretending to read a news-magazine.

Her throat closed, and something treacherous rippled through her stomach. "How did you get in here?"

Nathan smiled winningly, as though they'd never argued, as though an impassable barrier hadn't been erected between them. "I used the key," he said.

"Now you listen to me, Nathan McKendrick—"

But Nathan wasn't listening. He rolled easily off the bed, onto his feet, and pulled the soft cable knit sweater up over his head. After tossing that aside, he began undoing his belt, then the zipper on his slacks.

Finally, stark naked, he feigned an expansive yawn.

Mallory was gaping at him, as stricken by the bronzed, sculpted perfection of his masculine form as she had been the first night they were ever together. After a few moments, however, she regained her equilibrium and fled through the open door and into the living room. From there she rushed on to the kitchen.

She was perched on the cool, glistening yellow Formica of the counter, despondently munching on a chocolate sandwich cookie, when Nathan walked into the room. He hadn't bothered with a bathrobe, and Mallory averted her eyes stubbornly as he leaned back against the opposite counter and folded his muscular arms across his chest.

That, no doubt, was why she was so unprepared for his approach.

Facing her, Nathan placed the palms of his hands on the tender flesh between her knees.

Though the motion stirred treacherous sensations in Mallory, and she knew that her face had pinkened, she lifted her chin and summarily took another bite of her cookie.

Nathan laughed and shook his head. When he pushed her knees farther apart, it became much more difficult to sustain her indifference.

She groaned involuntarily as he caressed the secret of her

womanhood, cried out as he went on to claim a fiery preliminary possession.

"You and I should never talk, Mallory," he said in a hoarse, hypnotic whisper. "The minute we stop making love, it's war."

Mallory was writhing slightly, hating him for what he was doing and not wanting him ever to stop. "Damn—you—"

The thrust of his marauding fingers made her gasp; she was barely conscious of being lowered onto the counter, stripped of the T-shirt. She cried out in sweet misery as he nibbled endlessly at her tightening nipple.

His voice was a ragged, strangely vulnerable rasp. "You are so—soft—so warm—so sweet—"

Mallory was grasping at his bare muscle-corded shoulders now, wanting him, needing him. "Nathan," she pleaded. "Oh, Nathan, please—"

He chuckled hoarsely. "On a kitchen counter? Woman, thy name is wanton."

Mallory trembled, frantic and furious and dazed with passion. "You didn't mind the floor," she argued in a choked whisper.

He laughed and lifted her gently into his arms, then carried her back through the penthouse to the bedroom. There, they made sweet, fierce, sensual love.

When, at last, Nathan slept, Mallory watched him for a long time as she lay on her side in the big, tousled bed, one cheek propped in her hand. If she lived to be a thousand, she thought ruefully, she would never fully understand this man.

At the restaurant and then in the elevator, he had been hard and recalcitrant—almost cruel. And yet, as a lover, he was unfailingly gentle. Tenderness aside, Mallory knew that he would not change his mind. No matter how unpleasant their marriage might become, he would not release her from it easily.

Her feelings about this were mixed; on the one hand, she found the prospect of being near her husband, whatever his past sins, very appealing. On the other, however, she was insulted by his imperious attitude. No matter what, it was wrong for one person to control another in that way, to dictate where someone would live and with whom.

Sleep eluded Mallory, and she finally got up to read over her lines for the next day. It proved a difficult task, since her thoughts kept sneaking back to Nathan, alternately tender and furious.

11

In the morning, Nathan was up and dressed and already charming the housekeeper when Mallory ambled sleepily into the kitchen and helped herself to a cup of coffee. Nathan immediately exchanged the mug of steaming brew for a glass of orange juice, and while the housekeeper was amused, Mallory wasn't. She glared at him in surly challenge.

Paper bags rustled crisply as the housekeeper began unpacking all the groceries she'd apparently brought to work with her, and Nathan folded his arms across the front of his green velour shirt and grinned. "From now on, you're off caffeine," he said.

Mallory scowled, but since her concern for the child growing inside her was as great as Nathan's, she cast one baleful look at the forbidden coffee and drank her orange juice without protest.

The huge and ghastly breakfast Nathan and the housekeeper eventually assembled was another matter, though—Mallory's stomach was threatening mayhem. She managed one piece of toast, but no power on earth could have coerced her to eat more.

When Nathan sat down across from her, prepared to consume two eggs, hash brown potatoes and link sausage, she leapt to her feet and fled inelegantly to the nearest bathroom. Nathan followed, refusing to respect her privacy.

"Go away!" she gasped in wretched desperation.

But he wouldn't. He held her hair and was ready with a cool washcloth when the violent spate of sickness finally ended.

"See?" he drawled companionably. "You need me."

Mallory glared at him. "If it weren't for you, fella, I wouldn't *have* this problem!"

He laughed and then shrugged. "I am a man of many talents, pumpkin."

Mallory couldn't help grinning. His talents were undeniable. "You're not going to follow me around with a washcloth all day, are you?"

"Certainly not," he answered, his dark eyes bright with tender amusement. "But tonight is another matter. I've got rehearsals today, but I'll pick you up at the studio when you're through."

True to his word, he was there at the appointed time.

That day set the pattern for those to follow; each day, while Mallory was taping the show, Nathan went to a rented hall to rehearse with the band. They spent their evenings together in unaccustomed solitude, listening to music, watching television, making love. There was a tenuous sort of peace between them, but, in the last analysis, the only deep communications they shared were expressed by their bodies.

Mallory was reluctant to rock the proverbial boat by bringing up sensitive issues, such as Diane Vincent or Nathan's unreasonable decree that she would live with him at Angel Cove. As attractive as the idea was, it was *still* unreasonable, and she sensed that he felt the same way.

Mallory's commitment to the soap was completed the day before Nathan's concert, and there was a huge party that evening, given by Brad Ranner, to bid her farewell. It seemed that everyone Mallory had ever met was invited to that party, with the notable exception of Diane Vincent. The banquet room of the posh hotel where it was held was packed to the rafters.

Secretly, Mallory dreaded the fuss of it all, but she was determined to play this final role well. She wore a simple white silk caftan, bordered with glistening silver stitching, a sumptuous blue fox jacket and a slightly shaky smile.

"Star treatment," Trish Demming whispered in awe, looking appreciatively at the great crystal chandeliers and the embossed silk on the walls, her hand linked comfortably to the crook of Alex's arm. "Wow, Mall, I'm impressed."

Kate Sheridan's assessment of the affair was typically acerbic. "Don't let her stay in this madhouse very long," she ordered Nathan in a stage whisper. "She's about to drop as it is."

"I'll hold up," Mallory said, but her tone lacked conviction.

Nathan grinned, making no comment. He was a breathtaking sight in his tailored black tuxedo, which he hated, and impeccable white silk shirt.

Trish drew Mallory aside briefly to tell her that her things had been packed and removed from the little house on the island, and that the trees along the driveway had been cut down without incident. The Johnsons would be moving in any day. Mallory felt sad and slightly bereft. Cutting herself off from that part of her past was the wise thing to do, and she knew it. But that didn't make the parting any less painful.

The rest of the evening dragged on, seeming endless to Mallory. First, a dinner worthy of a Roman banquet was served, and she couldn't choke down so much as a bite. Following that, Brad made a flowery speech that brought stains of embarrassment surging into her cheeks.

Throughout that first segment of the night, Nathan sustained Mallory with well-timed touches, comical looks of wonder when the praise grew to ridiculous proportions and an occasional wink. "Give 'em hell, McKendrick," he whispered, when it became clear that Brad expected her to join him at the podium and speak.

Embarrassed almost beyond speech (somehow, this was so different from performing in front of cameras) Mallory made her way to Brad's side, graciously accepted an engraved plaque and an innocuous kiss on the cheek, and managed a few faltering words of gratitude and farewell. Returning to her seat beside Nathan was a vast relief, and she tossed a slightly frantic look in his direction as he stood and drew out her chair for her in a quiet display of chivalry.

He bent to brush his lips provocatively against her earlobe. "Pardon me, lady," he whispered, "but you wouldn't happen to have a chocolate cookie, would you?"

Mallory laughed, glad of the fact that the lights had been lowered, thus hiding her blush.

No protest was forthcoming when Nathan insisted that they leave the party early; from the looks of things, it was going to continue until all hours. And, as the Porsche navigated the dark, rain-slickened streets, Mallory was grateful to be on her way home.

Home. A corner of Mallory's mouth lifted in a reflective smile. Home had always been the island, but now it was wherever Nathan happened to be at the moment.

"What are you smiling about?" he asked, looking away from the road for only a moment.

"Nothing," Mallory lied. "So tomorrow is the big concert. What happens after that?"

"We go into seclusion for the promised year," Nathan answered without meeting her eyes again. "Mallory—"

Their constant lovemaking had lent the relationship an intimacy it had never had before, in spite of the odd distances that often intruded, and Mallory reached out, without thinking, to lay one hand on the muscular length of his thigh. "What?"

"I'm sorry for telling you that you had to live on the island with me, whether you wanted it or not. I know that wasn't right." He paused, shifting the car into a low gear to make a stop at a traffic light, and turned to look at her. "I was desperate."

Mallory's heart climbed into her throat. "Desperate?" she whispered.

"Losing you and that baby doesn't bear considering, Mallory. I know we've got a long way to go before we get this marriage back on its feet, but please—don't leave me."

Hot tears glistened, scalding, in Mallory's eyes. Never in the six years she'd been married to Nathan had she seen him reveal so much open vulnerability. "The other night you said we should never talk, just make love. Why is it that we fight the way we do, Nathan?"

The traffic light changed to green, and the car was moving again. Nathan appeared to be concentrating on the road, but a muscle flexed and unflexed at the base of his jawline. "I don't know. Maybe we'd better start by finding that out, Mrs. McKendrick."

At the apartment complex, Nathan surrendered the silver Porsche to the night doorman and ushered Mallory quickly across the elegant lobby and into an elevator. During the swift, silent ride to the penthouse, he studied the changing numbers over the doors with solemn interest.

After their showers, taken separately for once, they made love in the bed beneath the magical, ever-changing view presented by the skylight. Both reached shattering levels of fulfillment, and yet there was a hollow quality to their joining, a sense of never really touching.

Knowing that Nathan was still awake, and brooding, Mallory laid a cautious hand on the mat of dark hair covering his hard chest. "What is it?" she asked softly.

There was a long, discomforting silence before he answered, not with a statement, but with a question. "Did you really want to quit the show, Mallory?"

She raised herself onto one elbow, her free hand still moving on Nathan's chest. "Yes," she replied in complete honesty.

Even though it was dark, she could feel his ebony gaze touching her, searching her face. "I've hated the whole thing from the first," he said in a low voice, and the words had the tone of a reluctant confession. "All the same, if I forced you to give up something you really wanted—"

Mallory had a dreadful, inexplicable feeling. It was almost as though they were survivors of some horrible shipwreck, clinging to the flimsy debris of some hopelessly mangled vessel foundering in deep and threatening waters. "You didn't," she said quickly, but she knew, even as she leaned over to kiss him, even as her lips brushed his, that he wasn't convinced.

It was a very long time before Mallory slept, and the meter of Nathan's breathing revealed that he was awake, too. Underneath all her happiness about the baby and her freedom from the grueling hours on the set and the new closeness she and Nathan seemed to be establishing, was a layer of solid pain. Nathan might really love her, as he claimed. On the other hand, he was a gifted performer and it would be easy for him to pretend such feelings.

Mallory sighed and turned away from him, afraid that he would somehow sense the tears that were gathering on her cheeks. He wanted the child growing within her, and, remembering that intimate scene she'd stumbled upon in the island boathouse, Mallory had a suspicion that he was merely accepting her as a necessary part of the bargain.

When sunlight streamed through the huge window in the roof, Mallory awakened to find herself alone in the spacious bed and numb with a cold that bore no relation at all to the temperature of the room. Thanks to a medication Dr. Lester had given her, which she swallowed before even getting out of bed, Mallory did not suffer her usual bout of violent illness. That was a mercy, she reflected, since she already felt sick on some fundamental, half-discerned level.

She was startled when Pat appeared in the bedroom doorway, a fetching blonde, her slender frame regal even in blue jeans, a T-shirt and a pink hooded running jacket. Roger's diamond engagement ring flashed, like silver fire, on her left hand.

"Hi, there, pregnant person!" she chimed in greeting.

Mallory burst into tears.

Pat approached slowly. "Wow. What did I say?"

Mallory sniffled and dashed away the evidence of her doubts and fears. "Nothing," she reassured her sister-in-law quickly. "You know how it is—my hormones are suffering from the Cement-Mixer Syndrome."

Pat laughed, looked vastly relieved and sat down on the end of the bed, her hands balled in the pockets of her jacket. "Nathan is walking the customary two feet off the ground," she commented. But then there was an almost imperceptible change in her startlingly pretty face. "So why does this place have all the ambience of a battlefield?"

Mallory sank back on her pillows and studied the skylight. It was still beaded with dew, and tiny rainbows framed each droplet. When she said nothing, Pat continued bravely.

"Something is amiss here. You and Nathan are living together again—you're expecting a baby—but something is definitely wrong. And don't try to throw me off the track, sister dear, because I'm wise to all your routines."

Mallory summoned all she'd learned in her year as an actress and fixed a bright smile on her face. It ached, trembling as though it might fall away to lie among the hundreds of miniature rainbows reflected from the skylight onto the white satin comforter on the bed. "Both Nathan and I are still a little raw from all the troubles we've had lately, Pat—that's all."

"Sure," Pat said with angry skepticism.

Mallory had let slip the disaster in the boathouse to Brad, but she had no intention of dropping it on Nathan's sister. The burden would be both unnecessary and unfair. "Your brother has already left for one last rehearsal, I take it?" she hedged.

"You know Nathan. If it isn't right, fight."

Mallory sighed, nodded. Nathan could probably have given a dazzling performance with no rehearsal at all. But he was, where his music was concerned, a raging perfectionist. She certainly didn't envy the band the demanding day and night ahead. "How were the ticket sales?"

Pat shrugged. "What tickets? They've been gone since day one. Mallory, you are going, aren't you? To the concert, I mean?"

Mallory's eyes shot back to Pat's face. "Why wouldn't I?"

"Nathan said you might be—well—busy."

Busy? On the night of what could be his last concert ever? It was inconceivable, and Mallory was stung to think that he would doubt her that way. The hurt gave her words a biting edge. "Gee, it is my bowling night," she said sardonically. "But the league will surely forgive me if I don't show up."

"Mallory—"

But Mallory knotted her fists and pounded them down on the bedding in furious frustration. "Damn that man! What kind of wife does he think I am?"

"Oh, Mallory, shut up!" Pat snapped, neatly stemming the

flow of her sister-in-law's diatribe. "It's no big deal and I'm sorry I said anything!"

Mallory flung back the covers and swung herself to a sitting position on the edge of the bed. "That *rat!*"

Pat was instantly on her feet, her face flushed with responding anger. "Mallory, it's too damned easy to make you mad, you know that? Is temperament a fringe benefit from the soap or did you have it all along?"

Ignoring Pat, Mallory stormed into the bathroom to fill the intimidating tile bathtub that always reminded her of a small swimming pool. When she returned, a half hour later, she was chagrined to find that Pat was gone.

Now you've done it, McKendrick, she berated herself as she slathered cream cheese onto a sliced bagel with fierce, jerky motions. *Pat's always there for you, and you repay her with your best bitch act!*

After choking down most of the bagel, Mallory exchanged her flannel robe for jeans, a cotton blouse and her gray rabbit bomber jacket. She hadn't intended to intrude on the final rehearsals, but now she would have to; Pat would almost certainly be there, and Mallory wanted to extend an immediate apology.

Probably because they were Seattlites, the guards already posted at the Kingdome entrance Mallory selected recognized her and allowed her inside unchallenged. She made her way quickly into the auditorium itself and was instantly transfixed by the swelling, poetic tide of the ballad Nathan was singing. When the song was over, she walked down a wide aisle, her hands in her coat pockets, toward the small group of people sitting in the first row of seats. Nathan, busy conferring with the drummer and the lead guitar player, did not notice her approach.

Her guess had been correct—Pat was there, along with several other women, her sneakered feet propped unceremoniously on the edge of her seat. Mallory touched her shoulder tentatively. "Pat?"

Pat stood up and turned to face her brother's wife with shy eyes. "Hi, Mall."

"I'm so sorry!" Mallory blurted, tears brimming in her lower lashes, her chin trembling.

"Me, too!" Pat cried, flinging her arms around Mallory, in spite of the seat back rising between them.

"This is all very touching," Nathan drawled irritably, into his microphone, "but we're trying to work here."

Mallory grimaced, but Pat turned and put out her tongue with all the impudent aplomb reserved for a younger sister.

Some of the tension left Nathan's face, and he laughed. At his cue, the band and members of the sound crew dared to laugh, too.

"So *that's* how you handle the dreaded Nathan McKendrick!" Mallory grinned, watching her sister-in-law with bright eyes.

"An occasional kick in the shins works, too," Pat confided in a loud whisper.

Mallory chuckled and again touched Pat's shoulder. "I'm getting out of here. Kicked shins or none, he'll be a beast all day. Am I forgiven?"

Pat's eyes glistened. "If you'll forgive me, too."

"Done," Mallory said softly, and then she turned to leave.

Just as Mallory left the main part of the auditorium, Diane Vincent stepped into view, her face a study in sadness and resignation. She tossed her head toward the swinging doors, beyond which the band was already playing again.

"I hope you're happy now, Mallory," she said.

Mallory lifted her chin, "What's that supposed to mean?"

"You've clipped his wings," Diane replied with an eloquent little shrug. "He'll rot on that damned island of yours. But it all went your way, didn't it?"

Mallory started to reply, and then stopped herself. Diane might be Nathan's favorite playmate, but she, herself, owed the woman nothing—not explanations, not reassurances.

"You're ruining his life, Mallory."

Mallory moved to leave, but Diane cut her off in one agile step. Something soft and broken haunted her bewitching powder blue eyes.

"At least I loved him enough to let him be himself," she went on when Mallory didn't speak. "For God's sake, Mallory, Nathan *needs* his music!"

"You're certainly an expert on what he needs, aren't you, Diane?" Mallory retorted finally, in acid tones.

A responding smirk shimmered in Diane's eyes and danced briefly on her lips. "You really didn't think you were woman enough for a dynamic, vital man like that, did you?"

Mallory had had the same thought herself, many times, but she was damned if she would let Diane Vincent see that. Green eyes shooting fire, she leveled a savage retort at her beautiful enemy. "Ever notice that while men like Nathan fool around with your type, Diane, they marry mine?"

The shot was a direct hit: Diane wilted visibly, and a look of pain trembled briefly in her eyes. Mallory wasn't the least bit proud of herself as she walked briskly away.

She spent the next few hours browsing in the baby departments of Seattle's finest stores, but the activity lacked the quiet glow Mallory had anticipated. The encounter with Diane had cast a shadow over her day, if not ruined it entirely.

Her heart looking forward to the peace and pine-scented sanity of the island where she and Nathan would, at last, be alone, Mallory finally hailed a cab and went back to the penthouse. There, the part-time housekeeper, Mrs. Callahan, was marauding through the spacious rooms with her vacuum cleaner, singing Nathan's latest hit in a loud, exuberant and off-key soprano.

Mallory crept past her, unseen, to the bedroom. She locked the doors and huddled on the bed for half an hour, like a hunted creature with no place to hide. She was tormented by images of Diane and Nathan making love in posh hotel rooms, on Australian beaches kissed with moonlight, in auditorium dressing rooms—images that would no doubt be deftly described, for all the world to read, in Diane's forthcoming book.

Mallory closed her eyes and rocked back and forth in helpless hatred. How would she bear seeing that book on display everywhere? How would she stand knowing that Diane lived so near the villa on Angel Cove?

When it was time to eat supper, Mallory had no appetite. Instead of consuming the meal Mrs. Callahan had left for her, she dressed for the concert, selecting jeans, a woolly gray sweater and a colorful lightweight poncho. Her mood was dark indeed by the time she met Trish and Kate and Pat at an agreed place and entered the Kingdome with them.

The crowds were so thick backstage that Mallory despaired of catching so much as a glimpse of Nathan before taking a seat in the third row with her friends. She didn't know whether to be disappointed or relieved. But, suddenly, despite the crush of people, Nathan was there, looking magnificent, as always, in his simple black tailored slacks and gleaming white silk shirt. Mallory suppressed a wifely urge to button the shirt, which was gaping provocatively to his muscled, ebony-matted midriff.

"Hi," she said shyly as Kate and Pat exchanged conspiratorial looks and slipped away to find Trish again.

Nathan laid his gifted hands on Mallory's shoulders and his smile warmed his dark eyes and softened his lips. "You came," he said in a gentle, surprised voice.

Mallory bridled a little, hurt. "Nathan, why wouldn't I?"

He shrugged slightly, but a shadow of pain moved in the depths of his eyes. "I guess I thought you would be anxious to get back to the island."

Mallory barely stopped herself from flinching, and Diane's bitter words echoed in her mind. *He'll rot on that damned island of yours—he needs his music—*

"Not so anxious that I'd miss something this important, Nathan," she said in a voice tight with doubt. She stood on tiptoe to kiss him lightly. "Break a leg, babe."

He smiled and raised both hands to the dark softness of her hair. "Everything is going to work out," he said gruffly. "I promise."

Mallory longed for that same certainty the way a drowning swimmer longs for a life preserver, but she knew better than to let wild wishes overwhelm her reason. Outside the enthusiasm of the crowd was rising to a deafening roar. They were claiming him now, those thousands of faceless women, and Mallory felt a wrench at giving Nathan up to them, even temporarily. Silently, she touched his lips with an index finger, turned and walked away.

"The natives are getting restless," Trish observed dryly as Mallory sank into her seat on the aisle. "What's he doing back there?"

Mallory shrugged and looked around at the surrounding concertgoers with a tremor of alarm. Their mood was petulant— almost hostile—and some of them were crying.

They don't want Nathan to retire, even for a year, she thought, and, at that moment, nothing in the world could have made her admit that she was his primary reason for turning his back on them.

The stage went dark, and suddenly the auditorium was throbbing with an almost tangible expectancy. When the lights came up again, Nathan was there and the crowd seemed to call to him in one discordant voice. With lithe motions of his powerful arms, he reached out for the microphone, pretending a slight difficulty with the trailing black cord. When he held the small electronic marvel in both hands, he muttered, "Hi, group," in a rumbling, sensuous voice. "Fancy meeting you here."

The audience went wild—shouting, applauding, stomping their feet.

Nathan lowered his dark, magnificent head, and waited, the very picture of patience. When the thunderous welcome ebbed a little, a female voice from several rows behind Mallory pleaded plaintively, "Nathan, don't go!"

"I'll be back, baby," he promised, and, as another wave of screaming madness swept through the crowd, Mallory felt a small spike of jealousy puncture her heart. It was beginning then, this strange, spiritual lovemaking between Nathan and the adoring horde.

When Nathan slid into a gruff, sensuous ballad, Mallory felt like flotsam adrift on a sea of communal grief. She was grateful for the darkness that lent her what would seem to be a very timely anonymity, and she wasn't surprised when Kate nudged her during a brief lull between songs, and whispered, "Maybe you should have stayed backstage, Mallory."

Mallory was glad to have someone so sensible confirm her own sense that the mood of this multitude of fans was unfavorable toward her. But she brought herself up short. In the press conferences preceding the concert, Nathan had not given any specific reason for his unexpected sabbatical. It wasn't as though someone had circulated fliers imprinted with Mallory's face and the words GET THIS WOMAN, SHE MADE HIM QUIT!

Despite this logic, the mood of that audience was the mood of a spurned and vengeful lover. Mallory slid down in her seat, dreading the time when the concert would end and the auditorium lights would come up, revealing her in all her guilt to the furious masses.

Three songs later, Mallory's worst suspicions were confirmed when the woman in front of her whispered to her companion that Nathan's defection could be laid at the feet of his "bitchy wife." She'd read it in one of the supermarket scandal sheets and regarded it as gospel.

The atmosphere seemed to pulse more dangerously with every song after that—finally, it was so tangible, this rising fury, that Nathan raised both his arms in the air, perspiration glistening on his face, to stop the music midbeat. To the accompaniment of a petulant rumble from the crowd, he strode to the side of the instrument-cluttered stage and spoke inaudibly to someone just out of sight. In a moment, however, he was back, speaking soothing words, moving easily into another song.

The horde was calming down a little when two security guards came and quietly collected Mallory from her seat to usher her out through the nearest exit. In the glaring light of the empty passageway, the hum of the crowd was muted, though it was still as frightening as the swarming sound of enraged bees.

Standing there, between the two middle-aged men appointed

as her protectors, Mallory marveled at the change in the mob's mood. It was almost as though Nathan's fans knew that she had been removed.

One of the security guards took her arm gently. "Mrs. McKendrick, we have orders to take you home immediately. I'm sorry."

A shaft of terrible disappointment impaled Mallory. "Couldn't I just wait backstage?" she asked, stricken.

"I'm sorry," the man repeated, and he had the good grace to sound as though he meant it. "Mr. McKendrick wants you off the premises as soon as possible, and I can't say I blame him."

Mallory stiffened for a moment, but then she knew that there was no use in arguing. Rather than defy Nathan, these men would probably remove her forcibly. As they discreetly squired her outside to a waiting limousine, she resented Nathan's fans as never before.

Back at the penthouse, Mallory took off the casual clothes she'd worn to the concert and slipped into a sleek white cashmere jumpsuit. With quick, angry motions of her hands, she brushed her hair up and pinned it into the Gibson girl style Nathan liked. Maybe that faceless horde had won by sheer number, but that was the battle, not the war. No one would stop her from attending the party that would follow the concert, from taking her rightful place at Nathan's side—no one.

At eleven-fifteen, the concert ended; Mallory saw the headlights of thousands of cars leaving the Kingdome in splendid, jewel-like tangles.

The sudden, shrill ring of the telephone made her start. But, after a moment of recovery, she pounced on it. Nathan's voice was hoarse with exhaustion and worry. "Are you all right?" he demanded without preamble.

"Yes," Mallory managed after an awkward moment. "Nathan, just tell me where to meet you, and—"

"No."

Disappointed fury jolted Mallory. "What?"

"Stay exactly where you are, Mallory," he bit out in tones

that brooked no argument. "I'll be home as soon as I possibly can."

Before she could object, he summarily hung up.

Frustrated, hurt and outraged, Mallory had no choice but to obey his dictate. The party could be held in any one of a hundred places; searching would be fruitless. She paced for a time and then, in desperation, strode into the study and snapped on the seldom-used television set.

The late news was on, and the entertainment commentator couldn't say enough about the performance of Seattle's own Nathan McKendrick. Alone, Mallory sputtered out a commentary of her own, and it was not so flattering as that of the man on television.

There were a few feet of footage showing the high points of the concert itself, and then a shot of a harried, annoyed Nathan striding into the wings from the stage, his eyes flashing, his face glistening with the exertion of more than two hours on stage.

"Enough already!" Mallory shouted at the flickering screen. "Can't you talk about a war or something?"

And as if to spite her, there was Nathan on the screen again, now showered and clad in a navy blue blazer, dress shirt and slacks. At his shoulder bobbed the glistening, proud blond head of Diane Vincent. Weak with shock, Mallory reached out, snapped the set off and sank dispiritedly onto the study sofa, too stricken to cry or shout or even move.

It was three o'clock in the morning when Mallory felt the bed shift slightly under Nathan's weight. He sighed and fell into an instant, fathomless sleep.

"Not tonight, Diane," he muttered.

Nathan awakened late the next morning. Even so, he was fully conscious for several seconds before he dared to open his eyes. When he did, he was met with a fierce sea green gaze and an intangible, bone-numbing chill. Mallory was beside him in bed, but she might as well have been ten thousand miles away. Everything about her relayed the message: Don't talk, don't touch.

She had definitely seen last night's newscast.

Nathan swore and reached out for her, intending to explain that Diane, with her usual audacity, had purposely fallen into step beside him and smiled into the camera, that he'd gotten rid of her in a hurry. But Mallory drew back ferociously, her eyes wild.

"Babe," he began awkwardly. "Listen—"

She slapped him.

The blow stung fiercely, but Nathan did not flinch, did not look away. He caught Mallory's wrists in his hands and pressed them down, over her head. "About the newscast," he said evenly. "Diane didn't go to the party with me, Mallory. She simply chose an inopportune time to walk beside me."

Mallory's splendid oval chin lifted defiantly, and she glared up at him in sheer hatred. "I realize that," she said in acid tones.

"Then why the assault and battery?" Nathan demanded, watching her closely, still holding her prisoner.

"I don't want to talk about it!"

Nathan swore in frustration and released her. *"Mallory."*

"Drop dead, you bastard!"

He reached out again, this time to grasp her upper arm, hard, although he was, as always, careful not to hurt her. Even now, the savage desire for her was stirring in his loins, but he suppressed it even as he pinned her beneath him. "Start talking, lady. Right now."

She struggled and squirmed, clearly furious, and the motion intensified the desire Nathan was trying to ignore. "Leave—me—alone!" she sputtered.

Frightened, Nathan bore down on her harder. "Mallory, for God's sake, talk to me!"

"You liar—you *cheat*—" she mourned, and tears seeped through her thick, tightly clenched eyelashes. The sight wounded Nathan, transformed the need to possess into an equal or greater need to comfort and protect.

"How did I lie?" he asked with gentle reason. "Or cheat?"

She was turning her head from side to side, and sobs escaped her throat in soft, breathless gasps. Nathan remembered the precious child within her and eased the pressure he'd been exerting with his body.

"Please, Mallory," he pleaded, in a raw voice. "Please tell me what's wrong."

She cried out like something wounded and shoved at him with her small, frantic, furious hands. But he would not be moved. Not until he knew.

"I hate you, Nathan—dear God, how I hate you—"

Nathan's raw throat constricted, and he closed his eyes momentarily against the fierce sincerity in her voice, in her face. "Please," he said again, and if that constituted begging, he didn't care.

Mallory was watching him when he opened his eyes again. "You act so innocent!" she hissed in a sharp undertone.

Defeated for the moment, Nathan released her and rolled away. "I *am* innocent," he answered dejectedly.

"Liar!" she choked. "You talk in your sleep, Nathan!"

Nathan sighed, sat up, his back to Mallory, and braced his head in his hands. "What, pray tell, did I say?"

There was a brief, awful silence. "'Not tonight, Diane,'" she finally replied, her pain blunt and savage and hopeless in her voice.

He turned back to look at her. "You're getting pretty desperate for something to hate me for, aren't you, Mallory?"

She would not meet his eyes or answer, and, in that moment, Nathan knew that there was no hope of convincing her that the remark, made in his *sleep* for God's sake, had meant nothing. He had never slept with Diane, never actually even considered it.

Slowly, he rose to his feet and walked into the bathroom, where he wrenched on the shower spigots and stepped under the hot, piercing spray. He would lose her now, lose the baby. Bracing himself with both hands against the tiled wall of the shower stall, Nathan McKendrick lowered his head and cried.

The coming week was a wretched one for Mallory. Without her role in the soap opera, she had no reason to stay in Seattle.

And yet she had no island house to flee to either, for it was the Johnsons' house now, and not her own. She could not go there to hide and cry and be close to things and memories from another, less complicated time in her life. Besides, Nathan lived on the island and she didn't think she could bear to encounter him after the way she'd made such a fool of herself and driven him away.

Day by day she fought down her senseless, fathomless love for him, and day by day it grew, like a flower forcing its way up through asphalt.

"I want to hate you," she said aloud one grim winter afternoon to the photograph taken at Pike Place Market that day, the one that portrayed Nathan as a marshal and Mallory as a dance-hall girl. "Why?"

In her mind, she heard his voice. *You're getting pretty desperate for something to hate me for, aren't you, Mallory?*

"Yes," she said aloud, putting the framed photograph back onto the study's fireplace mantel and taking up another, one that showed her mother and father standing on the deck of their boat, displaying huge, freshly caught salmon and enormous grins.

She was angry with them, these cherished people in the photograph. How dare they die and leave her, when she'd loved them without reservation?

The question made Mallory draw in a sharp breath. She'd been deliberately sandbagging her own marriage, for weeks and months and years because she was afraid, afraid that if she loved Nathan completely, he would die.

In a flurry to reach him, she grabbed her purse and coat and fled the penthouse without looking back.

12

The villa overlooking Angel Cove was almost as imposing in the darkness as it was in the light of day. Mallory's heart caught in her throat at the sight of it, just as it had when she had first seen the place during childhood explorations of the island. It had been a place of wonder and mystery then, standing empty for so many years, and Trish and Mallory had worked up any number of fascinating fantasies concerning its past. Then, seeking refuge from the insane pace of his life-style, the famous Nathan McKendrick had bought the property and brought in an army of carpenters and decorators to refurbish it.

Mallory had met Nathan that summer at an island picnic and fallen in love with a soul-jarring thump that still vibrated within her whenever she even glanced at Nathan. Before winter, they had been married.

Now, standing forlornly on the sweeping front porch, Mallory wedged her hands into the pockets of her coat and swallowed hard, trying to work up the courage to knock. Oh, it would be so easy just to dash back to her car and drive away—

But no. She was through running.

Suddenly, one of the heavy front doors opened with a soft creak, and Mallory could feel Nathan's dark gaze upon her, even though her own eyes were clenched tightly shut in preparation for harsh rejection.

But the rejection didn't come. "Open your eyes, Mallory," Nathan ordered, not unkindly, but not warmly, either.

She obeyed but could only stare at him.

"It always helps if you knock," Nathan commented, taking her arm in a gentle grip and drawing her into the dimly lit entry hall with its black-and-white marble floor and tastefully papered walls.

She looked up at him and her throat constricted painfully, but she still could not manage so much as an offhand "hello."

Nathan clearly suffered from no such problem, but he wasn't inclined to make things easier for her, it seemed. He simply watched Mallory, his arms folded across his chest.

Mallory bit her lip. *Get on with it, say something!* she told herself.

"Is my dog here?" she choked out after several torturous seconds.

A tender smirk curved one side of Nathan's mouth upward. "Is that why you're here, Mrs. McKendrick? You're looking for your dog?"

Mallory squeezed her eyes shut for a second, and then opened them again. "If you're trying to make this difficult, it's certainly working."

He laughed and took her hand in a warm grasp. "I'm sorry," he said, leading her along the darkened hallway and into the brightly lit kitchen at the back of the house. There the fickle Cinnamon was gnawing at an enormous soup bone.

Nathan gestured grandly toward the beast. "Your dog, *madame.*"

"That animal has no scruples!" Mallory complained, only half in jest.

"None," Nathan agreed in a low tone that seemed to reach inside Mallory and caress her weary heart.

Mallory turned to face her husband squarely and lifted her chin. "I love you very much, Nathan McKendrick," she announced in an unsteady voice.

Deftly, Nathan reached out and drew her close. The pale blue cashmere of his sweater made her nose itch.

With one finger, he caught the underside of her chin and lifted it so that she was looking at him again. She saw the words in his dark eyes even before he voiced them. "And I love you."

Compelled by forces older than creation, Mallory pressed

close to him, comforted by the hard strength of his body, but disturbed by it, too.

Nathan moaned low in his throat. "Talk about no scruples. Lady, do you know what it does to me when you hold me like this?"

Mallory knew that her eyes were bright with mischief. "I have an idea," she confessed.

He tilted his head to one side and studied her with cautious, weary eyes. "Far be it from me to rock a very promising boat, sweet thing, but if you came over here to do me some kind of retaliatory number, I'll tell you right now that I can't handle it."

Mallory frowned. "Number? Nathan, what are you talking about?"

"This. It's going to wipe me out if we spend the night loving and then you leave again."

She lifted a gentle finger to softly trace the outline of his lips. "You really think I like to hurt you!" she accused.

Nathan shrugged, an action that belied the fierce and sudden pain darkening his eyes. "Nobody does it quite like you, lover. If revenge is what you want, kindly get it through your lawyers."

Mallory drew back at the sharp impact of his words; if he'd slapped her, he couldn't have caused her more anguish. "My lawyers?" she echoed. "Nathan, what—?"

His embrace tightened, and it was no longer tender. "Listen to me," he said in harsh, measured tones. "I love you. I need you. But I'm through playing stupid games, Mallory—either you're my wife and you live with me and share my bed or you're just somebody I used to know. The choice is yours. If you decide to stay, remember this—I've never made love to Diane—I've never been unfaithful to you at all—and I don't intend to be tortured for some imagined transgression from now till the crack of doom. Do we understand each other?"

Mallory's lips moved, but not a sound came out of her mouth.

Nathan's hands were moving in sensuous, compelling circles on the small of her back. "Go or stay, babe," he went on, "but if you walk out of here tonight, don't ever come back."

The hardness of his words chafed Mallory's proud spirit, but she knew he was right. A final decision had to be made and then abided by. Her voice trembled when she spoke.

"Aren't you being just a bit arbitrary, Mr. McKendrick?"

Nathan sighed, and his hands moved down to cup her firm, rounded bottom and draw her closer still. "Umm," he said, closing his eyes for a moment. "Stop stalling, woman. Do I take you back to Seattle or do I just take you?"

Mallory's cheeks brightened to a deep pink. The hard evidence of his desire for her was pressed against her abdomen, making it difficult indeed to think clearly. "This is coercion," she accused in a whisper.

Nathan's lips coursed warmly over her temple to nuzzle the soft, vulnerable place beneath her ear. "I didn't say I was going to fight fair," he reminded her, his voice gruff with need.

Mallory trembled; in truth, her decision had been made before he had opened the front door, before she'd left Seattle. What was the use in pretending, playing childish games? She swallowed hard.

"If you don't mind," she said softly, "I'll stay."

Trish and Mallory watched with comically serious faces as Pat modeled one of several wedding gowns she was considering.

"Too many ruffles," Mallory commented.

"Too few," Trish countered.

Pat paused, a vision bathed in spring sunlight, to glare at the spectators lounging on the living room sofa. "You two are no help at all!"

Mallory and Trish exchanged a look and then burst into a simultaneous fit of giggles.

Mallory, her stomach well rounded with the cherished weight of her child, Nathan's child, sat cross-legged, like a small, plump Indian. Beaming, she reinspected Pat's beautiful gown. "You look lovely. Yes, indeed, I think that is *definitely* The Dress."

"Me, too," Trish admitted. "Of course, I looked much better in mine, you know. Some of us just have better bodies than others."

Mallory and Pat both laughed, and Mallory glanced eloquently down at the dome of her stomach. Though it was only April, she was big enough that she couldn't join in the good-natured teasing by claiming any superiority for her own figure. "No comment from this quarter!"

"I should say not, fatso," Pat answered.

Trish rolled her eyes and sighed theatrically. "And it's April, for heaven's sake. By August, they're going to be transporting El Tubbo here with a block and tackle!"

Mallory gave her friend a good-natured shove and pretended to pout. "Nathan thinks I'm beautiful!"

"What does he know?" Trish countered.

Pat laughed. "Maybe we should ask Weight Watchers to send over their emergency squad."

Eyes twinkling, Mallory shot to her feet in dramatic indignation and summoned up her most imperious glare. "When are you two going to let up on the fat jokes?" she cried. "You'll destroy my ego!"

Pat lifted her chin and grinned. "If you run out of ego, sis, just borrow some from Nathan—he has plenty. As for the fat jokes, we'll let up when you can see your feet again, Mc-Kendrick. You remember—those things south of your knees?"

Mallory laughed and the child moved within her and she thought, in that moment, that she had never been happier in all her life.

Pat and Trish exchanged a look and giggled. A moment later, Pat was off to an upstairs bedroom to change out of the wedding gown and back into jeans.

Trish patted Mallory's hand with affection. "All jokes aside, old friend, you look wonderful. I know it's corny, but you actually *glow*."

"Thanks," Mallory replied, sitting down on the sofa again and resting her hands lightly on the protrusion beneath her blouse.

Trish frowned, looking briefly in the direction of the distant room where Nathan was locked away. "What's that man of yours up to these days? Rumor has it that you clubbed him over the head with a package of frozen shrimp and stuffed the body under the cellar stairs.''

Mallory smiled at Trish's remark and turned the simple wedding band on her finger, so that it caught the invading spring sunshine and transformed it to golden fire. ''He has been something of a hermit lately, hasn't he?'' She lowered her voice to a whisper, unable, in her pride, to keep the secret to herself. ''Trish, he's writing a soundtrack for a movie, and it's wonderful.''

Trish made a funny face. ''What else would it dare be but wonderful? But what about you, Mall? Do you miss all that glamor?''

Decisively Mallory shook her head. ''I taught the fourth grade yesterday,'' she confided, beaming at the memory. ''The regular teacher was sick and they called me. It was so much fun, Trish!''

Trish grinned. ''You are easily entertained, my friend. Since when is a raging horde of preadolescents considered *fun?*''

''Trish, they're darling,'' Mallory protested as the residual joy of the experience came back to her, full force. ''It was show-and-tell day, and this one little boy brought a sandwich bag full of hermit crabs—''

Trish was shaking her head slowly in amused, affectionate wonder. ''You are something else, McKendrick,'' she broke in. ''My God, you don't even miss the soap one little bit, do you?''

''It wasn't the way selling real estate is for you, Trish—I never enjoyed it. I never got excited about it, like I do about teaching.''

Just then Pat returned, clad in battered blue jeans and an old sweatshirt, her potential wedding dress in a box under her arm. ''Could I catch that ride back to the ferry terminal now, Mall?''

Trish rose quickly from her seat on the sofa. ''I'll take you over. I'm late for the office, anyway.''

''Great,'' Pat answered, the prospect of another evening with Roger shining clear in her eyes. Quickly, she bent and planted a kiss on Mallory's forehead. "See you around, sis. And don't let that brother of mine write himself into collapse, okay?"

It was May, and the weather was glorious. Sitting at the very end of the boat dock in front of the villa, her feet dangling between water and wharf, Mallory reveled in the singular splendor of Puget Sound. The clear sky cast its cobalt blue reflection onto the receiving waters, and the Olympic mountains were like snow-clad giants in the tree-lined distance, their peaks craggy and traced with jagged purple streaks. And everywhere, gulls sang their contentious songs, swooping and circling against the pearlescent sky.

Mallory laid gentle hands on the folds of her well-filled madras maternity blouse and smiled to know that her baby would grow up in this marvelous place. She glanced toward the duplex where Diane had lived until a month or so before, when she'd suddenly given up her writing aspirations and gone off to do press work for a punk rock group.

"Is this a private daydream or can anybody join in?" Nathan asked softly from just behind her.

Mallory hadn't heard his approach. She turned to look up at him; he was framed in a dazzling, silver aura of sunlight.

When she said nothing, Nathan sat down beside her, Indian-style, on the creaking, spray-dampened wooden wharf. He sighed, shoved his hands into the pockets of his worn blue running jacket and turned his dark eyes to the panorama of trees, sky, sea and mountains.

"If you could paint a picture of God's soul," he said quietly, "it would probably look just like this."

Mallory nodded, loving the man beside her even more than she had before he spoke. "How's the movie score going?" she asked, sliding her arm through the crook of his and resting her cheek against the warm rounding of his strong shoulder.

Nathan laughed wearily. "Who can work in that place? Every time I try to set a note to paper, some caterer shows up, flanked by two legions of florists."

Mallory smiled and kissed his rough, fragrant cheek warmly.

"I'm glad the wedding is tomorrow," she confided. "Pat is hysterical."

Nathan grinned and draped an arm around Mallory's ample waist, drawing her close. "*Pat* is hysterical?" he teased. "*I'm* hysterical. What if I blow my lines?"

Mallory laughed. "All you have to do is walk your sister to the front of the church and say 'I do' when the minister asks—"

"Who giveth this woman in marriage?" Nathan boomed, in a comically ponderous, clerical voice.

"Right. Considering that you've dazzled the crowned heads of Europe with command performances, you shouldn't have all that much trouble with two words."

Nathan's eyes were suddenly serious, almost brooding. They rose to a distance well beyond Mallory's reach. "Do you think Pat will be happy?" he asked.

Mallory gave him an affectionate shove. "Stop worrying. Pat isn't some besotted teenager, you know—she's a grown woman, perfectly capable of recognizing the right man for her."

He brought his gaze back from the unreachable hinterlands to sweep Mallory's face with tenderness and hope. "How about you, Mrs. McKendrick? Are you happy? Did you choose the right man?"

Mallory pretended to search the shoreline behind them. "Sure did. He's around here somewhere—"

Nathan caught her chin in his hand. "Mallory, I'm serious," he said, and the anxiety in his features bore witness to his words.

Something ached in Mallory's throat. "I've never been happier," she vowed. And it was true—she hadn't thought it possible to feel the wondrous things she felt, not only during their now-cautious lovemaking, but at mundane times, too, like when they walked the island's beaches or ate breakfast on the sun porch or watched the old movies they both loved.

He bent his head to brush her lips tenderly with his own. "You weren't always happy, were you?" he asked.

Mallory sighed and searched the sun-dappled waters dancing before them. "No. I remember thinking, one winter day, that we were like snowflakes on the sea, you and I. Our love was so beautiful, so special, but, like the snowflakes, when it touched something bigger, it dissolved.''

Poetry was an integral part of Nathan's nature, and he smiled, somewhat sadly, at the imagery in her statement. ''Snowflakes on the sea,'' he repeated thoughtfully, his eyes locked now with hers. ''Did it ever occur to you that that snow didn't really cease to exist at all? Mallory, it became a permanent part of that 'something bigger'—a part of something eternal and elemental and very, very beautiful.''

A smile trembled on Mallory's lips, and sudden tears made the whole world sparkle before her like a moving gem. ''I love you,'' she said.

Nathan bounded to his feet and drew his wife with him, pretending that the task was monumental. And Mallory's laughter rang out over the whispering salt waters like the toll of a crystal bell.

Mallory stood on tiptoe in the pastor's study, trying to straighten Nathan's tie. Beyond, in the main part of the small, historical building, the voices of guests and a few intrepid reporters hummed in expectation.

''Stop wiggling!'' Mallory scolded, as Nathan fidgeted before her, impatient with the doing and redoing of his tie. ''It's Roger's job to be nervous, not yours.''

He glared at her enormous flower-bedecked picture hat. ''Does that thing have a sprinkler system?'' he scowled.

Mallory laughed and then pirouetted to show off the rest of the outfit—a flowing pink organdy dress, strappy shoes and a bouquet of mountain violets.

Nathan was still uncomfortable. ''Everything has to be right,'' he grumbled. ''What if—?''

Mallory caught his face in both hands. ''Nathan, relax. Just *relax!*''

He laughed suddenly and shook his head. ''I can't.''

With a sigh, Mallory gave his tie one final rearrangement. ''Think of it as a performance,'' she suggested.

Just then the door leading into the main sanctuary opened with a creak, and Roger came in, flanked by the pastor. The groom shot a terrified look in Nathan's direction and swallowed hard.

Seeing his own discomfort mirrored in Roger's face seemed to ease Nathan. Mallory felt his broad shoulders relax under her hands, and saw a sudden mischief dance in his eyes.

"Don't you dare tease that poor man!" she whispered tersely, giving her husband a slight shake.

Nathan smiled down at her wickedly. "Would I do a thing like that?"

"Absolutely," Mallory replied.

The pastor, himself an aged and revered institution on the island—he'd married Mallory and Nathan, too, in that same small church—cleared his throat in an eloquent signal that the time was nigh.

"Be nice!" Mallory admonished her husband in a fierce whisper before leaving the room to join Pat in the tiny adjoining social hall.

At the sight of her sister-in-law, Mallory drew in a sharp breath and fought back tears of admiration and love. The other bridesmaids quietly slipped out, to wait in the sunny churchyard.

"Oh, Pat, you look wonderful!"

The tiny pearls stitched to Pat's gown and veil caught rays of stray sunshine from the fanlight window high on the wall behind her and transformed them to tiny rainbows. Even their splendor could not compete with the happy glow of the bride's face or the shine in her eyes. "Mall," she choked softly, "oh, Mallory, I'm scared!"

Mallory embraced this woman who seemed as much her own sister as Nathan's. "Take a deep breath," she ordered with mock sternness.

Pat complied, but her blue eyes looked enormous and a visible shudder ran through her slender lace-and-tulle-clad figure. "What if I faint? Mallory, what if I can't remember what to say?"

Mallory chuckled. "You're as bad as Nathan. You're not going to faint, Pat, and you know your vows inside and out."

Pat shivered. "We shouldn't have written them ourselves!" she cried in a small rush of last-minute panic. "We should have let Pastor Holloway read from his book! Then it would only have been a matter of repeating what he said—"

"Patricia!"

Pat closed her eyes tight and swayed a little inside Mallory's hug, but then she opened them again and smiled. The first strains of the elderly church organ wafted into the little, sunlit room.

"Mall—we're on!"

Mallory laughed. "Knock 'em dead, McKendrick," she said softly, and then she led her trembling sister-in-law outside into the fragrant spring day and around to the front doors of the church. There, she surrendered Pat to Nathan.

Being the matron of honor, Mallory walked proudly down the sun-and-stained-glass-patterned aisle, on the arm of Roger's best man. She thought what a picture she must present, with her flowered hat, flowing dress and bulging stomach, and bit her lip to keep from giggling. Out of the corner of her eye, she could see the occasional reporter scribbling on a notepad, but there were no bursts of blinding light from flash cameras—Nathan and Pastor Holloway had seen to that personally.

At the orchid-strewn altar, Mallory and the best man parted ways, both turning, as Roger did, to watch Pat's magnificent entrance.

Mallory's heart ached in her throat as Pat and Nathan proceeded slowly toward the front of the church—his face with a touching, concentrating grimace, hers hidden beneath the glistening white net of her flowing veil. When Nathan's sleeve brushed Mallory's, she looked up at him and winked discreetly, in silent reassurance. He grinned in response.

"Who giveth this woman in marriage?" Pastor Holloway demanded, raising his bushy white eyebrows and bending forward slightly to stare at Nathan expectantly.

Nathan drew a deep breath, and his arm slipped casually

around Mallory's waist. "We do," he said in a clear voice, and, at the pastor's crisp nod, he withdrew to take his place in a front pew.

Mallory was still grinning at the way Nathan had included her in that important moment when the minister began to speak. "Dearly beloved, we are gathered here—"

The house and garden at Angel Cove were positively overflowing with wedding guests and those who had been invited to the reception. Mallory's feet were throbbing, and she was beginning to feel cornered and slightly frantic when Nathan suddenly appeared beside her and took her arm. He ushered her into the outer hallway with dignity, but, there, he swept her suddenly up into his arms. "I think you've had all the celebration you can take in one day," he announced in a gruff yet tender voice.

Mallory started to protest that Pat would expect her to stay, but her husband's determined look silenced her. She was very tired, and she longed for a little quiet solitude, so she didn't challenge him.

Without drawing any apparent notice from the crowds gathered to wish Pat and Roger well, Nathan carried Mallory out the front door, down over the lawn and onto the wharf. When he finally set her down, it was on the deck of his impressive cabin cruiser, the *Sky Dancer*.

"What—" she muttered, looking around in amazement.

Nathan grinned and deftly freed the cruiser from its mooring. "We're escaping," he said.

And only minutes later the boat was cutting majestically through the Sound, casting wakes of diamond and sapphire behind her. Mallory sat patiently in the seat beside Nathan's, filled with a sort of amused wonder.

At last, the *Sky Dancer*'s powerful engine died, and they dropped anchor in a secluded cove they had visited many times before. Gently, Nathan gripped Mallory's arm and led her below into the vessel's well-appointed cabin.

It was even more well-appointed than usual, that day—the covers on the wide berthlike bed were turned back to reveal inviting pink satin sheets, and a pine-and-sea scented breeze billowed the new white eyelet curtains covering the portholes.

Nathan gestured grandly toward the bed. "Much as I'd like to undress you," he said with a speculative lift of one eyebrow, "I don't dare. I'll be back in five minutes, Mrs. McKendrick, and when I return, I expect to find you sleeping." With that, he turned and left the cabin.

Feeling lushly loved and shamefully pampered, Mallory removed the dress she'd worn in the wedding, along with her fussy picture hat and the dainty shoes that had been cutting into her swollen feet without mercy. Her tired flesh hungering for the restful, cool smoothness of those satin sheets, she took off her under things, too, and crawled into bed with a sigh of fathomless contentment.

Nathan returned, as promised, in five minutes, and he frowned sternly when he saw that Mallory wasn't sleeping.

"My feet hurt," she complained.

He sat down on the end of the bed, still clad in the elegant shirt and trousers he'd worn in Pat's wedding ceremony, and deftly brought both Mallory's feet onto his lap. When he began to massage them with strong, gentle hands, she sighed with sheer pleasure.

In spite of the cool breeze of the day, a powerful heat surged through Mallory's body as he caressed her toes, her heels, her aching arches.

"Make love to me, Nathan," she said in a sleepy, languid whisper.

"Wanton," he teased. "You're too tired and too pregnant."

"Too *fat,* you mean," she pouted.

With a sudden motion and a comically evil laugh, Nathan was standing beside the bed, leering. "Too fat, is it?" he boomed, and then he flung back the covers, baring her pear-shaped form, and knelt to kiss her satiny knees tantalizingly, first one, and then the other.

Mallory moaned, lulled by soft, insistent passion, by the delicate scent of the summery breeze from outside, by the caress of the smooth sheets and the gentle rocking of the boat itself.

Nathan's lips travelled up one thigh to the small mountain that was her stomach, scaling it with a series of soul-jarring, butterfly kisses.

"Nathan—"

His hands stroked her stomach gently, possessively. "No," he said.

"You made me want you," Mallory argued. "How do you expect me to sleep now, you brute?"

Nathan laughed gruffly, but one of his hands was already caressing the silken vee between her thighs. "Too much lovemaking is bad when you're so tired."

Mallory tilted her head back, wordless with weary need, and, of their own accord, her hips rose and fell in rhythm with the motion of his hand.

Nathan swore hoarsely and, with gentle fingers, bared the pulsing bud hidden from all eyes but his. Mallory cried out and entwined her fingers in the richness of his hair as he pleasured her.

August. Nathan could hardly believe that so much time had passed so quickly.

He stared at the squalling infant beyond the thick glass barrier, searching the tiny, crumpled face for some subtle resemblance to himself or Mallory. As far as he could tell, the kid looked like Don Rickles.

"Well?" Mallory prodded from her wheelchair beside him. "What's the verdict?"

Nathan smiled at his wife, at the returning light in her fatigue-smudged eyes. Delivering their baby had been difficult for her, and Dr. Lester had recommended rather forcefully that they forget having more.

Mallory had taken that decision hard, though with typical courage, and there were now faint traces of color in her pallid cheeks and a quickening flickered within her spirit that Nathan could feel in his own.

"Who does Baby McKendrick look like?" Mallory pressed, looking up at him, a mischievous twitch pulling at the corner of her mouth.

"What kind of name is 'Baby McKendrick'?" he stalled.

"Nathan."

He turned to study the child again, ponderously and at great length.

Persistent to the end, Mallory tugged at the sleeve of his corduroy suit jacket. "Say it. Your daughter is a dead ringer for Ike Eisenhower."

Nathan laughed uproariously, but when he looked at Mallory's face, her eyes were serious again, and wretched. He ached inside, all his amusement vanishing like vapor. He squatted beside the wheelchair to cup her trembling chin in one hand. "Come on," he teased hoarsely. "She'll grow out of it."

Mallory sniffled miserably. "There won't be any more babies," she reminded him in broken tones.

Nathan released her chin to smooth back a tendril of her taffy-colored hair. "What are you, woman—greedy? We've got Ike!"

Mallory's smile was like the first glimmer of light in a dark sky, shimmering and brave and full of hope. "And each other."

He kissed her briefly, tenderly. "And each other," he confirmed.

Mallory stood in the sound booth, Brittany perched on her hip, and watched the darkened stage below with as much anticipation as any of the other thousands of fans packing the Kingdome that rainy February night. When the stagelights were turned up to reveal Nathan, the auditorium rocked with a roaring, pounding welcome.

Looking splendid in his flashy red shirt and tailored black slacks, he raised both his arms in response to their greeting and lowered his head slightly. The gesture was both triumphant and humble, and Mallory felt tears of pride and wonder burn in her eyes. Their carefully considered decision had been the right one; she knew it in that moment as never before. Nathan McKendrick was back where he belonged.

At his almost imperceptible signal, the regathered band, which had been rehearsing at Angel Cove for a full month, began a skillful introduction to Nathan's greatest hit of all time, a throaty, sensuous love song. He sat down casually, on a high stool, and reached for his guitar. When he began to sing, the crowd was finally silent.

Mallory swallowed hard. *He's mine,* she exulted silently. *He's mine.*

Brittany babbled happily and pointed toward the distant stage.

Mallory chuckled and then whispered, in order to avoid bothering the technicians working in the booth. "Yes, that's Daddy."

One of the sound men looked up at Mallory and grinned, shaking his head. "One song and he's got them on their knees," he marveled.

Mallory only nodded, since the man was wearing earphones and probably wouldn't hear anything she said anyway.

Nathan was clearly in command, clearly glad to be performing again. Throughout the long concert, he wove his singular spell. During the livelier numbers, the audience clapped and stomped and sang along, while the ballads stilled them to a silence Mallory wouldn't have believed possible.

By the end of the performance, Nathan's face shone with sweat, as did the ample, darkly matted portion of chest revealed by his half-open shirt. Once again, he had given everything, and the massive audience roared its appreciation.

When he sprinted offstage, they summoned him back. The adoring mob clapped and shouted and stomped their feet. As was his custom, Nathan did not reappear.

Mallory could envision him backstage, toweling his face, his neck, his chest, congratulating the band. She felt the distance between them keenly, but did not leave the sound booth. She had promised Nathan that she and Brittany would remain in that remote bastion until the crowds had dispersed and someone came for them. He had not forgotten the mood of the audience at the last concert, and he was taking no chances.

The friendly sound man removed his earphones and stood up.

"Hi," he said, chucking Brittany's plump little chin. "That daddy of yours really brought down the house, didn't he?"

Brittany's Nathan-brown eyes widened, and her soft, dark hair tickled, fragrant, against Mallory's cheek. A moment later, she tossed back her head and began to scream.

"What did I say?" The sound man grinned, looking a bit abashed.

Mallory shook her head in reassurance and went to the back of the booth, where there was a narrow bench. From the looks of things, there were still a lot of people milling in the aisles below. It might be a while before they could leave.

Brittany was sound asleep when Pat and Roger and two security men came to claim them. They rode to the penthouse in a limousine, Pat protectively holding the sleeping baby, Mallory anxious to change clothes and rejoin Nathan.

The two security guards were waiting discreetly in the lobby when Mallory hurried out of the elevator again, feeling beautiful in her slinky powder blue dress, strappy shoes and silver fox jacket. By their own choice, Pat and Roger had stayed behind in the penthouse to look after Brittany.

Her escorts delivered her to the door of the private hotel suite where the party was to be held and left her only when Nathan pushed his way through the crowd of promoters, musicians and press people, grinned, and held out his hand.

Mallory McKendrick's heart sang a sweet song of its own as she hurried toward him.

BEWITCHING

Carla Neggers

1

THE PINKS AND ORANGES of dawn sparkled on the bay beyond Marsh Point, off a stretch of southern Maine that was still quiet, still undiscovered by tourists. Hannah Marsh stood on a boulder above the rocky coastline. The wind blew raw and cold, although the calendar said spring had arrived. In defiance of the weather, daffodils bloomed in the little garden outside her cottage.

In Boston the tulips would be out, perhaps even a few leaves budded. It wouldn't be so bad.

"You're going," a gruff voice said behind her.

She turned and smiled at Thackeray Marsh, aged seventy-nine, owner of Marsh Point, fellow historian and her cousin several times removed. He was a stout, fair-skinned, fair-haired man, although not as fair as herself, and kept in shape with dawn and dusk walks along a loop-shaped route that took in most of Marsh Point.

"I have no choice," Hannah said. "Most of the documents I need to examine are in Boston, and anything new on Priscilla Marsh will be there. It's where she lived and died, Thackeray. I have to go."

He snorted. "The Harlings catch you, they'll string you up."

"You said yourself there's only one Harling left in Boston, and he's even older than you are. I'll be fine."

Her elderly cousin squinted his emerald eyes at her. He was wearing an old tweed jacket patched at the elbows and rubber boots that had to be older than she was. His frugality, Hannah had learned in her five years in Maine, was legendary in the region.

"The Harlings and the Marshes haven't had much of anything

to do with each other in a hundred years," he said. "Why rock the boat?"

"I'm not rocking the boat. I'm going on a perfectly ordinary, honorable research expedition." She tried not to sound defensive or impatient, but she had gone over her position—over and over it—with Cousin Thackeray. "It's not as if Priscilla Marsh died yesterday, you know."

Judge Cotton Harling had sentenced Priscilla Marsh to death by hanging three hundred years ago. Hannah hoped to have her biography of her ancestor in bookstores by the tricentennial of the execution. Not only would it be good business, but it would pay a nice tribute to a woman who had defied the restrictions of Puritan America—of the Harlings of Boston.

And paid the price, of course. Hannah couldn't forget that.

The wind picked up, and she hugged her oversize sweatshirt closer to her body. Her long, fine, straight blond hair was, fortunately, held back in a hastily tied ponytail. Otherwise it would have tangled badly. Cousin Thackeray barely seemed to notice the cold.

"Hannah, the Harlings resent that we won't let them forget it was a Harling who had Priscilla hanged. We, of course, say they *shouldn't* ever forget. The feud has been going on like this for three hundred years."

She refused to let his dark mood dampen her enthusiasm for what was, after all, a necessary trip—and no doubt would prove boring and routine, involving nothing more than musty books and documents and hours and hours in badly lit archives.

He made her trip sound like some kind of espionage assignment. "At least," her cousin went on, "don't let anyone in Boston know you're a Marsh. It's just too dangerous. If Jonathan Harling finds out—"

"That's the name of the last Harling in Boston?"

Cousin Thackeray nodded somberly. "Jonathan Winthrop Harling."

She grinned. "I look at it this way. What could one little old man who happens to be a Harling do to me?"

J. WINTHROP HARLING climbed the sloping lawn of the gold-domed Massachusetts State House above Boston Common with a sense of purpose. He had come to look at the statue of the infamous Priscilla Marsh. Her tragic death three hundred years ago at the hands of a Harling still colored his family's reputation. It was a part of what being a Harling in Boston was all about.

The wind off the harbor was brisk, even chilly, but he didn't feel it, though he was only wearing the dark gray suit he'd worn to the office.

Although he'd been born and raised in New York and had lived in Boston only a year, he was a stereotypical Harling in one sense: he made one hell of a lot of money. Sometimes the size of his income, his growing net worth, staggered him. But the Harlings had always been good at making money.

Priscilla Marsh's smooth marble face stared at him in the waning sunlight. She looked very young and very wronged, more innocent, no doubt, than she had been in fact. The sculptor had managed to capture the legendary beauty of her hair, supposedly an unusual shock of pale blond, fine and very straight. She had been hanged on the orders of Cotton Harling when she was just thirty years old.

"Good going, Cotton," Win muttered.

But had she lived and died an ordinary life, Priscilla Marsh would never have inspired an oft-quoted Longfellow poem or a famous 1952 play. Nor would her statue have stood on the lawn of the Massachusetts State House, either.

Win brushed his fingers across the cool stone hair and felt the tragedy of the young Puritan's death. She had been dead less than a day when evidence of her innocence had arrived. Priscilla Marsh hadn't been teaching the young ladies of her neighborhood witchcraft, but how to cure earaches.

Her death should have been a lesson to future Harlings.

A lesson in patience, humility, faith in one's fellow human beings. A warning against arrogance and pride. Against believing in one's own infallibility.

But, Win thought, it hadn't.

HANNAH ARRIVED IN BOSTON without incident and set up house-keeping in a cramped apartment on Beacon Hill. She had traded with a friend, who would get two weeks in Hannah's Maine cottage come summer. The friend, a teacher, was off to Paris with her French class. Things, Hannah decided, were just meant to work out.

Her first stop, bright and early the next morning, was the New England Athenaeum on Beacon Street, across from the Boston Public Garden. It was a private library, supported by just four hundred members and founded in 1892 by, of course, a Harling.

Hannah indicated she was a professional historian and would like to use the library, a renowned repository of New England historical documents.

Preston Fowler, the director, a formal man who appeared to be in his mid-fifties, informed her that the New England Athenaeum was a private institution. Accordingly, she would be permitted into its stacks and rare book room only when she had exhausted all other possibilities and could prove it was the only place that had what she needed. And even then she would be carefully watched.

Hannah resisted the impulse to tell him other private institutions had opened their doors to her in her career. Arguing wouldn't get her anywhere. She needed something that would work. She sighed and said, "But Uncle Jonathan said I wouldn't have any trouble with you."

"Who?" Preston Fowler asked sharply.

"My uncle." She paused more for dramatic effect than to reconsider what she was doing. Then she added, "Jonathan Winthrop Harling."

Fowler cleared his throat, and Hannah was amused at how rigid his spine went. Ahh, the Harling factor. "You—your name is…?"

"Hannah," she said, not feeling even a twinge of guilt. "Hannah Harling."

WIN SETTLED BACK in his soft leather chair and took the call from the elderly uncle whose name he bore. "Hey, there, Uncle Jonathan, what's up?"

Jonathan Harling, who had just turned eighty, got straight to the point. "You going to the New England Athenaeum dinner on Saturday?"

"Wild horses couldn't drag me. Why?"

"Friend of mine says he saw a Harling on the guest list."

"Well, it wasn't me," Win said emphatically. "I haven't even been inside that snooty old place. Your friend must have been mistaken. What about you? You aren't going, are you?"

Uncle Jonathan grunted. "Some of us don't have unlimited budgets, you know."

"I would be happy to buy you a ticket—"

"Damned if I'll accept charity from my own nephew!" the old man bellowed hotly. "Why don't you go, meet a nice woman who'll inspire you to part with some of that booty of yours? How much you worth these days? A million? Two? More?"

Win laughed. "It's more fun to keep you guessing."

Still grumbling, his uncle hung up. Win turned his chair so that he could see the spectacular view of Boston Harbor from his fourteenth-floor window. He watched a few planes take off from Logan Airport across the water. It was a clear, warm, beautiful May afternoon, the kind that made him wonder if he shouldn't call up the New England Athenaeum and get a ticket to its fund-raising dinner, just to see who showed up.

But meeting women was not a problem for him. Contrary to his uncle's belief, Win did not live the life of a monk. No, he had no trouble at all finding women to go out on the town with him, occasionally to share his bed. It was finding the *right* woman....

"Romantic nonsense," he muttered.

By HER FOURTH DAY in Boston, Hannah had settled into a pleasant routine of research. Preston Fowler himself had invited her to the New England Athenaeum's fund-raising dinner and she'd accepted, despite the rather steep price. But she was supposed to be a Harling and therefore have money. Besides, Fowler himself had begun to help her ferret out information on the Harlings;

she had told him she was researching one of her ancestors, Cotton Harling. No point in stirring up trouble by mentioning Priscilla Marsh or the truth about her own identity. She was enjoying the perks of being a Harling.

"Is this your first trip to Boston?" Fowler asked on a cool, rainy morning. He had brought a couple of books to the second-floor table he had reserved for her at a window overlooking the Public Garden.

"Yes," Hannah lied, not without regret. He was being helpful, after all.

"Are you a member of the New York Harlings?"

The New York Harlings? Fowler's eagerness was impossible to miss—the New York Harlings must be rich, she thought—but she had never heard of them. She would have to remember to ask Cousin Thackeray, who still didn't know she was running around Boston claiming to be a Harling. But he had been the one to tell her not to reveal she was a Marsh.

She shook her head. "The Ohio Harlings."

"I see," the New England Athenaeum's director said. He was dressed in a Brooks Brothers suit today, a white on white shirt, wing tip shoes. There was never a hair out of place.

Hannah had invested in a couple of Harling-like outfits in an hour of rushing around on Newbury Street. Now she was afraid to dig out her charge-card receipts to see how much she'd spent. Would the IRS accept them as a business deduction? Preston Fowler would never believe she was a Harling if she kept showing up in her collection of leggings, jeans and vintage T-shirts. Once or twice she might get away with it, but not every day.

As for any real Harlings…well, there was only one in Boston, and she wasn't worried about him. Jonathan Winthrop Harling would be old, knobby-kneed and nasal-voiced, with a wardrobe of worn tweeds and holey deck shoes that he would be too cheap to replace. He would have bony hands with a slight tremble, and he'd wear thick glasses with finger smudges on the lenses.

She had him all pictured.

Fowler told her about a painting at the Museum of Fine Arts that she must see, a portrait of Benjamin Harling, the eighteenth-century shipbuilder. Hannah promised to have a look.

Finally he left.

She resumed her scan of a late-nineteenth-century newspaper account of a fistfight between some Harling or other and Andrew Marsh, Cousin Thackeray's grandfather. It involved their divergent opinions about the Longfellow poem on Priscilla Marsh, the Harling insisting it clearly romanticized her, the Marsh insisting it did not. A big mess.

Half paying attention, Hannah suddenly sat up straight. "What's this?"

She went back and reread a blurred, yellowed paragraph toward the end of the article.

In a long-winded way, it said that the Marsh had challenged the Harling to open up "the Harling Collection" to public inspection.

The Harling Collection?

Hannah's researcher's heart jumped in excitement. Now this was news. Something worth checking out. She read further.

Apparently Anne Harling, deceased in 1892, had gathered the family papers from the past three centuries, since the Harlings' arrival in Boston in 1630, into a collection.

What Hannah wouldn't give to get her hands on it!

She carefully copied the information into her notebook and sat looking out at the rain-soaked tulips and budding trees of the Public Garden, wondering what her life had come to that locating a bunch of old documents excited her.

"MR. HARLING?"

Win looked up from his computer and sighed. His young secretary, fresh out of Katherine Gibbs, was clearly determined to shape him into her idea of a suitable executive. He wasn't sure just what his failings were. "You can call me Win, Paula," he said, not for the first time. "What's up?"

"It's the impostor again."

"Where?"

"The Museum of Fine Arts."

"Uncle Jonathan called?"

"While you were in a meeting," Paula confirmed, all business. Win wondered if it had been a good idea to tell her about the unknown Harling who was supposedly attending the New England Athenaeum's fund-raising dinner. She had been convinced right from the start that they were dealing with an impostor. "He said to ask you if you had signed up for the lecture series on seventeenth-century American painting that is being offered by the museum. A friend of his knows the instructor and—"

"Yes, I understand. Uncle Jonathan knows everyone." Win tilted back in his chair. "He doesn't think it's a practical joke?"

"No." From her look, neither did Paula. She was tawny-haired and twenty-two and very good at what she did. "It's a woman, Mr. Harling. Trust me."

"Why would a woman pose as a Harling?"

Paula made a face that said what she wanted to do was groan, but groaning didn't fit her code of conduct. "May I speak freely?"

"What is this, a pirate ship? Of course you may."

She took a step closer to his desk, a black modern thing his decorator had picked out. "Mr. Harling, if you don't mind my saying so, I've been with you almost a year now, and it seems to me you don't have much of a clue as to how people around here view your family."

"The Harlings, you mean," he said.

"That's right." She was very serious. "Lots of people, given the chance, would like to take advantage of your wealth and reputation, your position in the financial community. You have breeding—"

"Breeding? Paula, I'm not a horse."

She was too sincere to be embarrassed. "As I said, you don't have a clue."

"Okay, suppose you're right. Suppose someone is trying to

take advantage of me. First, why me and not my uncle? Second, why a woman?''

''In answer to your first question,'' she said, obviously disgusted by his ignorance, ''because you are thirty-three and single and your uncle is eighty. Ditto that for the answer to your second question.''

''Why can't there be a third Harling in Boston?''

''There isn't.''

Win glanced at his computer; his work was beckoning. ''So a supposed Harling signed up for a class at the MFA and plans to attend a fund-raising dinner. That doesn't make a conspiracy.''

''You wait,'' Paula said confidently, heading for the door. ''There'll be another.''

WIN ARRIVED a few minutes late for his weekly lunch with Jonathan Harling at his elderly uncle's private club on Beacon Street, just below the State House. It was a musty, snooty old place with cream-colored walls, Persian carpets, antique furnishings and an aging, largely male clientele. Win would bet he was the youngest one in the place by forty years. The food, however, was passable, if traditional New England fare, and he always enjoyed his uncle's company.

''Sorry I'm late,'' he said, approaching Uncle Jonathan's table overlooking a stately courtyard. ''It's been one of those days. No, don't get up.''

Jonathan Harling sank gratefully into his antique Windsor chair. Always a model of integrity and responsibility for his nephew, he was a tall, thin man with eyes as clear at eighty as they had been thirty years ago, when he had been an acclaimed professor of legal history at Harvard. Win knew it had almost killed his uncle when he'd opted for Princeton.

''Name me one day in the past six months that hasn't been 'one of those days,''' the old man grumbled.

Win decided to sidetrack. ''It's a busy time of the year. Is the chowder good today?''

Uncle Jonathan already had a bowl in front of him. ''It's never good.''

"Then why do you keep ordering it?"

"Tradition," he said in a tone that indicated he damned well knew his nephew had no patience with such things.

Win deftly changed the subject. "Any news on our Harling friend?"

"The impostor, you mean. Nothing yet. He's taking his time, making sure he doesn't make a mistake."

"My secretary is convinced it's a she."

Uncle Jonathan mulled that one over. "Good point. I've alerted a number of my friends to keep on the lookout. We don't want him—or her—to start charging fur coats and fast cars to our name. *You* might be able to afford such things, but I can't."

Win let that comment pass. "Have you talked to Preston Fowler at the Athenaeum?"

"Not yet. I just heard about the Museum of Fine Arts incident today. I don't want to start ruffling feathers and end up looking like a fool if it's all just a coincidence."

"But you don't think it is," Win said.

Uncle Jonathan shook his head, serious. "No, I don't."

The waiter came, and Win ordered the roast turkey, his uncle the scrod. Out of the corner of his eye, Win spotted the maître d' leading a lone diner to the table directly behind him.

It was all he could do to remember to tell the waiter to bring coffee.

The lone diner was young and female, so that automatically made her stand out. But in addition she had hair that was long and straight and as pale and fine as corn silk, hair that would make her stand out anywhere. She was slender and not very tall, and she wore a crisp gray suit.

Uncle Jonathan had also noticed her. "Where did she come from?"

"I don't know," Win replied. "I've never seen her before."

"I don't think she's a member. Must be related to a member, though. I wonder who?"

Win shrugged and eased off the subject, having seen the sparkle in his uncle's eye. There was nothing he'd like better than to have his nephew attracted to a woman whose family belonged to the same prestigious private club the Harlings had been members of for all the one hundred fifty years of its existence. Lunch arrived, and Win brought up the Red Sox.

It didn't work.

"Look," Uncle Jonathan said, "she ordered the lobster salad."

The lobster salad was the most expensive item on the limited menu. Win couldn't resist turning in his seat. Her back was to him, maybe three feet away, but he could see her breaking open a steaming popover. Her fingers were long, feminine but not delicate, the nails short and neatly buffed. There was something strangely familiar about her, yet he knew he had never seen her before. He would have remembered.

Their meals arrived, and he turned back to his uncle. "The Red Sox," he said stubbornly, "had a terrible road trip. They're at home this weekend with the Yankees. Are you planning to go?"

"She must not eat lobster very often. She wouldn't stay that thin."

Win sighed. "Of course, the impostor could try to take over our box seats...."

That brought Uncle Jonathan around. "No, I doubt it. He's only left tracks at the Athenaeum and the Museum of Fine Arts. Probably not a baseball fan."

"I don't know, it's possible. I suppose there's not much we can do at this point, except remain on alert. As you say, it's too soon to act." Win tried his turkey; it wasn't very good. "But if there *is* an impostor running around Boston, capitalizing on our name...well, I'd like to get my hands on him. Or her."

Uncle Jonathan concurred.

By the time the waiter cleared their plates and brought fresh coffee, their conversation was back to the blonde. "Why don't you turn around and introduce yourself? It's not as if you're shy. Invite her over for coffee. Let's find out who she is."

"Uncle Jonathan..."

But he pushed his chair back and grabbed his cane, half getting up. "Miss, excuse me. Our saltshaker's stopped up, and I hate to bother the waiter. Mind if we borrow yours?"

There was nothing Win could do but indulge the old goat. He turned around, and the blonde was there facing him, her eyes huge and green and luminous. She looked a little startled. Who wouldn't? Win took in the high cheekbones and straight nose, the strong chin. Combined, her features made an angular, curiously elegant face. Her skin was pale and clear. Her arresting eyes and hair, however, dominated.

She looked intelligent enough to notice that their table had been cleared. Their waiter was approaching with the coffeepot and Uncle Jonathan's ritual dish of warm Indian pudding, which always looked to Win as if it had come from a cat box.

"Of course," the woman said, and handed over her saltshaker. Win took it.

She turned away.

So much for that.

Win shoved the saltshaker at his uncle. "You're incorrigible."

"Don't you think she looks familiar?"

"Yes," Win said, interested, "I do."

"I can't figure out why. Anyway, she's pretty. Invite her to dinner."

"Uncle..."

"You might never see her again. What if she's the one? You'll have missed your chance."

"If she's 'the one,'" Win said, speaking in a much lower voice than his uncle, who apparently didn't give a damn who heard him, "then there'll be another chance. I believe in fate taking a hand in matters of the heart."

Jonathan snorted. "Romantic nonsense." He waved his spoon. "There, she's leaving. Catch her."

"She's not a trout."

"If she were a tempting stock option you'd never let her get away. Can't you get excited about something that doesn't involve dollar signs?"

Win could. He most definitely could. He was right now. Watching the blonde's hair bounce as she left, the movement of her shapely legs, was not something that lacked consequences. Physical consequences, even. But he didn't share his reaction with his uncle. Instead he said sanely, "I won't come on to a perfect stranger. That could be construed as harassment."

"Only after she tells you to chew dust and you persist. The first time it's just an invitation to dinner."

"On what grounds do I invite her to dinner?"

"Who needs grounds?"

Win groaned. "If she had wanted to meet someone, she wouldn't have come here. This club's known for its elderly membership."

"It's no secret you and I have lunch here on Wednesdays, you know," Uncle Jonathan said thoughtfully. "Maybe she wanted to meet you. That ever occur to you?"

"If she'd wanted to meet me, don't you think she would have said something when you bellowed at her about the salt?"

His uncle was undeterred. "Maybe she would have if you'd said something first."

Win gave up. His uncle was the one indulging in romantic nonsense. The woman had given no indication she was interested in, had recognized or indeed cared if she ever saw either Harling again.

But those eyes. They were unforgettable. And her hair.

What was it about her that was so damned familiar?

Their waiter slipped Win the bill, which he would quietly sign and have put on his account. It was an arrangement they had, in order to keep his uncle from insisting on paying his half, which was just for show. Win knew Uncle Jonathan wouldn't part with a dime if he could get someone else to pay first.

Financially secure though he was, Win found the tab a bit staggering. "Wait just a minute! You've put an extra meal on my bill."

"Well, yes, your...Ms. Harling indicated..."

Win jumped to his feet. "*Who?*"

"The woman." The waiter nodded to the table just vacated by the silken-haired blonde. "If there's been a mistake..."

Uncle Jonathan was reaching for his cane. He was an intelligent man. He plainly knew what was going on. "She's our impostor!"

"Yes," Win said through gritted teeth. He looked at his uncle. "You all right?"

Uncle Jonathan waved him on with his cane. "Go, go. Track down the larcenous little wench."

Win didn't bother arguing with his uncle's choice of words, but simply signed the bill for the entire amount and went.

2

HANNAH WAS BREATHING hard and hoping she was sane again by the time she reached the modern building in the heart of Boston's financial district. Her name was Marsh, she repeated under her breath. Hannah Marsh, Hannah Marsh, Hannah Marsh. She *wasn't* a Harling.

This little visit would straighten everything out. She would go up to Jonathan Winthrop Harling's office, introduce herself, confess if she had to and explain if she could. She had put herself down for the New England Athenaeum's fund-raising dinner to keep Preston Fowler happy, had signed up for the lecture series at the Museum of Fine Arts on the spur of the moment, and realized only after she'd committed herself that she'd better be consistent and go as a Harling.

She didn't know how she'd explain lunch.

The Beacon Street club was one of Jonathan Winthrop Harling's hangouts, and she'd gone there hoping to meet him. Hoping to explain. Hoping to ask him about the Harling Collection. But she didn't even know if he'd been there because she'd frozen up, plain and simple.

That black-eyed rogue behind her had done it. Something about his looks had rattled her. Two hundred years ago he would have run guns for George Washington. Three hundred years ago Cotton Harling would have had him hanged. He had looked, she thought, decidedly unpuritanical. How could she think, much less confess, with him around?

So she hadn't. And then the waiter had asked if she wanted to put her lunch on the Harling account—she'd had to pretend to be one, of course, to get into the place—and not wanting to blow her cover, she'd said yes.

Now she was a criminal. If the Harlings were all as miserable as Cousin Thackeray had said they were, she could be in big trouble with Jonathan Winthrop.

Then she'd never get a look at the Harling Collection.

The time had come, she told herself as she went through the revolving doors, to come clean, plead for mercy and hope that an eighty-year-old man, even if a Harling, would understand that she was a legitimate, professional biographer. She would make him understand.

She glanced around the elegant wood and marble lobby, then bit her lip when she spotted the armed guards. There were four of them. One behind a half-moon-shaped desk, two mingling with the well-dressed businesspeople flowing in and out of the elevators and revolving doors, another on the mezzanine. He had a machine gun.

An easygoing place, Jonathan Winthrop Harling's office. Hannah had expected a nice old brownstone on Beacon Hill. But probably the old buzzard liked being surrounded by men with guns.

She approached the guard behind the half-moon desk. He was a big, red-faced man, tremendously fit-looking, with curly auburn hair and a disarming spray of freckles across his nose. He didn't look as if he would shoot a woman for pretending to be a Harling, but this was Boston and Hannah just didn't know.

He listened without expression while she explained that she had an appointment with Jonathan Winthrop Harling, but had forgotten which floor he was on.

"Your name?" he asked.

She gulped.

"Ma'am?"

"Hannah," she said. "Jonathan's expecting me."

His eyes narrowed. "Who?"

She'd made a mistake. "Jonathan Winthrop Harling. I'm— I'm Hannah Harling. From Cincinnati. The Midwest Harlings. We..."

She hated lying to men with guns.

The guard picked up the phone. "I'll call Mr. Harling."

"No!"

The old buzzard would swallow his teeth if the guard said one of the Midwest Harlings was here to see him. There were no Midwest Harlings.

"I just need his floor number," Hannah added quickly. "Really."

"And I need to call," the guard said coolly. "Really."

Good, Hannah. Get yourself shot.

She backed away from the desk. "Never mind," she told the guard, manufacturing a smile. "I'll come by another time. Don't bother telling Mr. Harling I was here. I—I'll call him later."

No one followed her through the revolving doors. Her heart was pounding when she reached the plaza in front of the building, but when she looked over her shoulder she didn't see any armed men coming after her.

But she didn't relax.

She wondered what had become of play-by-the-rules Hannah Priscilla Marsh. Cousin Thackeray had warned her about Boston. Maybe she should have listened.

Not wanting to look totally guilty, in case the guard was watching, she lingered at the fountain. It was a warm, beautiful day. Yellow tulips waved in the breeze and twinkled in the sunlight all along the fountain, which sprayed thin arcs of water every few seconds. The effect was calming, mesmerizing.

But she still had half an eye on the revolving doors. A flurry of activity, some shoving, people moving out of the way caught her eye. She turned.

And there he was.

"Oh, no!"

She was off like a shot, adrenaline surging. She didn't know who he was or what he thought she'd done, but she knew instinctively that he was after her, that she couldn't let him catch up with her.

It was her black-eyed rogue from lunch.

He looked fit to be tied. Determined. Dangerous.

Did he work with Jonathan Harling? Were they friends? Did he know she was running around town pretending she was a Harling?

There was no time to think.

She moved fast, pushing her way through a crowd and around the block, vaguely aware that Jonathan Winthrop Harling's building occupied the corner. She came to a side entrance.

She had no choice. None whatsoever. Looking back, she saw her pursuer pounding around the corner, straight for her. She had no idea if he had spotted her, was only aware that this wasn't her city and she didn't know where to hide, didn't want to meet him in a dark, unpopulated alley.

So back into the building she went.

WIN SPOTTED HER going through the revolving doors at the side entrance and moved fast to intercept her.

But when he got back to the lobby, she was gone.

He searched the place with his eyes. The red-haired guard came up to him. "Lose her?"

"She's in here," Win said.

"One of my men must have seen her."

"It's okay." This was his place of business, his space. He couldn't have a green-eyed blonde creating chaos here. "I'll find her myself."

"She doesn't know what floor you're on," the guard informed him. "I wouldn't tell her."

"Thanks."

Where could she have gone? The guard would have seen her if she'd tried to circle back to the front entrance. Win would have seen her if she'd doubled back through the side entrance. The only other options were the ladies' room and the elevators. Surely a guard would have questioned her if she'd tried to get onto an elevator. His was a financial building with moderately tight security.

Hannah Harling of the Midwest Harlings.

The blonde from lunch.

The larcenous little wench, Uncle Jonathan had called her. Win could think of other names.

He posted himself outside the ladies' room just off the lobby and waited.

HANNAH FINISHED booking a trip for two to Vancouver. Her plans, she told the agent, were tentative. The small travel agency off the main lobby was as good a hiding place as any and better than most.

She hated lying, but felt she had little choice.

"When I have everything finalized," the agent, a pleasant woman in her mid-fifties, said, "I should send it up to Jonathan Winthrop Harling. Is that correct?"

"Yes."

"And you're Hannah Harling," she went on.

Hannah didn't respond. She was going to get herself arrested if she wasn't more careful, but avoiding the truth about her real name was certainly preferable to facing the black-eyed man who was after her. He didn't look as if he would listen to any excuses she might have. Had he heard her say she was a Harling at the Beacon Street club? Was he protecting Jonathan Harling?

What if the old man with him at lunch had been Jonathan Harling?

She wished she had never listened to Cousin Thackeray. She wouldn't have been predisposed to say she was a Harling if he hadn't insisted so adamantly that a Marsh was doomed in Boston, "Harling country." But she knew her elderly cousin wasn't responsible. She was responsible for her own actions.

"I hadn't," the agent resumed, "realized Mr. Harling was married."

Married?

To some eighty-year-old man?

Hannah smiled and left without correcting the woman on any of her misconceptions. Surely she would be able to explain Vancouver for two to Jonathan Winthrop Harling. *Yeah, right.*

Given what you've demonstrated of your character so far, he'll just be delighted to give you access to his family's papers.

She'd dug one very deep crater for herself.

But what was done was done, and she couldn't hang around in the travel agency forever. Venturing carefully into the corridor, Hannah peered toward the main part of the lobby, where the security guard was posted behind his half-moon desk. She was out of view of the man on the mezzanine with the machine gun. *Thank heaven for small favors.* The other two she couldn't see. They didn't worry her nearly as much as her dark-eyed stranger.

Spotting him, she inhaled sharply.

He was posted at the women's bathroom at the far end of the corridor, not fifty feet from her.

Lordy, she thought, but he was a handsome devil.

Did he think she was hiding in the bathroom? Was he waiting for her? Maybe she was just being paranoid. Either that or she'd outwitted him, she thought, with a welcome surge of victory.

You're not out of here yet, she reminded herself.

She saw him glance at his watch and march toward the bank of elevators, his back to her. She held her breath at the sight of his clipped, angry walk. He did have broad shoulders. And his suit was so well cut it moved with him, made him seem very masculine indeed.... A modern pirate.

Telling herself she was playing it safe, not behaving like a coward, she ducked back into the travel agency to give the elevators time to whisk him back where he belonged.

The travel agent said happily, "I just faxed the information to Mr. Harling's office."

Oh, good, Hannah thought.

She decided to cut her losses for the day and darted out the side entrance before anyone so much as saw her, never mind pinned her to the nearest wall and called the police.

"I WARNED YOU," Paula said, handing Win the fax from the travel agency off the main lobby.

"What is it?" he asked, still too angry to focus on anything other than his frustration at having lost the blonde.

"Reservations for two to Vancouver next month."

"What?"

"You're going to Vancouver for a week. The agency's working out the details of your stay, but from what I can gather, it's going to be very luxurious."

"Paula, I'm not going to Vancouver."

"I know that." She jerked her head in the direction of the offending fax. "But tell Hannah Harling."

Win's eyes focused. He saw two names: Jonathan Winthrop and Hannah Harling. Then the little note from the travel agency downstairs, congratulating him.

On what? For what?

"She's not satisfied with being a long-lost cousin from Cincinnati," his secretary said scathingly. "She wants to be your wife."

THAT EVENING, Hannah opened up a can of soup for dinner, still too stuffed from lunch and too frazzled by her day to want a big meal.

She ate standing up, pacing from one end to the other of her borrowed, Beacon Hill apartment. It wasn't very far. At eye level, three shuttered windows looked onto the brick sidewalk and offered an uninspiring view, nothing like her view of the bay off Marsh Point. The friend who'd lent her the apartment kept a powerful squirt gun on the kitchen windowsill. Hannah had discovered the hard way that it was meant as a handy deterrent to particularly bold dogs, who occasionally did their business without benefit of leash, manners or master.

But the apartment was a quiet, functional place to work, and that, she reminded herself, was her purpose in Boston. Work. Nothing more. She had nothing to hide. She had no bone to pick with the Harlings.

Now she realized she'd blundered badly; she'd let Cousin Thackeray's hyperbole and paranoia get to her. She should never have posed as a Harling.

There was nothing to do but make amends. She had to confess.

First, however, she would lay everything out for her elderly cousin and see what he had to offer by way of advice. Her soup finished, she started for the wall phone in the kitchen.

And stopped, not breathing.

She was sure she recognized the charcoal-covered legs. The deliberate walk. The polished shoes. They were on her sidewalk, directly in front of her middle window.

She moved silently across the linoleum floor and leaned over the sink, balancing herself with one hand on the faucet. She peered up as best she could, trying to get a better look at the passerby as he moved toward the kitchen window.

It was him!

Her hand slipped off the faucet and landed in the sink, wrenching her elbow. Her soup pan, soaking in cold water, went flying. The thud of stainless steel on linoleum was loud enough to be heard at Boston Garden. There was water everywhere.

Hannah swore.

She heard the fancy shoes crunch to a stop on the brick sidewalk. Saw the handsome suit blocking her window. All he had to do was bend down and he'd see her.

She didn't breathe, didn't swear, didn't yell in pain. Didn't make a single, solitary sound.

He moved on.

I'm haunted, she thought, getting ice out of the freezer for her elbow. She threw towels on top of the spilled water and dumped the soup pan back into the sink. How many people in metropolitan Boston? Two million? What were the odds against seeing the same man at lunch, in the financial district, and now, on Beacon Hill at dinnertime?

Hannah waited an hour before going out. She tied a scarf around her head, tucking in every blond hair in case her black-eyed rogue was still out and about and might recognize her. She had to risk it. She needed to walk, to think. She couldn't even concentrate enough to call Cousin Thackeray. What on earth would she tell him? How could she explain her peculiar day, even to him?

Beacon Hill was a neighborhood of subdued elegance, a lovely place to be at dusk, with its steep, narrow streets, brick sidewalks, black, wrought-iron lanterns and Federal Period town houses. Louisa May Alcott had lived here, the Cabots and the Lodges, Boston mayors and Massachusetts senators—and, of course, the Harlings.

Hannah barely noticed the cars crammed into every available parking space, the fashionably dressed pedestrians, but imagined instead the picturesque streets a hundred, two hundred years ago. She knew her ability to give life to the past was the central quality that, critics said, made her biographies not just scholarly, but intensely readable.

Less than a week in Boston, and already her reputation was in jeopardy.

When she came to Louisburg Square, Boston's most prestigious residential address, she turned onto its cobblestone circle. Elegant town houses faced a small private park enclosed within a high wrought-iron fence. Hannah made her way to the house the Harlings had built. It had a bow front and was black-shuttered, its front stoop ending right on the brick sidewalk. Any yard would be in back, one of Beacon Hill's famous hidden gardens.

According to her most recent information, now several years old, the house was owned by a real-estate developer. The Harlings had sold it during the Depression.

Hannah sighed and stared at the softly illuminated interior that was visible through the draped windows. Would the current owner let her have a look at the place? Would she have better luck as Hannah Marsh, biographer, or Hannah Harling of the Midwest Harlings?

She wasn't quite sure why she cared. After all, what did a house built more than a hundred years after Judge Cotton Harling had sentenced Priscilla Marsh to death have to do with her work?

The cream-colored, brass-trimmed front door opened, startling her. She jumped back.

Then felt her heart jump right out of her chest.

Her black-eyed rogue bounded out, wearing nylon running shorts and a black-and-gold Boston Bruins T-shirt.

Never mind getting to blazes out of there, as any sensible woman would have done, Hannah barely managed not to gape at the man's thighs. The muscles were hard and tight, and a thick, sexy scar was carved above the left knee. He looked tough, solid, masculine.

And he recognized her immediately, scarf or no scarf.

"Don't move," he said. "I wouldn't want to have to chase you."

Given that she'd only slipped on a pair of flats and he was wearing expensive running shoes, she doubted she'd get far. And his legs were longer.

She was at a profound disadvantage.

His eyes bored into her. They were black, piercing, intelligent, alive, the kind of eyes that sparked the imagination of a woman more used to examining the lives of dead people. "I won't have you arrested—"

"Good of you," Hannah retorted, just lightly sarcastic.

He was unamused. "You will stop posing as a Harling."

She blinked. "Posing?"

Still no sign of amusement. Whoever he was, he took her little ruse this past week seriously—too seriously for her taste. "Posing," he repeated.

His lean runner's body was taut, and he seemed very sure of himself.

Hannah couldn't let him get the better of her.

"I don't know what you're thinking," she began, doing her best to sound indignant, "but I am a Harling. I'm from Cincinnati. I'm in Boston on a genealogical expedition and—"

He leaned toward her. "Give it up."

"Give what up?"

"You're not a Harling, and if I were you, I'd cut my losses while I still could."

His words grated. "And just who are you to be telling me to do anything?"

He raised his head slightly, looking at her through half-closed eyes.

Something made her swallow and think, for a change.

"You're not..." she mumbled, half to herself, "you can't be..."

"I'm surprised," he said cockily, "you don't recognize your own husband."

For the first time in her life, Hannah was speechless. A hot river of awareness flowed down her back, burned into every fiber of her.

The black eyes had thrown her off. Cousin Thackeray had said the Harlings were all blue-eyed devils.

But this black-eyed devil said, "Name's Harling."

She swallowed hard, preparing herself for the rest of it.

"J. Winthrop Harling."

He wasn't eighty. He wasn't knobby-kneed. He didn't wear smudged glasses. And he sure as blazes wasn't harmless.

What had she done?

You'll be in Harling country, Cousin Thackeray had warned her. *Just never forget you're a Marsh.*

She pulled off her scarf, letting her hair fall over her shoulders, feeling a small rush of pleasure at the sight of J. Winthrop Harling's widening eyes. But the pleasure didn't last when she realized what she saw in them. Lust. It was the only word for it.

Right now, at that moment, he wanted her.

Cousin Thackeray would croak.

She tossed back her head. "You Harlings will never change. You're the same arrogant bastards you were three hundred years ago. I'm surprised you haven't threatened to have me hanged."

He frowned. "Hanged?"

"It's the Harling way," she quipped, and about-faced. She headed for her street, daring J. Winthrop Harling to follow her.

Win let her go.

He jogged down to the Charles River and did his three-mile run along the esplanade, his mind preoccupied with the fair-haired, green-eyed impostor. She had as much as admitted that she was no Harling.

Then who was she? A conwoman? A nut? Had one of his friends put her up to this charade as part of some elaborate practical joke?

What was that nonsense about hanging?

Her eyes had seemed even more luminous in the soft lamp-light, their irises as green and lively as the spring grass. Half of her had seemed humiliated by having met a real Harling, but the other half had seemed challenged, even angry. She hadn't, he would guess, chosen the Harling name out of admiration.

So what was her game?

Sweating and aching, Win returned to the drafty house he had bought a year ago. It needed work. He could hire the job out, but he wanted to do it himself, with his own hands.

He grimaced, turning on the shower, trying to erase from his mind the image of his hands, not smoothing a piece of wall-board, but the impostor's soft, pale skin...touching her lips... stroking her throat....

He turned the faucet to cold and climbed in, welcoming the shock of the icy water on his overheated skin. But the heat of his arousal was not easily quenched, and the image remained. Fund-raising dinners, art lectures, his uncle's club, Vancouver, even his own street. The woman had invaded every corner of his life. And now his mind, as well. His body was responding to the simple thought of her tongue intertwined with his.

"She must be a witch," he muttered.

Then he had it.

He no longer felt the cold of the shower. He shut off the

water and reached for a towel. He barely noticed the continued swollen state of his arousal.

A witch.

Of course.

The pale, silken hair...the green eyes...the anger...the accusation about threatening to have her hanged...

His impostor was a Marsh.

3

HANNAH WAITED until morning, when she'd fully collected her wits, before calling Cousin Thackeray in Maine. "Jonathan Winthrop Harling," she announced to him, "is not the only Harling in Boston."

Her elderly cousin didn't comment right away, and Hannah used the moment of silence to quickly close the shutters, an easy process, since she was on a cordless phone. There was no point in inviting trouble, in case her black-eyed Harling decided to search Beacon Hill for her. She didn't trust him to be above looking into people's windows to find a woman posing as a Harling.

"Well," Cousin Thackeray said carefully, "I could be a bit out of touch. I haven't been to Boston myself in...oh, it must be fifty or sixty years."

Hannah gritted her teeth. "Then for all you know Boston could be crawling with Harlings."

"No, no, I doubt that."

"Thackeray," she blurted, "I'm in big trouble."

She told him everything, start to finish. He listened without interruption, except for an occasional gasp or sigh. It wasn't a pretty story.

When she finished, he said, "You've been posing as a *Harling?* Oh, Hannah."

"What's done is done, Thackeray. And now I need to talk to the elder Harling—this Jonathan Winthrop. I still want to examine the Harling Collection."

"Hannah, I want you to listen to me." Her cousin sounded very serious. "The Harling Collection doesn't exist. It never existed. The Harlings made it up to drive folks like you crazy."

"But I have reason to believe—"

"Trust me on this one, Hannah. It doesn't exist."

"If it does, Thackeray, it could well contain information that could provide insight into Cotton Harling's thinking when he signed the order for Priscilla's execution."

Her cousin was apparently unmoved. "It doesn't exist. Give up your search for it at once. Come home, Hannah. If the Harlings find out a Marsh is in town..."

"I'm not finished with my research here," she countered stubbornly.

Cousin Thackeray sighed, clearly not pleased. "You have a plan, I presume?"

"No, not really. I just want to find this old Harling—Jonathan Winthrop—and try to explain everything to him."

"He won't understand."

"Just because he's a Harling?"

"And because you're a Marsh," Thackeray Marsh added.

"Well, I'll have to take my chances with him. I suppose I could have explained to this younger Harling last night...." She inhaled, remembering the black eyes fixed on her, the arrogance. "But it didn't seem the time or place."

Her cousin grunted. "What, was a good hanging tree nearby?"

Hannah made a face. "That's not very funny."

"It wasn't a joke." He sighed. "You'll do what you'll do. You always do. If you need help, give me a holler. You know where I am."

"Thanks." But she could feel her heart thumping, and knew she should heed his advice. "I know I can always count on you."

He muttered something under his breath and hung up. Hannah gathered her materials and stuffed them into her canvas bag, promising herself an ordinary day of research at the New England Athenaeum. No hunting down Harlings today...unless, of course, she got a really good lead on old Jonathan Winthrop, one that would allow her to bypass the black-eyed Harling. She suspected that he was most likely devising his own plan to track *her* down.

AS HE ENTERED the Tiffany reading room of the New England Athenaeum, Win noticed the dour portrait of an ancestor above the mantel. He had to admit there was a family resemblance. Although not a member of the venerable institution, he doubted he would be turned out on his ear.

He introduced himself to the middle-aged woman behind the huge oak front desk. She showed Win back to Preston Fowler's office immediately.

"Mr. Harling," Fowler said, rising quickly from a chair old enough to once have belonged to Ben Franklin, "what a pleasant surprise. What can I do for you?"

"Win, please." He turned on the charm. It was midmorning, and he had already shocked his secretary by phoning in to say that he'd be late and she should reschedule his morning appointments. "I believe one of my relatives is in town."

"Well, yes, of course. I assumed you knew. I understand she's your cousin...."

"We're not close." His wife in one place, his cousin in another. She should keep her story consistent, Win thought.

"So I've begun to gather. She's been trying to locate your uncle. I haven't given out his private address, of course, but I did tell her she might find him at his club. I hope there's no problem."

"Not at all."

So she was after Uncle Jonathan. No wonder she'd been so shocked when she'd run into him yesterday instead. They were both called Jonathan Winthrop Harling, something Win would guess she hadn't realized.

"She's from Ohio—Cincinnati, I believe."

Like hell. "I see. And she's attending Saturday's fund-raising dinner?"

"Yes, she is. She's not officially a member of the library and wants to repay us for permitting her to use our facilities for her research."

"Her research?"

"She's a historian. I'm not sure precisely what her project is, but she's very interested in the Harling family."

No doubt, Win thought. The more she knew about the Harlings, the better chance she'd have of continuing her ruse of posing as one of them. "Do you have any idea what she wants with my uncle?"

"Just to meet him, I should imagine."

"And she hasn't mentioned me," Win said.

Fowler shook his head. He obviously didn't want any trouble with the Harlings. Win didn't judge the man. He had a tough job, trying to maintain an aging building and a priceless collection on what he could beg from a bunch of tightfisted Boston Brahmins. Uncle Jonathan's idea of a generous donation wouldn't keep the rare book room climate-controlled for a day.

"I'm not sure she's aware you're in Boston," the library director said carefully.

Undoubtedly not. Win spun an old globe, from the days of the British Empire. "Is it too late to purchase a ticket for the fund-raising dinner? I'd like to attend."

Fowler obviously struggled to contain his excitement: it was no secret Win had a hell of a lot more money than his uncle did.

"We would love to have you—I'll attend to the details myself. Oh, and if you would like to meet your cousin, she might be in the stacks. I'm sure I saw her earlier this morning."

Win felt his adrenalin surge, but said nonchalantly, "Really? If you don't mind, I'd like to see her."

"I can send someone after her...."

"No, that's all right. I'll go myself."

HANNAH WAS FLIPPING through a book of fasting sermons from the seventeenth century when she heard footsteps below her. The old-fashioned stacks had been formed by dividing the space between the tall ceilings in two, then making a floor in between of translucent glass and adding curving, wrought iron stairs and bookshelves. It was easy to detect another person wandering about. Only, she thought, this person sounded very purposeful...even sneaky.

She closed her book and set it back upon the shelf. She was sitting cross-legged on the thick glass floor, at the far end of a row of shelves. Below her, through the translucent glass, she could see the shadow of a tall figure. It wasn't one of the library staff. She was sure of that.

Listening carefully, not moving, Hannah heard the figure walk steadily up and down the stacks below her. The footsteps never paused, never varied their pace. It was as if whoever was down there was looking, not for a book, but for a person.

Me.

The figure reached the end of the row below her, then she heard the sound of footsteps on metal as it started to climb to her level.

Instinct brought Hannah to her feet. Launched her heart into a fit of rapid beating. Tightened her throat.

The footsteps came closer.

She slipped down to the end of her row and moved soundlessly past the next one, and the next, until she was at the far end, near the stairs.

The figure climbed the last stair and stepped onto her level. It was her black-eyed rogue of a Harling.

Oh, no....

Hannah slipped back behind the shelves and waited, not breathing, while he moved all the way to the end of the stacks. She knew he would then methodically walk up and down each row until he found her.

Then what?

Sweat breaking out on her brow, she heard him start on the far row. She ducked up her row so that he wouldn't spot her when he reached the end of his. She could try to keep this up, but he'd eventually catch up. Why not just pop out and hope she scared him to death? Why not just explain herself? Apologize?

Yeah, and you can get on your knees and beg a Harling for forgiveness while you're at it.

Priscilla Marsh hadn't begged. She'd gone to her death with her pride and dignity intact.

Hannah decided to take what little pride and dignity she had left and get the blazes out of here. He'd hear her on the stairs— no question about it. But she'd have a head start, she knew her way around the library, and if she was lucky…

Since when can a Marsh count on luck around a Harling?

She had to count on her wits…and maybe on a little gall.

Speed being more critical than silence, she darted down the row and hit the stairs at a full gallop, taking them two and three at a time.

Above her, she heard her pursuer curse.

She swung down to the next level and scooted through the stacks, zigzagging her way to the small corridor in the far right corner. Preston Fowler had loaned her the key to the rare book room. She came to the heavy door that marked its entrance, stuck in the key, and, relying on stealth, quietly pulled the door open and slipped inside.

Without turning on the light, she pressed her ear against the door and waited.

WIN FIGURED she'd locked herself in the rare book room. He also figured his uncle would never forgive him if he made a scene in the venerable New England Athenaeum by hauling a pretty, blond-haired Marsh out by her ear. Preston Fowler would have questions that Win couldn't answer and Hannah Marsh, if that was her name, no doubt wouldn't answer.

So he rapped on the door and said, "I know you're in there."

Naturally she didn't answer.

"You haven't stopped pretending you're a Harling," he went on. "Until you do, I have no intention of leaving you alone."

He waited, just in case she had something to say.

Apparently she didn't.

"By the way, I would say you have my uncle and me confused. We're both named Jonathan Winthrop Harling."

He heard a muffled thud. Had Ms. Hannah pounded her head against the door? He would guess he knew more about her and her devious plans than she expected him to know. Certainly more than she wanted him to know.

"You'd better leave my uncle out of this," he said in his deadliest voice. "I won't warn you again on that score."

Her voice came to him through the door, sounding very clear and surprisingly close: "What're you doing? Tying the noose even now?"

The woman was incorrigible.

In no mood to make her life any easier, Win tiptoed away, so she wouldn't know he had gone.

HANNAH SWEATED IT OUT in the rare book room for another hour.

There were two Jonathan Winthrop Harlings in Boston. All her leads had pointed her in the direction of the wrong one, and as far as she could tell, she was doomed.

Doomed.

But when she went back down to the main reading room, no one treated her like an impostor. Preston Fowler and his staff apparently continued to believe she was a Harling, which was a relief, if a small one. It meant, she knew, that the younger Jonathan Winthrop Harling planned to deal with her himself, in his own good time.

Hannah had no intention of waiting like the proverbial lamb for the slaughter.

On her way out, Preston Fowler said, "We'll see you tomorrow night at the dinner, Ms. Harling."

She smiled. "I'm looking forward to it."

She realized she would need a dress. Her Harling clothes were all for day, and her Hannah Marsh clothes—*my clothes,* she reminded herself—were too casual. So she headed off to Newbury Street, just a few blocks down from the New England Athenaeum. It was one of Boston's most chic and high-priced shopping districts. There wouldn't be much she could afford.

Her black-eyed Jonathan Winthrop Harling, however, could probably buy out the whole street and have plenty left over.

WIN HAD A HELL OF A TIME trying to concentrate that afternoon, and it was almost with relief that he greeted a grim-faced Paula bringing him news of another bit of larceny performed by Hannah of the Midwest Harlings.

"Is she my cousin today," he asked, "or my wife?"

His secretary didn't seem to appreciate his wry humor. "Your wife. The owner of the shop on Newbury Street where you buy your ties just called. A woman fitting the description of the impostor was in earlier and bought a black evening dress on your tab. He faxed me the bill." Paula handed it over. "You will note that she signed her name as Mrs. Hannah Harling."

"Arnie didn't believe her?"

"Oh, no, he believed her. He just called to congratulate you on your wedding. I think he's hurt he wasn't invited."

Win looked at the bill and inhaled, controlling an urge to pound his desk or throw things. The price of the dress was staggering. It was, he knew, Hannah Marsh's way of thumbing her nose at him.

"I was the one who had him fax the bill," Paula said.

"Did you give him a reason?"

She shook her tawny curls. "He should have asked for identification or at least called you before he let her have the dress. She must be awfully convincing."

For sure. Arnie was no pushover. Still, he wasn't alone in not wanting to annoy a Harling. "Call Arnie back," Win instructed her. "Tell him Hannah jumped the gun and we're not married yet."

Paula's eyes widened. "Yet?"

"The point is, I will pay for the dress. This impostor isn't Arnie's problem. She's mine."

THE DRESS WAS AWFUL, and Hannah decided she couldn't wear it. It was too…Boston. Too matronly. Too something. She stood in front of the full-length mirror in her borrowed bedroom an hour before the New England Athenaeum dinner and tried to figure out what wasn't right about a dress that had cost as much as this one.

She had bought it in a fit of pique, when she'd only wanted to strike out at Jonathan Winthrop Harling. Now the Harlings really had grounds for throwing her in jail. But better to hang for a thousand-dollar dress, she'd decided, than a twenty-dollar lunch.

Was she crazy?

Not only was the dress not her style, it also wasn't, in fact, hers. Never mind that it was in her possession. Harling money had—or would—pay for it. She hadn't even removed the tags.

And wouldn't. She would take the thing back on Monday. Twenty-four hours of sitting alone in her borrowed apartment, doing her work, being the studious, law-abiding biographer she was, had enabled her to think. Not even a Harling would turn her into an out-and-out thief.

A smarter decision would have been not to go tonight. The prospect, however remote, of bumping into her black-eyed Harling on his own territory didn't thrill her. But how could she just drop everything and head back to Maine? It just wasn't in her to run.

She rummaged around in her closet and found the dress she'd picked up at a vintage clothing store in Harvard Square. It was not a Harling dress, and it hadn't cost a thousand dollars. It hadn't even cost twenty.

But it was her.

"YOU'RE SURE she's a Marsh?" Uncle Jonathan asked when Win picked him up. Naturally his uncle had insisted on going to the Athenaeum's fund-raising dinner, once he knew their impostor was potentially a Marsh and would be there.

Win nodded grimly. "I'm positive."

"I should have guessed it myself. The blond hair's a dead giveaway."

"You can hardly suspect every blonde you see of being a Marsh without further evidence."

"You'd better watch yourself, Winthrop." Uncle Jonathan climbed into the front passenger seat. "If she's a Marsh, she's after something. Any idea what?"

"None."

"The Marshes have never let us forget Priscilla. They refuse to understand that Cotton was a man of his times, a flawed human being just doing his job.''

Win frowned at his uncle. ''He had an innocent woman hanged.''

''He wasn't the first, nor the last.''

There was no point in arguing. Win pulled into traffic, trying to concentrate on the road and not on what was coming up this evening.

''Think she'll risk showing up tonight?'' his uncle asked.

Win had already considered the question, given what had transpired yesterday morning, but it had only one answer. ''She wouldn't miss it.''

HANNAH ARRIVED EARLY at the exclusive seafood restaurant on the waterfront where the New England Athenaeum's fund-raising dinner was being held. Preston Fowler greeted her warmly. Before he could introduce her to anyone as a Harling, she slipped off to the bar, ordered a glass of white wine and found her table. Mercifully, it was at the far end of the room, but still had a good view of the entrance.

She sipped her wine, watching Boston's upper crust filing in, dressed in its spring finery. She saw a dress much like the one she had rejected. It looked curiously right on its owner, just as it had looked wrong on her.

What a long night she had ahead of her, she thought, if all she had to do was notice what people were wearing....

An old man with a cane shook hands with Preston Fowler. Hannah shifted in her chair, her interest piqued. She had seen him somewhere before.

Salt, she thought, for no apparent reason.

Lunch at the private club on Beacon Street.

Her heartbeat quickened, her fingers stiffened on her wineglass, and she said to herself, ''The old man with—''

But she didn't finish.

Across the room, the younger Jonathan Winthrop Harling's black eyes nailed her to her seat.

''Oh, no,'' Hannah whispered.

Her first impulse was to tear her eyes away and pretend she hadn't seen him, but she resisted just in time and met his gaze head-on. She even smiled. She made everything about her say he didn't intimidate her. She could take on him—a Harling— and win.

If ever a pair of eyes could burn holes in someone, it would be the two fixed on her. Hannah felt an unwelcome, unbidden, primitive heat boiling up inside her. There was something elemental at stake here, she thought, something that had nothing to do with Harlings or Marshes or three-hundred-year-old grudges.

She raised her wineglass in a mock greeting, then took a slow, deliberate sip.

He was past Preston Fowler in a flash, threading his way through the crowd, aiming straight for her. His steps were long and determined, as if he'd just caught someone picking his pocket.

Then he was upon her.

The man, Hannah thought, strangely calm, was breathtaking. His dark suit was understated, sophisticated, highlighting the blackness of his hair and eyes, making him look all the richer and more powerful. To be sure, he was a descendant of robber barons and rogues, but also of an infamous seventeenth-century judge who'd hanged one of her own ancestors.

"I like the daffodils," he said in a low, dark voice.

"Do you?" She fingered the two she'd tucked into her hair; it was an un-Brahminlike touch that went with her cream-colored, twenties tea dress. "I thought they were fun."

"They didn't go with your Newbury Street dress?"

So he knew already. She licked her lips. "Not really, no."

"You're a thief," he said simply, "and a conwoman."

She tilted her head to a deliberately cocky angle. "You know so much about me, do you?"

His eyes darkened, if that was possible. "I should, shouldn't I? We're supposed to be married."

Her mouth went dry. "I never said..."

"You didn't have to, did you? People assumed." He moved

closer, so that she could see the soft black leather of his belt. "I wonder why."

The old man with the cane stumbled up to them, saving Hannah from having to produce a credible response when she could still barely speak. "So you're our Cincinnati Harling," he said.

She managed a smile. "Word travels fast."

"This is my uncle," his nephew said, his tone daring her to persist. "Jonathan Harling."

She put out a hand to the old man. "I'm Hannah. It's a pleasure."

"Delighted to meet you. Welcome to Boston." He surprised her by placing a dry kiss upon her cheek, his eyes—Harling blue—gleaming with interest, missing nothing. He turned to his nephew. "You two have met?"

"Not formally," Hannah replied.

"No?" The old man clapped a hand on the younger Harling's shoulder. "This is my nephew, Win. J. Winthrop Harling."

So it was true. There *were* two Jonathan Winthrop Harlings in Boston. Oh, what a mistake she'd made.

"It's a pleasure," she said, refusing to let the situation get the better of her.

But Win Harling murmured, "The pleasure's mine," and bent forward, kissing her low on the cheek. To all appearances, no doubt, it was a perfunctory kiss, not unlike his uncle's. Hannah, however, felt the warm brush of his tongue on the corner of her mouth, his hard grip as he took her hand. And she felt her own response; it was impossible to ignore. Her mind and body united in a searing rebellion, imagining, feeling, that warm brushing, not discreetly, against the corner of her mouth, but openly, hotly, against her tongue, against other parts of her body.

"If Priscilla Marsh was anything like you, Hannah Marsh," Win Harling said in a rough, low voice, "I can see what drove Cotton Harling to sign her hanging order."

4

THE WOMAN WAS QUICK. Win would give her that much. She gave him a haughty look and threw back her shoulders regally, or as regally as anyone could manage in a silk tea dress from the twenties. The daffodils in her hair didn't help matters. But she said, "I don't know what you're talking about."

He laughed. He couldn't help himself.

She thrust her chin at him. He could still see the flush of pink, high on her cheeks, from his kiss. Obviously it had as powerful an effect on her as it had on him. "Why did you call me Hannah—who?"

He decided to indulge her. "Marsh."

"And Priscilla—it was Priscilla, wasn't it?"

"Yes."

"This Priscilla Marsh. Who is she?"

"Your great-great-great-great—oh, I don't know, I'd give it five greats—grandmother. She was hanged by a Harling three hundred years ago."

"I see," she said, apparently trying her damnedest to sound confused. Win knew she wasn't confused at all.

"Her statue is on the State House lawn."

"Oh!" Hannah smiled suddenly, as if finally getting it. "You mean the witch."

Look who was calling who a witch, Win thought, but kept his mouth shut. He was already out over two thousand dollars, thanks to Priscilla's great-whatever and was beginning to feel the bewitching effects of her eyes, her luscious, pink mouth.

"I've read about her," Hannah said.

"Every real Harling knows about Priscilla Marsh and Judge Cotton Harling."

"I don't."

"You're not a real Harling. You're a Marsh."

She sighed. "Well, I'm not going to argue with you. Shouldn't you and your uncle be finding your seats?"

Uncle Jonathan had busied himself tracking down a couple of drinks. Win sat down in the empty chair next to Hannah Marsh. "Preston Fowler thought the Harlings should sit together."

"How nice," she said, clearly not meaning it. She pursed her lips, trying to buy time, Win suspected, to think of a way to wriggle out of the tight spot she'd squeezed herself into. "If you're so certain of who I am, why haven't you told anyone?"

"You're a smart woman. Figure that one out for yourself."

"With a Harling, it usually boils down to reputation."

Win indicated his uncle, who was making his way through the crowd, carrying two drinks. "If it weren't for him, I'd stand right up on this table and expose you to everyone here for the lying thief you are. But Uncle Jonathan..." He narrowed his eyes on her and saw the spots of pink in her cheeks deepen under his penetrating gaze. "He deserves better."

"I can explain, you know. Or won't you give me the chance?"

"What mitigating circumstances might there be for you to charge an expensive dress to my account?"

Her lips parted slightly, her eyes shone. She dragged her lower lip under her top teeth, a habit, Win guessed, when she was caught red-handed. "You asked for it," she challenged him. "There isn't a court in the country that would convict me— unless a Harling was the presiding judge."

"You have to be a Marsh. Only a Marsh would hold someone responsible for what one of their ancestors did three hundred years ago."

She shrugged, neither accepting nor denying his accusation.

Uncle Jonathan arrived with the drinks. "Here you go, Winthrop. Did I miss any excitement?"

"No, not at all." His eyes didn't leave Hannah. "We were just discussing genealogy."

"Boring stuff." Uncle Jonathan sniffed. "Let the dead bury the dead, I say."

Since when? No one was more adamant on the subject of the Marshes' long-standing grudge against the Harlings than Win's uncle. Win glanced at him but said nothing.

"Well, Miss Harling," his elderly uncle said, "how do you like our fair city so far?"

She graced him with one of her beguiling smiles. Her eyes skimmed over Win, as if he were a cockroach she was pretending she hadn't noticed. "Please," she said, "just call me Hannah."

"My pleasure."

Win scowled at his uncle; he knew the woman was a liar and very likely a Marsh, yet he was still trying to charm her. She might look innocent, and she certainly was attractive, but Win wasn't fooled. She'd already cost him too much time and money.

Hannah gestured toward the glittering view of Boston Harbor. "Boston's a lovely city. I'm glad I can appreciate other places without wanting to give up my own life. I know people too afraid to appreciate somewhere else, because they believe it might make them think less of where they live, and others who can only appreciate places they don't live."

Uncle Jonathan stared at Hannah for a few seconds, blinked, sipped his drink and looked at Win, who from years of experience with his uncle already knew what was coming. "What did she say?"

"She likes Boston but doesn't want to live here," he translated, turning to Hannah. "Uncle Jonathan's a bit hard of hearing."

"I'm not. I just didn't understand what in hell she was saying."

Win wondered if he'd be as blunt in his eighties or have as tolerant a nephew. What Hannah was doing, he knew, was saying whatever popped into her head to keep the conversation going before one of the real Harlings at the table decided to call her bluff in public.

"I'm sorry," she apologized quickly, "I've had a long day."

"You're not going to plead a stomachache and make a fast exit, are you?" Win challenged her with an amused grin.

Her luminous eyes fastened on him, any hint of embarrassment gone from her cheeks. There was only anger. The zest for a good fight. "You'd like that, wouldn't you?"

"Just wondering how hot it will have to get before you bow out."

"I don't care what you think. I know who I am."

"And who is that?"

She gave him a small, cool, mysterious smile. "That's for me to know and for you to find out."

Before Win could respond, Preston Fowler came up between them and clapped a hand upon each of their shoulders. "You found each other all right, I see. Glad you could make it. People are delighted to have the Harling family active in the New England Athenaeum again. Hannah, have you talked to your cousin and uncle about your family history? Jonathan here is quite an authority. He might have family papers pertinent to your research that aren't part of our collection."

He spotted another couple entering late and made his apologies, quickly crossing the restaurant.

Uncle Jonathan looked at Hannah. "Didn't know I had a niece in Cincinnati."

Win watched her smooth throat as she swallowed. She said, "I sort of exaggerated our relationship, so I could use the library for my research."

"Sort of?" Win asked wryly.

She scowled at him. "Believe what you want to believe."

"I will."

"What kind of research?" Uncle Jonathan asked.

"Oh, I'm just looking into my roots."

"Why?"

"Curiosity."

Uncle Jonathan sniffed. He pulled at Win's sleeve and whispered, "She's a Marsh, all right. I know just what she's after."

Hannah was frowning, obviously certain Jonathan Harling

wasn't saying anything positive. Win, seated between them, turned to his uncle. "What's that?"

"The Harling Collection."

Win had never heard of it.

"I'll explain later," Uncle Jonathan told him, just as Hannah Marsh saw her opening and jumped to her feet.

Win grabbed her by the wrist with lightning speed. "Don't leave," he urged amiably. "You paid for dinner with your own money."

She licked her lips guiltily.

Win gritted his teeth.

"I started to pay with my own money," she explained, "but then I...well, one of the staff asked me if they should just send the bill along to you, and I said sure, why not?"

He didn't release her wrist. He didn't know how she managed to look so damned innocent. So justified.

"I also put you down for a hundred-dollar donation," she added.

"Sit."

"You won't make a scene. I know you won't."

"Sit down, *now*."

She batted her eyelids at him, deliberately, cockily. "Shall I beg, too?"

"It could come to that."

He spoke in a low, husky voice, and it was apparently enough to drop Hannah Marsh back into her chair. The spots of pink reappeared in her cheeks. Her breathing grew rapid, light, shallow. She drew her lower lip once more under her top teeth.

"I'm going to find out what you're after," Win said. "And if I have to, I'll stop you."

She gave him a scathing look. "Spoken like a true Harling."

It wasn't a compliment.

HANNAH GOT OUT her checkbook the moment she returned to her Beacon Hill apartment and wrote out a check to J. Winthrop Harling for every nickel she owed him.

When she had refused their offer of a ride home, Win Harling and his uncle had insisted on getting her a cab. She was quite sure they'd heard her give her address and wished, belatedly, she'd lied. But she was getting tired of lying.

She was not a liar. She was not a thief.

She had merely adopted an unwise strategy, that was all. Pretending to be a Harling had been a tactic. An expedient. She wasn't out to get the Harlings. She just wanted to write the definitive biography of Priscilla Marsh. She, Hannah Marsh, had always played by the rules. She didn't look for trouble.

But she'd found it in spades, hadn't she?

Her check made out, her bank account drawn down to next to nothing, she called Cousin Thackeray in southern Maine. She was still wearing her twenties tea dress.

Thackeray answered on the first ring.

"I'm in trouble," she began, then told him everything.

Her cousin didn't hesitate to offer his advice when she finished. "Come home."

It was tempting. She could picture him in his frayed easy chair, with rocky, beautiful Marsh Point stretched before him. From her own cottage nearby, she could see the rocky shoreline, tall evergreens, wild blueberry bushes, loons and cormorants and seals hunting for food. Even now she could conjure up the smell of the fog, taste the salt in it. Marsh Point was the closest thing she had ever had to a real, permanent home. She would go back. There was no question of that.

But not yet.

"I can't," she said before she could change her mind. "I have a job to do and I'm going to do it. I won't be driven from Boston by anyone."

"Driven?" There was a sharpness, a sudden protectiveness, in Thackeray's voice that made her feel at once wanted and needed, a part of the old man's life. He was family. "Have the Harlings threatened you?"

"Not in so many—well, yeah, in so many words. But don't worry. I can handle myself."

"Shall I drive down?"

Just what she needed. An eighty-year-old man who hated cities, particularly hated Boston, and really and truly hated the Harlings. He would, at the very least, get in the way. And she doubted he could do anything to get her out of hot water with Win Harling.

"No, I'll be fine."

He hissed in disgust. "You're not still after that Harling Collection, are you?"

She sighed. "I'd like to know at least if it exists."

"Can't you take my word for it that it doesn't?"

"Cousin Thackeray…"

"Come home, Hannah. You've done enough research on Priscilla. Just pack up and come home."

Although he was over a hundred miles away, and couldn't see her, Hannah shook her head. "You yourself have said that for the past three hundred years the Harlings have been tough on Marshes who don't kowtow to their power and money. Well, I won't. I'll leave Boston when I'm ready to leave Boston and not a minute sooner."

Cousin Thackeray muttered something about her stubborn nature and hung up.

Hannah was too wired to sleep. Work, she knew, was always the best antidote for a distracted mind. But when she sat at her laptop computer, she thought not of Priscilla Marsh and Cotton Harling, but of J. Winthrop Harling. His searing black eyes. His strong thighs. His sexy, challenging smirk.

Such thinking was unprofessional and unproductive.

Definitely not scholarly.

And as for objectivity… How could she be objective about a man who made her throat go tight and dry, even when she just looked at him? Win Harling could have passed for a rebel who'd helped rout the British, dumped tea into Boston Harbor, tarred and feathered Tories. He was tough and sexy and didn't fit her image of a Harling at all.

Clearly she needed to restore her balance and perspective. But how?

"Give the bastard his money," she muttered, "and hope it makes him happy."

"IT'S A SHAME," Uncle Jonathan said, having agreed to meet his nephew for Sunday morning breakfast, "that an attractive woman like that—bright, gutsy, clever—turns out to be a Marsh."

Win blew on his piping-hot coffee, then took a sip. The café at the bottom of Beacon Hill wasn't crowded, but he had still chosen a table at the back, in case Ms. Hannah, apparently also a Beacon Hill resident, blundered in. He needed to concentrate; he'd found he couldn't when she was near.

"If she wasn't a Marsh," his uncle continued, "she just might be the woman for you, Winthrop. She'd make you think about something besides work, I'd allow."

She already had, but Win said, "Uncle Jonathan, I didn't ask you here to discuss my love life. Now..."

"You need a woman."

Win sighed. "That's a rather blunt statement."

"It's true. You're waiting for fate to take a hand and present you with the woman of your dreams. I say she's out there somewhere and you need to hunt her down."

"Like a buffalo?"

"More like an antelope, I think. Maybe a tigress."

"Uncle Jonathan..."

"Well, Win, what can I say? You work too hard. You don't pay enough attention to your personal life. Dating women isn't the same as finding the woman meant for you. And don't tell me that's romantic nonsense, because it's not."

Win knew a change of subject was in order. He didn't want to argue, and not just because he didn't want to sit through another of his uncle's lectures on marriage and little ones. Anything Win said would bring up, however indirectly, Uncle Jonathan's own unhappy life. He had lost his wife to cancer twenty-five years ago, his only child, a daughter—a cousin Win had adored—to a car accident ten years back. The kind of life Jonathan wanted for his nephew meant that Win would have to set himself up for tragedy. Right now he preferred to keep his risks financial.

"Tell me about the Marshes," he said.

That distracted his uncle. He poured cream into his coffee and began a lecture on the Marsh-Harling feud of the past three hundred years, sounding like the history professor he'd once been. Win listened carefully.

"I wouldn't think," he said after a while, "that reasonable people would blame an entire family for the conduct of one of its ancestors. Right or wrong, Cotton's been dead a long time."

"The Marshes will capitalize on his mistake whenever they see an opening. That's how they ended up with a chunk of prime southern Maine real estate that's rightly ours."

"Ours? What do you mean?"

"About a hundred years ago the Marshes swiped a lovely piece of coastal land from the Harlings. They stole the deed from us and claimed they'd bought the land first. No one could prove otherwise. It's theirs to this day." He grimaced. "They call it Marsh Point."

"And the Harling Collection," Win said. "Tell me about it."

"About the same time the Marshes appropriated our land in Maine, a Harling—Anne Harling—gathered the family papers together into a collection."

"I never knew—"

Uncle Jonathan held up a hand, stopping him. "It's never been proven to exist. It disappeared not long after Anne finished putting it together. Nobody's ever produced a credible theory of what happened to it."

"And you think our Hannah Marsh is after it?"

"Yep."

Win shook his head. "It doesn't explain her behavior. Why would she lie to us and steal from us if she expected us to hand over the Harling Collection for her to examine?"

His uncle lifted his bony shoulders, then let them drop; he sighed heavily. "She doesn't expect us to hand it over."

"What do you mean?"

"I mean," his uncle announced, "she plans to *steal* it."

HANNAH ENDURED a disturbingly quiet Sunday. Twice she ventured into Louisburg Square. Nothing seemed out of the ordinary. But then, how would she know? The Harling House stood bathed in spring sunshine, giving away none of its secrets. She debated venturing up the steps and sticking her check into its mail slot. It would mean a lean winter ahead, but would restore her sense of pride. But she decided against leaving it. It had her name imprinted at the top, and she wasn't sure she wanted Win Harling to have her name confirmed for him, at least, not yet. First she had to find a way of explaining what she'd done, making him—or his uncle—understand her motives.

By Monday morning she'd decided Win Harling couldn't learn much more about her than he already suspected. But she remained on her guard. She couldn't relax. If anything, the fundraising dinner on Saturday could only have stimulated his desire to best her.

Stimulated his desire?

She cleared her throat, reacting to the unfortunate choice of words, and tried to dismiss the possibilities, but dozens of images flooded her mind.

Work. She had to keep working.

But when she arrived at the Athenaeum for a morning of what she'd promised herself would be disciplined research, a message was waiting for her. It was a note scrawled in black marker on a scrap of computer paper.

I suggest you come by my office in the financial district
today at noon. We need to discuss the Harling Collection
and Marsh Point. If you value your reputation, you won't
be late. I know who you are.

It was signed, arrogantly, just with Win Harling's initials, JWH.

Hannah stood rock still, feeling every drop of blood drain out of her. She read the note twice.

First of all, she now knew why he'd been in the well-armed

building in the financial district the other day; *his* office, not his uncle's, was there. Probably his uncle was retired and no longer had an office. Hannah hated making a mistake in her research, but never had one been as costly as this one.

"Well, no use crying over spilt milk," she muttered, reflecting that a lot more than milk could be spilled by the end of this affair.

Second, the Harling Collection. He'd figured out she was after it. Well, that she could understand. She had made no bones about looking into the Harling family history, and so could be expected to want to examine the Harling Collection, if it existed. Still, she would have preferred to have a chance to explain her real reasons for wanting access to it before Win Harling found her out. But so be it.

The mention of Marsh Point, however, she didn't understand. Why would he want to discuss Marsh Point? Did he know that was where she lived?

And just who did he think she was?

The library assistant who had handed her the note said, "He also left a book for you."

It was a copy of her biography of Martha Washington.

The bastard knew.

He knew!

"Well," Hannah muttered under her breath, "it's not as if you didn't see it coming."

But to threaten her reputation...

How like a Harling.

"Is something wrong, Ms. Harling?" Preston Fowler asked, emerging from his office.

"No. Not at all." She crumpled the note, stuffing it into the pocket of her squall jacket, and turned the book so that Fowler couldn't see the name of its author. She forced a smile. "Thanks for asking."

"Did you enjoy the dinner Saturday?"

"Yes—yes, I did. The food was wonderful, and I enjoyed

having the chance to be with my relatives.'' She smiled, hoping she didn't look as flustered as she felt, but knew she'd always been particularly good at thinking on her feet. A Marsh trait, according to Cousin Thackeray. Of course, if she had listened to him, she might not be in the crummy position she was in right now. She'd be home in Maine, where she belonged. ''If you'll excuse me, I'd like to get to work.''

''Of course. Let me know if I can be of any assistance.''

Would he be so willing to help if he knew she was Hannah Marsh and not Hannah Harling?

But she had a couple of hours before noon and refused to fall victim to obsessions about J. Winthrop Harling. Instead she tucked her notebook under her arm and proceeded to the second floor to the rare book room; the small, secure, climate-controlled space where Win Harling had trapped her the other day.

Amid her musty books, she began to relax. Come what might in her life, she always had her work.

She had already examined the most pertinent documents stored in the room, but there were several peripheral books and documents she wanted to look at. She got started.

After a relatively peaceful hour, disturbed only by moments of having to stomp on her unruly thoughts, she located a history of colonial Boston written in the early nineteenth century. On the inside front cover she spotted, in a faded handwriting, the name Jonathan Winthrop Harling and an address in the Back Bay section of Boston, just around the corner from where she was right now.

Win's uncle Jonathan. The old man with the cane. The man Hannah had intended to find in the first place, the only Harling supposed to be still in Boston. He must have donated the volume.

He had seemed reasonably charming on Saturday evening, and was still her best lead to the Harling Collection. If he hadn't moved, she could look him up herself, instead of going through his black-eyed, suspicious nephew. He might listen to her explanation of her behavior during the past week, to her legitimate reasons for wanting to examine the Harling Collection. He wouldn't threaten her reputation.

Neither would he threaten her peace of mind, create the kind of mental and physical turmoil his nephew did. He wasn't young and good-looking and too damned sexy for *her* own good.

She had time, if she hurried, to try and see Jonathan Harling before her summons to the Boston financial district and the offices of J. Winthrop Harling. She gathered her papers, stuffed them into her satchel and headed out, hardly stopping to say goodbye to Preston Fowler.

Built on fill from the top of Beacon Hill, the Back Bay consisted of a dozen or so streets beyond the Public Garden, within easy walking distance. Jonathan Harling lived in a stately Victorian brownstone on the sunny side of Marlborough Street. Once a single-family dwelling, the building had been broken up into apartments, probably shortly before or during World War II. The name HARLING was printed next to a white doorbell, which Hannah rang.

There was no answer.

Her spirits sagged. Just her luck. She had hoped she could explain her situation and get him to contact his nephew to have him call off his witch-hunt. If she were particularly persuasive, she might get the old man to talk to her about the Harling Collection and forgive her for her many transgressions. She *would* pay back his nephew.

She considered waiting on his front stoop until he returned, then realized that if she did, she would never make the financial district by noon. Win Harling would only hunt her down. She owed it not to him but to herself to find out what he knew about her, how he'd learned it, whom he'd told and—most important— what he'd meant by his reference to Marsh Point.

Uncle Jonathan would have to keep.

5

By THE TIME she reached the modern federal building and its armed guard, an appropriately blustery wind was blowing off the water and dark clouds had rolled in. Springtime in New England. Hannah hunched her shoulders against the cold. She had on a lightweight black squall jacket, black gabardine pants and a pale yellow silk shirt, a little less the proper Bostonian than on her previous visit to the financial district, but still not quite herself. Cousin Thackeray, she remembered, had insisted the Harlings and their crowd were a bunch of tightwads who considered new clothes tackily nouveau riche. Dowdy, worn-out, once-expensive clothes were the mark of a true Boston Brahmin. They'd accept her a lot quicker, he'd maintained, if she could show off a few moth holes. Hannah had refused his offer to beat her clothes on the rocks to make them look more authentically "old money."

Cousin Thackeray...

She couldn't have her feud with Win Harling touch him.

The red-haired guard grinned at her, not making a move for his gun as he might have been expected to, given their last meeting. "Go right on up. Fourteenth floor."

Hannah gave him an I-told-you-so smirk, but there was nothing in his expression that indicated he thought she had the upper hand. She dashed for the elevator and blamed its fast ascent to the fourteenth floor for the slightly sick feeling in her stomach and her sudden light-headedness. *Win knows about the Harling Collection...about Marsh Point....*

What could he have found out about Marsh Point?

Had Cousin Thackeray neglected to tell her something that he should have?

Checking the floor directory, she found her way to Win's office suite, entering a large, airy, L-shaped room, arranged so that both the reception area and corner office had windows with views of the city and the fountain plaza below.

A young woman greeted Hannah, who was a good ten minutes late. "Mr. Harling's waiting."

Hannah sensed the secretary's disapproval; she obviously didn't like anyone keeping Mr. Harling waiting. The younger woman led the way, pushing open his door in an exaggeratedly professional manner she'd either learned in secretarial school or had seen in old Joan Crawford movies.

J. Winthrop Harling's office was spacious, modern and spare, and Hannah was struck by its contrast to her own rustic, cluttered space overlooking Marsh Point. It was just more evidence that the two of them led totally different lives, and that she was an intruder. She was on his turf, and she wasn't the only one who knew it.

"Welcome." Win rose smoothly, his graciousness belied by the dark, suspicious expression in his eyes. He gestured to a leather chair in front of his gleaming desk. "Have a seat."

The secretary silently withdrew, shutting the door behind her. Hannah shook her head. "Thank you, I prefer to stand."

"As you wish."

"I got your summons," she said coolly.

His mouth twitched, and he sat down, eyeing her. He was wearing a white shirt, its sleeves rolled up to midforearm, its top button undone, and had loosened his tie. Very sexy. His suit jacket was slung on a credenza to his right. His jaw looked even squarer than usual, but if Hannah could change only one thing about him, it would be his eyes. She'd fade them out, water them up a little, add some dark shadows and red lines. That done, surely the rest of him wouldn't seem nearly as appealing...or as dangerous.

"So," she said, crossing her arms over her chest, "who am I?"

"Hannah Marsh, the biographer."

She shrugged, neither confirming nor denying, but her heart

was pounding. The man was relentless. But at least by leaving the Martha Washington biography for her, he'd given her fair warning of just what he knew.

He pushed a slender volume across his immaculate desk. It was her biography of three women married to famous robber barons of the nineteenth century. Like the study of Martha Washington, it had not been a bestseller. Win Harling would have had to dig to find her out.

"Okay," Hannah said unapologetically, "so I lied. In my position, wouldn't you have done the same?"

He made no apparent attempt to disguise his outright skepticism. After their rocky start, he was going to have a tough time believing anything she said. "Just what is your position?"

"Simply put, I'm a Marsh in Harling territory."

"There are just two Harlings in Boston." His tone was even and controlled, and all the more scathing for it. "My eighty-year-old uncle and me. Neither of us was disposed to harm or impede you in any way."

Hannah duly noted his use of the past tense. She decided she should keep her mouth shut until he finished.

Win sprang up and came around his desk, black walnut from the looks of it. Expensive. The man did know how to make money. "In my position, what would *you* do?"

She shrugged. "Leave me alone."

A smile, not an amiable one, tugged at the corners of his mouth. Hannah pushed aside the memory of that whisper of a kiss the other night.

"Wouldn't you want to find out what a woman posing as a member of your family was up to?" he asked. "Especially given the history between our two families."

"A lowly biographer? Nope. I wouldn't waste my time with her."

His eyes narrowed. In her mind, she washed out his black lashes. It didn't help. She still had to contend with the black irises.

"Wouldn't you think your behavior suspicious?" he asked.

"I'm not of a suspicious nature." She tilted her chin at him, unintimidated. They were fourteen floors up, in a well-guarded building. What could he do to her? "I'm a Marsh, remember? I don't think like a Harling."

He moved forward, so that they were only inches apart. She could smell his clean, expensive cologne and see a tiny scar at the corner of his right eye. It did not detract from the intensity of his gaze. "You're working on a biography of Priscilla Marsh."

"So?"

"So it's a nice cover for what you're really after."

"The Harling Collection," she said calmly. "I don't know what nefarious purpose you have attributed to me, but I only want to examine it for research purposes. I want to do as thorough a job as possible on Priscilla Marsh's life. Examining the Harling Collection could be very helpful in understanding Cotton Harling's thinking when he had her hanged."

Cotton's descendant stared at her in dubious silence. It was outrageous, Hannah thought, how sexy she found him. What would Priscilla have thought?

"That's the truth," she continued. "I didn't know it was even rumored to exist until I'd arrived in Boston and started doing my research, identifying myself as a Harling so I wouldn't arouse suspicion and might get better treatment. When I came here the other day, I tried to get in to see you without giving a name. I wanted to talk to you about my research first and explain. Of course, I thought you were your uncle. I had no idea..." She took a breath and glanced at him. "You don't get it, do you?"

"Oh, I get it. Your devious plan backfired."

She scowled. "No, you don't get it. You think I'm up to no good and I'm telling you I'm not. I was just doing my best under difficult circumstances."

"Of your own making. How do you explain the dress?"

"That was personal," she snapped. "I owed you for hunting me down like a dog."

His mouth twitched again, and this time she was sure he wanted to smile. At what? *She* wasn't having any fun.

She reached into her pocket and produced the check, by now wrinkled, she'd written on Saturday night, and thrust it at him. She could still return the dress, but she'd included its price in her check. "Here, take it. It's reimbursement for the lunch, the dress, the dinner, the donation to the New England Athenaeum—everything."

"I don't want your money, Hannah."

"Then what do you want?"

His eyes darkened and she stopped breathing. *Stupid question, Hannah. Stupid, stupid.* His answer was obvious in the heat of his gaze, the tenseness of his body.

What he wanted was her.

Just as she wanted him.

Their physical attraction was a fact, unpleasant, distracting, constant. And just as there was nothing they could do about their relationship to Cotton Harling and Priscilla Marsh, there was nothing they could do about the primitive longing that had erupted between them.

Well, Hannah thought, there was something....

But that was crazy. He was a Harling. He was the enemy. She couldn't think about going to bed with him!

Did he know that was what she was thinking? Could he even guess it?

"Okay, okay, fine," she said quickly, before he could respond. "Have it your way."

She spun around, preparing to leave. Wanting to leave. She would return to Marlborough Street, talk to Jonathan Harling about the Harling Collection, and bypass his know-it-all nephew altogether.

She got almost to the door before Win said, "The Harling Collection has been missing for at least a hundred years. Uncle Jonathan insists a Marsh stole it, just like a Marsh stole our land in southern Maine. Marsh Point, you call it now."

Stole Marsh Point? Damn, Cousin Thackeray! He must have known that was what the Harlings thought.

"Of all the—" Hannah whipped around, even more furious when she saw Win sitting calmly on the edge of his desk, watching her, waiting for her reaction. She pounded over to him, slinging her satchel. "That's what you think? That we've had the damned collection all along? Then why in hell would I risk life and limb trying to get in to see you to talk you into giving me access to it?"

"You tell me."

She groaned, itching to knock him off his high horse.

"So, you no longer deny that you're a Marsh," he said, rising.

It wasn't a question, but she said, "I never did deny it. I just didn't acknowledge it."

He touched her hair, wild from her mad dash across Boston, from the wind, from her anger. She fought the tingling sensation it caused. "A direct descendant of Priscilla Marsh?"

"The last."

He tucked a stray lock of hair behind her ear, letting his finger trace the outline of her jaw and creating a heat in her like none she'd known before. Then he dropped his hand to his side. "You're not from Ohio."

"I'm not from anywhere. I live in Maine now."

"Marsh Point."

"We didn't steal it." Her reply was based more out of loyalty to her cousin than on any certain knowledge.

"We have a case, you know. I've been looking into it. If we can prove the Marshes stole our deed, we can establish our right to the land." He remained close to her. "Until you showed up, I never paid much attention to Harling family history."

Hannah thought of Cousin Thackeray, who had been born on Marsh Point and wanted to die there. It was his home. Had he tried to talk Hannah out of going to Boston out of fear that she would rekindle the Harlings' claim to his slice of Maine?

Now Win Harling was on the case.

Thanks to her.

She faced him squarely. "What do you want from me?"

She saw the immediate spark of desire in his eyes and held her breath, wondering if he could see it mirrored in hers. But he didn't touch her, didn't act on the sexual tension hissing between them like a downed and very dangerous electrical wire. Neither did she.

"All I want," he said, "is the truth."

"I've told you everything I know." Her voice was hoarse; she paused to clear her throat. She wondered if his uncle had been filling him with the same kind of nasty tales about the Marshes that Cousin Thackeray had told her about the Harlings. "I understand you have no reason to trust me, but I'm not here to reignite the Marsh-Harling hostility. I'm just doing my work."

"If I knew you better, maybe I'd find it easier to believe you."

She tried to ignore the sudden softness of his voice. The fox coaxing the chickens to open the henhouse door. "Does your uncle know about me?"

"He suspects you're a Marsh, but that's all."

"He won't approve of my writing Priscilla's story, will he?"

"I'm sure he'll question your objectivity."

"Do you think he knows what happened to the Harling Collection, if it ever existed?"

Win smiled. "If he does, he'd never tell a Marsh."

She hoisted her satchel onto her shoulder, preparing once more to leave. She'd see what Jonathan Harling knew and didn't know, and what she could talk him into doing. "Truce?"

"Cease-fire. I'll talk to Uncle Jonathan this afternoon." Win stared at her for a moment. "Dinner tonight?"

It was more a challenge than an invitation. Hannah felt her throat tighten, but nodded. "Okay."

"You're not staying at any hotel in Boston," he said. She assumed he remembered the address she had given the cabdriver after the fund-raising dinner.

"No, I borrowed a friend's apartment on Pinckney Street, right around the corner from you."

His eyes held her. "So we are neighbors."

"I guess so," she said cheerfully and fled, wondering what she had got herself into. Why hadn't she listened to Cousin Thackeray to begin with and steered clear of Boston altogether?

"WIN HARLING KNOWS everything," Hannah told Cousin Thackeray from the kitchen phone. Her nerve endings were still on fire from her encounter with the wealthy Bostonian. She tried not to think of him simply as Win. That was too...personal.

Cousin Thackeray sniffed. "I told you this would happen."

"So you did."

"You coming home?"

"Not yet. Thackeray, what do you know about a Harling claim to Marsh Point?"

Silence.

"Thackeray?"

"They don't have one."

"Not a legitimate one, I'm sure. But—"

"But nothing's ever settled with a Harling," he grumbled, half under his breath. "Win Harling's after my land?"

"I don't think so. He says he doesn't know much about Harling family history, so all this stuff's fresh for him. He could laugh it off, or he could decide to take up the Harling cause. I just want you to be prepared." Not, she thought, that her dear cousin had paid her the same favor.

Cousin Thackeray laughed without amusement. "I'm always prepared for a Harling."

Hannah wished she could say the same for herself.

HOURS AFTER Hannah Marsh had left his office, Win was still trying to get her out of his mind. He walked home, hoping for distraction. The gusting wind, the traffic, the bustle of rush hour.

Nothing worked.

He made his way to Tremont Street off Boston Common, walking past the shaded grounds of Old Granary Burial Ground behind the First Congregational Church. Established in 1660, it was one of New England's oldest cemeteries. Thin, fragile, rectangular headstones stood at odd angles. Paul Revere was buried here, John Hancock, Samuel Adams, Ben Franklin's parents, the victims of the Boston Massacre.

And the man who had condemned Priscilla Marsh to death, Judge Cotton Harling.

He continued across Boston Common, welcoming its green grass and fluttering pigeons, its history. He crossed Charles Street and went through the Public Garden, where tulips and daffodils were in bloom. He didn't stop until he was in Back Bay, on Marlborough Street, letting himself into his uncle's brownstone with his key.

The door to his uncle's first-floor apartment was slightly ajar. Win creaked it halfway open. "Uncle Jonathan?"

He tensed when no response came.

Although Uncle Jonathan was not paranoid about city life, he was cautious and consistent about his personal security. He would never just step out for a quick walk and leave his door ajar, never mind unlocked. Had he been on his way out and stepped back inside because he'd forgotten something?

"Uncle Jonathan," Win called, raising his voice.

Still no response.

He went inside the apartment; its faded elegance made him feel as if he were taking a step back in time. Not wanting to startle his uncle, who might just be fine, Win shut the door hard and called him again as he headed from the small entry into the living room. Its bow windows looked onto Marlborough, and its Victorian style contrasted with the earlier Federal Period architecture of Beacon Hill.

"Good God!"

The place was a wreck.

Sofa cushions, drawers, shelves, the antique secretary; everything had been pulled out, tossed, scattered and left.

Win's heart pounded. *"Uncle Jonathan!"*

He leaped over books and magazines and papers and pounded down the short hall to his uncle's two bedrooms and bath.

Jonathan Harling was sitting on the edge of his four-poster bed, staring at the small fireplace. He looked unharmed, if gray-faced and stunned. He rubbed a hand through his thin hair and peered at his nephew. "I heard you."

Win squatted beside the old man. "Are you all right?"

His blue eyes focused on Win, betraying not fear, but anger. "She could have asked."

"What?"

"Your Hannah Marsh. She could have asked. I'd have told her no one's seen hide nor hair of the Harling Collection since around 1892."

Win jumped to his feet, stifling a rush of anger. He wanted to go out and track down Hannah and wring the truth out of her beautiful, lying lips. But he resisted the temptation. He had his uncle to see to. "Come on, Uncle Jonathan. I'll make you some tea and we'll talk. You're sure you're all right?"

"Oh, yes. I came in after the damage was done. Nearly had a damned heart attack on the spot. Wouldn't that have delighted the Marshes no end?" He reached for his cane, which lay on the bed, and used it to pull himself upright. He appeared, indeed, remarkably steady. "They'll never be satisfied until they've killed off one of us, the way they say we killed off Priscilla."

"Uncle…"

He shook his cane at Win. "She's a witch, I tell you!"

"Are you saying Hannah trashed your apartment looking for the Harling Collection?"

"Now you're getting it."

Win indulged his uncle's crotchety mood, given the scare the old man had just had, not to mention the circumstantial evidence that appeared to point to her. "Did you see her?"

"Nope. She's too clever by far for that. But I called the neighbors upstairs. They saw her. I gave them a description. She's easy to spot, you know."

Win knew.

"They said she came by this morning while I was at the club."

"Have you called the police?"

"Nope." He shook his head and pointed his cane again at Win. "This is between her and us Harlings."

Leaving it at that for the moment, Win helped his uncle, who kept grumbling he didn't need any damned help, into the kitchen, which had been spared the upheaval of the other rooms. Win filled a kettle with water and put it on the old gas stove.

Uncle Jonathan sat at his little gateleg table and heaved a long sigh. "And such a pretty woman to be such a scurrilous thief. I thought she was the one for you, Win, Marsh or no Marsh. Those eyes of hers…well, I should have known. She's got nothing but larceny in her heart."

"I'm having dinner with her tonight."

"Good. You can fleece the truth out of her."

Win thought he already had. He pictured Hannah Marsh standing in his office, proud, indignant, sexy, a woman to be reckoned with, who wouldn't project her own insecurities onto him. She hadn't looked as if she'd just ransacked an old man's apartment.

But then, what did he know about the real Hannah Marsh? She had already proved herself capable of lying and scheming to get her way, no matter how honorable her cause or understandable her reasoning. If indeed they were honorable and understandable. He had only her word to go on.

The kettle whistled, and Win made his uncle a pot of tea and even had a cup himself, though he was not a tea drinker.

"We need to talk," he said. "Then I'll clean up the place."

"Don't cancel with Miss Marsh on my account."

"Oh, no." He regarded his uncle's pale face with growing anger. What was worth terrifying an eighty-year-old man? "I'll keep our date on your account."

Uncle Jonathan grinned feebly. "That's the spirit."

HANNAH SIPPED at the glass of wine that Win had poured her and watched him whisk together raspberry vinegar and olive oil for the mixed green salad he'd thrown together. She hadn't expected dinner would be at his house. "What?" she'd asked upon entering the historic Beacon Hill mansion. "No maids?"

Win had smiled over his shoulder. "No furniture, either."

He wasn't exaggerating by much. Although the place retained its regal lines and potential, it needed work. Win Harling clearly could afford to have it done. Why didn't he?

There was a lot, Hannah admitted, she didn't know about the man. A lot mere prejudice couldn't explain.

"I haven't been here that long—I wanted the house back in the family and snapped it up when I had the chance. I keep thinking I'd like to do the work myself, but I haven't gotten around to it."

He swirled the contents of the glass carafe, then added pinches of dried herbs from small unmarked containers. "How do you know what's what?" Hannah asked.

"Who says I do?"

A seat-of-the-pants cook. "Dinner should be interesting."

"Always."

The kitchen was large and drafty, this morning's dark clouds now pouring forth a cold, steady rain. Expecting a restaurant, Hannah had put on a simple dress and flats. Now she wished she'd brought a sweater.

"You're shivering," Win observed.

"Not really."

He pulled off his cardigan and tossed it to her. "Here, put this on."

"Won't you get cold?"

"Nope. Cooking always makes me hot." He had his back to her, but Hannah didn't need to see his expression to guess what he was thinking.

The sweater was old but bulky, a thick, cotton knit still warm from his body. She slipped it on. He was wider through the torso than she was, and his arms were longer. She pushed up the sleeves, the fabric soft and well-worn, like a caress against her skin. She licked her lips, suddenly feeling self-conscious, even somewhat aroused. Wearing his sweater was too much like having him hold her. Dinner maybe hadn't been a good idea, but she had to find out what he knew—what he intended to do—

about Marsh Point. If anything. She'd stirred up this trouble; she'd see to it that it didn't reach Cousin Thackeray.

Win glanced back at her. "Better?"

"Yes."

He did not, she observed, look the least bit chilly himself in his close-fitting jeans and dark purple, short-sleeved pullover. She would bet it wasn't just the cooking that kept him warm, or even his all too apparent physical desire for her. There was also the fact that they were in his house, his city, on his turf. Easy for him to stay nice and toasty.

"What did you do today?" he asked casually.

"Not much. I spent most of the morning at the New England Athenaeum, met you, then headed up to the Boston Public Library. After that I went back to the apartment and entered my notes into my laptop."

Win got a small paper bag from the refrigerator and withdrew from it a mound of fresh linguine, which he promptly dropped into a pot of bubbling water. He scooped a cupful of the boiling water into a plain white pasta dish and swirled it around while the linguine cooked. "You didn't happen to wander over to Marlborough Street, did you?"

"Mmm...why would I?"

"I don't know." He stopped what he was doing and regarded her, his expression hard, challenging. "Why would you?"

Hannah licked her lips. "Am I being set up here?"

"Just tell the truth, Hannah."

"All right. I found your uncle Jonathan's address this morning in the rare book room. Before answering your summons, I took a walk over to Marlborough Street."

"Why?"

"To talk to him about the Harling Collection. I thought he'd know more than you would, and that he might be more reasonable than you would."

"Did you see him?"

"No, he wasn't in."

"How do you know?"

"What do you mean, how do I know? I rang his doorbell and he didn't answer. I assumed he wasn't home."

"Then you didn't go into his apartment?"

"No."

"What about this afternoon? Did you go back to Marlborough Street?"

She shook her head. "I decided to wait until we'd talked before trying to see your uncle again."

Win didn't say a word. Instead he picked up the bubbling pot and dumped the contents into a colander in the sink, steam enveloping him. He set down the empty pot. Hannah noticed the muscles in his back and upper arms, felt the raw sexiness of the man. Her careful preparations for dealing with the Harlings of Boston had been way off the mark.

He transferred the pasta to the warmed dish, then spooned on a herb and oil sauce and sautéed vegetables, tossing them with two forks.

"Why the interrogation?" Hannah finally asked.

"Because I don't know you." He brought the bowls of pasta and salad to the table, which wasn't set for dinner. "I don't know you at all, Hannah Marsh."

Suddenly he turned and lifted her by the elbows, slipping his hands under the heavy sweater and drawing her toward him. She didn't resist. To maintain her balance she let her palms press against his chest. It was even harder than she had anticipated. He drew her even closer, until she had little choice but to let her arms slide around his back. Now her breasts were pressed against his chest. She could feel the nipples turning into small pebbles. How much more of this could she stand?

How much more did she want?

Their eyes locked, just for an instant. She knew what he wanted. What she wanted.

Then his mouth closed over hers, hot and hungry, his tongue urged her lips apart, as if its probing would find all her secrets, answer all his questions. She felt herself responding. Her mind said she was crazy. He was a Harling, Cousin Thackeray had warned her, but her body didn't care. Her tongue did its own probing, its own urging. Her breasts strained against the muscles of his chest. He pushed one knee between her legs, pressing his hard masculinity against her, kneading her hips until she moaned softly, agonizingly, into his mouth. *Don't stop,* her body said, over and over. *Don't ever stop.*

But he took her by the shoulders and disentangled himself, pulling himself away. She felt swollen, frustrated, a little embarrassed. She couldn't read his expression. His eyes were masked, dark and mesmerizing.

"Did you ransack my uncle's apartment?" he asked hoarsely.

"What?"

"You heard me."

"No, I—of course I didn't!"

"You never went back to Marlborough Street?"

"I said no. What happened? Is your uncle all right?"

"Someone broke into his apartment. He's shaken up but otherwise fine."

She stepped back, increasing the physical and psychic distance between them. "So that's what this is about. You're trying to weaken my defenses and get me to admit to something I didn't do. Well, you're way off base, Win Harling. I've told you the truth."

He nodded curtly. "Fair enough." He picked up the two bowls that stood on the table. "We'll eat in the dining room."

"I don't know how I can have dinner with you after— My God, I can't believe you'd think I could rob an old man!"

"Why not? Think of all the things you believe I'm capable of doing." He grinned at her over his shoulder. "Come on, Hannah. My doubts about you aren't upsetting you nearly as much as that kiss."

She grew cool. "I've been kissed before."

"But have you ever responded like that?"

It was only nominally a question. He had got it into his head that she hadn't. That he'd been the first man she'd let get to her like that with a first kiss. The problem was, he was right. Ordinarily she held back. Deliberately, easily. She had never before permitted herself to respond with such abandon, such openness.

A serious mistake, perhaps?

Well, what was done was done. He had used her. Manipulated her. Lowered her defenses so that he could pose his nasty question and catch her off guard. He hadn't been anywhere close to out of control.

But he had been aroused. No doubt about that.

As he led her down a short hall, she noticed its cherry floor needed sanding. They entered a chandeliered dining room with the ugliest wallpaper she'd ever seen. Parts of it had been peeled back, revealing a clashing, but prettier, paper underneath. The only furnishings were an antique grandfather clock, a massive, gorgeous, cherry table and a couple of folding, metal chairs that decidedly didn't match. The walls were wainscoted and the ceilings high, the windows looking onto a darkened courtyard. The table was set with cloth place mats and simple white porcelain plates.

"I'll get the wine," Win said and disappeared.

Alone in the dining room, Hannah took the opportunity to restore her composure. She wiped her still-sensitized mouth with a soft cloth napkin and listened to the ticking of the grandfather clock, letting it soothe her. Although the Harling House was in the middle of the city, it might have been on Marsh Point itself for all its quiet and sense of isolation, its potential for loneliness.

Suddenly she wondered if she and Win Harling had more in common than either wanted to admit. Perhaps what had them groping for each other wasn't just a physical attraction gone overboard, but a subconscious understanding of that commonality.

He returned with their two glasses and the bottle of wine.

"I should go," she said.

"I know. I should make you go." He refilled her glass. "But there's another matter we need to discuss."

She could think of several. "What's that?"

"A rare copy of the Declaration of Independence, possibly worth hundreds of thousands of dollars."

6

"I DON'T KNOW what you're talking about," Hannah said simply.

Win lighted two tall, slender, white candles and sat on the folding chair at one end of the table, watching her in the flickering light. She was, he thought, a bewitching woman. "I figured that was what you'd say."

"It's the truth."

"Tell me," he said, pausing to sip his wine. "How did you learn about the Harling Collection?"

"It was mentioned in passing in something I read. I can't remember offhand exactly what it was, but I keep exhaustive records. I could look it up."

"Why don't you?"

"I don't like your tone, Mr. Harling." Hers was assertive, bordering on angry. "And I'm not under any obligation to obey any orders from you."

He set down his wineglass and passed her the pasta bowl, noting the slenderness of her wrists, the unself-conscious femininity of her movements. "Tell me again why you want to get your hands on the Harling Collection."

"I don't want to 'get my hands' on it. I want access to it—a chance to study it for anything it might contain pertinent to my work."

"Meaning anything on Priscilla Marsh or Cotton Harling."

"That's right."

"Then you're saying you didn't realize the Harling Collection is rumored to include a valuable, rare copy of the Declaration of Independence."

He could see his words sinking in, along with all their ramifications, and was suddenly glad they'd kissed before he'd brought up the touchy subject.

"Oh, I see what you're getting at." She bit off each word, anger visibly boiling to the surface. Her green eyes were hot, almost liquid. "You're accusing me of breaking into your uncle's apartment in an attempt to find the Harling Collection or some clue as to its location, in order to steal this Declaration of Independence and make a handy profit for myself at Harling expense."

Win scooped pasta onto her plate, and then onto his, maintaining his calm. "Only Uncle Jonathan doesn't know where the Harling Collection is. No one does. No one can even verify it exists, or ever did." His gaze fell upon her; it would be easier if she weren't so damned attractive. "Unless you have a new lead you're keeping to yourself."

She gave him a haughty look. "Why would you think that?"

He shrugged. "You're a scholar. You're good at doing research. Who knows what you might have ferreted out in the last week?"

"We're in quite a position, aren't we?"

Her voice rasped with not very well-suppressed fury, although, given her behavior this past week, Win couldn't understand why she was so irritated. Under the circumstances, he felt his suspicions were quite natural.

"By pretending to be a Harling," she went on, speaking tightly, "I shattered any trust you might have had in me, no matter how innocuous my intentions or how understandable my reasons. You still can't believe me. Won't believe me. Then there's the impact of three centuries of Marsh-Harling conflict...."

"It hasn't had any impact on me." Win tried his pasta; not bad. Hannah might calm down if she ate some. "Maybe it's had an impact on you, but not on me. I was hardly even aware of the extent of the grudge you Marshes hold against us."

"You're a Harling...."

"But not a Bostonian. I was born and raised in New York. I

only came to Boston last year, when I bought this house and moved my offices.''

She didn't seem particularly interested in his personal history, but he found himself wondering about hers. Where did Hannah Marsh live? How? And what made her tick?

''You had to know about Cotton and Priscilla,'' she said.

He smiled. ''You talk about them as if you know them.''

''That's my job, to feel as if I know the people I write about. It's pure arrogance to believe I do, but I have at least to have some sense of who they were. I have to feel that if they suddenly came to life in my kitchen, I'd recognize them.'' She caught herself and took a breath. ''Not that I have to explain myself to you.''

''Of course not. Yes, I was aware of Cotton and Priscilla, but I haven't participated in perpetuating three-hundred-year-old grudges.''

''Well, aren't you high and mighty? I've been doing everything I can to maintain my objectivity. I don't have a personal grudge against the Harlings. And if you don't have anything against the Marshes, why check into your family's absurd claim to Marsh Point?''

''It's not absurd,'' he said offhandedly. ''Actually, it's rather well-founded.''

Her look would have shot holes in him if it could have. ''There, you see? You're no saint, Win Harling.''

''Oh,'' he said playfully, ''that I'm definitely not.''

He could see her recognizing his words as the multipronged threat he'd intended them to be. Even with the pasta and more wine, he could still taste her mouth, imagine the taste of her skin.

''The point is,'' she said a little hoarsely, ''where do we go from here?''

His gaze held her. In the old, candlelit room, she could have passed for her doomed ancestor. But Win couldn't make up for the wrongs of Cotton Harling. He had his uncle to consider. ''Trust is earned.''

Hannah sprang to her feet, visibly indignant. "I didn't break into your uncle's apartment. I had no idea until tonight the Harling Collection might include anything of monetary value." She threw down her napkin, resisting an impulse, Win thought, to try to whip his head off with it. "There's nothing I can do to make you believe me. I'm not even going to try. Good night, Win. Please tell your uncle I hope he's all right."

And that was that.

Off she stomped to the front door, yanking it open and slamming it shut on her way out.

An angry woman, Hannah Marsh.

She hadn't eaten so much as a pea pod of her dinner. Win sighed and got up. He supposed he ought to go after her and apologize. But for what?

And what bothered her more? he wondered. His accusing her of breaking and entering or kissing her? Wanting her as much and as obviously as he did?

How the hell was he supposed to know for sure what she was up to? His first loyalty was to Uncle Jonathan, not to some fair-haired scholar with a bee in her bonnet about his ancestors.

Yet Hannah Marsh was so much more. He sensed it, knew it. There was a depth and complexity to her he hadn't even begun to probe.

He gritted his teeth at the unbidden thought of just how much of Ms. Marsh he wanted to probe....

"Damn," he muttered. Now it was his turn to throw down his napkin and pound from the room. He'd lost his appetite.

The doorbell rang.

"Hannah?"

He headed for the entry and pulled open the heavy front door, only to find his elderly uncle leaning on his cane and looking none the worse for wear for his day's ordeal. Without preamble the old man said, "The damned thief did get away with something."

"What? You don't have much of value...."

"Anne Harling's diary."

Win stared. Now what? "Who the hell's Anne Harling?"

"Your great-great-aunt, remember? The one who gathered together the Harling Collection. She died in 1892."

Wonderful. "Uncle Jonathan…"

"Invite me in, Winthrop. We need to talk."

THE NEXT MORNING, Hannah arrived at the New England Athenaeum within five minutes of its opening and asked to see Preston Fowler, in private. He brought her into his office, where she admitted to him that she was not Hannah Harling of the Ohio Harlings.

"I'm a Marsh," she said baldly.

He paled.

"Hannah Marsh."

"The biographer?"

At least he'd heard of her. She nodded.

He sighed, looking slightly ill. "My, my."

"I'm sorry I lied to you. It was just an expedient. I didn't think I could use the facilities here if you knew I was a Marsh." She swallowed. "I didn't think you'd risk offending the Harlings."

Fowler winced. "Your two families…the Harlings and the Marshes…"

"The history between us hasn't affected—and won't affect—my work," she said crisply, trying to sound like the professional she was. "I didn't want my being a Marsh to come into play. Hence my ruse. I'm very sorry."

"Oh, dear."

"The Harlings know the truth now, and I've made it clear to them that you were in no way a party to my deceit." She sounded so stuffy and contrite, but in fact she was neither. What she wanted to do was tell Win Harling to go to hell and Preston Fowler to have a little more integrity than to suck up to rich Bostonians for donations. "That's all I came to say."

Fowler tilted back his chair, placing the tips of his fingers together to make a tent. He sighed again. "How awkward."

"It's not awkward, Mr. Fowler. Not at all. I'm leaving Boston today. All you have to do is carry on with your work and pretend I never existed.''

He nodded. ''Very well. What about your biography of Priscilla? Will it go forward now that this has happened?''

''Of course. Why shouldn't it? Most of my research is completed.''

''But the Harlings...''

Hannah sat forward. ''I don't care what the Harlings want or think.''

With that she apologized once more, assured him no harm had been done to his venerable institution and headed out. Yesterday's clouds and rain had been pushed off over the Atlantic, leaving blue sky and warm air in their wake. Hannah breathed in deep lungfuls of it before crossing the Public Garden and cutting past the Ritz Carlton Hotel into Boston's Back Bay, straight for Marlborough Street.

Jonathan Harling asked for her name twice over the intercom. ''Marsh,'' she said both times. ''It's Hannah Marsh.''

He buzzed her in, anyway.

''Come on in,'' he said, opening his apartment door. ''I've been wondering when you'd show up. Think the roof'll cave in with a Marsh and Harling under it? Though I suppose if it didn't last night, with you and Win, we should be all right.''

The glitter in his eye suggested—although Hannah couldn't be certain—he had a fair idea that she and his nephew had more than simply shared the same roof. But she had vowed to stop thinking about Win's mouth on hers, his hard maleness thrust against her. She would not be at the mercy of her hormones.

Nonetheless, every fiber of her body—of her being—said she wanted more from Jonathan's nephew than a kiss, more than a heady embrace. She wanted to feel his skin against hers, his maleness inside her.

She wanted him to make love to her...with her.

There was no point in denying the obvious. Her abrupt departure last night had had less to do with his disgusting suspicion—his talk of the Declaration of Independence and of larceny—than with her ongoing, unstoppable, outrageous physical response to him. His dark, penetrating gaze had filled her with erotic notions. His hands, as he'd lighted the candles, had left her breathless, conjured up images of his touch on her mouth, her breasts, between her legs. Just looking at him had made her think of the two of them together in bed, or just right there on the dining room floor.

Such wild, irresponsible thinking had to stop.

It just had to. It was perverse to want a man she couldn't possibly have. A man who, even as her body ached for him, believed she was a thief, a grudge-holding Marsh, a woman he couldn't trust.

Jonathan Harling's apartment looked tidy, if cluttered, no evidence of a thorough ransacking still apparent. He offered Hannah a seat on an overstuffed, overly firm sofa. He himself flopped into a cushioned rocker. He was casually dressed, in a cardigan frayed at the elbows and chinos that must have seen Harry Truman into office. Hannah didn't feel the least bit out of place in her leggings and giant Maine sweatshirt.

"What can I do for you?" Jonathan Harling asked.

"I wanted to tell you how sorry I am about yesterday. Win told me. I hope you know I wasn't involved. I—" She broke off awkwardly, then decided she might as well get on with it. "You know by now I'm a Marsh and there are no Ohio Harlings."

He grunted and waved a hand. "I knew that days ago."

"Do you hate me for being a Marsh?"

"Nope. I don't trust you, but I don't hate you."

A fine distinction. Hannah let it pass.

"Be stupid to trust you," Jonathan added.

"I suppose, given the history of our two families, that's not unreasonable. Also given my own behavior. I'm leaving Boston today—"

"Win know?"

She bristled. "Why should he?"

"I didn't say he should or shouldn't," the old man replied, matching her gruffness. "Just asked if he did."

"No. I haven't seen him since last night."

"You going to tell him?"

"I don't see any reason to tell your nephew anything, and I didn't come here to discuss him. I..." She frowned. "What are you looking at?"

"You. Trying to figure you out. How come you go all snotnosed professor when someone asks you a personal question?"

"I'm not a professor."

He rocked back in his chair. "You and Win got something going?"

"Mr. Harling..."

"He threw me out last night after I started asking him personal questions. I do it all the time. Pride myself on being able to say anything I want to my own nephew, but I mentioned you, and out on my ear I went." He folded his scrawny hands in his lap. "Must be you two got something going."

Only Hannah's years of dealing with her exasperating Cousin Thackeray kept her from gaping at Jonathan Harling or throwing something at him. Or politely leaving. "Dr. Harling, I suspect your rather salty speech pattern is a total fake. You're a scholar yourself."

He waved a hand dismissively.

"Legal history. You taught at Harvard for fifty years."

"What, you writing a biography of me? I thought your only subjects were dead people."

She couldn't suppress a smile. "You're not dead yet."

"Glad you noticed."

"Look, I just came by to tell you I had nothing to do with yesterday's break-in. I only wanted to look at the Harling Collection for research purposes. I didn't know it might include a valuable copy of the Declaration of Independence. And I'm going home." She climbed to her feet. "It's been interesting meeting you. Should I send you a copy of my biography of Priscilla Marsh when it comes out?"

He lifted his bony shoulders, clearly feigning disinterest. "If you remember."

"Oh, I'll remember."

She told him not to bother seeing her to the door, but halfway there she felt his presence behind her and spun around. He was leaning on his cane, alert, still handsome in his own way. "Will you be mentioning Anne Harling?"

"Who?"

"You heard me."

"Yes, I did, but I'm not familiar..." She paused, searching her memory. "Cotton Harling's brother was married to a woman named Anne, wasn't he? She died before Priscilla was executed, as I recall."

"I'm talking about my great-aunt."

Hannah frowned, uncertain where he was leading her.

"She never married. Lived in the Harling House on Louisburg Square until her death, late in the last century. Interesting woman. She's the one who supposedly gathered the family documents together into the Harling Collection."

"I see," Hannah said, although she didn't.

Jonathan smiled knowingly. "Her diary was stolen from this apartment yesterday."

His words only took a few seconds to penetrate. "Oh, my. And you think...it would seem logical that I..."

"That you stole it, yes."

"But I didn't."

"So you say."

"Win... Have you told your nephew?"

"Told him last night."

And he hadn't broken her door down at dawn to demand an explanation. Maybe he didn't care nearly as much about her supposedly larcenous tendencies as much as he claimed. Or maybe hadn't liked the idea of dragging her out of bed at the crack of dawn. With his blood boiling and hers about to boil, who knows where it would have lead?

"I thought perhaps that was why you were leaving town," Jonathan Harling said, looking decidedly smug.

Hannah threw back her shoulders. "It isn't."

"Win's not going to scare you off, eh?"

"Nobody will."

"Then you're going to stay?"

She felt Jonathan Harling's trap snap shut around her and knew all she could do was wriggle and complain. Or chew her leg off. Figuratively speaking. "You haven't left me any choice."

He grinned. "That was the whole idea."

WIN WAS WAITING, slouching against Hannah's apartment door, when she rounded the corner of Pinckney Street. He could hear her sharp intake of breath when she spotted him. His own reaction was more under control; he'd had a few extra seconds to adjust to her imminent presence. He watched her slow down, saw a wariness creep into her gait. He also noticed how her hair tangled in the afternoon wind and glistened in the bright sun.

"I thought you'd be working," she said, coming closer.

"I left early."

"Is it costing you?"

He smiled. "In more ways than you probably would want to know."

"Try me."

Oh, lady, he thought. "I'd better resist. Let's just say I don't take many afternoons off. Mind if I come in?"

Without answering, she unlocked the heavy black door that led to the two basement apartments. The main entrance to the building was up the steps to their right, the first floor elevated, so that Hannah's borrowed apartment was almost at ground level. She unlocked that door, too. The apartment was predictably small, cluttered with her laptop computer, index cards, spiral notebooks, folders, papers, books.

"Look," she began, going straight into the kitchen area and filling a kettle with water, "if this is about Anne Harling's missing diary, I've already spoken to your uncle. He told me everything. I don't know what happened to it. I honestly don't. I didn't steal it.''

''Did he tell you she was the one who gathered together the Harling Collection?''

She nodded, setting the kettle upon the stove. She dried her hands and headed back into the living area, where Win was clearly considering just where he might sit. Not one surface was free. She settled the matter for him, lifting a pile of folders from a chair and dropping them onto the floor. ''Have a seat. Would you like tea?''

''No, thank you.''

What a life she must lead, he thought, sitting down. Steeped in the past. Inundated with books, documents, paper. Did she have friends? Romances? Or was her strength the past, not the present? He wondered about her and men.

''I borrowed this place from a friend of mine. She's taking my cottage on Marsh Point sometime this summer.'' Hannah returned to the kitchen area, banging around as she pulled out a cup, saucer, strainer and teapot—anxious, he thought, to stay busy. ''I can always stay with Cousin Thackeray if I can't get away when she wants the place.''

''Who's he?''

''Thackeray Marsh. He reminds me somewhat of your Uncle Jonathan.''

''Lucky you,'' Win said, amused.

She laughed. ''Thackeray would hang me out to dry for saying that. He's not much on Harlings. But...'' Her shoulders lifted, as if she couldn't quite express her feelings. ''I owe him.''

''For what?''

''Saving me.''

And she yanked open the refrigerator, blocking Win's view of her. She had said more than she'd meant to. More, certainly, than she felt he deserved to know. But it wasn't enough. He wanted to know more, everything.

''You're sure you don't want tea? I can make coffee, too. I have one of those one-cup drip things.''

"I'm fine. Thanks. How did your cousin save you, Hannah?"

"After my mother died five years ago—my father was already dead—I found myself wanting to see Marsh Point, and I met him. He's a historian, too. He understood me, knew I needed roots, a place to belong." She shut the refrigerator door and glared at Win. "I won't let you take Marsh Point away from him."

He said nothing. Her relationship with her cousin, he sensed, was much like his own with his uncle. What else might they have in common?

She set about her tea making. Win hated the stuff himself, but any more coffee today and he'd spin off to the moon. After Hannah's abrupt departure last night and Uncle Jonathan's peculiar visit, Win had taken a long walk up and down the meandering streets of Beacon Hill, trying to piece his thoughts and feelings into some kind of rational whole. But there were too many variables, too many bizarre, uncontrollable longings. Back home, he'd slept for a couple of hours, but had been up again at dawn, making a pot of coffee, seeing Hannah Marsh with him in his kitchen, imagining them up together at dawn after a night of lovemaking. Wondering if she really was a lying thief.

"So why," she said thoughtfully, carrying her tea into the living area, "do you think Anne Harling's diary was stolen?"

"I don't know."

"Come on. You have a dozen reasons why you think I stole it. I presume that's why you're here, to interrogate me on the possibilities."

"I'm here to talk to you. That's all. No accusations, no offensive questions, just straightforward talk."

"We'll be logical and rational."

He ignored her sarcasm. "Right."

"Is that what you tell your clients? Let's be logical and rational about your financial portfolio'?"

"Sometimes. Other times logic and rationality aren't at issue. Emotion is, wants and needs that go to the heart of a client's being, what he or she is about, what makes them feel alive.

Sometimes a client just needs my encouragement to go for the impulsive and outrageous.''

"All in a day's work, I suppose," she said lightly, but he could see that his words had had an effect. Their kiss had been impulsive and maybe even outrageous. It was still on her mind, just as it was on his.

She dropped to the floor and sat cross-legged amid her scattered research materials. Uncle Jonathan's apartment hadn't looked much worse than this yesterday, after it had been ransacked. But she seemed relaxed enough, setting her cup and saucer upon an enormous dictionary, muttering something about computer dictionaries just not being the same, no comparison. She ran her fingers through her hair, working out several small tangles.

"If I were going to break into your uncle's apartment specifically to steal Anne Harling's diary," she said, "don't you think I'd have gone out of my way to make it look like a real robbery and stolen a bunch of other stuff?"

"Not necessarily. You might have thought Uncle Jonathan wouldn't miss the diary until too late, if at all. You might have thought he didn't even realize he had it."

"Quite a risk."

"Maybe, maybe not. If Uncle Jonathan did realize the diary was missing, he would assume the other things had been taken as a smoke screen. If you were going to get caught, better with just an old diary in your possession than the family silver, so to speak."

"The 'you' here being a hypothetical you, not me."

He smiled. "Of course."

"So the thief took a chance."

"Possibly."

"It's also possible, wouldn't you say, that the diary isn't missing, that your uncle got rid of it years ago, or maybe never had it to begin with and just forgot."

"Obviously you don't know Uncle Jonathan, but never mind. How do you explain the break-in?"

She shrugged. "He's on the first floor of a nice building. He, or someone else in his building, could have left the front door ajar, and our would-be thief took advantage. He got into your uncle's apartment, pulled the place apart, didn't find any ready cash or easily fenced valuables and took off, cutting his losses."

"Highly coincidental, don't you think?"

"Life is full of coincidences." She drank some of her tea, watching him over the rim of her cup. "What's so special about Anne Harling's diary?"

"Nothing, so far as I know. That's the point. It's what *you* think is special about it that's important." Win stretched his legs. "Suppose you believe it contains a clue as to what happened to the Harling Collection."

She shook her head. "Ridiculous. The Harlings being the Harlings, they'd have discovered the clue decades ago and skimmed off anything of value in the collection themselves."

"I can't argue with that. But maybe it's a clue you—"

"Our thief."

"As you wish. Maybe you're the only one who understands the significance of the clue."

"Pretty farfetched."

"But the risk of breaking into Uncle Jonathan's apartment would have to be worth the potential benefit. Don't you agree?"

"I still like my idea about it being a coincidence."

"That's because it lets you off the hook." Win rose and walked over to where she sat, looking so casual and honest with her cup of tea. So unselfconsciously sexy. He lifted a manila folder marked Puritan Hangings of the 1690s. Charming subject. "You've been steeping yourself in Marsh-Harling history for how long?"

"I began work on Priscilla's biography last September."

"And you've been in Boston over a week, immersing yourself in three centuries of history that you can feel and touch. You've traveled the same streets Priscilla Marsh traveled. You've seen what Cotton Harling's descendants have become."

She set her teacup upon the floor beside her, a slight tremble in her hand. "I don't know what you're getting at, but I'm a professional historian. I don't get emotionally involved in my subjects."

"You're human, Hannah," Win said softly, reaching out and touching her hair. "Your mother's mother's mother's mother. How far back does it go? Does it even matter? Priscilla Marsh was wrongly hanged, and here in Boston you've been immersed in that wrong. It would be understandable if you let yourself get carried away."

"Into ransacking an old man's apartment?"

"And other things," he said deliberately.

She wriggled her legs apart and shot up. She appeared ready to bolt. But there was nowhere to go. This was her apartment, her space. And he hadn't moved an inch. To get past him, she would have to leap over stacks of books and files, a fact he could see her assessing, processing.

"You can't run from what's going on between us," he said, hearing his voice outwardly calm but laced with tension, desire—and determination. "Neither can I."

"I'm going back to Maine," she blurted.

"I figured as much."

"If you want to search my things before I leave..."

"If you did take the diary, you'd be too smart to leave it here. You wouldn't risk my showing up and tearing apart the place until I found it."

"Was that your plan when you came here?"

She held her chin raised, haughty and unafraid—or at least she was trying to appear so. Her eyes gave her away. But she wasn't afraid of him. He could see that. She was afraid, he thought, only of herself, of their muddled feelings about each other, on top of the very clear, obvious and tenacious physical attraction between them. Emotions, not just overexcited hormones, were at work and at stake.

"No," he said. "This was."

He tucked one finger under her chin, giving her a chance to

tell him to go to hell, but she didn't. He breathed deeply, knowing he was crazy. They both were.

"Hannah," he whispered, and closed his mouth over hers.

Her lips were smooth and soft and if not welcoming him, at least not turning him away. He tasted them. She tasted back.

"I wish I didn't want this to happen," she whispered into his mouth.

"I know."

But it was happening, and neither of them wanted it to stop. He pulled her to him, felt her hands around his middle, her slender body pressed against him. Her tongue slid into his mouth, tentatively at first, then more boldly. He could feel every fiber of him responding...aching...wanting....

And then it was over.

He couldn't say if it was he or she who pulled back. He wasn't sure it mattered. He only knew that within too short a time he was back on Pinckney Street's brick sidewalk, looking at the Charles River in the distance and wondering what in blue hell had happened.

She had wanted him. He had wanted her.

So why the devil wasn't he in there, making love to Hannah Marsh?

He raked one hand through his hair and heaved a sigh. He hadn't been motivated by any false nobility or nebulous impression that making love to her wasn't, deep down, what she wanted, as well. And it sure as hell wasn't the missing diary of some aunt who'd been dead for a hundred years or his eccentric, crotchety old uncle that had stopped him.

It was, he thought, very simple.

He was falling for Hannah Marsh and didn't want to make a wrong move.

And right now, taking into account not only the history that had brought them to this moment but all he didn't know about this woman, who could seem so outrageous and cocky one minute and so prim and proper the next, scooping her up and carting her off to bed would be a mistake. Never mind how much he wanted it. Never mind how much she wanted it.

First things first, he told himself. First he had to learn more about Hannah Priscilla Marsh. Find out what made her tick. Then...

By God, he thought. Then there'd be no stopping him.

7

"YOU'RE HOME EARLY," Thackeray said when Hannah reported in upon her return to southern Maine. "I knew your common sense would prevail."

She smiled. "It wasn't common sense, it was self-preservation."

"Whatever works."

When Hannah looked at her elderly cousin, she couldn't help but think of Jonathan Harling in Boston. On the surface all the two old men had in common was their age, but Hannah suspected they were much more similar deep down than either would care to admit.

He shoved a cat off the chair near the fire in his front room. It was cold, dank and foggy on Marsh Point, but Hannah had already been out to the rocks and tasted the ocean. She was home.

While she had a small winterized cottage close to the water's edge, Thackeray had a bona fide house, built in 1880, with high ceilings, leaded glass windows and four fireplaces. His wife, a native of Maine, had died ten years ago and they'd had no children, but still he'd managed to clutter up the place. He persisted in subscribing to a dozen magazines, plus *The Wall Street Journal* and *The New York Times*. He refused to read any of the Boston papers, lest he run across the Harling name, be it a reference to a live one or a dead one. Boston, he maintained, had never been kind to the Marsh family.

"Tea?" he offered.

"No, thank you. I just wanted to say hi."

"Anything to report?"

She decided not to tell him she had kissed a Harling, but filled him in on everything else, including the two Jonathan Winthrop Harlings' suspicion that she was after the rumored copy of the Declaration of Independence. Cousin Thackeray snorted at the very idea. She laughed, appreciating his unconditional support. But it had always been there, as consistent as the tide.

"What're you going to do now?" he asked.

Exorcise Win Harling from my mind....

"Start writing, I guess," she said, hating the note of melancholy in her voice. Her life would never be the same after Boston and her brush with the Harlings. "I've done more than enough research to get started, at least. I can't help but feel I ran away from Boston, but I hope that will pass."

"You exercised good judgment, that's all. You didn't run away from a thing."

No, not from a thing. From Win.

"You're not the type," Cousin Thackeray added, clearly convinced, as always, that any Marsh who deliberately avoided a Harling was just doing the right thing.

Hannah wished she shared his certainty. Instead she could only think about the desire Win Harling stirred up in her with his kisses, his touch, his very presence. And it was not just a matter of physical desire. In spite of their differences, she had felt an emotional connection starting to grow between them, something beyond flaming hormones.

But staying had become impossible. She simply hadn't been willing to risk the Harlings finding some way to blame her for Jonathan's ransacked apartment and the missing Anne Harling diary. She couldn't risk reigniting their outrage over having lost their beautiful point in southern Maine to a Marsh. She couldn't risk their finding some loophole—and Win was just the high-minded, bulldog type to find one—that would put it back in their hands.

She couldn't risk falling in love with Win Harling.

She shook her head. No. She really couldn't. She had her work. It would fill her mind, once she got into it.

"Hannah?"

Smiling, she kissed her cousin on the cheek and patted his hand. "It's good to be back."

UNCLE JONATHAN had spread a detailed map of Maine on Win's table when he arrived home from work, the evening after Hannah Marsh bolted. It was after eight. He could see his uncle had helped himself to the leftovers of the aborted dinner. The old man had also polished off the last of the wine.

"Trying to drown your sorrows in work, eh?" Uncle Jonathan said, cocking his head at his nephew.

Win slung his suit coat over the back of a folding chair. "I had to catch up on a few things."

"Distracting woman, that Hannah Marsh. If I didn't know better, I'd say old Cotton offed her ancestor, just so he could get his mind back on track."

"That's ridiculous," Win said.

"Of course it is, but if Priscilla Marsh looked anything like your Hannah, she made one hell of a Puritan." Uncle Jonathan abruptly turned his attention back to his map, running one finger down Maine's jagged coastline. "There's another helping of that anemic spaghetti in the refrigerator."

"Thanks, but I'm not hungry."

"Going to starve yourself over a woman?"

Win sighed. "I had a late lunch with a client. Uncle Jonathan, what are you doing here?"

"Besides acquainting myself with the pitiful existence you endure here?"

"Besides that," Win said, unable to stop his mouth twitching. He never quite knew when to take his uncle seriously.

"For heaven's sake, how much do decent chairs cost? You know, the Harlings have never been cheap. Frugal, yes, but not cheap."

"This from a man who hasn't bought a suit since 1970?"

"Don't need one."

"The map, Uncle Jonathan."

"Oh, yes." Placing one hand on the small of his back, he stretched, clearly a delaying tactic. He put the half-moon glasses he had hanging around his neck upon the end of his nose and peered more closely at the map. Then he tapped a spot in southern Maine. "That's Marsh Point."

Win leaned over and took a look. "So it is."

"You can take Interstate 95 north to Kennebunkport, then get off on Route 1. There'll be signs you can follow."

"'You' as in me?"

"Of course."

"Why would I go to Marsh Point?"

Uncle Jonathan exhaled, pursing his thin lips in disgust. "Do I have to spell everything out for you, Winthrop? Hannah Marsh is there."

"I know, but what—"

"She's probably curled up by the fire with her stolen view of the ocean, studying Anne Harling's diary for clues about where she can lay her greedy little hands on the Harling Collection and our copy of the Declaration of Independence."

Win stood back and crossed his arms over his chest, trying to figure out his uncle. "I thought you liked her."

"Did I say that? I'm strictly neutral. I don't like her or dislike her. I can objectively admit she's an attractive woman who might discombobulate a stubborn monk like yourself, but that's not to say I trust her." He yanked off his smudged glasses. "She can't help being born a Marsh. It's in her genes to want whatever she can get from us."

"How do you know what she wants is the copy of the Declaration of Independence?"

"I don't. Maybe it's just you."

Win scowled.

"The point is," Uncle Jonathan went on impatiently, "you can't wait for her to make the next move."

"Uncle, Uncle," Win said, "who says I'm waiting?"

WITHIN TWO DAYS Hannah knew she would have to take another crack at the Harlings of Boston. Specifically, at J. Winthrop Harling.

Although she'd resolved to put him out of her mind, she had

done a little research on him, thanks to computer modems, her local library and Cousin Thackeray's pack-rat habits. Most interesting was the article on him she'd unearthed in *The Wall Street Journal*. It painted the picture of a financial wizard even richer than Hannah had guessed. He had surprised no one by leaving New York for Boston. It was apparently his destiny to restore the Harlings' position as an active financial and social force in the community. Having a prestigious name wasn't enough for him. His purchase of the Harling House on Louisburg Square was, he was quoted as saying, only the beginning, a small step.

Cotton Harling's hanging of an innocent woman back in 1693 wasn't even mentioned. Steeped as she was in Priscilla's story, Hannah found this omission insulting. "How 'bout a little perspective?" she complained to Cousin Thackeray.

He sniffed. "Precisely what the Marshes have been saying for three hundred years. One doesn't begrudge the Harlings their successes or overly enjoy their failures, but putting them in context, it seems to me, isn't too much to ask."

All the same, the article wasn't about a seventeenth-century Harling, but a late-twentieth-century one. Hannah had to admit there was a difference.

She had also learned that J. Winthrop Harling had never been married. And when he did marry, he would—according to rampant speculation and unnamed sources—likely choose a woman who could further his dream of reclaiming his family's lost heritage. It sounded pretty calculating to Hannah, but then, Win Harling could be one formidably calculating man.

Except for their kiss. That hadn't been calculated.

Or had it?

"Thackeray," she said, "there's something I've been meaning to bring up. It's about the Harling Collection."

He groaned, throwing down his newspaper. He had the business section out, but Hannah knew he'd been reading the comics. "I thought you'd given up on that angle."

"Did you know a Marsh had been accused of stealing it?"

"Even were we all dead and gone for a hundred years, the Harlings will blame us for anything that happens to them that they don't like."

"I'm not talking about us. I'm talking about your Uncle Thackeray, the man you were named for. Not long after the Marshes moved to Maine, the Harlings accused him of having stolen a collection of valuable family papers."

"Where'd you hear this?"

"I found mention of it in an old Maine newspaper."

Her elderly cousin snatched up his paper and flipped back to the comics, not bothering to pretend he was reading about the latest stock market tumble. "So?"

"So I'm just wondering if things between the Harlings and the Marshes aren't exactly what they seem."

His eyes, as green as hers, narrowed at her over the top of his newspaper. "What have I been trying to tell you these past weeks?"

"Thackeray, did the Marshes steal the Harling Collection?"

He didn't even look up. Chuckling, he wagged a finger at her and made her read a comic strip he found particularly amusing. Hannah didn't laugh. She thought her cousin was being deliberately obtuse.

To clear her head and sort out her thoughts, she headed out to the rocks. The tide was coming in, and the wind out of the north was brisk and cold, but the sun glistened on the water. Hannah climbed down below the waterline, out of sight from Thackeray's house or her own cottage. Careful not to slip on the barnacle-covered rocks, she squatted in front of a yard-wide tide pool soon to be inundated. Waves swirled and frothed all around her. Wearing her jeans, sweatshirt and sneakers, she felt more like herself than she had in weeks.

A crunching sound on the rocks behind her startled her, and she started to fall backward, putting out a hand to brace herself. She felt barnacles slicing into her palm and cursed. It was probably just a damned sea gull. Obviously she wasn't used to being back in the country yet, away from the city of the Harlings.

"I thought for a minute there you were heading for the sharks," Win Harling said above her.

"You!"

He jumped lightly from a dry rock, landing next to her tide pool. He grinned. "Me."

Hannah regained her balance and shot to her feet, the wind whipping her hair. Caught completely off guard and seeing Win, so damned breathtaking, so incredibly sexy, so *unexpected,* she needed a few extra seconds of recovery time. "I thought you were a sea gull...."

He laughed. "I suppose people have thought worse about me. Are you all right?"

"Fine."

But he took her hand into his own and examined the scrapes from the barnacles. The skin hadn't broken. His touch was gentle, careful.

"I'll stick it in the ocean," she said, still breathless. "Ice-cold salt water's a great cure for just about anything."

"Anything?"

She saw the heat in his eyes. "Win, we need to talk...."

But talk, she knew, would have to come later. He lifted her into his arms while the wind churned the waves at their feet, spraying them with a fine, cold mist, but all she could feel was the warmth of wanting him.

"I'd hoped I could think with you out of town," he murmured, "but I couldn't. All I could think about was you—and this."

She tilted up her chin until her mouth met his, their lips brushing tentatively at first, then hungrily, eagerly. His hands slipped under her Windbreaker to the warm skin at the small of her back, and she sank against his chest, trying, even on the cold, windswept rocks, to meld with his body.

Then a wave crashed into the tide pool and soaked them to their ankles, its icy water a shock to their overheated systems.

Win swore.

Hannah smiled and brushed strands of hair from her face. "Welcome to Maine."

HANNAH'S COTTAGE was about what Win had expected. Its cedar shingles weathered to a soft gray, it stood amid tall pines above the rocks. In the tiny living room, the picture window provided a view of the ocean. A fire in the stone fireplace was just dying down as they entered. Hannah pulled off her wet sneakers and socks and set them in front of the fire while she stirred the red-hot ashes. She threw on some kindling while Win, also barefoot by now, wandered down the short hall, taking note of the two small bedrooms and bath, then back up the hall and into the kitchen, all knotty pine and copper-bottomed pans. The entire floor area would probably fit into his dining room and foyer. It would be sort of like sticking a map of New England inside a map of Texas.

In contrast to the sparsity of his furnishings and the impersonal, motel-like quality of his spacious rooms on Louisburg Square, every inch of Hannah's cottage was crammed with stuff. Pot holders, hummingbird magnets, wildlife wall calendars, samplers cross-stitched with silly sayings, old quilts, throw pillows, odd bits of knitting, photo albums, pottery bowls and teapots; all of it vied for space with the mountains of books, files, notebooks, clippings and office equipment.

The only order he could sense was indirect: Hannah Marsh seemed absolutely at home here. She padded about with an ease that he hadn't sensed in Boston.

He spotted a yellowed newspaper picture of himself, then saw that it was the vile profile from *The Wall Street Journal*. He hadn't agreed with the writer's highly subjective, not to mention uncomplimentary, slant on his motives for making money. Couldn't a man simply be drawn to a job that he did well and that also happened to pay well?

The fire caught and Hannah stood back, appraising her handiwork with satisfaction. Or relief? Perhaps it had occurred to her that he might have suggested they manage without a fire.

"Nice place," Win said. "How long have you lived here?"

"Almost five years."

"Before that?"

"Oh, here and there. I traveled a lot."

She wasn't so much being evasive, he thought, as cryptic, holding back a part of herself from him. But that was all right. He had conducted his own research into the life of Hannah Priscilla Marsh, finding a thorough, if brief, biography of her in *The New York Times Book Review*'s critique of her study of Martha Washington. Hannah, the only child of an army officer and his would-be artist wife, had led the peripatetic life of a member of a military family until her father's death in a helicopter crash when she was fourteen. She and her mother had then wandered from art school to art school, until Hannah had finally gone off to college. Her mother had eventually settled in Arizona, making her living as a painter and teaching as a volunteer in low-income neighborhoods. Her death five years ago had left Hannah alone, until she'd found her cousin and Marsh Point...and that elusive sense of belonging Win thought he understood.

These details were just a few important pieces of the puzzle that was Hannah Marsh.

"How's your uncle doing?" she asked, her tone conversational.

"Just fine, thanks."

"Did he ever report his break-in to the police?"

Win thought he detected a note of suspicion in her tone. "No, why?"

"Just curious."

More than curious, he decided. "You have a theory, don't you?"

"Nope."

She shoveled free a space on the sofa for him and disappeared into the kitchen without another word. Win sighed and sat down. The fire crackled, and he could hear the rhythmic crashing of the waves on the rocks. It was an almost erotic sound. Or maybe his mind was just being driven in that direction.

Hannah, Hannah.

She wandered back in a few minutes with a tray of mugs, teapot, English butter cookies and crackers. She set them down upon an old apple crate she used as a coffee table, atop a stack of overstuffed manila folders. "Be back in a sec," she said, and disappeared again. When she returned, she held a pottery pitcher, sugar bowl and a tea strainer, which she set over one of the mugs.

She poured the tea, and he immediately noted that it was purple. Honest-to-God ordinary tea was bad enough.

She smiled. "It's black currant—very soothing."

"Do I look as if I need soothing?"

Color spread into her cheeks. Seeing her discomfort—her awareness—was almost worth having to drink purple tea. "It's great with milk and sugar," she added quickly, "almost like eating a cobbler."

The "almost" was a stretch, but at least he could drink the stuff without gagging.

"Do you like it?" she asked, seating herself on a rattan rocker.

"It tastes like tea with something that shouldn't be in tea."

"I've been drinking more herbal teas lately."

"Not sleeping well?"

Her eyes, shining and so damned green, met his, and she smiled, knowing, he guessed, what he was thinking. "You flatter yourself, Win Harling."

"I'm not keeping you awake nights?"

"Nope."

He laughed. "That's two lies—or at best half truths—so far. Want to go for a third?"

She scowled at him, sipping her tea, clearly savoring it, rather than gulping it down, as he was his, in an effort to finish the job.

Leaning forward, he said, "Tell me you're not glad to see me."

"Are you asking me?"

"Yes, I'm asking you. Are you glad to see me?"

A smile tugged at the corners of her mouth. "What'll you do if you believe I'm lying?"

"That would be three lies in a row. I don't know. I guess I'd figure something out."

"Then the answer is yes. Yes, I'm glad to see you." She set her mug upon one knee, everything about her challenging him. "Now it's for you to decide if I'm lying or not."

He took one last swallow of the purple tea and set down his mug, then leaned forward again, so that his knee touched hers, and brushed one finger across her lower lip. It was warm and moist. Her eyes were wide with desire.

"I think a part of you isn't lying," he said, "and a part is."

"Do you know which part is which?"

He could hear the catch in her voice, the breathlessness. She had pulled off her sweatshirt; underneath it she wore a long-sleeved navy T-shirt. The fabric wasn't particularly thin, but he could see the twin points of her nipples, whether still from the cold or in reaction to him, he couldn't be sure. He made no attempt to disguise his interest.

"I think I do," he said, and this time he could hear the catch, the breathlessness in his own voice. He raised his eyes to hers. "Time for one part to listen to the other, wouldn't you say?"

"Should my mind listen to my body or my body listen to my mind?"

"Decide, Hannah. Decide, because your purple tea hasn't soothed me one little bit."

He skimmed her nipples with his fingertips, inhaling deeply, wanting her more than he'd ever wanted any woman. But he knew he had to hold back. Knew he couldn't touch her again, because if he did, he would be lost. He would never get Hannah Marsh out of his system.

Her breathing was rapid now, and he could see the pulse beating in her throat. But she didn't draw closer.

"It's your decision, Hannah. It has to be."

"Why?"

"You didn't invite me here. I came. I thrust myself back into your life. It's your decision if I stay."

She licked her lips, but pulled her lower lip under her top teeth. Didn't move.

"How long do I have?" she asked.

He tried to smile. "Now, Hannah." He knew how tortured he must sound, but couldn't help it. "Decide now."

8

HANNAH JUMPED UP, spilling her tea. She raked her hands through her hair. Every millimeter of her wanted to fall to the floor with Win Harling and make love with him, until neither of them had the strength left to accuse the other of anything. Instead she said, "You need to meet Cousin Thackeray."

Win remained seated on the couch. She wasn't deceived by his outward composure. His eyes were half-closed, studying her. His mouth was set in a grim, hard line. The muscles in his arms and legs were tensed. Everything about him was taut, coiled, ready for action.

And she knew what kind of action.

She wondered if his scrutiny would ever end. She watched the tea seep into her dhurrie carpet and wondered if the purple stain would forever be a visible reminder of her encounter with a real, live Harling. A warning of the perils of her own nature. A symbol of regret, of what might have been.

She should have stuck to dead Harlings.

Finally he slapped one hand on his knee and rose with a heavy sigh. "Okay, let's go."

"You're sure it's okay?"

"Hell, no. I'd rather carry you into your bedroom and make love to you until sunup, but—"

"That's not what I meant." She felt heat spread through her. "Cousin Thackeray—are you sure you want to meet him? He doesn't care for Harlings."

"Has he ever met one?"

"He says he did decades ago, but he won't give me a straight answer."

Win nodded thoughtfully, and Hannah grabbed her squall

jacket, glad to have the added cover. She could still feel the physical effects of wanting this man she had absolutely no business wanting. Even his gaze sparked pangs of desire in her. But she had to maintain control. She couldn't give in to her yearning...until she was sure she was doing the right thing.

"Well," he said, "let's go see if he decides to run me off with a shotgun."

"He doesn't own a shotgun. I'd watch out for a hot poker, though."

"A charming family, you Marshes."

They followed the narrow gravel path to the dirt road that connected Hannah's cottage to the main driveway. The wind made the air feel more like winter. Cousin Thackeray's few pitiful tulips seemed to be wishing they could close up again and come out when it was really spring. Walking beside her, Win didn't appear to notice the cold. Maybe he even welcomed it.

Thackeray's truck was still outside, but he didn't answer his door. Hannah pounded again. "Thackeray, it's me, Hannah."

No answer.

"He must have gone for a walk," she guessed. "Or maybe one of his buddies from town picked him up for a game of chess, although he usually lets me know when he's going out."

"He could be taking a nap."

"Are you kidding?" But she pushed open his back door, unlocked as always, and poked her head inside. "Thackeray?"

"We can look around out here," Win suggested, "or try again later. What have you told him about your trip to Boston?"

"Everything." She cleared her throat, feeling hot and achy with desire, and added quickly, "Except about you, of course."

He smiled. "Of course."

"It would only upset him."

"I understand."

She wondered if he did. "Does your uncle—"

"He knows to stay out of my private life. Not that it stops him."

"Does he really think I broke into his apartment and stole

Anne Harling's diary?'' But she didn't wait for an answer, springing ahead of Win to reach the driveway again. She cut over the side yard, heading toward the rocks. "You know, we only have your uncle's word for what happened."

"Meaning?"

"Meaning it's possible he made up the whole thing."

"You mean he pulled apart his entire apartment himself?" Win said dubiously.

Hannah knew she was on shaky ground; she could just imagine how she'd react if Win said something similar about Cousin Thackeray. "I'm not saying it's likely, just possible. I know *I* didn't do it."

He caught up with her. "What would be his motive?"

She shrugged, proceeding with caution. "Nothing devious, for sure. Cousin Thackeray would probably pitch me onto the rocks for saying this, but I actually like your uncle. I wouldn't want to believe he was up to anything truly underhanded."

"Such as?"

Inhaling, she went ahead and said it. "Getting Marsh Point back into Harling hands."

She continued walking, but Win stopped, not speaking. Up ahead, she could see Thackeray among the low-lying blueberry bushes with his binoculars, looking out at two cormorants diving for food.

"Thackeray!" she called, and waved.

He lowered his binoculars and turned, spotting her and waving back. She could see his grin.

"I've got somebody for you to meet!"

Behind her, Win said, "No."

She whipped around. "What do you mean?"

"I mean I'm not going to wait and see if I pass Thackeray Marsh's inspection. I'm not going to let you let him decide for you whether or not we—you and I, Hannah, no one else—go forward. I won't make it that easy for you." His black eyes searched hers for long seconds, and she saw in them not only physical longing, but a longing that came from his heart, maybe even his soul. "You're going to have to decide this one for yourself."

He about-faced and marched down the path toward her cottage.

Hannah gulped, not knowing what to do.

Cousin Thackeray was heading in her direction. Not fast—he never moved fast. Had she dragged Win out here to meet him, just so she could avoid making any decision about their relationship herself? What if Thackeray didn't like Win?

What if he did?

She sighed. It shouldn't matter how Thackeray felt. Win was right. "The bastard," she muttered.

But she didn't chase down the path after him. Instead she trotted across the windy point, toward the old man to whom she owed her loyalty, if not her life.

"YOU'RE SULKING."

"I'm not sulking."

Thackeray squinted at her in the bright sunlight, but didn't argue. He thrust his binoculars at her. "Look, a loon."

Hannah had no interest in his loon sighting and just pretended to focus the binoculars, while Thackeray gestured and gave instructions. "I see it," she said dispiritedly.

He hissed in disgust and yanked the binoculars away. "No, you didn't. There's no loon out there."

She pursed her lips. "That was a cheap trick."

"No matter." He gave her a long look. "Do you want to tell me about the Jaguar with Massachusetts plates parked at your cottage and that man I saw with the distinctly Harling build?"

Distinctly Harling build? What did Cousin Thackeray know? But she gave up before she even started. She was confused enough as it was.

"It's Win Harling," she told him.

"The younger J. Winthrop."

She nodded.

"Why's he here?"

"I'm not sure."

"They're after Marsh Point, aren't they, he and his uncle?"

Hannah hesitated only a moment. "It's possible. I have no proof, of course, but the uncle's story about his apartment being ransacked and Anne Harling's diary turning up missing strikes me as a bit fishy."

"Me, too. Think Win's a party to it?"

"It's hard to say. He's about as loyal to his uncle as I am to you."

Thackeray scowled and hung his binoculars around his neck. "What the devil's loyalty got to do with anything? A Marsh thinks for himself—or herself. You don't do what's wrong out of some skewed sense of loyalty. You do what's right for you."

But what if what's right for me is falling in love with J. Winthrop Harling?

"Hannah," Thackeray said when she didn't respond.

She turned to him. His nose was red in the cold air, his ratty corduroy jacket was missing a button. He was like a grandfather to her, a father, an uncle. Most of all, he was a friend. "I won't do anything that would make you hate me," she said.

"What in hell could make me hate you?" he scoffed.

She looked toward her cottage.

Then Thackeray Marsh surprised her with a hearty, warm laugh, one that reminded her he had led a long, full life. Still laughing, he headed through the blueberry bushes that were just beginning to get their foliage.

"What's so damned funny?"

"You and that Win fellow. My God, wouldn't that set three centuries of Marsh and Harling bones rattling?"

"I don't give a damn. We're talking about my life here, you know."

He stopped and spun around so abruptly that for a moment she thought he'd lose his footing. But she had never seen him so steady. "That's right," he said intently, his laughter gone. "It's *your* life."

With that, he pounded back to his house.

When Hannah returned to her cottage, Win was staring out

her picture window. She controlled a rush of desire at seeing his tall, lean body, at seeing him still there.

"I thought you might have cut your losses," she said.

He looked around, the corners of his mouth twitching. "Sounds a bit drastic, don't you think?"

She refused to blush. "Witty, witty."

"I try." But his humor didn't reach his eyes, and he asked, "Do you want me to leave?"

"No. No, I don't."

"Who decided?"

"I did."

He nodded. "Good."

"I owe Cousin Thackeray a lot, and I'd never deliberately hurt or disappoint him, but not making up my own mind about things..." She paused, searching for the right words, the courage to be honest. "Not making up my own mind about you—that isn't what he wants from me, even if it were something I could ever give."

Win was silent.

"Do you understand?"

"Yes," he replied.

"And you believe me?"

He smiled, the humor now reaching his eyes. "This time."

"Win Harling..."

"Shall we go talk to the old buzzard?"

She laughed. "I believe he used the same expression to describe your uncle. I thought we..." She felt blood rush to her face. "Never mind. I guess it's your turn to torture me."

"Hannah, Hannah," he said in a low, deliberately sexy voice, "you haven't seen anything yet."

THACKERAY MARSH PROVED as irascible as Win had anticipated. He and Hannah joined the old man at his drafty house for lemon meringue pie that must have been around for days and coffee that tasted as if it had been poisoned. Win later learned that Hannah's cousin had reheated it from his pot that morning. A waste-not, want-not family. Hannah, he noticed, drank every drop.

"So," Thackeray said, "how's that old goat of an uncle of yours?"

"He's quite well, thank you."

Win glanced at Hannah but couldn't will her to meet his eyes. She was sitting cross-legged on a threadbare braided rug in front of a roaring fire. Southern Maine's evening temperature had plummeted; there was even talk of frost.

"We met back before the war. He was a frosty old bastard even then. Heard a Marsh had dared set foot in Boston and hunted me down, warned me one day the Harlings would get Marsh Point back. He called it Harling Point, o' course." Thackeray fastened his intense gaze—his green eyes bore a disturbing resemblance to his young relative's—on Win, who didn't flinch. "That why you're here?"

Win worded his reply carefully. "I'm not interested in pressing the Harling case for Marsh Point, no."

Thackeray grunted. "They don't have a case."

"Then why worry?"

"Who said I'm worried?"

Definitely irascible. Hannah smiled, visibly amused, as she uncoiled her legs and rested on her arms. Win wished, not for the first time, that he hadn't been so damned noble and had instead made love to her before offering to chitchat with her elderly cousin.

Before heading out, she had insisted on taking a quick shower—he hoped she'd had to make it cold—and had twisted her hair into a long French braid that hung down her back. Win still didn't know how he'd stopped himself carting her off to the bedroom there and then. Even now it amazed him.

With her hair pulled off her face, her eyes seemed even bigger, more luminous. She had changed into leggings that conformed to every shapely turn of thigh and calf and left him imagining how her legs would feel entwined with his. Her top left much more to the imagination. It was a huge sweatshirt she must have picked up in Vermont; it had a Holstein's head on the front and its behind on the back, with Enjoy Our Dairy Air in black lettering. Apparently she collected T-shirts and sweatshirts. She had shown him one of the Beatles, circa 1967. It was another side of the scholarly Hannah Marsh, as was her Hannah of the Cincinnati Harlings. A complex woman.

"Win came to Maine to make sure I hadn't made off with Anne Harling's diary," she informed her elderly cousin, "which his uncle still insists I stole."

"He only wants to know the truth," Win amended. "So do I."

Thackeray waved them both off. "I'll bet you a day's work Anne Harling didn't keep a diary any more than I did."

Hannah shook her head. "It wouldn't surprise me. Upper-class women of that era quite commonly kept diaries...."

"*She* didn't."

But Hannah didn't give in, so Win sat back and observed while the two argued about the journal-keeping habits of late-nineteenth-century women. It was a spirited discussion, given, at least to Win, the dry nature of the topic. As far as he could tell, the two Marshes didn't even disagree.

"But back to Win's Uncle Jonathan," Hannah said, and Win's interest perked up. He saw the flush of excitement in her cheeks and smiled, not just wanting her, but liking her. "He indicated Anne Harling was the one who pulled together the Harling Collection, his theory being that I stole her diary to look for clues as to the collection's location."

"That's ridiculous," Thackeray said.

"Of course. The Harlings have had the diary—if it exists—for a hundred years, and certainly would have noticed any reference to a collection that could contain a valuable copy of the Declaration of Independence."

Win couldn't let that one go unanswered. "Maybe they never read it," he speculated. "Or maybe in your research you learned something that suggested to you a passage in the diary was really a disguised clue, something we wouldn't have recognized all these years. Maybe," he went on, ignoring Thackeray's snort of disgust, "you weren't looking for the diary itself, but stole it because it was the only thing of potential value in my uncle's apartment."

Hannah fastened her cool academic's gaze on him without an inkling, he suspected, of the elemental response it produced in him. He could have hauled her off to her cottage and made love to her all night.

He might yet.

No, he thought, not might. Would.

"I suppose," she said reasonably, "there are a number of reasonable theories to fit the supposed facts. But as I said, I'll manage my biography of Priscilla Marsh without the Harling Collection."

She climbed to her feet in a lithe movement that made him think of what they were going to be like in bed together. Considering her preoccupied state, Win thought, delaying the inevitable perhaps hadn't been wise.

"Thanks for the pie, Thackeray."

The old man jerked his head toward Win but addressed Hanna. "Is he going back tonight?"

Win shook his head, answering for himself. "No."

"You're going to stay at Hannah's cottage?"

She nodded, answering for her guest.

Thackeray Marsh thought that one over. "This fellow thinks you're a thief, and you still want to put him up for the night?"

"We've called a cease-fire," Hannah said steadily. "I've paid him back for every nickel I...appropriated."

And Win had already burned her check. Its ashes were in his fireplace in Boston.

Thackeray grunted. "I'll keep my shotgun loaded by my bed. You just give a yell if you need me."

Hannah had the gall to thank him.

On their way out, Win whispered into her ear, "I thought you said he didn't have a shotgun."

She grinned. "He's full of surprises, isn't he?"

Outside it was pitch-dark, the air downright cold, the wind gusting at at least thirty miles an hour, but Hannah Marsh seemed at ease, in control, downright perky. Win heard the gravel crunch under his feet. She seemed hardly to be hitting the ground at all. She darted ahead of him, familiar with every rock, every rut in the road to her cottage, while he stumbled along behind her.

He caught up with her. "I suggest," he said, slipping his arm around her slender waist, "you watch your yelling tonight, unless you want me blown to bits."

She turned her eyes upon him, luminous now in the starlight, and smiled softly, playfully. "Now what could possibly make me yell in the middle of the night?"

"I can think of several things."

He slipped one hand under her sweatshirt, touching the hot, smooth skin.

"Your hand's cold!"

"Serves you right."

But she didn't pull away. "Of course," she said, "*I* won't be the one Cousin Thackeray will shoot."

"Then the risk is all mine, isn't it?"

She shrugged, leaning against his shoulder. "I wouldn't say that."

"What's your risk?"

The gravel crunched under her feet as she came to a stop, staring at him with wide, serious eyes. "Falling for a Harling."

"Is that a bigger risk than getting shot?"

"It could be."

"Hannah…"

"But I'll take it," she said quickly, and darted away, into the night.

9

_____

NOW THAT DARKNESS enveloped the cottage, Hannah felt even more alone with Win Harling…and surprisingly content with the situation.

He lay stretched on the floor in front of the fire, staring at the blue and orange flames. She was on her rocking chair, rummaging through tins and old cigar boxes filled with scraps of paper, clippings, coupons and recipe cards. Mostly she was trying not to think how damned appealing Win's thighs looked.

"What are you doing?" Win asked finally.

"Looking for a recipe. I've got one last pint of wild blueberries from last summer in the freezer and thought I'd make blueberry scones. Thackeray gave me the recipe—it's from his mother. They're wonderful."

"Uncle Jonathan makes blueberry scones," Win said. "He insists they're only worth making with wild blueberries. The cultivated varieties won't work."

Hannah grinned. "Cousin Thackeray says the same thing. Do you suppose those two are twins, after all?"

"Don't ever suggest that to them."

"Scandalous, isn't it? They'd probably call a truce between the Marshes and the Harlings and string us up together."

"Hannah," Win said dryly, "no hanging metaphors tonight."

She felt a rush of warmth at the way he said "tonight," as if it were just one in a long string of nights they would have together. But she didn't want to dwell on thoughts of the future and the choices it might bring, only on the present. She concentrated on the familiar smell of oak burning in the fire, the familiar sound of the gentle ebbing of the tide just beyond her cottage.

Then Win moved, adding an unfamiliar sound, an unfamiliar presence as he put another log onto the fire.

"Here it is," she said, withdrawing a yellowed three-by-five index card. On it, in black ink now faded by time, Cousin Thackeray's mother had neatly printed her recipe for luscious blueberry scones.

Hannah jumped up and headed for the kitchen.

Win followed.

"You don't have to help," she told him.

"Okay." As he leaned against the sink, she noticed his narrow hips, the muscles in his thighs. "I'll watch."

She scowled. "You're in my way."

So he sat down at her small kitchen table, in front of a double window that looked onto her back porch. On the table itself stood only a wooden pepper grinder; there was neither cloth, napkins nor place mats. Hannah thought of Win's metal folding chairs and ugly dining room wallpaper and smiled, unembarrassed by her own simple existence. Never mind the fact that he could easily afford to turn the Harling House on Louisburg Square into a showpiece, that he wouldn't need a mortgage to buy Marsh Point.

He doesn't want to buy it, she thought suddenly. *He wants to prove the Marshes appropriated it from the Harlings....*

She wouldn't dwell on that little problem right now.

"Are you going to just sit there and watch me?" she asked somewhat irritably.

He shrugged, obviously amused, knowing just what kind of distraction he was. "Why not?"

Why not, indeed? She tore open the refrigerator door and dug around inside until she found a bottle of beer behind smidgens of leftovers of this and that she'd promised herself would go into a pot of soup. More likely they'd end up in the garbage.

She handed Win the beer. "It's my last one."

"Don't you want it?"

"I'm not much on beer. I bought a six-pack for friends who came to visit—oh, around New Year's, I guess it was."

"Your last company?"

"Hmm? I don't know...." She thought a few seconds. "No, I had friends over a couple of months ago."

"A couple of months ago," he repeated.

"I do more entertaining in the summer, and I've been so involved with my work I haven't had time for a lot of outside activities. I get out for dinner every once in a while with friends." She pulled her pint of wild blueberries from the freezer. "And I see Cousin Thackeray just about every day."

"Do you like living here in Maine?"

"Yes."

"Your cousin has no children," Win guessed.

She looked around. "Are you trying to ask me if I'm his heir? If so, yes, I am. He plans to leave me Marsh Point. Then, if you Harlings want to go toe to toe with me over who rightfully owns it, that's fine. I'll take you on. Just leave Thackeray alone."

Win didn't respond at once, but sat back in his oak chair and stretched his long legs, taking up more of her small kitchen than anyone had since she'd banished Cousin Thackeray's old Irish setter. The man simply wasn't built on the same scale as her cottage.

"So you're protecting your cousin," he said at length.

"I'm not protecting anyone. I have nothing to hide. I'm just giving you fair warning: I won't let Cousin Thackeray lose Marsh Point."

"Especially to a Harling."

"Especially."

She set to work on her scones. She got out her chipped pottery flour canister and her sugar container, of airtight plastic so the ants wouldn't get into it, the salt and baking powder. All the while she was intensely aware of Win's eyes on her. Finally she thrust the blueberries at him. "There might be a few stems and leaves floating around," she told him.

He insisted on doing a thorough job, spreading the blueberries on paper towels and examining every single one of them for stems, leaves, brown spots, bird pecks. Hannah was amused. "I usually just dump the lot into the batter and hope for the best."

"I'll keep that in mind," he said, "should I ever eat anything else I haven't supervised you cooking."

Besides the scones, supper included eggs, scrambled with fresh chives, and a carrot and raisin salad she threw together because she figured carrot sticks were too ordinary for company. Or maybe because she needed to do one more thing before sitting down kitty-corner to Win at her own kitchen table. She tasted none of the food, not even the scones. All her senses were focused on the rich, handsome, sexy rogue of a Bostonian who had come, it seemed, to dominate her very being.

"Are the scones like your uncle's?" she asked.

"Very much. It could be the same recipe."

But he was no more interested in discussing wild blueberry scones than she was. She could see it in his eyes, in the tensed muscles of his arms. He was as preoccupied with her as she with him.

It was not a comforting thought.

After dinner, they moved back into the living room, and for the first time in years, Hannah wished she owned a television set. She would have loved to turn on the news or have the idle chatter of a sitcom in the background. With just the crackle of the fire and the rhythmic washing of the ocean, it was as if there were nothing more in her world than the little cottage on Marsh Point and the man who'd come to visit.

Except that he hadn't come to visit. He had come to find out if her desire to examine the Harling Collection had prompted her to ransack his uncle's apartment and steal an old diary, so that she could later steal a rare and valuable copy of the Declaration of Independence.

He had come to find out if she was a thief.

"There are sheets in the bathroom," she said suddenly.

Win glanced at her from his spot in front of the fire. He had left plenty of room for her to join him, but she'd flopped into her rocker again, well out of reach. She could feel the warmth of the fire licking at her toes. Her fingers, however, were icy cold.

"For the bed in the guest room," she added.

"Ahh. I see."

She thought he did.

Still, she found herself trying to explain. "There's no point...your uncle...my cousin...this business about the Harling Collection and the Declaration of Independence..." She lifted her shoulders and let them fall again. "You know."

"I know," he responded. His voice was soft and liquid, filled with understanding. There was none of the hardness or defensiveness she would have expected.

Didn't he care?

She jumped up and snatched a tome on the Puritans from a pile of books next to her desk. "I'm done in. I've had a long day. I'll check the guest room and make sure everything's in order before I turn in. Do you want me to make the bed?"

"No," he said calmly, "I'll get it."

He doesn't care, she thought. She had been projecting her own desire onto him, thinking that because she wanted him that he must, therefore, want her. Which he had. Definitely. Only clearly not as much as she had him. Or at least he didn't now, which was the whole point.

I'm not making any sense.... I must be more tired than I thought.

As she flounced from the living room, she noticed he was hoisting a fat log onto the fire and arranging it with his bare hands, as if oblivious to the flames. "Don't set yourself on fire," she called over her shoulder.

"Too late," he said, half under his breath.

She slammed into the guest room. It was freezing. The curtains were billowing in the wind and the shade was flapping. Hannah quickly shut the window. When had she opened it? Not this morning. Yesterday? The day before? It had rained buckets one night.

She ran one hand over the twin bed.

Damp.

No, she thought, soaked.

She tiptoed out to the bathroom, got a couple of towels and hurried back, spread the towels on the mattress and patted them down so they could absorb as much moisture as possible. She let them sit a minute while she returned to the bathroom and grabbed sheets. If she made the bed, maybe Win wouldn't notice the wet mattress.

Her job done, she scooped up the damp towels and carted them off to her room, where her guest would be less likely to run into them. Given his suspicious mind, he'd think the worst.

"Making the man sleep in a wet bed *is* pretty bad," she admitted under her breath.

But what was the alternative?

She wouldn't think about it. The alternative, she knew, was too tempting...too much like what she really wanted. Instead she pulled on her flannel nightgown—it was a cool night, after all—and climbed into bed with her book on the Puritans. It was dry stuff. She gave up after a couple of paragraphs and picked up a mystery that lay on her night table.

About forty minutes later she was dozing between paragraphs, fighting nightmares, when footsteps in the hall startled her. Then she remembered she wasn't alone. It wasn't so much that she had forgotten Win's presence as that his footsteps were a tangible reminder of it.

"Good night, Hannah," he said softly.

"Good night. If you need anything, just give a yell."

In a few minutes he yelled, all right. *"Hannah!"*

He was back at her door in a flash, but Hannah casually dog-eared her page and yawned before she looked up. The door stood open now.

"Oh, dear," she muttered.

Send a man to lie on a cold, wet mattress, she thought, and pay the consequences.

J. Winthrop Harling was standing in her doorway in nothing but his shorts. As shorts went, they weren't much. But Hannah's attention was riveted on what they didn't cover. Long, muscular legs. A flat abdomen. A line of dark hair that disappeared into the waistband of his shorts.

He, of course, seemed totally unaware of his near-naked state.

"Is something wrong?" she asked innocently.

"The mattress is wet."

"It is?"

"Clammy, cold, wet."

"You aren't the sort of guest who would be too polite to point out something like that, I see."

His eyes seemed to clamp her against her headboard. "I'm never too polite."

"Well, I left the window open when it rained the other night. I suppose a little rain must have gotten onto your bed. I didn't notice when I made it up."

"Liar."

Succinct and accurate. She sighed. "Can't you make the best of the situation?"

"Oh, yes." He leaned against the doorjamb, suddenly looking quite relaxed, even more darkly sexy. "I can make the best of the situation."

Her heartbeat quickened. She waved her hand in the direction of the living room. "You can always camp out by the fire. I have a sleeping bag you can borrow. It's good to twenty degrees below zero."

"A good hostess," he said, "would give me her bed."

Her mouth went dry. "But I'm already in it."

As responses went, she could have done better. Win took a step into her room, her space. But just one step was enough. "Exactly."

There was no undoing, she thought, what she'd already done. She had told him he could stay. She had told him in effect that she wanted a relationship with him. A romantic relationship. A physical relationship. She had let him see a part of her she usually kept hidden. Oh, she could still send him packing. It wasn't too late. And he'd go. He'd already made it plain that he understood when no meant no.

But she didn't want him to go. She had made her choices and there had been reasons for them, even if there were also very good reasons for choosing the opposite.

She knew, with a certainty that had escaped her earlier, that she wanted him to stay.

Something in her expression must have told him so, for he took another few steps into her room. She didn't stop him.

Finally he stood next to her bed, staring down at her. "Flannel, hmm?"

"It's a year-round fabric in Maine."

"How practical."

"I bought Cousin Thackeray a nightshirt just like this one for his birthday last year. I've had this one for...I don't know, it must be going on four years. It's got a couple of holes." She held up one arm so he could see the burn hole in the sleeve. "The fire got me one morning."

"Hannah..."

"You know, don't make the mistake of thinking I'm a rube or anything. I've lived most of my life in the city. And here we're just a couple of hours from Boston. Just because I sleep in a flannel nightgown doesn't mean I'm unsophisticated. I've turned down teaching positions at Ivy League colleges."

"Hannah..."

"I'm sometimes torn between city and country."

"Hannah..."

"It's just that Marsh Point is the only real home I've ever known. My mother did the best she could after my father died, but she was chasing her own demons—and rainbows. We all do."

Finally Win just threw back the covers and climbed into bed with her. She stared at him. He grinned. "After getting into that snow cone you call a guest bed and standing here for ten minutes, I'm about to freeze."

She stuck out a toe and found his calf. "You don't feel cold to me."

"You're in the wrong place," he said, a little raggedly.

"Oh."

Even with the cold wind, Hannah had the curtainless windows in her bedroom open. Win said, "I guess I should have brought my own flannel nightshirt."

"Do you have one?"

He sighed.

"Well, they are toasty."

"I prefer," he said, "other methods of staying warm."

"Like electric blankets, I suppose. I don't believe in them, myself. I won't say they cause cancer, but they sure do waste electricity, and they're not very romantic. But I guess if you're allergic to down, or maybe if you turn down the heat in the house so low that you can justify the use of electricity…"

"Hannah."

"You had other methods of staying warm in mind?"

"Yes."

That silenced her. He looked so damned tempting and rakish beside her, a man who would stop at nothing to get what he wanted. Herself included? Did she dominate his list of wants tonight? But he was more complex than that. *They* were more complex than that.

But she didn't want to dwell on complexities now.

She moved closer, and he touched her mouth with his fingertips, just grazing her lips. "What do you want, Hannah Marsh?"

Without speaking, she caught up the hem of her nightgown and lifted it over her head, the cool night air hitting her warm skin. She tossed the nightgown onto the floor.

His black eyes were on her. She met his gaze head-on, without flushing.

"I've dreamed about this moment," she said honestly.

"So have I."

His mouth closed over hers, his hands skimming the soft flesh of her breasts, tentatively at first, then more boldly. She took a sharp breath when his thumbs found her nipples. The ache inside her was almost more than she could bear. But he didn't pause, merciless in his teasing and stroking, never letting up with either his mouth or his hands. She didn't want him to.

Still, it was a game two could play.

She reached forward blindly, a little awkwardly, but without embarrassment, until she felt him, already hot and ready, and before she could pull back or even hesitate, he thrust himself hard against her hand.

"I've never wanted anyone the way I want you," he whispered. "Never."

He drew back, just for a moment, sliding out of his shorts, then rolling back to her so that their bodies melded, so that she could feel the long length of him against her. She felt sexy, aroused.

"You're so beautiful," he whispered, before he began a deep, hungry, evocative kiss. He trailed his fingertips down her spine, captured her buttocks in his palms, then skimmed the curve of her hips until he found the hot, moist, ready center of her.

"Win...I..."

"It's okay," he whispered, "it's okay."

And it was. More than okay.

"I don't know if I can last...."

"That's two of us."

But he hadn't finished.

"You're not going to have mercy on me, are you?" she said playfully, already knowing he wouldn't.

She let him roll her onto her back. He moved on top, his torso raised while his eyes seemed to absorb every inch of her. She splayed her fingers in the hairs on his chest, feeling the lean muscle, then let them trail lower, until they closed around his maleness. He thrust against her with a rhythm that was as primitive as the crashing of the waves upon the rocks outside her window.

His mouth descended to hers, tasted, then moved down her throat, tasted some more, and to her breasts, tasting and nipping.

She wouldn't release him. Then he moved down her abdomen, tasting and licking now, not stopping.

"Let yourself go," he whispered. "Just let go."

As if she could stop herself.

But then she realized she'd never felt anything so erotic, so achingly pleasurable as his caresses.

He drew away from her, only for a moment to take precaution, before coming inside her, hard and fast, murmuring his encouragement, his love, until her cries mixed with those of the cormorants and the sea gulls and finally his body quaked with hers, rocking, shattering.

Afterward, in the stillness, she noticed the wind had died down, too, and the waves were making a gentle swishing sound, as if they had all the time in the world to get wherever they were going. Hannah listened to the ocean for a long time and smiled at the man beside her.

A Harling. In her bed.

"Do you suppose," she said, "three centuries of Harlings and Marshes are already planning ways to haunt us tonight?"

He grinned back at her. "If they are, we'll be ready for 'em, don't you think?"

After making love with him, Hannah figured she was ready for anything.

IN THE MORNING the only sign he'd been there was the blazing fire in the living room.

She was ordinarily not a heavy sleeper, so Hannah assumed that either their lovemaking at dawn had knocked her out or that Win had sneaked out on her very, very quietly. She made herself a pot of coffee, added another log to the fire, and told herself she didn't regret last night. If she had to do it over again, she would. The giving and taking, emotionally and physically, had been mutual, real, if also fleeting. She had decided last night to let tomorrow bring what it would.

And it had, hadn't it?

She called him a host of names, dumped the trash and changed her sheets, wanting a fresh start.

The name-calling didn't work. She kept seeing his dark eyes on her, hearing his deep laughter, feeling the strength and warmth of his arms around her. She kept remembering the things they had told each other in the night, about growing up and climbing trees and finding a rare piece of glassware at a yard sale for two dollars and not being able to take it, having to tell the new widow who was selling off her stuff to pay her property taxes with what it was worth. Mostly they had talked about little things. There had been nothing about Thackeray Marsh or old Jonathan Harling, nothing about the Harling Collection, the ransacked apartment, the missing diary or the Declaration of Independence.

"Oh, Hannah," Win had said, stroking her hips, the inside of her thighs. "There's never been anyone remotely like you in my life…never."

She remembered how she'd responded. Hotly, eagerly, more boldly than on the occasion of their first lovemaking, she had shown him where to touch her, let him show her where to touch him. They had made love with abandon. Without thought. Without inhibition.

Without commitment?

"Hannah, Hannah…I'll never stop wanting you," he'd added.

He had been inside her then, thrusting hard yet lovingly, and she'd had her hands on his hips, urging him on, thinking that her ache for him would never end, never be satiated, that he'd collapse first. But he hadn't. He'd murmured his encouragement, urged her to let go…and she'd felt his satisfaction when she'd exploded, rocked and moaned as he kept going….

Now, in the bright, cold light of morning, Win Harling was gone. Calling him names wouldn't bring him back or make her hate him.

Or regret a single second of what they'd done last night. It had been a deliberate, conscious, mature choice on her part. She'd known the potential consequences.

Just as she knew that, come what may, there would never be another man for her. Win Harling was it. She wasn't the sort of woman who jumped into bed with one man one night and just hoped for the best. She had gone to bed with him because she had wanted him and only him.

Now she had to pay the price.

"Damn," she swore under her breath. She grabbed a sweat-shirt, anxious for the solace of the sea, the rocks, the tide...for the solace of Marsh Point itself.

Outside in the chilly air, the dew soaked into her sneakers and she saw that his Jaguar was gone, too. It wasn't as if he'd ducked out for an early walk and planned to be back soon.

She didn't know if he planned to be back at all.

"The scoundrel," she muttered.

But what had she expected? She'd seen the two sides of Win Harling: the black-eyed rogue who'd chased her down in Boston and the sophisticated gentleman who hadn't pressed himself upon her yesterday, despite his plain sexual need. Had the rogue made love to her last night? The gentleman? Or some combination of the two?

"What does it matter? He's gone now."

She began her litany of names again, but none of them made her feel the slightest bit better.

10

AT SOME GREASY-SPOON diner not more than two miles from Marsh Point, Win and his uncle Jonathan sat over weak coffee and runny eggs. "You need to let me sort out this mess on my own," Win said in an attempt to reason with the old man.

Uncle Jonathan shook his head, soaking up a pool of egg with a triangle of pale white toast. "It's not your mess."

"Look…"

"I'm here, Winthrop. Make the best of it."

It was pointless to argue and Win knew it. Shortly after crawling out of Hannah's bed that morning and building a fire, he had slipped out to refill the wood box. He had planned to spend the morning with her, going over all the details of her trip to Boston, her research into Priscilla Marsh and Cotton Harling, her discovery of the possible existence of the Harling Collection. Everything. In turn, he'd tell her what little he'd learned from Uncle Jonathan.

Instead, out in the woodpile, he'd caught his uncle prowling about Marsh Point. Why the crazy old coot hadn't fallen and broken his hip in a tide pool was beyond him. Now there was nothing to be done but gather his things and cart Uncle Jonathan off to town, before one of the Marshes awakened and called the police.

So far, his uncle had yet to satisfactorily explain what he was doing in Maine. He had, he'd said, taken a bus from Boston and then a cab out to Marsh Point that had cost him double, he insisted, what it should have. He'd spent the night in a "disreputable" motel and had risen early and sneaked onto "the disputed property," where Win had found him.

"Has your apartment been broken into again?" Win asked.

"Nope."

"Did you find the Anne Harling diary under a couch cushion or something?"

"Nope."

"Uncle…"

"That cottage where I found you," Jonathan said, pouring still another little plastic vial of half-and-half into his coffee. "Hannah Marsh's, isn't it?"

Win sighed. "Yes, it is."

"She and you…slept together, did you?"

"Uncle Jonathan, you know I don't discuss my private life."

The old man grunted. "I'll wager you did more than sleep. My word, Winthrop. Falling for a Marsh." He let out a long breath. "No wonder I had trouble sleeping last night."

"You had trouble sleeping," Win muttered, controlling his growing frustration with difficulty, "because you know damned well you should have been home in your own bed. Uncle Jonathan, there's nothing you can do here except cause trouble. Go home."

The old man slurped his coffee and said, without looking at his nephew, "I wasn't the one who slept with a Marsh last night."

Win was at the end of his rope. "Cotton Harling and Priscilla Marsh lived three hundred years ago. I won't let them dictate to me what I should do with my life. And I don't give a damn whether we have a legitimate claim to Marsh Point or not. I don't even give a damn if Hannah would lie to her grandmother to get her hot little hands on the Harling Collection! You," he said, knowing he was losing control, "are going back to Boston."

Looking remarkably unperturbed by his nephew's outburst, Uncle Jonathan flagged the waitress for more coffee. She was back in a jiffy. Win let her heat his up. It was dreadful stuff. Almost worse than Hannah's purple tea.

Hannah, Hannah.

He had to keep Uncle Jonathan away from Thackeray Marsh

and Marsh Point, at least until he and Hannah had adequately compared notes.

His uncle began again. "I talked to a friend of mine from Harvard who deals in rare books and documents."

Continually amazed by the variety of people Jonathan Harling knew, Win indulged him. "About what?"

"The copy of the Declaration of Independence in the Harling Collection."

"Allegedly."

Jonathan waved off Win's correction. "It's worth even more than I had anticipated."

"You'd anticipated a lot. How much more?"

"If it's in mint condition..."

"And if it exists."

Uncle Jonathan sighed. "It would be worth seven figures."

"Seven—"

"A million dollars."

At that moment, with Win gritting his teeth at the figure his uncle had just named, Thackeray Marsh wandered into the diner.

Directly behind him, spotting the two Harlings at once, was his cousin, the blond and beautiful Hannah Marsh.

HANNAH GLARED AT WIN and his uncle, while Cousin Thackeray gave a victorious sniff. The two Harlings looked remarkably guilty. Still, Hannah felt a rush of excitement at seeing Win, though she had to fight back memories of last night. At the same time, she didn't regret one nasty name she'd called him.

"Thackeray Marsh," Jonathan Harling declared, eyeing his contemporary with exaggerated disdain. "So you're still alive. I'd heard you were killed in the Normandy invasion. Nothing heroic, of course. Drowned stepping over your own feet."

Win scowled at his uncle who, Hannah was sure, had heard no such thing.

It was equally clear that Thackeray wasn't in the mood to help matters. "At least I fought in the war, instead of using privilege to get me a safe stateside job."

Jonathan Harling reddened and nearly came out of his chair,

but Win clamped a hand on the old man's arm and held him down.

"Thackeray!" Hannah admonished her cousin.

He gave her a smug look for her trouble.

The diner was filling up with fishermen, in from their morning rounds. *All we need now is to start a brawl,* Hannah thought. "You two keep on like this," she told the two old men, "and you'll get us all arrested."

"Just stating the facts," Cousin Thackeray said loftily.

Jonathan Harling grunted. "A Marsh wouldn't know a fact if it smacked him in the face."

"Perhaps," Hannah said through clenched teeth, "we should go back to Marsh Point and discuss things."

Cousin Thackeray shook his head. "I don't want them on my property."

"*Your* property," Jonathan sneered. "Why, back in 1891—"

Win cut him off, his eyes pinned on Hannah. "How did you find us?" he asked quietly.

Before she could answer, Thackeray said, "That damned ostentatious car you drive sticks out around here like—"

Now it was Hannah's turn to do some cutting off. "My cousin found evidence of a prowler while on his morning walk and insisted it had to be a Harling. I indulged him in a spin around town, the result of which is our presence here."

"What evidence?" Jonathan demanded.

Thackeray gave him a supercilious look. "Nothing *you* would notice. I, however, who was raised out here, wondered if an elephant hadn't been through."

Win was on his feet, laying bills upon the table. His jaw was set, hard. He moved with tensed, highly controlled motions. An unhappy man. Obviously hadn't got enough sleep last night. Hannah watched him, pleased with herself. At least she wasn't the only one suffering.

"Let's go," he said, taking in both Marshes and his uncle.

"Oh, no, you don't," Cousin Thackeray replied, shaking his

head. "I'm not letting you two sneak off before I get a chance
to search your car and your persons."

"Fine." Win's tone was steely, but had no apparent effect on
anyone. "You and my uncle can drive together. I'll take Hannah."

The two old men argued all the way out to the parking lot,
but Win was adamant. He opened the passenger door to Thackeray's 1967 GMC Truck and told his uncle it was his choice: he
could be helped in or thrown in. Jonathan squared his shoulders
and climbed in without anyone's help. Thackeray muttered
something about wanting to ram the passenger side of his truck
into a tree, except for the fact that it had another five or ten years
left in it, might even outlast him. Win just looked at Hannah in
despair.

"We'll follow you," he told his uncle and her cousin. "No
tricks."

He turned away before either could say any more.

Hannah had opened the passenger door to his Jaguar. "Any
orders for me?" she asked coolly.

He glared at her. "Just get in."

She did so, slamming the door shut. He followed. His tall,
lean body filled the interior, instantly making her aware again of
last night, of her unceasing attraction to this man. She tried not
to show it.

"I take it," she said as he started the car, "that you found
your uncle snooping around this morning and sneaked out."

A muscle worked in his jaw. "That's about it."

"You made your choice, didn't you?"

"The way I see it," he said tightly, rolling into position behind Thackeray's truck, "I didn't have a choice."

"I'm not saying you shouldn't have gone with your uncle. All
I'm saying is, a note or a quick goodbye would have been...
courteous."

"And what would you have done?"

"If I knew your uncle was snooping around Marsh Point? I
don't know."

"You'd have raised hell, Hannah. At the very least you'd have hauled your cousin over, and he'd have called the police and had Uncle Jonathan arrested as a trespasser." He glanced at her. "Like me, you would have felt you had no choice."

He was crowding Cousin Thackeray on the winding, narrow road out to Marsh Point. Thackeray braked hard and Win cursed, just missing the truck's rear end. But he backed off. Hannah could almost hear her cousin's satisfied chuckle.

She sighed. "I don't know if you're right or you're wrong, and I guess we'll never find out. Did your uncle tell you why he's here?"

"We were just getting into it when you and Thackeray barged in. Nice timing." He exhaled, running one hand through his wild hair. His day obviously hadn't started out very well. Neither, however, had hers. "Hannah, I'm doing the best I can. Will you believe that much?"

She didn't answer right away. They had just rounded a bend, and she could see white-capped waves pounding the rocks of Marsh Point. The sun was shining. The temperature had begun to climb. It would be a splendid day in southern Maine. But her life here, Hannah thought, would never again be the same.

Finally she said, "I'll believe that much, yes."

In a few moments, he turned into Thackeray's driveway and followed the truck up to the house. Jonathan Harling seemed to jump out before the truck had even come to a full stop. He was waving his arms and shouting.

"This should be interesting," Win said grimly.

"Think I should keep a bucket of cold water handy, in case things get out of control?"

He looked at her and grinned. "A woman after my own heart." He nodded toward the house. "Shall we?"

"As I see it," she said, paraphrasing his earlier words, "we have no choice."

HANNAH, Thackeray Marsh and Uncle Jonathan were arguing a point of early American history that held no interest for Win, but at least, he thought, no one had yet come to blows. He noticed that Hannah held her own in the argument with the two men, whom she accused of agreeing with each other, even if they wouldn't admit it. Being no historian, Win couldn't comment.

Finally he rose, feeling it was relatively safe to leave them alone, and wandered from the living room to the dining room, preoccupied not with Puritans but with a document potentially worth a million dollars. If it existed. If it could be located.

Uncle Jonathan could use the money.

So could the Marshes.

Win exhaled, walking through the French doors onto a deck that overlooked a small cove he hadn't noticed yesterday. Here the land sloped gently to the water, where waves lapped over sand and marsh grass. He squinted against the sunlight.

Something had been shoved into the brush. It was dark blue; he could see just one end.

A canoe. A wooden canoe.

His uncle was capable of many things, but not of paddling from Boston or even Kennebunkport in a canoe. He had said he'd taken a bus and a taxi, and Win believed him. Maybe it was Thackeray Marsh's canoe. Or Hannah's.

But he didn't believe it. A dark suspicion started to formulate itself in his mind.

Returning to the living room, he grabbed his uncle. "Let's go for a walk."

Uncle Jonathan was red-faced with arguing. "These two"—he jerked his head at the Marshes—"know nothing about American judicial history."

"I'm sure they don't." Win didn't give a damn if they did. "Let's go."

"Hold your horses, there. I won't have you humoring me just because I'm an old man."

"Uncle Jonathan, we need to talk. I have a proposition I want to discuss with you before I present it to Hannah and Thackeray."

It was never easy for Jonathan Harling to abandon an argu-

ment, but he took the hint and followed his nephew outside.
They left behind Hannah and Thackeray, grumbling and looking
very suspicious, as well they might.

"What the devil have you got a bee in your bonnet about?"
Uncle Jonathan demanded. "I was being civil to those two."

"I think I know who ransacked your apartment."

The old man narrowed his eyes, then nodded solemnly. "I
was wondering when you'd figure it out."

"WHAT DO YOU SUPPOSE they're up to?" Thackeray asked.

Hannah sat cross-legged on the threadbare carpet, already contemplating just that question herself. "I don't know. But don't
you get the feeling they're holding more cards in their deck than
we are? And don't tell me it's the Harling way."

"Well, it is."

"Win's on to something." She climbed to her feet, feeling
oddly confident. Not outmatched. Not outwitted. Not as if Win
Harling and his cantankerous uncle were actual enemies. Not
allies, perhaps, but definitely not enemies. "I think I'll take a
walk, too."

"Don't let 'em catch you."

But he sounded distracted, preoccupied with something besides his natural inclination to doubt everything the Harlings said
or did. His eyes weren't focused on her. She said goodbye, but
he didn't answer, didn't even wave a hand.

Something was definitely up. Was she the only one who didn't
know what?

Outside the air was still and so clear that everything seemed
overfocused, outlined in sharp detail against a sky so blue that
it made a body appreciate life. Hannah went through the side
door, just as Win and her uncle had, but saw no sign of them.
She had no idea where they'd gone. Had they wandered toward
her cottage? She didn't want to eavesdrop, but her trust level
wasn't what it had been only a few hours ago. She wanted to
keep an eye on the two Harlings.

It was ridiculous, she thought, a Marsh like herself falling for a Harling, but there it was. And she wasn't falling, she knew that much. She'd already fallen.

She was in love with the man.

They weren't anywhere outside or inside her cottage. Hannah stared out the picture window in her living room, tapping her foot and cursing them. She forced herself to return to Thackeray's house, duly noting along the way that Win's car was still parked behind her cousin's old truck. Wherever they'd gone, it couldn't be far.

She headed back inside, determined to get some straight answers out of Thackeray Marsh about the Harling claim on Marsh Point and about the missing Harling Collection.

She would not let him or Jonathan Harling sidetrack her with their inflammatory comments on some obscure historical fact. She wanted answers.

When she had them, then she would figure out what to do about Win Harling.

And find out what he meant to do about her.

Cousin Thackeray wasn't in the living room. She checked the kitchen, but he wasn't there, either. She was getting really irritated now.

"Thackeray?"

Silence.

Had he gone for a walk, too? Let them all go off, she thought. She'd be damned happy, living all alone on Marsh Point! Who needed two old men and one know-it-all, black-eyed rogue?

She groaned. How the hell could she have fallen in love with J. Winthrop Harling? He made too much money. He'd had his life handed to him on a silver platter. He probably didn't know anything about the Deerfield Massacre or the influence of covenant theology on American democracy.

"Thackeray! Dammit, where are you?"

She flounced upstairs to check the bathroom; surely he must have heard her, for all the racket she was making?

The attic door was ajar.

Creaking it open, Hannah stuck her head inside and squinted

up the dark, steep staircase. She could smell the dust and mold. "Thackeray, are you up there?" she called, lowering her voice for no particular reason.

When there was no answer, she reached along the wall for a light switch, but found none. She didn't relish walking up there in the dark. But if Cousin Thackeray was up there, surely he had a flashlight and was just off in some corner? And even if he didn't, even if he wasn't up there, what else—who else—could be?

Bats, she thought. Spiders, cobwebs, mice.

"Coward," she muttered to herself and headed up.

The steps creaked and the musty odor worsened as she climbed the steep staircase. She had never been up to the attic. It was unfinished, there was no rail or wall built up around the stairwell; as her eyes adjusted to the darkness, she could see silhouettes of boxes and old furniture, but no beam of a flashlight. She was probably on a wild-goose chase, while Win and Jonathan and her cousin were all doing the real business of the day elsewhere.

"Thackeray," she called irritably, "are you up here?"

A shuffling noise came from the far corner off to her right, then a strangled cry. Her cousin's voice croaked, "Run, Hannah!"

"Thackeray!"

She lurched up the last three steps. The silhouette of a man emerged from behind a huge armoire. It wasn't her tall, thin, elderly cousin. Hannah quickly grabbed whatever was at her feet—a soggy box of hats, it turned out—and heaved it at the figure. It went wide. She scrambled for a stack of old drapes and started heaving them, too, but in a moment the strange figure had her, one arm clamped firmly around her middle. She kicked. He cursed viciously.

"What have you done with Thackeray?" she yelled. "Who are you? *Help!*"

But with one last, violent curse, he threw her against the armoire. She hit it hard with her right shoulder and spun into the darkness, out of control, breaking her fall with her left arm and landing unceremoniously in a heap in the pile of drapes. Her entire body ached. She let loose a string of curses herself.

"Thackeray, for God's sake, get away!"

She flung drapes at the figure behind her and leaped over the open stairwell to the other side of the attic, away from her cousin. Her pursuer followed. She could hear him breathing hard. She grabbed a ladder-back chair and shoved it into his path, knocking him off his feet.

Thackeray Marsh slipped down the stairs.

The man swore, scrambled to his feet and came after her again. "Bitch!"

There was a small, dirty window at the far end of the attic that Hannah was eyeballing for size. Would she fit? Could she make it through before her attacker caught up with her?

What happened if she did?

What happened if she didn't?

She dodged behind a metal clothes closet and dived for the window, tripping over a rolled-up rug. Adrenaline kept her from feeling any pain, any fatigue. She refused to panic. She got back to her feet.

Something to break the window... She needed something hard and within reach.

An old cane. Perfect!

Iron fingers closed around her left ankle and pulled her off her feet, sending her headlong. A heavy body landed on top of her. She felt the air going out of her lungs. Her right arm was twisted around to the small of her back, under him.

"Don't move, don't talk. I wouldn't want to hurt you."

She nodded her understanding.

And recognized his voice. The pieces of the puzzle fell together.

Her captor was Preston Fowler, director of the New England Athenaeum, to whom she had confided so much. He took a deep breath, then laughed roughly. "I might want to do other things to you," he said, stroking her hair with his free hand, "but not hurt you."

She kicked his shin as sharply as she could.

He bore down upon her twisted arm, and it was all she could do not to cry out. "You just bought yourself some pain, Miss Marsh."

"What do you want with me?"

"Don't talk."

"Tell me!"

He brought his mouth close to her ear, and she felt his breath against her cheek. "You're my ticket to a million dollars."

"I don't—"

"Shut up." He settled himself more firmly on top of her, sliding his free hand down her upper arm and just skimming her breast. "Just be quiet and still and nothing will happen to you."

She didn't move, didn't even breathe.

"You see," he said, "you're my hostage."

"WHERE THE DEVIL do you suppose he is?" Jonathan Harling asked.

Win regarded him with growing exasperation, though the feeling was directed not so much toward his uncle as the situation. They had combed the point for any sign of Preston Fowler, but found only the canoe and a single footprint in the mud. Both, they decided, had to be his. It was too early for tourists, and they had no doubt that Preston Fowler very much wanted first crack at the Harling Collection and the Declaration of Independence.

Win and his uncle headed back onto the deck off Thackeray's dining room, figuring to tell the Marshes everything.

"I don't know where he is, but if—"

Thackeray Marsh burst around the corner of the house, his thin hair sticking up, his face ashen. His clothes were covered with dust, and a cobweb dangled off one arm. He could hardly speak. "Hannah...the bastard's got her...he..."

A cold current shot through Win.

"Calm down, man," Uncle Jonathan ordered impatiently. "We can't understand what in blazes you're saying."

Win had understood. "Where?"

Thackeray pointed to the house. "The attic…"

It was all Win needed to hear.

Behind him, Uncle Jonathan hissed in annoyance. "Now don't go barging in up there before you get all the facts!" He pounded his cane on the ground. "Winthrop—Winthrop, we need a plan!"

But Win was already through the French doors. He grabbed the poker from the living room fireplace and headed upstairs, the cold current now a hot rage.

Fowler. If the stinking bastard even touched Hannah…

He ripped open the door and took the stairs two at a time, ignoring the darkness. He thought only fleetingly about how Fowler might be armed, what he had planned. His main concern was Hannah.

Hannah…

At the top of the stairs he stopped and listened, let his eyes adjust to the lack of light. He heard nothing, could make out nothing that resembled Hannah or Fowler. Had the bastard already sneaked off with her?

To his left he heard a soft moan.

"Hannah?"

Holding his poker high, he moved toward the sound. He had to fight his way through scattered drapes and past overturned furniture, but remained alert. The sun was angling in through the dirty window now, casting a faint light upon a figure that lay sprawled on what appeared to be a rolled-up carpet.

It moved, and the sun hit strands of long, silken, blond hair.

"Hannah," Win breathed.

Within seconds he was kneeling beside her, pulling a nasty-looking gag from her mouth, fumbling at the drapery cord that was tied around her wrists. Her eyes were huge and frightened, and damned beautiful.

She spat dust and cobwebs from her mouth, coughing, and finally sputtered, "It's a trap."

No sooner were the words out than Win felt something cold and metallic against his lower jaw. "Now I have two hostages," Preston Fowler said.

"Now," Win said tightly, "you have one hell of a mess on your hands. Let us both go, before you get yourself in any deeper."

"You arrogant, insufferable prig." Fowler laughed nastily, never moving the gun. "God, I've wanted to say those words to one of you for years. No, do not move, I warn you. As you have so accurately pointed out—as if I needed you to tell me—I'm in one hell of a mess. I intend, however, to emerge from it intact."

"He thinks Cousin Thackeray has the Harling Collection," Hannah told Win hoarsely. "He wants the Declaration of Independence. He's the one—" She had to pause to cough, so merciless had Fowler been in applying the gag. "He broke into your uncle's apartment."

"I know," Win responded gently. "I should have known from the beginning. He knew what you were working on. With your blond hair and reputation as a biographer, he probably figured out you were Hannah Marsh—Priscilla's descendant—right from the start."

Fowler smirked. "It was a simple matter to blow her cover story straight to hell."

"So he watched you, and knowing you were an expert researcher, he followed your leads to the Harling Collection...." Hannah shut her eyes, and Win could see pain and regret wash over her; it could be no worse than what he felt. He would give anything to see her smile. "Hannah, Uncle Jonathan knew it had to be Fowler who ransacked his apartment. Other than you, he was the only one who could have known about the diary or the Harling Collection."

"Oh, stop, both of you," Fowler ordered. "Let's get this over with. The Harling Collection, Miss Hannah. Where is it?"

She shook her head, not, Win could see, for the first time, and said wearily, "I told you, I don't know."

Keeping the gun pressed to Win's jaw, Fowler leaned over him and said to Hannah, "Suppose I start blowing holes in your lover boy here? Do you think that would improve your memory?"

Win made himself chuckle. "You've got that one wrong, Fowler. Give her the gun. She'll blow holes in me herself."

"Shut up!"

Win thought he heard a small, creaking sound on the attic stairs. Footsteps? Old men's footsteps?

Dear God, he thought.

He looked at Hannah and saw her eyes widen slightly. Had she heard the creaking sound, too?

Uncle Jonathan and Cousin Thackeray coming to rescue them.

It was almost more than Win could bear.

His fingers closed around the poker. One small opening was all he needed. He longed to knock Preston Fowler onto his greedy ass. But he had to cover for the two down on the staircase. Hannah, he noticed, was noisily shifting around.

"Can I untie her wrists?" Win asked.

"No, leave them. She's a vicious bitch, you know. Practically emasculated me. I'm sure you're disappointed she didn't succeed. But I won't be diverted from my task. The Harling Collection, Miss Marsh."

Behind them, Jonathan Harling's voice broke through the darkness. "It isn't hers to give away."

Then Thackeray Marsh said, "Drop the gun, Mr. Fowler. I have a loaded Colt .45 pointed at your lower spine and would be glad to pull the trigger to repay you for the thrashing you gave me alone."

"You're bluffing," Fowler sneered.

"So call my bluff. Find out what happens."

"He's a mean shot," Uncle Jonathan said. "He taught me how to shoot when we were at Harvard together in the thirties.

I remember he could hit a weasel from fifty yards, right between
the eyes—''

"I can blow your nephew's head off," Fowler interjected.

Thackeray sniffed. "Go ahead. He's a Harling. I'll get a bullet
into you before you get to Hannah."

Win's eyes locked with Hannah's. He could see she realized
her cousin was having a hell of a time.

"Drop the gun," Thackeray Marsh drawled. "Slowly."

He seemed to be taking his lines from old Clint Eastwood
movies, but Fowler, biting back what sounded like a curse, removed the gun from Win's jaw and slowly lowered it to the
floor.

"Bastards," he muttered, "all of you."

Then he whipped around, roaring like a madman, catching
everyone by surprise; he shoved the two old men aside and
leaped for the stairs.

"Shoot him!" Uncle Jonathan yelled. "Shoot the greedy bastard!"

"I can't bloody see him! I'm not twenty anymore, you know,
you old snot. Why the hell don't you go after him?"

"I'm eighty years old!"

"So? I'm seventy-nine."

"Take care of Hannah," Win growled. "*I'll* go after him.
Mind if I borrow your gun, Thackeray?"

"Not at all, but you'd better take care. It's not loaded."

Win forced himself to refrain from comment.

"If you hadn't gone off like a decapitated chicken," Uncle
Jonathan put in, "we'd have been able to take time to load the
gun. As it was, Thackeray couldn't remember where he'd put
the bullets. In fact, he'd almost forgotten he even had the gun.
I had to remind him...."

"The hell with it," Win muttered and dashed off with the
poker. Maybe Fowler hadn't loaded his gun, either.

He fought his way through the scattered drapes and overturned
furniture, choking on cobwebs and dust, warning himself not to
let his anger lead him into another trap. With a near-physical

effort, he dismissed the image of Hannah bound and gagged. It must have been a devastating experience for her. And it was all his fault. Would she ever be the same? Would she ever forgive him for not having shared his suspicions sooner?

No. You'll have to deal with that later.

Fowler had shut the attic door. Win pushed against it, but it wouldn't give. The bastard must have blocked it. He reared back and threw all his weight at the old door. It bounced and cracked a little, but still didn't give.

"Here," Hannah said, suddenly beside him, as pale as a ghost, "let me help."

Win saw the raw, bloody wrists, the spreading bruise on her jaw, and felt rage boil up inside him, threatening once again to overwhelm him.

Then he saw the gun in her hand.

"What's that?" he asked.

She smiled a little. "Fowler's gun."

Win grinned, suddenly reenergized. He pointed a thumb at the door and smiled at Hannah. "Shall we?"

She set the gun upon a step, and Win turned it so it wasn't pointed at either of them. He was taking no more chances.

Uncle Jonathan and Cousin Thackeray appeared at the top of the stairs. "Heave-ho!" they yelled.

It took Hannah and Win three tries, and the door splintered into three parts before the chair Fowler had anchored under the knob gave way.

They were out.

11

HANNAH IGNORED THE PAIN in her wrists and shoulders, her dry mouth, her fear. She concentrated only on keeping up with Win and trying not to shoot him or herself in the foot. Guns were not her thing.

They caught up with Fowler in Cousin Thackeray's truck. He must have snatched the keys from the hook by the back door; he was still fumbling with them when Win hauled him out of the cab and threw him onto the ground. Hannah controlled a wild impulse to fire the gun into the air.

"All right, all right!" Fowler yelled when Win twisted his arms behind his back. "I give up. Call the damned police."

Breathing hard, Win didn't let up. "You won't try anything?"

"Like what, running? You lunatics would shoot me like a dog." He spat a mouthful of grass and dirt. "Just let me go. I'll take what's coming to me."

"You're damned right you will."

Fowler glanced at Win, who still held his prisoner's arms pinned behind him. "I wouldn't have hurt anyone."

Hannah could see Win gritting his teeth. "You did hurt someone."

"She's a Marsh. One wouldn't think a Harling would go all soft over—"

He shut up when Hannah stepped forward, holding his gun. "One wouldn't think," she said, "a snooty Harling could knock you on your behind, either, but look at you now, Mr. Fowler."

"It's *Doctor* Fowler," he said loftily.

Win made a sound of pure disgust and let up, climbing to his feet. He looked at Hannah. "I'll call the police. You can keep an eye on him?"

"Sure. With pleasure."

Fowler sat up, his face red with anger, devoid of remorse. That was as far as Hannah would let him go. After her ordeal in the attic, she was taking no chances. But just as Win started for the house, they heard the wail of a siren, and Cousin Thackeray and Uncle Jonathan raced out of the back door, armed to the teeth with kitchen knives and skillets. They looked as if they were having the time of their lives.

"I've called the police," Thackeray announced.

"They're on their way," Jonathan added excitedly.

Fowler looked at his four captors and muttered, "Thank God."

The police came, explanations were made, and Preston Fowler was carted off. Charges were filed and the sorting-out process was begun. Through it all, Hannah noticed that Cousin Thackeray never once allowed that the Harlings and the director of the New England Athenaeum might be correct in their opinion that he knew the location of the long-missing Harling Collection.

She also noted that Win Harling never left her side.

The police seemed to be having a difficult time fathoming why a director of a prestigious institution like the New England Athenaeum would risk arrest to snatch a collection of old papers, even one that might include a valuable copy of the Declaration of Independence.

"How valuable?" the lieutenant in charge asked the group of people assembled in his small office.

The Marshes didn't answer. The Harlings, however, said, "A million dollars, give or take ten thousand or so."

The lieutenant, a rail-thin Maine native, whistled. "But there's no proof this thing exists?"

"None whatsoever," Thackeray Marsh replied, although the question wasn't directed at him.

Win smiled at Hannah, but said nothing. Then his gaze fell upon her bruised and raw wrists and his smile vanished, his expression darkening. The police had asked her if she needed medical attention, but she'd said no, largely because she didn't want to miss the Harlings' explanation of the day's festivities.

"And this Fowler character," the lieutenant went on, "learned about the collection—and presumably the Declaration of Independence—when Miss Marsh here was conducting research in Boston?"

"They weren't in cahoots," Thackeray put in.

"That's not what I was implying. I'm merely trying to establish the sequence of events. Miss Marsh, we'll need a statement from you on your trip to Boston and your association with Dr. Fowler."

"Certainly. I had no idea he would go to such extremes for personal profit. I myself had only an academic interest in the collection."

An eyebrow went up and the lieutenant asked, "Even though the subject of your new biography is one of your ancestors, who was wrongly executed by an ancestor of the Harlings?"

She smiled coolly. "Even so."

Jonathan Harling gave a small grunt that she managed to ignore.

Beside her, Win said, "Fowler broke into my uncle's apartment in an attempt to discover any materials that would provide him with a clue as to the location of the Harling Collection. He stole a diary written by—"

Win's elderly uncle cleared his throat and squirmed in his rickety wooden chair. "That's not quite the case. Fowler did break into my apartment, of course, and combed the place, but he didn't steal the diary. He just read it."

"He read it," the lieutenant repeated dubiously.

"That's right. It describes how the Marshes hoodwinked us out of our land here in southern Maine and stole the Harling Collection."

Thackeray was on his feet now. "It was never your land! The Marshes are the legitimate owners of Marsh Point and have been for a hundred years!"

The lieutenant sighed. "Could we stick to current history? The diary, Mr. Harling. You say it was never missing?"

"That's right. I only claimed it was gone to keep my nephew on the case. He and Miss Marsh…well, their relationship was about to go sour unless Winthrop did something, and I felt he was of a mind to do nothing at all, and therefore…"

Hannah could feel Win stiffening beside her and smiled. His uncle, she thought, was every bit as exasperating as her cousin. "I wouldn't," he said, "have done nothing."

Jonathan Harling shrugged. "Couldn't take that chance, m'boy."

The lieutenant continued. "How do you know Fowler read the diary?"

"Common sense," Jonathan replied simply.

Thackeray snorted. "A damned good guess is what it was."

"If you knew the Harlings knew the Marshes had the Harling Collection," the lieutenant asked, "why didn't they come after it before now?"

"We didn't know. Anne Harling was an eccentric and…well, she didn't care for the Marshes. She was aware of their grudge against our family and—"

"You—meaning the Harling family—didn't take her accusations seriously," the lieutenant supplied.

The elderly Harling pursed his lips and remained silent.

Hannah noticed a ghost of a smile on Win's face and felt a rush of pure affection for him.

"But Preston Fowler did," the lieutenant went on. "What made you suspect him?"

Jonathan squirmed.

"Tell him," his nephew ordered.

The old man grimaced. "I didn't think—I didn't believe Hannah, although a Marsh, was capable of ransacking my apartment. I knew my nephew didn't do it, and I knew *I* didn't do it."

"Why not a random thief?"

"Impossible."

His tone was so supercilious and dismissive that even the lieutenant didn't argue. He muttered something about not dealing with Nero Wolfe here and proceeded with his questioning, finally sending them all home with orders to stick around, because he was sure to need further clarifications. They began to head back toward the house.

"By the way, Thackeray," the officer said to his retreating fellow townsman, "what's this about you holding a gun on Fowler? Seems to me you don't have a weapon registered."

It was Jonathan Harling who spun around and replied, "Thackeray Marsh hold a gun on anyone? Don't be absurd. That old buzzard couldn't shoot a hole through the side of a barn at fifty feet."

"But you all said..."

"A ruse, Lieutenant, a simple ruse."

Then Jonathan marched out, shoulders thrust back, as if he'd made perfect sense and hadn't told a huge lie. For once Thackeray didn't contradict him.

Win seized Hannah by the waist. "I just know those two are both going to live to be a hundred," he muttered.

Back at the house, Thackeray rattled around in the kitchen and emerged with cups of hot tea laced with brandy and insisted they all drink up. For once, no one argued.

"Are you certain you don't want a doctor to examine your wounds?" Jonathan Harling asked Hannah.

She shook her head. "I'll be fine, thanks."

"It's a wonder Winthrop permitted Fowler to leave the property relatively intact."

Only the darkening of Win's eyes indicated he concurred with his uncle. All things considered, he was being remarkably untalkative. He never, however, left Hannah's side.

"Winthrop, hell," she said spiritedly. "It's a wonder *I* let him leave intact. Did he hurt you at all, Cousin Thackeray?"

"Only my pride. I have never done anything so difficult as leaving you in the clutches of that man, but I knew he had a gun, and I would be of no use to you, dead or maimed." He swirled around a mouthful of tea and then swallowed; gradually his face regained its color. "He sneaked into the house while Win and Jonathan were off plotting. You had gone, and I'm afraid he took me quite by surprise. Clearly he had no idea the Harlings were about. He thought he would just have to contend with Hannah and me. Of course, we would have managed."

Jonathan Harling opened his mouth, but his nephew cut him off before he could speak. "I'm glad things worked out."

"I just have one more question," Hannah said, her gaze taking in both old men. "You two were at Harvard together?"

Thackeray's face took on a look of pure distaste and Jonathan's matched it.

"Cousin Thackeray, you never told me you attended Harvard!"

"I'm not proud of it," he stated.

"He graduated magna cum laude," Jonathan Harling added. "Damned near killed my father, having a Marsh outdo a Harling, but I wasn't much of a student in those days. I reached my potential later, in graduate school. Thackeray had gone back to Maine by then, intent on being a Marsh."

Thackeray nodded. "Jonathan and I should have been great friends."

"And were for a while," his former classmate reminisced wistfully. He grabbed the brandy and splashed more into Thackeray's teacup, then into his own. "To our lost youth, my friend."

They drank up.

Win leaned toward Hannah and whispered, "Don't believe any of this. Uncle Jonathan's just leading up to demanding what in hell your cousin's done with the Harling Collection."

Sure enough, a few minutes later, Jonathan Harling leaned back, looking smug and content. "So, Thackeray, where have you had my family's papers hidden all these years?"

WIN FILLED HANNAH'S TUB with water as hot as he thought she could stand it and added white bath salts from a glass bottle. He had piled two fluffy white towels on the edge of the tub, where he sat, watching the water foam. He had abandoned Uncle Jonathan to dinner with Thackeray Marsh. The two would, no doubt, argue about the Harling Collection well into the night or perhaps reminisce about their days at Harvard. One simply never knew with those two, Win had decided.

"Going to take a bath?" Hannah asked, appearing in the bathroom doorway.

He shook his head. "You are."

She half smiled. "By your order?"

"It'll be good for your bumps and bruises."

And her spirits, he hoped. Since returning to her cottage she had been uncharacteristically reticent, and her skin, though normally pale, seemed almost ghostlike now. He had left her standing in front of her picture window, staring at the sea, while he filled the tub. A gulf had opened between them. He sensed it, hated it, but didn't know what to do about it.

He turned off the water. The silence that surrounded them felt damned unbearable. He felt Hannah's luminous eyes on him. He turned to meet them. "Are you going to be all right?"

She nodded, saying nothing.

"It was a hell of a scare, Hannah, for all of us. You just got the worst of it."

She nodded again. He rose from the tub and started past her, but she touched his arm, just a whisper of her fingers. "When Fowler had me pinned down..." She stopped and cleared her throat. Win could see the pain in her eyes, a pain that had nothing to do with cuts and bruises. "I wanted you to come, Win. It scares me how much. I've always been so independent."

"You still are," he assured her, then gestured to the tub. "Relax for as long as you want. Call me if you need anything."

And he left.

HANNAH SOAKED IN THE TUB until her skin was as pink as a lobster's, but couldn't boil J. Winthrop Harling out of herself. The hot water swirling around her only served to remind her of how much she still wanted him.

Fatigue weighed down her eyelids, while stress and the heat of the water made her feel drained and limp, without energy or purpose. She wanted only to sleep and when she woke up, to find that her life on Marsh Point was as it had been before she'd gone to Boston. Except that it wouldn't be, couldn't be…and if it meant losing Win, she didn't want it to be the same as before. She knew that.

Such contradictions! She groaned at her own confusion and climbed out of the tub, the stiffness in her joints and muscles eased for the moment. She toweled off, pulled her terry cloth robe from the hook where she kept it and wrapped it around her. Her reflection in the steamy mirror made her wince.

"You look like hell," she muttered.

Dark circles under her eyes made them appear even wider, nervous, afraid. Her skin looked splotchy and unnatural. Her mouth was raw from biting her lips. The bruises and cuts on her wrists had turned ugly shades of red and purple. She looked done in, as if the impact of what had happened earlier today had finally hit her squarely between the eyes.

And yet that was only a part of it.

The rest of what had hit her, she knew, was the impact of being in love with Win Harling…and of knowing she had no choice but to tell him to take himself and his uncle and head back to Boston, where they belonged.

WIN LISTENED to Hannah's request without interrupting. She had emerged from the bathroom in a robe that was surprisingly sexy and feminine, given her penchant for androgynous flannel nightshirts. "I know I look like hell," she'd said. That was the first inaccuracy he'd heard from her lips. Others followed.

But he let her talk.

Finally she finished and looked at him expectantly. He knew what he was supposed to say. Yes, she was absolutely right. Yes, he would collect Uncle Jonathan and leave immediately. But instead he said, "Let me see if I've got this straight."

"Okay."

. He moved over on the couch and made room for her. "Have a seat."

"I don't…"

"What are you worried about? Didn't you just say that last night was just the product of—how did you put it?"

"Adrenaline. The excitement of the moment."

"Right. Then you shouldn't be afraid of sitting next to me, should you?"

"I'm not."

He patted the spot beside him.

She flipped back her hair and sat down, as far from him as she could manage. He tried not to smile. *Adrenaline, my hind end!*

The tie on her robe had loosened, so it wasn't wrapped around her as primly and tightly as it had been. He could see the soft swell of one breast, still pink from her long, hot bath. Right now, even her feet looked sexy, designed just to torment him.

He wasn't leaving.

"Okay," he began. "You think Uncle Jonathan and I ought to leave because we belong in Boston."

"Yes."

"Does that mean we should never leave town? Never take a vacation? Nothing?"

She scowled. "It means you don't belong here."

"On Marsh Point," he concluded.

"That's right."

"And you and I. We don't belong together because I belong in Boston, I'm a Harling, I make too much money, I have a city job, and I would never live down falling in love with a Marsh."

She mumbled something that he had to make her repeat, which she did reluctantly, not meeting his eye. "I didn't say anything about falling in love with a Marsh."

"Ahh, correct. You said 'being with.' A fine distinction, don't you think?"

"No."

He leaned toward her. "Hannah, you're dead wrong on all counts."

She didn't say a word.

"I love Boston, but I didn't grow up there. I don't need to

live there. I am a Harling. You're not wrong about that, but you are wrong if you think it determines my outlook toward you or anything else. I do make a great deal of money, but how much is too much? And I don't, as you implied, exist to make money. I could not make another dime my entire life and find ways to be fulfilled and happy. As for a city job… With computers, I can do my work from virtually anywhere. I just happen to prefer Boston.''

Her top teeth were bearing down on her lower lip, already ragged from her ordeal with Preston Fowler. Win ran a forefinger gently over her lip, freeing it, while further tormenting himself. He shifted on the couch. Stupid to have made a fire; its heat was totally unnecessary, as far as he was concerned.

"And that last—never living down 'being with' a Marsh. Hannah, I don't give a damn what people think of who I want to be with. It's never mattered to me and doesn't now.'' He spoke in a low, deliberate voice. "And you know that.''

"Win…''

"You know all of it.''

She jumped to her feet. "I can't let you stay!''

"Fine. I'll go if you want me to go. Just tell me the real reason why.''

"Can't you just leave?''

"Hannah…''

"All you have to do is get your uncle, throw your stuff into your car and drive on out of here. It's really very simple.''

He got up. "Okay, if that's what you want. I'll go pack up. Can you run over and tell Uncle Jonathan to be ready to leave in fifteen minutes?''

"Sure. I mean…'' She narrowed her eyes at him, visibly suspicious. "You're going to leave, just like that?''

"It's not just like that. It's after listening to all your crazy reasons why I should and taking you at your word. You want me out. Okay, I'm out.''

He started down the hall.

"Now wait just a minute!'' she blurted.

Ignoring her—and his own incipient sense of relief—he walked into the guest room, where he'd deposited his overnight bag.

She was right behind him. "But you don't believe my reasons for wanting you gone."

"That's right," he agreed, shoving things back into his bag. "I don't."

"But you're not going to insist on the truth?"

"Nope."

"Why not?"

"Because I'm not a boor."

She was stunned into a momentary silence.

"If a lady orders me out of her house," he went on, "I go. It's the proper thing to do, you know. I don't plan to share a prison cell with Preston Fowler."

Hannah frowned.

Win resisted an urge to scoop her into his arms and carry her off. She looked so tired, so damned fragile. And yet he knew it was an illusion. Hannah Marsh was a strong and independent woman who was struggling with the fact that that strength and independence had been challenged.

"I wish I'd knocked a few of the bastard's teeth loose when I'd had the chance," he said. "You?"

Surprise flickered in her green eyes, then she gave a small smile and nodded. "More than a few."

"Damned humiliating, having to be rescued by those two old goats."

She almost laughed. "At least we got Fowler in the end."

"Yes, we did."

Then the laughter went out of her eyes, and she said softly, "It was terrifying, Win, finding him up in the attic.... I didn't know what he'd done to Cousin Thackeray, and then, when he tackled me...and touched me..." She inhaled. "But we got him."

"I'm not Fowler, Hannah. I'm not the enemy."

"You were," she reminded him quickly. "For a while you

were, and it was fun thinking that way, but after today…it's just not fun anymore.''

Win zipped his bag and straightened, his body rigid. ''Go warn Uncle Jonathan,'' he said.

She started to speak, then shut her mouth, nodded and went into her bedroom to get dressed.

COUSIN THACKERAY'S HOUSE was locked up and empty.

Hannah peered through a living room window. The only light visible was from the dying coals in the fireplace. A stiff wind gusted at her back. The contrast between the cool night air and her still-overheated skin was enough to make her shiver.

Where the hell was he?

Had Jonathan Harling gone with him?

She made a hissing sound of pure irritation through her gritted teeth and went around to all the entrances, looking for an un-locked door or a note, courteously mentioning where in blazes they'd gone.

There was nothing.

Indeed, her life had been different since the Harlings had erupted into it. Of course, that had been her doing. She had gone looking for them. It wasn't as if they had decided to hunt up the Marshes and demand Marsh Point and the Harling Collection after a hundred years. Now she was taking responsibility for her own actions.

But how could she send the two Jonathan Winthrop Harlings packing if she couldn't even find one of them?

Muttering and growling, she marched back to her cottage. On the way she noticed that Cousin Thackeray's truck was gone.

Win had set his bag by the back door in the kitchen and was scrambling some eggs, apparently unaware of her presence. She could smell toast burning. He cursed and popped it up, just shy of being ruined. Hannah observed the fit of his sweater over his broad shoulders, the place where it ended, just above his hips. She imagined his long legs intertwined with hers.

It wasn't fair, this longing for him. Making love last night had only made her want him more. Made her even more aware of him—and of herself, of her own capacity for love and desire.

Her throat tightened. She cleared it and said, "They've absconded for parts unknown."

Giving no sign of having been startled, Win looked around. "I wondered if they'd end up plotting something." He divided the eggs in the pan and dumped half onto one plate and the other half onto a second. "Jam on your toast?"

"Don't you think we should go look for them?"

He smeared butter onto the two slices of toast and put another two into the toaster. "Where would you suggest we begin our search? For all we know, they've decided to go fishing in Canada."

"They've gone after the Harling Collection," Hannah said. "You know it and I know it."

"To what end?"

"I don't know!"

"Maybe they've just gone out for lobster." He put the toast onto the plates and carried them into the living room. "Let's eat by the fire. It's always easier to endure being shot out of the saddle on a full stomach."

Hannah followed him into the living room. Except for the fact that his bag stood by the door, he didn't look like a man intending to depart anytime soon. She remained standing. "You haven't been shot out of the saddle. I've just asked you to leave."

"Then you plan to continue our relationship," he said.

"Well, yeah, I guess so."

His eyes darkened, looking as black and suspicious as the day he had run into her, outside his house. "That's not good enough, Hannah."

It wasn't. She'd known it when she'd said it. She changed the subject. "What about Cousin Thackeray and your uncle?"

"They're big boys. They can take care of themselves."

"But why didn't they tell us where they were going?"

"Maybe because it's none of our damned business."

He sat cross-legged on the floor in front of the fire, placing her plate next to him. He'd forgotten forks. Hannah went into the kitchen and got them, along with the second batch of toast, which had just popped up. It, too, was nearly burned. She slathered it with spicy pear butter and felt a sudden gnawing of hunger in her stomach. Dinner, perhaps, wasn't such a bad idea.

She took up her plate and sat at her desk chair in front of her computer. Win turned so that he was facing her instead of the fire. She groaned inwardly. Why did he have to be so damned good-looking? So rich. So successful. So *Harling*.

"You look more yourself," he said softly, the hardness gone from his eyes.

She nodded. "I'm feeling better."

"Hell of a day. If you want, I'll take a spin around the area and see if I can find your cousin and Uncle Jonathan."

"No, I'll go. I know the area."

He said nothing.

Suddenly she knew she didn't want to go alone. If she had to, she could do it. But she didn't have to. It was a choice, she thought, not a sign of dependence.

"We'll take my car," she said.

12

As cars went, Hannah's wasn't much. She explained to Win that in a rural setting high mileage, reliability and durability were more important than speed and prestige. He realized she was contrasting her car with his—in essence, her life with his. Or at least her understanding of his life. There was a difference, he thought.

They bounced along the narrow road that led from Marsh Point into town. "This is nuts," she muttered.

"So turn back."

She glanced at him; her hair seemed even paler in the darkness. "What about those two?"

"At worst, Uncle Jonathan is having Thackeray take him to the Harling Collection at gunpoint. It's far more likely they've gone into town for a drink after their ordeal today. Either way, if they had wanted us to interfere, they would have told us where they were going."

"Don't you feel responsible?"

"No."

The car slowed. Hannah gripped the wheel with both hands.

Win stretched his legs as best he could in the small vehicle. "You're not really worried, either. You're just looking for excuses, so you won't have to toss me, after all."

She shot him a look. "I am not."

"Then you still want me to head back to Boston tonight?"

"As soon as we find your uncle," she confirmed.

"Suppose he doesn't come back until morning. Suppose he and your cousin have taken off for Boston to see their old haunts in Harvard Square."

"Cousin Thackeray's not that crazy."

"Uncle Jonathan is," Win said mildly.

She braked hard, swerving onto the side of the dark road. The ocean was mere yards away. Win, however, assumed she knew what she was doing, and that whatever it was didn't include dumping him out for the seagulls to pick over.

After a few maneuvers, she had the car heading back toward Marsh Point.

"I'm not thinking straight tonight," she mumbled under her breath.

Win chose not to comment.

When they arrived back at the cottage, Win noticed that Thackeray Marsh's yellow truck stood in the driveway behind his house. He and Hannah looked at each other and sighed. "I wonder where they've been," she said, puzzled. "We were on the only road out of here."

The house's living room lights were on. Win climbed out of Hannah's car and started up the driveway without a word, assuming she would want to ease her mind and find out where the two old men had been.

She fell in beside him, not looking at him, not speaking. Watching her, Win nearly tripped over a rock. Her jaw was set...her eyes shining...everything about her was alive, focused, dynamic. The near depression, the preoccupation of earlier seemed to have vanished. And, Win thought, he hadn't even gone back to Boston yet.

As he'd suspected, he wasn't the problem.

He wondered if she'd figured that out yet.

On the stone path to Thackeray's side door, she darted past him and didn't bother knocking before bursting in.

"Ahh, the posse is back," Uncle Jonathan announced.

Hannah was having none of it. "Where were you two?"

Thackeray Marsh answered. "We took a spin out old Marsh Road. It's barely passable, but we managed."

"Thought we might see a moose," his contemporary added.

They were both seated near the fireplace, where Thackeray was poking at the coals, trying to restart the fire. Win saw that his uncle looked exhausted; he was also filthy and about as pleased with himself as his nephew had ever seen him. He doubted a moose sighting had done it.

Thackeray cursed the stubborn fire and gave up, flopping into his chair. He addressed his young cousin. "We'd have told you we were going," he said, "but didn't want to catch you...well, you know."

Win watched Hannah stiffen and her cheeks grow red. "I was asking Win to leave," she said starchily.

"Tonight? After what we have all been through today?" Thackeray snorted and waved a hand. "Even I wouldn't do that. Damned rude it is."

"It's okay," Win said. "She was bluffing."

"I was not bluffing!"

"Yeah, you were. You've just been slow to realize it." He smiled at her. "The perfect bluff is the one you do on impulse, when you're not sure it is a bluff or even why you're doing it."

Uncle Jonathan gave an exaggerated yawn. "Winthrop, what in hell are you talking about? Carry this woman off, will you? I'm tired. Thackeray and I have a big day tomorrow, and I need my rest. I'm not a young man anymore, you know."

Hannah threw up her hands. "These two are impossible!" she exclaimed irritably. "Carry me off, like he's some kind of Neanderthal. Moose hunting. Bluffs that aren't bluffs. Crazy Bostonians trying to kill me. Heck, I'm going to bed."

"Before you do," Thackeray said, "would you and your fellow here bring in the trunk from the back of my truck? I'm afraid Jonathan and I expended ourselves getting it into the truck in the first place. It's damned heavy."

"Set it in the kitchen," Uncle Jonathan added.

Thackeray nodded. "Yes, we'll have at it in the morning."

Hannah refused to play their game and started out without demanding an explanation, but Win didn't have her forbearance, or just hadn't reached total disgust the way she apparently had. "What trunk?" he asked.

"The one in the back of Thackeray's—"

"Uncle Jonathan..." Win warned.

The old man sighed. "See for yourself."

Thackeray sat forward and shook a finger at Jonathan Harling. "Now wait just a minute. We agreed to wait until morning."

"I'm not breaking our agreement. All Win has to do is look at the damned thing, and he'll recognize his name in brass letters on the front, don't you think? I sure as the devil did."

Hannah froze in the doorway.

"We'll be glad to get the trunk in," Win assured them.

He slipped his arm around Hannah's waist and urged her outside, where the wind was coming in huge gusts now. She had plenty of energy to jump up and into the truck bed, ahead of him.

Indeed, the name Harling was embossed in scarred brass lettering across the front of the trunk.

"The Harling Collection, I presume," he said.

Her luminous eyes fastened on him. "It must have been out at the old lighthouse on the other side of Marsh Point. It's been abandoned since 1900. I've never been out there because Cousin Thackeray insisted it wasn't safe."

Win decided not to mention the obvious: Uncle Jonathan was right. A Marsh had stolen the Harling family papers, just as Anne Harling had claimed in her diary of long ago.

"You know what's going to happen if we leave this thing in the kitchen," he said.

"Preston Fowler's in jail. He's no threat."

"Hannah, think about those two old men in there. Once each thinks the other's asleep, they're going to sneak downstairs and skim off whatever they don't want the other to see."

"Cousin Thackeray wouldn't—" She stopped herself, stared at the trunk, then said, "Yes, that's exactly what he'd do."

"And what do you think Uncle Jonathan was making such a big deal about getting to bed for? He never turns in before midnight. It's not even ten o'clock."

Hannah pursed her lips. "They can't be trusted with history."

So they each grabbed an end and lifted the trunk out of the

truck. After that Win offered to carry it himself, but Hannah was
having none of that. He grinned. "Don't trust me, do you?"

She held tight to her end of the trunk. "I do."

"But I'm a Harling."

"You can't help that. Look, it's not far to the cottage."

"Doesn't this hurt your wrist?"

"A little."

He could see in her expression that it hurt a lot. "Hannah, let
go."

For a few seconds she did nothing except stare at the brilliant
night sky. Then she looked at him, nodded and let go. Win carried the trunk into her kitchen and set it down next to his overnight bag.

"You were the one who was bluffing," Hannah said accus-
ingly, pointing at the bag.

"Me?"

"You never had any intention of leaving tonight."

"If you asked me to…"

"If I *made* you."

"I'm not a cad. If you didn't want me around, I'd have gone."

"Ha!"

He straightened, breathing hard…from carrying the heavy
trunk…from watching her prance ahead of him. From wanting
her. "I was just hoping I could call your bluff before you called
mine."

"Well, you didn't succeed."

"Yes, I did."

"How so?"

He picked up his bag. "Say the word, Hannah." His eyes
held hers. "Right now. Tell me to leave and I'll leave. No arguments. Nothing. I'll go."

"Your uncle won't leave without seeing the Harling Collection."

"This is between us. Just you and me, Hannah. I'll deal with
Uncle Jonathan if I have to. What's it going to be?"

She hesitated, staring at the floor, at anything but him. For an instant, Win wondered if he'd guessed wrong, if having him around was more than she could tolerate.

"You're making excuses," he said, "so I can stay."

Then she looked at him and grinned, the devil in her eye. "You noticed?" She glided toward him, confident. "You can stay, Win Harling, under one condition: I'm not going to let you sneak into the kitchen and have at that trunk before I do."

"How do you propose to stop me?"

"You know the saying: An Ounce of Prevention Is Worth a Pound of Cure." She slid her arms around him. "I propose that the only way for you to get to the trunk tonight is through me."

"Physically?"

She smiled. "Physically."

"TELL ME IF I HURT YOU," Win whispered, pulling her on top of him.

"You're not hurting...not at all."

Because of the thrashing she had received from Preston Fowler, Win was being gentle and cautious with his caresses, not that it was necessary. Hannah wanted him as much as she ever had. He stroked the curve of her hip, and she felt his maleness alive between them. The earlier fears had been dissipated by her desire for him, and his for her.

They kissed, a long, slow, delicious kiss that penetrated to her soul.

"I guess," she said teasingly, "old Cotton Harling would have us both hanged."

Win laughed softly, running his fingers through her hair, his eyes locked with hers. "I'm sure he could think of a number of offenses. Do you feel guilty?"

"Nope. You?"

He answered by lifting her gently, and she knew what he wanted. Slowly, erotically, she brought him inside her.

"I don't want to hurt you," he murmured close to her, "not ever."

Then he inhaled, letting her set the pace. She did so eagerly, believing once more in her capacity to confront the future, how-

ever different it might be from the one she'd imagined for herself
only a few weeks before.

DESPITE HER BEST efforts to avoid the predicament, Hannah had
fallen asleep, her body mercilessly intertwined with Win's. It
had been that kind of night. She woke with the first light of
dawn, impatiently taking a minute to plan her escape.

Finally, carefully lifting his arm from her waist, she peeled
her top half free and raised herself upon one elbow. He looked
so innocent in sleep. But he was a competent man, strong-willed,
caring, not one to cross. Locking the doors and pulling the
shades and curtains had been his idea; he hadn't trusted their
two elderly neighbors not to barge in on them.

She contemplated her next move. Somehow she had to extri-
cate the lower half of her body. How had she got into such a
position?

Then she remembered.

Oh, she remembered.

In the middle of the night she had stirred in the darkness, half-
asleep, the nightmare still swirling around her...Preston Fowler
on top of her...Cousin Thackeray in danger. She had cried out,
and Win had been there, wide-awake, pushing back the shadows,
he'd said, of his own nightmare. They'd clung to each other and
fallen asleep that way.

How could she go back to sleeping alone? An occasional night
or two, perhaps. But not permanently. Not because she had been
unhappy before she met and fell in love with J. Winthrop Harling. But because she *had* met him and fallen in love with him.

Still, there were his legs and other things between her and
freedom.

She bent down and listened to his steady breathing; he was
definitely asleep. Slowly, biting down now on her lower lip, she
eased her left leg free, holding her breath when he flopped over
and lay on his stomach. His hair brushed against her breasts. She
almost groaned, wanting him all over again.

Exhaling silently, she yanked out her right leg in one quick
movement. It was the only way to go. Given its delicate position,

anything else would have just started things up again and then she'd have been in a mess.

She was free.

On the wrong side of the bed.

With her spectacular view of the water and solitary sleeping habits, she had pushed her bed against the wall, so that she could just open her eyes and see out the window. It was almost like sleeping outside. Now, however, she was on the wall side of the bed.

Which meant crawling over her sleeping partner.

There'd be hell to pay if he caught her.

But how could she ever explain to Cousin Thackeray that she'd spent the night making love to a Harling, instead of doing her damnedest to get the first look at the Harling Collection? If there was anything in it that would cause him to lose Marsh Point, she owed it to him to find it and keep it out of Harling hands. Her biography of Priscilla Marsh was only a secondary concern.

She raised herself and carefully lifted one knee over Win's hips, his narrowest point. Quickly she lowered one hand to his side of the bed, all the while lifting her other knee. It was a tricky maneuver. She had to roll onto her side without rocking the bed and waking him up.

She kept on rolling, right out of bed, grabbed her robe and tiptoed down the hall to the kitchen.

The trunk was gone.

Gone!

"That sneaky old goat! Wait until Cousin Thackeray finds out. He'll..."

"He'll what?" Win asked languidly. He was leaning against the door frame behind her.

She whirled around. "Well, good morning. I was awake and thought I'd make coffee...."

"Then why the big production to get out of bed?"

"I didn't want to wake you."

"I'll bet the hell you didn't."

"Now, Win, I know what you're thinking, and I don't blame you...."

"Because I'm right."

"That's not the point. The point is, where's the damned Harling Collection?"

He came into the kitchen and leaned against the counter. She had already noticed he hadn't bothered with a robe or anything else, which made his presence even more distracting.

"Aren't you cold?" she demanded.

He smiled. "On the contrary."

Evidence to that fact was becoming increasingly apparent. Then Hannah realized she hadn't bothered tying her robe and it was hanging open, revealing everything. "The Harling Collection!" she cried hoarsely. "Where is it?"

"On its way to Boston."

"Boston! Win Harling, you double-crossing bastard! You took advantage of me so I'd sleep like the dead and you and that old goat of an uncle of yours could pull a fast one on us Marshes and—"

"And do you want the real story, or do you want to rant and rave for a while?"

She shut her mouth and tied her robe. Tightly. *So there,* she thought.

Win smiled faintly. "I carted the trunk back to your cousin's truck while you were sound asleep. He and Uncle Jonathan promised to leave at the crack of dawn—which it is—to take it to the Athenaeum, where it can be catalogued by qualified, neutral historians."

"I'm a qualified historian!"

"You're not neutral."

No, she thought, *I'm not.* It was a point she knew she needed to concede. An objective biography of Priscilla Marsh had never really been possible for her, either.

"They both agreed?" she asked.

"Not without a hell of a lot of arguing."

Hannah sighed. "Will wonders never cease? Cousin Thackeray must not be too worried about the collection corroborating the Harling claim to Marsh Point.''

"No, he's not.''

"You sound awfully confident.''

"I am.'' And he nodded toward a large, manila envelope on her kitchen table. "Open it.''

She did so, her fingers trembling. Inside were several sheets of yellowed, near-crumbling paper.

"It's tough going,'' Win explained, "but basically it lays out the details of how the Marshes managed to hoodwink the Harlings out of Marsh Point. I showed it to your cousin before he left and promised I would keep it separate from the collection. You know what he said?''

"Win...''

"He said, 'What the devil! You know damned well you Harlings used your power and influence to get your hands on Marsh Point, just when we were set to make our purchase.' He claims whatever the Marshes did, it was not without justification. He also said—and again I quote—'We won't sort out the legal mess until after I'm dead and then Hannah will have Marsh Point and you can fight *her* for it.' And then he grinned—you know that grin of his—and suggested it'd be a hell of a fight.'' Win laughed. "He's an old cuss, Hannah. He wasn't worried one bit about those papers. You know why?''

She shook her head.

He came to her and undid the tie on her robe, letting it fall open before he slipped his arms around her waist. His mouth descended to hers and he kissed her briefly, flicking his tongue against hers. "Because he knows the Marsh and Harling feud ends with us. He knows we're going to be together forever.'' Win lifted her to his waist, while she held onto his shoulders and let him ease her onto him, welcoming his heat. He kissed her hair, whispering, "And so do I.''

"Win...''

"Just say it, Hannah.''

"Forever.''

A MONTH LATER the Marshes and the Harlings made headlines once more.

It seemed, the newspaper reported, that the newly recovered Harling Collection included not only a rare copy of the Declaration of Independence worth over a million dollars, but an order signed by Judge Cotton Harling in 1693, exonerating Priscilla Marsh of the charges against her. She had, the judge said he'd come to realize, only been teaching young Boston ladies traditional herbal remedies, not witchcraft. But due to some unexplained mix-up, the order had come too late to save the doomed, fair-haired Bostonian.

The copy of the Declaration of Independence, it seemed, had been authenticated, its value assured. Its ownership, however, was in dispute. Jonathan Harling claimed it belonged to his family. Thackeray Marsh claimed it belonged to his. Neither would budge.

Reached for comment, Hannah Marsh, the newly appointed, part-time director of the New England Athenaeum—Preston Fowler was awaiting trial—had suggested the two elderly Harvard-trained historians sign a joint declaration donating the document to the prestigious institution.

Both men had replied, in effect, "In a pig's eye."

J. Winthrop Harling had had no comment, except to say he was planning to whisk Hannah Marsh away on a honeymoon, to a part of the world where they were not likely to bump into anything remotely historical.

Taking a break from her biography of Priscilla, Hannah read the entertaining article aloud to Win while he stripped wallpaper from the dining room of the Harling House on Beacon Hill. His parents were driving up next weekend from New York for a visit. Hannah was anxious to meet them. She and Win had invited Cousin Thackeray down for dinner, but he'd said that'd be too many Harlings in one room for him. Old prejudices died hard.

"Did you say 'historical' in a scathing tone?" she asked her husband.

"As scathing as I could manage."

She grinned at him. Marsh Point and Beacon Hill. Maine and Boston. A Marsh and a Harling. "It's a good thing we love each other, isn't it?"

He smiled. "A very good thing."

OUTRAGEOUS

Lori Foster

1

SHE HAD the biggest brown eyes Judd had ever seen.

She also looked innocent as hell, despite the ridiculous clothes she wore and the huge, frayed canvas tote bag she carried. Did she actually think she blended in, just because her coat was tattered and her hat was a little ratty? Did she think anyone would ever believe her to be homeless? Not likely.

So what was she doing here at this time of night? The lower east side of Springfield was no place for a lady like her. She strolled past him again, this time more slowly, and her eyes were so wide it looked as if they could take in her surroundings in a single glance. They took in Judd.

He felt a thrill of awareness, sharper than anything he'd ever felt before. She looked away, but not before he detected the faint pink blush that washed over her fine features. That blush had been obvious even in the dim evening light, with only the moon and corner street lamp for illumination. She had flawless skin.

Dammit. He had enough to worry about without some damn Miss Priss with manicured nails and salon-styled hair trying to fob herself off as a local. Judd had only stepped outside the bar to get a breath of fresh air. The smell of perfume inside was overwhelming, and enough to turn his stomach.

He could hear the music in the bar grow louder and knew the dancers were coming onstage. In less than ten minutes, he'd have to go back in there, baring himself in the line of duty.

Damn. He hated this cover. What decent, hardworking cop should have to peel off his clothes for a bunch of sex-starved, groping women? For nearly two weeks now he'd been entertaining the female masses with the sight of his body, hoping to uncover enough evidence to make a bust. He was now, at thirty-two, in his prime, more fit than ever and completely alone. Not only did he meet the necessary requirements to pull off such a ludicrous cover, he had a vested, very personal interest this time. He knew for a fact the room above the bar was the site for shady business meetings, yet he hadn't seen hide nor hair of a gun deal. Clayton Donner was laying low.

It was discouraging, but he wasn't giving up.

He was definitely going to get Donner, but that didn't mean he enjoyed displaying himself nightly.

Each of the strippers had a gimmick. He thought his was rather ironic. He played out the tough street cop, complete with black pants held together with strategically placed Velcro. They came off with only the smallest tug. He even had Max's original leather jacket—a prized possession, to be sure—to add to his authenticity. The women loved it.

He wondered if old Max had known how sexy the cop persona was to females. Or if he would have cared.

God, he couldn't think about Max and still do his job, which was to appear unscrupulous enough that Donner would think him available. Clayton always needed new pigeons to run his scams. Judd intended to be the next. It was the only way he could get close enough to make a clean bust.

And the last thing he needed now was a distraction with big brown eyes. Despite his resolve, his gaze wandered back to the woman. She was loitering on the corner beneath the street lamp, holding that large, lumpy bag to her chest and trying to fit in. Judd snorted. That old coat was buttoned so high she was damn near strangling herself. What the hell was she doing here?

He'd just about convinced himself not to care, not to get involved, when three young men seemed to notice her. Judd watched as they approached her. She started to back away, then evidently changed her mind. She nodded a greeting, but it was a wimpy effort. Hell, the men looked determined to get to know her, without any encouragement on her part. She, on the other hand, looked ready to faint.

Walk away, he thought, willing the woman to move. But she

stood her ground. He sensed, then he knew for certain, she was getting in over her head. His body was already tensing, his eyes narrowed, waiting for the trouble to start. They seemed to be talking, or, more to the point, she was trying to speak to them. She gestured with her hands, her expression earnest. Then one of the men grabbed her and she let loose a startled screech. In the next instant, those huge brown eyes of hers turned his way, demanding that he help her.

The little twit thought he was a regular street cop. At this rate she'd blow his cover.

Well, hell, he couldn't allow her to be manhandled. He pushed himself away from the doorway and started forward. The men were obviously drunk. One of them was doing his best to pull her close, but she kept sidestepping him. Judd approached them all with a casual air.

"Here now, boys." He kept his tone low and deep, deliberately commanding. "Why don't you leave the lady alone."

Judd could see her trembling, could see the paleness of her face in the yellow light of the street lamp. The man didn't release her; if anything, he tightened his grip. "Go to hell."

The words were slurred, and Judd wondered just how drunk they were. They might believe him to be a cop, but in this neighborhood, being a law enforcement officer carried very little clout and regularly drew vicious disdain. Damn.

He couldn't get into a brawl—he might literally lose his pants. Not that he wouldn't enjoy knocking some heads together, but still.... Where was a real uniformed cop when you needed one?

He turned his gaze on the woman. "Do you want their company?"

She swallowed, her throat working convulsively. "No."

One of the men shook his fist in Judd's face, stumbling drunkenly as he did so. "She's already made a deal with us." The man grinned stupidly at the woman, then added, "You can't expect a little thing like her to run around here without a weapon to protect herself...."

One of the other men slugged the speaker. "Shut up, you fool."

Judd went very still, scrutinizing the woman's face. "Well?"

Again, she swallowed. "Well...what?"

"Why do you need a weapon? You planning to kill someone?" Whisper-soft, his question still demanded an immediate answer.

Shaking her head, then looking around as if desperately seeking a means of escape, she managed to pique his interest. He couldn't walk away now. Whatever she was up to, she didn't want him to know. Because she thought he was a cop?

Disgusted, Judd propped his hands on his hips, his eyebrows drawn together in a frown. "Do you want the company of these men or not?"

She peered cautiously at the drunken, leering face so close to her own. Her lips tightened in disapproval and disdain. "Ah...no. Not particularly."

A genuine smile tipped his mouth before he caught himself. She had gumption, he'd give her that. She was no bigger than a ten-year-old sickly kid. The coat she wore practically swallowed her up. She was fine-boned, petite, and everything about her seemed fragile. "There you go, fellas. The lady doesn't find you to her liking. Turn her loose and go find something else to do."

"I got somethin' to do already." Her captor's hold seemed to loosen just a bit as he spoke, and taking advantage, she suddenly jerked free. Then she did the dumbest thing Judd had ever seen. She sent her knee into the man's groin.

Unbelievable. Judd shook his head, even as he yanked her behind him, trying to protect her from the ensuing chaos. He couldn't do any real damage to the men without attracting more spectators, which would threaten his cover. And the woman was gasping behind him, scared out of her wits from the sound of it. But damn it all, he definitely *did not* want to lose his pants out here scuffling in the middle of the sidewalk with common drunks. One of the men started to throw a punch.

Judd cursed loudly as the woman ran around him, evidently

not as frightened as he'd thought, and leaped onto his attacker's back. She couldn't weigh over a hundred pounds, but she wound her fingers in the man's hair and pulled with all her might.

Enough was enough. A glimpse at his watch told him it was time for his performance. Judd grabbed the man away from her and sent him reeling with a firm kick to the rear end, then stalked the other two, every muscle in his body tensed. Too drunk to persist in their efforts, the men scurried away.

Judd turned to face the woman, and she was... tidying her hair? Good God, was she nuts? He saw her look toward her canvas bag, which now lay in a puddle on the sidewalk, but she made no move to retrieve it.

"You don't want your bag?" he asked with all the sarcasm he could muster.

"Oh." She glanced at him. "Well, of course..." She made a move in its direction, but he shook his head. He could see more raggedy clothing falling out the opening, and if there was one thing this woman didn't need, it was hand-me-downs.

He took her arm in a firm but gentle hold, ignoring her resistance, and started her toward the bar. He automatically moved her to his right side, bringing her between his body and the building, protecting her from passersby. He held his temper for all of about three seconds, then gave up the effort.

"Of all the stupid, *harebrained*...lady, what the hell did you think you were doing back there?" He wondered if she could be a journalist, or a TV newswoman? She damn well wasn't used to living in alleys, or going without. Everything about her screamed money. Even now, with him hustling her down the sidewalk, she had a certain grace, a definite poise, that didn't come from being underprivileged.

She glanced up at him, and he noticed she smelled nice, too. Not heavily perfumed like the women in the bar, just...very feminine. Her wavy shoulder-length hair, a light brown that looked as baby soft as her eyes, bounced as he hurried her along. She was practically running, but he couldn't help that. He was going to be late. He could hear the music for his number starting.

Taking off his clothes in public was bad enough. He didn't intend to make a grand entrance by jumping in late.

She cleared her throat. "I appreciate your assistance, Officer."

Without slowing his pace, he glared at her. "Answer my question. Who are you? What the hell are you up to?"

"That's two questions."

He growled, his patience at an end. *"Answer me, dammit!"*

She stumbled, then glared up at him defiantly. "That's really none of your business."

Everything inside his body clenched. "I'm making it my business."

Digging in her heels as he tried to haul her through the front door, she forced him to slow down. She was wide-eyed again and he noticed her mouth was hanging open as he dragged her into the bar. "What are you doing?"

There was a note of shrill panic in her voice as she took in her surroundings. Judd had no time to explain, and no time to consider her delicate sensibilities. Everyone in this part of town thought of him as a money-hungry, oversexed, willing exhibitionist—Clayton Donner included. It was a necessary cover and one he wasn't ready to forfeit. Donner would show up again soon, and once he decided Judd was a familiar face in the area, the gun dealer would make his move. It would happen. He'd make it happen.

Still gripping her arm, Judd trotted her toward the nearest bar stool. *"Stay right here."* He stared down at her, trying to intimidate her with his blackest scowl. The music was picking up tempo, signaling his cue.

She popped right back off the seat, those eyes of hers accurately portraying her shock. "Now see here! I have no intention of waiting—"

He picked her up, dropped her onto the stool again, then called to the bartender. "Keep her here, Freddie. Make certain she doesn't budge."

Freddie, a huge, jovial sort with two front teeth missing, grinned and nodded. "What'd she do?"

"She owes me. Big. Keep your eye on her."

"And if she tries to pike it?"

Judd gave Freddie a conspiratorial wink. "Make her sorry if she so much as flinches."

Freddie looked ferocious, but Judd knew he wouldn't hurt a fly. That was the reason they had not one, but two bouncers on the premises. But the little lady didn't know that, and Judd wanted to find out exactly what she was up to. Gut instinct told him he wouldn't like what he found.

Suddenly the spotlight swirled around the floor. Cursing, then forcing a grin to his mouth, Judd sauntered forward into the light. Women screamed.

In the short time he'd been performing here, he'd discovered a wealth of information about his gun dealer...and become a favorite of the bar. The owner had promised to double his pay, but that was nothing compared to the bills that always ended up stuffed in his skimpy briefs. He refused, absolutely *refused,* to wear a G-string. His naked butt was not something he showed to more than one woman at a time, and even *those* exhibitions were few and far between. But his modesty worked to his advantage. The women customers thought he was a tease, and appreciated his show all the more.

As he moved, he glanced over his shoulder to make certain the lady was still there. She hadn't moved. She didn't look as though she could. Her eyes were even larger now, huge and luminous and filled with shock and disbelief. He held her gaze, and slowly, backing into the center of the floor, slid the zipper down on the leather jacket. He saw her gasp.

Her intent expression, of innocence mixed with curious wonder, annoyed him, making him feel more exposed than he ever had while performing. That he could feel his face heat angered him. He was too old, and too cynical now, to actually blush. *Damn her.*

Purposefully holding her gaze, determined to make her look away, he let his fingers move to the top of his pants. As he slowly unhooked the fly, one snap at a time, teasing his audience, teasing her more, she reeled back and one dainty hand touched her chest. She looked distressed. She looked shocked.

But she didn't look away.

OH, LORD. Oh, Lord. This can't be happening, Emily! It's too outrageous. There can't possibly be a large, gorgeous man peeling his clothes off in front of you.

Even as she told herself she was delirious, that the scene in front of her was a figment of her fantastical imagination, Emily watched him kick off his boots, then with one smooth jerk, toss his pants aside. She wouldn't have missed a single instant of his disrobing. She couldn't. She was spellbound.

Vaguely, in the back of her mind, she heard the crowd yelling, urging him on. He looked away from her finally, releasing her from his dark gaze. But still she watched him.

He was the most beautiful man she'd ever seen. Raw, sexual, but also...gentle. She could feel his gentleness, had felt it outside when she'd first walked past him. It was as if she recognized he didn't belong here, in this seedy neighborhood, any more than she did.

But they *were* both here. Her reason was plain; she needed to find out who had sold her younger brother the gun that backfired, nearly causing him to lose an eye. He would recover, but that wouldn't remove the fact that he'd bought the gun illegally, that he was involved in something he had no business being involved in and that he would probably be scarred for life. Emily had to find the man who'd almost ruined her brother's life. She couldn't imagine what kind of monster would sell a sixteen-year-old a gun—a defective gun, at that.

Her parents refused to take the matter to the police. Luckily, John had only been using the gun for target practice, so no one even knew he had the thing. And more important, no one else had been hurt. When she thought about what could have happened, the consequences...

But that was history. Now all she could do was make certain that the same man didn't continue selling guns to kids. She had no compunction about going to the police once she had solid evidence, enough that she didn't have to involve her brother.

Her parents would never forgive her if she sullied the family name. Again.

Her heart raced, climbing into her throat to choke her when the officer—obviously *not* an officer—started toward her. She couldn't take her eyes off his bare, hair-brushed chest, his long, naked thighs. The way the shiny black briefs cupped him... Oh God, it was getting warm in here...

Well-bred ladies most definitely did not react this way!

There were social standards to uphold, a certain degree of expected poise... The litany she'd been reciting to herself came to a screeching halt as the man stopped in front of her.

His eyes, a fierce green, reflected the spotlight. He stared directly at her, then moved so close she could smell the clean male fragrance of him, could feel his body heat. And God, he was hot.

Panting, Emily realized he was waiting for her to give him money. Of all the insane notions...but there were numerous dollars sticking out of those small briefs, and she knew, with unwavering instinct, he wouldn't budge until she'd done as he silently demanded.

Blindly, unable to pull her gaze away, she fumbled in the huge pockets of her worn coat until her fist closed on a bill. She stuck out her hand, offering the money to him.

Wicked was the only way to describe his smile. With a small, barely discernible motion, he shook his head. She dropped her gaze for an instant to where his briefs held all the cash. She'd watched the women put the money there, trying to touch him, but he'd eluded their grasping hands. He'd played up to the audience, getting only close enough to collect a few dollars, then dancing away.

She didn't want to touch him.

Oh, what a lie! She wanted to touch him, all right, but she wouldn't, not here in front of an audience, not ever. She was a respectable lady, she was... She squeaked, leaning back on her seat as he put one hand on the light frame over the bar, the other beside her on the bar stool. She was caged in, unable to breathe. She could see the light sheen of sweat caught in his chest hair, see the small, dark tuft of fine hair under his arm. It seemed almost indecent, and somehow very personal, to see his armpit.

Her body throbbed with heat, and she couldn't swallow. He stood there, demanding, insistent, so very carefully, using only her fingertips, she tucked the bill into his shorts. She registered warm, taut skin, and a sprinkling of crisp hair.

Still holding her gaze, he smiled, his eyes narrowing only the slightest bit. He leaned down next to her face, then placed a small, chaste kiss on her cheek. It had been whisper-light, almost not there, but so potent she felt herself close to fainting.

The audience screamed, loving it, loving him. He laughed, his expression filled with satisfaction, then went back to his dancing. Women begged for the same attention he'd given her, but he didn't comply. Emily figured one pawn in the audience was enough.

Though his focus was now directed elsewhere, it still took Emily several minutes to calm her galloping heartbeat. She continued to watch him, and that kept her tense, because despite everything she'd been brought up to believe, the man excited her.

His dark hair, long in the back, was damp with sweat and beginning to curl. With each movement he made, his shoulders flexed, displaying well-defined muscles and sinew. His backside, held tight in the black briefs, was trim and taut. And his thighs, so long and well-sculpted, looked like the legs of an athlete.

His face was beautiful, almost too beautiful. It was the kind of face that should make innocent women wary of losing their virtue. Green eyes, framed by deliciously long dark lashes and thick eyebrows, held cynical humor and were painfully direct and probing when he chose to use them that way. His nose was straight and narrow, his jaw firm.

Emily realized she was being fanciful, and silently gathered her thoughts. She needed to concentrate on what she'd come to do— finding the gun dealer. According to her brother, who at sixteen had no business hanging out in this part of town, he'd bought the gun on this street. It had been a shady trade-off from the start, cash for the illegal weapon. But John was in a rebellious stage, and his companions of late had ranged from minor gang members to very experienced young ladies. Emily prayed she could help him get back on the straight and narrow, that he could find his peace on an easier road than she'd taken. When she thought of the scars he'd have to live with, the regrets, she knew, deep in her heart, the only way to give him that peace was to find enough evidence to put the gun dealer away.

Though Emily planned to change his mind, John thought his life was over. What attractive, popular teenager could handle the idea of going through life with his face scarred? Then she thought of other kids—kids who might buy a duplicate of the same gun; kids who might be blinded rather than scarred. Or worse. The way the gun had exploded, it could easily have killed someone. And despite her parents' wishes, Emily couldn't stand back and allow that to happen. Her conscience wouldn't allow it.

The show finally ended, the music fading with the lighting until the floor was in darkness. The applause was deafening. And seconds later, the officer was back, his leather jacket slung over his shoulder, his pants and boots in his hand. He thanked the bartender, then took Emily's arm without any explanation, and rapidly pulled her toward an inside door. They narrowly missed the mob of advancing women.

Emily wanted to run, but she'd never in her life resorted to such a display. Besides, now that she knew he wasn't really a policeman, a plan was forming in her mind.

He pulled her into a back room, shut the door, then flipped on a light switch. Emily found herself in a storage closet of sorts, lined with shelves where cleaning supplies sat and a smelly mop tainted the air. A leather satchel rested in the corner. He didn't bother dressing. Instead, he tossed his clothes to the side and moved to stand a hairbreadth away from her.

"You gave me a fifty."

Emily blinked. His words were nowhere near what she'd expected to hear. She tucked in her chin. "I beg your pardon?"

He pulled the cash from his briefs, stacking the bills together neatly in his large hands. "You gave me a fifty-dollar bill. I hadn't realized my show was quite that good."

A fifty! Oh, Lord, Emily. She had no intention of telling him it hadn't been deliberate, that she'd been unable to pull her gaze away from him long enough to find the proper bills. What she'd given him was part of the money earmarked for buying information.

Maybe she could still do that.

Shrugging, she forced her eyes away from his body and stared at the dingy mop. "Since you're not a law enforcement officer, I was hoping the money would...entice you to help me."

He snorted, not buying her line for a second. Emily was relieved he was gentleman enough not to say so. He gave her a look that curled her toes, then asked, "What kind of *help* do you need, lady?"

It was unbelievably difficult to talk with him so near, and so nearly naked. He smelled delicious, of warm, damp male flesh, though she tried her best not to notice. But his body was too fine to ignore for long, despite her resolve not to give in to unladylike tendencies—such as overwhelming lust—ever again.

She licked her dry lips, then met his eyes. His gaze lingered on her mouth, then slowly coasted over the rest of her body. She knew she wasn't particularly attractive. She had pondered many disguises for this night, disguises ranging anywhere from that of a frumpy homeless lady, to a streetwalker. Somehow, she couldn't imagine herself making a convincing hooker. She was slight of build and her body had never quite...bloomed, as she'd always hoped for. She did, however, think she made an adequate transient.

She cleared her throat. Stiffening her spine, which already felt close to snapping, she said, "I need information."

"Your little trio of drunks didn't tell you enough?"

Since he appeared to have guessed her mission, she didn't bother denying it. "No. They didn't really know anything. And I had to be careful. They didn't seem all that trustworthy. But it's imperative I find out some facts. You...you seem well acquainted with the area?"

She'd said it as a question, and he answered with a nod.

"Good. I want to know of anyone who's selling guns."

He closed his eyes, his mouth twisting in an ironic smirk. "Guns? Just like that, you want to know who's dealing in guns? God, lady, you look like you could go to the nearest reputable dealer and buy any damn thing you wanted." He took a step closer, reaching out his hand to flip a piece of her hair. "I don't know who you thought you'd fool, but you walk like money, talk like money...hell, you even smell like money. What is it? The thrill of going slumming that has you traipsing around here dressed in that getup?"

Emily sucked in her breath at his vulgar question and felt her temper rise. "You have fifty dollars of my money. The least you can do is behave in a civilized, polite manner."

"Wrong." He stepped even closer, the dark, sweat-damp hair on his chest nearly brushing against the tip of her nose. He had to bend low to look her in the eyes, but he managed. "The least I can do is steer your fancy little tail back where you belong. Go home, little girl. Get your thrills somewhere else, somewhere where it's safe."

Suffused with heat at both his nearness and his derisive attitude, it was all Emily could do to keep from cowering. She clicked her teeth together, then swallowed hard. "You don't want to help me. Fine. I'm certain I'll find someone else who will. After all, I'm willing to pay a thousand dollars." Then, turning to make a grand exit, certain she'd made him sorry over losing out on so much money, she said over her shoulder, "I imagine I'll find someone much more agreeable than you within the hour. Goodbye."

There was a split second of stunned silence, then an explosive curse, and Emily decided good breeding could take second place to caution. She reached for the door and almost had it open, when his large hand landed on the wood with a loud crack, slamming it shut again. His warm, hard chest pressed to her back, pinning her to the door. She could barely move; she could barely breathe.

Then his lips touched her ear, whisper-soft, and he said, "You're not going anywhere, sweetheart."

2

SHE FELT light-headed, but she summoned a cool smile. He was deliberately trying to frighten her—she didn't know how she knew that, but she was certain of it. Slowly turning in what little space he allowed her, Emily faced him, her chin held high. "Would you mind giving me a little breathing room, please?"

"I might."

Might mind, or might move? Emily shook her head. "You have a rather nasty habit of looming over me, Mr....?"

For a moment, he remained still and silent, then thankfully, he took two steps back. He looked at her as if she might not be entirely sane. Emily stuck out her hand. "I'm Emily Cooper."

His gaze dropped to her hand, then with a resigned look of disgust, he enfolded her small hand in his much larger one, pumping it twice before abruptly releasing her. He stared at the ceiling. "Judd Sanders."

"It's very nice to meet you, Mr. San—"

"Judd will do." He shook his head, and his gaze came back to her face. "Look, lady, you can't just come to this part of town and start waving money around. You'll get yourself dragged into a dark alley and mugged, possibly raped. Or worse."

Emily wondered what exactly could be worse than being mugged and raped in a dark alley, but she didn't bother asking him. She felt certain he'd come up with some dire consequence to frighten her.

He was watching her closely, and she tried to decide if it was actual concern she saw on his face. She liked to think so. Things still didn't fit. He didn't seem any more suited to this part of town than she did, regardless of his crude manners and bossy disposition.

But now that he'd backed up and given her some room, she was able to think again. "I made certain to stay in front of the stores and in plain sight at all times. If mischief had started, someone surely would have offered assistance." Her eyebrows lifted and she smiled. "You did."

He muttered under his breath, and pointed an accusing finger at her. "You're a menace."

Glaring at him wouldn't get her anywhere, she decided. She needed help, that much was obvious. And who better to help her than a man who evidently knew his way around this part of town, and was well acquainted with its inhabitants. She cleared her throat. "I realize I don't entirely understand how things should be done. Although I'm familiar with the neighborhood, since I work in the soup kitchen twice a week..." She hesitated, then added, "I bought this coat from one of the ladies who comes in regularly. On her, it looked authentic enough. That was even her bag I carried—"

"Miss Cooper."

He said her name in a long, drawn-out sigh. Emily cleared her throat again, then laced her fingers together. "Anyway, while I know the area, at least during the day, I'm not at all acquainted with the workings of the criminal mind. That's why, as I said, I'd like to hire you."

"Because you think *I* do understand the criminal mind?"

"I meant no insult." She felt a little uncertain with him glaring at her like that. "I did get the impression you could handle yourself in almost any situation. Look at how well you took care of those drunkards? You didn't even get bruised, and there were three of them."

"Yeah. But you'd already laid one of them low."

She could feel the blush starting at her hairline and traveling down to cover her entire face. "Yes, well..."

He seemed to give up. One minute he was rigid, his posture so imposing she had to use all her willpower not to cower. Then suddenly, he was idly rubbing his forehead. "Let's get out of here and you can tell me exactly what you want."

Oh, no. She wouldn't tell him that, because what she wanted from him and what were proper were two very different things. But she forgave herself the mental transgression. No woman could possibly be in the same room with this man without having a few fantasies wing through her mind.

Trying for some vagrant humor to lighten his sour mood, she asked, "Wouldn't you like to change first?"

Staring at her, his jaw worked as if he was grinding his teeth. Then he gave one brisk nod. "Turn your head."

Emily blinked. "Turn my... Now wait just a minute! I'll go out to the bar and—"

"No way. I can't trust you not to disappear. Just turn around and stare at the door. I'll only be a minute."

"But I'll know what you're doing!"

He smirked, that was the only word for it. "What's the matter, honey? You afraid you won't be able to resist peeking, knowing I'll be buck naked?"

That was a pretty accurate guess. Emily shook her head. "Don't be ridiculous. It just isn't right, that's all."

"Afraid one of your society friends might meander along and catch you doing something naughty?" He snorted. "Trust me. Not too many upper-crust types visit this part of town. You won't catch yourself in the middle of a scandal."

But she had been caught once, and it had been the most humiliating experience of her life. She'd been alienated from her family ever since.

She thought of that horrid man and nearly cringed. She'd thought herself so above her parents, so understanding of the underprivileged. And she still believed that way. A gentleman was a gentleman, no matter his circumstances. Decency wasn't something that could be bought. But the man who had swept her off her feet, shown her passion and excitement, had proven himself to be anything but decent.

She'd nearly married him before she'd realized he only wanted her money. Not her. Never her. He'd used her, used her family, made a newsworthy pest of himself, and her parents had never forgiven her for it.

She could still hear herself trying to explain her actions. But her mother believed a lady didn't involve herself in such situations, under any circumstances.

A lady never lost her head to something as primal as lust.

Lifting her chin, Emily gave Judd the frostiest stare she could devise. "I can most certainly control myself." Then she turned her back on him. "Go right ahead, Mr. Sanders. But please make it quick. It is getting rather late."

Emily heard him chuckling, heard the rustle of clothing, and she held her breath. It was only a matter of a minute and a half before he told her she could turn around.

Very slowly, just in case he was toying with her, Emily peered at him. He was dressed in jeans, and had pulled on a flannel shirt. He was sitting on a crate, tugging on low boots. When he stood to fasten his shirt, Emily noticed he hadn't yet done up his jeans. She tried not to blush, but it was a futile effort.

He ignored her embarrassment. "So, Emily. Where exactly are you from?"

Her gaze was on his hands as he shoved his shirttails into his pants. "The Crystal Lakes area," she said. "And you?"

He gave a low, soft whistle. "The Crystal Lakes? Damn. No kidding?"

Annoyed, she finally forced her attention to his face. "I certainly wouldn't lie about it."

He took her arm and led her out of the storeroom. He had stuffed his dance props into the leather satchel he carried in his other hand. "I'll bet you live in a big old place with plenty of rooms, don't you?"

Emily eyed him with a wary frown. She wasn't certain how much she should tell him about herself. "I have enough space, I suppose."

He asked abruptly, "How did you get here?"

"Actually, I took the bus. I didn't think parking my car here would be such a good idea."

"No doubt. What do you drive, anyway? A Rolls?"

"Of course not."

"So?" He pulled her out the door and into the brisk night. "What do you tool around in?"

"Tool around? I drive a Saab."

"Ah."

"What does that mean? Ah?" He was moving her along again, treating her like a dog on a leash. And with his long-legged stride, it was all she could do to keep up. He stopped near a back alley, and Emily realized they were at the rear of the bar. "Why didn't we just go out the back door instead of walking all the way around?"

"'Ah' means your choice of transportation shouldn't surprise me. And we came this way so I could spare you from being harassed. Believe me, the men working in the back would have a field day with an innocent like you."

Don't ask. Don't ask. "What makes you believe I'm an innocent?"

Judd opened the door to a rusty, disreputable pickup truck and motioned for her to get inside. She hesitated, suddenly not certain she should trust him.

But he only stood there, watching her with that intense, probing green gaze. Finally, Emily grabbed the door frame to hoist herself inside.

Judd shook his head. "And you ask how I know you're an innocent?"

Before Emily could reply, he slammed the door and walked around to get in behind the wheel. "Buckle up."

She watched his profile as he steered the truck out of the alley and onto the main road. The lights from well-spaced street lamps flashed across his features. Trying to avoid staring at him, she looked around the truck and she saw a strip of delicate black lace draped over the rearview mirror.

Judd noticed her fascination with the sheer lace and grinned. "A memento of my youth."

Trying for disinterest, Emily muttered, "Really."

"I was sixteen, she was eighteen."

Sixteen. The same age as her brother—and obviously into as much mischief as John.

Judd ran his fingers down the lace as if in fond memory. "We were in such a hurry, we ripped her panties getting them off." He flashed her a grin. "Black lace still makes me crazy."

Emily went perfectly quiet, then tightly crossed her legs. *There's no way he can know what your panties look like, Emily,* she told herself. But still, she made an effort to bring the conversation back to her purpose. She had to find a way to help John.

Reminded of the reason she was with Judd in the first place, Emily turned to him. Taking a deep breath, she said, "I need to find out who's selling semiautomatic weapons to kids. I...I know a boy who had one blow up in his face. He was badly injured. Luckily, no one else was around."

The truck swerved, and Judd shot her a look that could have cut ice. *"Blew up?"*

His tone was harsh, and Emily couldn't help huddling closer against her door. "Yes. He very nearly lost an eye."

Judd muttered a curse, but when he glanced at her again, his expression was carefully controlled. "Did you go to the police?"

"I can't." She tightened her lips, feeling frustrated all over again. "The boy's parents won't allow him to be implicated. They refuse to realize just how serious this situation is. They have money, so they took him out of the country to be treated. They won't return until they're certain he's safe."

"Yeah. A lot of parents believe bad things will go away if you ignore them. Unfortunately, that's not true. But Emily, you have to know, there's nothing you can do to stop the crime on these streets. The drugs, the gangs and the selling of illegal arms, it'll go on forever."

"I refuse to believe that!" She turned in her seat, taking her frustration out on him. "I have to do something. Maybe I can figure out a way to stop this guy who sold that gun. If everyone would get involved—"

Judd laughed, cutting her off. "Like the folks who whisked their baby boy out of the country? How old was this kid, anyway? Old enough to know better, I'll bet." He shook his head, giving her a look that blatantly called her a fool. "Don't waste your time. Go back to your rich neighborhood, your fancy car and your fancier friends. Let the cops take care of things."

She was so angry, she nearly cried. It had always been that way. She never shed a tear over pain or hurt feelings, but let her get really mad, and she bawled like an infant. His attitude toward her brother infuriated her.

Judd stopped at a traffic light, and she jerked her door open, trying to step out. His long hard fingers immediately wrapped around her upper arm, preventing her from leaving.

"What the hell do you think you're doing?"

"Let me go." She was proud of her feral tone. "Did you hear me? Get your hands off me." She struggled, pulling against his hold.

"Dammit! Get back in this truck!"

The light had changed and the driver of the car behind them blasted his horn. "I've changed my mind, Mr. Sanders," she told him. "I no longer require your help. I'll find someone else, someone who won't choose to ridicule me every other second."

He peered at her closely, then sighed. "Aw, hell. Don't tell me you're going to cry."

"No, I am not going to cry!" But she could feel the tears stinging her eyes, which angered her all the more. How could she have been so wrong about him—and he so wrong about her? She didn't have fancy friends; she didn't have any friends. Most of the time, she didn't have anybody—except her brother. She loved him dearly, and John trusted her. When the rest of her family had turned their backs on her, her brother had been there for her, making her laugh, giving her the support she needed to get through it all.

She couldn't let him down now, even if he didn't realize he needed her help. He was the only loving family she could claim, the only one who still cared about her, despite her numerous faults. And she knew, regardless of the gun incident, John was a good person.

Several cars were blaring their horns now, and Judd yanked her back inside, retaining his hold as he moved out of the stream of traffic and over to the curb. He didn't release her. "Look, I'm sorry. Don't go and get weepy on me, okay?"

"You, Mr. Sanders, are an obnoxious ass!" Emily jerked against him, but he held firm. "I always cry when I'm angry."

"Well...don't be angry then."

Unbelievable. The man had been derisive, insulting and arrogant from the moment she'd met him, but now his tone had changed to a soft, gentle rebuke. He had a problem with female tears? She almost considered giving in to a real tantrum just to make him suffer, but that had never been her way. The last thing she wanted from Judd was pity.

"Ignore me," she muttered, feeling like a fool. "It's been a trying week. But I am determined to see this thing through. I'll find the man who sold that gun. I have a plan, a very solid plan. I could certainly use your help, but if you're only going to be nasty, I believe I'd rather just find someone else."

JUDD WAS AMAZED by her speech. Then his eyes narrowed. No way in hell was he going to let her run loose. She was a menace. She was a pain.

She was unbelievably innocent and naive.

Judd shook his head, then steered the truck back into the street. "Believe me, lady. I'm about as nice as you're going to find in these parts. Besides, I think I might be interested in your little plan, after all. I mean, what the hell? A thousand bucks is a thousand bucks. That was the agreed amount, right?"

Emily nodded.

Lifting one shoulder, Judd said, "Can't very well turn down money like that."

"No. No, I wouldn't think so." She watched him warily, and Judd thought, what the hell? It would be easier to work with her, than around her. If he turned her down, she'd only manage to get in his way, or get herself hurt. That was such a repugnant thought, he actually groaned.

He'd have to keep his cool, maintain his cover, and while he was at it, he could keep an eye on her. Maybe he could pretend to help her, but actually steer her far enough away from the trouble that she wouldn't be any problem at all.

Yeah, right.

It would probably be better to try to convince her to give up her ridiculous plan first. He glanced at her, saw the rigid way she held herself, and knew exactly how to dissuade her. "There are a few conditions we should discuss."

Emily heaved a deep breath. "Conditions?"

"Yeah. The money's great. But I'll still have to work nights at the bar. Actually, only Tuesdays and Thursdays. *Ladies'* nights."

Emily hastened to reassure him. "I don't have a problem with that. I wouldn't want to interfere with your...career."

His laugh was quick and sharp, then he shook his head. "Right. My career." He glanced at her again, grinning, wondering if she could possibly realize how uncomfortable he was with that particular career. "That's not the only thing, though."

"There's something else?"

"Yeah. You see, we'll need a place to meet. Neutral ground and all that. Someplace away from prying eyes."

Emily stared.

"You stand out like a sore thumb, honey. We can't just have you traipsing around in that neighborhood. People will wonder what you're up to. It could blow the whole thing."

"I see."

"My apartment is close to here. No one would pay any attention to you coming in or out. It wouldn't even matter what time we met. We'll need to work closely together, finesse these plans of yours. What d'ya say?"

Her mouth opened, but all that came out was, "Oh God."

Lifting one dark eyebrow, Judd felt triumphant. She was already realizing the implications of spending so much time alone with him. He hid his relief and said, "Come again?"

Emily shook her head, then at the same time said, "Yes, that is…I suppose…" She heaved a sigh, straightened her back, and then nodded. "Okay."

Judd stared at her, trying not to show his disbelief. "What do you mean, okay?" He'd thought for certain, since everything else had failed, that this would send her running. But no. She seemed to like the damn idea. She was actually smiling now.

"I mean, if you think we could successfully operate from your apartment, I'll agree to meet you there."

Contrary female. "Emily…" He faltered. He liked saying her name, liked how it sounded, all fresh and pure. She looked at him, with those huge, doe eyes steady on his face. She was too trusting. She was a danger to herself. If he didn't keep close tabs on her, she'd end up in trouble. He was sure of it.

"You were going to say something, Mr. Sanders?"

Nothing she would like hearing. He shook his head. "Just be quiet and let me think."

Obediently, she turned away and stared out her window. He wasn't buying her compliance for a minute. He had a gut feeling there wasn't an obedient bone in her slim body. He also suspected she was as stubborn as all hell, once she'd set her mind on something. And she was set to find a gun dealer.

The truck was heating up. It was late spring and even though the nights were still a little chilly, the days were warming up into the seventies. Without any fanfare, and apparently trying not to draw undue attention to herself, Emily began unbuttoning the oversize coat. Judd watched from the corner of his eye.

Just to razz her, because she took the bait so easily, he asked, "Would you like me to give you a drumroll?"

She turned to face him. "I beg your pardon?"

She looked honestly confused. He tried to hide his grin. "Every good striptease needs music."

"I'm not stripping!"

He shrugged, amused by the blush on her cheeks that was

visible even in the dark interior of the truck. She was apparently unused to masculine teasing, maybe even to men in general.

He snorted at his own foolishness. It was men like himself, coarse and inelegant, that she wasn't used to. He imagined she had plenty of sophisticated guys clamoring for her attention. And that fact nettled him, even though it shouldn't. Grumbling, he said, "You should try it. Everyone should experience stripping just once. It's a rush."

She held her coat together with clenched fingers, her look incredulous. If she knew him better, she'd know what a lie he'd just told. He hated taking off his clothes in front of so many voracious women. But she didn't know him, and most likely never would. He should keep that fact in mind before he did something stupid. *Like what, you idiot? Like promising you'd take care of her gun dealer for her, so she could take her cute little backside and big brown eyes back home where it's safe?* No, he most definitely couldn't do that, no matter how much he'd like to.

They came to the entrance to Crystal Lakes. "Which way?"

He'd startled her. She'd practically jumped out of her seat, and he was left wondering exactly where her mind had been. "Which way to your place? You didn't think I'd take you to my apartment tonight, did you? In case you haven't noticed, lady, it's after midnight. And I've put in a full day. Tomorrow will be soon enough."

The truck was left to idle while they stared at each other. Finally in a small voice filled with suspicion, Emily said, "You're not just getting rid of me, are you? You'll really help me?"

Those eyes of hers could be lethal. He wanted nothing more than to tug her close and promise her he wouldn't leave her, that he'd take care of everything, that he'd... She looked so damn vulnerable. It didn't make a bit of sense. Usually people with big money went around feeling confident that money would get them anything. They didn't bother with doubts.

Irritated now, he rubbed the bridge of his nose, then said in a low tone, "Since I haven't gotten my thousand bucks yet, you can be sure I'll be sticking around."

After heaving a small sigh, she said, "Of course."

Now, why did she have to sound so disappointed? And why did he feel like such a jerk?

"Left, up the hill, then the first street on the right."

Judd knew he had no business forming fantasies over a woman who blushed every time she spoke. Especially since he'd have to keep her close, more to protect her than anything else. She didn't understand the magnitude of what she was tampering with, the lethal hold gun dealers had on the city.

An idea had been forming in his mind ever since he'd realized he couldn't discourage her from trying to save the world. He'd thought, if he became aggressive enough, she'd run back home to safety.

Instead, she'd only threatened to find someone else to help her. And he couldn't let that happen. She might get herself killed, or maybe she'd actually find out something and inadvertently get in the way. He'd worked too hard for that to happen. He wouldn't allow anything—or anyone—to interfere. He *would* get the bastard who'd shot Max. But damn, he'd never expected Emily to openly accept his plans.

Crystal Lakes, as exclusive and ritzy as it was, sat only about twenty-five minutes from the lower east side. It was one of those areas where you could feel the gradual change as you left hell and entered heaven. The grass started looking greener, the business district slipped away, and eventually everything was clean and untainted.

Emily pointed out her house, a large white Colonial, with a huge front porch. It looked as if it had been standing there for more than a hundred years, and was surprisingly different from the newer, immense homes recently built in the area.

There were golden lights in every window, providing a sense of warmth. A profusion of freshly planted spring flowers surrounded the perimeter, and blooming dogwoods randomly filled the yard. All in all, the place was very impressive, but not quite what he'd expected. Somehow, he'd envisioned her stationed in real money. Any truly successful businessperson could afford this house.

Judd stared around the isolated grounds. "Do you live here by yourself?"

She nodded, not quite looking at him, her hands clasped nervously in her lap.

"No husband or little ones to help fill up the space?"

"No. No husband. No children."

"Why not? I thought all debutantes were married off at an early age."

He didn't think she'd answer at first, but then she licked her lips and her skittish gaze settled on his face. "I was...engaged once. But things didn't work out." She rushed through her words, seemingly unable to stop herself. "I bought this house about a year ago. My parents don't particularly like it—it's one of the smaller homes in the community. But it was an original estate, not one built when the Lakes was developed. It's been renovated, and I think it's charming."

She said the words defensively, as if she expected some scathing comment from him. Judd didn't like being affected this way, but there was something about Emily that touched him. He could *feel* her emotions, had been feeling them since first making eye contact with her. And right now, she seemed almost wounded.

Very gently, he asked, "Did you see to the renovations yourself?"

"Yes."

He looked around the dark, secluded yard and shook his head. "Your parents approve of your living here alone?"

"No, but it doesn't matter what they think. When my grandmother died, she left me a large inheritance. My parents expected me to buy a condo near them and then invest the rest using their suggestions." Her hands tightened in her lap and she swallowed. "But I loved this house on sight. I'd already planned to buy it, and receiving the inheritance let me do so sooner than I'd planned. I don't regret a single penny I spent on the place. Everything is just as I want it."

"What if you hadn't gotten the inheritance?"

"I would have found a job. I'm educated. I'm not helpless." She gave him a narrow-eyed look. "But this way, I don't have to. I'm financially independent."

And alone. "How old are you, Emily?"

She raised her chin, a curious habit he'd noticed she used whenever she felt threatened. "Thirty."

He couldn't hide his surprise. "You don't look more than twenty." Without thinking, he reached out and touched her cheek, his fingertips drifting over her fine, porcelain skin. "Twenty and untouched."

She jerked away. "Are we going to sit in the driveway all night? Go around the back, to the kitchen door."

He shouldn't let her give him orders, but what the hell. He put the truck in gear and did as directed.

The darkness of the hour had hidden quite a few things. There was a small lake behind her property, pretty with the moon reflecting off its surface. Of course, there were some twenty such lakes in the Crystal Lakes community, so he shouldn't have been surprised.

"Is the lake stocked?"

"Yes. But it's seldom used. Occasionally, one or two of the neighborhood children come here to fish. My lake is the most shallow, so it's the safest. And it's the only one on this side of the community. Most of the lakes are farther up."

"You don't mind the kids trampling around your yard?"

"Of course not. They're good kids. They usually feed the ducks and catch a frog or two. I enjoy watching them."

Judd stared back at the house. There was a large window that faced the backyard and the lake. He could picture her sitting there, content to watch the children play. Maybe longing for things she didn't have. Things money couldn't buy.

Hell, he was becoming fanciful.

Disgusted with himself, knowing he'd been away from normal

society too long and that was probably the reason she seemed so appealing, he parked the truck and got out. The fresh air cleared his head.

He opened Emily's door to help her out, but she held back, watching him nervously. "I'll make sure you get inside okay, then I'll take off. We can hook up again tomorrow morning."

"Oh. Yes. That will be fine."

She sounded relieved that he didn't intend to come inside tonight, and perversely, he changed his mind. He'd come in, all right, but with his imagination so active, he couldn't trust himself to be alone with her any length of time. Anyway, he told himself, she wasn't his type—not even close. She was much too small and frail. He liked his women big, with bountiful breasts and lush hips.

As far as he could tell, Emily didn't have a figure.

But those eyes... She walked up a small, tidy patio fronted by three shallow steps, then unlocked the back door and flipped a switch. Bright fluorescent light cascaded through a spotless kitchen and spilled outside onto the patio. Judd saw flowerpots everywhere, filled with spring flowers, and a small outdoor seating group arranged to his right. Everything seemed cheery and colorful...like a real home, and not at all what he'd expected.

Damn, he'd have to find some way to dissuade her from her plan before he got in over his head.

She turned and gave him a small, uncertain smile. "About tomorrow..."

He interrupted her, coming up the three steps and catching her gaze. "Let's make sure we understand each other, Emily, so there won't be any mistakes."

She nodded, and he deliberately stepped closer, watching with satisfaction as she tried to pull back, even though there was no place to go. Good, he thought. At least she had some sense of self-preservation.

He braced his hands on the door frame, deliberately looming over her. "From this second on, I call the shots, with no arguments from you. If you really want my help, you'll do as I tell you, whatever I tell you." He waited until she'd backed all the way into the kitchen, then he added, "You understand all that?"

3

EMILY'S MOUTH opened twice, but nothing came out. She was too stunned to think rationally, too appalled to react with any real thought. Judd dropped his arms and stepped completely into the kitchen, watching her, and by reflex alone, she started sidling toward the hall door. She had made a terrible mistake. Her instincts had been off by a long shot.

Judd's smile was pure wickedness. "Where ya' goin', Emily?"

"I, ah, I just thought of something..."

Like a loud blast, his laugh erupted, filling the silence of the kitchen.

She halted, a spark of suspicion beginning to form. "*What* is so funny?"

"The look on your face. Did you think I had visions of taking you instead of the money?" He shook his head, and Emily felt her cheeks flame. He was still chuckling when he said, "It only makes sense that I'd be in charge—after all, that's what you'll be paying me for. Like I told you, a rich little lady like yourself would only draw a lot of unnecessary attention hanging around that area. You'll have to follow my lead, and do as I tell you if you want to stay safe. And another thing, we need to figure out some reason for you being there at all. I think we'll have to do a little acting. Your part will be easy, since you'll just be the rich lady. That leaves me as the kept man." He spread his arms wide. "As far as everyone will be concerned, I'm yours. There's no other reason why a woman like you would be around a man like me, unless she was slumming. So that's the reason we'll use."

She was so mortified, she wanted to die. Stiff-backed, she

turned away from him and walked over to lean against the tiled counter near the sink. She heard Judd close the door, and seconds later, his hands landed on her shoulders, holding her firm.

"Don't get all huffy now. We have things to discuss. Serious things."

"You mean, you don't intend to taunt me anymore? My goodness, how gracious."

"You've got a real smart mouth, don't you? No, don't answer that. I'm sorry I teased you, but I couldn't resist. You're just too damn easy to fluster." He turned her to face him, then tipped up her chin.

"Here, now, don't go blushing again. Not that you don't look cute when you do, but I really think we should talk."

Emily stepped carefully away, not wanting him to know how his nearness, his touch, affected her. Even after all his taunting, she still went breathless and too warm inside when he was close. And ridiculously, it angered her when he belittled himself, claiming she could have no interest in him other than as a sex partner. The physical appeal was there, but it was more than that. Much more. He had helped her. He'd actually taken on three inebriated men to protect her, even though he wasn't a real cop. And he was willing to help her again. She discounted the money; what she was asking could put his life at risk. He must be motivated by more than money to get involved.

But for now, she couldn't sort it all out. Especially not with her senses still rioting at his nearness. She drew a deep breath, then let it out again. "I thought we were going to wait until morning to make any plans. It is getting rather late."

"No, I've decided it can't wait. But I won't keep you long. Pull up a chair and get comfortable."

Emily didn't particularly want to get comfortable, but she also didn't want to risk driving Judd away. For the moment, he was the best hope she had of ever finding the man who'd sold her brother the gun. She knew her limitations, and fitting in around the lower east side of Springfield was probably the biggest of them. She needed him.

As she headed for a chair, Judd caught the back of her coat, drawing her up short. "It's warm in here. Why don't you take this off?"

He was watching her closely again, and she couldn't fathom his thoughts. She shrugged, then started to slip the shabby wool coat from her shoulders. Judd's eyes went immediately to the tiny camera she wore on a strap around her neck.

"What the hell is that?"

She jumped, then lost her temper with his barking tone. "Will you please quit cursing at me!"

He seemed stunned by her outburst, but he did nod. "Answer me."

"It's rather obviously a camera."

Closing his eyes and looking as though he were involved in deep prayer, Judd said, "Please tell me you weren't taking pictures tonight."

"No. I didn't take any." She lifted her chin, knowing what his reaction would be, then added, "Tonight."

"You just had to clarify that, didn't you, before I could really relax." His sigh was long and drawn out, then he led her to the polished pine table sitting in the middle of her quarry-stone kitchen floor. He pulled out a chair for her, silently insisting that she sit. "So when did you take pictures?"

"I've been checking that area for three nights now." She ignored his wide-eyed amazement, and his muttered cursing. "The first night, I took some shots of things that didn't look quite right. You know, groups of men who were huddled together talking. Cars that were parked where they probably shouldn't be. Things like that. Not that I really suspected them of anything. But I didn't want to come home empty-handed.

"I was hoping to find something concrete tonight, so I brought the camera again. Let's face it. If I did find out anything, I doubt the police would simply take my word for it. I mean, if they were at all concerned with that awful man who's selling defective guns, well...they'd be doing something right now." Judd cringed, but Emily rushed on. "If I had something on film, I'd have solid evidence. The police would have to get involved. But there wasn't anything incriminating.''

Judd's mouth was tight and his eyes grew more narrow with each word she spoke. "You've been hanging out in the lower east side for three days...rather, nights?''

"Yes.''

His palm slapped the table and he leaned forward to loom over her again, caging her in her chair. Emily slid back in her seat, stunned by his fury. And he *was* furious, she had no doubt of that.

"Never again, you got that!'' He was so close, his breath hit her face in hot gusts. "From this day on, you don't even think about going anywhere, especially to the lower east side, without me. Ever. You got that?''

Emily bolted upright, forcing him to move away so they wouldn't smack noses. "You don't give me orders, Mr. Sanders!''

"Judd, dammit,'' he said, now sounding merely disgruntled. "I told you to call me Judd.''

"I hired you, *Judd,* not the other way around.''

He grabbed her shoulders and pushed her into her seat. His tone was lower, but no less firm. "I'm serious, Emily. You obviously don't have the sense God gave a goose, and if you want my help on this, I insist you stay in one piece. That won't happen if you go wandering around in areas where you shouldn't be. It's too dangerous. Hell, it's a wonder you've survived as long as you have.''

Emily tried to calm herself, but he was so close, she couldn't think straight. She recognized his real concern, something money couldn't possibly buy. Satisfied that her instincts hadn't failed her after all, she tried to reassure him. Her voice emerged as a whisper. "I have been careful, Judd. I promise. No one saw me take the pictures. But just in case, I took shots of inconsequential things, too. Like the children who were playing in the street, and the vagrant standing on the corner. If anyone saw me, they'd just think I was doing an exposé. They'd be flattered, not concerned."

"You can't know that."

He, too, was easing back, as if suddenly aware of their positions. Slipping the camera off over her head, he said, "I'll take this, in case there is anything important on the film."

Emily started to object, even though she truly didn't believe she had photographed anything relevant. Then she noticed where his gaze had wandered. Very briefly, his eyes lit on her mouth, then her throat. Emily could feel her pulse racing there.

Still frowning, but also looking a little confused, Judd laid the camera on the table, then caught the lapels of her coat and eased them wide. He just stood there, holding her coat open, looking at her. He didn't move, but his look was so hot, and he was still so near she grew breathless.

She felt choked by the neck of her dress, a high-collared affair that buttoned up the front and was long enough to hang to midcalf. It was sprinkled with small, dainty blue flowers, a little outdated maybe, but she liked it. She'd long ago accepted she had no fashion sense, so she bought what pleased her, not what the designers dictated.

Judd lifted a finger, almost reluctantly, and touched the small blue bow that tied her collar at her throat. She could hear his breathing, could see his intense concentration as he watched the movement of his hand. With a slow, gentle tug, he released the bow, and the pad of his finger touched her warm skin.

Emily parted her lips to breathe. She wasn't thinking about what he was doing or why. She was only feeling, the sensations overwhelming, swamping her senses. She surrendered to them— to Judd—without a whimper, good sense and caution lost in the need to be wanted, to share herself with another person.

Judd lifted his gaze to her face. He searched her expression for a timeless moment, his eyes hard and bright. Then abruptly, he moved away. He stalked to the door, his head down, his hands fisted on his hips.

He inhaled deeply, and Emily watched the play of muscles

across his back. "I want your promise, Emily. I don't want you to make a single move without me."

Gruff and low, it took a second for his words to filter into her mind. They were so different from her own thoughts, so distant from the mood he'd created. She cleared her throat and tried to clear her mind. Judd still had his back to her, his arms now crossed over his chest. He sounded almost angry, and she didn't understand him. Could he, who barely knew her, truly be so concerned for her well-being? "You'll help me? You're not just putting me off?"

"I'll help. But we move when I say, and not before."

She wished he'd look at her so she could see his face, but he didn't. "Since I assume you know the best time to find information, I'll wait."

Finally, he turned to her. "This house is secure?"

"Very."

He picked up the camera, then opened the door. "I've got to go. I have a few things to do yet. But I want you to promise me you'll stay inside—no more investigating tonight."

Nervously, Emily fingered the loose ties to her bow. She considered retying it, but decided against drawing any further attention to the silly thing. Judd glanced down at her fingers, and his expression hardened. "Promise me you'll stay in your castle, princess. We can talk more in the morning."

"Yes. I won't go anywhere else tonight." She tried to make her tone firm, but some of her fear came through in her next question. "How will I reach you tomorrow?"

Judd stood silently watching her a minute longer. "You got a pen and paper anywhere around here?"

Emily opened a drawer and pulled out a pad and pencil. Judd quickly scrawled several lines. "This is my number at the apartment, and this is the one at the bar. And just in case, here's my address. Now, I mean it, Emily. Don't make a move without me."

She tried not to look too greedy when she snatched the paper out of his hand. "I promise."

He hesitated another moment, then stepped outside, pulling the door shut behind him. Emily watched through the window as his truck drove away, wondering where he was going, but knowing she didn't have the right to ask. Perhaps he had a lady friend waiting on him.

Of course he does, Emily, she told herself. *A man like him probably has dozens of women.* But they're not ladies. He wouldn't want a lady.

And for some reason, that thought sent a small, forbidden thrill curling through her insides.

ANGER AND FRUSTRATION were not a good combination. Judd didn't understand himself. Or more to the point, he didn't understand his reaction to Emily.

He'd been a hairbreadth away from kissing her. Not a sweet little peck. No, he'd wanted his tongue in her mouth, his lips covering hers, feeling her urgency. He'd wanted, dammit, to devour her completely.

And she would have loved it, he could tell that much from her racing pulse and her soft, inviting eyes. She may play the proper little Miss Priss to perfection, but she had fire. Enough to burn him if he let her.

It wasn't the time and she wasn't the person for him to be getting ideas about. But he'd taunted her without mercy, wanting to conquer her, to show her he was male to her female. To prove...what? That he could and would protect her? That he'd solve her problems so she could smile more? He didn't know.

He'd had women, of course, but none that meant anything beyond physical pleasure. None that he'd wanted to claim, to brand in the most primal, basic way. He didn't know what it was, but Emily was simply different. And she affected him differently.

That dress of hers...so feminine, so deceiving. He'd always heard other men joke about having a lady in the parlor and a wanton in the bedroom. The dress had looked innocent enough, but her eyes...

He knew, even though he wasn't happy knowing, that Emily

fit the descriptive mix of lady and wanton to a tee. It was an explosive fantasy, the thought of having a woman who would unleash her passion for just one man, that no one would ever guess unless they were with her, covering her, inside her.

Beneath her dress, he could make out the faint, delicate curve of her breasts, her narrow rib cage. She was so slight of build, but so feminine. She had the finest skin he'd ever seen, warm and smooth and pale. And loyalty. She must be damn loyal to this kid—whoever he was—to take such risks for him.

Judd's thighs clenched and his heart raced. He hadn't been able to resist touching her, and she hadn't protested when he did.

She was too trusting for her own good. And he was too intuitive to be fooled by her prissy demeanor. Emily Cooper had more than her fair share of backbone, and that was almost as sexy as her eyes.

Stopping at a corner drugstore and leaving the truck at the curb, Judd got out to use the lighted pay phone. He never used the phone in his apartment to contact headquarters, in case there were prying ears. To his disgust, his hands shook as he fished a quarter out of his jeans pocket. He made the call, and then waited.

Lieutenant Howell picked up on the first ring. "Yeah?"

"Sanders here."

"It's about time. Where the hell have you been?"

Judd closed his eyes, not relishing the chore ahead of him. This wasn't going to be easy. He took a deep breath, then told his boss, "We have a little problem."

"I'm waiting."

"I met a lady tonight."

"Is that supposed to surprise me, Judd? Hell, you're working as a male stripper. I imagine you meet a lot of broads every damn night."

"Not a broad," Judd said, the edge in his tone evident. "A lady. And she was actively looking for Donner, though she hasn't put a name to him yet. Seems she knows a kid who had a faulty automatic blow up in his face, and she's pegged Donner as the seller.''

There was a low whistle, then, ''No kidding?''

''The kid's alive, but from what I understand, he's in pretty bad shape. His parents have taken him out of the country.'' Then, in a drier tone, Judd added, ''They're upper-league.''

Judd expected the cursing, then the inevitable demand for details. The telling took all of three minutes, and during that time, Howell didn't make a single sound. Judd tried to downplay his initial meeting with Emily and the fact she'd seen him perform, but there was no way to get around it completely. When Judd finished, he heard a rough rumble from Howell that could have been either a chuckle or a curse. ''She could throw a wrench into the works.''

Judd chose his words very carefully. ''Maybe not. I've been thinking about it, and it might actually strengthen my case. Being a stripper in such a sleazy joint makes me look pretty unethical. And I've made it known I'd do just about anything, including stripping, to make a fast buck.''

''But Donner hasn't taken the bait yet.''

''He will.'' Judd was certain of that. Donner always used available locals. That was how he worked. ''It will happen. But maybe, with a classy woman hanging around to make me look all the more unscrupulous, Donner will buy in a little quicker.''

''You think he'll figure the little lady is keeping you?''

''What else would he think? We're hardly the perfect couple. As long as she's informed and close enough for me to keep an eye on her, she'll be safe. And Donner will definitely get curious. Besides, I don't have much choice. She made it real plain she'd investigate on her own if I didn't see fit to help her. It's a sure bet she'd tip Donner off and send him running.''

Howell chuckled. ''Sounds like you got everything nicely under control.''

No. He didn't have his libido under control, or his protective male instincts that had him wanting to look after her despite his obligations to the job and his loyalty to Max. ''I can handle things, I think. It would have been better not to have a civilian involved, but my options are limited now.''

''I could have her picked up for some trumped-up violation. That might buy you a little time to settle things without her around.''

The thought of Emily being humiliated that way, being harassed—by anyone other than himself, was unthinkable. ''No. I'll keep an eye on her. Besides, she's so clean, she squeaks. I doubt you'd find anything. And I already tried scaring her off, but she's sticking to her guns.''

''Determined, huh?''

Judd snorted. ''I almost think she wants Donner as bad as I do. She was taking pictures. Can you imagine? I took the film. I don't think there's anything important on it, but I don't want to take any chances. Not with this case.'' *And not with her.* ''So I'll let her hang around a while, and use the situation to our advantage. In any case, she'll probably be with me when I perform at the bar on Tuesday.''

''Keep me posted as soon as you know about the film. And in the meantime, watch your backside. Don't go getting romantic ideas and blow this whole thing.''

''Fat chance.'' He hoped he sounded convincing. ''I just wanted you to know what was going on.''

''You need any backup on hand, just in case?''

''No.'' Everything had gone better than he could have hoped. His performance was convincing, even superior to the other dancers'. But he didn't intend to share all that over the phone. It was humiliating. ''I don't want to take a chance on blowing it now. I'm accepted. No one suspects me of being anything but a stripper.''

''Yeah, you fit the bill real good.''

Judd ignored that taunting comment. They'd checked the place over in minute detail before setting up the stakeout. Donner definitely used the room above the bar to make his deals and meet contacts. So it was imperative that Judd be on hand. Unfortunately, the bar was such a damn landmark, having been there for generations, the only transient positions available were the dancers'. The bartenders had been there for years and the bar's ownership hadn't changed hands except within the same family. If Judd wanted Donner he was stuck stripping. And he wanted Donner real bad.

"As I said, it's a believable cover, but I hope like hell we can wrap it up soon. I don't want to take any unnecessary chances."

And he didn't want Emily to get caught in the middle of his own personal war.

"Judd? Is there something you're not telling me? Has something happened? Is it time?"

His instincts told him things would come to a head soon, but he kept that thought to himself. "Hell, it's past time, but who knows? Something's bound to break soon. Either a deal or my back. Those ladies can be real demanding when you're peeling off your clothes."

As he'd intended, his cryptic complaints lightened the mood. "You're the perfect guy for the job. Just don't start enjoying yourself and decide to leave us for bigger and better things." Howell laughed, then cleared his throat. "Stay in touch, and for God's sake, stay alert. Get the hell out if things go sour."

"I'll keep my eyes open."

Judd felt a certain finality settle over him as he replaced the receiver. His superior hadn't nixed his plans with Emily, and it was too late to call off the cover, regardless of his personal feelings. He'd be spending a lot of time in Emily's company. And that filled him with both dread and sizzling anticipation.

HE HADN'T SLEPT a wink. The combination of worry and excitement from his vivid dreams of Emily worked to keep him tossing all night. But the knock on the apartment door sounded insistent, so he reluctantly forced himself out from under the sheet, then wrapped it around himself to cover his nudity.

"Just a damn minute!" On his way out of the room, he picked up his watch and saw it was only eight-thirty. Just dandy.

Carrying his pistol, he looked out the peephole, then cursed. He stuck the gun in a drawer, just before jerking the door open.

He managed to startle Emily, who nearly dropped a large basket she was holding in both hands. "Are you one of those perverse people who rises with the sun?"

Emily didn't look at his face. She was too busy staring at his body. Judd sighed in disgust. "I'm showing less now than I did last night, and you didn't faint then, so please, pull it together, will ya?"

That moony-eyed look of hers was going to be the death of him. A man could take only so much.

And she was looking especially fetching this morning in some kind of light, spring dress. It was just as concealing as the one she'd worn last night, but there was no tie at her throat, only a pearl brooch that looked as if it cost a small fortune. This dress nipped in at the waist, and showed how tiny she was. He could easily span her waist with his hands. His palms tingled at the thought.

"What the hell are you doing here, Emily? It's still early."

"I...actually, I thought we might have breakfast. You did say we would talk this morning."

"Eager to get started, are you?" Turning away, Judd stared toward the kitchen, then back to Emily. "I wasn't up yet. If you want coffee, you'll have to make it."

Emily seemed to shake herself. "Ah, no. Actually, I thought...you know, to thank you for everything you did for me last night...taking me home and all that, well...I cooked for you."

She ended in a shrug, and Judd realized how embarrassed she was. Or maybe she thought he'd mock her again, ridicule her for her consideration.

He raked a hand through his hair, still holding the sheet with a fist. "What have you got in there?"

He indicated the basket with a toss of his head. Emily's smile was fleeting, and very relieved. She glanced around the room, taking in the apartment's minimal furnishings: a couch, a small table with two chairs, a few lamps, a stereo, but no television. His bedroom sat off to the right, where the open door allowed her to see a small night table and a rumpled bed. The kitchen was merely a room divided by a small, three-foot bar.

He liked the place, even though the neighborhood was rough and the tenants noisy. It wasn't home, but then he'd never really had a home, at least not one of his own. He'd lived with Max Henley a while, and that had seemed as close as he'd ever get to having a family. But that was before Max died. Ever since, his life had been centered on nailing Donner. Where he lived was a trivial matter.

He waited to see Emily's reactions to the apartment, but she didn't so much as blink. After a brief smile, she set the basket on the wobbly table, then opened it with a flourish. "Blueberry muffins, sausage links and fresh fruit." She flashed him a quick, sweet smile. "And coffee."

He was touched, he couldn't help it. "I can't believe you made me breakfast."

"It's not fancy, but you didn't strike me as a man who would want escargots so early in the morning."

He grimaced, then ended with a smile. "And you didn't strike me as the type who would cook for a man."

"I like to cook. My mother thinks it's some faulty gene inherited from my ancestors. But since I'm not married, I don't get to indulge very often."

"What about dates? You could do some real nice entertaining in your house."

She busied herself with setting out the food. "I don't go out much."

He wasn't immune to her vulnerability. He reached out and touched her hand. "No woman has ever cooked for me before."

She stared at him, shocked. "You're kidding."

Feeling a little stupid now for mentioning it, Judd shook his head. "Nope."

"What about your mother?"

"Left when I was real little. My father raised me."

"Oh." Then she tilted her head. "The two of you are close?"

He laughed. "Hardly. Dad stayed drunk most of the time, and

I tried to stay out of his hair, 'cause Dad could get real mean when he drank.''

"That's awful!'' She looked so outraged on his behalf, he grinned.

"It wasn't as bad as all that, Em.''

"Of course it was. I think it sounds horrid. Did you have any brothers or sisters?''

"Nope.''

"So you were all alone?''

That was the softest, saddest voice he'd ever heard, and for some fool reason, he liked hearing it from her. "Naw. I had Max.''

"Max?''

"Yeah. See, I wasn't all that respectable when I was younger, and Max Henley busted me trying to steal the tip he'd left for a waitress. With Max being a cop and all, I thought I'd end up in jail. But instead, he bought me lunch, chewed me out real good, then made me listen to about two hours' worth of lectures on right and wrong and being a good man. I was only fourteen, so I can't say I paid that much attention. When I finally got out of that restaurant, I didn't think I'd ever go back. But I did. See, I knew Max ate his lunch there every day, so the next day, when he saw me hanging around, he invited me to join him. It became a routine, and that summer, he gave me a job keeping up his yard. After a while, Max kind of became like family to me.''

Emily was grinning now, too. "He was a father figure?''

"Father, mother, and sometimes as grumpy as an old school-marm. But he took good care of me. I guess you could say he was a complete 'family figure.''' *And Donner had robbed Judd of that family.*

"He sounds like a wonderful man.''

"Yeah.'' Judd looked away, wishing he'd never brought up the subject. "Max was the best. He's dead now.''

"I'm sorry.''

Judd bit his upper lip, barely controlling the urge to hug her close. She had spoken so softly, with so much sincerity, her words felt like a caress. Somehow, she managed to lessen the pain he always felt whenever he thought of Max. God, he still missed him, though it had been nearly six months since Donner had killed him.

Judd nodded, then waited through an awkward silence while Emily looked around for something to do.

She went back to unloading her basket. As she opened the dishes, Judd inhaled the aromas. "Mmm. Smells good. Why don't you get things ready while I put on some pants. Okay?"

"I'll have the table set in a snap." Then she grinned again. "I hope you're hungry. I made plenty."

Judd shook his head. She was wooing him with breakfast, a ploy as old as mankind, and he was succumbing without a struggle. If he was ever going to keep her safe, he'd have to keep his head and maintain the control. The only way to do that was to make certain some distance existed between them. He couldn't be moved by every small gesture she made.

When he emerged from the bedroom two minutes later, Emily had everything on plates. He noticed there were two settings, so obviously she planned to eat with him. He also saw that, other than coffee mugs, she'd found only paper plates and plastic cutlery in his kitchen. But she didn't seem put off by that fact. A tall thermos of coffee sat in the middle of the table. It smelled strong, just the way he liked it.

"This is terrific, Emily. I appreciate it." Normally, he didn't eat breakfast, but his stomach growled as he approached the table, and he couldn't deny how hungry he was.

Emily poured his coffee, still smiling. "I thought we could talk while we eat. Maybe get to know each other a little better. I mean, we will be working together, and we're practically strangers."

He glanced up at her. "I wouldn't say that."

She blinked, then looked away. "How long have you been... ah..."

"Stripping?"

"Yes." There was another bright blush on her cheeks. Judd wondered how she kept from catching fire.

"A while," he said, keeping his answer vague.

"You…you like it?"

Good Lord. He laid down his fork and stared at her. She was the most unpredictable woman he'd ever met. Watching her eyes, he said, "Everyone should experience stripping at least once. It's a fantasy, but most people don't have the guts to try it."

She sucked in her breath. The fork she had in front of her held a piece of sausage, ready to fall off. She looked guilty.

Ah. He smiled, reading her thoughts. "Admit it, Emily. You've thought of it, haven't you? Imagine the men, or even one man, getting hotter with every piece of clothing you remove. Imagine his eyes staring at you, imagine him wanting you so bad he can't stand it. But you make him wait, until you're ready, until you're completely…naked."

She trembled, then put down her fork, folding her hands in her lap. Judd didn't feel like smiling now; he felt like laying her across the table, tossing the skirt of her dress up around her shoulders and viewing all of her, naked. For him. He wanted to drive into her slim body and hear her scream his name. It angered him, the unaccountable way she could provoke his emotions, leaving him raw.

"You want to strip for me, Emily? I'll be a willing audience, I can promise you that."

"Why are you doing this?"

Her tone was breathless, faint. With arousal or humiliation? He slashed his hand in the air, disgusted with himself. "Eat your breakfast."

"Judd…"

"I'm sorry, Emily. I'm not usually such a bastard. Just forget it, all right?"

She didn't look as though she wanted to. Instead, she looked ready to launch into another round of questions and he couldn't take it. He began eating, ignoring her, giving all his attention to his food.

He waited until she'd taken a bite of her muffin, then said, "I've decided if I'm going to help you, I'll need more information."

Emily swallowed quickly and looked at him, her eyes wide. "I told you everything."

"No. I need the whole truth now, Emily. How you're involved, and why. What really happened." He took a sip of coffee, watching her over the rim of his mug. "Who's the kid? But most of all, what does he have to do with you?"

4

EMILY KNEW her luck had just run out. And though it surprised her he'd figured her out so soon, she had expected it. Judd wasn't an idiot, far from it. And she supposed it was his obvious intelligence and insight that made her feel so sure he would help her.

How much to tell him was her quandary.

Judd evidently grew impatient with her silence. "Stop trying to think up some elaborate lie. You're no good at it, anyway. Hell, if I can tell you're planning to lie, you'll never be able to carry it off. So just the truth, if you please. Now."

Emily frowned at him. He didn't have to sound so surly. And he didn't have to look so...sexy. He'd shocked her but good, answering the door near-naked. Even now, with his pants on, he still looked sleep-rumpled and much too appealing. She cleared her throat and stared down at her plate.

"All I can tell you is that someone I hold dear was injured when that gun misfired. Since I know no one else is going to do anything about it, I have to. And the only thing I can think of is to make sure that the man who sold the gun is brought to justice."

"Is the guy a lover?"

Emily blinked. "Who?"

"The man who is *dear to you.*"

His sneering tone had her leaning back in surprise. "Don't be ridiculous. He's just a boy. Only sixteen."

Judd shrugged. "So who is he? A relative?"

Why wouldn't he just let it rest? Why wouldn't he—

"Dammit, Emily, who is he?"

He shocked her so badly with his sudden shout, she blurted out, "My brother!"

"Ah. I suppose that could motivate a person. Never having had a brother myself, I wouldn't know for certain, of course. But I can see where you'd want to protect a little brother." Judd rubbed his whiskered jaw, then added, "Why don't your parents just go to the police?"

Emily stood up and walked away from the table. How had he gotten her to reveal so much, so easily? She knew she had no talent for subterfuge, but she hadn't thought she'd crack so quickly. When she turned to face Judd again, she caught him staring at her ankles. Her silence drew his attention, and when his gaze lifted to her face, he didn't apologize, but merely lifted a dark eyebrow.

Trying to ignore the heat in her face, Emily folded her hands over her waist and said, "My parents hate scandal more than anything. They'd rather move to another country than have their name sullied with damaging speculation."

"Don't they love their son?"

"Well, of course they do." Appalled that she'd given him the wrong impression, Emily took her seat again, leaning forward to get his attention. "It's just that they've got some pretty strident notions about propriety. Their reputations, and the family name, mean a lot to them."

"More than their son, evidently." Then Judd shook his head. "No, Emily, don't start defending them again. I really don't give a damn what kind of parents you have. But it seems to me, if they're willing to sweep the incident under the carpet, you should be, too. What can you hope to prove, anyway?"

This was the tricky part, trying to make him understand how important it was for John to see now, before it was too late, exactly what road he was choosing. She didn't want to see the same disdain in Judd's eyes when she mentioned her brother as he apparently felt for her parents. Why his opinion mattered to her, she didn't know. But it did.

Keeping her voice low, she said, "John bought the gun, I think, because he wanted my parents' attention. You'd have to understand how hard he tried to find his...niche. I remember last

Christmas, John was crushed when my parents sent him a gift from Europe." Her lips tilted in a vague smile. "It was a check, a substantial check, but still, it was only money. John sat in front of the stupid Christmas tree, seven feet high and professionally decorated, and he cried. I didn't let him know I was there because I knew it would embarrass him."

Judd looked down at his feet. "I never had a Christmas tree until Max took me in. It was only a spindly little thing, but I liked it. It beat the hell out of seeing my father passed out drunk in the front room where the Christmas tree should have been but wasn't."

"Oh, Judd."

"Now, don't start, Em. We're talking about John, remember? I only mentioned that memory because I guess I always assumed people with money had a better holiday. I mean, more gifts, better food, a lot of cheer and all that." He shook his head. "Shoots that theory all to hell, doesn't it?"

"People usually think having money is wonderful, but that's not always true. Sometimes...money spoils things. It can make people self-centered, maybe even neglectful. Because it's so easy to do what you want, when you want, it's easy to forget about the others who...might depend on you. It's easy to forget that everyone can't be bought, and money doesn't solve every problem."

Judd didn't say a word, but his hand, so large and warm and rough, curled around her fingers and held on. Emily started, surprised at the gentleness of his touch, at how comforting it felt to make physical contact with him. She glanced up, and his eyes held hers. There was no more derision, and certainly no pity. Only understanding.

It was nearly her undoing.

"My...my brother, he's a good kid, Judd, just a bit misguided. And though he's trying to play it tough right now, he's scared. He doesn't know if he'll ever look the same as he did before the accident. My parents keep assuring him they'll find a good plastic surgeon to take care of everything, but he's hurting. Not physically, but inside. He wanted my parents' attention, but all he's gained is their annoyance. They never once asked him why he bought the gun or how. They only complained about him doing something so stupid. And they made it clear, had he wanted a gun, they could have bought the finest hunting rifle available, and supplied him with lessons on how to handle it.''

"They missed the point entirely."

Emily felt his deep voice wash over her, and she smiled. "Yes, they did."

"Okay. So what will nailing the guy who sold him the gun prove to your brother?"

"That I love him. That I know what's right and wrong, and that he knows it, too, if he'll only open his eyes and realize that he is a good person, that he doesn't need affirmation from anyone but himself."

"Is that what you learned, honey? Do you understand your brother so well, because you've gone through the same thing?"

Emily forced a laugh and tried to pull her hand free, but Judd wouldn't let her go. He wouldn't let her look away, either. His gaze held her as securely as his fingers held her hand. "I've never felt the need to purchase a gun, Judd."

"No, but you must have wanted approval from your family as much as your brother does. What did you do, Emily, to get them to notice you?"

She cleared her throat and tried to change the subject. "This is ridiculous. It doesn't have anything to do with our deal."

"To hell with the deal. What did you do, Em?"

Panic began to edge through her. Not for anything would she lay the humiliation she'd suffered out for him to see. Besides, she'd buried the memory deep. It was no longer a part of her. At least, she hoped it wasn't.

"I've made my fair share of mistakes," she told him. "But I've forgiven myself and gotten on with my life. That's all any of us can do." Once she said that, she came to her feet, knowing she had to do something, occupy herself somehow, or she'd become maudlin. A display of emotions wouldn't serve her purpose.

But as she stood, so did Judd, and before she could move away, he had her tugged close. The morning whiskers on his jaw felt slightly abrasive, and arousing, as he brushed against her cheek. The warmth of his palms seeped through her dress to her back where he carefully stroked her in a comforting, soothing manner. She could smell his musky, male scent, and breathed deeply, filling herself with him, uncaring what had brought on this show of concern. It simply felt too good to have him hold her.

"You should always remember, Em, what a good person you are. Don't let anyone convince you otherwise."

His raspy tone sounded close to her ear, sending gooseflesh up her arms. And her emotions must have been closer to the surface than she'd wanted to admit, because she could feel the sting of tears behind her lids.

Not wanting Judd to know how he affected her, she hid her face in his shoulder and tried a laugh. It sounded a little wobbly, but it was the best she could produce. "You hardly know me, Judd. What makes you think I'm such a fine specimen of humanity?"

He rocked her from side to side, and she could hear the smile in his voice when he spoke. "Are you kidding me? You're obviously damn loyal since you're willing to risk your pretty little neck for your brother, just to keep him on the right track. You've opened your property to the neighborhood kids, not caring that they might trample your flowers or muddy up your yard. And you told me you volunteer at the soup kitchen. I'll bet you've got a whole group of charity organizations you donate to, don't you?"

Emily squeezed herself closer, loving the solid feel of his chest against her cheek, the strength of his arms around her. She couldn't recall ever feeling so safe. "I'm the one who benefits from the organizations. I've met so many really good, caring people, who just need a little help to get their lives straightened out. We talk, we laugh. Sometimes…I don't know what I'd do without them.''

Judd groaned, and then his hand was beneath her chin, tilting her face up. Emily smiled, thinking he had a few more questions for her, when his mouth closed over hers and she couldn't think at all.

Heat was her first impression. The added warmth seemed to be everything, touching her everywhere. She felt it in her toes as he lifted her to meet him better, to fit her more fully against him. She felt it in her breasts, pressed tight against his chest. And in her stomach, as the heat curled and expanded.

His mouth was firm, his tongue wet as he licked over her lips, insisting she open. When she did, he tasted her deeply, his hands coming up to hold her face still as he slanted his mouth over hers again and again.

Emily had never known such a kiss. She'd thought she'd experienced lust while she was engaged, but it had been nothing like this. She made a small sound of surprise, wanting the contact to go on forever—and suddenly Judd pulled away.

Emily grabbed the back of the chair to keep herself grounded. Judd stared at her, looking appalled and fascinated and…hungry. *Oh, Lord, Emily, now you've really done it.*

She should have felt guilty for behaving so improperly, but all her mind kept repeating was, *Let's do it again.* She shook her head at herself, dismissing that errant notion and trying to remember her purpose. Judd must have misunderstood, because he turned away.

"I'm sorry," he said.

Emily blinked several times. "I beg your pardon?"

Judd whirled to face her, once again furious. "I said, I'm sorry, dammit. I shouldn't have done that. It won't happen again."

Oh, darn. "No, of course not. It was my fault. I shouldn't have been telling you all my problems and—"

"Shut up, Emily."

She did, and stared at him, waiting to see what he would do, what he wanted her to do.

"Damn." He snatched her close again, pressed another hard, entirely too quick kiss to her lips, then set her away. "I take it back. It probably will happen again. Hopefully, not for a while, but...I'm not making any promises. If you don't want me ever to touch you, just say so, all right?"

Emily remained perfectly still, unwilling to take a chance that he might misunderstand her response if she moved. She prided herself on the fact she wasn't a hypocrite. No, she wanted Judd, and she was thrilled beyond reason that he apparently wanted her, too. And since he held rather obvious scorn for her background—that of money and privilege—he wouldn't expect her to play the part of the proper lady. No, Judd had already made it clear where his preferences lay. Any man who could strip for a living was obviously on the earthy side, primal and lusty and...her heart skipped two beats while she waited to see what he'd do next.

He laughed. It wasn't a humorous laugh, but one of wonder and disbelief. "You're something else, Emily, you know that? Here, sit down." He loosened her death grip on the chair back and nudged her toward the seat. "Don't go away. I'm going to shower and finish getting dressed, then we'll make some plans, okay?"

She sat. She nodded. She felt ready to explode with anticipation.

Judd ruffled her hair, still shaking his head, and left the room.

HE MADE CERTAIN it was a cold shower, but the temperature of the water didn't help to cool the heat of his body. Never could he remember being hit so hard. Holding her felt right, talking to her felt right. Hell, kissing her had been as right as it could get— bordering on blissful death.

He could only imagine how it would feel to...no. He'd better not imagine or he'd find himself right back in the shower.

How could one woman be so damn sweet? He'd have thought all that money and her parents' attitudes would have soured her, but it hadn't. Emily loved. She loved her brother, she loved the children in her neighborhood. She even loved the homeless who visited the kitchen where she volunteered. He'd heard it in her tone, seen it in her eyes.

God, she was killing him.

He had to stay objective, and that meant getting back to business. He finished dragging a comb through his damp hair and left the bathroom.

Emily hadn't moved a single inch. And if he hadn't already had a little taste of her, he'd believe her prissy pose, with her knees pressed tightly together, and her slim hands folded in her lap. Ha! What a facade. He dragged his eyes away from her wary gaze and began stuffing her thermos and empty dishes back into the basket. "You ready to go?"

"Ah...go where?"

He flicked an impatient glance her way. "To find your gun dealer. I thought we'd hit some of the local establishments. The pool hall, first. Then maybe the diner. And tonight, the bar."

"Are you...dancing tonight?"

"No. I've got all weekend free. I only dance on Tuesdays and Thursdays, remember?" He noticed her sigh of relief and frowned at her. "But you will be there when I dance, Em. To pull this off, you're going to have to be my biggest fan. Everyone will have to believe I'm yours. You can be as territorial as you like. Besides, I can use you as a smoke screen. If the ladies all believe I'm already spoken for, they might not be so persistent."

Emily pursed her lips, her shoulders going a little straighter. "Are you certain that's what you want? I don't wish to interfere in your social life."

"You know, Em, you don't sound the least bit sincere."

She looked totally flustered now, and it was all he could do not to laugh. "Come on, let's get going."

Holding her arm, a manner that felt as right as everything else he did with her, Judd hustled her down to the street and into his truck. He waited until she'd settled herself, then asked, "Did your brother mention what the guy who sold him the gun looked like?''

Emily shook her head. ''He wasn't in much condition to talk when I saw him last. I did get him to tell me where he'd bought it, though. But all he said about the man was that he'd grinned when he sold him the gun.''

Judd noticed she'd tucked her hands into fists again, and he reached over to entwine her fingers with his. ''When was your brother hurt?''

''Not quite a month ago. I saw him right afterward and then my parents took him away as soon as the hospital allowed it. I didn't even get to say goodbye.''

''So you have no idea how he's doing?''

Emily turned away to stare out the side window. Her voice dropped to a low pitch, indicating her worry. ''I've talked to him on the phone. He...he's very depressed. Though my parents evidently refuse to believe it, the plastic surgeons have already done all they can. The worst of the scars have been minimized. But the burns from the backfire did some extensive damage to the underlying tissue around his upper cheek and temple. He claims his face still looks horrid, but I don't believe it's as bad as he thinks. He's...he's always been popular in school, especially with the girls. I guess he thinks his life is over. I tried to make him look on the positive side, that his eyesight wasn't permanently damaged, but I don't suppose he can see a bright side right now.''

Her voice broke, but Judd pretended he hadn't heard. He instinctively knew she wouldn't appreciate her loss of control. For such a small woman, she had an overabundance of pride and gumption, and he had no intention of denting it.

He squeezed her fingers again and kept his eyes focused on the road. ''When will he be home again?''

''I don't know. I haven't spoken with my parents.'' She sent him a tilted smile. ''They're blaming me for this. They say I'm a bad influence on him.''

''You?'' Judd couldn't hide his surprise.

"I work with the underprivileged. I don't own a single fur coat. And I live in an old house that constantly needs repair."

"Your house? I thought your house was terrific."

She seemed genuinely pleased by his praise. "Thank you. But the plumbing is dreadful. I've had almost everything replaced, but now the hot-water heater is about to go. Either the water is ice-cold, or so hot it could scald you. I thought my father would disown me when he burned his hand on the kitchen faucet. But even more than my house, my parents hate that I refuse to marry a man they approve of. They want me to 'settle into my station in life.'" Emily laughed. "Doesn't that sound ridiculous?"

"Settling down? Not really. I think you'd make a fantastic wife and mother." Dead silence followed his claim, and Judd could have bitten his tongue in two. It was bad enough that he still yearned for a real family. But to say as much to Emily? She was probably worried, especially after that kiss he'd given her, that he might have designs on her.

He slanted a look her way, and noticed a bright blush on her cheeks. Trying to put her at ease, he said, "You look like a domestic little creature, Em. That's all I meant."

Those wide brown eyes of hers blinked, and then she started mumbling to herself. He couldn't quite catch what she was saying. Judging from the tone, though, he probably wouldn't want to hear it, anyway. He had the suspicion she was giving him a proper set-down—in her own, polite way.

Judd was contemplating her reaction, and the reason for it, when they pulled up in front of the pool hall. It was still early, well before noon, so he didn't expect the place to be overly crowded. Only the regulars would be there, the men who made shooting pool an active part of their livelihood.

Clayton Donner was one of those men.

Judd didn't expect to see him here today, but he never knew when he might get lucky. And in the meantime, he'd find out a little more about Donner.

Emily was silent as he led her into the smoky interior. Unlike the lighting at the bar, it was bright here, and country music twanged from a jukebox in the far corner. Some of the men looked as if they'd been there all night and the low-hanging fluorescent lights added a gray cast to their skin. Others looked merely bored, and still others were intent on their game. But they all looked up at Emily. Judd could feel her uneasiness, but for the moment, he played his role and, other than put his arm around her shoulders to mark his claim, he payed her little attention.

Leaning down to whisper in her ear, he said, "Play along with me now. And remember, no matter what happens, don't lose your cool." Then he gave her a kiss on the cheek and a swat on the behind. "Get me a drink, will ya, honey?"

He gave a silent prayer she'd do as she was told, then sauntered over to the nearest table. "Hey, Frog. You been here all night?"

Frog, as his friends called him, had a croak for a voice, due to a chop to the larynx that had damaged his throat during a street fight. Frog didn't croak now, though. He was too busy watching Emily as she made her way cautiously to the bar, careful not to touch anyone or anything.

Judd gave a feral grin. "That's mine, Frog, so put your eyes back in your head."

Frog grunted. "What the hell are you doing with her? She ain't your type."

Judd shrugged. "She's rich. She's my type."

Frog thought that was hilarious, and was still laughing when Emily carried a glass of cola to Judd. He took a sip, then choked. Glaring in mock anger, Judd demanded, "What the hell is that?"

Emily raised her eyebrows, but didn't look particularly intimidated by his tone. "A drink?"

"Damn, I don't want soda. I meant a real drink." Actually, Judd never touched liquor. He knew alcoholism tended to run in families, and after living with his father, he wouldn't ever take the chance of becoming like him. Still, he handed the glass back to Emily, then said with disgust, "You drink it. And stay out of my way. I'm going to shoot some pool here with Frog."

Emily huffed. She started to walk away, but Judd caught her arm and she landed against his chest. Before she could draw a breath, he kissed her. It wasn't a killer kiss like the one he'd given her earlier, but it was enough to show everyone they were definitely an item. He drew away, but couldn't resist giving her a quick, soft peck before adding, "Behave yourself, honey. I won't be long."

Emily nodded, apparently appeased, and went to perch on a stool. Judd looked at her a moment longer, appreciating the pretty picture she made, waiting there for him. She dutifully smiled, and looked as if she'd wait all day if that was what he wanted.

It was the kind of fantasy he could really get into, having a woman like Emily for his own. But he couldn't spare the time or the energy to get involved with her or anyone else. He needed, and wanted, to focus all his attention on taking Donner off the streets. The man had stolen a huge hunk of his life when he'd killed Max. Judd wasn't ever going to forget that.

So instead of indulging in the pleasure he got by simply watching Emily, he turned away. He knew she didn't realize what he'd done, making her look like a woman he could control with just a little physical contact, but every man in the room understood.

And even though that had been his intent, Judd hated every damn one of them for thinking that about Emily. It was bad enough that he'd sold himself to trap Donner, but now he was selling Emily, too. It didn't sit right with him, but at the moment, his choices were limited, and the only alternative was to postpone his plans. Which was really no alternative at all.

EMILY HAD NO IDEA investigating could be so exhausting, though Judd did the actual work. All she did was pretend to be his ornament. It rankled, but until she could get him alone and set him straight about how this little partnership was going to work, she didn't want to take the chance of messing things up.

Judd had been shooting pool for quite some time when the door opened and three men walked in. One was a heavyset man, dirty and dressed all in black, with the name Jonesie written across his T-shirt. Another was a relatively young man, looking somewhat awed by his own presence.

It was the third man, though, that caught and held Emily's attention. There was something about him, a sense of self-confidence, that set him apart. He didn't look like a criminal, but something about him made Emily uncomfortable. He wore only a pair of pleated slacks and a polo shirt. His blond ponytail was interesting, but not actually unusual. In truth, Emily supposed he could be called handsome, but he held no appeal for her. He simply seemed too...pompous.

When his gaze landed on her, she quickly looked away and kept her eyes focused on Judd. And because she was watching Judd so intently, she saw the almost imperceptible stiffening of his body. He'd only glanced up once to see who had walked in, then he'd continued with his shot, smoothly pocketing the nine ball. But Emily felt she was coming to know him well enough to see the tension in his body.

She was still pondering the meaning of that tension when the men approached where she sat.

"Hey, Clay, you want something to drink?"

The blonde smiled toward Emily and took the stool next to her before answering Jonesie. "No. I'm fine. I think I'll just watch the...scenery, for a while."

Emily wanted to move away, but she didn't. Not even on the threat of death would she turn and meet that smile, though she felt it as the man, Clay, continued to watch her. When he touched her arm, she jumped.

"Well, now, honey. No need to be nervous. I was only going to get acquainted."

Emily shook her head and tried to shrug his hand away. Instead of complying with her obvious wish, his well-manicured fingers curled around her arm. His touch repulsed her. She jumped off the stool and stepped back...right into the younger of the three men. She was caught.

This was nothing like talking to the drunks the other night.

She'd felt some sense of control then. But now, as Clay chuckled at her reaction and reached out to stroke her cheek, she felt a scream catch in her throat. His fingers almost touched her skin— and then Judd was there, gripping the man's arm by the wrist and looking as impenetrable as a stone wall.

"The lady is mine. And no one touches her but me."

JUDD NARROWED his eyes, hoping, without the benefit of common sense, that Clayton would take him up on his challenge. He knew he wasn't thinking straight. He could destroy his entire case if he unleashed his temper now, but at the moment, none of that mattered.

He'd kept Donner in his sights from the moment he'd walked in, and he'd thought he'd be able to keep his cool even after Donner noticed Emily. But he hadn't counted on Emily's reaction.

When he'd seen her face and realized she was frightened, all he'd cared about was getting to her, staking his claim and making certain she knew there was nothing to fear. The fact that she was afraid should have angered him, and probably would once he had time to think about it. Didn't she know he wouldn't let anyone hurt her? Hell, he'd take the whole place apart before he'd see her hair get mussed.

But he supposed she couldn't know that, because even now, with him beside her, she still looked horrified. And then she got a hold of herself and smiled, a false smile, to be sure, and stepped to his side. "It's okay, Judd. Really."

Clayton looked down at his wrist where Judd still held him. The gesture was a silent command to be released, but Judd wasn't exactly in an accommodating mood. He tightened his hold for the briefest of seconds, gaining a raised eyebrow from Donner, then he let go. The younger man took a step forward, and Judd bared his teeth in a parody of a grin, encouraging him.

Emily seemed nearly frantic now, saying, "Come on, Judd. Let's go."

But he had no intention of going anywhere. Emily didn't know, couldn't know, the riot of emotions he was suffering right now. His desire to avenge Max mixed with his need to protect Emily, and he felt ready to explode with repressed energy. This was what he'd been waiting for. He could feel Donner's interest, his curiosity, and he knew he'd finally succeeded. If Donner's crony wanted to take him on, he was ready. More than ready. At this point, Donner would only be impressed with his ruthlessness. His muscles twitched in anticipation.

Then Donner laughed. "Don't be a fool, Mick. Our friend here is only trying to protect his interests. I can understand that."

The young man, Mick, moved away, but he did so reluctantly. Judd flexed his hands and tried to get himself under control. He stared at Clayton, then nodded and turned away, making certain he blocked Emily with his body. He knew Donner wouldn't like being dismissed, but he also didn't want to appear too eager.

Frog was standing at the pool table with his mouth hanging open, and Judd had to remind him it was his shot.

"No more for me," Frog said. "I'm done."

And in the next instant, Clayton was there, slapping Frog on the back and smiling. "So, what do you have for me, Frog?"

Frog pulled money out of his pocket, looking decidedly uncomfortable, and handed the bills to Clayton. As he counted, Clayton continued to smile, and then he asked, "That's it?"

Frog shifted his feet, glancing up at Judd and then away again. "I lost some of it."

"Is that so?"

Judd carefully laid his pool cue on the table then faced Clayton with a smile. He couldn't have asked for a better setup. "It seems I was having a lucky morning." His smile turned deliberately mocking, and he flicked his own stack of bills.

Again, Mick started forward, clearly unwilling to overlook such an insult to Clayton, and this time Jonesie was with him. But again, Clayton raised a hand. "Let's not be hasty." And to Judd, he said, "I'd like to meet the man who just took two hundred dollars of my money."

Judd heard Emily gasp, but he ignored her surprise. "Your money? Now, how can that be, when Frog told me he'd won that money last night shooting pool? And now that I've won it, I'd say it's my money."

Clayton lost his smile. "Do I know you from somewhere?"

Mick blurted out, "He's one of them strippers. I seen him at the bar the other night."

"Ah, that's right. I remember now. You've been something of a sensation, haven't you?"

Judd shrugged. "Hey, I make a buck wherever I can. A man can't be overly choosy."

"Obviously." Clayton looked down a moment, then his smile reappeared. "Maybe we can do business together sometime. I have several different ventures that might interest you. Especially since you're not choosy."

Again, Judd shrugged, careful not to show his savage satisfaction. Then he took Emily by the arm. "Maybe." He deliberately dismissed Clayton once more, knowing it would infuriate him, but probably intrigue him, as well. As he started out the door, he said, "You can look me up if anything really... interesting comes along."

They were barely out the door, when Emily started to speak. Judd squeezed her arm. "Not a word, Em. Not one single word."

The tension was still rushing through him, and he knew Clayton was watching them through the large front glass of the pool hall. Playing it cool had never been so difficult; no other assignment had been so personal. Playing up to Donner turned his stomach and filled him with rage. He wanted to hit something. He wanted to shout.

He wanted to make love to Emily.

But, he couldn't do any of those things, so he had to content himself with the knowledge he'd set Clayton up good. Not only had he more or less managed to steal two hundred dollars Clayton had earmarked as his own, but he knew damn well Clayton didn't consider their business finished. Not by a long shot. He'd hear from Donner again, and soon.

He only hoped he could manage to keep Emily out of the way.

5

EMILY THOUGHT she'd shown great restraint and a good deal of patience. But her patience was now at an end.

Judd had refused to talk to her while he aimlessly drove around the lower east side, burning off his sour mood and occasionally grunting at the questions she asked. Twice they had stopped while he got out of the truck and talked to different people loitering on the sidewalk. Emily had been instructed to wait in the pickup.

When she asked him what he was doing, he'd said only, "Investigating." When she asked what he'd found out, he'd said, "Quiet. Let me think."

It had been nearly two hours since they'd left the pool hall, and her frustration had grown with each passing minute. She tried to maintain her decorum, tried to keep her temper in check and behave in a civilized manner, but he was making that impossible. *You're the boss here, Emily. You hired him. Demand a few answers.* She decided she would do exactly that, when Judd pulled up in front of the diner.

Apparently, he expected her to get out and follow him like a well-trained puppy, because he stepped out and started to walk away without a single word to her. She refused to budge.

Of course, Judd was halfway through the diner door before he realized she was still in the truck. Then he did an about-face, and stomped back to her side, looking very put out. "What's the holdup?"

Emily gave him a serene smile. "I want to talk to you."

"So? Let's get a seat inside and you can talk. God knows, that's all you've done for the past hour, anyway."

She stiffened with the insult, but refused to lower herself to his irritating level. "You're not going to make me angry, Judd. I know you're just trying to get me off the track. But I want to know what that was all about in the pool hall. And don't you dare shake your head at me again!"

He looked undecided for a long moment, then let out a disgusted sigh. "All right, all right. Come in, sit, and we'll...talk."

Emily wasn't certain she believed him, he still looked as stubborn as a mule, but she left the truck and allowed Judd to lead her inside. They sat at a back booth, and a waitress immediately came to take their order. The woman seemed a little hostile to Emily, then she all but melted over Judd.

Judd treated her to a full smile and a wink. "You got anything for me, Suze?"

You got anything for me, Suze, Emily silently repeated, thinking Suze had just received a much warmer greeting from Judd than she herself had managed to garner all day.

The waitress looked over at Emily, one slim eyebrow lifted, and Judd grinned. "She's fine. Just tell me what you've got."

"Well..."

Emily rolled her eyes. Suze obviously had a flair for the dramatic, given the way she glanced around the diner in a covert manner, as if she were preparing to part with government secrets. She also patted her platinum blond hair and primped for a good ten seconds before finally exalting them with her supposed wisdom. *What a waste of time.*

Emily no sooner had that thought than she regretted it. Suze turned out to be a fount of information.

"He's been in twice since we spoke and something is definitely going down. He met with the same guy both times, that punk kid who distributes for him. I'd say something will happen within a week or two. That's usually the routine, you know."

"You couldn't catch an actual date?"

"Hell, no, sugar. If Donner caught me snooping, he'd have my fanny."

Judd reached out to smack the fanny-in-peril. "We wouldn't

want that to happen. But Suze? If anything more concrete comes up, you know where to find me."

She knew where to find him? Emily knew she had no right to be jealous. After all, her relationship with Judd was strictly business. But still, she didn't like the idea of him...consorting with this woman. Of course, Suze seemed to know a great deal about the gun dealer. In fact, she seemed to know almost too much. Emily narrowed her eyes, wondering exactly when Judd had contacted this woman, and what their relationship might be. Judd seemed to be on awfully familiar terms with her.

But Suze did appear to be helping, and Emily certainly had no claims on Judd. She decided to concentrate on that fact, but she couldn't keep herself from glaring at the waitress. Suze didn't seem to notice.

She was back to primping. "Of course I know where you'll be. I wouldn't miss an act. Do something special for me Tuesday night, all right?"

Judd laughed and shook his head.

Suddenly, Suze was all-business. "You two want anything to drink or something? It don't look right me standing here gabbing without you orderin' anything."

"Two coffees, Suze. That's it."

Emily barely waited for the waitress to go swaying away before she leaned across the table and demanded Judd's attention. "Was she talking about who I think she was talking about?"

"Who did you think she was—"

"That's not funny, Judd!"

"No, I guess it isn't. And yes, she was talking about our friendly, neighborhood gun trafficker."

Emily was aghast. "She *knows* him?" She couldn't believe the waitress had called him by name. Why, if he was that well known...

"Everyone knows who commits the crimes, Em. It's just coming up with proof that's so damn difficult."

Her breath caught in her throat and she choked. "You know who he is, too?"

Judd shrugged, his eyes dropping to the top of the table. Then he quirked a sardonic smile. "You met him yourself, honey."

"I did..." Suddenly it fit, and Emily fell back against the seat. "The guy at the pool hall?"

"Yep. That was him. Clayton Donner."

It took her a minute, and then she felt the steam. It had to be coming out her ears, she was so enraged. Judd had let her get close to the man who'd hurt her brother, and he hadn't even told her.

He was speaking to her now, but she couldn't hear him over the ringing in her ears. Her entire body felt taut, and her stomach felt queasy. No wonder she had reacted so strongly to that man. He'd been that close and...

Emily didn't make a conscious decision on what to do. She just suddenly found herself standing then walking toward the door. She somehow knew Judd was following, though she didn't turn to look. When she stepped outside, and started past his truck, he grabbed her arm and pulled her around to face him.

"Dammit, Emily! What the hell is the matter with you?"

"Let me go." She felt proud of the strength in her voice, though she knew she might fall apart at any moment.

"Are you kidding? I've tried every damn intimidation tactic I could think of—"

"Ha! So you admit to bullying me?"

"—to send you running, but you clung like flypaper. And now, with one little scare, you want me to turn you loose?"

Flypaper! How dare he compare her to... No, Emily, don't get sidetracked by a measly insult. The man deceived you. She lifted her chin and met his gaze. "I wish to leave now. Alone."

"No way, baby. You wanted in, and now you're in."

Her heartbeat shook her, it pounded so hard, and her fingers ached from being held in such tight fists. If she wasn't a lady, she'd smack him one, but good. "When were you going to tell me, Judd? When?"

Judd stiffened, and his jaw went hard. "Get in the truck, Em."

"I will not. I..."

"Get in the damn truck!"

Well. Put that way... Emily became aware of people watching, and also that Judd was every bit as angry as she was. But why? What possible reason did he have for being so mad? She was the one who'd been misled, kept in the dark, lied to...well, not really. But lies of omission definitely counted, and Judd had omitted telling her a great deal.

And after he'd insisted she bare her soul.

When he continued to glare at her, she realized how foolish they both must appear, and she opened the truck door to get in. It wouldn't do to make a public spectacle of herself.

"Put your seat belt on."

Emily stared out her window, determined not to answer him, to ignore him as completely as he'd ignored her all day. But then she muttered, *"Flypaper."*

She heard Judd make a small sound that could have been a chuckle but she didn't look to see. If the man dared to smile, she'd probably forget all about avoiding a scene. But then, thoughts of attacking that gorgeous body left her a little breathless, and she decided ignoring him was better, by far.

Judd reached over and strapped her in. He stayed leaning close for a second or two, then flicked his finger over her bottom lip. "Stop pouting, Em, and act like an adult."

It took a major effort, but she didn't bite that finger. She could just imagine how appalled her parents would have been by that thought.

Judd's sigh was long and drawn-out. "Fine. Have it your way, honey. But if you decide you want to talk, just speak up."

Fifteen minutes later, Emily was wishing she could do just that. Judd pulled into her driveway with the obvious intent of being well rid of her, and she desperately didn't want him to go. She felt confused and still angry and...hurt. If he could explain, then maybe she could forgive him and... *And what, Emily? Maybe he'd let you have one of those killer smiles like the one he gave Suze?* She'd been taken in by one man, and though she honestly believed Judd was different, she wouldn't, couldn't, put all her trust in him. Not on blind faith. Not without some explanations.

When all was said and done, he worked for her, and she deserved to know what was going on. She had to find evidence against Donner, and she needed Judd to do that. But only if he didn't shut her out.

He stopped the truck, and she sat there, trying to think of some way, without losing every ounce of pride, to talk things out with him.

But Judd saved her the trouble. He got out of the pickup, slamming his door then stomping over to the passenger side. She stared at him, her eyes wide with surprise, when he opened the door and hauled her out.

"What do you think you're doing?" His hold was gentle on her arm as he led her up the steps to her back door. She practically had to run to keep up with his long-legged, impatient stride.

"We're going to talk, Em. I don't like you treating me as if I've just kicked your puppy."

Uh-oh. He sounded even angrier than she'd first assumed. "I don't even have a dog—"

Judd snatched her key from her hand, unlocked the door and ushered her inside. "Do you need to punch in your code for the alarm system?"

It took her a second to comprehend his words since her mind still wrestled with why he was in her house, and what he planned to do there. "Oh, ah, no. I only turn it on when I'm in the house. The rest of the time, I just lock up."

Judd stared. "Why the hell would you get a fancy alarm system, and not use it?"

"Because twice I forgot to turn it off when I came in, and the outside alarms went off, and then several neighbors showed up at my door and the central office called, and it was embarrassing." Judd rolled his eyes in exasperation, and Emily felt her cheeks heat. She hadn't meant to tell him all that. "Judd? I don't want to talk about my alarm system."

Looking restless and still a bit angry, Judd paced across the kitchen. Then he stalked back to her. "Tell me this, Emily. What would you have done if I'd spoken up and introduced you to Donner?"

She watched as he propped his hands on his hips and glared at her. "I don't know what I would have done. But I know I would have done…something."

"Something like accuse him? Or something like demand he give himself up? I thought you needed proof? I thought that was what we were doing, trying to nail him."

His scowl was much more fierce than her own, and her anger diminished to mere exasperation. The man could be so remarkably impossible. "We?" she asked, lacing her tone with sarcasm. "There was certainly no 'we' today. You've refused to tell me anything." When he crossed his arms, looking determined, she added in a gentler tone, "Judd, I can't very well find evidence against this Donner person if I don't know who he is."

Judd came to stand in front of her and gripped her shoulders. "I was working on finding evidence. Or did you think I just enjoyed toying with that bastard? Besides, you were scared out of your wits, Em. And that was without knowing who he was. He had a damn strange effect on you, which now that I think of it again, isn't very complimentary for me. I thought you knew I wouldn't let anyone hurt you."

Emily swallowed, feeling a tinge of guilt. "I'm sorry. Of course I assume you'll protect me, but—"

"Don't assume, Emily. Know. As long as you do as I tell you and follow my lead, you won't get hurt."

"Just like that? You tell me what to do, and I do it, no questions asked? I'm not a child, Judd—"

"So I noticed."

"And… You noticed?" Emily quickly shook her head so she wouldn't get sidetracked. "If you want me to trust you, you have to be totally honest with me, not just expect me to sit around and watch you work, without telling me what you're working on."

"You're making too much of this. I was only shooting pool."

"But you had a goal in mind. And you kept that from me. I despise dishonesty, Judd. I won't tolerate it." He winced, but she didn't give him time to interrupt. "I had no idea today that you were deliberately taking money from one of Donner's men. If I had known, maybe I wouldn't have been so surprised..."

"Exactly. Do you think I want Donner or any other punk to look at you and think you know the score?"

That silenced Emily for a moment. Why would Judd care what other men thought of her? "I quit worrying about others' opinions long ago."

"Why?"

"What do you mean, 'why'?"

"Everyone cares what other people think, even when they know it shouldn't matter."

Busying her fingers by pleating and unpleating her skirt, Emily felt her exasperation grow. "Certain things...happened in my past, that assured me public opinion meant very little, but that honesty meant a great deal."

"Like what?"

When she didn't answer, he said, "Okay, we'll come back to that later."

"No, we won't."

"Dammit, Em. I'd much rather you come off looking like an innocent out for a few kicks, than to have some jerk assume you've been around."

Emily swallowed hard. Judd had evidently made some incorrect assumptions about her character, and it was up to her to explain the truth. "Judd, I don't know why you persist in thinking I'm...I'm innocent. I believe I told you once that I'd been engaged. Well..."

She couldn't look at him, her eyes were locked on her busy fingers. And then she heard him chuckle. Her gaze shot to his face, and she was treated to the most tender smile she'd ever seen.

"Honey, it wouldn't matter if you'd been engaged twenty times. You're still so damn innocent, you terrify me."

Emily didn't understand that statement, or the way he reached out and touched her cheek, then smoothed her hair behind her ear.

She felt disoriented, and much too warm. She wanted to lean into Judd, but she knew she had to settle things before she forgot what it was that she wanted settled. Once before she'd let her passionate nature guide her. That had been a huge error, and this was too important to be sidetracked by anything—including Judd's heated effect on her.

"The thing is, Em, this whole deal will work out better if your reactions to Donner and his men are real. You can't lie worth a damn, and I don't think, if Donner got close again, you'd be able to hide your feelings from him. You could blow everything."

She cleared her throat and spoke with more conviction than she actually felt. "You don't know that for sure."

His expression hardened, turning grim. "And I'm not willing to take the risk. Things could backfire real easy, and someone could get hurt."

She understood his reasoning, but she couldn't accept it. "This isn't going to work, Judd. Not unless you're willing to tell me everything."

He stared at her, hard, then muttered a curse and looked away. "No, you're right. It won't work. Which is why I've come up with an alternate plan. I decided I'd just find this guy for you, but on my own. You can stay in your little palace and play it safe."

"*What?*"

"You heard me. From here on, you're out of it."

Emily sputtered, then stiffened her spine. "You said I was 'in,' remember?"

"I've changed my mind."

"Well, you can just unchange it, because I'm not going to be left out."

"I refuse to risk your getting hurt, and your reaction today was proof positive you aren't ready to mingle with the meaner side of life. Let's face it, Em, you're just a baby."

"Oh, no, you don't." She propped her hands on her hips and glared at him. "You're not going to pull me into an argument by slinging horrid insults at me. We had a deal and you're the one who isn't following the rules. Well, you can just stop it right now."

He blinked at her in amazement. "I wasn't insulting you, dammit!"

Emily could tell by his expression he hadn't seen anything insulting in his attitude. But that only made the insult worse. She pursed her lips and tilted her head back so she could look down her nose at him. "I'm not entirely helpless, Judd. I can take care of myself."

There was a minute curving of his lips before he shook his head and spoke in a gentle, but firm, tone. "I'm sorry, Em. My mind's made up."

He acted as if he hadn't just dumped her, as if he hadn't just let her down and destroyed all her plans. But it was even more than her plans now. It was Judd, and she cared about him. She took one step closer and poked him in the chest with her finger. "Okay, fine. You don't want to help me, then I'll find another way."

Startled, he grabbed her finger and held on. "You already have a way. Me. I can do this, you know. I'm more than capable, and I damn sure don't need you looking after me. It'll be easier without you."

That hurt, but she didn't show it. She lifted her chin and met his intent gaze. "No. I won't let you risk yourself for me, not while I sit around and do nothing."

Judd bit his upper lip and his eyes narrowed. He suddenly looked…dangerous, and Emily shivered in expectation of what he might say. She knew it would be something outrageous, but she was prepared for the worst.

"So you'll pay me a five-hundred-dollar bonus. No big deal."

He had a very credible sneer. Emily frowned. She couldn't believe he'd just said that. And she couldn't believe he was really doing this only for the money. She couldn't have been that wrong.

A deep breath didn't help to relieve the sudden pain in her chest, or the tightness in her throat. She still sounded strained as she whispered, "Fine, if money's the issue, I'll pay you to forget you ever met me." She waited for his reaction, and though Judd remained rigid, she noticed his hands were now curled into tight fists.

There's a reaction for you, Emily. He doesn't seem at all pleased by being bought off. She decided to push him, just to see what it would take to force him to drop his charade. "Five thousand dollars, Judd. But I don't want you risking yourself. Take it or leave it." Then she opened the door and waited to see if he would actually leave.

"Damn you, Emily." The door slammed shut and she found herself pinned to the wall by his hard chest, his arms caging her in, his lips pressed to her hair. She could hear him panting, struggling for control of his temper.

Relief washed over her—and hot excitement. "Judd?"

He didn't answer. He kissed her instead, and if the first kiss had been hungry, this one was ravenous. Emily moaned and wrapped her arms around him, holding him tight as his tongue pushed deep into her mouth. How she'd come to care so much about him so quickly, she didn't know. Perhaps it was because she sensed the same emptiness in him that she'd often felt. When he'd told of his past, as different as it was from hers, she still saw a lot of similarities.

Emily knew she was being fanciful, but she couldn't deny the way she felt. It seemed to her sometimes there were no real heroes left in the world, people willing to do what was right— just because it was the right thing to do.

But Judd was a hero, despite his chosen profession, despite his lack of manners and sometimes overbearing arrogance. A hero was a man who could do what needed to be done, when it was needed. And Judd was as capable as they came.

"Oh, Em." His mouth touched her throat, her chin, then her lips again. "I have to stop."

She tried to shake her head, since stopping was the last thing she wanted, but she couldn't. His hands cupped her cheeks and he had her pressed flush against the wall, pinned from chest to knees, his erection hard and throbbing against her belly. It was glorious. She was well and truly trapped, and she loved it. "Judd..."

"No, honey." He was still breathing hard, his mouth touching soft and warm against her flesh, planting small biting kisses that tingled and tickled and stole her breath. "Neither one of us is ready for this. Hell, you've got me so crazy, I don't know what I'm doing. I need time to think. And so do you."

Don't beg, Emily. Don't beg. "Judd...I—"

He touched her lips with his thumb, then his eyes dropped to where she knew her nipples puckered tight against the front of her dress. His voice, when he spoke, was a low, raspy growl. "You're killing me, Em. Please understand."

"I've never felt like this before, Judd."

He groaned, then kissed her again, this time so soft and sweet, she trembled. He pressed his hips hard against her once, then forcibly pulled away. When he touched her cheek, his hand shook. "I'll call you later tonight, okay?"

She swallowed hard, not wanting him to leave, but knowing he was right. It *was* too soon to make a commitment.

It was difficult, but she managed to pull herself together. He was leaving; she knew that was for the best. But she had to recall what had started this whole argument and make certain he understood her position. "I was serious about what I said, Judd. I don't want you doing anything on your own. I don't want the...responsibility of your safety."

He pressed his forehead to hers and gave a loud sigh. "I know. I promise not to do anything until we've figured it all out." Then he chuckled, and it sounded so nice to her ears, she laughed, too. "I must be crazy." He gave her one more quick, hard kiss, then moved her away from the door. "I have to go before I forget my good intentions and ravish you right here. Any red-blooded male can only take so much provocation, you know. And honey, you're damn provoking."

She smiled again, and as he stepped out, Judd said, "Emily? Thanks again for breakfast."

Emily contained herself until she saw Judd drive away. Then she whirled and laughed. Her emotions had been on a roller coaster all day. Whether it had been good or bad, it had definitely been exciting. In fact, her time spent with Judd was easily the most exciting time she'd ever known.

He thought her provocative, and because of that, she felt provocative. That, too, was new, but decidedly delicious. She should feel guilty, since she hadn't done anything to help her brother yet. But she couldn't manage a single dollop of guilt. She simply felt too exhilarated.

HOURS LATER, Emily stood looking out her kitchen window, impatiently waiting for Judd's call. The house was dark and dim, just like her yard. She hadn't bothered to turn on the lights as she'd watched the sunset. The kitchen was her favorite room in the house. The pine cabinets had a warm golden hue, and the antique Tiffany lamp that hung over her table provided a touch of bright color. She thought of Judd sitting at that table with her, of the kiss he'd given her against the wall, and she wondered what he was up to, if he was safe…if he was with Suze.

That vagrant thought had her scowling, and she decided a soothing cup of chamomile tea was just what she needed. Without turning on the lights, she retrieved a cup from the cabinet and turned on the hot water. She knew her kitchen well and didn't need the light intruding on her warm, intimate mood.

It wasn't until she heard a sound and looked up that she realized she'd never reset the alarm. Her heart lodged in her throat as she saw a large body looming outside her kitchen door. Frozen in fear, she stood there as the hot water grew hotter and steam wafted upward around her face. A soft click sounded, and then another. When the door swung silently open and a man entered, his body a shadowed silhouette, she finally reacted. Emily let out the loudest ear-piercing scream she could manage. And after a stunned second and a low curse, the man pounced on her.

Emily didn't have time to run.

6

JUDD WHISTLED as he kicked off his shoes and dropped back onto the lumpy couch. God, it felt good to get off his feet. And to finally get home. He wanted to talk to Emily. He needed to make certain she'd understood his motives this afternoon. He'd seen the shock on her face, then the determination when she'd thought he was dumping her.

It had felt as if she'd snatched his heart right out of his chest. But what the hell else was he supposed to do? Watch her get involved? He hadn't counted on every guy around, including Donner, wanting to cozy up to her. He supposed that elusive sensuality he'd noticed in her right away was as visible to every other guy around as it was to him.

But he didn't like it. He didn't like other men looking at her and seeing tangled sheets and mussed hair and warm silky skin. He didn't like other guys thinking the thoughts he had.

He also couldn't hurt her. He'd just have to find a way to keep her close, and himself detached. That was going to be the real trick, especially when she did crazy things like offering him money just to keep him safe. He sure wasn't used to anyone trying to protect him, not since Max had been killed.

But he could get used to it, if he let himself.

His eyes narrowed at the thought. He couldn't get distracted from his purpose now, not when he was so close. Emily was a danger, and she didn't even realize it. She had the power to help him forget, and he didn't want that. Donner had hurt her brother, but he'd taken the only family Judd had ever known. Whenever he remembered Max's face, usually smiling, sometimes solemn, occasionally stern, his stomach tightened into a knot. Max was the finest, most honest person Judd had ever known, the only one who'd really cared about him.

Except for Emily.

Judd squeezed his eyes shut to block the thought. What Emily felt or didn't feel for him couldn't matter. Not now. Probably not ever. Judd wouldn't give up until Donner was put away. And after that, he'd have no more reason to be with her.

He was just reaching for the phone to call Emily, when the damn thing rang, causing him to jump. He snatched the receiver. "Yeah?"

"Judd, I'm glad I could reach you. Are you sitting down?"

Startled, it took Judd a second to answer. The lieutenant knew better than to call him at his apartment. It was a real breach of security. Something big must have happened. Trying to sound casual, he said, "As a matter of fact, I'd just propped my feet up. I've had a hell of a long—"

Howell interrupted. "Well, your day's about to get a whole lot longer." He hesitated, then added, "You remember that little lady you mentioned to me the other day? The rich one. She still hanging around with you?"

"Emily?" Judd didn't say that he couldn't forget her even if he tried. He cleared his throat. Even though he was as sure as he could be that no bugs existed in the apartment, he wouldn't take any chances. "Sure. In fact, I was just thinking about her. I guess we've got a regular thing going, at least for a while."

"I see." Judd could hear the restrained frustration in Howell's tone. "That being the case and all, I thought you ought to know, I just heard the little lady had her house broken into."

Judd felt his stomach lurch. "What?"

There was an expectant silence, then, "I recognize that tone, Judd. Just calm down and let me tell you what I know."

"Is Emily all right?"

"She's fine, just a little shaken up, I gather. It only happened a few minutes ago, but I thought... Judd?"

Judd cursed and pushed his feet back into his shoes, "I'm on my way."

He vaguely heard Howell protesting, and knew he'd catch hell later for hanging up on the lieutenant, but the only thought that mattered was seeing Emily. He raced out the front door, only stopping long enough to grab his jacket and his Beretta.

Ten minutes and three red lights later—which he ran—Judd decided he was too old to take this kind of stress. His palms were sweating and his head was pounding. He hadn't felt this kind of nauseating fear since the call telling him Max had been shot in the line of duty. But Judd hadn't made it then. He'd gotten to the hospital too late. Max had died only minutes before he arrived.

He stepped more firmly on the accelerator, pushing the old truck and thanking the powers that be for the near-empty roads that lessened the danger of his recklessness. His hands tightened on the wheel as his urgency increased. He could literally taste his fear.

When he sped into the curving driveway and saw the two black and whites parked there, he didn't stop to think about an excuse for his timely arrival. He simply busted through the door, his eyes searching until he found Emily.

She sat at the kitchen table holding an ice pack to her cheek. That alone was enough to make his blood freeze. She looked up, and the moment she saw him, her eyes widened, and then she smiled. "Judd."

He stalked toward her, sank to the floor beside her seat and took her hand in his. With his other hand, he lifted the ice pack so he could survey the damage. "Are you all right?"

She blinked away tears then glanced nervously at the hovering officers. "I'm fine, Judd. But how—"

Already her cheek was bruising and her eye was a bit puffy. Still holding her hand, Judd came to his feet and glared at the officers. "Who did this?"

"We don't know, Detective. We're still trying to find out all the details."

"Did you check the house? Has anyone searched the yard?"

He didn't wait for an answer, but bent back to Emily. "Tell me what happened, honey."

She gave a nervous laugh, then quickly sobered. "Really, Judd, there's no reason to yell at the nice officers. They came almost as soon as I called."

"Why didn't you call me?"

He realized what a ridiculous question that was almost as soon as he made the demand. Emily thought he was a male stripper. Why would she call him? That fact had his temper rising again.

She leaned toward him and patted his shoulder. "Shh. It's all right, Judd. Just calm down."

She was trying to soothe him? Judd gave her a blank stare, then shook his head. "Emily..."

"I was waiting for your call. I guess after you left...I forgot to reset the alarm, because I was making tea when suddenly someone started opening the door."

"Oh, honey." Judd wrapped her in his arms, lifting her from the seat at the same time. "You must have been scared half to death."

Emily had to speak against his chest, since he was still holding her tight. He couldn't let her go just yet. He was still suffering from all the terrible thoughts that had raced through his head after Lieutenant Howell's call.

"I suppose I was scared at first," she said. "I know I screamed loud enough to startle the ducks on the lake. Then the man sort of just jumped toward me. And without really thinking about it, I turned the faucet sprayer on him." She leaned back to see Judd's face. "Do you remember me telling you the water heater was in need of repair? Well, I had the water running hot for my tea, and when he came at me, I just grabbed the hose and aimed at his face. At least, I think I hit his face. It was dark in here and everything happened so fast. I do know he yelled really loud, so I think the hot water must have hurt him."

Judd touched his fingers to her bruised cheek. "How did this happen?"

Emily looked very sheepish now, and her cheeks turned a

bright pink. "It's really rather silly. You see, after the man yelled, I jerked away and ran for the library so I could use the phone. But, uh..." It was obvious to Judd she was embarrassed as her eyes again went to the two cops. "I tripped just inside the door. I hit my cheek on the leg of a chair."

Bemused, Judd asked, "The guy who broke in didn't do this to you?"

"No. I did it to myself. I think he left right after I shot him with the water. I locked the library door and called the police. When they got here, he was gone."

One of the cops cleared his throat. "We checked the water in her faucet. It's scalding hot. It's a wonder she hasn't burned herself before." Then he grinned. "You might want to get that checked."

Judd stared.

Emily pulled on his sleeve, regaining his attention. "Do you remember me telling you about my father burning his hand on the faucet? It really does get hot, hot enough to make tea without boiling the water. I wouldn't be at all surprised if the fellow has a serious burn on his face."

Feeling as though he'd walked into bedlam, Judd shook his head then turned his attention to the two officers. "Call Howell and tell him I'm spending the night here. And go check the area. With any luck, the bastard might still be out there if he's burned all that bad."

Both men nodded and started away. Judd turned to Emily, ready to lecture her on the importance of keeping her alarm set, when he felt her stiffen. She looked paper-white and her bottom lip trembled. He grabbed her arm and gently forced her back into her chair.

"Emily, I thought you said you were all right."

Her lips moved, but she didn't make a sound.

"Are you going to faint? Are you hurt somewhere?" He very carefully shook her. "Tell me what's wrong."

His urgency must have gotten through to her, for she suddenly cleared her throat, and her expression slowly changed to a suspicious frown. "One of the officers called you detective. And you're ordering them around as if you have the right. And even more ridiculous than that, they're letting you."

"Oh, hell." Judd wondered if there was any way for him to get out of this one. How could he have been so careless? Howell would surely have his head. His mind whirled with possible lies, but he couldn't see Emily believing any of them. She wasn't stupid, after all, just a bit naive.

He watched her face as he tried to come up with a logical, believable explanation, and he saw the confusion in her eyes, then the growing anger. One of the uniforms came around the corner and said, "Detective, I have Lieutenant Howell on the phone. He said he needed to talk to you, sir, uh...now." And Judd knew Emily had finally guessed the truth.

Before she could move, he cupped her cheeks, being especially gentle with her injury. "I can explain, honey. I swear. Just sit tight a second, okay? Right now, I have to pacify an enraged superior."

"Oh, I'll wait right here, Detective. You can count on it."

Judd didn't like the sound of that one little bit. But it was her look, one of mean anticipation, that had him frowning. This whole damn day had been screwy, starting with Emily cooking him breakfast. He should have known right then he wouldn't end it with his safe little world intact.

No, Emily had turned him upside down.

The hell of it was, he liked it.

EMILY LISTENED as Judd went through a long series of explanations over the phone. Yes, he could handle everything... No, his cover wasn't blown as long as Howell set things right with the two officers. Ha! His cover was most definitely *blown.* Emily wanted to interject at that point, but Judd watched her as he spoke, and so she kept herself still, her expression masked, she hoped.

Her cheek was still stinging, but not as much as her pride. *Lord, Emily, you've been a fool.* Hadn't she known from the start that Judd didn't belong in the east side of Springfield? He talked the talk, and dressed the code, but something about him had been completely out of sync. He could be every bit as hard and cynical as the other roughnecks, but his behavior was forced. It wasn't something that came to him naturally.

She closed her eyes as she remembered offering him money to drop the case. If he reminded her of that, she just might...no. She would not lower herself to his level of deceit.

That decision did her little good when Judd hung up the phone and came back to kneel by her chair. He lifted the ice pack again and surveyed her bruised cheek with a worried frown. "I wonder if you should go to the hospital and have this checked."

"No."

Her curt response didn't put him off. "Does it hurt?"

"No."

His fingertips touched her, coasting over her abraded skin and causing goose bumps to rise on her arms. He ended by cupping her cheek and slowly rubbing his thumb over her lips. Then he sighed. "Just sit tight and I'll make you that tea. After everyone's cleared out, we'll talk."

Emily watched him bustle around the kitchen, thinking he looked curiously *right* there. It was almost as if the room had been built for his masculine presence.

The quarry-stone floor seemed every bit as sturdy and hard as Judd, the thick, polished pine cabinets just as comforting. There were no frilly curtains, no pastel colors to clash with his no-nonsense demeanor.

Emily made a disgusted face at herself. Comparing Judd to a kitchen? Maybe she had hit her head harder than she thought.

When he sat the tea in front of her, she accepted it with a mumbled thanks. Moments later, the officer who'd been outside came in and shook his head. "Not a sign of anything. It doesn't even look as if the door was tampered with."

Judd turned to Emily with a stern expression. "It was locked, wasn't it?"

Since she was already mortified over the evening's events, she didn't bother to try to hide her blush. "I really have no idea. I can't recall locking it, but sometimes I just do it by rote."

"Emily..."

She knew that tone. "Don't lecture me now, *Detective*. I'm really not in the mood."

She was saved from his annoyance by the remaining officer coming downstairs. "I checked out the other rooms. They're clean. I don't believe he ever left the kitchen. Probably took off right after she splashed him, going out the way he came in."

Judd worked his jaw. "I suppose you're right. You guys can take off now. I'll stay with Miss Cooper."

Since Emily had a lot of questions she wanted answered, she didn't refute him. It took the officers another five minutes to actually go, and then finally, she and Judd were alone. Sitting opposite him at the table, Emily prepared to launch into her diatribe on the importance of honesty and to vent her feelings of abuse, when Judd spoke in a low, nearly inaudible tone.

"Clayton Donner shot Max about six months ago. I was out on assignment, and by the time I got to the hospital, Max was dead. I've made it my personal business to get Donner, and I'll damn well do whatever I have to until he's locked up."

Emily didn't move. She heard the unspoken words, telling her he wouldn't let her—or her feelings for him—get in his way. She'd thought she had a good personal reason to want Donner, but her motivation was nothing compared to Judd's. Without thinking, she reached out and took his hand. She didn't say a word, and after a few seconds, Judd continued.

"I told you Max had taken me in. He was everything to me, the only family I'd ever had. He was a regular street cop, and his run-in with Donner was pure coincidence. Max had only been doing a routine check on a disturbance, but he inadvertently got too close to the place where Donner was making a deal." Suddenly Judd's fist slammed down on the table and he squeezed his eyes shut.

"Judd?"

"Max got shot in the back." Judd drew a deep breath and

squeezed Emily's hand. She squeezed back. He wouldn't look at her, but she could see his jaw was rigid, his eyes red. Her heart felt as though it were crumbling.

"We all knew it was Donner, but we couldn't get anything concrete on him. And to try him without enough evidence, and take the chance of letting him go free...I don't think I could stand it. I have to see him put away. Regardless of anything, or anyone, I'll get him."

Wishing he'd told her all this because he wanted to, not because he'd been forced, wouldn't get Emily anywhere. And she couldn't, in good conscience, interfere. Not when she could see how much getting Donner meant to him. "I understand."

"Do you?" For the first time, Judd looked up at her, and that look held so many different emotions, Emily couldn't begin to name them all. But the determination, the obsession, was clear, and it scared her. "I left everything behind when I followed Donner here," he said. "Springfield is just like my own home ground. Every city has an area with run-down housing and poverty, a place where kids are forgotten or ignored, where crime is commonplace and accepted. I fit in there, Em. I'm right at home. Sooner or later, I will get Donner. But not if you blow my cover. What happened tonight can't happen again."

Emily knew he wasn't talking about the break-in. "What—exactly—did happen, Judd?"

"I lost my head, and that's bad. I can't be sidetracked from this assignment."

"You know I want Donner, too."

"Not like I do."

She would have liked to probe that a little more, but she held her tongue. She was afraid he was trying to find a way to say goodbye, to explain why he couldn't see her anymore. "What do you want me to do?"

Judd shot from his chair with an excess of energy. He shoved his hands into his back pockets and stalked the perimeter of the room as if seeking an escape. Finally, he stopped in front of the window, keeping his back to Emily. "I want you to understand that I can't let you get in my way. I can't...can't care about you. But when I think about what might have happened tonight..."

"You need me to stay out of your way?" Emily heard the trembling in her tone, but hoped Judd hadn't.

He whirled to face her. "No. Just the opposite, in fact."

She blinked twice and tried to still the frantic pounding of her pulse.

Again, Judd took his seat. "I work as a stripper in the bar because Donner does a lot of his business in the office upstairs. I've set myself up to get hired by him."

"That's what you were doing in the pool hall," Emily said with sudden insight. "You were impressing him, by being like him."

Judd nodded. "Everyone around there believes I'm out for a fast buck, a little fun, and not much else. That makes me Donner's ideal man. Making contact with him today was important. He'll be coming to me soon, I'm sure of it. He's intrigued, because he doesn't like people to refuse him, the way I refused him at the pool hall. I'd like to steer clear of you, to keep you uninvolved." He cast her a frustrated glance. "But it's too late for that."

Her stomach curled. "It is?"

One brisk nod was her answer. "I need you, Em. My superior thinks it's risky to make any changes now. He's already furious that you know my cover, but that can't be helped, short of calling everything off. And I don't want that. He'll pull the officers who were here tonight, because by rights, they screwed up, too. They shouldn't have acknowledged me as a detective, but they're rookies and..." He trailed off, then frowned at her. "If you suddenly stopped hanging around, after the scene we played out today at the pool hall, Donner might get suspicious. The whole deal could be blown. And it's too late for that."

Emily tried to look understanding, but she was still reacting to Judd's casual words. *He needs you, Emily.* She knew she would do whatever she could for him. "Has...has something come up? Something definite?"

"I think so. I visited Frog again after I left here. Next Wednesday night, Donner will be making a pickup."

"What kind of pickup?"

"He gets the guns dirt cheap since they're usually stolen. Then he sells them on the street for a much higher price. The man he buys from has a shipment ready. That would be the best time to bust him. In fact, it's probably the only way to make sure we nail him."

Seeing the determination in his eyes, Emily knew Judd would find a way to get Clayton Donner, with or without her help. But she wanted to be near him any way she could. "Since I still have my own reasons for wanting him caught, I'll be glad to help however I can." She hesitated, then asked, "You're certain Donner is the one who sold my brother the gun?"

"As certain as I can be. We traced him to Springfield by the weapons he sold. One whole shipment was faulty guns. I don't know yet how Donner got hold of them, but from what you told me, it's safe to say your brother got one of them."

A resurgence of anger flooded through her. So Donner had known the guns were faulty before he sold them? He had deliberately risked her brother's life, and that fact made her determination almost equal to Judd's. "I look forward to doing whatever I can to help."

Judd let out a long breath. Then he leaned across the table and took both her hands. "I don't want to have to worry about you. I want your word that you won't try anything on your own. I don't even want you in that part of town without me. Promise me."

"I work there at the soup kitchen..."

"Not until this is over, Em. I mean it. It's just too risky. Promise me."

"Judd—"

"I lost Max, dammit! Isn't that enough?"

His sudden loss of control shook her. She stared at his eyes, hard now with determination and an emotion that closely resembled fear. Reluctantly, she nodded. The last thing she wanted to do was distract him. Already, it seemed to her, he was too emotionally involved, and that weakened his objectivity, putting him in danger. It was obvious that Max Henley had been, and still was, the most important person in the world to Judd. Emily decided she might very well be able to keep an eye on Judd as long as he let her stay close. And evidently, the only way to do that, was to agree to his rules.

"All right. I promise. But I want a promise from you, too, Judd."

It took him a moment to regain his calm demeanor. Then he lifted an eyebrow in question.

"From now on, you have to be honest with me," she said. "There are few things I really abhor, but lying is one of them. You've lied to me from the start."

Judd turned his head. "I was on assignment, Em. And you just came tripping into my case, nearly messing everything up. I did what I thought was best."

"And of course telling me the truth never entered your mind?" When he gave her a severe frown, she quickly added, "Okay, not at first. But since then? Surely you had to realize I wasn't a threat?"

His stare was hard. "You're a bigger threat than you know."

Emily had no idea what that was supposed to mean. And while she did understand Judd's position, she couldn't help feeling like a fool. First she thought he was cop, then she believed he was a stripper. Now she finds out he actually is a cop. A small, humorless laugh escaped her. "I suppose it really is funny. Did you laugh at the irony of it, Judd?"

"Not once."

"Oh, come on. I must have looked like an idiot. And here you were, trying to keep the poor naive little fool out of trouble."

"It wasn't like that, Em."

She stood, suddenly wanting to be alone. "I should have learned my lesson long ago." She knew Judd had no idea what she was talking about, that she was remembering her sad lack of judgment so many years ago. She shook her head, not at all certain she'd ever tell him. Lord, she probably wouldn't have the chance to tell him. Once this ordeal with Donner was over— and, according to Judd, it would be over soon—Judd would go on about his business, and she would have to forget about him.

"I wonder if my parents were right."

Judd hadn't moved. He sat in the chair watching her. "About what?"

"About me being such a bad judge of character. They always claim I have a very unrealistic perception of mankind, they say that I should accept the world, and my place in it, and stop trying to change things. I suppose I ought to give up and let them have their way."

Judd stiffened, and his expression looked dangerous. "You don't mean that."

With a shake of her head and another small smile, Emily turned to leave. Just before she reached the hallway entrance, she stopped. "One more thing, Judd."

She turned to face him and her gaze locked with his. "The man who came in here? He mumbled something, just before I ran, about only wanting the film."

Judd shot to his feet. *"What?"*

Her smile turned a bit crooked. "I didn't want to tell the police, because I thought it might be important. I was going to wait and tell you so we could figure out what the man meant. But now, since you are the police..." She shrugged.

Judd was busy cursing.

"What are you going to do?" she asked him.

"First, I'm going to get someone over here to check your door for fingerprints."

"It won't do any good. He wore gloves. I felt them when he grabbed me."

"Another tidbit you were saving only for me?"

"Uh-huh. I honestly don't know anything else, though." She stifled a forced yawn. "I think I'll get ready for bed now."

Judd moved to stand directly in front of her. "I'm staying the night, Em."

"That's not necessary." *But, oh, it would be so nice.* She sincerely hoped he would insist. For some reason, the thought of being all alone was very unsettling. And even more unsettling was the thought of letting Judd out of her sight.

"I think it is. I won't bother you, if that's what you're worried about."

"I wasn't worried."

He accepted that statement with a smile of his own. "Good. Why don't you show me where you want me to sleep? Then I've got a few more calls to make."

Since Emily wouldn't show him where she really wanted him to sleep, which was with her, she led him to the room down the hall from her bedroom. Decorated in muted shades of blue, it had only a twin bed and was considered her guest room. There were two other bedrooms, one was John's room, since he dropped in often whenever there were problems with her parents, and the other room served as a small upstairs sitting room.

Judd nodded his approval, then took Emily's shoulders. "Try to sleep. But honey, if you need anything, don't hesitate to let me know."

He doesn't mean what you're thinking, Em. Didn't he just tell you earlier tonight it was too soon? "Thank you, Judd. Good night." Emily forced her feet to move down the hall, then she forced herself inside her room and closed the door. Her forehead made a soft *thwack* when she dropped it against the wood, and her cheek started throbbing again.

But none of it was as apparent as the drumming of her heart. It was all just beginning to sink in, from the slapstick beginning to the frightening end. Judd was an officer, who chose to take his clothes off in an undercover case, using a police uniform as a costume. It was too ironic. And Lord help her, so was her situation.

She was falling in love with a thoroughly outrageous man.

JUDD LAY in the narrow bed, stripped down to his underwear, with only the sheet covering him. His arms were propped behind his head and he listened to the strange sounds of the house as it settled. He'd left the door open in case Emily needed him.

God, what a mess.

Howell had raised holy hell with him, and for good reason. He'd behaved like a rookie with no experience at all. He knew better, hell, he was damn good at his job. But he just kept thinking of what could have happened. The thought of Emily being hurt was untenable. He had to find some way to wrap this operation up, and quickly. He didn't want to be involved with her, didn't want to care about her. But he knew it was too late.

Did two people ever come from more different backgrounds? Emily was cultured, refined, elegant. She had a poise that never seemed to leave her, and a way of talking that implied gentleness and kindness and…all the things he wasn't. That refined speech of hers turned him on. Everything about her turned him on.

He had to quell those thoughts. Emily wasn't for him. From what he knew of her parents, they would balk at the mere mention of her getting involved with someone like him. And he didn't want to add to her problems there. She evidently had some very real differences with her parents, but at least she had parents. And probably aunts and uncles and grandparents, all of them educated and smelling of old money.

The only smells Judd had been familiar with around his house were stale beer and unwashed dishes. Max had tried to teach him a better way, but Max had been a simple man with simple manners. He hadn't owned a speck of real silver, yet that was exactly what Emily stirred her tea with. And he couldn't be certain, but he thought the teacup she'd used earlier was authentic china. It had seemed delicate and fragile—just like Emily.

He squeezed his eyes shut, trying to close out the image of her lying soft and warm in her own bed, her dark hair fanned out on the pillow, those big brown eyes sleepy, her skin flushed. He wanted her, more than he'd ever wanted anything in his life. He hadn't known a man could want this much and live through it. She was right down the hall, and he suspected if he went to her, she wouldn't send him away.

But as bad as he wanted her, he also knew he had no right to her. So he continued to stare at the ceiling.

Somewhere downstairs he heard a clock chime eleven. Then he heard a different noise, one he hadn't heard yet, and he turned his head on the pillow to look toward the door.

Emily stood there, a slight form silhouetted by the vague light of the moon coming through the window. He couldn't quite draw a breath deep enough to chase away the tightness in his chest. When she didn't move, he leaned up on one elbow. His voice sounded low and rough when he spoke. "Are you all right, babe?"

She made another small, helpless sound, then took a tiny step into the room. Every muscle in his body tensed.

He couldn't make out her face, but he could tell her gown was long and pale and he could feel her nervousness. He didn't know why she was here, but his body had a few ideas and was reacting accordingly. He was instantly and painfully aroused. "Em?"

She took another step, then whispered in a trembling tone, "I know you said it was too soon. And you're right, of course. I told myself this wasn't proper, that I should behave with some decorum." Her hands twisted together and she drew a deep, shaky breath. "But you see, the thing is..."

Judd knew his heart was going to slam right through his ribs. He couldn't wait another second for her to finish her sketchy explanation. She was here, she wanted him, and despite all the reasons he'd just given himself for why he shouldn't, he knew he wanted her too badly to send her away.

He stared at her in the darkness, and then lifted the sheet. "Come here, Emily."

7

SHE MOVED SO FAST, Judd barely had time to brace himself for her weight. Not that she weighed anything at all. She was soft and sweet and she smelled so incredibly inviting—like a woman aroused. Like feminine heat and excitement. Her brushed-cotton gown tangled around his legs when he turned and pinned her beneath him. He felt her body sigh into his, her slim legs parting, her pelvis arching up. In the next instant, her hands cupped his face and she kissed him. It wasn't a gentle kiss. She ate at his mouth, hungry and anxious and needy.

So many feelings swamped him. Lust, of course, since Emily always inspired that base craving, even when she wasn't intent on seducing him. And need, a need he didn't like acknowledging, but one that was so powerful, so all-consuming, he couldn't minimize it as anything less than what it was.

But first and foremost was tenderness, laced with a touch of relief that he wouldn't have to pull back this time; she would finally be his. She had come to him, and she was kissing him as if she wanted him every bit as badly as he wanted her. That wasn't possible, but if her need was anywhere close to his, they both might damn well explode.

"Emily..."

Her kisses, hot and urgent, landed against his jaw, his chin, the side of his mouth. Her nipples were taut against his chest, her breath hot and fast. He wanted to touch her everywhere, all at once, and he wanted to simply hold her, to let her know how precious she was. He slid one hand down her side, felt her shiver, heard her moan, and he nearly lost his mind. He gripped her small backside with both hands and urged her higher against his throbbing erection, rubbing sinuously, slow and deep, again and again. He wanted to drown in the hot friction, the sensual feel of her warm body giving way to him. Her legs parted wide and she bent her knees, cradling him, offering herself.

Judd groaned low in his throat and went still, aware of the soft heat between her thighs now touching him. He knew she was excited, and the fact was making him crazy. "Too fast, honey. Way too fast."

Emily wasn't listening. Her hands frantically stroked his naked back and her legs shifted restlessly, rubbing against his, holding him. She continued to lift her hips into him, exciting herself, exciting him more. Judd dropped his full weight on her to keep her still, then carefully caged her face. She whimpered, trying to move.

"Shh. It's all right, Em. We've got all night." Then he kissed her. She tasted hot and sweet, and when he slipped his tongue between her lips, she sucked on him with greedy excitement.

Judd had never known kissing to be such a deeply sensual experience. To him, it had always been pleasant, sometimes a prelude to sex, sometimes not. But he'd never felt such a keen desire just from kissing. Emily was driving him over the edge, and he hadn't even touched her yet.

He caught her slim wrists in one hand and trapped them over her head. He had to take control or he'd never last. She muttered a low protest and her hips moved, rubbing and seeking beneath his, finding his erection and grinding against it. Her nightgown was in his way and he knotted one fist in the material and lifted, urgently. He needed to touch all of her, to explore her body, to brand her as his own. Emily squirmed to accommodate him, allowing the material to be jerked above her waist. When Judd felt her bare, slender thighs against his own, he growled and pushed against her.

It almost struck him as funny, the effect she had on him. Prim, polite, proper little Emily. He dipped his head and nuzzled her breasts at the same time he slid his hand over her silky mound, letting his fingers tangle in her damp curls. Emily stopped mov-

ing; she even stopped breathing. Judd felt her suspended anticipation.

He released her wrists long enough to jerk the buttons open
on the bodice of her nightgown so he could taste her nipples,
feel the heat of her flesh, and then he wedged his hand back
between her thighs. He pressed his face to her breast and kissed
her soft skin, his mouth open and wet. Emily shifted so her
puckered nipple brushed against his cheek and Judd smiled, then
began to suckle, drawing her in deep, stroking with his tongue,
nipping with his teeth.

Her ragged moan was low and so damn sexy he moaned with
her. His fingers slid over the tight curls, felt her slick and wet,
hot and swollen with wanting him, and then he slid a finger deep
inside her. She was incredibly tight and he added another finger,
hearing her groan, feeling her body clasp his fingers as he forced
them a bit deeper, stretching her.

He began a smooth rhythm, and with a breathless moan, her
body moved with him. His thumb lifted to glide over the apex
of her mound, finding her most sensitive flesh and stroking it,
while his mouth still drew greedily on her nipple, and Emily
suddenly stiffened, then screamed out her climax. Judd went still
with shock.

Her slim body shuddered and lifted beneath his, her face
pulled tight in her pleasure. He watched her every movement,
her intense delight expressed in her narrowed eyes, her parted
lips, the sweet sounds she made. Judd knew he had never seen
anything so beautiful, so right. It seemed to go on and on, and
as her cries turned to low breathless moans, he kissed her, taking
her pleasure into himself.

When she stilled, he continued to cuddle her close, his own
need now put on hold. A tenderness he'd never experienced before swirled through him, and he couldn't help smiling. Miss
Cooper was a red-hot firecracker, and he must be the luckiest
man alive. "You okay, Em?"

She didn't answer. Her breasts were still heaving and her
heartbeat thundered against his chest. Judd placed one last gentle

kiss on her open mouth, then lifted himself away to reach for his pants. He fumbled in the pockets until he found his wallet and located a condom. When he turned back to Emily, he saw her watching him, her dark eyes so wide they filled her face. Her bottom lip trembled as she slowly drew in uneven breaths. Damp curls framed her face and her expression was wary.

She was probably a bit embarrassed by her unrestrained display. He didn't have time to soothe her, though. He needed to be inside her, right now, feeling her body clasped tight around his erection just as it had clasped his fingers. With the help of the moonlight, he could see her pale belly and still-open thighs. He bent and pressed his mouth to her moist female flesh, breathing in her scent and his need for her overwhelmed him. His tongue flicked out, stroking her, rasping over her delicate tissues and he gained one small taste of her excitement before Emily gasped and began struggling away.

He caught the hem of her gown and wrestled it over her head, chuckling at the way she tried to stop him. She slapped at his hands, and when she realized he had won the tug-of-war, she covered her face with her hands. Once the gown was free, Judd tossed it aside and then immediately pulled her hands away from her face. The feel of her naked body, so warm and soft and ready, made him shudder. He covered her completely and said in the same breath, "You are so beautiful, Em. I've never known a woman like you."

She peeked one eye open and studied him. "Really?"

"Oh, yes," he answered in his most fervent tone.

She said a small, "Oh," and then he lifted her knees with his hands, spread her legs wide and pushed inside her. She was tight and hot and so wet... Slowly, her body accepted his length, taking him in by inches, her softness giving way to his hardness. Judd had to clench his teeth and strain for control. She made small sounds of distress, and he knew he was stretching her, but she didn't fight him, didn't push him away. Her small hands clenched on his shoulders and held him close.

It didn't take her long to forget her embarrassment once he

was fully inside her. He ground against her, his gaze holding her own, seeing her eyes go hot and dark and intent. She pulled her bottom lip between her teeth and arched her neck.

"That's it, sweetheart." He drew a deep breath and began moving. Emily rocked against him, meeting his rhythm, holding him tight. He pressed his lips to her neck, breathing in her scent. He slid his hands down her back and cupped her soft bottom, lifting her higher. He felt her nipples rasp against his chest. Every touch, every breath, seemed to heighten his arousal. When she tightened her thighs and sobbed, her internal muscles milking his erection until he wanted to die, he gave up any effort at control and climaxed with a low, rough endless growl.

It took him a few minutes to realize he was probably squashing Emily. She didn't complain, but then, she wouldn't.

He lifted up and stared at her face. His eyes had adjusted to the darkness, and he could see her fine, dark hair lying in disheveled curls on the pillow. Her eyes were closed, her lashes weaving long thick shadows across her cheeks. The whiteness of her breasts reflected the moonlight, and Judd couldn't resist leaning down to softly lathe a smooth, pink nipple. It immediately puckered.

He smiled and blew against her skin.

Emily squirmed. "You're still inside me."

"Mmm. I'm still hard, too."

"I noticed."

Her shy, quiet voice touched him and he smoothed her hair away from her forehead. "I've wanted you a long time, Emily."

"We haven't known each other a long time."

She still hadn't opened her eyes. He kissed the tip of her nose. "I've wanted you for as long as I can remember. It doesn't matter that we hadn't met yet." She shivered and Judd touched his tongue to her shoulder. "Your skin is so damn soft and smooth. I love touching you. And tasting you."

He licked a path up her throat, then over to her earlobe. "I could stay like this forever."

Emily drew in a shuddering breath. "No, you couldn't."

He laughed, knowing she'd felt the involuntary flex of his erection deep inside her. He wanted her again. "If I get another condom, do you promise to stay exactly like this?"

"Will you let me touch you a little this time, too?"

His stomach tightened at the thought. And he hurriedly searched through the wallet he'd tossed on the floor only minutes earlier.

But once he was ready, he still couldn't let Emily have her way. Watching her react, touching her and seeing his effect on her, was stimulant enough. He'd thought to go slowly this time, to savor his time with her. But every little sound she made drove him closer to the edge. And when he entered her, the friction felt so unbearably good, he knew he wouldn't be able to slow down.

He'd told her the truth. He'd been waiting for her forever. But now he had her, and he didn't want to let her go.

EMILY WOKE the next day feeling fuzzy and warm and remarkably content. Then she realized Judd was beside her, one arm thrown over her hips, his face pressed into her breasts. His chest hair tickled her belly and their legs were entwined. They were both buck naked.

She should have been appalled, but seeing Judd looking so vulnerable, his hair mussed, his face relaxed, made her heart swell with emotion. Very carefully, so she wouldn't awaken him, she sifted her fingers through his hair. It felt cool and silky soft. Emily wouldn't have guessed there was anything soft about Judd. She placed a very careful kiss on his crown.

He shifted slightly, nuzzling closer to her breasts and she held her breath. But he continued sleeping. She was used to seeing the shadow of a beard on his face, but feeling it against her tender skin added something to the experience. She looked down the length of their bodies, and the vivid contrast excited her. He was so dark, so hard and muscled, while she was smooth and pale and seemed nearly fragile beside him.

She almost wished he would wake up, but he appeared totally exhausted. His breathing was deep and even, and when she slipped away from him, he merely grumbled a complaint and rolled over onto his back.

Lord help him. The man did have a fine body. It was certainly shameful of her to stand there leering at him, but she couldn't quite pull her eyes away. Dark hair covered his body in very strategic places, sometimes concealing, sometimes enhancing his masculinity. And Judd Sanders was most definitely masculine. He took her breath away.

Emily might have stood there gawking until he did wake up, if she hadn't heard a knock on her front door. She gave a guilty start, her hand going to her throat, before she realized Judd had slept through the sound, and the person at the door had no notion she was presently entertaining herself with the sight of a naked man.

She snatched her gown, then ran to her own bedroom to retrieve the matching robe. By the time she got downstairs, the knocking had become much louder. "Just a minute," she mumbled.

When she peeked out the small window in the door, she couldn't have been more surprised. For the longest moment, she simply stood there, crying and laughing. When her brother shook his head and laughed back, she remembered to open the door and let him in.

She grabbed him into her arms, even though he stood much taller than herself, and squeezed him as tight as she could. She couldn't stem the tide of tears, and didn't bother trying. "Oh, John, it's so good to see you."

"You, too, Emmie. What took you so long to let me in?"

Emily froze. Uh-oh.

"Emmie? Hey, what's up?"

She shook her head. "What are you doing here, John? I thought you were still out of the country. Did Mother and Father come with you?"

He set two suitcases just inside the door then walked past her, heading for the kitchen. Ever since she'd bought the house, the kitchen had become a kind of informal meeting place. Whenever

John visited, they sat at the kitchen table and talked until late into the night.

"John?"

"Could I have something to drink first, Em? It's been a long trip."

Emily stared at John, trying to be objective. He looked better, so much better. The scars on his right temple and upper cheek had diminished, and now only a thin, jagged line cut through his eyebrow. He'd healed nicely, but his eyes still worried her. They seemed tired and sad and...hopeless.

"You look wonderful, John. The plastic surgeons did a great job."

He scoffed. "You call this a great job? This is as good as it gets, Em, though Mom keeps insisting she'll find a better surgeon who'll make me look as 'good as new.' She refuses to believe nothing more can be done."

Emily closed her eyes, wondering why her mother couldn't see the hurt she caused with such careless comments. "John, I never thought the scars were that bad. I was more concerned about your eyesight, and once we realized there wouldn't be any permanent damage there, I was grateful. You should be, too."

"Oh, yeah. I'm real grateful to look like a freak."

For one of the few times in her life, Emily lost her temper with her baby brother. It was so rare for her to be angry with John, she almost didn't recognize the feeling. And then she slammed her hand onto the counter and whirled to face him. "Don't you ever say something so horrible again! You're my brother, dammit, and I love you. You are not a freak."

John seemed stunned by her display. He sat there, silently watching her, his dark eyes round, his body still. Emily covered her mouth with her hand and tried to collect her emotions. Then she cleared her throat. "Are you hungry?"

A small, relieved smile quirked on his lips. "Yeah, a little."

"I'll start breakfast. The coffee should be ready in just a minute. There's also juice in the refrigerator."

John tilted his head. "Since when do you drink coffee? The

last time I asked, you said it was bad for me and gave me tea instead.''

''Uh...'' She'd bought the coffee for Judd, but it didn't seem prudent to tell John that. ''You're older now. I see no reason why you can't drink coffee if you like.''

''Okay.'' John still seemed a little bemused, but then he squared his shoulders. ''I ran away, Emmie. Mom and Dad refused to bring me home, and I couldn't take another minute of sitting around waiting to see which doctor they'd produce next.''

Suddenly, Emily felt so tired she wanted to collapse. ''They'll be worried sick, John.''

''Ha! I left them a note. You watch. When they can't reach me at home, they'll call here, probably blame you somehow, then carry on as if they're on vacation. We both know they'll be glad to be rid of me. Lately, I've been an *embarrassment.*''

Since Emily had suffered similarly at the hands of her parents, she knew she couldn't truthfully deny what he said. She decided to stick to the facts, and to try to figure out what to do. ''You came straight here from the airport?''

''Yeah. Mom and Dad probably don't even realize I'm gone yet. They had a couple of parties to attend.''

The disdain, and the hurt, were obvious in his tone. She wished she could make it all better for John, but she didn't have any answers. ''You know you're welcome here as long as you like.''

John stared at his feet. ''Thanks.''

''You also know you'll have to face them again sooner or later.''

''I don't see why,'' he said. ''They're disgusted with me now, but they won't say so. They never really say anything. You know how they are. I won't hang around and let them treat me the way they treat you. Do you remember how they acted when that fiancé of yours tried to scam them for money? Did they offer you support or comfort? No, they wouldn't even come right out and yell at you. They just made you feel like dirt. And they never forget. I don't think you've been to the house since, that

Mom didn't manage to bring it up, always in some polite way, that she'd been right all along about him, that you'd been used by that jerk, just so he could get his hands on your money." John shook his head. "No thanks, I don't want to put up with that. I can just imagine…how…I'd…"

Emily looked up from pouring the coffee when John's voice trailed off. She'd heard it all before, his anger on her behalf, his indignation that she let her parents indulge in their little barbs.

She didn't understand what had silenced him now until she followed his gaze and saw Judd leaning against the doorjamb. He had his jeans on—just barely. The top button was undone and they rode low on his hips. His feet were bare, he wore no shirt and his hair fell over his forehead in disarray. He looked incredibly sexy, and the way he watched her, with so much heat, instantly had her blushing.

Then John stood. "Who the hell are you, and what are you doing in my sister's house?"

JUDD WISHED Emily's little brother had waited just a bit longer before noticing him. The conversation had taken a rather interesting turn, and he wouldn't have minded gaining a little more insight into Emily. But he supposed he could question her later on this fiancé of hers and find out exactly what had happened.

He was careful not to look overlong at the boy's scars, not that they were really all that noticeable, anyway. But just from the little he'd heard, he knew John was very sensitive about them. He was actually a good-looking kid, with the all-American look of wealth. Now, however, he appeared mightily provoked and ready to attack.

Judd ignored him.

His gaze locked on Emily, and suddenly he was cursing. "Damn, Em, are you okay?"

Emily faltered. "What?"

He strode forward until he could gently touch the side of her face. "You've got a black eye."

"I do?" Her hand went instantly to her cheek.

"It's not bad, babe. But it looks like it might hurt like hell."

She cleared her throat and cast a nervous glance at her brother. "No, it feels fine."

Judd smiled, then deliberately leaned down to press a gentle kiss to the bruise. Before Emily could step away, he caught her hands and lifted them out to her sides. In a low, husky tone, he said, "Look at you." His eyes skimmed over the white cotton eyelet robe. The hem of her gown was visible beneath and showed a row of lace and ice-blue satin trim. It was feminine and romantic and had him hard in a heartbeat.

Leaning down by her ear, Judd whispered in a low tone so her brother wouldn't hear, "I woke up and missed you. You shouldn't have left me."

He could feel the heat of her blush and smiled to himself, then turned to greet her brother. The kid looked about to self-destruct. Judd stuck out his hand. "Hi. Judd Sanders."

John glared. "What are you doing in my sister's house?" he repeated.

"That's none of your damn business." Then in the next breath, Judd asked, "Didn't you notice Emily's black eye?"

John stiffened, a guilty flush staining his lean cheeks. "It's not that noticeable. And besides, Emily was asking about me, so I didn't have time—"

"Yeah, right." Judd turned to Emily. "Why don't you sit down and rest? I'll fix breakfast. What do you feel like eating?"

"Hey, wait a minute!" John's neck had turned red now, too. He apparently didn't like being ignored.

Judd sighed. "What?"

For a moment, John seemed to forget what he wanted. He opened his mouth twice, and his hand went self-consciously to his scar. Then he asked, with a good dose of suspicion, "How did Emmie get a black eye?"

Judd smiled to himself. He folded his arms over his chest and braced his bare feet apart. "Some guy broke in here—"

"It was nothing, John." Emily frowned at Judd and then rushed toward her brother. "Would you like to go freshen up, John, before breakfast?"

"Women freshen up, Em. Not men."

She glared at Judd for that observation.

Judd lifted his eyebrow. "He has every right to know what happened to you. He's your brother and you care about him, so it only stands to reason that he cares for you, too." Judd looked toward John. "Am I right?"

"Yeah." John stepped forward. "What did happen?"

Emily looked so harassed, Judd took pity on her. "Why don't you go upstairs and...freshen up, Em, or change or whatever. I'll entertain your brother for you and start breakfast." Then he leaned down close to her ear. "Not that I don't like what you're wearing. You look damn sexy. But little brother looks ready to attack."

Her eyes widened and she cast a quick glance at John. "Yes, well, I suppose I ought to get dressed..." She rushed from the room. Judd watched her go, admiring the way her delectable rear swayed in the soft gown.

"What did you say to her?"

Little brothers were apparently a pain in the butt, and Judd wasn't known for his patience. But he supposed, for Emily, he ought to make the effort. "I told her how attractive she is. I get the feeling she isn't used to hearing compliments very often." The way he said it placed part of the blame for that condition directly on John. Judd didn't think it would hurt him to know Emily needed comforting every bit as much as anyone else. "Emily's a woman. They like to know when they look nice."

As he spoke, Judd opened the cabinets and rummaged around for pancake mix and syrup. It was one of the few breakfast things he knew how to make. He wanted to pamper Emily, to make her realize how special she was.

Last night had been unexpected, something he hadn't dared dream about, something he supposed shouldn't have happened. But it had happened, and even though he didn't know what he was going to do about it yet, how to balance his feelings for Emily with his need to get Donner, he knew he didn't want her to be uncomfortable around him.

He thought breakfast might be a good start. Besides, he owed her one from yesterday.

John interrupted his thoughts with a lot of grousing and grumbling. "I'm good to Emily."

"Are you?" He pulled out a couple of eggs to put in the mix, his mind whirling on possible ways to proceed against Donner, while keeping Emily uninvolved. Perhaps having her brother here would distract her from capturing the gun dealer.

"She's been worried about me."

Judd glanced at John as he pulled down a large glass mixing bowl. "I don't see why. You seem healthy and strong. Hell, you're twice her size." He took the milk from the refrigerator and added it to the mix.

"I nearly lost my eyesight not too long ago. And now I've got these damn scars."

Judd gave up for a moment on the pancakes. He turned to give John his full attention. "That little scar on the side of your face?"

John nearly choked. "Little?"

"It's not that big a deal. So you've got a scar? You're a man. Men are expected to get banged up a little. Happens all the time. It's not like you're disabled or anything. You'll still be able to work and support yourself, won't you?"

"I'm only sixteen."

Judd shrugged. "I was thinking long term."

"My face is ruined."

"Naw. You're still a good-lookin' kid. And in a few more years, that scar will most likely fade until you can barely see it. Besides, you'll probably get all kinds of sympathy from the females once you hit college. So what's the problem?"

John collapsed back in his chair. "You really don't think the scars are all that bad?"

Judd went back to mixing the batter. "I didn't even notice them at first. Of course, with Emily around that's not saying much. I wouldn't notice an elephant at the table when she looks at me with those big brown eyes. Your sister is a real charmer."

There was a stretch of silence. "You and Emily got something going?"

"Yeah. Something. I'm not sure what. Hey, how many pancakes can you eat? About ten?"

"I suppose. I didn't know Emily was dating anyone."

"We aren't actually dating."

"Oh." Another silence. "Should I be worried about this?"

That brought Judd around. "Well, hallelujah. I didn't think anyone ever worried about Em."

John frowned. "She's my sister. Of course I worry about her."

"Good. But no, you don't have to worry right now. I'll take care of her."

"And I'm just supposed to believe you because you say so?"

He almost smiled again. John sounded just like his sister. "Why not? Emily does."

That brought a laugh. "My parents would have a field day with that analogy. They don't think Emily has very good judgment."

"And what do you think?"

"I think she's too naive, too trusting and a very good person."

Judd grinned. "Me, too."

"So tell me how she got the black eye."

Suddenly, John looked much older, and very serious. Judd gave one sharp nod. "You can set the table while I talk."

Fifteen minutes later, Judd had three plates full of pancakes, and he'd finished a rather convoluted explanation of Emily's exploits. It was an abridged version, because even though Judd admitted to helping Emily, he didn't say anything about going undercover as a male stripper, or his overwhelming attraction to Emily, or their newly discovered sexual chemistry. In fact, he wasn't certain yet just what that chemistry was, so he sure as hell wasn't about to discuss it with anyone, let alone Emily's little brother.

John was appalled to learn what steps Emily had taken to try to help him.

And he hadn't even noticed her black eye.

Judd knew he was feeling guilty, which hopefully would help bring him out of his self-pity. "So you can see how serious Emily is about this."

"Damn." John rubbed one hand over his scar, then across his neck. "What can I do to help?"

Ah. Just the reaction he'd hoped for. From what Emily had told him about John, Judd hadn't known for sure what to expect. By all accounts, John could have been a very spoiled, selfish punk. But then, he had Emily for a sister, so that scenario didn't seem entirely feasible. "You want to help? Stay out of the east end. And stay out of trouble."

"But there must be something—"

"No." When John started to object, Judd cursed. "I'm having enough trouble keeping an eye on Emily. And she has enough to do without worrying about you more than she already does. Give her a rest, John. Get your act together and keep it together."

"That's easy for you to say. You don't know my parents."

"No. But I do know your sister. If she turned out so great, I suppose you can, too."

John laughed. "That's one way of looking at it."

Emily walked into the room just then, and Judd immediately went to her. He tried to keep his eyes on her face as he talked to her, but she was wearing another one of those soft, ladylike dresses. But what really drove him insane was the white lace tie that circled her throat and ended in a bow. Without meaning to, his fingers began toying with it. "I told your brother what happened."

The frown she gave him showed both irritation and concern. "Judd."

"Hey, it's okay," John said as he took a plate of pancakes and smothered them in warm syrup. "I'm glad he told me. And I'm glad he's looking after you."

"Judd is not looking after me. He's a...well, a partner of sorts."

Judd lowered his eyebrows as if in deep thought, then gave a slow, very serious nod. "Of sorts."

The look she sent him insisted he behave himself. He wasn't going to, though. A slight tug on the bow brought her an inch or two closer. His eyes drifted from her neatly brushed hair, her slender stockinged legs and her flat, black shoes. Her attire was casual, but also very elegant. "You look real pretty in that dress, Em. Do you always wear such...feminine stuff?"

Trying to act as though she wasn't flushed a bright pink, Emily stepped out of his reach and picked up her own plate. She stared at the huge stack of pancakes. "Most of my wardrobe is similar, yes. This is one of my older dresses because I have some work to do today."

"I like it."

John suddenly laughed. "I think you've caught a live one, Emmie. I don't remember what's-his-name ever acting this outrageous. He always tried to suck up to Mom and Dad by being as stuffy and proper as they are."

After frowning at her brother and giving a quick shake of her head, she said, "I can't truly imagine Judd ever 'sucking up' to anyone. Can you?"

"It'll be interesting to see what the folks think of him."

An expression of horror passed over her face. "For heaven's sake, John. I doubt Judd has any interest in meeting our parents."

Judd narrowed his eyes at the way she'd said that. So she didn't want him to meet them? It was no skin off his nose. He wasn't into doing the family thing, anyway. He couldn't remember one single woman he'd ever dated who wanted to rush him home to meet her mama.

But somehow, coming from Emily, the implicit rejection smarted. "There wouldn't be any reason for me to meet them. Especially since they're out of the country, right?"

Emily stared at her fork. "Yes. And we should have everything resolved before they return if we're as close to finishing this business as you say."

And once everything was resolved, there would be no reason to keep him around? Judd wanted to ask, but he couldn't. It was annoying to admit, but he felt vulnerable. He couldn't quite credit Emily with using him; she simply wasn't that mercenary. But that didn't mean she wouldn't gladly take advantage of a situation when it presented itself. He'd known from the start that she wanted him. They'd met, and sparks had shot off all around them. And if she wanted to have a fling on what she considered "the wild side of life," Judd was more than willing to oblige. For a time.

He would get a great deal of satisfaction when Donner was taken care of, and he'd be able to return to his normal routine: life without a driving purpose. He'd be alone again, without Max and without the overwhelming need to avenge him. Actually, he'd have no commitments, no obligations at all, unless Emily...

Judd shook his head. With any luck, he'd be wrong in what he was feeling, and he wouldn't miss her. The time he had with Emily right now would be enough.

Hell, he'd make it enough.

With that thought in mind, he urged Emily to eat, and he dug into his own pancakes. When she was almost finished, curiosity got the better of him and he asked, "So who was this bozo who tried to schmooze your parents?"

Emily choked. He took the time to whack her on the back a few times, then caught her chin and turned her face his way. "Emily?"

When she didn't answer right away, John spoke up. "Emmie was engaged to a guy for a while. She loved him, but he only wanted to use her to get in good with my parents. Luckily, everyone found out in time, before the wedding."

"Thank you very much, John."

"Oh, come on, sis. It wasn't your fault. The guy was a con artist."

"Yes, he was. And that is all in the past. I'd appreciate it if we found something else to talk about."

Judd transferred his gaze to John. "Your folks are pretty hard on her about it still?"

"God, yes. And she lets them. I don't think I've ever heard her really defend herself, though I'd like to see her tell them where to go. They even try to bully her into giving up her work with the homeless. They keep reminding her how she got burned once. It was a real embarrassing event. The papers got wind of it and all of society knew." John made a face, then added, "My parents really hate being publicly embarrassed."

With a disgusted sound of protest, Emily stood and took her plate to the sink. Judd glanced toward her, then back to John. "She's still a little touchy about it."

"Yeah. It was pretty hard on her. But Emmie is tough, and she doesn't let anything really get her down. Including Mom and Dad. That's why she moved here, away from my folks. She won't argue with them, but she will walk away. Of course, they hate this house, too. I don't know why she puts up with them."

Swiveling in his chair, Judd saw the stiff set to Emily's shoulders, the way she clenched her hands on the sink counter. He wanted to hold her, to comfort her, but the time wasn't right. Later, though… "Did you love him, Em?"

It took her so long to answer, Judd thought she'd decided to ignore him. It wasn't any of his business, but he wanted to know. The thought of her still pining over some guy didn't sit right with him.

Then she finally shook her head. "I suppose I thought I did…maybe I did. But now, it doesn't seem like I could have. I was so wrong about him. He was out of work and needed me, and I thought he cared about me, too. But he turned out to be a really horrible man."

Judd was out of his seat and standing behind her in a heartbeat. "That was one incident."

She turned and smiled at him. "Are you thinking I might decide I was wrong about you, too, Detective?"

"Since I don't know what you think about me, how am I supposed to answer that?"

When it came, her smile was sweet enough and warm enough to make his muscles clench. He caged her waist between his hands and waited.

"I think you're probably a real-life hero, Judd, and unlike any man I've ever known."

The words hit him like a blow. He stared into her dark eyes, dumbfounded. He saw her acceptance, her giving. He was a man with no family, no ties, a cop out to do a job, and willing to use her to do it. He was certainly no hero. But if that was what Emily wanted...

John cleared his throat. "Maybe I should make myself scarce."

Remembering where they were and who was with them, Judd forced himself to release Emily and take two steps back—away from temptation. "No. You can help me do the dishes while Emily calls to see if she can get someone here to repair the hot-water heater."

"Do the dishes? But I don't know how..."

Judd smirked. "It's easy. I'll show you what to do."

"But—"

"Do you want to be able to take care of yourself or not?"

Emily laughed. "Well put. I'll leave you two to tend to your chores." But she stopped at the doorway. "By the way, Judd. What if there was something on that film?"

"I'm picking it up today. Then we'll know."

"I'll go with you."

"No, you won't."

"But..."

His sigh was exaggerated. "You're as bad as your brother, Em. I thought we had an agreement."

When she turned around and practically stomped away without a word, Judd decided she was mad. "Well, hell."

John only laughed. "Gee, I'm really tired. Too much traveling, I guess. I think I might need to spend a lot of time in my room, resting up."

"What's that supposed to mean?"

With a buddy-type punch in the shoulder, John said, ''I think you're going to have your hands full with Emmie. She can be as stubborn as a mule, and it's no telling who will win. I don't want to get caught in the crossfire.''

And I don't want Emily caught in the crossfire, he thought. *Which is why I'm leaving her here.* There was really no other choice. He would get Donner, one way or another. The past, and Max, couldn't be forgotten. And he couldn't pretend it had never happened, not without finding some justice.

It would be only too easy to get wrapped up in Emily's problems. *It would be much too easy to get wrapped up in Emily.* But he wouldn't. Judd was afraid Emily could easily make him reevaluate himself and his purpose. Arresting Donner and seeing him prosecuted had to remain a priority. But he was beginning to feel like a juggler in a circus, wanting his time with Emily, and still needing to seek vengeance on Donner.

He'd have all weekend to spend with Emily before anything more could be done on the case. His body tightened in anticipation with just the thought. Somehow he'd have to manage— without letting her get hurt.

He only hoped Emily understood his motivations.

8

"I WANT YOU, Em."

Emily jumped, her heart lodging in her throat. "Good heavens, Judd. You startled me."

His hands slid from her waist to her hips, then pulled her back against him. She could feel the heat of his body on her back, her bottom... "Judd, stop that before John sees."

His growl reverberated along her spine, his mouth nipping on her nape. "John's taking a nap. He's still suffering jet lag."

With shaking hands, Emily carefully laid aside the picture she'd been looking at. She already knew Judd wanted her. He'd made that clear with every look he sent her way. But her brother was here now, and she wasn't comfortable being intimate with John in the house. She cleared her throat and tried to come up with a distraction.

"I don't see anything in these pictures that would prompt anyone to steal them."

Judd pressed closer and his hands came around her waist to rest on her belly. She sucked in a quick breath. His deep voice, so close to her ear, added to her growing excitement. "You have innocent eyes, honey."

"What do you mean?"

"Innocent, sexy eyes." He leaned over to see her face, his gaze dark and searching. "You really don't know what sexy eyes you have, do you?"

It took her a second to remember what she'd been talking about. "No, I... The pictures, Judd?"

His gaze dropped to her mouth and he gave her a soft, warm kiss, then picked up one of the photos. His expression changed as he looked at it, turning dark and threatening. "The guy in the doorway of the deli is an associate of Donner's. My guess is, he only visits this part of town when making a deal. Since the deal surely concerns guns, I'd say he's the one who instigated your break-in.''

Emily gave the photo another look. "Really?"

Judd cursed, then tossed the picture back on the kitchen counter. "Unfortunately, I can't do anything about it yet without taking the risk of tipping off Donner and blowing my cover. If we grab this guy, we put a halt to the deal, and lose our advantage." He tightened his mouth. "That's not something I'm willing to do."

"I see." But she didn't, not really. Why was Judd so upset?

"Do you? Do you have any idea how I'd love to get my hands on that guy—*now*—for scaring you like he did?"

His possessive tone made her heart flutter, and she had to force herself to think about the case. "Then you think he was the one who broke in here?"

"Probably not. Like Donner, he has flunkies to do that kind of thing for him. But your taking this picture has obviously annoyed him. Hopefully, it'll help strengthen our case against Donner, too, and we'll be able to make another connection there once we prosecute."

Emily licked her lips and tried for a casual tone. "Do you think the picture alone will be enough to incriminate Donner?"

Judd shrugged. "Possibly. But I don't want to incriminate him. I want to nail the bastard red-handed."

Emily had known that would be his answer, but still… "Judd, maybe it's time to rethink all this. I mean, is it really worth risking your life—"

He laid his finger across her lips before she could finish. "I'm not giving up, Em. I've already gone too far, and I have no intention of letting Donner win. But in the meantime, until he's put away and everything's settled, I don't want you staying here alone."

So. There it was. Emily knew he was up to something the minute he came back in with the developed pictures. She'd been surveying the pictures, not seeing anything out of the ordinary, when Judd started acting amorous.

Acting, Emily? Can't you feel the man's body behind you? He's not acting. No, and as much as that tempted her, she had to remember he only wanted to stay at her house to protect her. It had nothing to do with actually wanting her. Well, maybe it had a little to do with that, but wanting her wasn't his primary motive. She had to remember that.

Smiling slightly, she said over her shoulder, "My brother will be here with me."

He opened his thighs and pulled her bottom closer to him, his hand still firm on her belly, now caressing. "Not good enough. I want to be certain you're safe."

"I...I'll remember to turn on the alarm system." *Lord, Emily. You sound as if you've run five miles.*

Apparently done with talking, Judd dipped his hand lower and his fingers stroked between her thighs, urging her legs apart and moving in a slow, deep rhythm. The material of her dress slid over her as his fingers probed. Heat rushed through her, flushing her face, making her legs tremble, her nipples tighten. She slumped back against him and her head fell to his shoulder. How could she let this happen again when she still felt embarrassed over her wild display the night before? It was as if she had no control of her reactions.

Judd lifted his other hand to her breast, his fingertips finding a taut nipple then gently plucking.

"Judd—"

"Let me." He nuzzled her throat, his warm breath wafting over her skin. "I love how you feel, Em. I love how you come apart for me."

But you don't love me. She almost cried out at the realization that she wanted his love. She wanted it so bad. All the old insecurities returned, the memories of how she'd tried, just as her brother was trying, to gain a modicum of real emotion, real affection from someone. They all swamped her and suddenly she couldn't breathe. She jerked away, hitting her hip on the counter and hanging her head so Judd couldn't see her face. She felt breathless and frightened and so damn foolish.

His hand touched her shoulder, then tightened when she flinched. "Shh. I'm sorry, babe. I didn't mean to push you."

He turned her to hold her in his arms, no longer seducing, but comforting. And that seemed even worse. The tears started and she couldn't stop them.

His palm cradled the back of her head, his fingers kneading her scalp, tangling in her hair. "Tell me what's wrong, Em. I'll fix it if I can."

Through her tears, she managed a laugh. He was the most wondrous man. She pulled away to retrieve a tissue, then cleaned up her tear-stained face before turning back to him. He looked so concerned, so caring, she almost blurted out, *I love you.* But she managed to keep the words inside. She had no idea how Judd would feel about such a declaration, but she couldn't imagine him welcoming it, not now, not while he had to concentrate on getting Donner.

"I guess I'm just a little overwrought," she said lamely. She quickly added, "I mean, with my brother being here, and worrying over him and the break-in."

Judd still looked concerned, but he nodded. "I understand. Would you like to take a nap, too?"

She'd never be able to sleep. "No. I have housework to do, and the yard needs some work. And I thought I'd put on a roast to cook for dinner."

Looking sheepish, and somewhat anxious, Judd asked, "You mind if I hang around and help?"

He could be so adorable... *Lord, Emily, are you crazy? The man is devastating, not adorable.* "Of course you're welcome to stay. But you don't have to help out. And I'm still not certain that it's a good idea for you to stay overnight."

"I think it's a hell of an idea. And I insist." When she frowned, he added, "It'll only be for a few days. I have to be back at the bar Tuesday. I have the feeling Donner will approach me then. He's getting restless, and he's made it clear he thinks

we'll work well together. Since he doesn't like losing, he'll probably make me an offer that no normal stripper could refuse.''

It was a small grab for humor, so Emily dutifully smiled. But
inside, she felt like crying. The thought of Judd getting more
involved with Donner made her skin crawl. They both knew how
dangerous he could be.

"Stop frowning, Em. I should be able to set something up
with him, find out when and where his next shipment will be,
and then I'll bust him. It'll be over with before you know it.''

And he'd go out of her life as quickly as he'd entered it. Emily
bit her lip. "I'm worried, Judd.''

"Don't be. I can take care of myself.''

She supposed that was true, since he'd been doing just that
since he'd been a child. But for once, she'd like to see him taken
care of.

Just that quick, she had a change of heart. Judd might never
love her, but he deserved to be loved. And she could easily
smother him with affection. She'd enjoy taking care of him, and
maybe, just maybe, he'd enjoy it, too.

They spent the day together, and though she tried, Judd didn't
let her do any actual work around the house. She couldn't convince him that she enjoyed getting her hands dirty once in a
while, and since he seemed so determined to have his way, she
allowed it. Judd followed her direction, and she simply enjoyed
her time with him.

He was a pleasure to watch, to talk to. He moved with easy
grace, his muscles flexing and bunching. It was almost a shame
he wasn't a real stripper, for he was certainly suited for the job.

When Judd suddenly stripped off his shirt, Emily thought he
might have read her mind. He didn't look at her, though, merely
went back to work. She heard herself say, "Are you performing
for me, Judd?''

She'd meant only to tease him, but he slowly turned to face
her, and his eyes were intent, almost hot as he caught and held
her gaze. "I could be convinced to…in a private performance.''

Not a single answer came to mind. She sat there, staring stupidly. Judd walked to her, pulled her close then kissed her. It was such a devouring kiss, Emily had to hold on to him. His tongue pushed into her mouth, hot and wet and insistent. Judd slanted his head and continued to kiss her until they were both breathless.

When he pulled away, she stared up at him, dazed. He drew a deep breath and tipped up her chin. "Anytime, Emily. You just let me know."

After that, she refrained from provoking comments. Judd might handle them very well, but she didn't think she'd live through another one. Instead, she asked about Max, Judd's past, and about his work. She wanted to know everything about him.

Emily went out of her way to show Judd, again and again, how important he was to her. At times he looked bemused, and at times wary. But more often than not, he looked frustrated.

She understood that frustration since she felt a measure of her own. But having her brother there did inhibit her a bit. Of course, so did her unaccountable response to Judd. It was scandalous, the way he could make her feel. But she suspected he didn't mind, even if it did embarrass her, so she decided she'd try to see to his frustration—and her own—once John had gone to bed for the evening.

That thought kept her flushed and filled with forbidden anticipation the entire time they worked.

Midafternoon, John joined them, and Emily was amazed to see how John reacted to Judd. It had startled her that morning when John had spoken so openly to Judd. Usually, her brother was stubbornly quiet, refusing to give up his thoughts, brooding in his silence. But with Judd, he seemed almost anxious to talk. And Judd listened.

Emily was so proud of Judd, she could have cried again. No one had ever reached her brother so easily. In a way, she was jealous, because she'd tried so hard to help John. But she supposed it took a male to understand, and Judd not only listened, he gave glimpses into his own past, allowing John to make a connection of sorts. They found a lot of things in common, though their upbringings had been worlds apart.

Emily decided she was seeing male bonding at its best, and went inside to give them more privacy.

She was starting dinner when they both walked in, looking windblown and handsome. Judd winked at Emily when he caught her eye, and John laughed.

"A man's coming tomorrow to replace my water heater." She more or less blurted that out from sheer nervousness when Judd started her way. He had that glint in his eyes again, and she truly felt embarrassed carrying on in front of her brother.

But Judd only placed a kiss on her cheek, and flicked a finger over the tip of her nose. "Good." Then he turned to John. "Make sure you're here when he comes. I don't think Emily should be alone in this big house with a strange man."

"I'll be here."

Emily might have objected to their protective attitudes, except that she heard a new strength in John's tone, that of confidence and maturity. She gave both men a tender smile. They stared back in obvious confusion.

Backing out of the room, John said, "I think I'll go watch some TV." But he glanced at Judd, then back to Emily. "Uh...that is, unless you need me to do anything else?"

"No. You can go do whatever you like."

Once he'd left the room, Emily turned a wondering look on Judd. "How did you do that?"

His grin was smug. "Do what?"

"Turn my little brother into a helpful stranger."

He laughed outright. "First of all, you could stop calling him your little brother. He's a head taller than you, Em. Respect his maturity."

"I hadn't realized he possessed any maturity."

"No, I guess you haven't seen that side of him. But I know Max had to work hard at getting me turned around. And the first thing he did was explain that I was old enough to know better. Put that way, I felt too embarrassed to act like a kid. And little

by little, Max pointed out ways to distinguish what it takes to
be an adult. Your brother's no different. He just needed some
new choices.''

Emily stood there feeling dumbfounded by his logic. She had
enough sense to know it wasn't that simple, to realize what John
needed was someone to identify with, someone who cared. That
Judd was that man only made her love him more. "Thank you."

Judd stared at her, his gaze traveling from her eyes to her
mouth, then slowly moving down her body. He muttered a quiet
curse, and started toward her. Emily felt her heart trip. But the
phone gave a sudden loud peal, and Judd halted.

Hoping she looked apologetic rather than relieved, Emily
asked, "Could you get that, please?"

It rang two more times before Judd turned and picked up the
receiver.

She knew right away that asking him to answer the phone had
been a mistake. The look on Judd's face as he tried to explain
who he was would have been comical if Emily hadn't already
suspected who her caller was.

When Judd held a palm over the mouthpiece and turned to
her, she braced herself.

"It's your father, and he wants to talk to John. By the way,
he also wants to know who I am and what I'm doing here answering your phone." Judd tilted his head. "What do you want
me to tell him, babe?"

Lord, Emily. You're in for it now.

"IT'S OVER and done with, Em. You might as well forget it."

Ha! That was easy for Judd to say. Emily had no doubt her
parents were headed home right this minute. Of course, it would
take them time to get here, but still, she was already dreading
that confrontation.

"Come on, Emily. You know John didn't mean to upset you."

"Of course he didn't. It's just that my parents could rattle
anyone." But why did John have to tell them Judd was her
boyfriend. Lord, if they showed up before everything was settled,
she'd either have to admit Judd was a detective, and accept their

unending annoyance for involving herself in something they'd expressly forbidden, or she'd have to tell them he was a...a stripper. She could just imagine their reactions to that.

"I wish I'd talked to them, instead of John."

Judd turned his face away from her. "I offered you the phone, honey. But you just gave me a blank look. I didn't think you wanted to talk to them. And even if you had, what could you have told them? That I was a traveling salesman who just picks up other people's phones?"

She shook her head. "No. But I might have thought of something. And John's been so solemn since he talked with Father. I have no idea what they talked about—other than their conversation about me—but I know it couldn't have been pleasant. John's been sullen and sulky ever since, barely eating his dinner and running off to bed early. I wish he'd talk to me about it."

"He's all right, Em. He just needs a little time to himself."

Emily barely heard him. She stood up and started to pace the room, her mind whirling. Then she threw up her hands in frustration. "Oh, this is just awful. What am I going to do?" She didn't really expect Judd to answer, since he'd only been watching her with a strange look on his face. "You can't possibly realize what a trial my father can be. He's so judgmental, so rigid. Once he takes a stand, he never backs down."

Judd put his hand at the small of her back and nudged her toward the stairs. "Come on. It won't do you any good sitting down here and worrying about it. I'd say you probably have a couple of days before your folks get here, and by then, I'll be gone. So you're probably worrying about nothing."

They were halfway up the stairs, when Emily realized what he'd said. She turned to him and gripped his arm. "What are you talking about?"

He wouldn't look at her, but continued up the steps. "I don't want to cause you any problems. So I'll make certain I'm out of the way before they get here. Maybe John can say he misunderstood the situation, or something."

Judd started to go to the room Emily had given him the night before. She rushed up the remaining steps to catch him. "Wait a minute."

Judd lifted one dark eyebrow in question. "What?"

What are you going to do now, Emily? Just blurt out that you want him? He doesn't really seem all that interested anymore. She swallowed and tried to find a way to phrase her request without sounding too outrageous. "I...um."

Judd frowned and walked closer to her. "What is it?"

She glanced toward her brother's room, then took Judd's hand and urged him away from the door. When they were outside her bedroom, she stopped. Judd made a quick glance at the door, and this time both his eyebrows lifted.

Emily drew a calming breath. "I don't want to disturb John. And I don't want you to misunderstand."

Judd waited.

"It's about what I said before. I didn't mean that I wanted you to leave. I was worrying about John, not myself. My parents might not approve of my having you here, but then, they approve of very little when it comes to me. I'm almost immune to their criticism. But John isn't."

"So you're worried about him, not yourself?"

She didn't want to lie to him, that wouldn't be fair. "I can't say I'm looking forward to explaining you. After all, if I tell them the truth, they might interfere, and then your case could be jeopardized."

"What will you tell them?"

Judd had slowly moved closer to her until he stood only a few inches away. Already she was responding to him, and he hadn't even touched her yet. "I don't know. But I don't want you to—"

He laid one finger against her lips. "You've told me all kinds of things you don't want, Emily. Now tell me what you *do* want."

"You."

The way his eyes blazed after she said it reassured her. Her fingers trembled when she reached up to touch his chest. "I want you, Judd. It's a little overwhelming, what you make me feel.

I've never felt anything like it before. But last night, you gave a part of yourself to me. Now, I want to do the same for you.''

His eyes closed and he drew a deep breath.

Emily took his hand and placed it against her heart. "Do you see what you do to me? It's probably wrong of me to like it so much—'' She had to stop to clear her throat as Judd's fingers curled around her breast. The heat in her face told her she was blushing, both with excitement and with her audacity, but she was determined to tell him all of it. "When I was engaged, I thought I knew what excitement was, and it was wonderful because it was forbidden. I felt wild, and just a little bit sinful. But that was nothing compared to how I feel with you.''

"How do you feel?''

"Alive. Carnal.'' She felt the heat in her cheeks intensify with her outrageous admission, but she continued, "Not the least bit refined.''

"God, Emily, you're the most refined, the most graceful woman I've ever seen.'' His tone dropped and his thumb rubbed over her nipple. "You're also remarkably feminine and sexy. Just thinking about how wild you get makes me so hard I hurt.''

She licked her lips, then stepped closer still so she could hide her face against his chest. "There are…things, I've wanted to do to you, Judd.''

His body seemed to clench, and his voice, when he spoke, was hoarse, "What…things?''

Smiling, Emily whispered, "Don't you think we ought to get out of the hall before we…ah, discuss it?''

She'd barely finished speaking before Judd had opened her bedroom door and ushered her inside. The light was out, but Judd quickly flipped the wall switch. Now that they were out of the dim hall and she had his undivided attention, Emily felt very uncertain about what she had to say. But Judd was staring intently, and waiting, so she forged ahead.

"The last time…well, I know I took you by surprise.''

He traced her mouth with a finger. "You can surprise me anytime you like.''

"That's not what I mean. You see, even though I try very hard to be proper..." She glanced at his face, saw his fascination, then carefully pulled his teasing fingertip between her lips. Her tongue curled around him as she gently sucked and she heard him gasp. She licked at his flesh, lightly biting him.

"Oh, Emily."

She forgot he watched her with intense scrutiny. She forgot that such displays could be embarrassing. She could only think of the many things she wanted...

She released his finger and he dropped his hand to her buttocks, cuddling her. With a deep breath and a nervous smile, she blurted out, "I'm afraid I'm a fraud. I'm not at all proper. At least, you see, not when I'm..."

"Turned on?" His words were a breathless rasp.

She gave a painful nod of agreement.

There was no smile now, but his eyes showed wicked anticipation, and a touch of something more, something she couldn't recognize. "Are you turned on now, Em?"

The rapid beating of her heart shook her. Heat pulsed beneath her skin, making her warm all over, making her nipples taut, her belly tingle. It was so debilitating, wanting him like this. "Very."

"And you want to do...things? To me?"

Again, she nodded, feeling the husky timbre of his voice deep inside herself. "If you wouldn't mind."

His long fingers curved over her bottom and began a rhythmic caressing. "Tell me what things, Em."

Pressed so close to his body, it was impossible to ignore the length of his erection against her belly, or the warmth of his breath fanning her cheek. She went on tiptoe and nuzzled her mouth against his throat. "I want to taste you...everywhere."

His hands stilled, then clenched tight on her flesh. Against her ear, he whispered, "Oh, yeah."

She pulled his shirt open, and rubbed her cheek over the soft, curling hair there. "I'd like to have you...beneath me, so I could watch your face. You are such an incredibly handsome man,

Judd. When you stripped for me…at least, it felt like it was just for me…''

"It was. It made me crazy, the way you ate me up with your eyes. I had to fight damn hard to keep from embarrassing myself that day.''

Not quite understanding what he meant, she tilted her head back and stared up at him. "How so?''

His lips twitched into a smile. "You make me hard, Em, without even trying. But watching you watch me… It was the first time I thought stripping was a turn-on. Before that, it was only damn embarrassing.''

"I'm looking forward to watching you again.''

He groaned, then kissed her, sucking her tongue into his mouth. Emily almost forgot that she wanted to control things this time, but with a soft moan, she pushed Judd away.

"Emily…''

"No, wait.'' She had to pant for breath, but she was determined. "Will you take your clothes off for me, Judd?''

He blinked. "Will I… How about we take them off together?''

Reaching for his shirt, she said, "Of course,'' but Judd stopped her hands.

"I meant, we should take *our* clothes off, Em. I want you naked, too. All those things you want to do to me, well, I want to do them to you.''

Her mouth went dry. Just the thought of Judd kissing her… She shook her head. "No. Not a good idea. This is my turn…''

"Let's not argue about it, okay?''

She could see the humor in his gaze, and his crooked smile. He was so endearing, so charming, so… "I've never undressed for anyone before.''

There. She'd made that admission. She knew her face was scarlet, but she simply hadn't considered that he might want her to display herself. He was the stripper, not her.

Even as his fingers went to the waistband of his jeans, Judd murmured, "Fair's fair, Em.'' His eyes challenged her, and while her fascinated gaze stayed glued to his busily working fingers, Emily nodded.

She started to untie the bow to her dress, but Judd caught her hands. "No. This one is mine. I thought about doing this—so many times—since we first met." He took the very tip of the lace tie between his finger and thumb, then gently tugged. It pulled open and the ends landed, curling around her breasts. Judd carefully separated the looped strips, while the backs of his fingers brushed over her nipples again and again. Then he slid the tie—so very slowly—out of her collar. Through it all, Emily didn't move.

It was the most erotic thing she'd ever had done to her.

She barely noticed when Judd tucked the lace tie into the back pocket of his jeans. And then he began stripping again, prompting her with a look to do the same. She felt horribly awkward, and very self-conscious. Her body wasn't perfect like his, but rather too slim, too slight. Where Judd looked like every woman's vision of masculine perfection, she was a far sight from the women's bodies displayed in men's magazines.

After unbuttoning her dress, she stepped out of her shoes, trying to concentrate on what Judd was doing, rather than on her own actions. Next, she took off her nylons, tossing them onto the chair by her bed. She saw Judd go still for a moment, then saw his nostrils flare. It hit her that her disrobing excited him. He'd already removed his shirt, and now his jeans, along with his underwear, were shoved down his legs. He stepped out of them, then fully naked, he turned his attention to watching her. There was no disguising his state of arousal. His stomach muscles were pulled tight, and his erection was long and thick and throbbing.

She drew a shuddering breath. "Judd?"

"Go on, honey." When she still hesitated, he said, "You're doing fine, Em. Now, take off the dress."

His words hit her with the impact of a loud drumroll, and she couldn't swallow, her throat was so tight. She saw a slight smile hover on his mouth, and he said, "I've had some fantasies, too, babe. And seeing you strip is one of them."

"I can't."

"I'm not talking about doing it in front of an audience. It'll just be you and me." Then he lowered his gaze to where her hands knotted in the dress. "Take it off, Em."

She wanted to, she really did. But it wasn't in her to flaunt her body, not when she felt she had nothing to flaunt. She looked away, feeling like a failure, afraid she'd disappointed him. Tears of frustration gathered in her eyes, and just when she would have begun a stammering explanation, Judd touched her.

"Shh. It doesn't matter, honey." He pulled her close again. Emily kept her face averted.

Judd pushed the dress down her shoulders, then worked it lower. The soft material slid over her arms and caught, for just a heartbeat, on her narrow hips, then went smoothly to the floor.

Judd's breath left him in a whoosh as his gaze dropped to her black lace panties and stayed there. Emily suddenly didn't feel quite so awkward, not with the intense, heated way he watched her, as if she were the most fascinating woman he'd ever seen. She skimmed off her bra, then offered him a small, nervous smile.

"Incredible." His gaze finally lifted from her panties to her face. "If I'd known what you were wearing under that dress, I never would have lasted this long." He lowered his head for another long, heated kiss, and at the same time, slid his hands into her underwear, his large warm palms cradling her bottom. His fingers explored, probing and stroking, and Emily clung to him. Before the kiss was over, her panties had joined the rest of their clothes and then she urged Judd to sit on the side of the bed. She dropped gracefully to her knees before him, then reached out and encircled his erection with both hands. He was breathing hard, his thighs tensed, his hands fisted on the bed at his sides. Emily leaned forward, feeling her heart pound, and took a small, tentative lick. He jerked, and a rough broken groan escaped him.

Emily felt encouraged and anxious and excited. She leaned forward again, rubbing her breasts against his thighs, her nipples tingling against his hairy legs. Then she closed her mouth around him, gently suckling and sliding her tongue around him, feeling him shudder and stiffen. Judd gave a long, low, ragged groan and twined his fingers in her hair, leaning over her and holding her head between his large palms, urging her to the rhythm he liked. His hands trembled. So did his thighs.

For the first time in her life, Emily was able to indulge in her sensual nature. Judd encouraged her, praised her, pleaded with her. She loved the scent of his masculinity, the texture of his rigid flesh, so silky smooth and velvety. She gave him everything she could, and he gave her the most remarkable night of her life. She knew, if Judd left her now, she wouldn't regret a single minute she'd spent with him.

And she also knew she'd never love another man the way she loved Judd Sanders.

9

THE BAR WAS CROWDED as women waited for the show to begin. Emily felt a twinge of jealousy, thinking of all those women seeing Judd in his skimpy briefs, but she kept reminding herself it was necessary for him to perform.

She'd left John, still acting contrary and withdrawn, at her house. It seemed it only took one phone call from her father to destroy all the headway Judd had made with her brother. Judd told her not to worry, that he was certain John would work everything out. But John was her little brother, and she couldn't help worrying about him any more than she could stop worrying over Judd.

He was obsessed with catching Donner. Anytime Emily tried to discuss it with him, he went every bit as silent and sullen as John. She supposed he had to get into a certain mind-set to be able to work his cover. After all, not many men could pull off being a stripper. But she hated seeing him act so distant. Even now, as he lounged beside her sucking on an ice cube he'd fished from her cola, she wanted to touch him, to somehow reach him. But he ignored her.

"There aren't any men here tonight. It doesn't seem likely that Donner will come."

She knew Judd had heard her, despite her lowered voice. But he didn't look at her when he replied, "He'll come. I feel it. And there aren't any men because it isn't allowed. It's ladies' night. But Donner has free run of the place. He'll be here."

The look in his eyes, the way he held himself, was so different from the Judd she knew. She felt alone and almost sick to her stomach. She had wanted Donner so badly, but now, she only wanted to protect Judd. From himself. From his feelings. And most especially from his self-designed obligations to a dead man.

Before Emily could comment further, Judd glanced at the watch on his wrist, then said, "I have to go get ready."

He straightened, and Emily tried to think of something to say, anything, that would break his strange mood. Then Judd leaned down and lifted her chin with the edge of his fist. "Do me a favor, babe. Don't watch. If you do, I'll start thinking about last night, and I might not make it."

Emily blinked. "I thought you wanted everyone to believe we had an...intimate association."

"Oh, they'll believe." Then he kissed her. Emily heard the bartender hoot, and she heard a few of the women close by whistle. One particularly brazen woman offered to be next.

Judd practically lifted her from the bar stool, one hand anchored in her hair, the other wrapped around her waist. The kiss was long and thorough, and couldn't have left any doubts about their supposed relationship.

Pulling back by slow degrees, Judd said, "Damn, but I want to be home with you. Alone. Naked."

Emily hastily covered his mouth. "Hush. You'll have me so rattled, I won't remember what I'm doing here."

He kissed her fingers, then straightened again. "Stay out of trouble. And stay where I can see you."

"But don't watch?"

"You've got it." Then he flicked a finger over her cheek and walked away to his "dressing room." Emily couldn't hold back a smile. *He wasn't as indifferent as you thought, was he, Emily? Who knows, this may all work out yet. Maybe, if enough time passes without Donner showing, Judd will finally give up and let someone more objective handle the case.*

Emily was daydreaming about having a future with Judd, when Clayton Donner strolled in the front door, along with his bully boys. Emily sank back on her stool to avoid being noticed. Not that she was all that noticeable, with so many women in the room.

Donner stopped inside the door and spoke with one of his men. He checked his watch, smoothed a hand over his hair, then opened a door leading to a set of stairs. Mick, one of the men from the pool hall, stayed at the bottom. Minutes later, another man entered and spoke quietly with Mick. Emily sucked in a sharp breath as she realized he was the man from the photograph. Fear hit her first, knowing this man had deliberately sent someone to break into her home. But anger quickly followed.

Whoever he was, he could be no better than Donner. And Emily wanted to see them both put away—preferably without involving Judd.

Their heads were bent together in a conspiratorial way, and Emily wished she could hear what they were saying. When Mick led the other man upstairs, she decided she would follow. She felt a certain foreboding, not for herself, but for Judd. She had to protect him.

Her heart pounded with her decision.

Judd was probably the most capable man she'd ever met, but his love for Max would make him vulnerable in ways that could endanger his life. If there was some way, any way, to help predict Donner's actions, she could use the information to help Judd.

With that thought in mind, she waited until Judd had been cued by his music and walked onto the dance floor, then she slipped away. Judd didn't notice since he seemed to be making every effort not to look her way. Women screamed in the background and the music blared. But above it all, Emily heard the rush of blood in her ears and her thundering heart. She tried to look inconspicuous as she made her way to the door.

It opened easily when she turned the knob, and she held her breath, waiting to see if anyone would be standing on the other side. She could always claim to be looking for the ladies' room. But once the door was open, she was faced with a narrow flight of stairs, with another door at the top.

Oh, Lord, Emily, don't lose your nerve now. And stop breathing so hard or they'll hear you. Each step seemed to echo as her weight caused the stairs to squeak. As she neared the top, she could make out faint voices and she strained to listen. Donner's tone was the most prominent, and not easy to miss. He had a distinctive sound of authority that grated on her ears.

Trying to draw a deep, calming breath, Emily leaned against the wall and concentrated on picking up the discussion, hoping she'd hear if anyone moved to open the door. Gradually, she calmed enough to hear complete sentences, and minutes later, she started back down the stairs.

Her hands shook horribly and she thought she might throw up. When she opened the door and stepped back into the loud atmosphere of the bar, her vision clouded over and she had to shake her head to clear it.

Nothing had ever scared her like eavesdropping on Clayton Donner. But she now had what she needed to protect Judd. She knew when, and where, the next shipment would be bought. A plan was forming, and she'd have a little more than a week to perfect it. She'd make it work, and best of all, it wouldn't include Judd.

JUDD FINISHED UP his act just as Emily slid back onto her stool. She was stark white and her face seemed pinched in fear. He felt an immediate surge of anger. Something had upset her, and he wanted to know what.

Ignoring grasping hands as he left the floor, he strode to Emily and stopped in front of her. She met his gaze with wide brown eyes and a forced smile. A crush of women began to close in behind him and he took Emily's arm without a word, then started toward the room where he changed. As he walked, he glanced around, hoping to catch sight of Donner or one of his men. He saw only grinning women.

When he closed the door behind them, she began to chatter. "The crowd seemed especially enthusiastic tonight. It's a shame you're not really a performer. You're obviously very good at it."

Judd didn't offer a comment on that inane remark. He studied her face, saw her fear and wondered what had happened. "Where did you go, Em?"

"Where did I go?"

"That's what I asked." He tossed his props aside and picked up a towel to rub over his body. Emily watched his hands, as she always did, with feminine fascination. "You were gone the entire time I danced."

"Oh." She pulled her gaze up to peer into his face, then shrugged. "I went to the ladies' room."

"Uh-uh. Try again."

She tried to look appalled. "You don't believe me?"

"Not a bit." Maybe she had seen Donner. Maybe the bastard had even spoken to her. Judd felt his shoulders tense. "Where did you go, Em?"

She gave a long sigh, then looked down at her feet. "All right, if you must know, I was jealous."

That set him back. "Come again?"

She waved her hand airily. "All those women were ogling you as if they had the right. I couldn't bear to watch. I suppose I'm just a...a possessive woman."

Judd narrowed his eyes, mulling over what she'd said. She sounded convincing enough, but somehow, her explanation didn't ring true.

Emily gave him a defiant glare when he continued to study her. "How would you feel if the situation were reversed? What if that was me dancing, and other men...were ogling me?"

She blushed fire-red as she made that outrageous suggestion, and Judd felt a smile tug at his mouth, despite his belief she was keeping something from him. He pulled on his jeans and then said to her, "I suppose I'd have to take you home and tie you to the bed. I sure as hell wouldn't sit around while other men enjoyed the sight of you. I'm a little possessive, too."

"There! You see what I... You are?"

Shrugging into his shirt, Judd said, "Yes, I am. And because I'm so possessive, I'd like to know what you're up to."

She immediately tucked in her chin and frowned. Judd was

just about ready to shake her, when a knock sounded on the door. He went still, his adrenaline beginning to flow, then he moved Emily out of the way and opened the door.

Mick stood there, an insolent look on his face.

"Yeah?" Judd forced himself not to show any interest.

Mick frowned. "Clay wants to talk to you."

"Tell Clay I'm busy." As he said it, he reached back and wrapped an arm around Emily. She seemed startled that he'd done so.

Mick's gaze slid over Emily, then came back to Judd. "He said to tell you he'd like to discuss a little venture with you."

"Ah. I suppose I can spare a few minutes, then. Where is he?"

"Upstairs. I'll take you there."

"I can take myself. Tell him I'll be there when I finish dressing." He shut the door in Mick's face.

Emily immediately started wringing her hands. "Don't go."

"What? Of course I'm going." He leaned down and jerked on his socks and shoes. His hands shook, the anticipation making simple tasks more difficult. He looked up at Emily. "This is what we've been waiting for. Don't go panicking on me now."

As he was trying to button his shirt, Emily threw herself against him. "It's too dangerous. You could get hurt."

"Em, honey." He didn't want to waste any time, but he couldn't walk out with her so upset. He drew a deep breath to try to collect himself. "Em, listen to me." When he lifted her chin, she reluctantly met his gaze with her own. "It'll be all right. Nothing's going to happen here in the bar. I'm only going to talk to him. I promise."

Her bottom lip quivered and she sank her teeth into it to stop the nervous reaction. Judd bent to kiss her, helping her to forget her worry. "I want you to wait at the bar for me. Stay by Freddie until I come back out. Promise me."

"I'll stay by Freddie."

"Good." He opened the door and urged her out. "Now, go. I won't be long."

Judd leaned out the doorway and watched until Emily had taken a stool in the center of the long Formica bar. He signaled Freddie, waited for his wave, then went back into the room, stuffed his props into his leather bag and hoisted it over his shoulder. He took the steps upstairs two at a time. He rapped sharply on the door. His jaw felt tight and there was a pounding in his temples.

Mick opened it, peeked out, then pulled it wide for him to enter.

Donner stood and came to greet him. "Well, if it isn't our friend, the stripper. Tell me, do the ladies ever follow you home?"

Judd forced his muscles to relax. "They try sometimes. But my calendar is full."

"Ah, yes. I almost forgot. The little bird from the pool hall."

Judd didn't reply. He wanted to smash his fist against Donner's smug, grinning face. Instead, he forced a negligent smile.

"Do you enjoy dancing…Sanders, isn't it?"

"That's right. And no, not particularly." Then he pulled a wad of money from his pocket, all of it bills that had been stuffed into his briefs. "But it pays well."

"I can see that it does. There are easier ways to make money, though."

Judd settled back against the wall and folded his arms across his chest. He was so anxious, his mouth was dry. But he kept his pose, and his tone, almost bored. He gave a slow, relaxed smile, then said, "Why don't you tell me about it."

JUDD WAS still trying to figure out how he was going to keep Emily out of the picture. He couldn't risk her by taking her along, but if she was told the truth, she'd insist on coming with him. They'd argue, and she'd end up with hurt feelings.

He couldn't bear the thought of that. Her feelings were fragile, and she was such a gentle woman, the thought of upsetting her made him feel like an ogre. But dammit all, he had to keep her safe. *Max was dead, but Emily was very much alive.* He had to make certain she would be okay.

Eight days. Not long enough, but then, no amount of time would be enough with Emily. The way he felt about her scared him silly, and it had been a long time since he'd felt fear. Growing up in the wrong part of town, with his father so drunk and angry and unpredictable, he'd gotten used to thinking fast and moving faster. Which was maybe why he'd never settled down with any one woman.

He wouldn't settle down now, either.

He couldn't. Not with Emily. She deserved so much more than he could ever give her, more than he'd ever imagined possessing. Not material things—she had those already, and he wasn't exactly a pauper. He could provide for her. But emotional things? Family and background and happy memories? He couldn't give her that. But he wanted to. So damn much.

She reached over and touched his shoulder as he drove through the dark, quiet streets of Springfield. "What happened, Judd? You've been so quiet since talking with Donner."

He couldn't tell her the truth, so he lied. And hated himself for it. "Nothing happened. He questioned me a little. Tried to feel me out. But he didn't give me a single concrete thing to go on."

"So…" She swallowed, looking wary and relieved. "So you don't know yet what his plans are?"

"No." He flicked her a look. The streetlights flashing by sent a steady rhythm of golden color over her features. She was so beautiful. "I guess we'll have to keep up the cover a little longer. I, ah, suppose I can let you out of it if you think it'll pose a problem. I mean, with John being home now and all."

"No!" She gripped his arm, then suddenly relaxed. "No. I don't mind continuing…as we have been."

A little of his tension eased. He desperately needed a few more days with her. Once it was over, he'd have no further hold on her, and he wouldn't be able to put off doing the right thing. But for now… He tugged on her hand. "Come here, babe."

Emily slid over on the seat until their thighs touched and her seat belt pinched her side. She laid her head on his shoulder.

Judd felt a lump of emotion that nearly choked him, and he swallowed hard. For so long, he'd been driven to get Donner and to avenge Max's death. He'd thought doing so would give him peace and allow him to get on with his life. But he realized now, after claiming Emily as his own for such a short time, there would be no peace. His life would be just as empty after Donner was convicted as it had been before. Maybe even more so, because now, he knew what he was missing.

EMILY FELT like a thief. She was getting rather good at sneaking around. It still made her uneasy, but with Judd always watching her so closely, the subterfuge was necessary.

In order to "protect" her, he'd sort of moved in. It was a temporary situation, prompted by Judd's concern over the break-in. He'd never once made mention of any emotional involvement, but his concern for her was obvious. And though it made her plans that much more difficult to follow, she was glad to have him in her home.

During the day he teased her and talked with her; he made her feel special. And at night...the nights were endless and hot and carnal. Judd touched her in ways she'd never imagined, but now craved. The shocking suggestions he whispered in her ear, the things he did to her, and the greedy, anxious way she accepted it all, could only be described as wicked—deliciously wicked. She loved his touch, his scent, the taste of him. She loved him, more with every day.

They had to be discreet, with John in the house, slipping into bed together after he was asleep, and making certain to be up before him. But John seemed to take great pleasure in having Judd around, even trying to emulate him in several ways. The two men had become very close.

Emily had thought long and hard about her situation with Judd, and her main priority was to take every moment she could with him. She suspected John might be aware of their intimate relationship, but since she would never ask either man to leave, there was no help for it. And she simply couldn't feel any shame in loving Judd.

Now, as she slipped from the bedroom an hour before the sun was up, Emily thought of her plan. She knew Donner would be making his deal tomorrow at the abandoned produce warehouse on Fourth Street. She had her camera loaded and ready. If she could get a really good, incriminating picture, there would be no reason for Judd to continue his investigation. He would be safe.

Giving Judd the evidence he needed would be her gift to him, to help him put the past to rest. Then maybe he'd want her to be a part of his future.

She was at the kitchen table studying a map when she heard Judd start down the steps. Seconds later, when he entered the kitchen, she tried not to look guilty. The map, now a wadded, smashed ball of paper, was stuffed safely in a cabinet drawer.

"What are you doing up so early, babe?"

Emily drank in the sight of him, standing there with his hair on end and his eyes blurry. There was so little time left. After tomorrow, his case would be over, the threat would be gone and Judd would leave her. She rushed across the floor in her bare feet and hugged him.

Judd seemed startled for a moment, and then his arms came around her, squeezing tight. "What's wrong, Em?"

"Nothing. I just couldn't sleep."

He set her away from him. "Take a seat and I'll start some coffee."

She sat, and fiddled with the edge of a napkin. "Judd?"

"Hmm?"

"I have some stuff I have to do tomorrow. Around two."

His hand, searching for a coffee mug, stopped in midreach. When he turned around, he wore a cautious expression and his posture seemed too stiff. "Oh? What kind of stuff?"

"Nothing really important. I have a load of clothes to drop off at the shelter, and some packages to send to an aunt for her birthday." She held his gaze, striving for a look of innocence. "And I think I'll do a little grocery shopping, too."

All at once he seemed to relax and his breath escaped in a sigh, as if he'd been holding it. He gifted her with a small smile.

"Well, don't worry about me. I'm sure I can find something to occupy my time. In fact, I should go check on my mail and maybe pay a few bills."

Emily congratulated herself on her performance. She'd been brilliant and he'd believed every word. Now, if she could only get him to leave before her so she wouldn't have to try to sneak out. He'd surely notice her clothes, dark slacks and a sweater, since he'd never seen her wear anything like them before. She liked the outfit. It made her feel like 007.

An hour later, all three of them were finishing breakfast. It was a relaxing atmosphere, casual and close, like that of a real family. Emily smiled, thinking how perfect it seemed.

That's when her parents arrived.

THE INTRODUCTIONS were strained and painful. Judd remembered now why he'd never done this. Meeting a mother, especially when you were barefoot and hadn't shaven yet could make the occasion doubly awkward. He thought about bowing out, letting Emily and John have time alone with their parents, but one look at their faces and he knew he wasn't going to budge.

"What is he doing here, Emily?"

"I told you, Mother, he's a friend."

"What kind of friend?"

"What kind do you think, Father?"

Judd winced. He'd never seen Emily act so cool, or so defensive. And her smart reply had Jonathan Sr. turning his way. "I think you should remove yourself."

Judd raised an eyebrow. Well, that was blunt. Before he could come up with a suitable reply, Emily fairly burst beside him.

"You overstep yourself. This is my house, and Judd is my guest."

That startled Judd, but evidently not as much as it did Emily's family. They all stared, and Emily glared back. "Uh, Em..."

"No." She raised one slim, imperious hand. "I want you to stay, Judd."

Evelyn Cooper stepped forth. She was an attractive woman, with hair as dark as Emily's and eyes just as big. For the briefest moment, Judd wondered if this was what Emily would look like when she got older—and he felt bereft that he'd never know.

"We have family business to discuss, Emily. It isn't proper for a stranger to be here."

John snorted, "He isn't a stranger, he's a very good friend. And he already knows all about me. I trust him."

Evelyn narrowed her eyes at her son. "I wasn't talking about your irresponsible behavior. You will, of course, return with us. We've found the perfect surgeon." Then her gaze traveled again to Judd. "I was speaking of Emily's...unseemly conduct."

Judd was still reeling over the way John had just defended him. He was a friend? A very good, trusted friend? He felt like smiling, even though he knew now wasn't the time. Then Evelyn's words sank in. *Unseemly?*

John had told him that Emily never stood up to her parents, that she took their insults and their politely veiled slurs without retaliating. Probably because she still felt guilty for misjudging her fiancé and causing her parents an embarrassment. But to put up with this? He didn't like it, but he also didn't think he should interfere between Emily and her parents. He drew a deep breath, and tried to remain silent.

Emily lifted her chin. "I'm not entirely certain John wants to see another surgeon, or that it's at all necessary."

"John will do as he's told."

"Despite what he wants?"

Jonathan Sr. harrumphed. "He's too young to know what he wants, and certainly too irrational at this point to make a sound decision. It's possible the scars can be completely removed. Appearances being what they are, I think we should explore every avenue."

Judd stood silently while a debate ensued. John made it clear he didn't want any further surgery. The last doctor had been very precise. The scars would diminish with time, and beyond that, nothing more could be done. Judd thought it was a sensible decision on the boy's part, but John's father disagreed. And though he'd told himself he wouldn't interfere, Judd couldn't stop himself from interrupting.

"Will you love your son any less with the scars?"

Both parents went rigid. Then Jonathan shook his head. "This has nothing to do with love!"

"Well, maybe that's the problem."

That brought a long moment of silence. Evelyn looked at her husband, and then at her son. "We only want what's best for you."

"Then leave me alone. I'm sick of being picked over by a bunch of doctors. I did a dumb thing, and now I have some scars. It's not great, but it's not the end of the world, either. They're just scars. I'd like to forget about what happened and get on with my life."

Jonathan frowned. "What life? Skulking around in the slums and getting into more trouble? We won't tolerate any more nonsense."

"Is that why you wanted to keep me out of the country? Dad, I could find trouble anywhere if that's what I really wanted. But I don't." He looked at Judd, then sighed. "I'm sorry for the way I've acted. Really. But I want to stay here now. With Emmie."

Jonathan shared another look with his wife, then narrowed his eyes at Emily. "I'm not certain that's a good idea. Emily's always been a bad influence on you."

Judd waited, but still, Emily offered no defense. It frustrated him, the way she allowed her parents to verbally abuse her. Again, he spoke up, but he kept his tone gentle. "It seems to me Emily's been a great influence. Didn't you just hear your son apologize and promise to stay out of trouble? What more could you ask for?"

Evelyn squeezed her eyes shut as if in pain. "Good Lord, Emily. He's just like the other one, isn't he? How much will it cost us this time to get you out of this mess?"

Judd froze. They couldn't possibly mean what he thought they meant. He looked at Emily, saw her broken expression and lost any claim to calm. But Emily forestalled his show of outrage.

"How dare you?"

She'd said it so softly, he almost hadn't heard her. The way her parents stared, they must have doubted their ears, too.

"How dare you even think to compare them?" Her voice rose, gaining strength. She trembled in her anger. "You don't know him, you have no idea what kind of man he is."

Judd was appalled when he saw the tears in her eyes. He touched her arm. "Emily, honey, don't." She hadn't defended herself, but she was defending him? He couldn't bear to be the cause of dissension between her and her family. It seemed to him they had enough to get straight without his intrusion.

Emily acted as though he weren't there. She drew herself up into a militant stance and said, "I would like you both to leave."

Jonathan glared. "You're throwing us out?"

"Absolutely. I've listened long enough to your accusations and disapproval. I won't ever be the daughter you want, so I'm done trying."

Evelyn laid a hand to her chest. "But we just got here. We came all the way from Europe."

Emily blinked, then gave a short nod. "You may have ten minutes to refresh yourselves. Then I want you gone." And she turned and walked out of the room.

Judd started to go after her when he heard Jonathan say, "You're not good enough for her, you know."

He never slowed his pace. "Yeah, I know."

But before he'd completely left the room, he heard John whisper, his tone filled with disgust, "You're both wrong. They're perfect...for each other."

WHAT DID KIDS KNOW? Judd asked himself that question again and again. So John liked him. That didn't mean he could step in and do something outrageous like ask Emily to marry him. No, he couldn't do that.

But he could let her know how special she was, how perfect...to him.

When he found her in the bedroom, she was no longer crying.

She sat still and silent in a chair, her back to the door, staring out a window.

"You okay?"

"I'm fine."

She wasn't and he knew that. He made a quick decision, then knelt beside her chair. After smoothing back her hair, he brushed his thumb over her soft temple. "Maybe you should go talk to them, babe. No yelling, no silent acceptance. Talk. Tell them how you feel, how they *make* you feel. They love you, you know. They don't mean to hurt you."

She didn't look at him. "How do you know they love me?"

Because I love you, and I can't imagine anyone not loving you. "You're a beautiful, giving, caring person. What's not to love?"

Her face tilted toward him, and he saw a fresh rush of tears. He kissed one away from her cheek. "Talk to them, Em. Don't let them leave like this." He stroked her cold fingers, then enfolded them in his own. "Anything can happen, I learned that with Max. Time is too short to waste, and there are too many needy people in the world to turn away those that love you."

She squeezed her eyes shut and tightened her lips, as if trying to silence herself. Judd stood, then pulled her to her feet. "Go. Talk to them. I'll get showered and dressed."

"In other words, you intend to stay out of the way?"

He grinned at her grumbling tone. "I think that might be best. But I'll be here if you need me."

She stared up at him, her eyes huge, her lashes wet with tears, and Judd couldn't stop himself from kissing her. He'd wanted to spend this last day with her, to fill himself with her because after tomorrow, he'd have no reason to be in her house, no reason to keep her close. No reason to love her. He pulled back slowly, but placed another kiss on the corner of her mouth, her chin, the tip of her nose.

"You'd better get a move on before they leave. The ten minutes you gave them is almost up."

She laughed. "If you knew my parents, you'd know how little

that mattered. They think I'm on the road to ruin. I doubt they're about to budge one inch." Then she hugged him. "Thank you, Judd. You're the very best."

As she left the bedroom, he grinned, hoping she'd work things out, and wondering at the same time...the best of what?

10

UNFORTUNATELY, it rained. Emily felt the dampness seep through her thick sweater and slacks. But she supposed the rain was good for one thing—it made her less conspicuous lurking around the back of abandoned warehouses.

Leaving today hadn't been too difficult. Judd had gone on his errands before her, and her parents, though they had stayed in town, hadn't remained at her house. They had talked a long time yesterday, and her mother had said they hoped to "work things out." They'd been apologetic, and they'd listened. Emily wondered at their change of heart, and if they'd still feel the same after she went against their wishes and brought charges against Clayton Donner.

This particular produce warehouse had several gates where a semi could have backed up to unload its goods. Three feet high and disgustingly dirty, the bottom of the gate proved to be a bit of a challenge as Emily tried to hoist herself up. The metal door was raised just enough for her to slip through, and although she still had time before Donner was due to arrive, she wanted to be inside, safely ensconced in her hiding place so there'd be no chance of her being detected.

The flesh of her palms stung as they scraped across the rough concrete ledge. Her feet peddled air before finding something solid, and then she slid forward, wedging herself under the heavy, rusting door. She blinked several times to adjust her vision, then wrinkled her nose at the stale, fetid air. Donner had certainly picked an excellent place to do his business. It didn't appear as though anyone had been inside in ages.

Emily got to her feet, then hastily looked around for a place where she could hide, and still be able to take her pictures. The warehouse was wide-open, so she should be able to capture the deal on film. The entire perimeter was framed with stacks of broken crates and rusted metal shelving, garbage and old machine parts. Not a glimpse of the vague light penetrating the dirty windows reached the corners, so that's where Emily headed. She shuddered with both fear and distaste. But she reminded herself that it could easily have been Judd here, risking his life. That thought proved to be all the incentive she needed.

Just as she neared the corner, she heard the screeching whine of unused pulleys and one of the gates started to move. With her heart in her throat, she ducked behind the crates and crouched as low as she could. She wondered, a little hysterically, if they would hear her heart thundering. She listened as footfalls sounded on the concrete floor, and voices raised and lowered in casual conversation. Then she forced herself to relax; no one was aware of her presence.

When Donner and the man from the picture came to stand directly in front of her, not twenty feet away, Emily silently fumbled for her camera. A van backed up to the gate, and the driver got out—Emily recognized him as Mick—and began unloading wooden cases. She almost smiled in anticipation, despite her nervousness.

Just a few more minutes and… A soft squeaking sounded near her. Emily didn't dare move, her heart once again starting on its wild dance. Then she heard it again. She very carefully tilted her head to the side and peered around her. Then she saw the red eyes. *Oh my Lord, Emily!* A dark, long-bodied rat stared at her.

She drew a slow deep breath and tried to ignore the creature. But it seemed persistent, inching closer behind her where she couldn't see it. She felt the touch of something, and tried not to jerk. The camera was in her hands, she had a clear shot between the crates where she hid, and Donner was winding up his business. All she needed was a single picture.

The rat tried to climb the crate beside her, using her leg as a ladder. Emily bit her lip to keep from breathing too hard. And she was good, very good. She didn't make a single sound.

But the damn rat did.

A broken crate collapsed when the rodent tried to jump toward her, and in a domino effect, other containers followed and Emily found herself exposed. She fell back, trying to hide, but not in time. Within a single heartbeat, she heard the click of a gun, then Donner's voice as he murmured in a silky tone, "Well, well. If it isn't the little bird. This should prove to be interesting."

JUDD CURSED, not quite believing what he'd just seen. How had she known? He'd been so damn careful, even going as far as faking frustration to make her believe that the deal had been called off. But somehow she had found out. And now she was inside, with Donner holding a gun on her. He lowered himself away from the window, then swiped at the mixture of rain and nervous sweat on his forehead. His stomach cramped.

Cold terror swelled through him, worse than anything he'd ever known, but he pushed it aside. He couldn't panic now, not if he hoped to get her out of there alive. His men were stationed around the warehouse, but at a necessary distance so they wouldn't be detected. Judd had planned to make the deal, recording it all through the wire he wore, then walk out just as his men arrived, making a clean bust. Now he'd have to improvise.

Speaking in a whisper so that Donner and the others wouldn't hear, he said into the wire, "Plans have changed. We'll have to move now, but cautiously. There's a woman inside, and I'll personally deal with anyone who endangers her." He allowed himself one calming breath, then said, "I'm going in."

With icy trickles of rain snaking down his neck, he took one final peek through the grimy window, then lowered himself and inched forward until it appeared he'd just arrived directly at the back entrance of the warehouse. His stance changed to one of nonchalance, and he walked through the door beside the gate.

Emily looked up at him in horror. Mick, his grin feral, held her tightly, with her arms pulled behind her back. Donner and the other man stood beside him. Judd feigned surprise, then annoyance. "What the hell is she doing here?"

Donner smiled, then inclined his head. "I'd thought to ask you that when you arrived. You're late."

With a casual flip of his wrist, Judd checked his watch. "Four o'clock exactly. I'm never late. Now, what's she doing here? I didn't want her involved."

"As you can see, she's very much involved." Donner held up a camera. "I believe she had some photography in mind."

"Damn." Then he stomped over to Emily. "I thought I told you to knock that crap off?"

He gave an apologetic grimace to Donner. "She's been thinking of doing a damn exposé on the east end. She's taken pictures of every ragtag kid, every gutter drunk or gang punk she can find. Annoys the hell out of me with that garbage."

Donner gave a lazy blink. "I think she's stepped a little over the line this time."

Judd lifted an eyebrow. "Got some interesting pictures, did she?" He turned to Emily, chiding her. "You just don't know when to quit, do you?"

"Actually," Donner persisted, "I don't think she took a single photo. But that's not the point, now, is it?"

Judd crossed his arms over his chest. "If you mean what I think you mean, forget it. I'm not done with her."

"Oh?"

"She promised to buy me a Porsche. I've been wanting one of those a long time."

Donner moved his gaze to Emily. With a nod from him, Mick pulled her arms a little tighter. The dark sweater stretched over her breasts and her back arched. Judd had to lock his jaw.

"After today, you won't need her. We can make plenty of money together." He dropped the small camera and ground it beneath his heel, then paced away from Emily. "Get it over with. We've been here too long already and there's plenty more to do." As he spoke, he watched Judd.

Knowing Donner was waiting for a reaction, Judd did his very best to maintain an air of disgust. But his mind raced and he tried to gauge his chances of taking on all three of them. He planned his move, his body tense, his mind clear.

The man from the picture grinned. He hefted an automatic weapon in his hand, the very same make that had been sold to Emily's brother. He held the gun high in his outstretched hand and aimed at Emily. Judd roared, lurching toward him, just as the gun exploded.

EMILY SQUEEZED her eyes shut, so many regrets going through her mind, all in a single second. She'd been a fool, a naive fool, thinking she could help, thinking she might make a difference. She'd ruined everything, and now Judd would die, because of her.

She heard the blast of the gun and jerked. But she felt no pain. A loud scream tore through the warehouse, echoing off the stark walls. She opened her eyes and realized the man who'd intended to shoot her was now crouching on the cold floor, his blackened face held in his hands. Blood oozed from between his fingers. The gun had backfired?

Judd reacted with enraged energy. His fist landed against Donner, who seemed shocked by what had just happened. She felt Mick loosen his hold and she threw herself forward, landing hard on her knees and palms, her shoulders jarring from the impact.

And then the room was flooded with men.

There was so much activity, it took Emily a moment to realize it was all over, that Donner and his men were being arrested. Judd appeared at her side, helping her to sit up.

"Are you all right?"

His voice sounded strange, very distant and cold. She brushed off her palms, trying to convince her heart that everything was now as it should be. Her throat ached and speaking proved difficult. "I'm fine. Just a little shaken."

Lifting her hands, Judd stared at her skinned palms, and his eyes narrowed. "I think you should go to the hospital to get checked over."

After flexing her shoulders, still sore from the way Mick had held her and the impact on the hard floor, Emily rubbed her knees. "No. That's not necessary—"

"Dammit! For once, will you just do as I tell you?"

Her heart finally slowed, in fact it almost stopped. He sounded so angry. She supposed he had the right. After all, she'd really messed things up and nearly gotten them both killed. *You might as well begin apologizing now, Emily. From the looks of him, it's going to take a lot to gain his forgiveness.* She reached out to take his hand. "Judd, I—"

He came to his feet in a rush and his eyes went over her, lingering on the dark slacks. He ground his jaw and looked away. An ambulance sounded in the distance, and when Emily looked around, she realized the man who'd been about to shoot her was very seriously wounded. Donner looked as though he wasn't feeling too well, either. He'd been close enough to receive some of the blast from the gun, and he bore a few bruises and bloody gashes from his struggle with Judd.

A passing officer caught Judd's eye, and he was suddenly hauled over to stand before Emily. Judd seemed filled with annoyance. "See that she gets to the hospital. I want her checked over."

"Yes, sir."

Remarkably, Judd started to walk away. Emily grabbed for him. Her hands shook and her heart ached. "Judd? Will I see you later at the house?"

He didn't look at her. "I already got my stuff out. Your house is your own again. Go home and rest, Em. We can question you later."

She watched him walk away, not quite believing her eyes, not wanting to believe it could end so easily. And then it didn't matter anymore. She wasn't giving up. She may have been a fool, but she refused to remain one. She wanted Judd, and she'd do whatever it took to get him.

HE CUT HER COLD. Emily tried numerous times to reach Judd. Three weeks had passed, and the police no longer needed her as a witness. Evidently, Judd no longer needed her...for anything.

She had no reason to seek him out, but she still tried. He'd remained at the small apartment. She'd been there several times, but he either didn't answer the door, or he was so distantly polite, asking her about her brother, wishing her well, that she couldn't bear it. They might have been mere acquaintances, except that Emily felt so much more. She loved him, and even though her parents tried to convince her not to make a fool of herself, she couldn't give up.

She had tried apologizing to him for mucking things up. That had made him angry all over again, so she'd refrained from mentioning it further. John had gone to him once, to see how he was doing. Judd received her brother much better than he'd received her, and Emily felt a touch of jealousy. It bothered her even more when John claimed Judd was "absolutely miserable."

"He wants you, Emmie. I know he does. He just doesn't realize you want him, too."

Much as she wanted to believe that, she couldn't allow herself false hope. "I've made it more than clear, John. I can't very well force the man to love me."

But John had shrugged, a wicked grin on his face. "Why not? At least then you'd settle things, one way or another."

She thought about that. How could she "force" a man who was nearly a foot taller and outweighed her by ninety pounds? She decided to try talking to him one more time, and went directly to his apartment. His old battered truck sat out front, and as Emily passed, something different caught her eye. At first, she had no idea what it was, and then it struck her.

She bent next to the driver's window and peered inside. The black lace that used to hang so garishly from his rearview mirror had been replaced by the tie from her dress. Emily vaguely remembered that night when Judd had shoved the pale strip of material into his back pocket moments before they'd made love.

And now it had a place of prominence in his truck.

It was ridiculous how flattered she felt by such a silly thing, but she suddenly knew, deep in her heart, that he did care. At least a little.

She remembered the day he'd allowed her to indulge her fantasies. He'd said he had fantasies of his own, and he'd whispered erotic suggestions to her while they made love, wicked things about her really stripping—performing for him. She had been mortified and excited at the same time. Some of the things he'd suggested had been sinfully arousing, and she'd promised herself, once she could gain the courage, she'd fulfill every single one of his fantasies.

But she hadn't. She'd let inhibitions get in her way, even though she knew how wild it would make him. But maybe it wasn't too late. Maybe she could still set things right between them, and show him how much she loved him by giving him everything she possibly could.

She started away from the truck, her confidence restored. But she stopped dead when a little old lady blocked her path.

"What were you doing there, girl?"

"I..." What should she say? That she was admiring an article of her clothing, strung from a rearview mirror like a masculine trophy? That she intended to seduce a man? *Get a grip, Emily.* "I was just about to call on my...brother. I see his truck is here, so I know he must be—"

"He ain't home. He's taken to walkin' in the park every evening. Usually picks up a few necessaries for me while he's out."

"I see." Emily's disappointment was obvious.

"I'm the landlady here. You want me to give him a message?"

"No. I had hoped to...surprise him." Her mind whirled. "It's his birthday today. And since he doesn't have any other family, I thought maybe I could make this day...special."

"His birthday, you say? Well, now we can't let it go by without a little fun, can we? I could let you into the apartment, if that's what you're wantin'."

Already Emily's pulse began racing. "Yes, that would be wonderful. And I promise, he'll be so surprised."

JUDD DRAGGED himself up the steps to his apartment. The weather had been considerably mild lately, and he wore only a

T-shirt with his jeans. The early-evening air should have refreshed him, but he still felt hollow. He'd felt that way ever since Emily had been endangered—by his own design.

His drive, his need to see Clayton Donner sent to jail, had clouded his reason and cost him his heart. He'd thought losing Max had been the ultimate hurt, but knowing he'd endangered Emily, knowing he'd risked her life, used her, loved her, was slowly killing him. He couldn't bear to face himself in the mirror.

He also knew he'd love her forever, and it scared the hell out of him. Time and distance hadn't helped to diminish what he felt. But what could he do? Ask her to forgive him, to spend her life with him? How could he? She deserved better than him. Her grace was always with her, whether she was working at the soup kitchen, or sneaking into a warehouse full of danger. She was elegance personified, and he was a man who went to any extreme to get what he wanted, to see a job done, including stripping off his clothes for a pack of hungry women.

Self-disgust washed over him. He rubbed his face, wishing he could undo the past and be what Emily deserved.

Mrs. Cleary met him in the hallway, a huge smile spread over her timeworn features. Struck dumb for a moment, Judd stared.

"Did you fetch my bread and eggs?"

"Here you go, Mrs. Cleary. Are you sure you don't need anything else?" Judd had taken to the older woman with her gruff complaints and constant gossip. He figured she was probably every bit as lonely as he was.

"No, I got all I need. Now you run on home. And happy birthday."

Judd blinked. "But..." She winked at him, and he decided against correcting her assumption. Age could be the very devil, and if she wanted to believe it was his birthday, for whatever reason, he'd let her. "Thanks."

When he reached his apartment and stepped inside, he knew right away that something was different. He could feel it. All his instincts kicked in, and he looked around with a slow, encompassing gaze. His bedroom door was shut.

That seemed odd. Then odder still, music began to play. He recognized the slow, brassy rhythm as one of his favorite CDs, and his instincts took over. Without real thought, he inched his way to the cabinet where he kept his Beretta, slowly slid it into his palm, and crept forward.

The beat of the music swelled and moaned, and Judd flattened himself beside the door. Then, with his left hand, he slowly turned the knob and threw it open.

He waited, but no bodies came hurdling out, and he cautiously, quickly, dipped his head inside then jerked back to flatten himself against the wall.

No. It took his mind a second to assimilate what he'd just seen, and still, he didn't believe it. He blinked several times, then peeked into the room again.

Yes. That was Emily.

Standing in the center of his rumpled bed.

He moved to block the doorway, his gun now held limply at his side. The black leather jacket he'd used as part of his stripping costume hung around her shoulders, the sleeves dropping past her fingertips. It wasn't zipped, and he could see a narrow strip of bare, pale flesh, from her black lace bra to her skimpy lace panties. Her navel was a slight shadow framed by the zipper and black leather.

Max's hat sat at a rakish angle on her head. She grinned.

Sweat on his palms made it necessary for him to set the gun aside. He stumbled to the dresser, then took two steps toward her before he stopped, unsure of himself, unsure of her.

With her eyes closed, her hips swayed to the music. As he watched, her face blossomed with color—and the jacket fell away.

He licked his lips, trying to find some moisture in his suddenly dry mouth. It had been three long weeks, three *endless* weeks, since he'd made love to Emily. She lifted her arms over her head, her nipples almost escaping the sheer lace, and he felt his body harden. His erection grew long and full, pressing against his suddenly tight jeans.

She turned on the bed, not saying a single thing. Judd breathed through his mouth as his body pulsed, his eyes glued to the sight of her small bottom encased in black lace. Her hips swayed and his erection leaped, along with his heart.

Emily reached behind her back to unhook her bra. He took another step closer. He wanted to ask her what this meant, but he was afraid to speak, afraid she'd stop—afraid she wouldn't. When she turned around, she tossed the bra to him.

It hit him in the chest and fell to the floor. He couldn't move. He couldn't blink. He could barely force air past his restricted lungs.

The hat fell off when she bent slightly at the waist, hooking her thumbs in the waistband of her panties. The blush had spread to encompass her throat, her breasts. Her pointed nipples flushed a dark rose. The music picked up, hitting a crescendo and crashing into a final, raging beat.

Emily released the panties and they slid down her slender thighs, landing against his disheveled covers and pooling around her feet.

Judd stared at the triangle of dark glossy curls and his nostrils flared. He started toward her.

She raised one hand and he stopped. "We need to talk, Judd."

"Talk?" His mind felt like mush, his body, like fire.

"I realized desperate measures were necessary to get your attention."

"Believe me, Em. You have my attention." It was an effort, but he managed to force his gaze to her earnest face.

She lifted her chin. Her lips trembled for a moment. "I hope you'll understand. Sometimes we have to do outrageous things to meet our ends. Just as you had to strip to trap Donner, well, I had to strip to…trap you." She clenched her hands together, and then she blurted out, "I love you."

"You…" He'd been engrossed with her odd comparison, and the fact she'd evidently understood his motives all along. And she hadn't blamed him for doing whatever needed to be done. He'd been wrong about that.

But now his thoughts crashed down. She couldn't have said what he thought she'd said. "You...love me?"

"Yes. I love you. I want you. Forever. I realize I'm not quite what you had in mind for a...a woman."

"A wife?"

"Well, yes. That would probably be the most logical thing, considering how I feel."

"You love me?"

She made an exasperated sound and propped her fists on her naked hips. His body throbbed.

"Didn't I just say so? Twice?"

"I believe you did."

"Well? Do you think you can come to love me? I realize this is probably not very...fair of me. To try to seduce you—"

"You passed 'try' when the music began."

"Oh. I see. Well, then, you should know, I expect everything. Our...reactions to each other are...very satisfying, but I want more."

"You want me to marry you?"

She tromped over to the edge of the bed, bringing her breasts a mere foot from his face. He swallowed, then gave up trying to keep his gaze focused.

He put first one knee, then the other on the bed and wrapped his arms around her, pressing his mouth to her soft naked belly. "I love you, too, Em. God, I love you."

Her fingers clenched in his hair. "Really?"

"I was afraid to love you, but it happened, anyway."

"You were afraid?"

He nodded, then nuzzled one pointed nipple. "You deserve so much better."

Her fingers tightened and pulled. Wincing, he looked up at her. "Don't you ever say that again! You're the finest, the most caring man I've ever known."

He saw her intent expression, her anger, and felt himself begin to believe. "Our backgrounds—"

"Damn our backgrounds!"

Judd blinked. Cursing from Emily? He felt shocked, and ridiculously happy.

"You rose above your upbringing, Judd. Despite all your disadvantages, you're a hero." Her fingers tightened again and she brought his head against her. "You're my hero."

"No."

"Yes! I'm not giving you pity, because you don't need it. I'm only giving you the truth. I love everything about you." She swallowed hard, then gentled her hold on his hair, smoothing her hand over his crown. "And you make me feel loved. Nothing else matters. We can work out the rest."

"The rest?"

"I love my house, Judd. I'd like us to live there."

"I'd...I'd like that too. But Emily, I'm not a pauper. I've never had anything to spend my money on, so I have a hefty savings—"

Her fingers touched his mouth. "I never thought you were helpless, Judd. And we'll support each other, okay? That is, if you can tolerate my parents. They do seem to be trying."

He pulled her down until she knelt in front of him. "Marry me, Emily."

Her eyes, those huge, eat-a-man-alive eyes, fairly glowed with happiness. She kissed him, all over his face, his ear, his shoulder. "Yes," she shouted, "Oh, Judd, I love you."

As they both began trying to wrestle his clothes from his body, Judd said, "Promise me you'll strip for me again later. You took me so much by surprise, I think I might have missed something."

Her blush warmed him, and she smiled. "Whatever you say, Detective." And then he made love to her.

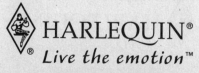

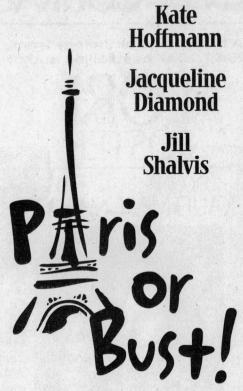
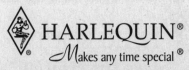

This February—2003—
Silhouette Books cordially invites you
to the arranged marriages
of two of our favorite brides, in

The
Wedding
ARRANGEMENT

A man fulfilling his civic duty finds himself irresistibly drawn
to his sexy, single, *pregnant* fellow juror. Might they soon be
sharing more than courtroom banter? Such as happily ever
after? Find out in **Barbara Boswell's** *Irresistible You.*

She *thought* she was his mail-order bride, but it turned out
she had the wrong groom. Or did she? The feisty beauty had
set her eyes on him—and wasn't likely to let go anytime
soon, in **Raye Morgan's** *Wife by Contract.*

Look for The Wedding Arrangement *in February 2003
at your favorite retail outlet.*

Where love comes alive™

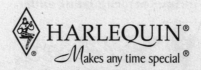